FORGOTTEN MASTERS 11

ECHOES OF ENGAGEMENT

SCOTT M. SWAINE

Primix Publishing
East Brunswick Office Evolution
1 Tower Center Boulevard, Ste 1510
East Brunswick, NJ 08816
www.primixpublishing.com
Phone: 1-800-538-5788

This is a work of fiction. Names, characters, places, and incidents either are the product of the author's imagination or are used fictitiously, and any resemblance to any persons, living or dead, is entirely coincidental.

Published by Primix Publishing: 10/01/2024

ISBN: 979-8-89194-131-1(sc)
ISBN: 979-8-89194-254-7(hc)
ISBN: 979-8-89194-132-8(e)

Library of Congress Control Number: 2024906018

Because of the dynamic nature of the Internet, any web addresses or links contained in this book may have changed since publication and may no longer be valid. The views expressed in this work are solely those of the author and do not necessarily reflect the views of the publisher, and the publisher hereby disclaims any responsibility for them.

CONTENTS

Chapter 1

PROLOGUE, THE ESCAPE

Screams echoed through the streets of the city as the orcish army surged forward. The attack was unexpected. There was no prior warning. The orcs had never exhibited any outward aggression before this. In fact, there were relatively few interactions between their primitive tribal culture and the much more enlightened inhabitants of the city, the Daanen-Aryku, other than some minor trade and small fragments of cultural exchange. But today, all that changed.

The initial onslaught killed thousands. Orcish shamans could be seen casting their foul magic at any hapless victim who came into their line of sight. This devious spell-craft represented a mysterious force to the scientifically adept Daanen-Aryku. Their advanced technological society understood many extraordinary inventions, but magic was unknowable to them. The entire concept of it, prior to their discovery of this world some fourteen centuries ago, was largely myth. None of their sciences allowed them to properly define it. Even after they first arrived, they considered the strange manners of the native orcs to be little more than a practice of superstition and mysticism conducted at fireside rituals.

Nevertheless, the orcs saw them as a powerful society, perhaps even on the level of gods, when they first arrived. They established a tentative peace and permitted the Daanen-Aryku space to build a home. These travelers had become a nomadic society since their departure from their ancient home world. This represented only the most recent in a long chain of worlds they discovered where they hoped to find peace and a place to rest.

Unfortunately, this would not come to pass, as once again they came under attack. As the shamanic conjurations struck their targets, the unfortunate quarry would collapse into a heap on the ground. Their screams echoed through the streets, bellowing out the unmentionable suffering they would now need to endure as their bodies begin to transform into hideous mutations. The obscene rending twisted their minds and dulled their keen intellect, barely allowing them to produce intelligible thought. They became atrocities to their own dignity, a race once proud of its highly evolved nature, but now reduced to nearly mindless servants enslaved by their new masters.

"Run, Kali! Hurry!" comes the shout from the girl's mother. "We need to get to the ship!"

The two of them ran feverishly through an alley and onto the main avenue in the direction of an enormous structure rising up in the background of the city skyline not far ahead. The feature dominated the scene for its size alone, standing almost like an artificial mountain of technological mastery. It was the famed Naarg uy'Sodrad, a massive colony ark that once brought their people to this remote world in an effort to escape from a monstrous evil that has pursued them relentlessly across the cosmos…a being known only as Sargeras.

"Why are they doing this?" screams the young girl. "How dare they attack us…those beasts!"

"Just keep running! Don't look back!"

"Where is Father?" Kali demands. "Why isn't the militia here helping us? Why are we always running? All we do is run, and more people die!"

The child's frustration was well-known to both her parents, having been raised in an environment often influenced by desperation and anxiety. Her people had been graced by a rare glimpse of reprieve from the chase, having made a frantic jump from their last home to this new world. They had hoped to have finally evaded Sargeras and his armies, but it was a hollow dream for some.

"Please, Kali, not now! Just run, it's all we can do!"

Their hunters, known as the Suuden-Aryku, the original population of their ancient home world of Azgarén, had been pursuing these people for many millennia after they ran away from Sargeras shortly after his arrival. But the reasoning, often lost on the minds of their pacifistic society, was generally interpreted as being they refused to submit to him like the others did. Time and again, they would run to a new world, only to be discovered sometime later, and the chase resumed. Today's attack didn't seem rational that it could be them again, not after that last leap, but for some, it couldn't be anything else. They were too heavily conditioned by now to run like frightened animals.

With each of these attacks, their numbers would be diminished. They were not a militant society, instead one of scientists and scholars. Therefore, they did not have a proper military to fight with, only a security force to serve as law enforcement. And their cultural philosophies largely denied violence. As the result, despite the young girl's rage, they simply could not fight back, they could only run... each and every time.

Kali and her mother continued to charge along the roadside, the outline of the great ship clearly visible only a few blocks ahead. Explosions caused by soaring fireballs rocked the buildings near them as they passed. Magical fire rain hailed down onto homes and offices, setting everything ablaze.

A row of militia, the security forces known as the Sentinels, had formed a blockade line, trying to hold back the encroaching invaders. They fired defensive weapons in an effort to delay the attackers long enough for the last few survivors to retreat behind the line to safety.

"Try to get behind that line, Kali!" her mother shouts as she points at the row of guardsmen.

Barely a moment after she finishes her command, she lets out an abrupt shriek. She was hit. A shamanic conjuration bolt had slammed into her back and was now spreading throughout her body.

"Mother!" the girl screams as she observes the fallen figure.

Already, her mother's body was beginning to deform. Grotesque tendrils could be seen slithering beneath the skin. She writhed on the ground, moaning fiercely, clutching at her skin as though it burned.

"R-run Ka-li!! D-don't s-stop!"

Her voice groaned, becoming gruff and thick as the vulgar influence coursed its way through her body.

Kali looked on in horror. She screamed. Her mother's form was changing, right before her eyes, becoming hideous, a grotesque perversion of the woman she loved, defiled by the workings of lesser beings, creatures that never once earned a symbol of respect in the girl's mind, despite their cultural teachings to the contrary. And this display simply finished it for her.

Now, as she looked down at the altered form of her mother's body, what used to be the familiar comfort of home and family was now a monster, and her unwavering disgust for those who committed this deed had escalated a hundred-fold. During the raid, she had seen others turned like this, and then used by the orcs to pursue and assault other people. They appeared unnatural, like something from out of a nightmare, freakish and offensive machines of macabre horror. Their science could never imagine such a thing by rational means, so in her young mind, it simply had to be supernatural.

Nothing could be done to change it. The transformation could not be halted. The woman twitched and struggled hopelessly against the violation of her body, and the young girl standing over her was traumatized by the assault. Kali let out a desperate wail for her loss, and slapped her hands over her eyes. She stumbled backwards and then turned and ran away.

She dodged amongst the trees along the sidewalks, hoping to confound the orcs from targeting her on the next attack. The row of guards was not far from her now, but she knew to keep off to the side, not cross between them and the orcs, thereby putting herself in the line of fire. She turned down another alley, hoping to circle around the next building and come up the other side, closer to the defensive line. But as she ran along the alley, she came upon a high wall. It was a dead end.

The wall was easily twice her height. From the appearance of the buildings around her, she presumed the alley should continue on the other side, but the challenge was to get over the wall. She studies it carefully. It was made of a dark fabricated brick, and the top was a smooth crown.

"All right, girl," she mumbles to herself. "Let's see if any of those gymnastic courses in school taught you anything."

Kali judges the obstacle in front of her. She walks up to it, turns, and paces off a calculated number of steps, then turns back to take another look. She recalls her school practice. Over the years, she had conditioned herself through lengthy rehearsals on floor exercises and acrobatics. Her legs were well-toned, and she held honors on the outdoor track as having amongst the best sprinting records within her age group, as well as her high jump.

She takes a deep breath and measures her angle, then launches forward. She bounds along towards the wall, makes a minor leap and coils down on her haunches, then springs upward using her tightly wound muscles to propel her to the top of the wall. She hooks her hands over the crown to assist, then using the remainder of her momentum, she vaults over in a somersault. As she comes back down on the other side, she lands firmly on her hoofed feet, flinging her arms out to the sides to deflect her inertia in a classic triumph pose.

Looking over her shoulder, she smiles briefly at her achievement, realizing her time spent in practice has paid off with tangible results. But the moment of self-tribute was short, as the wails of fleeing citizens once again reached her ears, and she was forced to return to her frenetic dash to safety.

She started running once again, cornering around the large civic building and up the other side back to the main avenue. She estimated that she should come out just behind the line of guards. She was very close to the ship now. It was just across the street and around a final set of buildings on this side of a short masonry wall separating the city bounds from the original landing site. She pushed herself to run even faster. Adrenaline tingled in her veins as she closed in on the next corner. She could now see the guards, but only in time to witness a fiery explosion smashing through the line.

Screams rang out as bodies went sailing into the air. A couple of guards who were sheltered by the structure returned fire. One of them heard the pounding of small, hoofed footsteps behind him. He turns with his weapon raised, but pulls back at the sight of the young female racing toward him.

"Get to the ship, girl!" he calls out to her, pointing to the other side of the street. "Hurry, before they break through!"

Kali halts and turns to cross the street. She could hear the shouts of the orcish horde coming up in the distance. She dashes across, quickly reaching the other side, then angling sharply to continue up towards the intersection. She rounds the next corner and darts along the sidewalk towards a gate that passed through the masonry wall. The ship was just in sight, only a moment away.

Another explosion was followed by more shouts from the guards. They were falling back. The order had been given for the remaining troops to move to the ship. All was lost now. The only thing that remained was to get inside and launch.

Kali continued forward, now nearing the ramp that would lead into the vessel. She could see only a few other survivors at this late moment, themselves franticly trying to escape the orcs. Most had already boarded the ship, and any who were too slow or late in leaving the safety of their homes, were likely either dead or…like HER now.

As Kali arrived on the ramp, she ascended into the security of the ship. The sounds of explosions reverberated around the city, but fortunately the ship was made of a more durable material than the surrounding buildings.

The huge vessel was not their own creation, but instead apparently the gift of an advanced, but otherwise unknown entity or civilization. All they understood was it had been delivered, perhaps even to say donated to them by a group of strange entities they described as the cu'Nar. These cu'Nar arrived on their original home world at around the same time as Sargeras, delivering a message of a sort, along with instructions to run away. The whole scenario seemed planned, perhaps even engineered by someone, but without any clue as to who or why, they simply took the hint and followed. But unfortunately, this would culminate with the chase.

Her people were once part of the Suuden-Aryku, a society of high scientific achievement representing a civilization roughly two million years old. This, in itself, was a proud statement, if not for the fact of being hunted for so long and losing so many of their numbers along the way. They carried portions of their knowledge and history with them, but the attacks had a habit of destroying some part of it each time, diminishing them slowly and painfully.

In their language, they might sometimes use a special form of suffix, 'kai, affixed to a word, like their race name, to symbolize a reference or a relationship to the owner of the word. This world they found belonged to a local race of beings. And the Daanen'kai city was something of an easement, an allowance granted to them to take up their residence. Here they hoped to finally be rid of their aggressors, and described themselves as being in exile from their ancient origins.

Their name, Daanen-Aryku, carries the meaning of the Exiled Ones, and this was yet another insult to their former glory as Suuden-Aryku, the Lifted Ones. This name describes the ascension from their primeval origins. And this home they made for themselves, a world they called Ruuki uy'Daan, a land of exile, was in itself offensive, as it was not their own. Even to describe it as a place of exile was demoralizing.

Kali's grudges were compounded by all of this, and now to have her fragile innocence violated with the attack, tipped her over the brink. Her people stood on the edge of extinction, with what they believed to be the last of their culture, their history, their prestige as lifeforms that once held so much sense of purpose and accomplishment. This was further exasperated by those so-called Lifted Ones appearing as monsters by now, with their own mutation and cold-mannered behaviors.

More explosions echo outside, but the ship holds fast as the last of the guards file through the hatchway. The doors begin to close, but even with the subsidence of the sound of battle outside, another commotion is heard deeper within the bowels of the ship. Shouts ring through the local corridors, and weapons' fire ricochets off the walls. An alarm sounded, and this rang up to the bridge.

"What's happening down there?" responds the comms officer.

"Intruders! Three of them!" shouts the voice over the speaker. "We don't know who they were, but they were found in Engineering."

The disturbance draws the attention of a ranking officer.

"Orcs?" he responds. "How in all the nether-space could they possibly get down there!"

"No Sir, not orcs. These were different. They had an advanced anthropoidal body frame, pale-skinned, light-colored hair. We've never seen anything like them before."

"That's not even a native inhabitant! Where did they come from?"

"Sir," the comms officer interjects. "This might indicate external involvement."

"It would, and this is the last thing I want to hear right now. You say they were in Engineering?"

"Yes Sir," the voice replies. "They attacked us on their way out."

"Cu'Nar's pity! As if we needed that climbing our tails. Check for damage! Now!"

Kali was coursing her way through the corridors. The ship was nearly a maze of rooms and hallways, but an internal directory service assisted the people in finding their way. There was also a transport chute service, a little like a subway system that provided rapid transit from one area of the ship to another. She used this to find her way up to the bridge, which is where she expected to find her father, among others.

Along the way, she passed by several areas where she saw people cowering from the disturbance outside. Some simply stood along the walls, while others retreated to staterooms and public meeting areas.

As she arrives on the bridge, she sees a myriad of officers standing at the various control stations trying to power up the ship. Orders were being given to run checks on the ship's systems and to bring more functions online. The ship, which in their language carried the name Naarg uy'Sodrad, Pursuit of Freedom, had been dormant for too long. Bringing it back to life became a struggle.

Glancing around the room, her eyes finally came upon an ornately clad form wearing the robe of an elder statesman. She moved determinedly to meet with him, her gaze filled with fire and rage over what happened outside.

"Father!" she screeches.

The large figure, leaning partially on a tall, gilded staff set with a glowing crystal on top, turned slowly to face the young girl, his stiffened motions betraying his great age.

"Kali! Thank the cu'Nar, you're safe. Where is your mother?"

"Gone! No thanks to you!"

Kali's eyes welled up with tears as she fought to hold her composure.

"She was hit in the back by those horrible beasts with their magic," she continues. "I saw it all. She's...she's not... And all you can do is run! Now mother is gone! She might as well be dead for what they did to her."

"Oh no..." he moans. "But Kali, they took us by surprise..."

"Surprise? Yeah, just like always. Cu'Nar's pity, how many times can someone 'take you by surprise' before you start to expect it. And you just run! We have all these machines, but people die, and still you run!"

"Kali, these...machines...are not weapons to fight with. And those people chasing us have apparently invented new and more powerful forms. And then this out here, well..."

"I don't care anymore. Mother is gone. I hate you! It's all because of you! You and the rest of the Council. I'll never speak to you again. You're no longer my father!"

With this, Kali storms away, leaving the bridge and heading to one of the staterooms, where she looks for a quiet corner to sit down and wait.

The elder male watches her as she moves away, his mouth agape at the surprise of the violent lashing from his youngest child. His heart grows heavy and sullen. He has lost his wife, and now his daughter. Many people have been lost over the years, though never has he felt as wounded as he did now.

Across the room, he glances up briefly to catch the eyes of a young male, one of the junior officers attending a security station. The man looks back at him mournfully, his eyes crossing between the girl and the elder.

"I'll try to talk to her later," he offers. "I'm sure she's just as hurt as the rest."

"Thank you, Kailen. You know her temper, but it seems this attack has seriously affected her. I can only hope...but then, she is probably right," he sighs and shakes his head. "In the end, we should never NOT expect something out of them."

"The long duration of peace we had here probably softened us up too much."

"Yes, and after that last jump..."

"Excuse me, my pardons," the ranking officer interjects. "But we have a problem."

The elder man's thoughts are unexpectedly forced out of their depression, now shifting to the voice of the officer.

"Yes, Commander?" he responds softly.

"We got a call from Engineering a moment ago about intruders... some new race who shouldn't otherwise be here."

"How..." he frowns.

"I don't know, and I don't have the time to speculate on it. According to the engineers down there, we think they were trying to sabotage something."

"Do we know if they were successful? And what were they trying to sabotage?"

"Almost anything is possible, but there doesn't seem to be any clear damage to any of the controls. So, we could possibly say they didn't have time to finish anything. Still, I don't think I can take that chance. If they were down there, they must've known a thing or two about what they were doing."

"Are we able to lift off? Do we still have power to escape from here?"

"The helm reports we do seem to have functioning control of the engines. Nav also tells me they have a lock on a potential jump point."

"Good. What about the people outside? Did everyone make it?"

"As far as I know, everyone within sight…or at least until the orcs were in view."

"There was that one patrol that stayed behind as a last defense," Kailen adds.

"I still disagree with that strategy," the Commander argues. "We are too few in number to begin with to leave stragglers behind."

"I understand, Commander," the statesman nods sympathetically. "I spoke with him as we were coming to this conclusion, um…" he pauses as if lost in a personal thought. "Captain Lapäli understood his role to keep them at bay while we escape. I cannot be sure why he was chosen, but there has to be a purpose to it. They never misled us in the past, and I must trust their judgment. They seem to possess a form of knowledge which I cannot fully interpret."

"I sure hope you're right. He's a good man, and I don't want to lose any more like that."

"Sir!" Kailen issues abruptly. "I'm showing sensor readings here that the orcs are arriving outside and are apparently trying to attack the ship directly now."

"Naturally!" he snaps. "I wish them good luck with that, but in the end, even with their primitive weapons and this magic of theirs, we might still take damage if they work hard enough at it."

"This simply means we need to launch immediately," the statesman concludes. "As for the Captain, whatever role he must serve, I pray to the cu'Nar it is not in vain."

"I'm still thinking of those saboteurs. Whatever they did to the place, we might not get far. There's no telling what might happen."

"True, Commander, but I'm afraid we have no choice. Give the order. And may the cu'Nar watch over us."

The Commander bows his head and turns back to a large tactical projector table in the center of the bridge. It displayed a 3D image of the local space.

"Helm, take us up," he calls to one of the crewmen. "Bring us to a suitable altitude and power up the jump drive."

"Yes, Sir!"

The immense ship shudders as it lifts off the ground. It lethargically orients skyward, departing the immediate area of hostilities and rising up through the atmosphere.

"Sir," the helmsman inquires. "Do you wish us to jump from here, or try taking it into orbit? Jumping directly from this point will cause quite a disturbance on the ground."

"As if I care about that, after what they did to our people. Also, with the involvement of external agents, there's no telling what's waiting for us up there, especially if THEY found us again. Better not to give them the chance of taking any shots at us. We'll jump from here. Give us the numbers, Ensign."

"Affirmative, Sir! Charging... Ten percent... Twenty... Thirty..." the count proceeds forward as the powerful ship comes to life once more.

Subtle tremors are felt rumbling through the walls and flooring. The ship, for all of its incredible technology and apparent durability, was at the same time ancient by now. Whispers begin to flow along the corridors from the frightened refugees. They spoke of fears over the ship exploding, or perhaps of the dimensional rift folding inward and collapsing down to a singularity.

The count continues.

"Forty... Fifty percent... Sixty... Seventy... Nether-space generator engaged... Eighty... Ninety... Phase-shifting active! The rift is open! We're passing into the conduit."

Travel through trans-dimensional space carries a different sensation than movement through physical space. There is no property of inertia as the ship doesn't actually experience a change in velocity. The ship phase-shifts through a dimensional warp, as if to cut a hole in space, pass through the hole, and reemerge at a new location. To accommodate this, the ship wraps itself in a distortion pocket called nether-space, where the ship is held motionless, without any physical mass relative to the outer domain. Space itself is then pulled around the field, dragging the pocket, including the ship and its contents, along for the ride.

Initially, all seems to be running well, but then an error signal comes up on one of the panels. The ship begins to shudder violently.

"Sir, we have an energy spike!" shouts the helmsman. "The tunnel is convulsing! We're experiencing a spontaneous formation."

"That shouldn't be possible! Try to hold the field integrity. Give it more power!"

"Yes, Sir! I'm diverting power from the secondary reactor."

"Sir!" the navigator calls out. "Our course is altering. It looks like some kind of override from our previous trajectory."

"And here we go!" the Commander growls. "No doubt this is the little gift from our unwelcome visitors!" he turns to a local intercom panel. "All hands, prepare for a rough reentry. Grab hold of whatever you can!"

Shouts and screams begin to well up inside the ship, as the panicked refugees strain to find anything solid to hold onto. The wavering of the nether-space field causes the ship to rock to one side, throwing passengers across the floor. It rocks back again, and they tumble the other way. Suddenly, another alarm rings out, more imperative than the first.

"Sir!" reports the helmsman. "I'm showing a feedback loop! We've lost containment! The drives are going critical!"

Seconds later, a massive shockwave pulses through the ship as the engine nacelles explode, tearing through the hull and ripping a portion of the underside of the ship away. The nether-space field suddenly collapses, and all who are aboard now feel the full return of inertia as the ship finds itself in a flat spin.

"We're emerging from the tunnel! I can't hold it!"

"Stabilizers!" shouts the Commander. "Try to keep the nose up! Nav, where are we?"

"Unknown, Sir!" he shrieks. "The nav system is scrambled.

The screens are dead. It looks like a total wipe. But I'm showing something under us. We're coming in hot. Brace for impact!"

Somewhere above an otherwise peaceful valley, a tremendous flash of light rips across the sky, followed by a fierce sonic shock that flattens trees for miles around. Within the gaping maw of the otherworldly blast, a strange object hurtles outward. Shards of debris mixed with jets of flame follow. The great glowing hulk of the Naarg uy'Sodrad, barely under the management of its guidance control, descends rapidly, crashing into the ground and carving a deep groove into the land. Waves of heat ignite spontaneous fires in the surrounding area, and a wide arc of vegetation mingled with soil is hurled away as the noble ship comes to its final rest...never to fly again.

Chapter 2
PROLOGUE, THE PROPHECY

"Master Velen, you summoned me?"

A young attendant rushes into the room, called to the side of an aging male resting in his bed.

"Yes, I had a vision while I slept. I need to record it. I think the cu'Nar spoke to me again. It's been so long since the last time."

"A message? I'll bring your journal at once!"

The attendant rushes over to a writing desk where he picks up a hefty book and a pen. He brings it back to the Daanen'kai elder and sets it on his lap. Here, Master Velen begins to scribe the visions he received to the best of his recollection, and interpretation.

From a circle of light, He shall come.
The Divine Justice, One divided by Two.
In His hands He carries:
The Power of Infernal Destruction,
And the Power of Blessed Life.
Evil will crumble under the weight of His majesty.
The Child will find its Gift.

The Lost will be found.
And the Sundered will be Restored,
As Vengeance arrives on silver wings.

As Velen proceeded through the course, he struggled to recall the details clearly enough to write his interpretations, but the visions were already fading. Then, as he finished scribbling his notes, he relaxes back onto his pillow. The attendant picks up the book and returns it to the desk.

"It's been many decades since our…arrival," Velen begins. "Our people suffered heavily from the crash. So few now… So few…"

He looks up at the attendant.

"I remember the days back on Azgarén," he continues. "It was peaceful, we had our studies, and there was so much to offer. It seems like a full Age ago now. I am too old. I have seen too much."

"Master Velen, without you, we may not have survived even this long. It was you who warned the Council of the dangers of following Sargeras. And it was you who led us away from his treachery."

"Yes, but to what end? Look at us. Once, we were a civilization, a population measured in billions back in our ancestral homes on Azgarén. We could only bring with us a paltry few that could fit inside the ship."

"Three hundred thousand isn't really a paltry few, but yes, I understand."

"And since that time, we have been pursued and slaughtered by those who stayed behind, now twisted by his will, malformed into this horrid army. Each time we find a moment's respite, they appear again."

He glances lazily around the room.

"And now," he continues. "We are but a shadow of ourselves, what we struggled so hard to maintain. Barely ten thousand remain from our last home. We lost so much this time. For many of us, our children were the worst of it, in the old school…too young to die, and too young to know how proud we once were, just as it has been so many times before."

The attendant waits several moments to see if the man has anything else to say.

"That is all for now," Velen relents. "Please go. I need to return to my rest."

"Of course, Master Velen, sleep well."

The attendant turns and exits out the door, closing it gently.

"If only I had time to save my work," Velen reminisces quietly to himself. "I labored so hard and for so long, but now it's gone...lost on Ruuki uy'Daan. And with the damage to the ship and so much more loss, there is nothing left for us. Dearest Tyanna, forgive me. I wish I could've foreseen this."

Velen slides back under the covers and attempts once again to find peaceful slumber, a chore he has been unsuccessful at for many years.

+·+◆+·+

"Mother...?" the softly rasping voice calls into the cavernous rocky chamber. "Is your meeting... Completed...?"

"It is... My ssson..." she returns in a gentle but solemn maternal tone. "The messssage is sssent..."

"What is wrong...?" he asks as he studies her expression. There was sorrow in her eyes.

"I weep for them... But it is nothing new... And they are not the firssst..."

"As it has been... Many timesss before..." he reflects discreetly.

"Ssso many have been losssst... And they knew not why. How could they...? When they know not even... What he is... Or where he comesss from..."

"No one knowsss... Except for usss... And the Great Powersss..."

"They are a forgotten memory..." she retorts brashly. "As they should be! All except for him. But his day will come... And I shall be... The one who bringsss it!"

"What musssst we do now...?"

"We can do no more... But to wait. We are not ready. Not yet. Time will passss. Thisss world musssst grow... Jusssst a bit more..."

"Do we have time to wait…?"

"Barely enough… I have foressseen it. He mussst crossss our path… Before he can make… His approach. But he will ssstumble… And thisss will awaken… Our watch. The ressst will fall… Into place… As we make… Our resssponse. From there… We will follow… The tracksss… He ssset down… During his own journey. And the circle… Will finally close. He will be… His own undoing…"

The great silver wyrm snickers silently as her long-time plans come into fruition. She had spent the greater part of her lifetime on this. And in her case, that equates to nearly an eternity. Her son, barely a mature dragon in his own right, had left the room while she was engaged in her recent meeting with her spies, a group of beings who made occasional visits into the chamber to report their sightings to her. These beings were a most unusual sort, not made of flesh, but instead of elemental light and energy. She had been using them since the beginning of this pursuit to keep a vigil on her prey while she focused on other matters closer to home.

For almost a millennium and a half, she had been monitoring the progression of events as she moved from place to place during her corporeal reinstatement on the world that was once her ancient native home, but now donated to a younger generation of beings. She used her spies as her eyes and ears, though the term is very loosely applied as these beings don't technically have eyes or ears in the traditional sense. Through them, as well as her potent prophetic visions, she could observe events in such far distant places as other worlds, and even other universes. But her visions were often unsettling, as she witnessed such occasions as the Daanen-Aryku and their torment.

The great beast rested quietly in contemplation, a creature of almost immeasurable wisdom and age, though virtually none of it truly acquired during her current incarnation. Her son sat next to her hoping to comfort her. She glanced at him as he gazed into her eyes consolingly.

"Fear not… My ssson…" she appeals. "For I have ssseen… Far more… Than what they have sssuffered…"

"But your ssstory... Of their lassst attack... It leavesss their numbersss... Precariousssly thin..."

"It does... But they are not... The lassst of their kind. The othersss... Can ssstill be redeemed..."

"How do we do that...?"

"Before all elssse... The circle mussst close. I will firssst sssee... My turn with him... To remind him... And to inform him... That he is not forgotten. Not by those... Who felt his touch... When his kind once ruled..."

"And after he has fallen...?"

"Then we will sssee... To the ressst... And repair the damage... Left in his wake. Thisss will be the time... When my Children return..."

The two rest from their discussion, with nothing else to do but allow the passage of time to carry her plans to the next step.

Chapter 3

ARRIVAL OF FATE

"So, where are they coming from?"

A young dark-skinned female elf addresses her two companions, her charged voice carefully tempered to remain at whisper level so as not to be overheard by the nearby line of enemies.

"It doesn't make any sense to my eyes," she continues. "They're just coming right out of the bleedin' rocks!"

"Hush, Relissa," the male member mumbles. "They're too close."

"Don't you hush me, you round-eared spark-thrower. I'm more to knowing how to be quiet than you ever were!"

"Relissa! Haran! Both of you be silent!"

The last of the group, a tall female Daanen'kai soldier, speaks sternly under her breath.

"At least wait for them to pass before you have at each other's necks again."

The three companions, who often teamed up together, were on a scouting mission, each for their own respective commissions. In their own ways, each was something of a misfit amongst their kind, so they fit together perfectly as friends. They had been sent into a region known locally as the Badlands, a territory recently discovered to be taken over by a large orcish settlement. Furthermore, reports have been coming in of an increase in activity in the area, so the demand for more information was evident.

Relissa Moonshimmer was a scout runner for a faction known as the Night Elves. She was dressed in a snug suit consisting of a mottled black and green leather tunic, leggings, and boots. The outfit also included a hood, but at present it was folded back along her shoulders, leaving her short, pale gray-white hair exposed.

Haran Carronel, a mage acolyte, served as a member of the human faction's Academy of Arcana. He wore the robe of a mid-classman student, a dark red fabric with delicately embroidered silver stitching along the lapel, cuffs, and hemlines.

The acting leader of the group was Petty Officer Kaliya Nazég, a soldier dressed neatly in synthetic partial plate composite armor embedded with several monitoring sensors and a control interface cuff on one arm. She also carried a hefty two-handed lightning lance strapped across her back. This was a ranged weapon capable of discharging pulses of electric shock. She wore the heraldic symbol of the Naarg uy'Sodrad Sentinels Force, the militia service of the Daanen-Aryku faction.

Between the three of them, they accounted for the majority of the allied races on this world, with the only exception being the dwarven community which did not seem to involve themselves in military activity.

They had positioned themselves behind a row of low-lying boulders near the base of a small knoll, and further camouflaged themselves with bits of shrubbery gathered from around the area. From there, they could safely observe a column of orcs emerging seemingly out of nowhere from a crevice within a large rock formation jutting out of the ground atop the knoll. There was nothing on the other side of the formation except open space, and there were no known cave entrances in the area.

"It must be a portal of some kind," Kaliya conjectures. "More damnable reinforcements, as if they ever needed those."

Kaliya strained to look for evidence to support her theory. She could see faint flashes as each new appearance took form.

"See there! Did you see that flash of light?" Kaliya states as she gestures at the latest arrival.

"Right," Relissa admits. "So, it's more of the smelly beasts from Ruuki uy'Daan, is it?"

"If it is, they found themselves a new coordinate index to arrive here. How do these portal things actually work, like if you try to aim one?"

"Unfortunately," Haran responds. "I'm the wrong one to ask that question. They don't teach us this level of magic at the academy."

"By the sound of it, they barely even teach you the word 'magic' in there."

"Yeah," he chuckles feebly. "And then we have that."

The column of invaders begins to slow, with only a few appearing at long intervals now.

"It's slowing," Kaliya notes. "How many does that make now? Anyone care to guess?"

"A frightening number, to be sure…" Haran suggests. "Look down there. The canyon floor is black with them."

Below the observers was a wide river canyon. The line of orcs had been making their way along a ridge descending into it and across roughly to its center where it flattened out into a plain. There, one could see a vast army forming into a large mass. At least three primary encampments could be distinguished.

"This is most disturbing, Kaliya," Haran confesses, wincing at the sight of the immense gathering. "Such a powerful invasion force so close to our own cities…"

"That's got to be at least a good two hundred thousand, no less," Relissa considers as she surveys the size of the assembly. "Although I can't say I ever saw that many bodies at one time and in one place."

"To be honest," Kaliya muses. "I find it hard to believe they might have that many as a full population count. How do you feed that many mouths when you don't even have any organized farming or mass food production?"

"Either way," Haran concludes. "I think it hardly matters, whether more or less by one thousand or ten, it's a dangerous amount, simply by looking at it."

"And arriving so close to us…" Kaliya ponders as she turns to her companions. "We'll need to report back on this. I doubt any of our superiors will be pleased, but they'll need to know. Maybe we could arrange a joint preemptive strike. If we hit them hard enough by surprise, we might be able to..."

"What in all the bleedin' hells is that?" Relissa exclaims as she points back up the hill.

Kaliya and Haran both turn their focus to see what the young elf has spotted. For a brief instant, they thought they saw the forms of three new arrivals, but then they vanished almost as soon as they appeared.

"Huh?" Kaliya whispers. "Did I just see something go poof?"

"Aye! They went invisible, I'll bet."

"A magical cloak?"

"Maybe...but I thought I saw them put something up to their mouths."

"Perhaps they took some manner of potion," Haran muses. "We have something like this back home. But then the question becomes, who are they? I've never heard of orcs using potions of any kind."

"Relissa, did they come out of the rocks?" Kaliya asks.

"Aye, I think so," she nods. "But they didn't look orcish...too small for that, their girth was more like that of a human, but wearing leathers...black leathers. I didn't see any skin showing."

"That sounds like a covert group to me," Haran muses. "Black outfits for stealth, although it's broad daylight here, and that's something better left for a nighttime thing. And again, unlike orcs, or at least as I understand their manners."

"Maybe it was nighttime wherever they came out of," Kaliya considers. "But there are no humans on Ruuki uy'Daan. At least, that is, there never were before. So unless something new has occurred..."

"Maybe it was some of those Flame Elves?" Haran wonders.

"Possibly," Kaliya considers. "They're known to be taking sides. But what were they doing over there and why arrive in such a way as this?"

"We're seeing an awful lot of bodies coming into the region. Maybe there's something special going on. If they're part of some sort of covert operation, maybe this is a return of forces from somewhere. Maybe it's not from Ruuki uy'Daan after all."

"Oh great, Haran, and thank you, but you could be right. This could be a return of a special operation somewhere, and using Flame Elves to make trouble for yet another society, like they did once with us."

"This is bad, peeps." Relissa groans. "But now, I hate to break it to you, but shouldn't we be a little bit fizzed about where they just went?"

"Um, actually…yeah," Haran shudders. "And if it's a return of some kind, why did they go into a cloak? That's still covert, and they essentially own this territory."

"Cu'Nar's pity, you two…" Kaliya moans. "You're going to cause me to pull my horns out before this day is done. They could be anywhere by now."

Suddenly, the three of them began to realize that whoever these new arrivals might be, if they went under an invisibility cloak, they could be scouting the local area, leaving the three of them suddenly vulnerable.

"Duck low and be silent!" Kaliya whispers urgently, though it seemed in vain.

Their hiding place was designed to conceal them from the orcs up the hill, a line of workers, so it seemed, that were bringing supplies into the camps below. It did nothing to cover their backsides, however. If these scouts were not travelling to the same location, this left a lot of possibilities open.

Kaliya moves close to Relissa's ear to whisper into it.

"Look sharp. Maybe you can catch of glimpse of their movements."

"I'm spying, but these buggers are too good for my eyes," she responds quietly.

They carefully scan the surrounding area, looking for any sign of movement. Relissa's eyes trace the ridgeline into the canyon while Kaliya tries desperately to see evidence of footprints in the dusty soil just in front of her. Haran turns his focus over his shoulder to see if anything is coming up behind them.

"Um, ladies?" he pronounces nervously.

"Haran! You idiot, what are you…" Relissa begins as she turns her attention to the mage.

"Yes, Relissa, I'm fully aware of that. Still, I hardly think it matters at this point. Look there."

Positioned directly behind the trio at a comfortable distance, squatting low to the ground stood the figures of three darkly clad individuals. The only truly visible parts of them were their eyes peeking out from narrow slits in their masks. They wore what appeared to be black leather suits, very trim and tight-fitting. On their belts was a pair of daggers, several pouches, and some odd-looking clips that held some manner of stone-like objects. Everything appeared to be designed for stealth and quick movement. They held their positions, watching the companions, but made no offensive movements.

"I'm not going down without a fight!" Relissa announces sternly as she starts moving her hands to her daggers.

"Relissa, stop!" Kaliya intercedes. "Don't go for your weapons yet. They could've taken us, but they didn't."

Relissa stares at Kaliya for a moment, clearly frustrated at the suggestion.

"And that's reason enough to just sit here?" she balks, returning her gaze to the three visitors.

"Look at them. They're not close enough to pose an immediate threat, and I think it's intentional."

"Uh huh, so are you going to suggest we all sit for a nice cup of tea next?"

"Relissa, please… There's something different about this group. I can almost feel it."

"Right, and I know about you and your…feelings. How many times did I pull you out of a pinch because of them?"

Haran shifts his position, feeling a bit exposed as he was previously sitting behind the other two while facing through the blind, but now he was stationed in front where these visitors were concerned.

It was only a short moment passing, but it seemed like an extended lull to the three friends. The strangers looked them over carefully, as though they were the subject of a laboratory study. Not knowing what to expect, the companions waited, their muscles tensed, ready to reach for any weapon to serve in their defense. The strangers began to make a series of odd gestures with their hands, what looked like some form of silent communication. Then they abruptly rose up and moved off, travelling down an embankment away from the cliffside, and away from the group.

Kaliya and the others watched intently, breathing only a very slight sigh of relief, but unsure how to interpret the actions of the figures.

"Well, that was convenient," Haran muses. "All right, so what now? They didn't seem to care about us being here, but that still doesn't answer the one about who they are."

"It couldn't be Flame Elves then," Kaliya suggests. "Covert or otherwise, I think they would've attacked."

"Unless we're just not that important to bother with…"

"I suppose that depends on the stories people tell about them."

"Right, and also who tells them. Some folks back home like to brag things up a lot."

"Well, whatever it is," Relissa argues. "I'm not ready to get myself planted with the sticks just yet. Where are they off to?"

Kaliya unconsciously gets up and begins to follow the strangers, keeping a fair distance away so as not to provoke anything unpleasant.

"And just what are you doing, you blue-skinned cliff-runner?" Relissa demands.

Her reference was a hidden tease relating to the Daanen'kai's cloven hooves, and their similarity to certain animals known to the local races.

Kaliya ignores the comment and moves onward. Her two friends are forced to follow close behind to back her up, as foolish as it may seem.

The three strangers moved some distance away from the canyon cliffs, and therefore out of sight of the orcish settlement below. There, they lined themselves up in a row, spacing themselves apart at roughly the distance of two arm-lengths. All the while, they seem to be watching the three companions and their movements, but apparently content that the three are not a serious threat. Satisfied with their positions, they each pull out one of the odd stones from their belts.

Kaliya looks on, halting at a distance so as to appear nonthreatening, and wondering what these small tokens represented, with her two companions watching at her side. She cautiously glanced back at the canyon, but by this time, they were no longer in easy view.

The strangers held the stones in one hand and began making circular motions over them with the other one. The onlookers could hear chanting, as a small glowing disc formed around each of the strangers at their feet. The shimmering discs intensified and erupted into vertical showers of energy, rapidly enveloping the individuals. The showers swirled around their bodies, up over their heads, and into funnel-like shapes spiraling back down into the glowing stones in their hands. The glowing subsides and all is quiet again.

"Haran," Kaliya asks. "That was some of that magic stuff, right? Did you pick up on any of it?"

"Sorry, I didn't understand a word of it. It may not be a language I'm familiar with."

"But can you tell what they were doing?"

"I wish I could, but other than apparently enchanting those things, I couldn't say for what purpose. Those look like some manner of rune stones. But even more curious is that these people do not give the general appearance of mages."

"Maybe they're a special class."

"Compared to me, even my grandmother would be that much. And she was a dressmaker," he chuckles ironically.

He pauses briefly in thought as he continues to observe the strangers.

"And I should probably again point out that they do not seem to care that we are standing here in plain view."

This detail was not lost on Kaliya or Relissa. These three odd visitors were performing unrecognizable acts seemingly without care or concern of the group who is watching.

The strangers placed the stones back into their pouches and they each pulled out a new one. They began weaving another chant and the stones started to glow, but there was no circle of energy at their feet this time. It is the stones themselves that are circled in energy. As the chant proceeds, the circles form into small columns, jumping up for an instant in their hands, and then settling back into a broad ring around the stone. The stones appear to glow brightly.

Kaliya glances at Haran, but he can only shrug. She then turns back to the strangers.

Each of the strangers then claps their free hand over the stone they are carrying. As they do this, they are quickly engulfed in a sphere of energy. A muffled sound of gushing air and muted thunder issues forth as the three strangers vanish.

"Very well," Haran sighs. "Now I think I have your answer, for whatever good it does."

"Aye," Relissa returns sardonically. "I'll bet you do."

"Portals…" he reasons. "If I'm not mistaken, we just saw the three of them vanish into portals departing away from here," he glances at his two friends to gauge their expressions. "To this end, I would further suggest that the previous display was the enchanting of additional rune stones, possibly to serve as an entrance back into our space."

"Buggers!" Relissa yelps as a chill runs down her spine. "And why do they need more of those! If they're Flame Elves, their city is just over those hills to the south. They could run the distance."

"Wait a minute!" Kaliya interjects. "They made new portals? Then what is this thing up here in the rocks, if not a portal?"

"Um, good question," he titters. "Maybe they didn't like the location?"

"I…well…" she grumbles softly. "And regardless, they didn't seem at all interested in us. At least, it didn't look that way if they were so content to do all this in full view. But then, why are they here?"

"Yeah," Haran adds. "Relissa, I'm actually siding more with Kaliya for this point. I don't think they were Flame Elves at all. Why would Flame Elves use covert means for any reason out here in the middle of nowhere? Are they hiding from us, or the orcs? They should have no real reason to suspect we could be out here. After all, it's almost suicide to be here right now."

"Aye, I suppose," she admits reluctantly.

"Maybe you were closer to the real answer, and this is the reason they went covert. They're not elves, but humans after all, and they followed the orcs through their own portal. This could also answer Kaliya's question, to create their own as a backup. Did you happen to notice no new orcs have arrived? Maybe there aren't any more on that side by now. Maybe, if these people are going covert, something happened on that side and these orcs are running from it, not returning from some operation."

"Running from it? But with humans on the other side?"

"Yeah, that last group was bringing in a lot of supplies, so it could be more like an evacuation. What if whoever it is they're running from found them and are using cloaks to spy on them, especially if they're passing through a portal to places unknown?"

"Bloody hell, Haran, while I'm not against your idea, this doesn't help by much. So, are we looking at a new invasion? Who are these peeps, and do we need to worry about them now? Maybe…um… maybe…oh grand…" Relissa whines as her breath quickens. "I think we'd best be skittering out of here, like now!"

"I would normally agree, but one must also wonder how far we'd get if their return is imminent. If those were elite mages in leather outfits, they looked like they could probably catch us fairly easily. And I'm not an especially fast runner without one of our speed potions."

"Oh wonderful…"

"I could easily outrun both of you," Kaliya admits. "But you know I would never leave you behind. And we still have unanswered questions about this. Although I'm certainly no more anxious to stick around to find the answers if things go bad. And yet, I'm also reminded that there is the issue of our superiors. You know as well as I, they'll want a report."

"Aye, fine!" Relissa grumbles. "But they can hear about it some other day! What good is a report if your bum's tied to a post over a roasting fire?"

"You're right again, Relissa," Haran relents. "However, I must wonder whose roasting fire is the worse…theirs, or our superiors."

This minor reckoning brought into focus the unpleasant memories within each of them of how poorly viewed they were in their professions back home by their seniors.

Relissa momentarily recalled the casual disregard of her supervisor, Enforcer Baeleron of the Guild of Wardens in her home city of

Solinaia. He barely had any faith that she could carry out the work assigned to her. Instead, he would chastise her for her excessive fondness of animals and the time she spent playing with them.

Haran had his problems with the Dean of the Academy in the human city of Rolsklinde, who was commonly demeaning of most of the lower and mid-classmen, but had a particular affinity to berate Haran.

Kaliya was an underdog amongst her ranks in the Sentinels force. Her commander was typically hard on her. Although his meaning might be intended to toughen her against the enemies they faced, she often took it personally as criticism over her failures in past assignments. She also held poor esteem within the eyes of the governing Elder Council.

None of them favored the idea of returning home with only half a story just to hear the traditional scolding over yet another botched exercise. But the pause for consideration would be short-lived, as a disturbance was soon heard off to the side and down the embankment from them.

The three of them turned to look at the new sight. Lumps formed in their throats as they quickly realized that any chance of escape was now gone, for what they now beheld were three separate portals opening up in those places where the darkly clad scout-mages once stood. Their eyes were fixed and unblinking, waiting for the first figures to emerge, almost certain their doom was near. Then they came, row after row jumping into view. Soldiers! They each exited a portal, and then darted off to one side, allowing space for the next to appear. It was a neatly choreographed dance of armor glimmering in the sunlight.

"Humans…" Haran notes. "They do appear human!"

"Well, Relissa," Kaliya accedes. "You got that one right."

"Aye, fine," she mutters softly. "I'm happy they're human, but not so happy for how they're dressed."

"That's a military force," Haran offers. "This much you can be certain of."

"But it doesn't make sense, Haran," Kaliya refutes. "Where in all the nether-space would humans and orcs find common residence?"

"Better to ask, why would they want to?"

Relissa mulls the suggestion based on their previous discussion.

"Maybe the orcs invaded some other world and stepped on someone's toes?"

"That doesn't sound too hard...for orcs. And these toes are attached to a strong military body. Just look at those people!"

The soldiers were all dressed in brightly gleaming armor and colorful heraldic tabards depicting the shape of a dragon head and wings. The wings merged into the shape of a shield, and emblazoned within that shield was the image of a sturdy hammer crested by a set of weighing scales, and a laurel of vines held in claws underneath.

A good two dozen of these troops, composed of both male and female members, arrived on the scene followed by archers. Next came several people in robes with arcane symbols, and lastly followed by another group, also in robes, but with priestly hoods.

"That's a healthy assortment," Haran muses. "They look like they could take on a hefty opponent even for their small number."

"But not this bunch in the valley, I'll bet," Relissa smirks.

"An infiltration team," Kaliya considers. "And covertly positioned out of view from the valley. It's the orcs they're after."

"And what about us?"

As she pondered these words, a small group of soldiers formed up and ran towards the three companions. Startled by the sudden attention, they stumbled backwards and instinctively moved their hands to their weapons ready to draw and fight. But the soldiers did not make any aggressive movements to attack. Instead, they simply created a line a few paces in front of the three observers, with their shields drawn and firmly planted in the soil, and their swords exposed and held in a relaxed posture alongside.

"Hold still, everyone," Kaliya urges. "That's a defensive wall formation! Don't do anything to provoke them. They're forming a line of some kind."

"Are you sure we're not going to end up on the ends of their pikes?" Relissa complains while nervously fidgeting with her daggers.

"I think I can say..." Haran advises cautiously as he glances around, "...at least with some certainty, the answer is likely no."

"Oh?" Relissa yips as she glares at him. "And just how do you figure that one?"

"Simple. Look behind you. What do you see?"

Relissa was already overly nervous about what was in front of her, but she took a cautious peek over her shoulder anyway. The space was empty.

"Our escape," Haran continues. "They're leaving it open. In other words, they're not trying to surround us."

"Yet!" Relissa adds defiantly.

"He's right," Kaliya agrees. "This is a statement: Don't come any closer. It's just to keep us away from them."

"Well, um…all right, maybe."

They watched as more troops take up a defensive formation in the general direction of the canyon.

"Yeah," Kaliya continues. "They have their eyes on those orcs down there. We're simply extras. But now, who are they? Haran, do you recognize that heraldry pattern? Maybe we have some survivors out there who chased these orcs off their land."

"That would be a remarkable suggestion, but no, I don't recognize it in the least."

Haran looked closely at the markings.

"A dragon symbol," he observes. "That's ancient. And then a hammer and a balance, and some kind of vine? Such a peculiar assortment! We have some really old books in the academy on icons and glyphs. I recall Tristeen telling me a few things she saw once. If I were to try to guess by the symbolism, the balance often refers to Law, and the hammer might suggest Judgment. Dragon images are often depictions of physical might or ferocity, but the vine thing… I wouldn't expect to see that on a military emblem. Such things as that typically represent nature, or a peaceful devotion. It doesn't seem to follow in the general context here, especially on soldiers."

"Strength, Law, Judgment and Peace…" Kaliya speculates. "Could this be a message depicting a process?"

"That's one bugaboo of a process," Relissa winces. "Be nice to us or ba-bam, we do it the hard way," she chuckles.

"Heraldic symbols of this sort," Haran surmises, "may be used by an order of knights or perhaps a religion. I would hardly imagine they describe a process...more like a belief."

Relissa was surveying the assortment of people in front of them, now being drawn to the priests and mages in the rear. But as her eyes settled on one cluster, her body became tense, and she started fidgeting nervously.

"Oh buggers!" she cries with her voice suddenly trembling. "Um, peeps... Can I start panicking again?"

"What, Relissa?" Kaliya urges.

"There, those peeps in the robes...mages, I think. They're elves! And not any of us..."

The trio was drawn to a group of mages forming on one side of the assemblage. They appeared as pale-skinned elves.

"What, by the grace of the cu'Nar, are they doing here?" Kaliya gasps. "Those look like Flame Elves!"

"But they're wearing the same heraldry as the others," Haran notes. "Smallish badges on their robes, do you see it?"

"They're the bleedin' enemy! I know it!" Relissa yelps. "These traitorous buggers are teaming up with them!"

"Hold onto yourself, Relissa." Kaliya cuts in as she tries to calm the nervously twitching elf. "They still haven't made any aggressive moves against us. Remember, they're facing the orcs!"

"Buggers to that, I say! So they suddenly got tired of the smelly wankers."

"Maybe, maybe not... Like I said earlier, maybe this is a rogue group of survivors."

"From both sides?" Haran muses. "That's an interesting thought, but it doesn't fully explain this heraldry and why both sides are wearing it. We don't have elves living in Rolsklinde, and I don't recall any humans ever living in Solinaia, right Relissa?"

"Aye, we don't mix things up like that around here. So, I have to admit, why are they doing it?"

As the flow of troops through the portals comes to an end, those same three darkly clad scouts reappear, along with two other people.

The first was a tall, ornately dressed man with a moderately pale complexion and shoulder-length silver-white hair. Although the hair might suggest age, his complexion foretold anything but that. His broad form was covered in brilliantly shining armor composed mainly of plate and chain. A long flowing cape ran down his back, partially covering what appeared to be a large two-handed sword. He also sported a dagger on his belt, along with several pouches and clips of various sizes, not unlike those of the scouts standing next to him. His armor seemed to glow, even beyond what the natural daylight would normally afford.

The second was a woman, perhaps the same size as Relissa. Her complexion was perhaps the palest of all the strange visitors, and her long hair was the color of spun gold, neatly braided and wrapped so as not to cause any inconvenience with her movements. Her features included deeply slanted crystalline blue eyes and gracefully pointed ears. But as appealing as these may be, her most prominent feature was a pair of huge snow-white feathered wings folded up behind her back, reaching from the ground to well over her head.

"Bloody flippin' hell," Relissa croons. "What is that business?"

"Have either of you ever seen anything like that before?" Kaliya asks hesitantly. "That…woman…over there…"

"Gods' pity, look at her!" Haran exalts quietly. "Look at her gown!"

Ever the mage acolyte, Haran always could point out the blatantly irrelevant to the greater general concern. Kaliya and Relissa both glare at him, astounded that he could find any interest at this moment in time to one's fashion apparel.

"Buggers, Haran," Relissa barks. "Has it been so long since your last little tryst with your girl that you forgot what to look at?" she giggles. "What about the rest of it?"

"Well, all right, the wings do tend to stand out a bit, but they're obviously foreign at this point, so I think the idea of rogue survivors is out by now."

"Foreign…like from another world?" Kaliya wonders. "All right, I suppose I have to agree, but it only offers up new questions now.

What world would have all this in one place? But now, what about that gown? Why does that catch your eye over the prospect of wings?"

"Granted, the wings are a remarkable sight," he offers. "But as for the gown, do you know what that stuff is? Mithril! An entire garment made of it!"

"Mithril?" she asks. "I don't think I've heard of that before."

"I'm not at all surprised! It doesn't exist in our world. I know of it only from a few precious examples held at the Academy."

"Haran, that's a contradiction. It doesn't exist except for a few precious examples that do apparently exist."

"Well, all right, Stretch," he smirks. "Let me clarify. Native deposits don't apparently exist, or at least no one has ever found any that I'm aware of. But these artifacts are said to be very old, so maybe they have another origin."

"That's better…"

"Which lends me now to wonder about his armor. See how it gleams?"

"More of the same?"

"I don't think so. The color is a bit off. I can see how mithril may be used for a chain weave, perhaps, but not as likely for plate."

"Why?"

"Rarity, if my understandings are correct, but that doesn't answer the other question, as his would be even more of an anomaly."

"What do you mean? What else can it be?"

"I can't be sure, but one name comes to mind. The trouble is it's little more than a legend…a material called adamantium."

"Never heard of it…"

"It's supposed to be similar to mithril, but found much deeper. Of course, this doesn't necessarily help as for the rarity issue, but both of these are said to be highly magical, many times stronger than steel, and much lighter."

"I'm not aware of this material ever being found on Ruuki uy'Daan, not that any of us might know what to look for, and certainly never used by orcs, or anyone else I know of. Which means, whoever these people are, they're from some completely new world, and by what we're looking at here, they must be very well resourced. But still, back to my original question. What about the woman herself? What race do you think she is? Does anything from your study come to mind?"

"By the physical features, she would appear elven, but with those wings..." he shakes his head.

"Wings..." Relissa mutters silently and lost in thought. "Elves with wings...from the Ancients, the time before the Flowering..."

"Relissa?" Kaliya inquires as she turns her attention to see what the girl is mumbling about.

"I don't know..." she relents. "I'm trying to remember something my Dah once tried teaching me. A piece of me is now wishing I had actually paid attention to any of it."

"Have you ever heard of anything like this?" Haran asks.

The girl sighs feebly.

"As you probably know, my people seem to delight in keeping up their ancient traditions and babbling. Personally, I can't see the point of it! Not when we're at war and all the hells are coming down in our ears. Who'll be left to remember anything after that, I say!"

She pauses for another sigh.

"But if you must know, I can just barely remember something mentioned about some kind of elves with wings. It's from a long time ago...a very long time ago."

"How do you define 'a long time' as compared to 'a very long time,' hmm?" Haran asks jestingly.

Relissa sneers at him mockingly.

"A long time would be well before my years, and maybe even before that of my Great Grand-Dah. A very long time goes back to before my people ever came to this skank of a world. There was a time we once called the Flowering. It was a time when many of the elven races began moving here and there to find new homes. We call them the Ancients. Some of them went to other places, but ours came here...not that it served us. We got lost and never found our way back. We've been alone ever since, and don't you go about itching me on the why of it," she finishes angrily and shaking a finger at him.

"All right, enough, you two," Kaliya intervenes. "I swear! Keeping you two apart is becoming a full-time job. Listen... Let's see if we can overhear some of their conversation. That man over there," she points discreetly to the tall one in the ornate armor. "I'm going to guess he's a commander of some sort."

"He looks more like a noble to me," Haran comments.

"Whatever, he's giving orders. Can either of you understand what he's saying? I don't recognize it."

Both Haran and Relissa strain to listen to the words being spoken by the new arrivals. Unfortunately, neither of them is able to interpret anything. The language they were using seemed completely foreign.

A soldier wearing a crest, with the appearance of a ranking officer, walks up to the trio after speaking briefly with the tall nobleman. He passes around the line of soldiers forming the defensive wall to step directly in front of Kaliya. He carefully studies her, from horn to hoof, even peering around her form to examine her tail. He next moves on to Relissa. His expression furrows somewhat as he studies her face. He takes special note of the positioning of her hands, which are still gently gripping the hilts of her daggers. He utters a word with a serious demeanor.

"Drow?"

He glances into her eyes, and then back to her hands.

"Relissa!" Kaliya commands in a hushed tone. "Pull your hands off your daggers, girl. Don't make him nervous, we're not in a position to start a fight."

"I doubt your daggers would even cause any harm to him," Haran adds. "Not with that armor."

Haran's eyes were locked onto the officer's chest plate. He couldn't help but notice how it glistened, but it wasn't simply because of a bright shine. Up close, he thought he saw waves of energy flowing through it, as if it was charged somehow. He also paid attention to a series of badges and tokens decorating the upper right quadrant, probably awards of valor, and another one on the left with some writing on it. The language of the writing seemed as strange as the spoken form.

Relissa stares at the officer. She was nervous. Deep down, she knew she was outmatched by this assembly. She cautiously rolls her eyes first to Haran, then to Kaliya. Reluctantly, she returns back to the officer, closes her eyes in a show of submission, and pulls her hands away from her daggers in an open-palmed gesture of non-hostility, afterwards clasping them in front of her.

The officer nods and moves on to Haran. He examines the mage up and down. He looks back at the two women, then returns to Haran. He tries to initiate conversation, but the words are unrecognizable. Haran can only shrug his shoulders and shake his head. He then tries to offer his own greeting, but the man shakes his head in a similar fashion, and then begins to walk away.

"Um!" Kaliya blurts to get his attention.

The officer turns around abruptly to focus on the gesture. He strolls back casually to assess her.

"Relissa," she offers privately. "Your people have a native language, right?"

"Now wait a minute, you!" the girl protests. "Didn't I just say a bit ago I never paid any attention to my Dah and his Elven Tradition babbling?"

"You may be one of the very few possibilities for us to communicate with these people. I can't let it go without at least trying. And we do need to find a way to talk to them."

Relissa grumbles something unintelligible as she folds her arms across her chest and pouts.

"She does have a point, Relissa," Haran adds. "You should at least try."

Realizing words were useless, Kaliya tried using gestures to signal her intent. She points a thumb at Relissa and gesturing to highlight her elven features, like her pointed ears. Then, looking across at the crowd, and especially the winged elf, she points again, finishing with a speaking gesture.

The officer studies her and picks up on her intent, swinging his glance at the others behind him before nodding and moving away.

"Well," Haran notes. "It looks like he got the message."

"That's a good sign," Kaliya replies. "That he's willing to try."

The nobleman had already moved forward by this time to survey the canyon and the large orcish settlement. He was crouching low on the ground peering over the cliff and shaking his head, laying it in his hands for a moment, as though he was despairing. A moment later, he pulls himself away and moves back with the others. The woman steps up to him and lays her hands on his shoulders. She speaks softly to him.

He composes himself, calls up the three scouts and begins giving some manner of instruction. He gestures with his hands in several directions outward from their position. One scout then runs off at blazing speed to the south parallel to the river canyon, while another takes off to the north, and the last disappears due east.

"There's your answer to those scouts and their running speed," Haran observes. "Potion or no, they're clearly augmented with some sort of enchantment. These people seem to make no small use of arcane spell-craft."

"They must be very advanced as compared to your people," Kaliya notes.

"That really isn't saying much, Kaliya, all things considered. We simply don't have that much."

Haran pauses briefly in contemplation, silently debating what he had seen of the actions of these visitors so far. He turns to the other two with his thoughts.

"All right, so let's consider they're at war with these orcs on their world. Relissa mentioned them possibly invading someplace and stepping on someone's toes. If these are the toes they stepped on, and they're so well resourced, and now those same people are here on our world, this might mean they completely wiped them out on theirs."

"Jiggers," Relissa moans. "Now there's a thought."

"And further, if they're chasing them back here, these people don't simply give up once their home soil is clean."

"And that's another, even scarier thought. So, what do you think comes next? They finish the job here?"

"Maybe..."

"But again, what about us?"

"I think it would be prudent for us to make sure what side we're on, don't you?"

"Aye!" she yips enthusiastically.

"But Haran," Kaliya interjects. "This might be fine against the orcs, but we still have all the rest, the worst of it being the Suuden-Aryku. They don't go down as easily."

"Maybe, but we don't know the full extent of these people, either. Whatever the case, we should try to investigate. If they're going up against the orcs, they may step on a few other toes along the way."

"Yeah, you're right, so we should warn them, at the very least. But I also took notice of his face a moment ago. He doesn't look so happy about what he sees out there."

"Perhaps it's simply that he didn't expect to find so many in one place. I can't be sure. That's a tight clustering with a lot of bodies. It would be a hard fight to clean it all out."

"A messy one, too..."

The officer walks over to the nobleman with the message from Kaliya suggesting a parley between the two elves. As he does, they both glance over at the companions standing expectantly behind the defensive line.

"I'm going to be bad at this, you know that?" Relissa mourns.

"Do the best you can, Relissa," Kaliya replies reassuringly. "It's all we can ask. I'm also thinking I could try something of my own if this becomes too difficult."

"What's that?"

"Well, I can maybe recall a little bit of Orcish. It's a leftover from...well, from a long time ago. A time I'd much rather forget."

"You mean from Ruuki uy'Daan, right?" Haran asks soberly.

She doesn't answer.

"That must've left a really deep mark on you, Kaliya. I worry for you sometimes."

"Thanks, Haran. It's good to have friends, and I don't have too many these days."

"It may also be subjective if these people can actually speak it."

"True."

The nobleman and the woman approach the companions. Moving around the formation, they bring themselves squarely in front of the small group. As with the officer, they both make careful examinations of each member, conversing with each other as they go along. No doubt, the details of this revolved around the peculiar physical features of the Daanen'kai female, the nervous look on the dark-skinned elf, and the feigned look of calm on the human's face.

"Relissa, it's your game now," Kaliya encourages.

Relissa casts a brief look of anxiety at Kaliya and turns to the strange, winged form of the fair-skinned elf. She sees that the woman is wearing a rather expensive-looking necklace of gold and colored gems which sparkle in the light. The necklace looks to be fashioned into sections that are clasped together, where each of the sections is ringed with some manner of symbols that give off their own light. Yet more enchantments…Haran was right about these people; they do seem to use a prolific amount of magical effect.

The woman looks at Relissa, waiting for her to speak. The girl sighs heavily and takes a tiny step forward with an agonized look forming on her face.

The man and the woman both stood waiting, clearly giving the nervous young elf the first word. Relissa never liked being the center of attention, and she fumbled with her pronunciation.

"Uh, m-mah…meh…" she sighs. "Uh, my…MY! My…my… gah…goh… Dammit Kaliya," she scorns discreetly. "I can't even remember the standard greeting!"

There was a mild chuckle, but not from either of her two friends. It was from him, the nobleman.

"Mae govannen?" he mentions humbly.

His voice was deep and carried a powerful presence.

Slowly, a memory stirred, as if awakening from a slumber. Relissa's eyes grew wider, and her jaw went slack as she angled her head up to look into his face.

"Aye…" she replies softly. "I understood that."

"Great!" Kaliya applauds enthusiastically. "Now, what else can you do for us?"

Relissa cranked her head around to her Daanen'kai friend and looked at her with a staggered expression, as if she wanted to speak. But then, thinking better of it, she turned away.

"Lle quena i'lambe tel'Eldalie?" the nobleman offers, seemingly enjoying the spectacle.

She stared at him blankly. He smiled and tried again.

"Lle…" he begins, pointing at Relissa, "quena…" gesturing speech from his mouth, "i'lambe…" making a waving motion outward from his mouth, "…tel'Eldalie?" he finishes by pointing at both Relissa and the other woman, again directing their attention to their elven features.

Relissa paused to consider the words.

"I wouldn't expect him to be the one talking," she mutters.

"Obviously," Haran suggests, "they must've shared this knowledge at some point."

"Right, I suppose that's a natural. Why didn't we ever do that?" she chuckles softly. "Um, so he says you speak, um, something… Elvish. Is he telling me, or asking me?" she briefly ponders the missing word. "Oh buggers! Language! Right! Do you speak the Elvish language! You need to turn the words around."

"How do you turn those around?"

"Well, technically, it's more like 'do you speak the language of the elves.' But it takes a little interpretation."

"Fair enough, but I think you should answer as no. You definitely need help," he grins.

She looks at him crossly, and then sighs in reluctant admission.

"You're right. I hope these two are more patient than my Dah. Maybe I can do this, but it's been a lot of years. I never imagined I'd actually need any of this."

Relissa looks back towards the man.

"Um… L-Lau… Uh…amin naa…n'quel."

"What was that?" Haran asks.

"Hopefully to say I'm bad at it."

"Fine and good, at least now there's no more question to it…as if there ever was to begin with," he snickers.

Relissa nudges him on the shoulder for his little rub.

"Relissa," Kaliya suggests. "We should ask him his name."

"Oh sure, put some more pressure on me," she gripes before turning back to the nobleman. "Um..."

Relissa ran her fingers through her hair as she was trying to think of the phrase. This was one of many simple phrases she remembered having to study as a child, but that childhood was many decades ago.

"Uh, mani...naa...something. Wait, I have to go formal on this, which means to use en lle," she mumbles to herself trying to recall the right words.

Kaliya observed the nobleman as he looked at the winged elf next to him and smiled. He looked mostly human, though he was significantly taller than average. But at this range, she was able to notice a feature which suggested there was something else to him, maybe not so human after all. He had gold-colored eyes, and not just the deep yellows she had seen in other creatures. These appeared as nearly true metallic gold! She then looked at the woman, and hers were similarly strange, appearing as though they had a glittering effect, like actual crystals.

Relissa tried again.

"Mani naa... Name, girl, what's the word for name... Essa! Mani naa essa...um...en lle?"

"Heru Thaelyn naa essa amin," the man declares proudly with a smile and giving a slight bow.

"Arwen Aerlie naa essa amin," the woman replies just after him, followed with a polite curtsy.

Haran pulls up close to Relissa's ear, though she appeared to be going into shock at this moment.

"Should we assume their names are Heru Thaelyn and Arwen Aerlie, then?" he asks.

The girl gasps and quickly throws a hand over her mouth, nearly jumping back a step with her eyes bulging wide.

"Oh buggers..." she squeaks. "Aye, close enough, but it's in Elvish, remember..."

She quickly lowers her head and makes a courteous bow to the visitors.

Haran stares at her, feeling a shiver for the implications.

"And the translations?" he asks briskly.

"Those first words were Lord and Lady."

"Great gods, two nobles?"

Haran quickly follows her in a bow. At the same time, he looks over to Kaliya, who is still standing upright.

"Kaliya!" he calls to her, trying to maintain a humble demeanor in his voice. "Do your people hold any special service when confronted with nobility?"

Kaliya had been watching Relissa in her atypical display of reverence, but quickly jerked her head around to Haran, then back to the two people standing in front of them.

"Huh? Oh, I…uh…technically no. We don't have any."

She nervously adjusts her posture for her own show of deference, displaying a traditional Sentinels' salute of a wing gesture with her hands raised just below her neckline and a subtle bow of the head.

Thaelyn and Aerlie both smiled at the clearly unprepared display, and he followed on this topic by pointing at Relissa.

"Mani naa essa en lle?" he asks.

Though shaken slightly, she pulls herself up and replies.

"Relissa…naa essa…amin."

She was barely able to choke it out, but she let out a pleasant smile when she realized she really could do this.

"Ar' en lle mellonea?" he continues.

Relissa holds up a gesture of pause while she tries to interpret the words. As she does, she begins unconsciously speaking to herself again.

"Ar'…that's the word 'and', then to me, and last is mellonea… Mellon is friend…oh yeah, plural! So, what is it? He's asking about my friends."

She looks to both sides of her. Kaliya was the ranking officer, so she intuitively takes her first.

"Um, oh, I don't know the word for the rank. In fact, I'm not even sure if we have one for yours."

"Just use our given names for now," Kaliya suggests. "That'll do well enough."

"Good, thanks," Relissa replies.

She turns back to the two nobles and points to the tall Daanen'kai member.

"Kaliya naa essa…" she begins, but fumbles on the last word.

"…he," Thaelyn finishes for her.

She smiles at him, and then turns the other way.

"Haran naa essa…" she fumbles again, but looks to Thaelyn for help.

"…ho," is his response, with a gentle smile.

"Good work!" Kaliya applauds. "You up for one more? Then maybe I can try a little to give you a break."

Relissa looks up at Kaliya with eyebrows raised in anticipation, as her confidence is inspired by now.

"See if you can ask him where he's from."

"I'm not right and proper sure if I can remember that one, but I'll try."

She looks back at Thaelyn, struggling with her memories to form the new question.

"Manke, uh…manke naa…lle…"

She lays her hand on her forehead as she tries to think of what comes next.

"Tuulo'?" he finishes.

Relissa looks up at him, thankful for the help.

"Diola…lle," she responds.

"Lye naa tuulo' Tae'Eladar!" he exclaims as he waves his hand across his assembled troops.

Haran had always considered himself to be a rather clever student, so he decides to take a moment to interrupt the conversation.

"Relissa, what part of that last one was the name of the place they're from, the word Tae'Eladar?"

"Aye, I think he said, 'we are from', and that name. Although I can't be sure what kind of place they're talking about. I don't remember ever hearing that name before."

"My guess is it's the name of a world," Kaliya submits. "Based on everything else, and our earlier conversation, it simply makes the most sense. But it still demands a lot of questions for the composition of their troops, these orcs, how and why they're here, and so on."

"And let's not forget that armor," Haran adds. "It has to be from somewhere else, rather than around here."

Kaliya now realizes it's her turn. She looks into the faces of her two friends, sighs, then prepares to clear her throat to see if she can recall something she had hoped she would never hear herself use again.

◆◆◆

"Aerlie…"

Thaelyn turns to speak to the lovely, winged form of his wife standing next to him.

"As much as I would adore standing here refreshing this dear lost child on her ancestral heritage, which she truly should have learned before she outgrew her first set of britches, we have more pressing matters to attend, and using Elvish on her is not going to prove productive anytime soon."

"I agree, so what do you suggest?" she replies. "We find ourselves in a strange new world, and they don't seem to recognize our native tongue, to say nothing of anything ancestral."

"And this simply begs the question of who they are, where they came from, and then how they found their way here. You did take notice of that dimensional membrane we passed through during the portal jump, correct?"

"Yes, and that was certainly unexpected. And then to find these people here. All I can say is it must have occurred a very long time ago if they do not speak our modern tongue, and worse, if she has forgotten even the ancient one."

"Indeed," he nods. "And we do not have the luxury of time to teach anything at length," he glances in the direction of the canyon and the large body of orcs. "Therefore, I find myself with a dwindling number of options."

"You mean like what, perhaps a melding?" she asks.

"It would certainly offer a solution. But my concern is that these three are clearly too agitated for such an elaborate exercise. This man, with respect, does not look sturdy enough to withstand the pressure, and this young elven Child's mind leaves a few issues of concern simply to grasp the nature of it."

"Clearly, they're nervous. We're probably a surprise to see in their midst, and if they were previously spying on these orcs, then to see us arriving…"

"Yes, so the situation is poor all around. But this simply leaves…" he gestures with a hand to the tall, blue-skinned figure, which seemed curiously lost in thought at the moment. "And I am unsure even of her."

"Her figure is indeed a new one…" Aerlie observes. "Just look at how tall she is! Gracious."

"Yes, she certainly holds an impressive stand. I might say between seven and a half to eight feet."

"And with ram-like horns projecting out of her temples, a smooth slender tail, and cloven hooves for feet. These are features you might normally find on a creature living in Sigil, or maybe from the Lower Planes."

"Her skin color, that pale blue, is not so common, though," Thaelyn continues.

"Abishai have that color sometimes, right?"

"Yes, but typically it runs with deeper tones. And she does not match the other features, at least not perfectly. Not as I recall them. She is too, well, appealing for that," he admits jestingly.

"Be careful, my love, or you might find another lightning bolt in your back," she winks.

Thaelyn grins and coughs gently.

"Yes, and this time I am fairly sure it would hurt," he chuckles. "But needless to say, I would sense her origin in that case, and we would not be discussing it. We might already be at each other's throats," he muses at the thought.

"What about the eyes?"

"Yes, and then there are the eyes. That glow…a pale blue-white, almost like a background illumination. Not something you would see from any creature of the Lower Planes…perhaps from the upper realms but not the lower. The spiritual energies involved are of a different polarity there. Though, you would not likely find such a creature as her in the Upper Planes, either."

"But this might indicate a positive alignment, rather than negative. I can sense it. She seems like a pleasant soul."

"This is fair enough," he nods. "So, clearly, she is charged with positive essence. But where it comes from, I know not. This is not something I would expect to occur naturally, not with such potency, and not on a Prime world."

"Not on a Prime world…" she muses. "Could she even be native to this place? If she cannot be from the Outer Planes, at least not those you might be familiar with, can there be another? Or are we simply speaking of an unusual sort to be found here?"

"Well, I am aware the Powers do enjoy overseeing the great variety of life as it arises on one or another Prime world, so we might have found one such example."

"Maybe, but an odd lot it is, to be combined with humans and elves, themselves who ought not to be native to this place."

"True enough," he declares. "And a Morier on top of that. I would not expect to see one such as her to be standing so casually alongside any other race without planting a dagger in their backs," he sighs softly. "The migration must have found a detour somewhere, if to bring them here. Maybe this place belongs to the tall one, and the others intruded upon it. But it must have occurred at a very early moment."

"Early enough for them to grow together," she considers. "But Thaelyn, if this Morier is peaceful, it had to be from the time of the Flowering, maybe even before. The Crown Wars spoiled a lot of things for them, as you know."

"This is true. We might have found a pure example of their original breed."

Kaliya and her friends listened to the exchange, although it was all foreign to them, but the extended conversation clearly implied the two nobles were just as curious about them as she and the others were about their visitors. She also took notice that she was once again the focus of another careful study, and is pulled from her recollection. She finds herself feeling a bit uncomfortable by this time.

"Relissa," she whispers. "I realize I'm a lot different from the rest of you, but am I really so strange that I draw so much attention?"

"Well, you're a good bit taller, and your skin tends to stand out, along with your horns, and such. I personally don't think much of it, but then I've known you for a long time. They're new here. So, I'll just say, don't let it get to you."

"I suppose…"

Aerlie was still in contemplation of their discussion when she returned to one particular aspect of their subject matter.

"Thaelyn," she offers. "Regardless of who originally belongs to this world, how in all Creation did these others find their way here? Where are we that these people could find access to this world? I mean, if we consider the migration to Tae'Eladar, they used that old artifact to link the two. But that's still on Tae'Eladar!"

Thaelyn skims his view across the plain, and then up to the sky.

"This is a good question. Look there, above us."

He points towards the western horizon about a quarter of the way up.

"Their local moon?" she guesses. "All right, I see it's not Selûne, and this simply exacerbates the situation. This is one more indication we're not on Tae'Eladar anymore."

"And there are too few other options for the answer when you consider our journey. So let us test a theory. Follow my mind."

Thaelyn closes his eyes and moves his hand up to his temple in a moment of concentration. Aerlie mirrors the gesture.

Relissa and Haran are both waiting for Kaliya to pull together enough courage to produce the first words of orcish she's used since childhood. The continued conversation between the two nobles, which was spoken in their native language, delayed the inevitable. Then they began to notice the strange gestural activity.

"What are they doing?" Relissa whispers to Haran.

"Interesting," he responds. "The gesture suggests some kind of psychic projection. What are they looking at, the moon?"

Kaliya listened to the whispers made by her two friends. She briefly glances at them, then back to Thaelyn and Aerlie, trying to follow their gaze.

"Is this sort of thing known to either humans or elves?" she asks.

"To my understanding," Haran replies. "Very few humans have any serious psychic abilities. Some might claim a few odd things, but I don't pay much mind to it, personally. Then again, I was noticing during our conversation that he doesn't look entirely human, certainly not like any we have back home."

"Don't look at me," Relissa shrugs. "I don't see this sort of thing with my people."

"My...he...him..." Kaliya sighs tensely. "V-Velen..."

"Girl..." Relissa soothes. "Why do you always have so much trouble with that name?"

"It's old now, you know this. Anyway, I know he once studied telepathy...it was part of our old factional studies...but these people look like they're trying to envision something out there. I doubt even he was that good."

Thaelyn and Aerlie both project their minds outwards as they reach for the distant lunar body.

"Come with me, Aerlie." Thaelyn communes telepathically. *"I will take us to the surface of that body. From there, we can see better what is around us."*

Psychic travel tends to move rather quickly, as Thaelyn leads the two of them ascending a clairvoyant stairway to the nearby lunar surface. Almost as soon as he mentions it, they arrive at their destination, where Thaelyn refers back to Aerlie again.

"See here. We are above the skies of the world, no longer obscured by the aura of daylight. Do you see?"

"Stars!" Aerlie exclaims. *"Then, we are inside a natural plane. Good gracious, I thought I'd never see the like, certainly not for a long while until our people were ready to depart from home."*

"But they would still need an exit from the Shell that surrounds us. Although, at this point, I might suggest we have found one."

"Yes, and so conveniently, if also unfortunate for the circumstances. But Thaelyn, we did this due to those orcs. What about those people down there, how did THEY do it?"

"Indeed, this is yet another curiosity, made worse for the fact of crossing

a dimensional bound, not simply a space between local destinations. And at the same time, referring back to the orcs, it is also rather disturbing. Not only can these foul heathens open portals of any kind, and not simply to a new world within a plane, but to a new plane entirely!"

"Granted, 'tis powerful magic, to be sure, much more so than might be expected of such creatures. But take ease, my love. We'll not let them escape us again," she declares, trying to comfort him.

"Yes, but this is not my full concern. It is not that we might see them escape again, but rather that they can perform such feats at all. Where did they learn this skill, I wonder? It was never my proper understanding that they could wield so much power."

"Could it be related to this uprising and the ultimate source of it? Maybe they befriended someone or something that gave them forbidden knowledge?"

"This could possibly answer it, although it is still disturbing to think that any such creature portraying itself as a god would hand out such knowledge so frivolously. And then we have the other implications. They could use this against us, if they so desired, possibly to open portals inside our cities and wreak havoc before we could mount a proper defense."

"Intolerable, to say the least...and especially after their behavior in the past. This actually reminds me of Master Zharaden, but in this case a real threat using portals."

"Indeed!"

Thaelyn gradually withdraws them from the mental projection back into their physical selves. On returning, Aerlie glances back to Relissa and Haran, both of whom are staring in wonder at them. She smiles innocently and shrugs.

Kaliya seizes the moment and clears her throat to draw the focus of attention. In her best manner to vocalize the rough tones, she tries to pronounce her words.

"You...speak...orc?"

Thaelyn feels a slight shiver run through him as he stares into the tall female's eyes.

"Aerlie, she knows Orcish."

"Badly, but true," she replies.

"This does not bode well for us, Dear."

"That she can speak it, or that she is so bad with it?" she smirks tenderly.

"Are you aiming for another mark, my dear?" he retorts playfully. "No, I mean to learn a language takes time...time and exposure. And orcs are not known to give out free lessons."

Now Aerlie felt cold.

"Meaning, she's been around them long enough to pick up something. And that means..." Aerlie suggests, now pausing to look into the canyon. "Those over there may not be refugees after all, at least not all of them. Some of them may have pre-existed in this world."

"This would further explain their source, and that of the corruption. And our war may not be as close to an end as we had hoped," he concludes.

Kaliya could see the sudden looks of consternation in their eyes, and this made her feel a little worried.

Relissa gives a playful slap on the warrior's back.

"Well, love, it looks like you've dropped your boots on this one!" she proclaims, looking down at Kaliya's otherwise bare hoofed feet. "Well, in a manner of speaking, that is," she finishes.

Kaliya recomposes herself and tries again, putting more of an imperative tone to the statement.

"You...speak...orc. Yes?"

"Yes," Thaelyn answers smoothly. "How do you know this language?"

Kaliya quickly realizes she is outclassed in her skills by the ease of his pronunciation.

"Well, so much for simply knowing it," she muses softly. "This guy sounds like an expert."

"They must have a lot of experience behind them," Haran suggests. "But this also defies a simple invasion and stepping on someone's toes."

"Yeah."

Now she finds herself trying to interpret the question.

"Me…talk…learn…girl."

"Gods, help us," Aerlie moans with a strained chuckle. "She's simply awful. Let us hope this is a sign of her lack of time in study."

"Yes," Thaelyn agrees. "I also took notice of her reaction. She did not apparently expect my fluent response."

"All right, so they might not know of the orcs and their long occupation in our world."

"Possibly. But what about more recently?"

"If they have their own troubles, I might say it was behind their backs."

"Good enough. But this now demands us to know the sequencing. Which came first in this world? And then, I am wondering about something new. Is she suggesting she learned this as a child? And how could this be from such creatures as those?"

"All I can say is to ask her," she suggests.

Thaelyn glances at Aerlie with a smirk. He then looks back to Kaliya.

"How did you learn this as a child? How long ago?"

Kaliya now found herself recalling old memories of her youth… the attacks, the screams in the streets. But she had to go beyond that, to a time before…a time when things were calmer. Once, on Ruuki uy'Daan, she recalled her people associated with the primitive orcish clans. There was trade, communication, and Kaliya learned a few words here and there from these otherwise peaceful interactions. But now, how to explain this?

"Um…" she begins. "Me…girl…home…not here. Um…orc home… Orcs…friends…old days."

"Aerlie!" Thaelyn exclaims softly with his face flushing slightly.

"Calmly, my dear, her diction is badly muddled."

"Granted that, but those statements leave me with several distinct new fears. Orc home? Not here? And then, old days."

"Yeah, and this could answer the one about your sequencing. The orcs don't belong here, maybe like so many others."

"And therefore, our troubles back home. Whoever taught them to use portal magic is driving them across multiple worlds."

"Kaliya…" Relissa mutters imperatively as she notices Thaelyn's shift in tone. "You'd better say something else, fast. He didn't like that one. What did you just say?"

"He was asking how I knew Orcish. I was trying to explain about my childhood and the old days when my people once held relations with them. Well, sort of, at least back home on Ruuki uy'Daan."

"Well, explain it better, before he cuts you a new opening."

Kaliya snaps back to Thaelyn. Nervously, she fumbles with something further to say.

"Uh…me…people…not orc friends…eh, now days. Um…old days…uh, go bad. Yes, orcs go bad, old days…um…"

"Yes," Thaelyn soothes. "I understand…"

Kaliya nods anxiously, "Yes. Uh, not…not orc friends, now days. Me people…run…here…" she points figuratively at the ground and glances around the area. "Orcs come. More bad."

She holds her breath and waits for a response.

"This sounds even worse," Thaelyn muses. "They are being chased."

"She's certainly scared," Aerlie concludes. "Probably of us and what we might represent, at least as much as anything else."

"Indeed, and her usage leaves much to be desired," Thaelyn admits. "And she knows this. Not here, old days, and a friendship gone bad, as if orcs could be friends with anything to begin with. Interesting."

"Could this relate to that change in behavior?"

"Perhaps. Something polluted it, and it spilled over into our world for some reason. But this simply means we have more questions to answer. I think I will have no choice but to do a meld, but I will need to consider my selection carefully."

Thaelyn looks calmly into Kaliya's eyes.

"I understand. But your Orcish is bad, Child. Not a good way for us to speak. Wait here."

Thaelyn raises a hand in gesture to reinforce the command.

He turns to walk away with Aerlie in tow. By this time, the scouts would be returning from their circuitous route to examine the surrounding area. His attention is caught by the obedient line of soldiers that stood in his path forming the defensive line in front of the companions.

"Formation dismissed!" he commands.

The three friends look on as the soldiers break formation and return to the rest of the detachment, feeling somewhat relieved by the sight.

"Kaliya, what was the final verdict?" Haran asks. "We're still alive, so I guess you got it under control?"

Kaliya breathes a sigh of relief, though a bit disappointed as Thaelyn strolls away.

"Well, yes and no. I got the message across, but I think he doesn't want to use Orcish with me, not that I can blame him. But dammit! I didn't even get to ask anything!"

"Relax, my friend, there are other ways, perhaps not as glamorous, but I suspect we are far from done here."

"Like what, drawing pictures in the dirt?"

"Maybe. At least it's something."

"Whatever the case," Relissa moans. "There he goes, walking away from us."

"Look there," Kaliya directs. "His scouts are returning. No doubt his attention will be occupied as they report in. I guess we'll have to take a back seat to that for now. He's obviously a very business-oriented person. My guess is he has to be part of this military body, nobility or otherwise."

"Well, fine then! Are we at least free to move around a bit?" the elf huffs as she looks over the scene.

"The guards were called off," Haran surmises. "So, I guess that means we're no longer restricted."

The three of them carefully take a few steps forward, taking note to see if anyone else might step in their way. No one does.

Kaliya places her attention on Thaelyn, who is currently involved with the scouting patrol. She moves in a little closer, but keeps a comfortable distance so as not to appear like she's tailing him, rather just trying to move into the general proximity.

Haran, not really sure what to do with himself, tries to give the impression of innocently meandering about, hoping to observe more of the troop deployment at closer range. His fascination with their armor and the magical devices and enchantments he's been observing draws most of his attention.

Relissa felt a little more confident now than before, and gradually steps towards some of the other elves she saw earlier. She was beginning to remember some of her old lessons by now and found herself curiously drawn to them. Clearly, these weren't Flame Elves, as the descriptions entailed a rather distinctive appearance. She could see members of this group that looked similar, but others were very different.

She came near to a small gathering that had become engaged in conversation. There was an assortment of professions represented here. Some wore robes, like those of a mage. Others had hoods and what she interpreted as holy symbols draped on cords around their necks. A few others were clearly archers. Some appeared to be of elven character, while others were human.

She didn't approach very near, just enough to get a clear look at a few of them, but she was noticed, nonetheless. Several of them turned to face her. Suddenly, she felt very self-conscious and ducked her head to turn away.

"Child, do you wish to come closer?" calls a priestess.

Relissa pulled her head back up to look at where the voice came from. She didn't immediately recognize what was said, but knew it was in the Elvish tongue. She smiled shyly, realizing instinctively that she was in the presence of something greater than herself.

"Come," calls the priestess again, waving her hand to attract Relissa's attendance.

"All right, girl, you're in for it now," she mumbles under her breath as she slowly steps closer to the group.

"What is your name, Child?" asks the priestess.

Being somewhat practiced by the exchange from her earlier experience with Thaelyn and Aerlie, she answers back much more easily this time.

"My name is Relissa."

"Are you a lost member of the Ssri clan?"

Relissa goes blank, not understanding most of that, so she fumbles to explain her poor skills.

"I…not speak…Elvish…um, not good…"

Aerlie, with her keen ears, overhears the introduction and marches over to assist.

"This one has very poor skills in the old ways," she reports. "We'll need to coddle her until she can learn anything useful. Keep the expressions simple and try to help her fill in the missing pieces."

Aerlie smiles at Relissa and places a hand on her shoulder to reassure her before turning away again.

The priests smile and try again, starting from the beginning and working to help the inexperienced young female reconnect with her heritage.

Kaliya stood not far from Thaelyn, hoping to get another chance at speaking with him. She waited patiently for him to finish with the scouts. But then, surprisingly, he seemed to be issuing new orders, this time pointing directly through the orcish camps. The scouts lined themselves up, and each began a brief chant. After only a few seconds, they waved the arcanic energies around their bodies and vanished, as if pulling a cover around them to hide from view.

Kaliya looked on in amazement. Being up close like this gave her a good view to watch, although it didn't help her to understand what she saw, other than to say they went invisible again. Now the question was where they were off to this time that they needed to be cloaked for it. She needed answers. More and more of these questions were building up inside of her, and she needed to know. She decided to take this moment to see if she could get his attention again.

"Thaelyn?" she calls.

On the announcement of his name, he turns his focus away from the settlements in the canyon to face Kaliya.

"Um…where…you…go?" she asks loosely.

Kaliya tried once again using her badly pronounced Orcish to see if she could get a response. To help augment her intention, she attempts to gesture the disappearance of the scouts and the apparent direction she thought they took.

By now, Aerlie was returning from the gathering of priests helping Relissa. She joined by Thaelyn's side.

"How do you think you'll answer this one, my dear?" she asks jovially.

Thaelyn paused for a moment.

"This will be complicated," he sighs. "And surely too much for this young lady to understand with her poor language skills. There can be only one effective way, at this moment," he states determinedly.

He turns to Kaliya to give his response.

"Listen to me…here…" he points at his head.

Thaelyn takes in a deep breath and closes his eyes briefly to collect himself. When he reopens them, there is a soft glow inside. He stares deeply into Kaliya. She had only enough time to make a slight gasping sound, and then darkness surrounded her.

Gradually, an image begins to form in Kaliya's vision again. As it grows stronger, she is able to make out forms. The vision initially wavers somewhat as her natural inclination to resist the effect tries to override it. The focus weaves in and out until finally it forces its way into view. Shapes and sounds now come into clarity, and she begins to realize she is centered inside an orcish camp!

Her instincts took over immediately. She felt around on her back for her weapon, but it was missing. She quickly examined herself, only to find she was stripped of her armor and now wearing commoners clothing. She started to panic.

Frantically, she looked for an escape route. Around her, she saw workers tending to fires with large cooking pots, and warriors honing their weapons. Some were engaged in conversation, a few even playing some sort of brutish game, battering each other to see who could stay standing the longest.

Strangely, although she was standing in plain sight, none of them seemed to be paying any attention to her. Orcs were walking around the camp, passing right by her, and not giving so much as a sideways glance at her.

And then, darkness came again as suddenly as it did before.

Another image began to form. Now she found herself in a village of some kind. She saw humans walking along the streets. There were children at play, men working in shops, and women carrying baskets. All seemed cheerful and content, until she began to hear a rumbling sound off in the distance.

She turned to find the source of the disturbance and observed a mass of orcish warriors stampeding into the village from across an open plain. War cries and death chants followed the horde as they trampled carts and set torches to buildings. The villagers shrieked and ran.

Chaos ensued as the orcish raiding party hacked their way through the populace, carrying off crates, barrels, and other supplies, and even a few bodies. She also noticed some of them dragging away several of the remaining villagers, kicking and screaming as they slid along the ground. The image seemed to transform before her eyes, from a peaceful village to charred ruins. All was quiet again when darkness fell one more time.

Kaliya then saw the image of the orcish camp appear before her again. As with the previous vision, she saw cooks and warriors at their various tasks, but now there was something new. She saw humans, badly beaten and forced into servitude. She watched in horror as the orcs abused the poor victims, kicking them down and laughing. A large commotion came up behind her and she turned to face it. A short distance away, a man had fallen, and the basket of food he was carrying had spilled onto the ground. He looked too weak to stand up anymore, worked nearly to death by his captors. A large orc struts over carrying a heavy club. He raises it up and brings it down hard on the man's skull, crushing it in one blow. The orc then lifts the body and places it on a table near one of the cooks, who had just finished carving up another one prior to that. Kaliya felt ill and covered her face, and the image faded to black yet again.

Light returned and she found herself standing on the edge of the canyon, directly overlooking the settlement she and her friends had been scouting earlier. Then the image deformed, as if she were made to look through a scope. Sections of the landscape magnified, and she could see forms moving quickly across the land. They were the scouts, but made visible and glowing, as if to highlight them against the background. They scattered throughout the large encampment and seemed to be looking for something.

At distinct intervals, she could see regions of the camp enlarged, focusing first on a scout, and then another nearby body which would be highlighted amongst the orcs, but it appeared human, instead. At another moment, the body might be elven. She even saw the generic form of a Daanen'kai, similar to herself. Then, the image faded one final time.

✦✦◆✦✦

Haran felt like he was visiting a carnival, although he could only browse and not touch. He admired the glimmering of the armor and the radiance of the weapons in their sheaths and slots. So much of it seemed to glow. There were only a few dozen troops present, but he studied each one carefully with a bright grin on his face. He was lost in the spectacle of the parade. A few of the soldiers even offered to show off a little.

His experience with mithril was limited to only a few occasions within the academy when the Dean would display a small collection of figurines that had been in their possession for as long as anyone can remember. Adamantium, on the other hand, was virtually unknown, revered only in stories passed along from a nearly forgotten history. But what he saw here was like a festival of dancing light. He could barely comprehend how much was on exhibit. Chain and plate, swords, and shields, it all sparkled.

"How is it possible," he muses distantly. "Kaliya was right, they must be very well resourced. In fact, they would need exclusive access to their own mines for this much. But how much would all this cost in the end? I should think it would cost a king's ransom, at the very least, from what I ever heard of it. And yet, look at how commonly they wear it. Did they in fact pay so much for it, or is it actually so abundant in their world that it doesn't carry such high value to begin with?"

As he made his rounds, his mind continued to drift away.

"Maybe this is just an elite guard. Yes, that makes sense, actually. A noble lord goes out into untamed lands, so naturally he would bring the best protection money could buy. Of course!"

But there was still a nagging little voice in the back of his mind.

"An elite guard, maybe. Or is this only the tip of something bigger. If we recall what we were saying earlier, and they were at war on that other world, and now they're here, then this could simply be an advance guard. Elite or otherwise, if they are so determined to drive them to another world...great gods!" he halts his motion abruptly. "If we say they drove the orcs completely off that world, what if he actually owns that world, or at the very least, he's a military leader for the owner. Then we could be looking at a significant military force here. What if they're all like this? Oh my..." he croons dreamily.

His mind drifted into the realms of his imagination, marveling at the possibilities of a powerful army stocked in such a manner, numbering in the thousands...no, tens of thousands, as he expanded his visions. He could not possibly know what a true world power might have for an army, so his imagination was limited to only what he could comprehend for the local societies. Nevertheless, what a grand sight that would be. His eyes beamed in a dreamlike gaze. No other army would be able to oppose it!

"If this could be the case," he surmises fondly. "Those orcs likely wouldn't stand a chance. No wonder he drove them away. My goodness, even by comparison to our own..."

His mind is suddenly yanked out of his dream state.

"By comparison..." he contemplates now more seriously, "...to us? Make allies? Oh dear gods, yes, we should make allies with this man. He could conquer our entire world with such an army! And the Flame Elves...and the Suuden-Aryku...hmm... What about them? He'll no doubt encounter them along the way, especially if he starts attacking the orcs. They'll surely get nervous after a while. Gods be blessed, we could be speaking of an apocalypse if we foul this up!"

The reality of the world suddenly returned to him of the war he and the others were currently fighting…and losing. His captivation with the marching opulence faded. An idea started to burn itself into his consciousness. He searched around to find Kaliya, wanting to share this with her. Spinning around, he spies her standing over near Thaelyn. But she looked a bit…odd.

Haran trotted briskly across to the small group. He pulled up alongside Aerlie, who was standing pensively, observing the other two. He looked at her, almost ready to speak when he remembered she used a completely different language.

Aerlie was in careful observance of the telepathic communion between Thaelyn and Kaliya. She took care not to disturb them. She saw the arrival of Haran next to her. When it looked as though he was attempting to communicate, she put a finger to her lips to instruct him to be silent.

He backed off as he continued to gaze at his tall friend. She appeared to be in some sort of trance, barely able to stand upright. He also took note of Thaelyn's glowing eyes. This now frightened him. He turned to Aerlie again, and then back to Kaliya, but without any other recourse, he nervously dashes off to find Relissa.

✦✦✦

The priests were finding it a bit of a challenge to educate Relissa, and so they called over a few of the mages and a couple of archers to join in. In the tradition of elven society, they made something of a game out of it. She actually started to enjoy herself. Such a light-hearted attitude was relatively uncommon amongst her people. Years of war had taken their toll and dampened much of their spirit.

The mages found it of value to use a form of demonstrative magic to help illustrate certain ideas and concepts, conjuring up images and giving them names. Relissa had never seen the use of magic in this fashion before. It changed the entire learning experience for her.

Among the basic lessons, the mages brought up orbs of colors, hovering in place. Then they would call them out.

"Calan *(red)*... Malen *(yellow)*... Calen *(green)*... Elu *(blue)*."

They refreshed her at the simple art of counting on her fingers, which she also lost over the course of years.

"Er... tâd... nêl... canad... leben... eneg... odog... toloth... neder... cae."

Soon, they were helping her to assemble simple sentence structures.

"Mani naa tanya *(What is that)*? Manke naa lle autien *(Where are you going)*? Tenna' ento lye omenta *(Until next we meet)*."

She recalled when she was a child in the stuffy libraries of her home, listening to the boring monotones of her instructors. The idea there was simply to fill your head with as much tedium as you could tolerate during one sitting. It was no wonder she couldn't learn anything. Her mind would tend to freeze up after only a short while.

Here, with these people, the lively atmosphere generated enthusiasm for learning, and she didn't even feel as though she was in school. She picked up the words quickly, as much from the recollection of her original studies as what she was receiving now. In time, however, she did start to notice a few differences in certain phrases and words from what she recalled of her old lessons. It would seem the language has changed somewhat over the millennia since her people left their ancestral home.

After a while, she felt empowered enough to try asking a few questions. Like Kaliya, she had her own desires to learn what these people were about, but she found her interests drifting more towards personal goals than professional. Her people were the only remaining...friendly...elves in this world, detached from their ancestry and feeling forgotten. Now, she had something new to look at.

"Tell me of your people. Who are you?" she asks with the words coming slowly and carefully chosen.

"We are the Children of the Flowering," responds one priest.

"The Flowering..."

Relissa could not help but recall what she said only a short while ago to Haran. The Flowering was an important moment in Elven history. She suddenly felt very meek at the blatant mention of it.

"Do you know of the Flowering?" he asks.

"I know a little bit of the Flowering. Old stories… What place are you from?"

"Our world is called Tae'Eladar. Do you know this name?"

"No, I don't. Is that name to say Beloved Green World?"

"It is! In the words of our people. We gave this name to the world we discovered, but if your people came here so long ago, maybe you do not remember. What about this name, the land our people first came to…Sein'amar, New Home."

Relissa struggled to recall her father's lessons on the Ancients. Although the first name was lost on her, this other one made her feel faint. Only one thought rang out by now.

"Sein'amar…" she wheezes. "Yes! I know that word. But…all of you? Them too?" she points at a group of humans nearby.

"Our world has many people in it. It has been this way for a long time. It was originally the home of humans, and ours came later."

"Really! But you…um, you're elves. We have a name, it's old… Tel'Quessir."

"This is the ancient name of our people, even from before we came to Tae'Eladar."

Relissa moans wistfully as she nearly doubles over and drops her head into her hands.

"The Ancient Ones…" she mumbles, now using her native tongue. "They've found us! Buggers to bugaboos… Oh, Father, I'm so sorry. I am in shame before these people. Why must I be the first to make contact?"

She understood now. These were no migratory elves, as her people became. They were the originals, or at least they were the descendants of them, which placed them in the ancestry of their early beginnings, the core of their society.

Her people had tried desperately to hold on to whatever scraps of their heritage they had left, trying to keep with the proper traditions. But having no more contact with their homelands or their kin, they were isolated from the growth of the society of Tel'Quessir.

Similarly, before the war, the Flame Elves were in the same

situation. But the war turned them into horrible fiends, which isolated both groups even further.

"Relissa, Child, are you well?" the priest asks.

By this time, Relissa had collapsed fully to the ground and was now sitting. She tried to speak again.

"My people...your people...we came here in the old days, the days of the Flowering. We do not know where from now. We have a name, but only a name."

"You are lost?"

"Lost? Aye, we're lost! So lost that some of us think it was a dream. We call them the Ancient Ones."

She looks up into their faces with tears moistening her cheeks.

"You are not the same as me. Why?"

"We are many people and many clans," the priest responds as he turns to one of the mages. "He is a Calaer, a High Elf."

"Right, I know them. Some of them came with us once."

"Are they still here?"

"Um, aye, but not the same now. Something bad happened to them, now we're at war."

"Oh dear, I'm sorry to hear that. Anyway..." he next turns to an adjacent mage. "She is an Ithiler, a Moon Elf."

He turns to one of the archers.

"And here is a Taurer, a Wood Elf."

"Wow, but no elves like me?" she asks with a forlorn look on her face.

"There are those whom we call Morier. From the stories we hear, they look a little different from you...darker, and with red eyes. But they are evil in our world."

Relissa's expression turns to horror. Could it be that her people were the evil ones on that world just like the Flame Elves had become here?

"We call them Drow," the priest continues.

She remembered hearing that word before. It was the word the officer used on her after the soldiers first arrived, when he was inspecting her and the others.

"I heard this word from that man. But I am not a Drow," Relissa pleads as she hangs her head low.

"We know this, Child. We can see this in you."

"How did this happen? What did they do?"

"We had a series of wars. We call them the Crown Wars."

"Wait, I know that name. We have some history that talks about a Crown War."

"Only one? Interesting, and this helps us to understand the timing. But there were four more after that, and during this time, the Morier turned wicked on us."

"Four more...five of them? Oh grand...I'll bet that hurt..."

"Relissa!" Haran shouts as he approaches. "I need you! Something is up with Kaliya."

He kneels down by her side to meet with her.

"Are you alright?" he asks. "What are you doing down here?"

"I sort of collapsed when I realized who I was talking to here. It's a bit of a shocker."

"Um, them...these people?" he thumbs at the nearby group of elves. "All right, I suppose I simply must ask this, but I'm also in a bit of a fix."

"That doesn't surprise me, you round-eared spark-thrower," she attempts a small grin.

"Cute, so what is it that got into you?"

"Do you recall what I said about the Flowering and the Ancient Ones? Well, you're looking at them. This is where my people came from, once upon an eternity ago."

"Really! That's actually very interesting, and maybe it could answer a few questions. But can we call them friend or foe after all this time?"

"Well, they seem nice enough. They were helping me relearn a bit of Elvish just now."

"All right, that's a good sign. Maybe we can build on that."

"The thing of it is, I'm simply a disgrace in front of them for all I represent. Look at me, Haran. Would you think me to be a proper representative of my people in front of them after all this time?"

"Relissa, honestly…um, well…" he hesitates.

"Aye, I know the answer already," she gripes. "You don't need to rub it in."

"Now wait," he retorts. "Don't go putting words in my mouth. We're friends, and I would never want to say something to hurt you. Sure, you're a bit rough around the edges, but then look at me. Am I any better? And yet, here I am in a similar spot where my people are concerned, and probably not much better for it."

"All right, fair enough…sorry, Haran. So, what's the bit with Kaliya? Has she gone and done something wacky again?"

"I'm not sure how to answer that, but I think as friends, we both need to do our part and offer a shoulder to lean on, in case she needs it."

"Aye, that's one thing I'm good at. And thanks, Haran, for your shoulder just now."

"Of course, Relissa," he smiles.

They stand up together, and Haran motions to where Kaliya still seems to be standing in a trance. They run off to join alongside Aerlie, just as Haran did before.

"What's going on here, Haran?" she whispers in his ear.

"I came over a few moments ago to speak with her, and I found her like this. Aerlie bade me to be silent, not that I could do much about anything to begin with, so I went looking for you. She looks to be in some sort of trance, and I think Thaelyn is responsible. Look at him…his eyes."

"Aye, now there's a sight for you!" she winces. "So, what do we do about it? Do we wait? And for how long?"

"At this point, I couldn't say, but I don't think we want to disturb it. So, unless your new Elvish skills can ask a question or two, my only option is to wait and see."

"Aye…um, but it makes me wonder now."

The two of them wait, and during this time, Relissa takes a moment to glance discreetly at Aerlie. She studies the lines of her face, the color of her skin and hair, and finally the large white wings. She also notices an interesting tattoo mark on her forehead. It looked like a swirling wind pattern. Her newfound ambition causes her to try a small exchange.

"Um…" she gently taps the woman on the arm.

Aerlie turns and looks at Relissa as the nervous girl makes a new attempt at speaking.

"What is this?" she points at Thaelyn and Kaliya.

"Thaelyn is teaching her something."

"Teaching? How? And what?"

"She asked a question, but words are no good for us here. Thaelyn must use another way."

"But…um…I…wait. We have many questions."

"I know, as do we, but words are hard for us now. Your Elvish is better, but not great. But Thaelyn and I have an idea to help."

"Uh huh…more of this, is it?" she points more assertively at Kaliya.

Aerlie giggles softly as she composes her reply.

"We don't know yet. We're still thinking about it."

"Right…"

A few moments pass, and they notice movement in front of them.

Kaliya rocks forward, and then jerks back, seemingly unstable. She moans and displays a dazed look in her eyes.

"Haran! Get to the other side!" Relissa orders as she moves up to support the tall woman.

Haran circles around and takes an arm over his shoulder.

"Funny, you did say something about shoulders to lean on," she quips.

"Yes, and I should probably pay closer attention to my wording," he grunts. "This girl isn't one of your daintier examples."

Thaelyn closes his eyes for a moment and draws a new breath. When they open, they appear normal again. He waits for Kaliya to regain her composure.

Kaliya takes a moment to find her feet. She's only barely cognitive of the two people under her arms supporting her. She clamps her hands around her head, latching onto her horns as leverage. She was pale and felt a cold sweat after her ordeal.

"Whoa…" she wheezes lethargically. "Cu'Nar give me strength! I've never felt anything like that before!"

"Are you alright, Kaliya?" Haran asks.

"Huh?" she looks around. "How long have you been there?"

"We just arrived and found you like this. What the bloody hell happened?"

"Wait, give me a moment. I'm still trying to pull myself together. Is this the real world again?"

"Real world?" he winces. "Well, what's left of it, to be sure."

"Yeah, and thank you for the reassurance. Wow, that was a powerful link."

"A link?" Relissa muses. "What do you mean, link?"

Kaliya shakes her head in an effort to clear it. She feels her brow and tries wiping away the sweat as she struggles to catch her breath.

"Telepathy…it had to be. One minute I'm asking something, and the next thing I know, the whole world turns into a dreamlike scenario to explain my answer."

"But you look like your explanation turned into a nightmare," Haran frowns.

"Jiggers, girl," Relissa groans. "I hope this doesn't become a habit for how we talk to these peeps."

"Yeah," Kaliya nods. "I swear, it took complete control of me. Utter domination…I was simply along for the ride. I was scared at first, but once I realized what it was, I just let it go. It was fascinating, at least as much as it was frightening."

"Kaliya," Haran lectures. "That sort of power is not to be trifled with. I can't say I'm any sort of expert on it, but you really should be more careful."

"Yeah, well, under the circumstances, I guess it couldn't be avoided. If my orcish is so bad, and he needed to explain something complex, he might have no other choice but to do it this way. But it was surprising that he could do it at all!"

"How would this compare to that Velen fellow of yours?"

"Not even close," she shakes her head. "As far as I know, he's only able to pass a few thoughts this way and that. This would dwarf him by comparison."

As her focus returns, she relaxes her arms, giving the others a pat on their shoulders in thanks.

"Kaliya," Thaelyn pronounces in orcish again. "Do you understand?"

"Yes," she responds. "You go look…see people. Uh…us people, not want there."

Relissa places her hand on Kaliya's arm to get her attention.

"What was that?"

"He was simply asking me if I understood his visions."

"Would you care to share it with us," Haran jokes. "Or do we make a game of it?"

Kaliya couldn't help but crack a smile at the obvious attempt at levity.

"He's looking for potential prisoners out there. But beyond that, let's move over here to the side and I'll fill you in."

The three of them moved back over to where they started, just behind the small clutch of rocks that once served as a hiding space. Kaliya tells the tale of her visions; the orcish camp, the village, the slaves, and finally of Thaelyn's scouts with their current assignment.

"Well, I must admit," Haran declares. "I don't think I've heard of such brutality before by orcs, but maybe those in their world behave differently. Or, perhaps ours simply aren't as hungry."

Relissa wipes away a bit of sweat from her face.

"Or maybe humans don't taste so good," she jests. "The orcs tend to be sitting more to the south and west of here. Our people see them a bit more often, so we get more stories out of it."

"Anything like this?"

"Nothing as nasty as this, not that I ever heard, but I recall a few scouting reports of how they live, and it isn't pretty. Keep in mind…we don't have any more of the little towns here. The war has already dusted them all. And the city walls are too thick, making them too hard to hit."

"So, not as much opportunity for such raids, I guess. Ours is more of a kill-or-be-killed war, rather than a food fight," Haran surmises with a mild chuckle. "But what if he does find any prisoners? What can he do about it? There are too many orcs down there to mount a rescue. The hostages would be killed long before he could ever get to them."

"I need to get more out of him," Kaliya reflects. "I need another one of those telepathic visions."

"Don't you dare!" Relissa scorns. "I'm not picking up your oversized bum after another of your crazy schemes."

"Do you have a better idea, Relissa? Do you think you can rediscover the entire Elvish language in one afternoon to help us figure out what these people are up to?"

Relissa sighs heavily.

"Well, maybe not, but I'll have you know that while you were off in dreamland, I did find some help with it. I also had a few words with that Aerlie dame. She said they're putting together some kind of idea for better communication. This means they're also anxious to fix this, since they also seem to have a lot of questions. Maybe we should see what they have in mind first."

"Well, maybe… They might have some new trick to play, or at least better resources to work with. I'm just concerned about time. It's getting late, and I'm sure each of our superiors will be getting anxious to see us come home soon."

"Aye, that too…and I'm already thinking of what mine will say about all this. I learned these people are those same ones from our ancient homeland. They finally found us."

"Is that a good thing?"

"I certainly hope so! All I have is ancient history, but they look organized, so maybe they have something to say about it."

"And I also had a rather interesting thought occur to me," Haran interjects. "A desperate one, at least, and we need to talk about it."

✦✦✦✦✦

"Aerlie, that was a most enlightening experience," Thaelyn recalls.

"Oh? What did you find?"

"Well, if you were monitoring, you will know that I portrayed visions of the orcish atrocities to her. Her mind seemed remarkably sturdy, although I might also say undisciplined, as you could see from her withdrawal."

"Her first time... Everyone starts out a virgin, you know," she smiles.

Thaelyn leers at her, and she giggles from the thought.

"You spoke of lightning bolts before..." he muses jovially.

"Yes, well," she shrugs.

"Anyway, I found I had to place some effort in the beginning to contain the link, she was resisting so fiercely."

"Resisting?"

"Yes, she actually held enough capacity that I had to exert myself in order to enforce the link. How interesting..."

"She must come from a rather well-developed society then. Maybe this also explains the eyes. But does this mean you would consider her a good candidate for a meld?"

"Possibly..." he nods. "If she understands the process and would accept it, it will certainly provide for a more predictable result. Nevertheless, we should measure ourselves carefully. She may have a strong mind, but it is clear she is unconditioned. You saw her as she came out, and that was a simple thought link."

"You're right. So, the next time should be sitting down, especially for a meld."

"There are no benches or chairs here, and the ground might not be appropriately accommodating. I need to be within comfortable reach. Are there any decent rocks or old logs around?"

They look around the local landscape.

"I see a few rocks here and there," Aerlie responds. "But nothing suitable to sit on. There's a lone tree over there, but no logs. This place is desolate! I can see it all the way to those mountains, both there in the north and those on the eastern ridge."

"No doubt from the orcs stripping it bare. You always did have the eyes, my dear."

"And don't forget the ears!" she smirks. "You can never escape those."

"Perhaps for as long as you keep them clean," he teases and flashes a haughty grin at her.

"Oh! You!" she feigns disparagement. "One of these days, I'm going to beat you at this game."

The two of them shared a quick laugh and a hug.

"Very well," Thaelyn asserts. "Since I do not care to go all the way back home for a simple set of chairs, I suppose I will need to make use of that tree, as much as I hate cutting down trees for such meager wants. But then again, in the longer term, it truly makes no difference."

Aerlie looks at him inquisitively.

"When we lay down the orcs," he responds in answer to her stare.

"Then, you are thinking of using Mystra's Fury on this one. Yes, it would be the most obvious choice, the orcs being so tightly clustered down there."

"We will need shield mages," he declares. "Once we get word back from the scouts, we should start reorganizing the troops. Let us hope we have no further complications."

Chapter 4
A LITTLE HOUSEWORK

"Haran, my people know a thing or two about this," Kaliya asserts. "As I said, some of our elders have studied this," she pauses to consider her words. "Although not very often…and not for actual use, mostly in theory these days… And technically, not since leaving Azgarén…" she chuckles feebly. "In fact, Elder Vankkar is particularly avoidant on the topic. He simply hates the idea. He says it's a major security risk."

"Aye," Relissa interjects. "And what do you think he'll have to say about you going off and doing something he wouldn't approve of to begin with?"

"He'll scream at me, what do you think? But if I can avoid telling him…" she smirks timidly.

"Uh huh…right. So, you're thinking of going out there to do this telepathy bit again and ask all these questions, and when you go home to report, you'll say you met with people from another world who don't speak our local tongue, and then what?" she grins impishly.

"Relissa, let's not make this any more complicated than it has to be. We need this information. Someone needs to do it, and we're already here. There's no point in going home just to make someone else…or maybe us again…come back out here to finish it."

"You know, Kaliya," Haran offers. "I might suggest there are those who are better qualified in these matters than we are."

"Maybe, but it still requires more effort, and a delay in time, when we may not have that much to begin with. Just remember these orcs out here. There's too many to waste time on with diplomacy. Whatever he has in mind, we need to know about it, and where we stand in the meantime. And I doubt he has in mind to wait for us."

"All right, fine, but now let's consider the repercussions. Like I said earlier, if this man has an army as well outfitted as this group out here, or anything similar, and if he has enough of them back home to push every orc off his world, as we were suggesting a short while ago, this represents a force to be reckoned with, no matter how you label it."

"Yes, but if you want to consider things, we should probably also consider how many orcs there were to begin with. If we're speaking of a simple invasion, it might not be that much to push off."

"Granted, unless you look at this out here, if we say this is a refugee camp of whatever remains. But next is this: Depending on his overall motivations, he may eventually discover and, well, for lack of a better term, step on the toes of the rest of them here."

"Aye, you got that one right," Relissa nods. "And what will he do about it, or they do about him?"

"This could erupt in an all-out war to finish off whatever remains of our world…which isn't much by now. I don't really know how to approach this, but I feel certain we need to take sides here for our own survival."

"And this just brings us back to our supers," Relissa moans. "Jiggers, how do I tell this to the Enforcer? He'll flip when he hears of yet another invasion force coming in, no matter who it is."

"My brother won't be too happy either," Kaliya admits. "We're already so badly frayed from all the skirmishes we take."

"I think the Dean will laugh at me for most of this," Haran surmises. "He never did take me seriously for anything. But he has to admit that this could offer a significant difference in how we approach the war effort."

"In any event, it comes down to doing it and bringing it home, whatever the repercussions, because I think those repercussions will be there one way or another."

"I hate to admit, but you're probably right. Regardless, we'll just be bringing home the details. You're the one taking the big risk here actually doing it. I worry for you, Kaliya."

"Well, I don't think he would actually want to hurt me. If they have so many of their own questions to ask, I think they would get better responses out of people who are still alive to talk about it, right?" she grins softly.

"Well, yes…but you didn't see the look on your face on that last effort."

"My best is to say, sit down for it next time," Relissa jests.

"Yeah, this much I think I'll agree on," Kaliya smiles.

"So, where do we start? You try asking him in your bad Orcish, or me with my bad Elvish? Then see if he'll fill up your empty head with more goofy visions?" she smiles playfully.

"Maybe… It might be the only way. Telepathy is not unknown to us, just an early concept. If only we had more time, opportunity, and people who actually trained it, rather than losing everyone to this damnable war…well, who knows."

"This actually makes me wonder about something," Haran adds. "Humans don't carry much…ehm…" he catches himself and looks at Relissa. "What I mean to say is they don't…project…much mental power, like for performing psychic abilities and such, and certainly not on the scale we saw."

He glares at Relissa waiting for a response from her, but she simply looks away innocently. So, he continues.

"However, this Thaelyn doesn't necessarily look fully human to me. Those eyes, for instance…"

"Right…" Kaliya admits. "And it didn't feel that way either. I have never had any first-hand telepathic experience with another person, and well, no disrespect, Haran, but I don't think your people have what it takes to do what he did to me."

Now Relissa lets out an uncontrollable giggle.

"Oh shush, girl!" Haran demands. "I knew that was coming out sooner or later."

"Sorry, Haran," she chortles. "It's just me. So, what do you think he is?" she asks as she tries to choke back her cheeky outbreak.

"I don't know," Kaliya accedes. "But it can't be human, at least not fully. I saw his eyes light up, and as far as I understand it, normal beings shouldn't do that. Not unless you can tell me this was more of that magic stuff. But I didn't see him do anything other than call on what I assume to be an innate ability. And for the power he put out, that ability must be big."

"All the more reason to be very cautious," Haran intones warily.

"I agree, but it doesn't help matters if we need our answers. And this is better than drawing pictures in the dirt. So, let's go. Maybe they also have that idea of theirs ready by now."

Kaliya gets to her feet with thoughts and ideas flowing through her mind on how she might go about her impending telepathic exchange. She was determined to find a way to learn more, though she felt some trepidation over what to expect from it. Her two companions rise up along with her, and together they begin to seek out Thaelyn again.

Thaelyn and Aerlie had been speaking to the three scouts, who had just recently returned from their mission. They reported no unusual sightings.

"Captain Hagmaert!" he commands.

The officer in the crest, the same one that had been so carefully examining the trio earlier, rushes up to him and salutes.

"Yes, my Lord!"

"We are moving forward. Inform the troops to collect together. We will be calling in shield mages, so you will need to organize them in a circle."

"Shield mages?" he ponders, looking over at the canyon. "Oh dear, may the gods have mercy," he mutters softly. "Absolutely, my Lord!"

He salutes again and charges off, commanding troops as he goes along.

Kaliya and the others notice movement occurring all around as they hike back across to find Thaelyn. They see the Captain running across the field giving orders.

"Something's happening," Kaliya suggests. "Does anyone see those scouts?"

"Over there, moving into the cluster of guards," Relissa replies.

"I wonder what the report was like."

Their eyes follow the three scouts as they move among the troops. And then they observe as the troops begin to cluster into a tight circular formation.

"What the…" Haran mutters. "What are they doing now? What sort of formation is that?"

As Kaliya makes her approach, she prepares to speak.

Thaelyn watches the reorganization of the troops. Aerlie stands close to him, casting an occasional glance at the canyon behind them to check for any unusual activity. She sees Kaliya and nudges Thaelyn, who then turns to meet her gaze.

"People with orcs?" she asks in orcish.

"No, only orcs…"

She nods contentedly, knowing there will be no barbeques today.

"You me talk?"

"Not in Orcish, this is not good for us."

"Um, yes…but, you…uh…" she flusters. "Relissa, you ask him. Ask about that idea of theirs. We need to get some information here before he goes off and does something bad."

"Aye…" she replies.

Relissa steps forward and tries her best in her own language.

"Please, we have many questions to ask. We must talk before you do something here."

"Relissa," Thaelyn advises. "I agree, but your Elvish is not very good either."

"Thaelyn," Aerlie interjects gently but imperatively. "We should do this now. Doing so will take time, and I know we do not wish to extend our stay here overly long," she emphasizes by glancing at the canyon. "But these people will not likely understand what is occurring or how to cooperate under the conditions we use. It also occurs to me, if they are so eager to talk, there may be a few details we should become aware of beforehand."

"Very well, I suppose I must agree. So, let us hope we have the time for it."

He nods and turns back to Kaliya and Relissa.

"Relissa, tell her we must teach you our language. More of this..." he points at his head, and then to Kaliya.

"Buggers!" she yips. "Kaliya, you're going to get your wish. Get ready for another head spanking. He says he's going to try teaching you his language using more of that telepathy gibberish. Well, girl, it was nice knowing you," she takes the girl's hand and shakes it vigorously. "I'll call for a wagon to pick you up later."

"Oh, thank you, Relissa," Kaliya retorts nervously. "You're such a wonderful pal. But cu'Nar help me if it's anything like that last one. How does he hope to teach me a full language telepathically?"

Thaelyn points assertively toward the rocky nook where he first found them, and he begins directing the group back in that direction.

"I don't know about the rest of you," Haran observes. "But he's doing something new out here. Look at the troops. They're forming a circle, which seems very specific, and I thought I saw someone depart through another portal for some reason."

"Maybe he's preparing for action against those orcs?" Kaliya muses. "The one leaving could be to call for reinforcements. But in all the nether-space, how can he make an attempt on them with so many out there?"

"I don't know. I'm not military, but if he is calling for reinforcements, he'll need a lot of them. I just hope he really is planning to do something, and not simply leave, thinking his world is safe with all of them over here now."

"Oh buggers," Relissa moans. "Don't even suggest that, Haran! He could change the war for us around here."

"Not to worry, Relissa. Once Kaliya gets her gift of mind-numbing wisdom, and assuming she can still speak afterwards, we'll try to resolve this."

"You know," Kaliya mumbles. "Between the two of you, you instill me with a tremendous amount of confidence."

"Well, look at it this way. If you're going to get in trouble with your Elder Vankkar, at least make it memorable."

"Oh, is that how it goes now?"

They walked briskly back to the rocks, where Thaelyn points to a location on the ground. The trio moves to that location and halts, waiting to see what he has in mind next. He then strolls over to an old tree a short distance away around the side of the knoll, where it stood opposite the location the orcs had first been seen exiting through the rocks earlier in the day. He steps up to the tree and examines it closely, placing his hand against it and moving along the trunk.

"Why is he looking at a tree?" Haran asks. "I thought he was going to teach her something."

"Well," Relissa quips. "If he were stepping around the other side of it, I could offer a reason."

"Oh, thank you, Relissa, and with us watching it?"

"Aye, well, two of us are girls, so maybe he figures we'd like it?"

"Um, somehow I doubt it, actually."

"All right, other than that, can a person be telepathic with a tree?"

"I've heard where druids may have some weird ideas about that, but not I."

"You have druids in that city up there?"

"Well, no, but I hear you have a few."

"Aye, that we do, but don't be itching me about it. I don't fall into that, either."

Thaelyn pulls out his two-handed sword and holds it firmly in his hand at arm's length. The blade is composed of a dark shiny material that seems to glow softly.

"Wow, I guess he really doesn't like that tree," Haran jokes as he continues to observe.

"Now wait a bleedin' minute here," Relissa yips. "No way! Not on this side of right thinking! If he has any ideas bouncing between his ears about that..."

"Why? What do you think he's doing?"

"Maybe to cut it down for a place to sit…? But with a bloody sword?"

"That looks like a very special sword, actually."

"Special or otherwise, do you know what kind of tree that is? That's an ironwood tree! And those live up to the name. You can't cut that with a sword! Not even an axe! You might spend the whole day whacking at it and barely put a scratch in it."

Kaliya remained quiet during the brief exchange, simply observing, and wondering what would come next.

Haran recalled some of the extraordinary equipment these people carried. He stared intently at the sword. It seemed different from the other gear he was looking at earlier.

"I don't know what that thing's made of," he mumbles to himself. "It's not a metal I recognize, and not the same as the rest. Kaliya?"

"Uh-uh…no idea."

"But it does look enchanted. Very enchanted."

Just then, Thaelyn backs away one step from the tree in military prose. He pulls up the sword close to his face and seems to mutter a word softly into it. Suddenly, the sword erupts in a fantastic display of magical blue flame, shooting fully along its length and out past the end.

"Gracious!" Haran yelps. "It's not just enchanted. It's activated by a Word of Power!"

"Um, Haran," Kaliya mutters urgently. "What does that mean?"

"What it means, girl, is don't get in the way of it!"

"Yeah, I can see that much. Cu'Nar's pity, look at that thing."

Now, with the grace of a master swordsman, Thaelyn makes a series of one-handed twirls, followed by a loop and a low spin of his body to the right, sweeping the blade close to the ground in a rapid slice. The blade whooshed through the air as it went.

He spins a full circle with the blade cleaving through the air until it makes contact with the base of the tree. An explosion of sparks flies out in all directions as it passes through seemingly without resistance. The swing comes to an end in line with his outstretched arm to the side.

The tree moans as it lethargically topples over, tipping away from Thaelyn to fall behind the knoll, and striking the ground with a heavy thud. Branches snap from the force of the impact, and bits of splintered wood shoot out along its length.

He returns upright and pulls the sword back into a salute. He mumbles another word, and the magical energies subside. All that remains is the soft glow of its resting state. Another deft twirl brings the sword home to the sheath on his back.

Relissa's jaw drops, and her eyes nearly pop out of their sockets as she lets out a minor yip. When she recovers enough to say something, she can barely push the words out.

"Bloody...hell..." she groans.

Haran could just barely gulp down the lump in his throat as he tried to speak.

"Folks, I don't know what that thing is made of," he advises. "But clearly, if this is how these people play the game back home, beware. That thing must have some nearly godlike enchantments on it! That blade might just be able to cut through any material known to man...and maybe a few that aren't!"

Kaliya is stunned as she observes the dazzling finesse. She looks over her shoulder at her own weapon, and then back to Thaelyn.

"He did that with just one hand...using a greatsword!" she murmurs. "But you know... That blade kind of resembled a plasma torch to me."

"Oh? Where might you normally use one of those?"

"Most often in an industry to make clean precision cuts through thick plates of metal..."

"Aye then," Relissa asserts tensely. "So, here he used it on a tree. That's fine enough," she titters. "I feel a wee bit sorry for the tree, though. That was the last one out here. But now, what's he going to do next, huh? Throw it over his shoulder and carry it off?" she wonders while straining a chuckle.

Thaelyn glances at the group, but is unconcerned with their expressions. Rather, he searches the local area for a convenient location, and settles his gaze on a suitable spot on the ground to one side. He returns to the log and extends a group of fingers towards it.

"Aye, peeps, we have a fresh new log there," Relissa jests. "Are you going to try throwing a few sparks at it to polish it up now?"

"Relissa," Haran suggests mildly. "No offence, but maybe you should stifle it. I think he has something else in mind."

Just then, the log twitches and lurches off the ground, held by some invisible force of immense power. Thaelyn brings his hand up, and the log follows to about shoulder height. He then strolls along casually, as if on a walk in a park, moving towards the spot he had selected, with the hulk of the tree hovering just off to his side until he sets it down again.

"Criminy!" Relissa whines. "All right, you got me, Haran. I won't be saying another word."

"Kaliya," Haran offers worriedly. "Are you sure you want to do this? You do understand what that was, don't you? Or at least what it appeared to be...in theory?"

"Unbelievable!" she replies softly. "In theory, sure. But I've never actually seen it before. This is simply mythical! My...my...he... dammit!" she scorns silently.

"Him again, right? That name you can never pronounce?"

"Yes, Haran, I'm sorry. Anyway, he would lose his horns if he ever saw that. In fact, I already lost mine. I think they ran off under those rocks over there," she thumbs over her shoulder.

"Right, and do you understand the implications?"

"Well, we've generally agreed he isn't exactly human."

"Isn't exactly..." he huffs. "Dear, if he's got that much power inside that noggin of his...good gracious, he could be a full mentalist! Do you know what that means? I can barely perceive of it, even in theory!"

Kaliya looks at Haran, then back to Thaelyn, who was now cleaning up some of the loose bits on the log. Haran continues, now animating his words.

"He could be able to reshape matter, alter the flow of energy, perceive of places and objects beyond his reach..."

Suddenly, a memory flashes back to Kaliya.

"The moon, when we were first trying to talk to him," she recalls.

Haran jerks his head around to look at her.

"Dammit, you're right," he muses. "But why, do you think?"

"Maybe for a bird's eye view, or even an orbital view of where we are? He's in a new world…to him, at least. That would make a great vantage if you could get up that high."

"Yes, I suppose it might, at that. But then…" he sighs and lowers his voice as he returns to Thaelyn. "What else? As a mentalist… he could perhaps even have the power to foresee future events…in theory, that is."

All Relissa could do was make whimpering noises as he spoke.

"So, what does that make of him, then?" the girl squeaks.

Haran looks over at the distraught young elf. He wraps an arm around to comfort her.

"Probably more than anything people like us are meant to see."

Thaelyn took a position straddling one end of the log. He looks up at Kaliya and waves her over to join him, patting on a space just in front of where he was sitting.

She reluctantly trudges over to him, each step building a level of anxiety like she had never felt before. She turns to face him, hesitating a moment to gaze longingly at her friends before straddling the log to sit down. She could feel a cold sweat coming over her again.

"No…hurt…me," she whispers ever so slightly under her breath in Orcish.

He places his hands on her shoulders and squeezes gently, offering a tender smile.

"We have much work here," he whispers. "But I will try to be soft."

He then gestures for her to pull in closer. Their knees bumped together, and their legs were nearly overlapping. Haran winced at the arrangement.

"That looks a bit awkward, Kaliya. You're nearly sitting in his lap, just for him to gain good access to you."

"It's my legs, mostly," she replies. "After all, we're so tall in relation to you."

Aerlie settled in next to them, sitting cross-legged on the ground with her wings splayed out in a wide angle.

"Aerlie," Thaelyn mentions. "We know we want to teach her ours, but it would behoove us to learn hers as well."

"It would…" she turns toward Relissa. "Relissa? We think it would be wise to trade yours and ours. What do you think?"

"I'm not the one sitting there," she diverts briefly to Kaliya. "Kaliya, they want to trade both ways. How do you feel on that?"

"I don't know if I can even hold up one way," she mumbles nervously. "But I suppose, ultimately, if we can do it at all, and they feel it's alright, then I guess I'll try to struggle through it."

Kaliya turns to Thaelyn and nods.

"Relissa," Thaelyn wonders. "Does she have more people here?"

"Aye, she does. Why?"

"Do you all speak the same?"

"Many of them, I think… Um, wait… No, her Elders don't."

"Elders?"

"Her…um, what word is it…a Council."

"Ah, and they have their own language?"

"Aye, her people have their own language. They're not from here."

"Most interesting…and this might complicate things if we need to work any political agreements."

"They probably have a spokesperson," Aerlie offers.

"Probably, but I wonder if we could include this extra piece. She has a strong mind, so if we can work this delicately enough…"

"Wow, so are we speaking of one in and two out? That'll put a lot of pressure on her."

"It would. Let me try to test her as we go in to see how it feels. I have never done three before…or even two, for that matter…"

"Have you ever done this even once?"

"Um, well, yes…in practice up in Mount Celestia," he smirks gently.

"Uh huh," she muses playfully. "And here you want to try it officially with not one, not even two, but three, and on someone as frightened and inexperienced as this young lady."

"Well," he shrugs. "In a time of war, we find ourselves pressed to some rather extreme demands."

"Gods be blessed. Relissa, ask her how she feels about including her native one as well. We'll try to take them one-by-one to ease the pressure."

"Oh buggers," she moans. "Um, you know, she's a good friend of mine. I'd like to keep her that way."

"Not to worry, we'll leave a few pieces for you to play with. Just tell her to be strong."

"Are we ready, Dear?" Thaelyn asks.

"I'm ready. I'll share the exercise to reinforce yours. I didn't get the chance to practice it up there," she giggles.

"Of course, so for you it is mostly theory. This should be interesting. Then let us begin. For the volume alone, this will likely be turbulent."

Kaliya listened to the exchange, as well as Relissa's translations for her part. The dark elf's low skills were just barely enough to catch these simple words in her language, but they were all nervous.

Thaelyn placed his fingertips on the young Daanen'kai's head, moving them bilaterally across different regions of her cranium.

"Kaliya," Haran invokes hesitantly. "This looks serious. Are you really sure about this?"

"Haran, I think I'm committed by now," she replies while vainly trying to conceal her own heightened tensions. "There's no easy way out, and I'm pretty sure I need this. We all do."

"But girl," Relissa interjects. "Every time you go out needing something, you come home to another royal bashing by your bleedin' Elders. We already spoke about this, but by the looks of it…jiggers."

"Relissa, I would rather you try telling me everything will be alright, not how bad it's going to be later."

"Aye, sorry. He said to be strong, so do your best, girl. I'm here for you, even if I do need to call on that wagon later," she chuckles.

"Uh huh…"

Kaliya tried to focus herself on her work. She didn't care to think about what might come later. It would probably come anyway by now. She really didn't have much more to lose after all the previous occasions. Maybe, she thought, after all was said and done, it would be a blessing, and she would no longer have to worry about a future she had so little control over.

Thaelyn found several satisfactory spots on her head and began positioning his fingers across them, wrapping over and around her horns in the process. When he appeared ready, he looked into her eyes and gave a slow nod.

"Relissa, please," Kaliya whimpers. "Can you offer me anything special before I go in?"

"Kaliya," she places a hand on her shoulder. "You're not the religious sort...then again, neither am I for that matter. But the best I can offer is to let the Seldarine watch over you. My Mum is a priestess, remember, so she would certainly offer a prayer for you."

"All right, thank you. I'll take it."

Kaliya drew in one more difficult breath and made a long blink. She looked back at him and nodded.

Thaelyn closed his eyes and breathed in deeply, held it, and let it go. Similarly, Aerlie closed her eyes and imitated his actions. Then they both began chanting something in perfect synchronization. And all physical sensation left Kaliya's body.

She felt herself falling, but she couldn't have been falling, as there was nothing under her pulling her down, and neither was there anything alongside her floating upwards. All was dark, initially. She was aware of herself, but it seemed like a distant memory lost in a great void. She strained to peer deeper into it, but it was thick as ink. The space around her seemed motionless...stiff, as a jar filled with jelly, unable to flow.

In a moment, it seemed to grow denser. There was something akin to pressure being applied, but she could not see from where. She felt squeezed on all sides. It grew in intensity until she felt she may pop, but then the sensation relaxed, and there was a pause.

Soon after, she could feel a pulling. It was an inversion of the former sensation, distending her, trying to stretch her into new proportions. As before, it grew until she reached her limit, and subsided again, until all was calm once more.

She waited for what seemed like several moments, until she began to see movement, little flecks of light, like particles of sand, all aglow. She tried to reach out to one, but she had no limbs. She forgot what sort of appendages she should be expecting anyway, though she was fairly certain there should have been something. The sand came in around her, first drifting, then swirling, more and more until it grew into a minor storm, and soon to a blizzard. All the while, they simply swirled around her at a distance, a dusty ring orbiting her shape but not coming close enough to make contact. She wanted them to touch her, she felt a passion for it, an unnatural desire welling up inside, begging them to come closer to share their comfort.

Suddenly, one of them deviated and merged with her. There was a brief flash and a sound, like a voice. It felt good and she wanted more. Then another one collided. She saw another flash, like that of a portrayed image. She felt one more hit, and then another. More sounds, more images. They were coming faster, and it was wonderful. Soon she found herself bathed in the joy of the dance, a whirlpool of pleasure, the musical symphony of sight and song acting as a harmonious aphrodisiac filling her senses.

Still more came, faster and more furiously. She reveled in their charm, but the sensations were reaching their capacity. The flow did not ease, it continued to rise. The pleasures were becoming a burden. She soon felt overloaded by the intense rush of visions, sounds, words, and meanings. It was nearly suffocating, if only for the apparent lack of a true need to breathe.

The barrage seemed to peak, but the bombardment continued incessantly. She felt as if she was being buried alive underneath a mountain of details. The visions were bizarre in some cases, as concepts, notions, and cogitations of a mystical wonderland with strange shapes and purposes.

Her mind was straining under the pressure of the delivery, filling her with a virtual encyclopedia of knowledge. She felt as if she had become a bottomless vessel, and someone was pouring in a large influx of content without care or concern for how much she could actually hold. She struggled to contain herself, simply to hold on until it finished. There had to be an ending to it somewhere.

It continued this way for what seemed like a minor eternity. Then, something new occurred, a sudden interruption, like a shocking snap of the fingers to transition from one sensation to a completely opposing one. But as this transition broke through, she felt something else occur, something…collateral. It was strange, as if a wall had fractured and crumbled away, and a forgotten specter came peeking through, if only briefly. It had the face of a lonely child on an empty street in a half-destroyed city. But the image was fleeting, as by this time, memories started flooding outward.

The tide had reversed, with a torrent of new imagery and definitions more familiar to her senses, but circulating away in this perpetual maelstrom. The flows mingled in multiple tongues. She felt as if she was being siphoned of knowledge, like a book with the pages being torn out, though it did not leave a lasting impression of a true emptying.

This new onslaught continued as she writhed in the deluge, a sensation of nearly drowning in her own memories, seething of interpretations and definitions both old and new. And somewhere, in the back of her mind, she recalled a faint memory to simply hold on until it was complete, even though it seemed to go on forever.

✦✦✦✦✦

Relissa and Haran looked on, though there didn't appear to be much to see. The initial chanting that Thaelyn and Aerlie were performing had settled to a low mumbling of what seemed like random words. As for Kaliya, her face was a mask of stone, with her gaze fixed at Thaelyn, and her body was rigid.

The soldiers had completed the reorganization and were waiting patiently. They occasionally looked over at the group to see if any new activity was occurring on the log. They seemed to understand the process, perhaps from previous experience, or some other form of reckoning.

"Such a strange arrangement," Haran muses. "It looks like a circle of mages around that group now. Are those their reinforcements? Just another group of mages? And all of them waiting for something."

"Aye, waiting for him, I'll bet," Relissa responds. "But then what? What's this bleedin' army going to do next, I wonder? No way can they hit the orcs by these numbers, not even with that fancy sword of his."

"Not unless those mages have something up their sleeves. They do seem to use a lot of spell-craft, and those are dressed differently."

The troops had organized themselves in a cluster formation closer to the top of the embankment for a better view of the canyon floor and the orcish settlement, though neither of the two companions could figure out why.

"There must be more to it," Haran conjectures. "So far, they're just waiting for him, and keeping an eye out down below. We just have to wait till he's finished with Kaliya."

"Right. And after that, I'm wondering if she'll have any marbles left to throw together. We may actually have to carry her home."

"But the problem with that is," he chuckles softly. "She must weigh more than both of us combined. Do you think you can drag her over those mountains?"

"Not in this lifetime. I may have been joking with the wagon bit, but jiggers if I would actually need to do it," she giggles.

"Still, this telepathic process looks to be taking a while. I just hope we don't get any surprises while we wait."

"Aye, I'm feeling a wee bit exposed right now. What if a patrol comes up here sniffing around?"

"Exactly! Let's hope these soldiers can deal with it promptly. We surely don't need the whole floor moving on us."

Relissa gazes at the cluster of soldiers and recalls her earlier experiences with the elves. She hears the echoes of her conversation reverberate in her mind.

"In all the bleedin' hells, I never would've thought of it," she mumbles.

"What now?"

"Oh, Haran, it's just that, well, we have our stories, and the others hold on to them like a bloody drunkard with his beer. I never put much faith in it. I mean, what good is it to us now? Those days are long dead and buried."

"It's a curious thought. While you were busy burying your past, it looks like someone else was pressing forward with their future. These people are organized, and not just elves, but humans, too."

"Aye, I wonder how it all happened. To think of it, another world, people live and die, and times change. When I was talking to those elves before, I learned a few things. The language is a mite different now…my Dah will have fun with that, I'm sure."

"There's probably a lot of new history for him to study too."

"Oh, don't even start with that! He already crawls so deep into his books that Mum can't find him half the time."

"But now, Relissa… What about you? Are you happy they're here? You were speaking earlier about how much you hated your people clinging to so many lost traditions. This simply proves they're not so lost after all."

She turns to look at him, staring pleasantly into his eyes. She pauses briefly to consider his words.

"When they first told me who they were, it was like the gods themselves spoke to me, calling out my suffering. It might not mean the world will be a different place tomorrow, but the stories seem a little closer to home now."

She turns back to the soldiers, who were still patiently waiting for Thaelyn to finish his meld with Kaliya.

"Haran," she continues. "Thanks."

"For what?"

"For being a friend and listening to all my bickering," she finishes. "It's more than a lot of folks back home ever did."

"I've always believed that friends are the most precious of commodities, and something that is often very difficult to come by."

They were broken out of their discussion by a deeply strained groan that rose into a faint whimper. It was Kaliya, the meld had ended, and she was out. But almost as soon as she was released, she passed unconscious.

Kaliya felt exhausted, or so she thought. She held the sensation of weariness, as if she had run a very long distance, or exerted herself with a lengthy and vigorous amount of work, but it didn't carry the same as a physical sensation. Her mind seemed empty, with her previous experiences rapidly fading into the background. Now, only a few dreamlike flashes popped into view: Classrooms, study halls, libraries. Some of these lingered and carried echoes of voices. One of these stood out, and it sounded like a distant memory of an instructor giving lessons.

"The theorem of our teachings goes like this… Perception enables recognition, existence demands definition, and from this, substance becomes our reality."

The voice faded, but its echo still rang in her thoughts.

"What does he mean by that?" she wonders.

As her thoughts struggled to coalesce, she hears the voice again.

"And then we have the axiom. In a metaphysical reality, nothing unknown exists. It only exists after it is known."

"Huh?" she muses. "But isn't that a contradiction? To know of it, it must first be there to have something to know about."

She finds herself trying to reconcile this concept.

"To know it exists…to perceive of it, to recognize it. Yes. In order to recognize it, I must first perceive it. The mind is the center of perception, and therefore, the center of recognition. And with recognition, comes knowing."

She mulls these strange thoughts some more, recalling the words again.

"Existence demands definition. Of course, all things must hold definition, their physical parameters, size, mass, volume, velocity, trajectory…these are definitions, and from this is defined the property of existence. But one must also perceive of these in order for them to exist in the mind. Otherwise, they are unknown, and to the mind they do not exist."

The concepts were suddenly becoming fascinating to her, although she couldn't fully explain why. It was as if something new had arrived that invoked a different perspective.

"Substance," she continues. "All things in reality represent substance. This is what carries definition, and therefore, explains their existence. This existence is then perceived by the mind and thereby recognized. And to the mind, it is now known."

At this moment, another odd voice whispers from the recesses of her mind, like that of a mature woman giving gentle instruction.

"In this space you have Will, and your Will can alter this space."

Kaliya looks around, but there is no one present. The origin seemed like a lost memory.

"That was strange..." she muses. "Where did it come from? Will...from the mind... To apply Will, and this Will can alter... the definition? Yes! This is the answer! The mind is the center of perception. If a thing can only exist after it is known, it must first be perceived by the mind. Our perception enables recognition by giving it definition, and this definition establishes its potential for existence. This is then demonstrated by the resulting substance being generated as an alteration of reality due to this same perception."

She reflects on her astonishing revelation, but there was something uniquely strange with the idea.

"Wait a minute, that's backwards!" she balks. "Are we saying the mind makes reality? In a physical reality, things exist...wait, no. Those words...a metaphysical reality... Nothing unknown exists. It only exists after it is known. It must be Known first!"

Now another echo emerges from the depths.

"What is a thing? What can be said to exist? These are the principles of Ontology."

She muddles this new concept.

"What is a thing? As if a thing must first be defined before it can exist? Yes! The mind governs its definition of existence. In a physical space, it may carry definition based on its recognizable substance. But in a metaphysical space, it would only carry recognizable substance after it is defined, and the mind is the center of this perception. First, we perceive it, and then we apply this to affect the alteration of this space to form our reality."

She relaxes from her argument for a moment, trying to imagine a space that can be altered by the Will. But the moment is short-lived, as a new series of echoes emerges. Screams and shouts erupt in the space around her. She begins to witness fiery explosions conjured out of what seems like thin air. Shadowy figures are running in all directions.

She spins around, trying to focus on these frightening new images. She is standing on a street in a city on fire, with panicked citizens and an advancing line of brutish figures in the background.

"No!" she screams. "How could they? Those beasts! How dare they attack us! What did we ever do to them?"

She instinctively turns as if to run away, when she is unexpectedly halted by a smallish figure standing right in front of her. It was a young girl staring discontentedly up at her. Kaliya glares at the figure, only partially recognizing it.

"You!" she shouts. "What are you doing here?"

"Why isn't the militia here helping us? Why are we always running? All we do is run, and more people die!"

"It's all we can do! They took us by surprise."

"Surprise? Yeah, just like always. Cu'Nar's pity, how many times can someone 'take you by surprise' before you start to expect it."

"Yes, I know this! And I tried!" she begins to break down. "But every time I went out there, I made some horrible mistake, and more people got hurt."

"They tried to teach you, but you were too dull-horned to listen."

"Listen to what! How to fight a losing battle? There's too many of them!"

"No Kaliya, it's not about that. Don't you remember? We have a secret."

As the girl speaks, Kaliya begins to hear a bizarre alteration of her voice.

"In this space you have Will…" her voice now deepens to that same maternal tone. "…and your Will can alter this space."

Kaliya grimaces at the supernatural vision and stumbles back. She lets out an impulsive yelp, and the vision ends. She wakes up.

Her eyes popped open suddenly and she gasped. Her breathing was shallow for the unexpected release. She found herself leaning against another body, seemingly in an embrace, but more like she must've collapsed, and someone was now holding her. Under her cheekbone was a plate spaulder, the shoulder piece to plate armor. Her face seemed to be pressed into a fold of a silver and blue cape, and lightly tickled by a lock of flowing silver-white hair.

She laid there for a few moments, trying to understand what had just happened. Her mind seemed dull and confused. The area was mostly quiet now. No more screams and shouts, no explosions. So, she slowly lifted an arm to push herself off this other body, though she was disoriented to find her mark immediately. She felt around the other side of the body for another shoulder to support her. Sluggishly, she straightens herself up to a seated position.

She wobbled slightly at first, but her balance returned soon enough when she got a feel for it again. Her head drooped, and her eyelids were heavy, as if waking up from a deep slumber and having trouble shaking it off.

She tried looking into the face of the person sitting before her. The image was fuzzy at first. It came into focus to be that of a man with golden eyes. She gazed at him, as he looked like someone she should know, but the memory was lost in a sea of bewilderment.

"Kaliya?" a female voice speaks softly. It sounded familiar.

She turned slowly to find the source, almost losing her balance and falling over in the process. Her eyes came to focus on a slender dark-skinned female. Next to her was a fair-skinned male in a robe. She stared at the duo briefly, raising a finger as if she wanted to speak, but her focus drifted off before she could think of anything to say.

"Can you say something," the girl offers gently.

Kaliya turns again to refocus on her.

"Say…something…?" she mumbles distantly.

The female turned apprehensively to look at the male and shook her head.

Kaliya fought with herself. She moved her eyes around the scene, trying to identify individual items. Her eyes landed on the figure of a winged female sitting on the ground next to her, but nothing firm came to mind yet. She moved on to rocks, shrubs, soldiers, anything that might distinguish itself.

"Well, Relissa," Haran notes privately. "I think your idea of that wagon may come to pass after all."

"Aye," she admits. "Poor thing... But we'll need ropes and pulleys to lift her into it," she giggles.

Thaelyn smiled gently at the two who were still sitting on the side, waiting for the next step in this curious visitation. He then turned to Kaliya to begin his interaction.

"Can you understand my words?" he speaks in the native tongue.

"Jiggers," Relissa moans. "Does that mean it worked?"

"On my side, I might say it did, but now to test her. She is rather undisciplined to manage herself on such occasions, but she does have a remarkably strong mind."

Kaliya returns her gaze to Thaelyn as they sat there on the log. Her voice seemed unnaturally sluggish.

"I can...understand...you, but...my thoughts...are...confused."

"The sensation is temporary. Let us try to bring you into focus with a few exercises. Can you give me your proper name?"

"Name..."

She made a few turning motions of the head, as if the memory rolled off into a corner somewhere and she needed to find it again.

"My name is...Kaliya..."

She pauses as if trying to assemble the rest of it from a number of disjointed pieces.

"...Officer... Petty... Nazég..."

She halts as if to realize this didn't sound right. She closes her eyes and tries again to shake off the last of her dizziness.

"No, wait...let me try again. My name is... Petty Officer...

Kaliya...Nazég," she nods sleepily. "Yes, better. And I serve the Daanen-Aryku Sentinels."

"How interesting, but that would represent a naval rank, would it not? Are we near a seaport of some sort?"

"No, not ours... Ours is a longtime tradition for a space navy."

"A space navy..." he croons. "Oh, I would love to speak more on this. And you call it the Sentinels? Is this some kind of service?"

"Militia...what's left of it."

"Very well, but is this to say you are not faring well due perhaps to these orcs? That seems like a bit of a contradiction if you are so advanced that you can travel the stars."

"Maybe... It goes back a long way for us. The orcs aren't really the problem."

"I see. Perhaps we can discuss this in a moment. Let us now test your new skills if we may."

He now changes to the Tae'Eladaran common form.

"Do you understand me when I speak like this?"

She glares at him for the clearly foreign language, but which now seems strangely familiar to her.

"Fascinating... Yes, I do. Cu'Nar's grace, how did you do that?"

"Where I come from, we have a number of very curious and useful qualities, though I will admit, it is not often when I may need to apply myself in this particular way."

"Is that before or after the one and only practice session you took?" Aerlie teases.

"Indeed, and thank you, Dear, in front of this poor young lady who became my one and only...official...example."

"Grace of the cu'Nar," Kaliya winces. "And I thought these two were bad," she thumbs at her friends. "Is this how you usually do things?"

"No, as I do not typically find myself in such places as this, and under such conditions as these."

"Thank the cu'Nar for that. So, this is more of an exception to the rule than the norm?"

"Mostly, and largely for those occasions where we are pressed upon by desperate circumstances."

"Like where we are now."

"Indeed, but now let us return to your tongue to involve your friends."

"Of course, and thank you."

Thaelyn now turns to the rest of the group, where Relissa and Haran watched and waited expectantly, as well as with fascination over the obvious results.

"If I didn't see it," Relissa muses. "I don't think I would've believed it. Kaliya, how do you feel after that?"

"I'm getting better, but wow, that was a hit like nothing I could ever imagine."

"Aye it was. You just fell right over. You were out for a long while too."

"I was? Oops... Well, I guess there's nothing I can really do about that. But now that we're here, um, we have a lot of ground to cover, I think."

"We do," Thaelyn admits. "And worse is that we have time pressing down on us for it. So, let us try to be on with it as expediently as we can. Aerlie?"

"Yes Dear..."

"Yes...Dear?" Haran mumbles as he raises his brow.

Aerlie smiles as she makes a set of downward squiggly lines with fingers on both hands, followed by a circle and angling sharply upward, which quickly levitates her off the ground to a standing position.

"Now there's a new way to bring yourself up," Haran comments.

"Aye," Relissa retorts. "Maybe you could add that to your finger-waggling and show your Masters a new trick."

"I think my Masters would scoff at it, more than anything."

Aerlie flutters her wings and ruffles her feathers to shake off the dust from the ground before stepping around the log for better interaction. Thaelyn lifts himself up from the log and they join in front of the group.

"Now that we have this opportunity," he begins. "I think we should begin with a more appropriate introduction. My proper name is Lord Thaelyn, and this is my wife, the Lady Aerlie."

"A husband and wife?" Haran yelps. "Great gods, you're not even the same race! Do people do this back where you come from?"

"Indeed, you might see this from time to time between humans and elves, though her example might be an odd one, as ours would be the first. But now, to continue, we are the King and Queen of our home world, which we call Tae'Eladar."

Relissa gasps and whines sharply. She nearly collapses from what was already a seated position to a grovel stance.

"Bloody hell," she wheezes. "I didn't know you were royals. I got the Lord and Lady part, but royals?"

She is quickly joined by Haran as he also repositions himself to a proper kneeling pose. Once again, he glares at Kaliya, who was still sitting on the log, and seemingly in a daze.

"Kaliya, do I need to remind you of your manners?"

"Do not trouble yourselves," Thaelyn soothes. "We already attended to this, so there is no need to return to it. This is simply a formality to clarify a few terms."

"Clarify..." he chuckles nervously. "He's the King of an entire world, and he's simply clarifying the point. Gods pity us."

"Yes, well... Relissa, for all her efforts, leaves a few things to be desired for her language skills, and it is rather unfortunate that we have this situation to begin with. But now, let us move forward. Perhaps the two of you would wish to share your proper names?"

"Oh, right!" Haran blurts as he pulls himself upright again. "My name is Haran Carronel and I'm just a simple mage...or trying to be as I'm still enrolled in our academy up north. This here is Relissa Moonshimmer, and she's a scout serving her people in their home city, which is more to the west."

"A Morier, such a curious sight to see in a place like this. But then, so are you. How did you find your way here?"

"Um..." Haran frowns at the curious question.

Relissa speaks up to help answer.

"My people have some really old history behind us that tells of our travels from a place that's almost legendary to us by now, called Sein'amar. As I recall the tale, there were my people, a bunch of other elves, and the humans, all travelling together, when we found ourselves here."

Haran now turns his glare at the girl for her statement.

"You never told me that before."

"Well, I would think you round-ears would remember a wee bit of it on your own, you know?"

"I didn't ever learn of it in my old school."

"Well, don't look to me about that."

"Relissa," Aerlie ushers. "What do you call your people here?"

"We're called Night Elves these days. But I learned from those peeps over there that you have more of us back home, as nasty as it sounds, and you call them Drow, I guess."

"Indeed, we do, which is part of the reason for our surprise to see you here. You must've diverged from their clan a long time ago to preserve your better temperament. You also appear slightly different from them."

"Aye, I suppose so, but jiggers, I'm sorry to hear about the rest of them. But now, I'm wondering about you. I recall an old tale about elves with wings. Are you one of those?"

"I am," she smiles. "My people are the Aril clan of the Tel'Quessir. We are commonly known as Avariel elves."

"Incredible, just wait till I tell my Mum and Dah about this. She's a priestess, and he's a scholar and historian, and I'm sure they'll both flip when they hear this."

"How curious! So are mine, and in that same order."

"Um…" Haran interjects cautiously. "But anyway, shouldn't we be getting on to the more important matters of the reason you're here and about these orcs down there? I get the impression you might be at war with them. Am I right?"

"Indeed," Thaelyn nods. "I can certainly appreciate you have your questions, no different from we have ours, so perhaps if we relate our story, this can bring us better in line. But I should again emphasize that we have already spent a fair amount of time on this when we have work ahead that does not endear habits of waiting," he glances at the canyon.

"Naturally…"

"First, to recapitulate, we come from a world called Tae'Eladar. On that world, we have endured a plague of orcs for a great length of time. In the past, they were little more than a bother, easily controlled by a few well-placed guard patrols on highways and in outposts throughout the land. They would mostly raid merchant caravans and wayfarers, but not typically the organized settlements."

"Uh," Relissa raises a finger. "You had them over there previously?"

"Yes, they apparently arrived on Tae'Eladar many thousands of years ago from places unknown, as part of what we assume to be a kind of migration. Similarly, we are unsure how they arrived, other than to say it was likely using portals, and further, they likely had help. Our history with them tells us they were never that good at applying the magical arts to produce these themselves."

"Jiggers, that doesn't sound good already, especially when you consider our history with them here."

"Indeed, but let us come to that in a moment."

"Thousands of years?" Kaliya frowns. "But that…well, never mind for now. Please continue."

"So here we are with them occupying space on our world. But then, something changed. Several decades ago, we saw a transition of behavior. What was once simply bad became worse. Villages came under attack, even some of the smaller towns, those that were not a target previously. It began as raids for food and supplies, and initially we thought they had run out of their local stocks, so we tried negotiation to see if we could finally settle our long-standing differences."

"How did that work out for you?" Relissa wonders.

"Badly… They refused to cooperate, which was nothing new to us, and soon these attacks increased in frequency and severity to include our citizens. Orcs care little for anything that is, well, not orcish. The hostages were used as forced labor until they were too weak to continue, and then ultimately, they would end up on a platter."

"Like in those visions you gave me," Kaliya mentions.

"This is correct. Up until this time, we were willing to tolerate them if their only crime was theft, hoping to quell this in a more polite manner. We had tried to maintain vigilance to keep the orcs under control, but they did not take well the message. Then we had an attack in one particular region, where they took to abducting and cannibalizing our citizens. This was an atrocity I could not permit."

He turns to scan the canyon valley below as he continues.

"I united the people of my world to create a better future for all, but these heathens would have no part of it. This final straw would represent the last of my patience. As such, I was forced to make a rather grim decree: There can be no peace in our world for as long as orcs exist alongside of us."

"Ouch…" Kaliya grimaces.

"We have seen this as our history teaches us of their absolute refusal to cooperate. They do not negotiate with that which they regard as fodder, and I will no longer make the attempt. Therefore, I set myself and my military Order to their absolute destruction. Genocide."

He lowers his head briefly as he catches his breath. He again turns and points a finger at the massive horde down below for emphasis.

"They once occupied a large nation on our world, but we beat them back. Our war has persisted for a few years by now, but this is largely due to their numbers, not their threat potential. We drove them against the sea and into the last pocket of their lands. But in these final few months, we began to take notice of how few they were suddenly becoming. We had hoped this was because they had used up most of their best warriors and had nothing left to throw at us."

The three friends look on in fascination of the tale while Thaelyn continues his oratory.

"We would soon find our answer, however, and it was surprising to us. In the last of their settlements, we happened upon an underground chamber with several shamans maintaining a portal while workers carried supplies through. They were escaping! We had never seen them use portals before, so this was new. I realized instantly that I could not simply allow them to run to some hidden location where they could possibly regroup for a later return. Therefore, I rushed three of my elite scouts into the portal with instructions to make a quick survey and report back, bringing away portal runes leading to the local area at all reasonable costs. We then dispatched the shamans so they could not pass this knowledge on to others."

"Excuse me, Your Lordship," Haran interrupts. "You are speaking of those people who showed up here. But scouts using magic?"

"Many of our people study magic to a rather high level of prestige within our military Order these days, and especially scouts in order to make and use portal runes. It simply makes the craft that much more versatile," he shrugs.

"Oh! Well, my goodness, how could I possibly miss that," he chuckles satirically.

"Indeed, but our society back home does not follow as it once did if you originally came from there. Back before my arrival, and of course my influence to teach the people, only a scarce few might study anything, and mostly for their own personal gain. I changed that."

"Wow, all right. So, do you use these things often where you come from?"

"Quite often, and for a long time, as well. Their utility is easily apparent."

He now makes a passing glance at his assembly of troops before returning his gaze out onto the valley.

"It was my initial hope that the shamans might simply be performing a conjuring to another location within our own world. This would have been a much simpler form of magic for them to use."

He now turns his stare at Kaliya.

"But when the scouts returned with the report of a strange creature they had not seen before, at least not on our world, nor anything else I might recognize, I began to wonder where these beastly cretins were taking us. Portals to other worlds, and indeed to other planes, are far more complex, particularly to know where to aim one. This further complicates matters as it now virtually demands outside help. We had suspected this uprising was inspired by something new to us, although granted it was still believed to be local. And yet, now we find ourselves standing on a new world, and in a new universe, leaving me to wonder what that something truly was."

"A new universe?!" Kaliya yelps. "You came from yet another one? Cu'Nar help us all."

"Yet another?"

"My people are also from another universe. This isn't our native home."

"How interesting. This plot seems to be thickening with details that will demand their own explanation soon. Let us begin here. What name do you give to this place?"

"We call this wreck of a world Therinë, Your Lordship," Relissa grimaces. "Not that any of us here are too pleased about it these days."

"An elven name? Very nice. But due perhaps to these orcs?"

"Due to a lot of bunk that's happened to us over the years."

"I see. Then we should add this to the list of things to discuss momentarily. My next greatest concern is this… I feel reasonably certain, if only by guessing, that within yon accumulation of orcs there may be, in parts large or small, refugees of the armies I have chased off Tae'Eladar. But if they have portals leaving Tae'Eladar and returning here, I must also suspect this population may be the original inspiration of the uprising back home. And yet, Kaliya, you used the words 'orc home' in one of your statements. Are we looking at the point of origin for these creatures? Or is this located elsewhere?"

"No, um…Your Lordship," Kaliya offers, borrowing from her friends for the manner of address. "Their native home is one jump backwards on the path my people took to arrive here. It's a world we call Ruuki uy'Daan."

"Wonderful, and also such an interesting name, between that and yourself…people and a place in exile… Are you turned out from somewhere?"

"We had to run away from our ancient home due to something

big and bad that came to visit. That's all. We're not criminals or anything, just running for our lives, what's left of us."

"And here we have yet another anomaly. All right, one at a time… These orcs are apparently occupying this world, correct?"

"Yes."

"But their native home is another one, and this further denotes the application of what I must assume to be outside help to allow them to move around like this."

"Yes. He's a very powerful being, so it's likely he taught them a few things."

"This does not bode well. They may also revere him as a godlike entity. Their society would naturally follow such a thing if it were influential enough."

"Probably, and they've been making incursions using what we suspect to be portals from there for a few centuries so far."

"Centuries! Powers pay witness, and no doubt this reflects on Relissa's displeasures of this world."

"Yeah, part of it."

"Only part? There is more? And is this where you learned to speak Orcish, if only just barely," he smiles gently.

"Yeah, barely…" she chuckles. "I learned as a child on Ruuki uy'Daan, but in those days we held peaceful relations with them, at least until they got up and hit us in the back, forcing us to flee to this place."

"Interesting, but then, if they lived in peace with you, being who you are as a society, they might have also seen you as a rather extravagant example worthy of respect. What caused them to turn on you?"

"That same being that probably sent them at you. His name is Sargeras, the one who came to our ancient home and corrupted the rest of our people."

"Gracious, Kaliya!" Aerlie yips. "What sort of trouble did you get yourselves into? What kind of being is it that could turn a whole society as enlightened as you into such beasts that they would chase you across dimensional bounds just to hunt you?"

"I don't know. We have no idea where he came from or what he is, just that we were told to run when he arrived."

"All right, this is one more issue for a later moment," Thaelyn sighs. "Let us continue. Relissa, you were hinting at other concerns here on this world. Perhaps we should touch on this now."

"Aye, but you're not going to like it."

"Understood, but give it to me, as I should probably be made aware of it regardless."

"Aye, you should, because if you have plans on hitting those orcs out there, they have friends. This is our bugaboo of a problem on this skank of a world. There's nothing left of it after a four-century long war dusting the whole of it."

"Powers pay pity, Child," he winces. "How can a world of any sort survive a siege of that magnitude? Very well, who are these others?"

"Firstly, how…we didn't. My home is the sole survivor city for my people. His, the same," she thumbs at Haran. "As for who, part of it is those other elves I mentioned earlier. That Sargeras bugger corrupted them and turned them against the rest of us."

"Oh, how nice of him!" Aerlie blasts. "He would do this to our people? What sort of elves are we speaking of here?"

"They call themselves Flame Elves nowadays. They have a city just south of here past those hills down there," she directs to the southern end of the valley.

"Flame Elves," Aerlie frowns. "That is a rather curious, if also unsettling name."

"Aye, and they have manners to match. But my schooling told me once they were called High Elves, like some of yours over there," she glances at the circle of troops.

"High Elves? So, you and a group of Calaerea were travelling together?"

"Aye, I suppose, but this was forever ago by now. Then the war hit us, followed by the orcs by about half a century, I think, along with her people," she now thumbs at Kaliya.

"Uh oh…so the hunters are present alongside the hunted?"

"The Suuden'kai, aye. They have camps to the east, behind

those mountains, to the best of my knowing, but no one ever goes over there because they're simply too dangerous."

"What sort of weapons do they use, can you tell us?"

"Um, Kaliya, this is your bit."

"They use what we call plasma rifles," she informs. "Do you know what those are?"

"Indeed, I do," Thaelyn considers. "And this could present a problem. We may need to step carefully around those if we should ever come to blows. I wonder how our mage shield would hold up to that," he muses as he glances at Aerlie.

"I would imagine it should suffice," she returns casually. "It can handle Mystra's Fury easily enough, even at close range. If it can take that, I doubt we should have anything to worry about."

"Yes, so a simple energy weapon ought not to be much of a bother. But we will need a portable form of the shield to apply it here."

Kaliya watched the curious, if also seemingly casual disregard to the seriousness of the technology referenced here. She then glanced at the contradictory appearance of the soldiers with their medieval-appearing armor and weapons.

"Excuse me, but are you sure you know what I'm talking about? These things blast stuff to bits, and I should know because I've seen it!"

"Young lady," Thaelyn encourages. "I do know of the technology. High energy physics...plasma, the fourth state of matter, and here as what, a ranged pulse-like weapon, perhaps?"

"Yes, that."

"Very good. But we also have a few tricks to play. So, tame your skepticism a tad until we can gain a better understanding together. What are these people called?"

"Our original name is Suuden-Aryku, although the name is something of an insult by now, especially where they are concerned."

"Suuden-Aryku..." he muses. "The Lifted Ones? Lifted in what way? And would this hold any relation to your eyes, by the way. You seem to have a rather peculiar glow," he smiles.

"As far as the name goes, it's the ancestral name for our people, lifted from our primeval beginnings as a civilization. We are…or were…a society founded on science and intellectual pursuits. At least until HE came along. As for the eyes, um, no… The eyes are what we call the Blessing of the cu'Nar."

"And here we have that word again, cu'Nar. You have used that word on a few occasions so far. Is this some form of deity for your people?"

Relissa suddenly erupts in a boisterous laugh at the suggestion. She doubles over briefly and covers her mouth. Her eyes dart across to Kaliya, who simply smirks and sets her hands on her hips to wait it out.

"Buggers to that, I say," she chortles. "If that doesn't just tie it! Her people aren't at all the religious type, Your Lordship. This is some wacky thing that helped them escape from home."

"Indeed," he smiles. "But then, how do we define it? And why this curious name…cu'Nar, they who follow. Follow what?"

"To begin with," Kaliya answers. "We call them cu'Nar because, for lack of a better name, they seemed to be following Sargeras shortly after he arrived. They tried to explain themselves, but their language, if you can call it that, is simply weird. It's telepathic."

"Ah! Very well, so we might say they are using a conceptual form to represent themselves. This is how a true telepathic society might do it."

"If you say so, it's just weird to me. But now, they are a strange form of life which we interpret to be a pure form of light and energy. We encountered them on our ship when it was delivered to us on our home world of Azgarén. The ship is called the Naarg uy'Sodrad, but it's not something we built. It was apparently donated to us by…someone…and just at that moment when we had to leave. The cu'Nar once came to us with a message that Sargeras was bad and to run away. Then they delivered the ship and we loaded up as many people as we could, and left home. Along the way, they gave us this strange gift, which we interpreted as a blessing to serve as a form of protection, or cleansing, or something. Since that time, our eyes glow."

"Indeed! Aerlie, what do you think of this?"

"This sounds most peculiar," she admits. "And I think you would agree, Thaelyn. Are we speaking of some manner of positive energy elemental?"

"We could be, and therefore the coloring, as well as that positive aura she emits."

"But Thaelyn, what would a band of…well, Positive Primes, I suppose…be doing outside their native realm, and more so to interact with people like hers in any way?"

"And especially this level of interaction. This is yet another curious mystery."

Haran glared at them for the blatant terms being applied here.

"Elementals?" he wonders openly. "These cu'Nar are some kind of elementals? But, um…I thought those were only, well…I'm not entirely sure."

"You are a mage student, are you not?" Thaelyn inquires. "Do they not teach you this in your academy?"

"No, actually… They barely teach us how to light candles, they're so chintzy in the lessons. I recall this briefly mentioned in a book once in our library, but the Masters don't let us do much more than brew potions for people like me sent out in the field on suicide missions like this," he thumbs aggressively at the mass of orcs in the canyon.

"Good gods, Haran," Aerlie winces. "Why do you even take lessons there if they don't treat you with any level of decency?"

"It's all I have," he moans and hangs his head.

"Kaliya," Thaelyn resumes. "Help me to understand more of your home and these Suuden-Aryku. You say you come from another universe. What brought you to this one? Are your people so adept that they cover so much territory by now?"

"No, as far as I understand it from my own history, Sargeras and his loyalists chased us all around our local galaxy back home, at least until we made what we call a wild jump to this universe. And before you ask, as I'm fairly sure you will," she smiles delicately. "A wild jump is literally to program a random set of coordinates into our nav computer and let it go."

"Great Powers, Child!" he wheezes. "I may not be one to travel across Prime domains in such a manner, but even I know the dangers of such a maneuver as that! Why would you do this?"

"One word, desperation… We were tired of moving across so many worlds and getting hit so many times, only to move elsewhere to be discovered and hit again. We decided to make this one in the hopes of going so far away, he couldn't find us again. Unfortunately, it didn't seem to work in the end."

"This sounds as if he was playing with you, and further that he must have some means of following you."

"Generally, yes, we believe this also. The ship never took any hits. We might see an occasional ground assault or a few pot shots here and there from orbit into the city, just to bump us along."

"That's despicable!" Aerlie growls. "And for how long?"

"Um, according to my history, this was…uh…well, not quite ten full millennia."

Both Thaelyn and Aerlie went slack jawed at the outrageous figure. They turned to gaze at each other, and then back to the girl still sitting on the log.

"Excuse me," Aerlie mutters. "Did you say millennia just now?"

"Yeah, millennia…thousands of years," she grins shyly.

Thaelyn covers his eyes and stumbles a few steps away.

"How, in the names of all the Great Powers, and in all of Creation, can a body of populace survive being hunted in such a fashion and for such a measure of time? And for that matter, the one who is pursuing them to find continued interest in such for that same period."

"I wish I could answer that," Kaliya moans.

"And further to think, how many generations have passed along the way! Those who began the journey, then they who would come after, and so on, down to where you are now. The sheer numbers are potentially staggering."

"Well, I don't know the actual count, and staggering would certainly be a good word for it, but, um…you should also ask about our lifespans, since we're on the subject."

"Oh? Very well, if you think this is important. Um, young lady, perhaps you would like to tell us how old you are?"

"Sure! Four..." she smirks cutely.

"Four..." he frowns at her.

"My, my..." Aerlie muses wittily. "You grow up fast."

Relissa was displaying a wide grin by this time, as she knew what was coming up next. Thaelyn couldn't help but notice the smug expression, and he nudged his wife to examine it also.

"Yes..." he clears his throat tenuously. "I feel as though I should ask this, although I do not know precisely why, but four what?"

"Centuries!" Kaliya croons.

"Indeed! This is most curious. So, you hold a habit of measuring your age in centuries, or are you simply playing a little game with us," he grins.

"Oh no, this is how we do it, at least once we pass our first... out of two hundred!"

Now Thaelyn lets out an exacerbated wheeze, and nearly doubling over, while Aerlie covers her face as her eyes bulged.

"Two...hundred...centuries?!" he gasps. "Powers behold, dear young lady, how does your society rate such an outlandishly extended longevity? How old is your civilization overall?"

"According to my history, about two million years..."

Thaelyn pulled himself upright, and recomposed his posture as he contemplated this new figure.

"Two million...and with lifespans of twenty millennia..."

"Thaelyn," Aerlie considers. "I can already find something strange in those numbers."

"Strange, yes, but without a careful examination of their history, and how they came to possess this level of longevity, we are limited to make any conclusions. But simply to possess it in the first place! This would place their trek within only half a lifetime for the original excursionists. Who amongst your people still survive from the initial population?"

"My...um," Kaliya coughs briefly as she fumbles her reply. "Our leader is one we call…Velen. Right now, he's really the only survivor of the original group. He's one hundred eighty-two by now…"

Both Thaelyn and Aerlie wince at the figure as Kaliya continues.

"Everyone else, including myself, were born on one or another world along the way. Many of us are of a younger age range, meaning a few or several millennia, and some are many generations away from those who originally left Azgarén."

"So, we do have a fair number of people who are separated from the originals, even so."

"Velen is the one the cu'Nar contacted, and they gave him the message. He was a member of our governing Council back on Azgarén. When Sargeras arrived, Velen tried to warn the others not to listen to him, but I guess no one listened to the warning instead. Then the cu'Nar brought us the ship and we left. Sometime after that, we started to see these attacks, and we noticed the Suuden'kai forces had been transformed somehow."

"Suuden'kai?" Aerlie wonders. "According to those lessons I just received, this is a familiar term to reference the name, correct?"

"Yes, it's a part of our language. The 'kai suffix is added to offer a form of respect to an individual or a thing when used as a descriptor…although it's just as much an insult in this case."

"I see."

"Transformed…" Thaelyn asks. "How, precisely?"

"We don't know how, precisely," Kaliya responds. "He must've done something funny to them. But on those few occasions we saw them, like during a ground assault, they appeared mutated, and they behaved almost like machines, with no apparent emotions or compassion."

"That sounds like some sort of mind control," Aerlie muses. "Perhaps these mutations altered them in some fashion as to dominate their original capacity."

"Possibly," Thaelyn offers. "But if we are to fight them here on this world, I would like an opportunity to examine them to see how it was applied and if there could be a treatment of some sort."

"Jiggers," Relissa emits. "You think you might want to try turning this around?"

"Relissa, we are not such that we simply go out and destroy everything we see. These orcs may have raised our ire for their deeds, but these others are another matter. If an artificial influence was applied, especially by a malignant factor, my first thought is to understand it, not simply destroy any and all examples of it. I will take that course only if I can find no other option."

"Well, fine, but first you need something to look at, and I doubt you can just whistle, and they'll come running like a pet dog."

"Perhaps, but this is a topic for later, I am sure."

"Whatever the case, Your Lordship," Kaliya adds. "They're a very highly technological society, so be careful."

"Very well, I will take this under advisement."

"Um, Your Lordship," Haran interjects tenderly. "I certainly don't wish to present myself as someone who may appear excessively brash, but we've answered a good many questions for you so far, and yet we still have a sizable number for ourselves."

"This is fair, Haran, and I would surely wish to accommodate, but as we are already taking some time with this, I am growing increasingly nervous about our friends down there in that canyon," he thumbs over his shoulder. "Let us see if we can finish this up quickly so we can relieve ourselves of that much."

"Fine and thanks… First, you tell us you are at war with them, and for that matter, so are we, among those others we spoke of. But we simply don't have the means to fight any longer, we've been at this for so long. Poor Kaliya has seen her fair share of misfortune during her lifetime, both on Ruuki uy'Daan as well as here, and my understanding is her people take constant hits from these others as little more than skirmishes just to keep them hiding indoors. I hope you will understand from our side, we are rather desperate from our experiences in this war."

"If you have been at this for a period on the order of centuries, I am amazed to see you still standing at all. You say you are down to your last cities, but what condition are they in?"

"Well, to my knowledge, I don't think we've seen any assaults within my lifetime. Relissa?"

"Nah," she offers. "A few hits on the outer fringes with orcs playing games on our watch towers, but not the city itself."

"Just one moment here," Thaelyn asserts. "So, they whittle you down to one surviving city each, and then halt?"

"There's something wrong with that," Aerlie muses. "That sounds more like a purging effort, and then a form of population control to keep them that way."

"Bloody hell!" Relissa yips. "So, what do you mean by that, they're keeping us in reserve for something?"

"If they wanted you dead, I think you would be dead, and in much less than four centuries, especially if we are speaking of a society with orbital bombardment capacity."

"She's right, Relissa," Kaliya agrees. "She's actually got a point, same with us."

"Buggers!" she barks. "Fine, but I don't like the sound of it."

"And no doubt this would only exasperate the condition of their desperation," Thaelyn adds. "As well as to demoralize them."

"Well, anyway," Haran continues. "I'm not much of a spokesperson for my people, I don't carry that sort of authority, but as I look over here at your troops, and by the way, I'm not sure what you have in mind with all those mages, but I'm asking myself what your overall plan is, and if it could somehow give aid to each of us. I don't want to sound like I'm trying to grub for offerings, but surely you can see our situation."

"Haran, relax. I am not one to leave people out in the cold. It is clearly evident what we have here, and if I can give aid, I will. But I must also admit to a need to take this on an official level with proper political support."

"Oh, but of course! Naturally..."

"But so far we have a more imperative need, and that is this hazard over yon," he again glances at the canyon. "In order to secure my position up here, I must dispose of them first. Once done, I should have some breathing room to apply myself on other sides. The difficulty is in their numbers."

"Oh, you don't need to tell me that. Clearly, we have a lot of them down there."

"Aye," Relissa interjects. "I'm guessing a good two hundred great in that batch, even though I've never seen that many in one place before."

"That is not a bad guess. How do you make your estimates in this case?"

"I'm taking a small bunch and compare how close they are, and then I multiply for the larger seas of them by trying to measure the scale of it."

"Not a bad method. You must have learned your lessons well in this regard. Personally, I was judging about the same, maybe as much as a quarter million or so."

Relissa smiled at her achievement and the commendation he offered. It was the first real credit she had ever received during her service, even by her own superiors. She glanced at her friends to see their faces before returning to him.

"But how do you plan on doing this?" Haran wonders. "Like I said, you will surely need more forces than this to take on all of that."

"If I were to use a common ground assault, yes..." Thaelyn affirms. "But we have other means at our disposal here, and several additional concerns that need attention. You must understand something, and that is I am no stranger to warfare. I am the King of a full world, but it did not come about by accident, and neither by simple inheritance. I built it with my own two hands out of a congregation of nations that in many cases did not cooperate well, and in some cases did not even go willingly."

"Jiggers!" Relissa yips. "Suddenly, I'm a little scared of you."

"Relissa, the reasons for this became clear to me after a while as I came to fully understand my intended purpose in that world, and it was precisely to unite the masses into one collected society in peace and harmony, so that we may travel the road to the future together. There could be no exceptions."

"And who told you this load of bunk?"

"The owner of that world. It was a divine mandate, dear Child. I was sent there by one of the Powers."

Now it was Relissa and Haran who went slack jawed. Kaliya wheezed softly as she tried to fathom the meaning of this statement, but not being religious, she couldn't really imagine something like a god directing the show. She began pulling herself off the log to join her friends.

"When you say, the Powers," she intones warily. "What do you actually mean? You talk about me and my reference to the cu'Nar, but my people aren't religious, like Relissa said. And yet, you have also used this word several times, and now in such a way that it makes them appear as physical bodies giving orders."

"Indeed, and sometimes they do. Um..." he hesitates as he scans the local area and one more time down into the canyon. "Aerlie, we are taking a while on this. Do you see anything down there?"

"I see movement here and there, but nothing significant coming this way, like a patrol. But I'll keep watch. Go ahead, you may as well finish this part, at least. At this point, I think they may need to know, at least partially, so we don't get any backtalk when we drop Mystra's Fury on the place. We'll need their cooperation in this, and not have them running around like frightened children."

"What's this Mystra's Fury bit?" Relissa asks timidly.

"A type of weapon..."

"Uh huh...and do I need to remind you how many we decided were down there?"

"Well, no, but it's a big weapon, also," she smiles innocently.

"Oh, right. Did I say you peeps scare me? Well, I'm asking myself which is the worse for it now."

"Kaliya," Thaelyn resumes. "And Relissa, and Haran, in answer to your question, I feel I must explain exactly who...and for that matter...what I am. But..." he emphasizes with a finger. "Promise me this. This is private just between us here. I am a stranger in strange lands, and surrounded by unknowns on multiple sides, most of whom are apparently unfriendly. Keeping this secret is paramount, as I could use it as a tactical advantage. Do you understand?"

"Aye! You got my word on it. Haran?" she elbows him in the ribs.

"Yes, absolutely," he nods eagerly. "I certainly wouldn't want to spoil something that could ultimately help our people."

Kaliya had arrived next to the others by now. She was feeling a little nervous, not so much due to the need for security here, but how she might ultimately hold up under it with the Elder Council back home demanding information, as well as her track record in general.

"I will offer my best support," she mutters. "But I hope you can explain what…exactly…you mean by it, because we don't believe in divine entities."

"Very well, then let us approach it in this way," he surmises. "With your people living in this world, you have likely, if also inadvertently, influenced their culture with your advanced presence."

"Yeah, I suppose you could say that," she chuckles softly. "They were really surprised to see us drop out of their sky that one day."

"Indeed! So, perhaps we could jumpstart this a bit if they are already partway there. If you cannot accept the superstitious definition, would you perhaps believe in entities of such a supremely high level of advancement that they could potentially represent gods to other…younger…societies, like theirs perhaps?"

"In all the bleedin' hells," Relissa moans under her breath. "How do you mean that, exactly?"

"Um…well," Kaliya responds cautiously. "I suppose I could. But I think I would still need some kind of definition. Because the way they talk about it…well, you know."

"Of course, many people of their sort are like this. But for this point, and since this dear young lady is about to have her innocence shattered, we should give it our full attention. Relissa, do your people still worship the Seldarine?"

"Aye, we do."

"Very good. They are but a small chapter of a larger body we call the Estelar."

"Jiggers…"

"In all the Seas of Creation, which represents the myriad of dimensional planes and other bodies, meaning such things that people like you would most often refer to as universes, there exists a grand body of beings on a scale that very literally reaches godhood. They are called the Estelar. This is essentially a conglomeration of many different races of beings who each independently scaled the evolutionary tree to such extremes, that they no longer even hold corporeal form, and neither do they inhabit what we refer to as Prime domains...a universe like this one," he waves to the general space around him. "They live on the outside by now in a place some call the Fifth Fold."

"What's a Fifth Fold?" Kaliya asks.

"The term 'fold' is what some use to represent a dimensional plane. This universe would be one example. Your original home would be another, mine yet another, and so on, on a three-dimensional scale. But they make their homes in that higher domain, and from there they might have access to anything and everything that is technically beneath that perch, meaning to say those dimensional planes of lesser proportions."

"Um, wait. I feel my horns sagging now. Is this to describe something like five-dimensional space?"

"It is."

"Wow, this goes a little beyond my education now. But it also contradicts with what I'm looking at over there with your people, who look a little, um..."

Thaelyn glances at his troops, who were still patiently waiting for the meeting to close.

"Perhaps you might be thinking of the word primitive?"

"Um, well, no offence, but...uh..."

"Ours is a rather unique situation," he nods pleasantly, "as we hold a special relationship with that body of Estelar in our local space. They have a strict principle of rule not to evolve a younger society by artificial means, instead allowing them to grow naturally, and only when they are ready for it. But ours holds such a relationship that they might know more about the nature of these beings than your average example," he directs to Relissa and Haran. "And then we have such as the two of us," he directs at himself and Aerlie. "We are also exceptions to the rule."

"And how do you describe this?"

"We are no simple…mortal…creatures. If you can give your age in terms of centuries, so can we, though it is uncommon for us to see this used elsewhere outside our own."

"In all the nether-space…would this also relate to this telepathy of yours, and that telekinesis we saw earlier?"

"To say nothing of his trip to the moon," Haran notes. "Is that another one, perhaps?"

"And does this relate to your eyes being gold?" Relissa wonders.

"You are very astute," he smiles. "Then I must admit to each of these, as they are a part of my being, which we describe as a Celestial. My race is called Aasimar, while Aerlie is called Eladrin. These are ascended forms, in our cases being hybridized, whereas other Celestials, natural ones, are more like you, but on a much higher scale approaching, but not yet attaining that divine ascension. We are born directly of the Estelar themselves."

"Cu'Nar's Grace," Kaliya whimpers. "Am I getting an education now! But how, in all the nether-space, am I going to explain any part of this to the Elder Council. They'll want to know what's going on out here, especially if you want any kind of political interaction."

"Perhaps we can develop a plan together once we have some time to ourselves."

"You know," Relissa submits. "My Mum told me a few things about where babies come from, but um… How does a god, and um…well…one of us…um…"

Thaelyn grins and raises his brow at her, then turns to Aerlie for help.

"You are the priestess and medical professional here, my Dear. Perhaps you can indulge?"

"Oh, am I supposed to be giving out lessons now on the nature of things?"

Aerlie smiles and steps forward a nudge.

"The gods do not reproduce quite the same as we, but they can and do sometimes reproduce. However, in the case of creating a hybridized Celestial, which is actually a rather rare and precious gift, they most often bring it forward from within a mortal female's body. But unlike your traditional male contribution, like from that of a man giving his seed to a woman, the Estelar must use alternate means to create a body. Between the two of us," she glances at her husband, "we actually have two very different examples, as he does not technically have a mother at all. His body was simply produced by his Father, and then given life."

"Bloody hell," Relissa covers her face. "That blows it for me."

"How?" Kaliya asks. "Are we speaking of fabricating it somehow?"

"In your case," Aerlie responds. "Since you must surely be high enough in your medical science to know this much, it was genetically engineered based on a human framework."

"And cu'Nar's pity again! So, they just make something and ZAP! There you go."

"Generally so," she smiles. "His Father, one of the Estelar in our local domain called Tyr, is the one who did this for us. I, on the other hand, was also created by Tyr, but I was essentially a clone of my mother's body, and then ascended to a Celestial condition."

"And that basically blows it for me now."

"Um," Haran hesitates. "So, this Tyr is a Father to both of you? Eh, doesn't that make you brother and sister?" he smiles bashfully.

"Of the spirit, perhaps," Aerlie replies, "as we do contain some of his divine essence. But of the spirit is not the same as of the body."

"So, if I'm getting any part of this, the Celestial side is mostly a form of ascension from your more common mortal form to something partway to godhood? Like, as if to say, you are half god due to this?"

"Yes, this would be a fair estimation. But that half we possess is rather potent, as you could see here," she directs her gaze at the tree.

"Yes, I think that would certainly stand out. What else are you people capable of, or do I dare ask?"

"This is where we tend to keep our secrets, as most mortals are simply not in the position to know too much about it. But you can be sure there are gifts some of us possess and may even focus on as a kind of specialization."

"Is there some special reason he did all this? You said this is a special and rare thing. Was it solely to bring your world together?"

"Jiggers, Haran," Relissa winces. "Someone must've been really hot to settle all those squabbling nations of theirs, if that's the case."

"In a manner of speaking," Aerlie resumes. "You may be right. Although, if the statement, 'the gods work in strange ways', holds any meaning, it also applies to us sometimes. We each have a curious history, and a path of Fate we've been following, so only part of it is revealed to us thus far."

"This is truly fascinating…" Kaliya muses. "To think that an actual being we can call a god would create something that brings a world together, and then one day I might have a chance to speak to someone about this. It almost makes me believe in…well, actually…"

"Believe in what, Kaliya?" Haran asks.

"Oh, Haran, nothing… It's absolutely silly, and like we keep saying, I'm not religious. What do I know about anything? For instance, do these gods take up anything like, oh, professions?"

"Indeed, they do!" Thaelyn asserts proudly. "Just as with any other society, they may specialize in certain principles and philosophies, in this case largely for the purpose of presenting themselves to the younger societies as a means of guiding them along certain precise paths. Look at Relissa here, for example. If her people follow the teachings of the Seldarine, you have a selection of deities, each with their own portfolio of teachings, which can offer a variety of pathways for their followers to choose from."

Kaliya suddenly found her voice catching in her throat as he continued to speak.

"Then, we have others who are outside that group, such as what the human society might follow, and those for some of the other races we have on Tae'Eladar. Some of these might overlap in their specialization, but for different races and perhaps in different manners to suit the occasion. Tyr, for example… Although we lost him a few centuries ago to an unfortunate event that took his life…"

"They can die, too?!" she screeches. "I thought they were supposed to be all-powerful, all-this, all-that…and such."

"Yes, the common depictions you might so often see with many societies tend to grant this impractical definition to the gods, where impractical, in this case, is to grant an infinite quality to what is otherwise a finite form. You cannot. They may be greatly this, and greatly that, but infinite? No, this is not reasonable. The Estelar are still people, simply people of such extremely high potential that to someone of a lesser station, they might seem as so much more."

"And there goes the last of it for me," Relissa moans.

"Now, now…they are every bit as much as you could hope for, but we must also be realistic if we are to interpret them as people, not as some mystical body of unfathomable proportions."

"Aye, I think I follow, but you were right, this is a wee bit of a shocker."

"What happened to this one called Tyr that he died?" Kaliya wonders.

"It was an unfortunate, as well as a very painful loss for us. He and a group of others were out and about trying to enact a sentencing of judgment against a rival, when he fell in battle."

"Oh, I'm terribly sorry, and he was essentially your Father."

"Yes, his station was replaced by another we call Torm, the new Lord of Justice over our local domain."

Kaliya glared at him as he mentioned those words. She suddenly felt a chill, and her face turned pale, although it might not show unless you could determine paleness in bluish skin. At the same time, her mouth fell open and her eyes were growing wide.

"As for me," Thaelyn continues. "I chose to rededicate our Order of Knighthood to his honor. We call ourselves the Order of Tyr, in honor of his principles of Justice and Law, and the strength to uphold it in the face of any uncertainty," he pauses to gaze out onto the canyon again. "ANY uncertainty…" he asserts firmly.

"Dear cu'Nar…" Kaliya whispers and clamps her hands over her face. "Could it be? Can it actually be? The Divine Justice?"

"Thaelyn," Aerlie interrupts urgently. "I'm sensing something."

"Wonderful. How many?"

"I foresee four of them. They will be arriving shortly on the edge of the cliff."

"All right, listen to me," he directs to the group. "Get behind those rocks and hide. Stay out of sight. Let us handle this. As much as I enjoyed our chat, we must now get to work. I cannot wait any longer. Perhaps later, we may find more time."

The two of them pulled back abruptly. The suddenness of their movements called the immediate attention of the circle of troops. The small company pulled itself to attention as they waited for instruction.

Aerlie turns herself around to the canyon and begins panning the rugged cliffside, while Thaelyn turns to the troops with hands raised, snapping fingers on both sides, and making a set of rapid gestures.

First, he put his hands up with open palms facing each other, making circular motions, as if sliding the palms around, although they were not actually touching. He follows by drawing his hands to either side of his head, and like pulling curtains over a window, slides them across over his eyes.

Haran and Relissa jump back behind the rocks to take shelter. But they soon realize Kaliya is apparently in some form of shock, so they rush out again to drag their tall companion down into their former hiding spot. Haran eyes Thaelyn, with his peculiar hand gestures, and now he observes the troops as they begin some form of spell-weaving.

The mages on the front line begin conjuring something. Waves of energy were flowing through their hands and around their bodies, coalescing into an outline just in front of them. A moment later, the entire group vanishes behind a curtain that remarkably resembles the empty terrain under them.

"A group invisibility field?" he muses privately. "Gods be blessed, these people are way ahead of us where their magical studies are concerned."

"If you have a half-god teaching them," Relissa suggests. "I guess you can do that."

"But didn't he say they have a policy of some sort?"

"Aye, but do we actually know how long they've been doing it over there? Look at us. My people don't do that much, and yours do even less. If he owns the whole world, he's probably giving them all sorts of leverage."

"But how does this relate to things like science," Kaliya adds. "And anything I might be able to recognize?"

"Don't ask me. Maybe we can find out later."

Thaelyn and Aerlie now take up stands out in the open, seemingly the only people in easy view on the field. Aerlie pulls her wings back in what resembles an attack pose, and together they wait.

"She looks serious," Haran notes. "But I'm wondering now how she knew they were coming."

"I heard her say something about foreseeing it," Relissa offers. "So, you may have another one for the list, a kind of Sight."

"That's simply scary. To hold that much power, what does it do to a person?"

"If you're the child of a god, my guess is you already have half the answer. You do as they do, but maybe a wee bit closer to our level."

After a short pause, a small orcish patrol of four warriors comes up the ridge into view of the two nobles. As they were the only ones visible on the field, the orcs focused exclusively on them. Thaelyn exclaims angrily in a harsh form of Orcish.

"Look at this!" he taunts. "A challenge of two to one, how delightful! But do you even have the loin meat to come forward? Ha-Ha!"

The orcs were enraged by the insulting display and lurched to the attack. They crossed the space from the cliffside to the two nobles in rapid succession. But before they could get within reach, Thaelyn waved his hand, and two of them went sailing across the field to fall behind the invisible wall. Aerlie also waved hers, and the other two followed close behind.

"Folks," Haran mutters feebly. "Please don't make those people angry, whatever you do."

"Aye," Relissa whines.

A few moments later, the cloaking wall came down to reveal the troops hauling the dead orcish bodies out of their circle.

Thaelyn snaps his fingers to draw the attention for the trio to come back over. Haran rushes up, determined to be first in conversation.

"Your Lordship," he asks hurriedly. "Um, I would really like to know how you intend to defeat that mass down there, if you please. This up here…" he glances at the guard troupe. "Well, unless you're going to tell me they're all like you, I personally don't see it happening."

"True, although I might at the same time suggest we could certainly do a fair bit of damage. These are not your ordinary troops here. Regardless of that, I intend to use a magical construct called Mystra's Fury. It is a difficult and complex spell that requires some time for the casting. As such, I must ask you to take up occupancy with my troops in the circle and wait. Do as they do…no more, no less. Understood?"

"All right, but magic you say? I thought you were much more a warrior class…by your dress, that is."

"As a Celestial, I hold a much deeper affinity with the natural elements. Therefore, I am a master at both."

"Gracious…all right, I won't argue anymore."

"Kaliya, you speak our language. If you receive further instruction, follow it, and relate it to your friends. Do you see that man with the elevated headdress?"

"Yeah, the one who was inspecting us earlier?" she replies.

"His name is Captain Hagmaert, and he is part of my Royal Guard. He is in command outside of me for the moment."

"Got it…"

"If you're thinking of using magic," Relissa jests. "You'll need one grand bugger of a spell for all that. No way can you kill all those with some dinky bit of sparkling."

"Trust me, young lady, you will not be disappointed, but you must do as you are told."

"Aye, fine."

The three of them walk away towards the circle to join the others while Thaelyn and Aerlie turn towards the canyon.

"So many out there…" he mourns. "And here I was hoping our war was nearly finished. Now we have another world to fight."

"And worse, with new enemies," Aerlie submits. "At least some of whom might take exception to us being here fighting these orcs."

"These Suuden-Aryku may be a problem."

"And I want to know what that heathen did to our brethren."

"You are not the only one, Aerlie. This would amount to a grave insult, although it might also stand as an insult to the others, as well."

"Yes, I suppose I must agree…each in their own way."

"I was hoping to keep a low profile by coming here, but I suppose this is not to be."

"Thaelyn, a low profile? Mystra's Fury? Ahem."

"Yes, well," he smirks mildly. "But it is either that or a bloody ground campaign. And that ground campaign will take time that could be precious on other sides. If to show Mystra's Fury, however, perhaps this could afford us a window with a potential deterrent."

"Maybe, but if our enemies are just on the other side of these mountain ranges," she passes her gaze around the area.

"Very well, a low profile on some aspects, for instance if we keep to a narrow focus. We clear the local area, set up an outpost, and solidify our foothold. Then, if we do not give them any immediate cause to march on us, they might instead hold back to study us."

"And the orcs?"

"We will use stealth tactics at first, and in such areas that might not be as quickly noticed."

"All right, and this could give us time to plan the rest, may the gods actually grant us this time."

"Indeed! Are you ready for this, my Dear?" he asks.

"I suppose. Standard procedure as before," she replies. "That shield application bothers me a bit, we are so close to the center."

"Just make sure you hold your focus, unlike with that lightning bolt you graced upon me once," he winks.

"Oh! Are you ever going to let me live that one down?"

"Not for as long as you keep giving lectures in the Third Circle opening course. Besides, it gives us something unique to reflect upon in our lives."

"Indeed, it does. I just wish it didn't become one of my defining titles at our wedding."

"Personally, I think it is rather quaint. Who else could possibly earn such a degree?"

"Oh, so are you now going to give me a badge for it?"

"Hmm, the Merit of Accidental Lightning Bolts," he muses jovially.

Aerlie jabs her elbow into his side.

"Anyway," he continues. "We should begin before we receive any more company up here."

"Yes, and may the Powers forgive us for this sacrifice."

"On the one hand, they made their choice for their devotion. We are simply fulfilling our role in the Measure of Balance. But on the other hand, between Tae'Eladar and this place, if they feel themselves brazen enough to wreak such havoc without justifiable cause," he shakes his head. "They do not belong here, and yet they came here explicitly to bring destruction upon innocent people. Measure of Balance or no, this is simple injustice."

"Perhaps, but it does not change the feeling of leaving so much destruction in our wake."

"I fully understand, my Dear. But I think we are not the original instigators of this destruction. We are simply a response mechanism."

The two of them move over in the direction of the cliff.

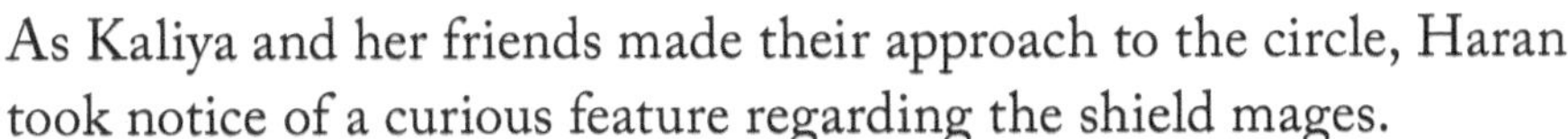

As Kaliya and her friends made their approach to the circle, Haran took notice of a curious feature regarding the shield mages.

"Look at them, under the hoods of their robes. They're wearing some kind of mask."

"Aye, that's an odd one," Relissa admits.

"It looks like a tight cowl wrapping around their head, covering the eyes, the ears, and most of the face."

"Is that some sort of ritual covering?" Kaliya suggests.

"No idea, but their manner of dress is a bit different from the others."

They entered the circle and found a convenient location to sit. But then Kaliya felt perhaps she should check in with the resident officer. She steps over to speak to the man.

"Um, excuse me, are you the Captain?"

"Aye, good lady," he replies politely. "Is there something you need?"

"I'm just wondering if you have any special instructions as we take up space here with you."

"Nothing of unusual import… We are simply going to relax a bit and enjoy the sights while His Lordship attends to this unfortunate matter of the local refuse."

"Uh huh, and is this how you usually describe bringing down a quarter million orcs in a single shot?" she grins softly.

"Well, perhaps not precisely, but with no better way available, and for all the experiences we've had back home, cleaning house is certainly a fine way of putting it."

"All right, I'll try to keep calm. But I'm telling you, if I see those orcs start climbing that cliff wall, I'm grabbing my friends and running as fast as I can."

"Jolly good!" he grins boldly.

Kaliya feels a witty pucker coming on as she retracts from the conversation. She returns to her friends and sits down.

Haran had been observing her interaction, and then her face as she turned around.

"So, did you make a new friend?" he inquires cheerily.

"Haran, I've never met someone like that before, but I'm starting to build a picture of what happens when you have a half-god leading your people."

"Oh, and how does that appear?"

"They go tail-crazy with overconfidence."

"Buggers, girl..." Relissa moans. "And here I am sitting on the ground waiting for the end of...something...to come around. I just hope it's not me."

"Well, let's do as he says, because I suspect these people must know what he's capable of that they're so casually sitting here waiting for the same."

They now set their eyes on Thaelyn and Aerlie, who have come up to the edge of the cliff.

Aerlie steps to one side, slightly apart from Thaelyn. She begins spreading her wings fully outward and up, to their maximum visibility.

"What in all the bleedin' hells is she doing?" Relissa blasts in disbelief. "Overconfidence is one thing, but jiggers! With those wings of hers popped out, they'll see her for sure!"

Then Thaelyn spoke.

"THIS PLACE SHALL BE CLEANSED!!"

Thaelyn's voice was supernaturally loud. It thundered across the plains, like the sky itself opened up and threw it down. The force of it could be felt physically through the air. Relissa and the others shuddered under the weight of it.

"Bloody hell!" she yelps. "Right! Kaliya, you said something about being overconfident. Well, half-god or otherwise, that was overconfident!"

Thaelyn then began a rhythmic motion, a movement of arms and hands, sweeping in arcs from the ground up over his head and back again. Swirls of energy welled up at his feet and spun around him, accumulating into an orb hovering over his head.

"How is he doing that?" Haran gripes. "He's got plate armor on him. You can't do that with plate! Not even with chain! That's warrior's garb. A mage needs free-flowing motion. Cloth only... robes! Well, at least that's what they teach us in the academy."

"Like he said," Kaliya offers. "He's special, I guess. Personally, I don't know how any of you do it. It's all nonsense to me."

Thaelyn continued conjuring, and the orb was growing. The swirling patterns around him grew denser, almost opaque.

"Haran," Kaliya inquires while keeping her eyes on the spectacle. "Anything you might recognize?"

"You must be kidding me!" he retorts sharply, then sighs. "Sorry, Kaliya…no, not a thing, this is completely outside my skill level… assuming they actually taught us anything to begin with."

He pauses a moment to consider the prospect.

"But I will mention this… The duration he's taking so far suggests a very powerful spell. Long-casting would equate to power. And by the size of that orb he's conjuring up, I'd say we're in for a show."

"I just hope we're still around to see it," Relissa squeaks. "I hear rumbling from the canyon!"

The three companions felt chills running through them as cries, shouts, and beating drums were heard emitting over the canyon walls. It seemed like the entire canyon floor began to move, a mass charge in their direction.

"Peeps, I've got a really bad feeling about this!" Relissa whimpers.

She darted her eyes around hurriedly to see what the other soldiers were doing. They only sat, seemingly indifferent to the events unfolding before them.

"Overconfidence, my shiny bum! Kaliya…"

"Steady, girl…"

Thaelyn's orb was growing to substantial proportions by now, much larger than himself. He had become completely enveloped in the flow of energy as it moved around him.

Relissa turned to look over her shoulder, hoping to see an easy escape route, anywhere to run to get away.

"I don't know what that is," Haran admits as he watches the orb grow. "But you'd better be ready when he throws it!"

"Hold still!" Kaliya commands, as she notices Relissa and her nervous movements. "You heard him tell us to stay here and follow with the others, right?"

"Kaliya!" she groans. "There's a horde of orcs charging our way and…and only…" she passes her eyes around at the group trying to gauge numbers. "Only a couple score of us up here. What do you think's going to happen, ay?"

"He said to stay here with the others, and also to trust him, although I'm with you at least part way on this overconfidence bit. But without anything better, and if these people are so content to do it, I feel I have to at least try."

"Try, nothing! They're all suicidal nits kissing up to some wanker with an oversized napper."

"Relissa," Haran cautions. "I would be really careful about using such words. We have no idea what's inside that thing, and it could be the very answer to your troubles. That thing is growing to huge proportions, so can you please stifle it...again? Remember that tree?"

She turns a scowl at him, but then softens up slightly.

"All right, fine...I'm sorry. But Haran, you know how I feel about this war. I fully expect to die in it. I'm just struggling for a little bit longer, and today's not the day for it. And as for you, you oversized doorknocker," she glares at Kaliya. "I can't believe you can sit there so quietly and take it. What's holding you together so neatly?"

"Who ever said I was holding together?" she sighs feebly. "But he said something earlier in that last part of his conversation. And, well, it reminded me of something. I need to see if it's true."

"You've got to be kidding me!" Relissa snaps. "Now's not the time for you to be testing theories, girl!"

"I'm sorry, but all that talk about gods and such. It hit something personal."

"Personal...to you? You're not even religious!"

The forward line of the mass of bodies in the canyon was beginning to reach the crags at the bottom of the cliff. It would be only a matter of moments before they found the trail leading up the side.

Thaelyn finished the sweeping motions, and the swirling ceased. He made a set of circles underneath the orb with one hand, followed by a firm clap. The orb seemed to ripple slightly from the inside, as if something was inserted into its core. Lastly, he made one final gesture, circling a set of fingers as a bullseye at a location out on the field and swinging the other arm around like an overhanded toss. This caused the giant orb to launch away, sailing across the landscape.

"There it goes!" Haran cries.

Thaelyn buckled over from the strain, while Aerlie, having already retracted her wings, moved quickly to his side. She turned and pointed affirmatively to the group.

"Bring up the shield!" the Captain shouts.

The shield mages circling the cluster of soldiers began chanting furiously. Haran also noticed Aerlie doing the same over herself and Thaelyn.

"A shield?" Kaliya mutters unconsciously.

"Huh?" Haran blurts through his own tension. "What do you mean?"

"He called for a shield just now."

"Oh dear gods…" he gasps as he turns to observe the mages. "They must specialize in this, therefore their appearance."

The orb flew over the canyon, travelling farther with each passing moment. The war cries on the floor died down as the orcs stopped their movement to observe the strange sight passing high over their heads. Some of them began shrieking. The mass of bodies so closely gathered together and charging with unified purpose was now scrambling in all directions. Screams and cries of panic could now be heard. The mass separated down the middle, moving off to the sides in a vain effort to escape.

Haran tries to peer over the edge of the cliff to see the action below.

"Some of them seem to know what this is, I think."

"Maybe they saw it before on his world," Kaliya muses.

"Then it can't be good, especially if it's causing them to part ways in such a panic, regardless of their numbers."

The shield mages continued their chanting. Swirling energies were circulating around the outer rim of the circle and over the heads of the soldiers. An instant later, a boisterous crackling of thunder issued forth as bolts of energy raced across between the mages. The energies expanded and coalesced into a continuous shield surrounding the cluster on all sides, forming an umbrella-like bubble encasing the group. The chanting lessened and altered into a new repeating pattern.

"A maintenance chant," Haran mumbles. "May the gods give them strength."

Kaliya jolted as the potent energies coalesced, and then studied the result. She tried reaching up tentatively to test the form of the shield.

"It's solid! Hard as rock!" she announces incredulously. "How is that even possible?!"

"Well, one thing's for sure," Haran mutters, shuddering as he speaks. "Whatever's inside that orb, it's worse than just bad."

"But how do you make something seemingly physical out of essentially nothing?"

Kaliya kneeled down again and turned her attention back to the orb as it reached a high point in its arc and was now on its way down only a few miles away in the center of the canyon. She noticed Thaelyn and Aerlie covered by the same type of shield as the group, though smaller and with Aerlie apparently maintaining it.

"Shadow blinds down!" comes a firm command from the Captain.

Movement stirred all around the group as soldiers pulled something down from under a compartment inside the front of their helmets to cover their eyes. It appeared like a mask with heavily tinted lenses.

Haran examined the activity and saw the strange black mask being pulled into view, although the aspect of the lenses was not immediately clear for the shading. Being puzzled at first, the meaning soon struck him like a hammer, as he recalled the circle of mages and their masks.

"Gods pity us!" he shrieks. "Now I understand these mages. Cover your eyes!"

He tried pulling up any loose cloth he could find in his robes and buried his face in it.

Relissa's nerves, which were already badly frayed, began to spike. She first whimpered, and then yelped as she shot her eyes to-and-fro searching for anything to help her, and finally to lurch to Haran's side.

"'Ere now! Save some for me!" she screeches.

She grabs some of his robes and buries her face in it while curling up into a fetal position. Haran wrapped an arm around her to pull her in.

Kaliya observed in disbelief the activity around her.

"I swear," she whispers silently. "I simply don't understand. What are you talking about now? We're not allowed to see it or something? Like a vision of some holy thing we little people aren't permitted to look upon?"

Confused and perplexed, she watched the actions of the soldiers, and that of her friends, but still she could not dissuade her childlike curiosity. What could possibly be inside that orb to cause such a reaction? She did not understand the principles of magic, as it represented an unfathomable concept to her people. Therefore, she again glanced at the soldiers and their masks, by now developing an idea of their purpose. Here she begins to take notice of the intense shading of the lenses.

"Uh oh..." she mumbles. "Protective eyewear. But wait, we can't be saying... These people... And using magic?!" she blurts.

But her realization came too late, and too slow to hide from it, as the others did. She instead reflexively returned to observe the orb as it made impact.

At first, it seemed as if the orb buried itself into the ground, penetrating below the surface with barely even a puff of dust. Then a glow began to radiate outwards. A split second later, and a dome of light many times brighter than the sun burst over the land, filling the canyon, and quickly engulfing the entire valley. Kaliya screeched as she tried to cover her eyes, then falling to the side and quickly turning away from the blinding glare.

In the next moment came a titanic boom that roared through the region. The ground vibrated and rattled. The sound of hurricane force winds battered the shield bubble, and the outside world turned many shades darker.

Several difficult moments pass until Kaliya is able to pull her arms away from her face. She had turned herself over, away from the canyon, in an instinctive move to protect herself from the blaze. She was dazed, and there were many spots in her vision, but fortunately it was not serious enough to cause permanent damage. After several blinks, and a short pause to make sure they recovered, she found her vision returning.

"Dammit, girl," she whimpers privately. "There's your answer. Blast it, you need to start listening to people more often. How dull-horned can you be after all, and how many times now. You nearly went blind on that one."

She looked at the soldiers, trying to see them through the blur. All was the same as before the explosion. They simply sat and waited.

"Overconfidence, my crinkled tail! These people are rock solid stoic! No wonder that Captain called it a simple house cleaning. To him, it probably is."

She takes a moment to catch her breath, and for her eyes to return their focus.

"But then, how could you possibly be expecting something like this? They wear metal armor and use swords, for cu'Nar's sake. How could you expect them to have anything like atomic science, and especially applied through this crazy mysticism? Just what was he saying about that policy of his!"

The continued shaking of the ground made it challenging for her to maintain her stability. The roaring and violent rushing of wind outside brought her attention to the image of flame and molten rock racing past the shield, deflecting around it on all sides while the shield itself seemed unaffected by the power of the forces acting upon it.

"These people seem medieval, but they have shield technology that's better than us!"

She tried to sit up again, searching for better support on the shifting ground and hauling herself back around in the direction of the canyon. The sight she beheld took her breath away. It was a broad column of flame and ash reaching far into the sky above, combined with an enormous cloud of debris blasted out of the earth, and then capped by a wide dome, like that of a large mushroom.

"Cu'Nar's pity, what has he done."

She stretches out a hand to find Relissa, unable to take her eyes off the incredible sight. She feels around, but the young dark elf was just out of reach. Kaliya moved in closer to pat her on the back, hoping to get the girl's attention. There was no reaction, as the girl was frozen with fear. Kaliya tried pulling her away from Haran to see her face, but it was a simple mask of terror emitting sobbing noises. So, she picked her up to cradle her in her arms.

"Relissa!" she yells into the girl's ear, trying to be heard over the noise outside.

The elf gave no response, except to continue whimpering.

"Relissa! Come to! Breathe, girl! We're still alive, and you've got to see this!"

Bending over Relissa's stiff body, Kaliya reaches out to pound on Haran.

Haran shifts slightly, pulling away his robes a tiny bit to test the view, and then more as he gained confidence that it was safe to open up again.

Relissa started to move, with her face relaxing and her whines slowly fading. Her hands slid away cautiously as she experienced the disturbance from Kaliya over her.

The noise was subsiding, as was the shaking of the ground, while the winds outside died down. Haran's gaze followed the giant mushroom cloud hanging over the valley.

"Um, right..." he mutters almost inaudibly. "Well, I think it goes without saying, we don't need to worry about those orcs anymore."

Relissa unfolds herself from Kaliya's embrace and turns to look at the canyon, which was now glowing bright orange and with a gaping hole in the center. Tears were flowing from her eyes, due as much from the shock as from the awesome scale of the display.

"Dear Gods of Old, what happened out there?" she whispers.

"Incredible!" Kaliya murmurs breathlessly. "And absolutely frightening, especially to be this close to it. But cu'Nar's Pity, Haran! How can someone do this with that nether-wild fantasy stuff of yours?"

"Kaliya, I've tried on several occasions to teach you, but I guess my own lessons just aren't good enough to relay anything useful. You know how bad they are in our academy to actually teach anything."

"Yes, of course, and I don't blame you, either. I'm probably just too iron-horned to catch anything out of it. But with such a demonstration as this, clearly, whatever it is, there's a lot more to it, and it has to be very powerful."

"And they actually study it, which to me says they're a lot more liberal with their lessons."

"But Haran, if that means they teach this on any similar level to a larger body, whether military, or even on a civilian level…"

"That would be a sight to see, an entire society using magic in their common everyday lives. But now, Kaliya, do you recognize anything out of this from your side of wisdom?"

"Yes," she sighs reluctantly. "This would represent a type of science applied in a weaponized form, and it's every bit as dangerous as it looks. From a utility perspective, it could revolutionize many other productive sciences, but if you use it wrong…"

"Everything has a right and wrong way to it, Kaliya. I think I can appreciate this much."

"But it still doesn't make sense when I look at the rest of it," she glances around the group. "These people don't represent the type of society that should be in possession of this level of knowledge, the same as with this shield," she looks up at it, "which is clearly a counter to it, and a very effective one at that, and it surpasses even what WE have."

Haran couldn't help but let out a minor chuckle at the notion.

"I recall lessons from our old school on Ruuki uy'Daan," she continues. "That is, what little I actually got out of it before the attack. It's mostly ancient history to us by now, but it would still be above where you are, and I wouldn't really know where to begin to explain it to you in technical terms."

"That's alright, I'll let it pass this time," he retorts soothingly.

"But again, how can you do it with this thing you call magic? What powers it? Everything needs a power source…well, at least according to my understanding. And with respect, Haran, those lessons you get don't answer enough of this to help me understand on my level of empirical science."

"All I can say is, maybe you can ask HIM one day..." he points out onto the field. "He clearly has a better technique for teaching."

The conversation pauses as they continue to scan the scene.

"Peeps," Relissa wonders. "If you can quit your bickering over the existence of magic, maybe you can help me with a wee bit. Why is everything so dark?"

The three examined the area, and indeed everything did seem many shades darker outside the bubble. The brightly glowing flames of the cloud, the molten rock outside, even the light of day, all appeared as though it had been eclipsed by a heavy shadow.

"My first guess," Kaliya surmises, "is this shield became tinted due to the extreme glare outside. Much like these masks with heavily tinted lenses, as eye protection. This would be necessary even with our application."

"So, some things are the same all around," Haran muses.

She crawled on all fours to the edge of the bubble to take a closer look. On her side the ground felt cool, or at least what would be normal to the region. She picked up a handful of sand and studied it, then examined the glowing mass on the other side. It formed a perfect line along the edge of the shield, but the light passing through was clearly darkened.

"It must be incredibly hot out there," Haran notes, "with all that molten material lying about."

"Oh, no doubt!" she admits. "But being this close to it, I don't actually feel the heat. This shield is remarkable, but I wonder how long these mages intend to keep it up."

She pulled back and turned to look at the sky above. Beyond the edge of the great cloud it was still generally clear. She then looked eastward to the mountains in the distance. Everything was black and orange, the barren landscape now devastated, charred, and partially molten.

Many minutes pass, and the companions wait, watching the cloud slowly dissipate. The fires had cooled and only smoke and ash remained. The glowing land around them slowly turned black as it cooled into a form of glasslike rock. Across the way, they could see Thaelyn and Aerlie waiting under a similar shield.

Soon after, they saw the fallout hailing down rock and ash excavated from the huge blast crater. Kaliya watched as it came down from above, pelting the shield and sliding off.

"This thing really does represent a solid surface," she muses. "Even from the outside."

She stood up to make a closer inspection of the ash and dust particles coming down, hoping to examine them as they settled on the shield surface, but she soon noticed a curious effect.

"Haran, look at this with me. This dust here... This should represent a fairly level surface on the outside, but this stuff isn't sticking in place. It's still moving off to the side."

"It's sliding away," he considers. "It's still a dome-like shape, as broad as it is, so it's sliding off to the nearest side.

"But it's so fine! I should think friction would hold it in place, even on a slanted surface."

"Keep in mind, this isn't your common surface."

"Of course...and for it to move at all...all of it...no single particle is holding still. Grace of the cu'Nar, Haran, do you know what this resembles to me? Something that's only theoretical in our science...a true frictionless surface."

"So, no matter what it is, and no matter how carefully you place it there, it'll still slide off?"

"Basically, yes."

"Fascinating... If I could learn even a few lessons from these people, it could place me in an entirely new skill level compared to our academy back home."

"Yeah, but don't get your hopes up too high. We don't know how eager they are at sharing."

"By the way," Relissa emits. "How does all this fit with that theory you were yipping about earlier?"

"Theory?" Kaliya wonders.

"Aye, before all this hullabaloo got started, you mentioned he said something, and you wanted to see it for yourself."

"Oh!" she snaps and quickly clamps her hand over her mouth. "Right. My mind went blank for a while there."

"Aye, I can't blame you for that much," she smirks mildly.

Kaliya feels a shudder rush through her as she recalls her earlier anxiety. As she surveys the scene one more time, the sheer magnitude of the ruin begins to manifest itself into her mind, and a suggestive thought returns to her.

"The prophecy…" she whispers.

"The what?" Relissa balks. "You peeps don't believe in magic, and yet you have a prophecy of some kind?"

"Yeah, I suppose it sounds weird, but this comes in the form of a message from the cu'Nar."

"Aye, and there's the other thing," she grins impishly. "You don't believe in a god, but you speak of them almost the same way."

"All right, Relissa, but at least they're an entity we can associate with, and they helped us on many occasions…or at least tried to. They're known to come to us…well, to him…"

"Him?" Haran wonders. "You mean Velen again, right? You said he's the one who got this message to run away once."

"Yeah, that."

"But Kaliya, why do you have so much trouble pronouncing that name? He's the leader of your people, right?"

"Yes. It's personal, and it's old, and it hurts."

"All right, easy does it, Kaliya. So, what does this thing say?"

"It was not long after we arrived in this world. They passed a message, which allowed him to offer a new prediction to us. But after everything else, I think I lost most of my faith by then. I didn't want to believe it, not after so much tragedy. But now, with Thaelyn and the things he said earlier…and then this," she waves a hand at the scene outside. "I don't know what to think any more."

"Can you clue us in on it a little?"

"I'm really hesitant to say anything. Maybe I really am too iron-horned to trust anything anymore…a lot like Relissa with her issues. This piece included two parts, neither of which we're able to interpret, assuming we could interpret any part of it, they're so cryptic. Like Relissa said, you almost need a religion to believe in it. For all I know, this is simple coincidence...it doesn't actually mean anything at all."

"Well, while that's a reasonable suggestion, if this really is that prophecy, my advice is to soften up those iron horns of yours and pay close attention. If he can blast that canyon to all the gods, I would wager he's got a few other tricks hidden away. Just looking at these soldiers of his, and then his statements earlier, is impressive enough on its own."

"Maybe... But still, there's more to it, and its source is someone I..." her voice trails off as she looks away.

"...Don't like," Haran concludes. "Got it. But this sounds like another thing you need to clear up."

Haran pats his tall friend on the back as they take up seating again and wait.

A short while passes, and the mages cease their chanting. The shield makes another crackling sound as the bubble separates back into bolts of energy and quickly fades away. Everyone is greeted with a blast of heat from the surrounding terrain as the air mixes.

The shield mages, ever vigilant, proceed to their next task. They each begin conjuring up new spells, joined by others who were previously sitting in the group. Ice shoots out from their fingertips over large sections of the land in front of them, covering the space with a layer of frost which rapidly melts and turns into steam, issuing out a loud hiss due to the heat still held within the rocks below. The clouds rise up and waft away, building in density as they merge with other clouds from other melting frost sprays, creating a warm fog. The mages proceed outward from the circle in all directions. Several moved in the direction of Thaelyn and Aerlie, laying down a path that was safe to walk upon, though the rock crunched under their footsteps.

Haran was inspired by the activity and wished to try a little of his own. He moved up along one of the mages and conjured his own spell of ice magic, throwing it down on the ground in front of him. It wasn't quite as spectacular a spread as with the other mages, but he was proud, nonetheless. He looked across to the mage standing next to him with a broad smile on his face. She raised a hand and tilted it side to side in a gesture of so-so quality. His expression straightened and he raised an eyebrow at her. She returned with a pleasant smile, gently nudging him to try harder. Realizing she was trying to encourage him, he responded with a mannish grin while stretching his arms out and folding his hands together to crack his knuckles, preparing to try again. She returned to her work with a subtle giggle.

Relissa wasn't sure what she should do. She looked around at the scenery, the canyon, the valley, the mountains to the north, and to the east. Much of it was black. The entire region, all the Badlands was scorched. She had visited this place often during her lifetime, but now she felt like she had been transported to an alien landscape.

Kaliya waited for the mages to press forward in the direction of the canyon. She began to follow them, keeping a fair distance to make sure the ground was safe. It fractured and crumbled loudly under her weight, leaving telltale impressions behind, unique to her hoof prints. Other soldiers worked their way along as well, moving up to the cliff's edge.

As she slowly crept up to the edge of the canyon, she took note of the gigantic bowl-shaped depression that had been carved into the canyon floor. It looked to be perhaps a mile or more across. There was no evidence of the settlement or the orcs, just blackened earth.

She could see Thaelyn and Aerlie, now free from their bubble and kneeling in reverence of the extraordinary sight. They were joined by the other soldiers, and soon the mages, as more space was cooled and made available for the service. Soon, the full assembly was kneeling as if in prayer.

"What are they doing?" she whispers to herself.

She needed to find an answer. And so, believing it to be a religious ceremony, she looks around for a likely candidate and sees a nearby priestess. She moves in closer and kneels down beside her.

"Excuse me, what are you doing?" she asks humbly.

The priestess, a light-skinned elf, turns to respond.

"We mourn for the dead."

"But these were orcs, your sworn enemies!"

"The dead are still the dead, Child. Evil is our enemy here, not life. The orcs may demonstrate their wickedness in our eyes, but they are still living souls. We mourn for them out of our respect for life. But they are not the only ones harmed here. Because of our actions, this land has also been injured, and now it must be healed."

"Actions…" she pauses to examine the land again. "Well, fine, but mourning for the orcs?" her voice escalates. "Excuse me, but these orcs are horrible beasts! They're not worthy of being mourned. They're so primitive and filthy…"

"Hold, Child!" the priestess interrupts harshly. "We do not judge those around us by their gifts, or the lack of them. We may judge them by their deeds, and if those deeds are wicked, we may apply ourselves to correct this according to our own values."

"Deeds? Let me tell you something about their deeds. They attacked my people on our home world, killed most of them, and what's more, used some kind of horrible magic to change others into mindless abominations to attack even more. I can't see how anyone would pay tribute to them as anything worthy of living."

"Indeed, this would pose a justifiable cause for your rage, but I suspect this is not the only thing in play here. You also seem to hold something personal. But despite their deeds, they hold just as much right to exist as you and I. They are a part of Creation, no different from the rest, and must coexist as their component in the Measure of Balance."

"The what? Measure of Balance," Kaliya muses inquisitively. "Is this some sort of religious doctrine?"

"It is better described as a philosophical doctrine taught to us by our gods, which we describe as a society of beings called the Estelar. All things in Creation must balance. This includes matter and energy, and even life and death, and these forces divide themselves along the polarities of positive and negative persuasion. Despite where we may sit within this Balance, we need both sides to oppose each other fairly. It is a functional demand of existence."

"Wow, you look like a priest, but I would never have expected something like that out of someone like you."

"What would you normally expect?" she smirks gently. "That I instead say a god demands us to follow some simplistic manner of behavior based on a doctrine that we are not intended to know the greater wisdom of Creation?"

"Um, something like that," she hesitates. "Although he told us a little about these Estelar of yours. But this sounds more like a science lesson than a religious one."

"Indeed, perhaps it is," the priestess diverts her gaze into the canyon. "We serve as their apprentices in some ways, even though we are still a very young society. But you will always find conflict between good and evil, and the polarities also conflict on occasion. We are simply travelers along this path. Those of us who take one side will always combat those of the other, the same as they will always combat ours. Sometimes we win, sometimes we lose, much to our own sorrow."

"So, what are you trying to say about these orcs then? We were in the wrong place at the wrong time, or something?"

"I cannot say with precision in your case, but our experiences back home tell us they did not get along well with most other bodies. As for our recent war, this became our breaking point. Their deeds were intolerably criminal. And crime is still crime, whatever side of the equation you may stand on. Instead, it is the underlying spirit beneath the crime that I speak of when I say we must honor the essence of life."

"And therefore, you're telling me…um…" she glances briefly at the canyon.

"Life, by itself, is not a thing to be judged for its simple existence. What we do now is weep for the loss of life, and there was a considerable amount down there."

"Yeah, you're right, actually."

"Now, this life could have been positive as much as it could have been negative, if only for the influence placed upon it by its governors. And yet, we cannot let this deter us, even if we are on the same side.

Their deeds, which we must oppose more than anything else, must be reconciled."

"Really. So, it has to be universal? But what do you mean by influence? These things were always primitive and brutal. I often thought they were born like that."

"When I speak of influence, I mean to say their overall culture and breeding. Who they are as a society, and where they stand with their internal beliefs and principles. Their actions may be based on this, or they can be based on another influence that is external to their culture, and this may offer some form of motivation."

"Motivation… Like crime, I suppose, right?"

"Precisely. Look at your own society, for instance. Can you tell me that who you are in the present day is the one and only manner of your existence throughout your long history?"

"Um…" her voice trails off.

Kaliya was beginning to see the direction of this conversation, although it didn't necessarily relieve her of her own woes. The orcs were a society with their own way of life as opposed to her people's example. Now she tried to recall some of her history lessons in school on her people's ancient past for comparison.

"There was a time in our history…" she considers. "Yeah, ours is a very old society, but if you go back far enough, we also had our problems. But I don't think we were ever as bad as these orcs…I don't think."

"Regardless of that, you are what you are, the same as they are what they are…except for these recent crimes."

"Right, and these crimes were simply awful. And they were all equally responsible. I honestly can't see why we should excuse them for what they did to us, or to your people, regardless of their nature. Thaelyn showed me a vision of what they did to you. This isn't worth paying homage to them as living bodies."

"For their deeds, perhaps, but we generally believe they must've taken up a new religion of some sort, and this caused a deeply influential movement. If this is the case, it would probably transcend beyond whatever culture they had previously."

"A religion...oh...uh oh..." Kaliya delicately covers her mouth and leans back.

"Does this trigger something within you?"

"Um...yeah, actually, and I guess I didn't include this before. We were speaking earlier on this. On Ruuki uy'Daan...that's where we first met them...and initially we were at peace. But then they turned on us like animals. It was sudden and devastating. Since then, we see them siding with our long-time enemies here on this world. That's probably where the religion came from. Sargeras. If he got inside there behind our backs..."

"Who is this Sargeras?"

"A very evil godlike thing that arrived on our ancient home world once, and he's been chasing us ever since."

"Then you should direct your ire at him, not the orcs. They are simply his pawns."

"Pawns..." she muses. "But...all right, I suppose I can accept this for the attack, but the brutality of their actions...on our people, on yours...and that bit with the cannibalism. You don't excuse that, no matter who it is and what religion you credit them with. On Ruuki uy'Daan, they used some sort of horrible magic stuff on our people to mutate them and turn them against the rest of us."

"I will agree with you on some part of this. The cannibalism was truly villainous, and ultimately the cause of our war. In fact, from what we understand of their normal culture, this would violate even that much."

"It would?"

"Indeed, as even in orcish culture, I think this would be a vulgar act. And while I cannot advise on this magic of theirs, as orcs are not well-known for their proclivity in the Art, we did observe them opening portals on Tae'Eladar, and that in itself is a potent application. Therefore, if they were corrupted by something external, and at this point, it sounds as if they were, almost anything is possible if they received outside help."

"Outside help..." Kaliya muses. "Meaning to say he taught them a few new tricks...really nasty ones, too. And if they regard him to be so powerful that they're willing to throw away even their native cultural values…cu'Nar help us all."

"Absolutely! This is a troubling aspect. But do you at least recognize why we must give our respect to the essence of life, regardless of who or what it belongs to? If these orcs did not come under the influence of this Sargeras, you might never have seen this trouble in the first place."

"But how might it be possible to cause this mutation? They were all good people, and then they started chasing us like…well, like more animals."

"Magic is a potent natural force in Creation, and if applied by those who know its ways, it can cause as much havoc as it can bring benefit. This can include altering the body and mind in ways that make it unrecognizable. And since we are all essentially living machines that can be rebuilt, if one has the right means, many things become possible, especially bad ones."

"You know…" Kaliya frowns softly. "You people, with respect that is, don't look like you should be advanced enough to have this level of understanding. And yet you seem to have more than some of my own people."

The priestess giggles and smiles delicately.

"You probably never can, and never should judge something by its exterior. Our society is rather unique in a few ways for how we developed, and even we know this by the teachings we receive regarding certain other societies we know about and how they once developed."

"And there's another thing, the way you talk, these statements of yours… Do you people normally have the means to travel to other worlds?"

"I would probably have to answer no, in the general sense of it. Unless we happen to come upon the most extraordinary event of a portal leading off somewhere, this would count as a very unusual case for us."

"Uh huh. Unusual, and yet here you are. You just recently arrived, and yet you look like this is old news to you," she chuckles.

"Maybe so," she smiles. "But we are aware that the Seas of Creation are vast, and one day, we will eventually find our way out to them. It is simply a matter of time."

"Incredible! And then you speak of other people and societies out there…well, um, you sound a little like my mother when I was a girl."

"She was wise if she believed in this. But then, if you hold more experience in this, it might become a given quality. There are certain truths in the realms that are consistent to all beings. They are not dependent on who we are, where we come from, or how we developed as a society. The only stipulation might be our experience, and maybe the teachings we are privileged to receive."

"Kaliya," Relissa interjects. "Finding a new religion now? Is this finally a turning point for you? Jiggers, if ever I would see the day."

The young elf plopped herself down next to her tall Daanen'kai friend, with Haran settling in after her.

"Relissa," Kaliya emits. "If only you could understand this language. I don't know what you might say to it, but I'm sure it would astonish you. I'm talking to this woman trying to find out why they seem to be in prayer here."

"Aye, I was wondering that too. Maybe you'd like to share it with us?"

"It's complex, you can be sure of that much. Not simply a religion, but apparently a way of life for them to respect all things they come across, simply for the fact that they are living beings, and despite any evil deeds they perform. Crime is still crime, of course, and so this sounds like a religion that might be based at least as much in law enforcement as it is a respect for life."

"This would likely follow with that god he was talking about earlier," Haran notes.

"Yes, it would. But these people seem far more enlightened in a lot of things than what they appear to be on the outside. Simply to be standing on what, to them, would be a foreign world, is like a walk in the park for them…just a matter of time, as she was saying. Like, as if to say…oh look!" she animates. "That might be fun to try out!"

The three friends join in a subtle laugh.

Kaliya continues, "So far, she's managed to shoot down just about every argument I threw at her about how I feel over the orcs, and she's now explaining the meaning of life on a scale not even our own people would know about. And now I'm starting to question my own feelings."

"Jiggers, girl, that's got to be a rough one."

"Child," appeals the priestess. "Perhaps, if you are so interested in learning our ways, you would wish to join us in the service? I can still see some turmoil in your eyes. Maybe, if you were to join me in prayer, it could be cleansing for your own spirit."

Kaliya turns back to the woman, uncertain how to answer.

"My people aren't religious," she admits softly. "I don't really know how to pray to something."

"Religious or not, to offer oneself in memoriam to the fallen can often release our burdens and lift our souls, that we demonstrated ourselves to uphold a higher principle that is more becoming of our underlying creed."

"Yeah, and that does sound very religious."

"It is as much a state of mind and spirit as it is a belief, and it should extend beyond our opinions of any deeds. And I can actually feel within you a kind of conflict where you are wavering on these principles."

"You can? How?"

"Perhaps you have a very strong spirit, and I can feel an empathic emanation coming out of you."

"Oops! Well, maybe… I had a rough life."

"And all the more reason for you to cleanse yourself and find a truer path to follow."

"All right, but how do I do this?"

"I will show you how," the priestess offers with a caring smile.

Chapter 5
A HEALING WIND

"Captain Hagmaert! We need druids and a life-seed!"

Thaelyn was dismissing the prayer ritual and began issuing orders again. The mages went back to work on the remaining area that was still too hot to step on.

"Aerlie," he turns to her. "Return back and organize our people."

"Yes, Thaelyn. Should I also return to B.T. for supply trains? We will be assembling an outpost, correct?"

"Indeed, and let us also bring parts for a spire, and of course a gateway as well. And do not forget food. It will be nightfall before we are finished, and our people will need to eat."

"Naturally, then I should leave immediately. After all, I would not wish to be present for your next performance. The winds are terrible on my wings," she smirks.

"Of course, my Dear, and we all know how much you adore your wings. I still recall that moment in the courtyard," he grins.

"Now wait a moment!" she protests teasingly. "I told you before, I truly have no idea where that came from. It just popped into my mind as something to attract your attention."

"Oh, so it simply popped into your mind, did it?" he eyes her suspiciously. "You know, I still recall your mother's statement of how she had no idea where you could pick up that little trick."

"Yes, well, she was also a priestess and rather conservative."

"As were most of your people up there in those mountains," he smirks. "And this only complicates matters, unless…oh wait…" he grins mischievously.

"Uh oh…now what?"

"Well, of course, we may also wish to consider your performance in that circus."

"Hey! I was locked in a cage on that occasion."

"So you say…" he winks. "But you are also known for being very outspoken, especially that one occasion in my office with that bottle of blue. Do you recall that?"

"Oh great, here goes the other one now," she sighs.

He leans in to plant a gentle kiss on her cheek.

"And we will always cherish these moments."

"Yes…" she shrugs. "And I suspect they will follow me for a long while, the same as that lightning strike."

The two of them shared a moment of humor. Then Aerlie turned to the assembly of soldiers.

"Who has a rune back to the last camp?" she shouts. "Open for me, please."

One of the mages stops the ice conjuring to pull out a rune from his belt. He rushes up to Aerlie and chants a summoning spell on it. It sparkles and swirls with energy, just as it did before with the scouts. When he is ready, she brings her hand up and touches the stone lightly, and is quickly enveloped in a ball of energy, vanishing from sight. The mage then cancels the enchantment and returns the stone to his belt before resuming his former duty.

Haran's attention had been attracted by the summons, and so he observed the affair.

"Interesting," he mumbles quietly. "So, they seem to have a first-person as well as a second-person application."

"What do you mean?" Relissa asks as she overhears his personal note.

"Those rune stones, they would appear to have some versatility to them."

Captain Hagmaert calls up the remaining troops and another of the mages with a return rune stone. He issues an order to the mage, who pulls out the rune and begins conjuring, but this time he is holding it upright facing outward to an open space. As he finishes the invocation, a two-dimensional circular aperture forms in front of him, allowing the others to jump through the trans-dimensional vortex and out of sight.

"And that makes three," Haran remarks. "Does anyone ever walk on their world?"

Thaelyn begins striding away from the canyon, moving down the embankment and across the field. He seems to be focusing his attention at some point far off in the distance. A cluster of mages charge ahead to throw down more ice magic along his path. He progresses across the field, moving ever further from the canyon into a broad area of open land. Kaliya and the others start following behind, curious as to why he's moving out this far.

Haran cannot help but to look back again at the swirling vortex as the last soldier passes through. The mage holding the rune then makes a gesture to dismiss the anomaly, followed by reengaging it for his personal departure.

"I suppose he doesn't need them anymore, but now what is he planning?"

"Whatever it is," Relissa considers. "It can't be because of those orcs. If he came here to finish them, that much is done by now."

"Right, but if he has in mind to continue pursuing them..."

"Well, personally, I wouldn't be against it. It'll give the rest of us a nice little breather."

"He'll need a base of operations for that," Kaliya suggests. "And so, he'll need to establish an outpost of some kind. Maybe he's looking for a nice spot to settle in."

Thaelyn and the others marched ahead slowly, with the delay caused mainly due to the need to cast ice magic before proceeding. After a while, perhaps a mile away from the canyon wall, Thaelyn seemed satisfied with the location. He waves to the mages to spread out and cover the area with ice magic, preparing it for occupation.

"Um, Your Lordship?" Kaliya mutters tenderly. "What are we doing here?"

"We will be establishing a camp here, but first I need to heal the land and make it ready."

"What do you mean…to heal the land? How do you heal land?"

"Firstly, in case you had not noticed, the explosion caused a considerable amount of damage," he waves to the charred and crusty rock below.

"Right, that much I can see."

"I maintain a strong responsibility for what I leave behind me, and this is no different. For this, I will need their help," he points to a group of strangely clad people rushing up from the now-distant cliff side.

There was a moaning sigh from Haran as he turned to look.

"Oh great… Druids… Please, anything but that!"

"Do you have something against druids, Haran?" Thaelyn wonders.

"I'm not a religious man, Your Lordship, and the druidic faith is one of the most ridiculous, in my mind."

"Curious. What is it about their faith that disconcerts you?"

"They have a tendency to talk to trees. Doesn't that seem a bit odd to you?"

"Ah, but of course, such foolishness," he smirks gleefully. "But they do have their uses on occasion."

The mages worked hurriedly at cooling the surrounding area. Once a sufficient amount of space had been prepared, they reassembled back with Thaelyn.

"Over there," he points off to the side. "Mark a way-line, thirty-wide. Then return back and wait. We will call for you when the area is ready."

The mages run off to the far end of the prepared space, forming up in a line at its edge. They each opened up an elongated pouch on their belt, just behind the row of rune stone clips. From within, they pulled out yet more rune stones.

"Just how many do these people keep on them?" Haran ponders openly, though not really expecting a reply.

"Like I believe I said before," Thaelyn responds. "We tend to use these often, and for a variety of reasons. And each of those pouches holds six extra stones, for occasions like this."

"Should I ask why?"

"Possibly…" Thaelyn affirms with a smile as he turns and walks over to the druids.

"Well that…"

Haran stares blankly at the retreating noble, and then looks up at Kaliya, who can only shrug.

"Well, I suppose you only asked half a question, so you get what you paid for."

"Indeed!" he huffs. "Note to self: If you want anything out of that man, be direct!"

Thaelyn meets with one of the druids. She is ornately decorated with forest green leather leggings reaching only to her knees, and a similar style cropped vest. Strips of enchanted bark line the front, back, and outer sides as a form of natural armoring. She has wristlets and anklets made of feathers, and a necklace adorned with a variety of carved wooden charms. Around her head is a wreath made of vines and leaves, but unlike the others standing next to her, hers was crowned with a set of tall, brightly colored feathers protruding up on both sides. She also had a medium-sized pouch attached around her waist.

Thaelyn begins speaking with her and waving to an area off to his left. She nods and opens the pouch, pulling out a rather large object that looks a bit like an oversized nut. She cradles it gently in her hands as she displays it to him.

Kaliya strains to overhear the conversation.

"I'm hearing a few words out of that, but they're strange."

"What are they?" Haran wonders.

"Something about a circle, a seed, and forming up for a ritual of some kind."

"Uh huh…like I said, druids," he shakes his head.

"Relissa, those people look like elves, but their skin is not the same as the others."

"Aye, I met one of them earlier as an archer. Those are the Taur clan, Wood Elves."

"Wood elves?"

"Aye, I think they must be one of the old clans, but I don't recognize the name. My Dah tried teaching me of the old clans, but they used different names back then."

"So something has changed since then," Haran surmises.

"And that nut thing?" Kaliya asks. "Could that be the seed he's talking about?"

"Maybe, but don't ask me what it is," Relissa shakes her head vacantly. "I'm not a farmer."

Another druid steps up to Thaelyn and hands him a long wooden staff made of twisted vines. He takes it and walks over to the location he had just pointed to a moment ago, where a wide circle of druids was now forming. He steps into its center.

Kaliya steps forward impulsively. She eyes the circle of druids tenuously, but she feels she needs some clarification.

"Um…" she calls while waving a hand. "Can you tell us what you're doing?"

"Kaliya," he returns. "This involves a rather difficult holy ritual, the nature of which may be impossible to explain at this time. My best advice is to keep back and prepare for a few unexpected anomalies. And hold on tight until it is done."

"Oh wonderful… Did I mention I wasn't religious?"

"You may wish to reconsider that notion by the time we are finished here," he smiles.

Thaelyn now returns to his work, first by pulling out a small flat object from a pouch on his belt. He holds it in his hand and stares intently at it, turning himself around part way to the right. He then puts it away back into the pouch.

Relissa watches and turns her head to see where he's facing.

"That's a strange one; he's turned to the north."

"Then that thing must've been a compass of some kind," Kaliya surmises.

The circle adjusts itself to his new orientation and the druidic high priestess approaches, now holding a small pouch tied with drawstrings. Thaelyn sets the staff standing just off to the side and releases it. The staff seems to hold itself upright without falling. He then forms a cup with his hands to receive the priestess's gift, and she opened the pouch to pour out a fine dust, which was clearly enchanted, as it emitted a soft glow.

"Yeah, ritual is right," Kaliya muses. "I've seen the orcs and their crazy mysticism do stuff like this, although I'm surprised to see someone who can drop a bomb like that now performing a religious rite."

"If he's half-god," Haran offers. "He could hold a background in things we can only dream of. So I might suggest you take his advice and simply hold on. If he's speaking about fixing all this burnt land…gods help us for what's coming up next."

"Aye, but whose gods, Haran," Relissa shudders.

With the pouch now empty, the priestess backs away penitently while Thaelyn raises his hands to the sky and holds his posture briefly. The druids begin a low murmuring chant. He shifts the dust to one hand and brings his free hand through a wide semicircular motion to clamp down on the strange material, then gently rubbing it as the contents trickle out. The dust creates a glowing shower in a downward swirl around him into the ground at his feet, temporarily illuminating the earth just below. He then relaxes his posture and the chanting ends.

"Well, that was exciting," Relissa quips. "And for an encore?"

"Be careful what you ask for, Relissa," Haran mentions subtly. "I seriously doubt he's finished. That was just a primer, and there's no shield over us this time."

"Oh, please! You got it right the first time. These are druids, ay? What are they going to do? Here, look at this stuff…"

She bends down to pick up a shard of the glassy rock at her feet. It was hard and brittle.

"What do you think it'll take to fix this? This here is burnt to a crisp and then some. Kaliya, from your side of it, what would it take to make this right again?"

"Well," she considers. "My first thought is to bulldoze the entire area, using heavy equipment to turn the soil, and probably grind up all the burnt portions and mulch it to return it to a viable condition for planting again. But this would take an extreme amount of time and labor, especially if you're thinking about the entire valley. Even just for a modest area to use for a settlement, it would take days to prepare it, maybe several weeks or more to mulch it and lay down a new layer of topsoil. And that's assuming you had the people and equipment to invest into it in the first place."

"Right, whatever that means," she chuckles ironically. "And he's got druids out here dribbling dust on the ground. So, unless they're thinking of opening up the bleedin' sky over our heads and pelting us with lightning, I say pfft!"

Thaelyn could overhear the young dark elf's outburst, and deep down he understood her doubt. Nevertheless, his amusement caused him to form a mildly mischievous grin. He jerks his hand open, and the staff abruptly jumps into it. The druids follow the gesture with a much more vocal chant, more like a song than a series of rhythmic words. They begin to sway side to side with their hands moving in minor arcs around them. He waits while holding the staff upright in both hands.

The chanting continues a few moments longer, charging the air with a distant vitality. He raises the staff vertically and pauses, then thrusts it back firmly to the ground. As the staff strikes the crusty soil, one can hear a faint echo through the rocks.

Relissa's attention suddenly turns to the disturbance as she scans the earth at her feet.

"Uh oh..." she murmurs silently.

The druids and their chanting now take on a new level, louder and faster, with their arms swinging fully around, and the swaying turned to jumping and hopping. A breeze begins to stir, and the once clear sky turns hazy.

Relissa's eyes now turn skyward. She can feel a cold shiver moving up her spine.

"And uh oh again… Jiggers, maybe I should learn to keep my mouth shut."

"Yes!" Haran agrees sternly as he studies the scenery.

The druids carry on the heightened fervor of their dance, and their voices rise and fall like the ebbing of a strong tide. The hopping and jumping occasionally turns them in slow circles. The breeze strengthens into a moderate wind and clouds begin to form, filling the sky with a billowy veil, a dance of nature in tune with the music, until finally the sun is blotted out.

Relissa gulps in anticipation, along with Kaliya and Haran.

"Haran," Kaliya emits nervously. "Do they teach anything like this in your academy?"

"My dear," he replies solemnly. "They barely teach us how to light a candlestick, and not by praying to it. Although the result might be the same."

"Relissa, what about you…your mother is a priestess, right?"

"Aye, but I doubt she ever did anything like this."

Thaelyn prepares himself for another strike. He crouches low to the ground with the staff turned outward in one hand. He makes a powerful leap, reaching over the heads of the druids. Once more, he brings the staff up, and as he comes back down, he pounds it strongly at his feet. Thunder rolls through the land as the rocks quiver from the force.

"Buggers!" Relissa shouts as she jolts in surprise.

This latest hit sends the druids into a new frenzy, now twirling and bowing, then leaping and spinning, with their arms flailing through the air, waving high and swinging low. As the dance increases in vigor, the wind turns violent, the sky grows dark, and lightning begins to spark in the distance.

Haran looks at Relissa with scorn in his eyes. She returns with fear in hers.

The druids are now at a frenetic pace, with their voices virtually screaming. The dance carries them in arcs around the circle, twirling with arms outstretched in one direction, then throwing them skyward, followed by twirling the other way and repeating. Each time they throw up their arms, they let out an enforced bellow.

The winds grew to near gale force, and the rushing sounds began to overwhelm their ears. The sky is now black and foreboding and it races with streaks of lightning, tracing webs from one side to the other without intermission. With each new spark, the sky illuminates briefly, and among these countless flashes is revealed a swirling vortex forming in the clouds directly overhead, inverted like an upside-down whirlpool of spiraling doom. As the maelstrom forms, the winds start taking on the same circular motion on the ground.

"Curse you, Relissa, and your insolent words!" Haran shrieks to be heard over the uproar.

"Grace of the cu'Nar!" Kaliya shouts. "This is a bad place to be right now. Both of you, to my sides! Get down and hold on tight!"

The lightning sprays across the face of the storm furiously, first in all directions, then slowly aligning itself into the vortex. The entire sky lights up as hundreds of bolts arc across it simultaneously in a continuous stream funneling into the core. The vortex begins to glow from the insurgence of energy.

"This is simply irrational!" Kaliya screeches. "In all the netherspace, this is really, really bad!"

Finally, Thaelyn brings the staff to bear one more time, and as he does, the lightning begins to change color, from the typical white to a pale yellow-green.

"What in all the nine hells is that?" Haran screams, but his words are lost in the winds.

Thaelyn drops into another crouch as he prepares to jump again. The druids halt the reckless prancing and stand perfectly erect, with their arms reaching fully upward like pillars of flesh, and letting out one final screech. The winds abruptly change course, being sucked directly into the circle and upwards. Thaelyn leaps into the turbulent updraft as it carries him aloft, causing him to soar high above the ground. As he reaches the apex, the winds die off, the lightning ceases, and for an instant, all is eerily quiet, as though time itself has stopped.

"Relissa?" Haran trembles.

"Aye?" she replies sheepishly.

"If I survive this day, I'm going to kill you."

"Aye…and I'll even help."

Thaelyn now makes his descent, and a new wind begins to flow, this time downward and out from the circle, increasing rapidly to match the previous one. At the same time, great shots of yellow-green lifeforce energy race downward from the perimeter of the vortex into the bodies of each of the druids, penetrating through them and into the ground. The vortex itself also plunges downward, following Thaelyn's motion and racing to catch up.

As he meets the ground, he slams the staff down violently. Rock and soil are ripped apart, spraying out in a high arc. Ripples surge through the earth as a heavy shockwave passes underneath. Then the downward tip of the funnel cone makes impact, pummeling the ground around Thaelyn and expanding outwards, encompassing the druids and everything else. The rushing force of the howling winds blasts the three companions as they desperately huddle together on the ground. Flying bits of rock sting their faces within the dense cyclonic cloud, and the ground rumbles under the downward pressure, while waves of energy wash past them inside the druidic storm.

Kaliya holds on as best she can to her two friends. Using all her might, she wraps her arms around them and forces them into the ground, hoping to reduce the drag produced by their bodies. She furrows her hooves into the earth behind her, though it does little to help as she still feels herself driven back by the powerful wind. Her only hope is to hold out long enough before they're all carried away like kites.

The tempest passes rapidly, moving at an unreal rate as the inner eye expands outwards, leaving the group open to calm air and warm sunlight on their backs. When Kaliya felt the stillness returning, she pulled her head up, spitting out bits of dirt from between her teeth.

"I swear, I'm not going to survive long enough to report this in. I'll die of a heart attack before that happens…and I'm only four!"

She looked up and saw a clear blue sky. She turned to look over her shoulder and saw the black wall of the tempest moving away across the Badlands, deeply saturated by flashes of energy. It formed a full circle expanding out in all directions, resembling something like a huge waterfall, but here in the form of dense clouds pouring down upon the land. She stared at it in awe.

Relissa and Haran were detecting it might be safe to move again. They pulled out from under Kaliya's embrace and turned to examine the retreating storm and clear skies above.

"You mentioned something about mysticism, Kaliya," Haran mutters softly. "But can you explain that with your science?"

"I couldn't begin to, and I don't think I'd want to try. I might actually have to admit, this would indeed take the power of a god, because any level of science to do this would have to be godlike in itself."

Relissa glanced over at Thaelyn and the druids. Thaelyn was sitting on the ground, wearily gripping the staff, and using it for support. The druids were all lying motionless on the ground, seemingly blasted outwards from the center of the circle.

"Are they dead?" she asks.

"Gods, I hope so!" Haran states longingly. "Not that I would actually wish something like that, but just for good measure to bring peace again."

Kaliya continues to look around and spies Captain Hagmaert slowly standing up and brushing himself off. He had been positioned off to the side. Next to him was one mage, also standing up and straightening out his robes. There were no other people to be seen.

"What happened to those other mages that were here?" she wonders.

"Do you honestly want to know?" Haran responds hesitantly.

"Well, under the circumstances, I think it might be useful."

"Maybe. I saw them enchanting more of those runes, and then I think they went home."

Kaliya nodded and repositioned herself to stand up. But as she placed a hand down to lever herself, she noticed the ground felt abnormal, unlike what she expected. It was soft and squishy. She turns her gaze down to look at it, pausing for a long blink as she struggled to understand what her eyes were telling her. The texture of the landscape had changed. It was no longer black and crusty…it was now rich brown and loose. She grabbed a handful and brought it up to her face to sniff it. It smelled fertile, like the soil in an old woman's herb garden.

"Cu'Nar's pity, look at this!" she gasps.

The other two looked into Kaliya's handful of dirt, and then to the ground under them, each of them astonished by what they saw. But then, something else catches their eyes. There was movement within the soil just in front of them. They jerked back, unsure what to expect next.

Kaliya jumps to her feet, followed immediately by Relissa and Haran. They stared at the tiny disturbance in anticipation. Then another piece starts to move, and more after that. The longer they watched, the more movement they saw. Tiny bits of dirt started popping off revealing something slender and green underneath. It slithered and writhed as it tried to reach upward. Dirt was dislodging everywhere by now, and under each piece was another of these thin green snaking tendrils.

"That's grass!" Relissa yelps. "But, jiggers, how is it moving so fast?"

They extended their view across a larger area. Everything was erupting in fresh young shoots of green grass, growing at a phenomenal rate. Then Kaliya spies something new, growing thicker and taller. She gives a slow pat on Relissa's shoulder to draw her attention, and the group turns to see a young sapling stretching up out of the ground, nearly as tall as a man and still going.

Grass, trees, shrubs, and flowers are all blossoming with nearly as much fury as the storm that put them there. The Badlands, formerly a desert waste, was transforming into a prairie, with meadows of bright colors, and groves of lush woodlands.

"Haran," Kaliya mutters softly. "You said something about druids and religion?"

"Yeah…"

"How do you feel about it now?"

"Shaken to the core… You?"

"I'm probably even less religious than you, and right now I'm ready to get on my knees and start praying."

As they stood there, the air mixed with the fresh new scents. Kaliya took a deep breath to sample it.

"Do you smell that? It smells like…"

"…Springtime," Haran finishes.

Relissa was shaking her head at the extraordinary scene.

"Those druids brought the wrath of the gods into this place, only in reverse."

"But Relissa," Kaliya wheezes. "If we try to say a god can create something out of nothing, um, wait a minute."

Kaliya halts her words as a sudden flashback hits her.

"That riddle…" she whispers distantly.

"A riddle? You have a riddle now?"

"Well, maybe it's not a true riddle, but I always regarded it as such…a lot of us, actually, kind of like a generational thing. This is something from my old school, a part of our old science faction, but it's so obscure. Maybe I just didn't get as much time in study as I should have to understand how to apply it. We had the attack, and then, well…"

"Aye, I'm with you. What's it about?"

"It comes in two parts, the first of which is a theorem. Perception enables recognition, existence demands definition, and from this, substance becomes our reality."

"Jiggers, this is what they teach you in school over there?"

"Well…" she shrugs. "It's part of our studies in Metaphysics, which is the foundation of our faction. But the study is very abstract. The next part was an axiom, which says that in a metaphysical reality, nothing unknown exists. It only exists after it is known."

"Isn't that a little bit backwards?"

"Yes and no, depending on how you look at it. Take a physical object. You can study it, and therefore, define its properties, such as size, texture, weight, and so on. This defines its existence in a physical reality. The mind is what creates these definitions, as we need first to perceive of the object, and then assign measurements to it, which therefore represent the definitions of the substance it's made from."

"Uh huh, I think you lost me when you first called it a riddle," she grins.

"But the metaphysical aspect is always what got to me, as it's mostly theoretical. There's no way in which to prove anything."

"So, how would you apply it here," Haran wonders. "Or are you simply talking about your studies for the fun of it?" he smiles.

Kaliya pauses in contemplation. She could only vaguely recall elements of the dream she had earlier.

"What is a thing…" she muses.

"A thing?"

"Take any object you can imagine, but then ask yourself, how do you define it? How do you define reality, and that which is a part of it? The mind determines the definitions based on its perceptions."

She pans her view around the scene again, as the memory slowly returns to her.

"Perception! If you have a physical object, you can derive its definitions based on its substance, and the mind will perceive of its existence as the result. This is our empirical science speaking."

"That sure sounds like it."

"But in a metaphysical reality, the mind first perceives of a thing, gives it definition, and THIS is what governs its existence by altering the substance of that reality to serve its needs. This is the power of a god. He perceives of it and invokes this by overlaying his perceptions onto the space around him."

"Congratulations, Kaliya, I think you just made a breakthrough. This is how I apply my magic…if you can call it that."

"But this is still theoretical to me, as I wouldn't really know how to apply this myself."

"Maybe so, for now at least, but it's a step in the right direction."

"That's a wonky bit, if ever I did see," Relissa smirks. "And so, this guy brought the reverse wrath of his gods down here, and altered the reality of this valley to overlay all this sparkling new life. That's a dandy one!"

"A god… Life…" Kaliya mumbles. "Blessed Life… Great cu'Nar!" she shouts.

Kaliya felt a sudden shiver rush through her, and she grabbed her horns to steady herself. Her knees became weak, and she crumpled to the ground, catching herself as she slowly slumped into the fresh new grass.

Relissa and Haran were both startled by the sudden reaction, so they rushed to her side. They wrapped their arms around the girl as she began to weep softly.

"All right, so what got inside there this time, girl?" Relissa whispers in her ear.

"I'm sorry…so sorry…I was so bad," she moans.

"Um, Kaliya?"

"I think I'm going to need therapy before this day is out."

"Aye, right along with the rest of us, to be sure. So, what happened?"

"That prophecy again…the second part."

"Can you tell us what it is now?" Haran inquires.

"It's just one piece of a larger message, but maybe they reference different moments, and it may be impossible to measure the timing. But I think this one has just come true. It goes like this: From a circle of light, He shall come, the Divine Justice, One divided by Two."

"Thaelyn, perhaps?"

"If you consider two bodies, maybe to say two children, him and Aerlie, and their Father being one of those gods, in this case with the professional center of Law and Justice, which in itself is a weird thing to think of for someone like me. A god who works for a living," she chuckles faintly.

The other two feel a similar moment of humor as Kaliya continues.

"Maybe also if you think of this circle of light being that portal they came out of."

"Aye!" Relissa admits. "That's a good one. You peeps don't use those…neither do we, for that matter. So, we might not see it right away."

"They might represent this Divine Justice with their relationship, or maybe this military body he dedicated."

Kaliya turns to face Thaelyn, who is now beginning to stand up again.

"Whatever. The rest of it is certainly pointing at him for the moment, although I'm sure Aerlie has her roles, if it talks about two of them."

"They both describe themselves as Celestials," Haran suggests. "That ought to involve something."

"Yeah, but then the prophecy continues with another section. In His hands, He carries the power of Infernal Destruction, and the power of Blessed Life. Evil will crumble under the weight of His majesty."

"You got the majesty part right," Relissa suggests. "He's a King, after all."

"And half god, to boot," Haran adds. "That's certainly majestic enough."

"The destruction part would have to be that bomb," Kaliya muses. "And the Life part has to be all this."

"And this would go a little beyond simple coincidence. I could see one, but not both in sequence…and this is certainly a sequence, and no small demonstration of it."

"Yes, Haran!" she nods assertively. "But how could a person possibly interpret all this out of those words?"

"Maybe it's not up for interpretation, but more of a wait-and-see so it blows your horns off, as you people like to say," he snickers.

"Thank you, Haran, and not only for usurping one of our favorite expressions and using it against me," she grins softly. "But if this is the case, how do we know what to expect from the rest of it?"

"There's more?"

"Yeah, and it's generally interpreted to represent a salvation of some sort, though I've never actually believed it."

"Well, from my perspective, that's certainly encouraging. What does it say?"

"Like I said, it's very cryptic. It talks about a child finding some kind of gift, lost ones being found, and something sundered being restored. The last part is the most mysterious."

"And what is that?"

"It mentions vengeance on silver wings, but no one understands what that can be. A few have speculated with some rather wild ideas, but no one is willing to accept any of this without more study, and preferably some evidence. As for me, it was all just a lot of talk, or so I thought."

"The way it sounds to me, it sounds like a kind of notice to watch out for something, but without the details to say exactly what…not that I would expect any of you, or us either, to really understand anything, even if we did see it."

"Aye," Relissa nods. "I'll give you that much."

"But now, what's next?"

"What's next is whatever he's up to, I guess," Relissa offers as she points at the circle. "Look!"

The druids were recovering from the shock of the energy strikes. They gathered themselves up off the ground and back into the circle formation around Thaelyn.

"Gods be blessed," Haran demands. "What does it take to kill these people? Um, again, not that I would actually wish it, but you have to lay down a line somewhere," he glances at the sky again.

The druidic high priestess approaches once again, now presenting the nut she held out earlier.

"Oh dear gods, now what?" Haran barks. "Are they planting a garden next?"

She reverently steps up to Thaelyn while holding the nut in front of her. Thaelyn forms his hands into another bowl to accept it. She places it inside and again backs away out of the circle. He holds it up to the sky briefly while the circle begins another low murmuring chant. He then kneels to the ground and scoops out a few handfuls of dirt, placing the nut gently into the hole, covering it, and carefully packing the soil around it. He stands up, takes his staff again, and waves it in circles over the seedling. A stream of yellow-green sparkles falls from the staff onto the mound to empower the soil, and then he steps back.

At first, it seems as though nothing is happening, but then the mound begins to stir. A delicate shoot of growth presses upward through the soil, pushing away the surrounding material. It bears the resemblance of a young sapling.

"All right, so what is that now?" Haran sighs. "All this, just for a tree?"

"I'm guessing this could be something symbolic," Kaliya mentions. "So, Haran, try not to mock it too harshly. After all, he just finished cleaning house and remaking reality."

Haran glares at her for a moment before returning to the scene.

The sapling continues to grow rapidly, as with most other things around them. Its height reaches well over Thaelyn's head before slowing to a halt. He moves around in front of it and kneels.

"Now let me get this straight..." Haran begins. "He's a warrior, a mage, and what else, a druid?"

"This is becoming ridiculous," Kaliya sighs. "What purpose does this serve? And what else can he possibly do out here."

A sound is heard off to the side. They turn to see the lone mage conjuring up an exit portal. An instant later, and he's gone.

"Uh oh..." Relissa moans. "That can't be good."

"Can it be any worse than anything else we've seen so far?" Haran poses.

"All right, no more of this," Kaliya asserts sternly. "I think by now we need to bring this into better context."

Haran carefully eyes his tall friend for the change in her vocal tones. Her stress levels were starting to show, not that it surprised him, but under the circumstances, this was a bad time for it.

"Kaliya," he urges. "Try to control yourself. I've seen this mood of yours before."

"Haran, I'm in control. I'm only slightly perturbed this time, if only due to him being a half-god who could probably smite me to ashes with a wave of his hand."

"Yeah, but this isn't how things usually turn out for you. That would actually be a good thing, in your case."

"Please, Haran, whenever we see these people passing through their portals, all of nether-space comes unraveled."

"Personally, I can't see how much more of it can come unraveled. He just finished putting the last of it together again."

"Fine, but as you humans like to say, balderdash! The day is getting late, and I...we need answers! He comes in here, takes over the place..."

"Kaliya..." he utters sharply.

"...And like so many others, he thinks he owns everything. We can't afford to lose any more! Not you, and not us."

"Kaliya, wait!"

She lurches to her feet and prepares to charge up to Thaelyn.

Haran and Relissa both jump up and grab her arms to hold her still. But the tall Daanen'kai's general strength was a bit overwhelming for them, as she started dragging them behind her.

"Kaliya!" Relissa snaps discreetly so as not to make a scene. "You just stop! Remember how many times I had to pull your tail out of trouble? This guy has a bleedin' army behind him. Now just hold on a wee bit and take a deep breath. We'll get our answers, but not by jumping on the son of a god for it, ay?"

Kaliya halts and glares at Relissa. Her breathing had quickened, and her determination drove her to continue, though at this time she stopped moving.

"In addition to that," Haran adds. "He did say something about establishing an outpost, didn't he? Maybe in their world this... symbolic...tree represents something like a foundation stone."

Kaliya halts at this curious statement. She turns to glare at him now.

"A tree as a foundation stone?" she muses incredulously.

"Well, if druids are such an integral part of their society that they can do all this, it goes without saying they're a little bit, um, odd."

"And that mage just now?"

"If I were to guess, he's a messenger going home to call the rest of them here."

"Oh great, but now what… All right, Haran, you got me, but this doesn't forestall us to finish our own work."

"This much I'll agree on, but at the same time, if he's your prophecy coming true, the last thing you want to do is make an enemy out of him."

"You're absolutely right. Forgive me. All right, let's take this slowly."

The three of them now proceed in a more orderly manner, with Kaliya in the lead.

"Your Lordship," she calls, hoping to keep her voice calm. "Can you please allow some time for more talk. We're getting a little frayed over here."

"Only a little frayed?" he muses kindly. "I could hear some of that argument you shared just now, as well as Relissa's curious remarks during our ritual."

"Uh oh…" Relissa moans. "So, does that mean I'm in trouble now?"

"I think you found your own reconciliation. As for your nerves, I do not blame you, but you must also see it from my side."

"Right," Kaliya responds. "It's just that you brought some very potent forces into this valley, and I think we would like to find some peace before you do anything else to us."

"Very well, I believe I can afford a few moments. My people need time to assemble themselves, now that the land is attended to. From here, we will be importing people, supplies, and materials to build a camp. So, let us take a little walk to relax ourselves."

They move away from the area of activity to find a quiet place to talk.

"The first thing I think we should touch upon," Thaelyn muses, "is your lack of understanding of our ways. As I said before, I am a stranger in strange lands, and with potential enemies on multiple sides. I play this game my way, according to my own rules, to give me and mine the advantage over such foes. I dare not waste time or resources if I find myself in such a situation where lives could be at stake."

"Naturally..." Kaliya nods. "I should expect as much. I'm sure we would do the same if we ever had the opportunity...maybe also the inclination."

"Inclination?"

"Well, as I think we said earlier, my people are largely scientists... intellectuals, and not military in any way. So, inclination, meaning to actually get our tails in motion to do the deed."

"Ah, I see," he chuckles. "As if to say a largely pacifistic society. Very well, but the orcs that were offending our people seem to be coming from this world, and further that they seem to possess portal magic. This represents a serious threat to the security of my home. This is something I cannot and will not tolerate."

"Yes, again, I understand. We actually have the same here, if only we could do anything about it."

"It would also appear there is an external force at play here in the form of this Sargeras of yours, as he may be the driving force behind some or all of this. This is yet another complication to the rule. Combine this, and anything else that falls into the equation, and further compounded by your lack of understanding of our countermeasures, and we may find ourselves in this situation, to which I will apologize, but it is unavoidable."

"Yes."

"These...forces...I applied here are the result of our rather extensive development in various forms of study on Tae'Eladar. If they seem excessive to you, and I will certainly admit to this for these two examples, it is just as likely due to your severe lack of development in similar areas. Haran mentioned his academy studies. If this is the extent of your magical talents, then Powers help us for whatever else you might think if you were to visit Tae'Eladar proper," he chuckles.

"Really!" she smiles feebly. "Now I'm curious to see it for myself."

"You have your science; we have our magic. You developed your way; we developed in ours. But unlike you, we do not as often require machines to do our work, not unless we should develop actual science for the occasion, and instead we can apply our magic as an alternative."

"Wow, so you can do things we might need machines to do, but simply with magic. That's fascinating, but also frightening, if all you need to do is conjure something up out of thin air."

"It can apply in many forms. But now, as for…taking over the place…while I would not wish to impose myself on any of you, this valley was previously owned by orcs, not your people. I am only taking over the spoils of my wartime victory here, and with good reason as I must continue my campaign to protect my people. This must be my highest goal, regardless of anything else. I am sure you would do no less for your own."

"Absolutely…and again if we had the inclination for it," she sighs.

"Interesting. Is this to say you are so extremely pacifistic that you tend not to fight even if your very lives depend on it?"

"This is how it seems to work for us much of the time, so yes."

"Powers help us, this is actually not a good thing to hear. But regardless, I would hope my previous interaction would present itself as one who is more interested in polite interactions, not hostile ones."

"That's my fault, Your Lordship," Kaliya begs. "I sometimes lose control of myself, and this can get me in trouble. We're in a very fragile position here, all of us, fighting for our lives for centuries on end and not getting anywhere with it. This does things to a person after a while, and my people have taken some really bad losses since that attack on Ruuki uy'Daan."

"What sort of losses are we speaking about in your case that you are so delicate now?"

"We had a very nicely developed city over there once. I was born on that world, and life was good for us, at least within reason if it weren't for the hidden fear of being discovered again. Then came the attack and boom! There goes my innocence."

"How old were you at the time?"

"About half a century, which for us is early childhood."

"Powers behold, young lady. How long does it take for you to reach maturity?"

"Two centuries."

"Incredible," he shakes his head.

"We had something like a hundred thousand people, but only a small fraction made it to the ship, and maybe half of those died in the crash."

"A crash?"

"Yeah, saboteurs were found inside tampering with our nav and engineering systems. This caused an explosion, and we lost control, then we crashed here."

"I am very sorry for this."

"Since then, the Suuden-Aryku have laid siege on us such that we can barely even go outside. I suffered a bad childhood trauma as a result of that attack, and this has played a number of roles on me ever since. It's the main reason I haven't progressed very far in my service, as I tend to make a lot of bad choices."

Thaelyn turns to examine her carefully.

"Do you suffer from violent dreams or nightmares?"

"Sometimes..."

"...Of perhaps a young child running through ruined streets?"

"Huh?" she glares at him. "How would you know this?"

"During our meld, Aerlie and I were monitoring your thoughts as we finished, simply to ensure you made a proper recovery. This process, in your case at least, was a complex one for the volume of information we were hoping to exchange. During this time, I could hear your inner voice debating a most curious review of some science principle, and with a remarkable conclusion, but this was apparently interrupted by one of these visions."

"A debate? Wait a moment. I had a flashback not long ago where I think I recalled that. It was concerning metaphysics. This is the science foundation for our faction."

"A faction? Does your society divide itself along such lines?"

"For this, we would need to go all the way back to Azgarén.

Our society was composed of a variety of science factions, and further represented by a Council of Elders, where each of these was a representative leader for his or her faction of scientific dedication."

"Wait, are we speaking of scientists serving a political station here? A form of technocracy? How interesting."

"Yes, this is our government body, or at least it was. But our faction wasn't very highly regarded, as I understand it, as it didn't involve the traditional empirical study the others so often favored. Metaphysics was regarded as too abstract and fanciful."

"Really!" he chuckles. "I know of a young lady up in the city of Sigil, a location we Celestials might find of interest on occasion, who would find your story fascinating. She does not get out much, but to bring this to her would surely put a smile to her face."

"Well, anyway, these visions come to me quite often, and I have trouble sleeping on occasion as a result. I also lose control due to my impetuous nature at seeing my people suffering so many losses, and this just makes me angry…as these two know by now," she directs fingers downward to point at her two friends.

"You know, Aerlie is trained in psychology, among other things. Perhaps the two of you should sit down together for a chat."

"My brother has already tried this on many occasions, along with his wife, Ankhia, our chief med-tech at the Naarg uy'Sodrad. So far, it hasn't helped."

"This may be, but it would not hurt to try."

"What is this tree?" Haran asks. "Does it hold some special purpose for your people?"

"In a manner of speaking, it does," he nods. "Our people are tightly bonded with a reverence for the natural world. We hold a great respect for our native environment and a responsibility for the impact we make on it as we build our homes and cities. For all that we take, we must still allow something for the natural realms to flourish, along with their native wildlife. We must remember to share our home with everything else out there. It is not ours alone to do with as we please."

"Wow, all right."

"The tree, in this case, is a special variety. It is a symbol of our culture and a source of our prosperity. It gives our people direction, focus of spirit, and a sense of duty to the needs of the natural world around us. We plant these in each of our cities and towns, and across the land to enrich it and allow it to flourish."

"Does this mean your whole society is populated by druids?"

"No, people are still people, but our dedication might run deeper than in some examples. One does not need to worship nature to appreciate it. We are all creatures of the world we live in. Our lives follow the same cycles as everything else. We draw from it for our sustenance, but we should also realize a responsibility to give back to it. The food you eat, the clothes on your back, the materials you use in your craft or simply to furnish your home…everything has its origins, and those origins often have other origins."

"Gracious, that suddenly sounds very complex."

Haran is taken aback by this perspective, having never considered it this way before. He begins pondering the implications.

"All right, I think I can see it, at least a little bit," he considers. "For instance, the herbs and reagents we use in the academy have to be grown in gardens by herbalists, but space is limited inside our walls to grow food as well."

"You cannot grow food outside your walls?"

"Not with the war out there. Going outside is forbidden."

"Indeed! Perhaps due to these orcs in such close proximity?"

"That and everything else…like those Flame Elves."

"Where is your home located from here?"

"Mine is a city we call Rolsklinde. It's just to the north past those mountains."

"And these Flame Elves?"

"South, on the other side, and past some hills…"

"Well, with me here in the middle, you should find some relief from that direction. What about these orcs?"

"Mostly west of here, and I believe they extend south, right Relissa?"

"Aye," she affirms. "My people are the ones to see those most often. Our home is Solinaia, a city hidden in a grove of trees west of his by about half a day's walk. We sometimes see a few skirmishes on our outer towers, but not on the city itself. I think the city is too tough for them. But we think they take up everything from here to the sea."

"Indeed," Thaelyn nods. "And this might be a problem, if only for the numbers again. Kaliya, what about your people? Where are they located?"

"The remains of our ship, which we had to convert into a type of citadel, is half buried under a hillside east of Rolsklinde by about a hundred clicks."

"And for reference, how do we measure a…click?" he grins.

"Oh, right. You wouldn't be familiar with our measurements, would you," she chuckles.

"I can help with that," Relissa smiles. "Figure a good two-day jog or so, for those of us who don't skitter around in those fancy hover-thingies of theirs."

"Ah, but of course," Thaelyn laughs. "Hover-thingies… And I suppose we should be on the watch for those during our leisurely jogs to prevent accidents."

They all share a moment of humor together.

"Speaking of which," he continues. "Kaliya, how did you arrive here? By one of those…ahem…hover-thingies? I did not take notice of any vehicles as we first arrived."

"No, they don't let me drive any of those on my scouting runs. Not that they don't trust my driving skills, but when going into hostile territory like this, they tend to stand out. And by the way, they're actually called hover-coaches or hover-shuttles, depending on the size and configuration."

"I see. Very well. So how did you find your way out here? By foot?"

Relissa suddenly let out a compulsive giggle at the idea.

"She…hoofed it!" she laughs boisterously.

Their attention is impulsively drawn to the tall Daanen'kai's hoofed feet.

"I swear…" Kaliya jests as she lays her hands on her hips.

"I might have to agree," Thaelyn eyes the young elf suspiciously. "I get the impression you are the mischievous sort, young lady."

"Aye, I like to rib her a lot," Relissa admits. "It's all fun, and she knows it."

Thaelyn smiles at the gesture.

"Even if I did drive one out here," Kaliya adds. "It'd be gone by now."

"Not necessarily," he admits. "Such a thing as that I might wish to relocate first."

"Oh, well, that's nice of you."

"It represents personal property, and I would not wish to be accused of disrespecting it."

"Right, I probably should've thought of that. And speaking of which, that explosion, you called it Mystra's Fury?"

"Yes," Thaelyn nods solemnly. "It is a magical invocation where I hold the dubious honor of its creation. It is based on my Celestial teachings. War can sometimes breed the most contemptuous of inventions. In my efforts to destroy an entire nation of these accursed orcs, I was forced to think of ways to bring mass destruction down upon them as an alternative to the pain of a long and bloody campaign. And despite the durability of my people, I would not wish to engage them in such as that unnecessarily."

"My people once had a science that described such a process as what I believe I saw. Is yours the same?"

"While I might suggest it could be, depending on what sort of knowledge you actually possess, I must again defer to the rules we must abide by for the sharing of knowledge to younger races. Therefore, my answer would depend greatly on your own teachings and what I could disclose accordingly."

"Is this to say you can't talk about things we don't already know about?" Haran asks.

"Generally, yes. The Estelar have a strong principle that the younger races, what we most often refer to as the Child Races, must grow and mature over time as a natural process. To impart any advanced wisdom to them when they are not otherwise ready for it could result in havoc. Let me draw an example for you."

He strolls in front of the three listeners as he begins his lecture.

"On my world, though I cannot grant my people this privilege directly, I can still inspire them to find it on their own, if the effort is carefully measured and timed to give them opportunity to relax into it once they learn. I will often give quests and challenges to find answers to specific problems. The reward to this is an aspect of new knowledge. In this way, my people have moved far and overcome many difficulties."

"Sounds nice. So, this means you can give them the inspiration to learn something without actually revealing it to them directly."

"Precisely. However, let us now create a hypothetical circumstance. Say, for example, a being comes to a world and provides superior wisdom to a lesser society. Then, let us say this lesser society goes out to an opposing faction. They use this power, and it feels overly good to them. They become corrupt and perverted. Soon, they begin setting themselves upon all that is within their reach, unleashing this power with wanton disregard for its inherent danger, destroying all others and eventually themselves. Who is to blame here?"

He studies each of their faces, reading concerned stares all around.

"Jiggers," Relissa moans. "That sounds bad just by the sound of it."

Thaelyn nods, "This philosophy can apply from any superior form of life to any lesser form of life, no matter where they are found. The Powers simply have some very strict rules for it concerning their own."

"So," Kaliya proposes. "Is this to say your people understand such powers as what we just saw?"

"The short answer to that is no, not fully in the present day. The people of my world are only partially adept in these studies, to the point of understanding the basic principles of matter and energy, but not to the degree of using them to create such a weapon as this. However, I did share a few of its concepts with some of my higher-ranking officers and military personnel to prepare them for it. I consider it reasonably tolerable if it can be kept as a military secret for now, leaving only Aerlie and myself the responsibility of its application."

"And the shield? There were other mages using that."

"Yes, that was an invention resulting from a quest challenge I gave, in part due to my own creation, to oppose it. My people earned that one. It is also largely a military application, but I consider the gift of a defensive conjuration to be far more tolerable than an offensive one for this point."

"Right, I understand."

"What about all this stuff going on around us here, ay?" Relissa asks. "How did you go about making that wacky storm and changing the land?"

"This is a special topic, and also due to our war, and again due to my development of Mystra's Fury. I needed a counteragent to restore what I harmed. Do you recall my mention of a responsibility to repair the damage I leave behind? Well, this is the product of that responsibility. I share a relationship with what I will describe as a rather special, as well as potent being, that provides a unique bond with the natural elements. It is due in part to this that our society holds our beliefs where the natural world is concerned, in which we must honor her for her gifts to us. In fact, that tree over there is the gift she donates to us as the result."

"She gave you a tree? That's an odd one."

"She is one part out of three, including myself, who joined forces to build our world. And we watch over this with my military Order."

"How long have you been at this? It sounds like you've been a mite busy over there."

"Indeed! At this moment, I have spent about three-quarters of a millennium on Tae'Eladar building our society to where we stand now."

"Three-quarters of a millennium," Haran whistles. "So, how old are you overall?"

"I was a full millennium when I first arrived there."

"So, one and three-quarters... Wow, not bad...for a half-god," he grins.

"Perhaps, but I know of a few who belong to other denominations who are much older," he smiles. "So, we might say I am still a bit young by comparison."

"But you're immortal, correct? And that means…well, you just keep on going, I guess."

"Yes, Powers permitting, and assuming no catastrophes. But I think I would see most of those coming before that would happen."

"And that simply exaggerates the issue! Nothing can stop you, save maybe those same Powers you mention."

"Perhaps…"

"Jiggers," Relissa hangs her head. "That just finishes it for me. What about Aerlie?"

"She is rather young at four centuries, which is still within the frame of her mortal kin. But as you look at her, you will not see any signs of aging, as we tend to stop once we hit our physical maturity."

"Lucky you!" she quips.

Thaelyn now straightens his stance and turns to Kaliya.

"Now, my turn, if I may," he asserts. "I noticed a curious mention from you, Kaliya. You mentioned your people once had some of this science. Is this to say you lost it at some point? Knowledge is not something to be lost under a rug or in a closet."

"Um, well," she reflects. "We were speaking of that Mystra's Fury thing of yours, which I'm assuming to be based perhaps on the atomic sciences. This would count as ancient history to us, so I'm just speaking in past tense on that one. But actually, yeah, we did lose a lot in that last attack. Our libraries, and other things, were all on Ruuki uy'Daan, and probably destroyed. We try to keep backups on the ship, but some of that was also destroyed in the sabotage, and then the crash. This generally leaves us crippled, outside of personal knowledge, and then with the Suuden-Aryku on our tails, we're unable to rebuild anything."

"By the sound of it, this Sargeras is playing a game of cat-and-mouse with you, taking as much pleasure out of it as he can before you finally succumb."

"Yeah, and over a long period of time, too…"

Thaelyn taps a finger on his chin to think.

"We will need to attend to these political meetings as soon as possible, I should think, if we want to accomplish anything. Perhaps, as part of this, I could offer some aid in one form or another, be it defensive to give you some space, or perhaps resources to help bolster your own. But I must proceed carefully so as not to violate any of my previous oaths."

"Fine by me," Relissa nods eagerly. "But in the long of it, how do we actually fight this bleedin' war? You want to do away with the orcs, which is fine, but what about the others, especially these Suuden'kai peeps. They just keep on coming, as far as I know."

"If their source is off world," Thaelyn admits thoughtfully. "That can make it a challenge to defend against, a challenge I can relate to with the threat of these orcs. One must find the source if one is to win such a battle."

"This would be our ancient home world of Azgarén," Kaliya relents. "But there's no way for us to reach it from here. First, it's in another universe, which I suppose doesn't matter as much by now. Whether another universe, or simply another star system, our ship is dead and all our nav logs are wiped due to the sabotage. We're essentially stuck here with no way home…not that I would call it a home by now."

"I can most certainly appreciate this aspect of things, but I am not one to simply give up hope on such matters. While I may consider it a moment of good fortune to find that group of orcs and their portal leading us here, I would rather choose to apply whatever skills and opportunities may present themselves to see our way through the rest of it, and not simply depend on luck alone."

"Oh dear… Does this mean you might actually choose to fight this war all the way back to Azgarén?"

"If they should dare force it upon me, I will, even if I have to steal one of their own starships to do so."

"Cu'Nar help us," she winces. "So, this means you Celestials don't take no for an answer. Wow."

"Kaliya, I feel it is my duty to perform this service. This comes down from my Father's teachings. If you are being hunted, or simply offended by errant manners and deeds, I will fight for you. The rules of the Estelar are rather strict, and there is little margin for leniency."

"Yeah, just wait till I try to explain that one to our Council. We're not much of a warrior society, so warfare is repulsive to us."

"Be that as it may, but for now, let us focus on our most immediate needs, and attend to the rest as it becomes an issue. First, we will establish an outpost. Then, we will survey the land for our enemies and plan our actions accordingly."

He pauses to study Relissa, taking note of her clothing and gear.

"You bear the resemblance of a scout-class operative, is this correct?" he asks.

"I know the land well enough; I've been up and down it enough times."

"Perhaps we could make a bargain together. Naturally, I would need to discuss this with your superiors, but if you would be willing to assist me, I could use your knowledge of the land to start me off in this campaign. How do you feel about this? I will gladly compensate you for your efforts."

Relissa felt at first excited for the suggestion, but this was quickly muted by her memories of her experiences back home. She sighed deeply at the prospect.

"Personally, I wouldn't mind it, and maybe I would live a wee bit longer standing next to you…well, unless you start remaking reality again," she chuckles. "But I'm not a favorite with my…superiors. I doubt they would give me this much grace to represent something."

"Can you explain what you mean? You seem like a fine enough example to me, if also a tad on the mischievous side," he smiles.

"Aye, and thanks for being so nice about it," she returns the smile. "I actually like standing here talking to you, which is more than I can say for my super. He doesn't like me at all. I don't seem able to live up to his expectations."

"Is he simply so demanding, or is he displeased for other reasons?"

"Well, for one thing, this war, running on for so long, has been grating on my nerves ever since I was little. It got in the way of a lot of things, like my instructors trying to teach me the ways of our people, and this turned up a lot of noses at me."

"Ah yes, this could pose a contributing element. Elven tradition, at least on Tae'Eladar, is rather demanding. I suppose this also accounts for your poor language skills. But I will not hold this against you. In fact, if you are so far behind, perhaps you might try our schools. They can teach you in a more enthusiastic way such that you might actually enjoy the lessons."

"Really! Jiggers, is it anything like those mages you had here earlier trying a few things on me?"

"That and perhaps more… Is there anything else involved here?"

"Well, um…he often complains that I spend too much time with my little friends."

"Little friends…" he raises his brow. "How little are we speaking of here?"

"Furry little critters I sometimes like to play with. People poke at me for it a lot, but I really enjoy animals."

"Most interesting. Is this largely for pleasure, or do you teach them to do tricks?"

"Well, there's pleasure, of course, but aye, I can talk to them, if just a wee bit," she giggles briefly. "There was this one time when I had this squirrel run up to a window and throw nuts on the head of my super after I got a really heavy bashing from him. People don't believe me when I tell them this, but I can almost hear them talking back to me."

"Indeed!" he intones enthusiastically. "How extensive is this?"

"Um, well… Are you really so interested? It's probably just a load of bunk, really."

"Not at all! Some elves hold this special affinity, and you could be one example. Do your people have such a profession that we call a ranger? It is a form of scouting profession that uses animal companions to aid them in their work."

"A what? No, nothing like that… Why? How does it work?"

"A ranger is specially trained to interact with animals in such a way as to form a bond where they can join as a pairing. They can communicate with each other using a special, if also simplistic language, where the animal companion can serve as an extension to the ranger's scouting efforts. Smaller ones can be your eyes and ears in places the ranger might find inaccessible or too risky to venture into personally, and you can also train larger animals for companionship and protection."

"Jiggers, now that's a bugaboo of a trick to play. But risky places? I wouldn't want to hurt the little guys."

"No, but a bird in a tree is much less noticeable, to say nothing of conspicuous, than to see you standing there personally."

"Aye, it is! Wow. Do you teach this?"

"We do. We find mostly elves who sign up for these lessons as they hold this natural bond with nature more so than humans. Perhaps you might be interested."

"But I'm not even part of your world. Can I actually do this?"

"It is certainly a possibility. I hold a reputation to seek the greatest strength in those around me, and I support them until they achieve their highest potential. Then, well, if we speak of my own citizens, I employ them to our most productive combined purpose. In your case, I would certainly not waste such talent."

"Aye, maybe, but what about the rest of it, I'm not exactly prime goods here."

"Relissa, where do you get this impression from?"

She takes another deep sigh and turns away.

"A lot of things... My boss, the people back home, my Mum and Dah for my bad behavior..."

"But this is where your elven traditions are concerned."

"Aye, I'm not exactly in their best favor."

"While I am sorry for this, perhaps it can be corrected if I can convince you to take some advice from me."

"Advice?"

"Indeed, as it would seem I need to spend a bit of effort here to educate you on the manners of a Celestial."

"Uh oh..."

"Firstly, we do not throw people away, and certainly not those who hold potential. In our case, we are aligned with the positive side of the Measure of Balance, and generally incompatible with the negative side. As such, they whom we hold in our favor become our students. This is to say we encourage them to grow and overcome their shortfalls."

"How does this compare to the other side?" Haran wonders.

"Theirs would be adversity and discord, to apply a challenge in which to test the veracity of life to survive in the face of that which would otherwise bring it down. And Kaliya, in your case, dare I say it, but your people are not faring well in this regard."

"Figures," she shrugs. "But I suppose I would need to agree."

"And secondly," he continues. "We have very literally the patience of the gods built into us," he chuckles.

"Aye, fine then," Relissa breaks a tiny smile. "We'll see about that."

"I am sure we will, as I enjoy a good challenge. And to emphasize this, despite your superior and his opinions, I would ask for you specifically to join at my side, if for no other reason than out of spite for your lack of self-confidence. You give the impression of one who has given up on yourself, as much as others have apparently given up trying to help you. This is a waste I would never permit."

As the words sink in, Relissa looks up into his eyes. Somewhere within her, a tiny flicker of self-esteem ignited, and her expression softened with a glimmer of hope.

Kaliya and Haran exchanged glances as they listened in. They also felt something stirring within as they each recalled moments of their own difficulties.

"You seem like a very powerful influence," Haran mutters. "Is this how you do things back home?"

"It is," he nods. "And I will do no less here in this world."

A disturbance catches their attention from off in the distance. It came from the area where Thaelyn had organized the row of mages.

"Ah, here they come..." Thaelyn announces.

Their eyes turned to a row of portals that were beginning to open up. At first, only a handful, but the numbers rapidly expanded as more appeared, until finally a total of thirty stood in a long line.

"Criminy!" Relissa exclaims at the sight.

"Now that's an invasion," Kaliya muses wittily. "That would scare the horns off a few people, if ever they had the chance to see it."

"Gracious…" Haran mumbles, staring in disbelief until he catches himself again. "More portals… You people seem to use those quite often, don't you."

"Yes," Thaelyn affirms. "And for a long time in our history. They are a valuable tool for us. We use them to cross our world, both for travel and commerce."

"Everybody?"

"Indeed, our citizens need to move about just as much as our armies, though we use permanent fixtures called Gateways as the means, not the stones."

"That reminds me," Kaliya recalls. "All those mages that were here…"

"They marked a row that we call a way-line and departed back to our world in preparation for our people to come through. This is the result."

The row of portals glimmered on the field. Haran gazed at it, so many of them. Never has he seen such flamboyant use of magic. Then an odd sound came to his ears, the sound of marching and, he thought, singing?

Row by row, they came through; soldiers, marching in unison, carrying banners and drums, and singing some sort of marching song as they went. Entire companies filed through the portal rifts. The portals seemed to be grouped as twelve on each end, and six in the middle. The larger groupings produced troops while the middle group had large, winged beasts coming through. They were enormous, with bodies like lions, and the head, wings, and claw-like talons of birds. They were equipped in full armor barding and carrying riders in the first of two saddles. One of them had Aerlie riding in the second mount. She instructs the rider to pull aside briefly so she can hop off and return to the group.

"Egads!" Haran screeches. "What are those?"

"Gryphons!" Thaelyn proclaims. "They are specially bred for use within our Order, larger and stronger than the feral sort, and capable of equipping plate armor and two mounts. Deploy a few handfuls with either a mage or an archer in the rearward mount, and you can rule the sky."

Relissa makes an uncontrolled giggle.

"And if not the mage," she muses. "Just fly them over the buggers after filling up on a nasty meal."

Haran casts an unpleasant look at her. She returns with a playful smile.

"An air force?" Kaliya muses incredulously.

"In a manner of speaking," Thaelyn responds. "And a most valuable tool. We have used them for several centuries now."

"Just how advanced are your people at this time? I'm still thinking of those soldiers we saw earlier. They didn't look like the sort to carry a lot of science with them…at least not anything I would otherwise recognize."

"Perhaps, but the advances we made might not appear the same as yours. We are recently entering into an early form of Industrial Age back home, where we are just beginning to make use of a limited form of mechanization and electrical services."

"And you have an air force of mounted troops. Well, that beats a few things in our history."

"Especially if you can put mages in the back seat," Haran notes. "They could possibly toss fireballs down on you from up there."

"Yeah, and I thought those orcs were bad. But those soldiers were using swords. Do you use anything like guns or rifles?"

"Not so far," Thaelyn affirms. "We still favor the use of bows, but in our case, most often highly enchanted to use elemental ammunition rather than physical."

"I don't even know what that means."

"I do…" Haran considers. "And it sounds nearly as bad as your plasma weapons, Kaliya, so don't underestimate it. Imagine a fireball as ammunition."

"In all the nether-space, so you use bowlike weapons that evolved with your magic in some ways like our technological forms, and just as dangerous."

Kaliya pauses briefly to imagine the scenario of Thaelyn's men going up against the Suuden-Aryku, and the resulting chaos that might follow.

"No wonder you put down the idea of our weapons that first time," she relents. "If you were to use that shield of yours, combined with your bows, the Suuden-Aryku are in trouble."

"Perhaps," he admits. "But as with all things, I would wish to study my opponent before I launch against him."

"Of course..."

As the troops continued to pour through, Haran again paid attention to their armor. It appeared as more of the same as what he saw on the small assembly that was here earlier, mithril and adamantium, gleaming with their own brilliance. But these were measuring as thousands, and more came through after that, a sparkling sea of it. The entire area was filling up, a full legion of them.

"Dear Gods, man," he gasps. "Look at all that metal. How many do you have out there?"

"I am currently travelling with a full division, which amounts to ten thousand troops."

"Only currently?" he wheezes. "How many do you have altogether?"

"Technically speaking, this would amount to classified military information, but I will admit, my full army numbers in the millions, with a good many of them as inactive reserve, though many others are assigned to civilian roles. I will also be allowing many of my active troops to return home for temporary leave. They have worked hard for it."

"Man...many...mil...mil..." Haran's legs buckle, and he collapses, letting out an audible moan as he goes down.

The others turned to look at the place where he was standing, only to have to angle downward to find him.

"There he goes," Relissa quips. "The bugger just couldn't take all the shiny bits. But to be fair, I'm not too far away from it, either."

"You and me both, Relissa," Kaliya accedes. "I'm looking at all this, and the only thing that comes to mind is an old saying: And here comes the Knighthood."

"You have a saying about knighthoods?"

"It's ancient, I think. People use it sometimes, but I don't really know where it came from."

The center columns of animals halted after a while and now caravan wagons started coming through loaded with supplies. They included crates, barrels and sacks, cords of firewood, and some also carried prefabricated building components fashioned with metal fittings.

"What are those for?" Kaliya asks as she points to the most recent arrivals.

"The outpost components," Thaelyn admits. "I have educated my people in ways to create fabrications of materials for the rapid deployment and construction of common buildings. It is a form of modular construction. It was another necessity of this war as we were covering a large area of our continent and needed to build forward bases quickly. With these, we are able to establish defensive walls, towers, barracks, mess halls, and more in just a short time."

"Ingenious!" she mutters as she takes it all in. "And again, entirely unexpected..."

"Why is that?" he wonders curiously. "Surely, a lesser society might use portable building components, just not of this particular design. Tents, for instance..."

"Well, all right, I suppose I have to agree, and maybe to use pieces that can be erected quickly in mounting brackets and such."

"Exactly."

"Obviously, I'm not nearly as experienced in this level of mobilization, so I guess I'm showing my lack of wherewithal on this point."

"Maybe. You did say you were only a Petty Officer, correct? That is rather low on the ladder."

"Yeah, but I should be much higher, if only for the mistakes I so often made along the way due to my personal troubles."

"And here we have that mention again. Aerlie?" he calls out to her as she makes her approach. "We seem to have a potential patient for you."

Aerlie rushes over to join the conversation.

"Oh? Which one, and what sort?"

"The tall one with the peculiar complexion, and she seems to suffer from a number of unfortunate psychological traumas. Do you recall those visions we saw in that dream of hers?"

"Yes! I was worried about that, and I also happened to take notice of something else, which very quickly flashed by us during the meld."

"Oh, which one was that?"

"It was a rapid flash of a young girl on a ruined street. I think it occurred when we reversed direction on the polarities."

"Most interesting…yes, I recall this, if only barely. How would you interpret this?"

"Without a proper study, I can only speculate so far. Kaliya, what are these traumas of yours?"

"The orcish attack on Ruuki uy'Daan," she responds. "Watching my mother get hit in the back by one of their mutation magic things, buildings exploding, fire everywhere, people screaming…should I go on?"

"And how old were you?"

"A young child, half a century…"

Aerlie winces and shakes her head at the number. She lays a hand on her forehead and turns away in surprise.

"Yeah," Kaliya smiles gently. "That's what a lot of people think around here. But this is just who we are."

"Well, right off the top, if you were so young, surely all this would leave a very deep mark on you, especially the image of your mother going down. Where were you at the time?"

"Standing right next to her… We were running to the ship when she was hit."

"And what were they using on this occasion, do you know?"

"Some kind of awful magic thing, we think, but we don't understand magic, it's all mysticism to us. Anyway, we saw this used on our people as we were trying to run. It mutated them into some kind of monsters who then got up and apparently started chasing everyone else, which only added to the panic."

"All right, my first impression is you would suffer no less than at least a few very disturbing images of the affair, and as a young child, this would likely cause trauma, which could result in repressed feelings, violent dreams, vivid memories, and finally some sort of blockage as a defensive reaction. That dream we witnessed could be one symptom, but that rapid flash…that felt different. I may need to think about this a little to see if it holds any meaning. It was almost like something was released during the pressure of the meld."

"How about mood swings," Haran offers as he returns to the group. "She has those on occasion."

"Oh yes, most certainly, if she has anything bottled up inside of her, and especially after that tirade she shared with the priestess at the prayer we held over there," she glances back towards the canyon. "Her ire towards orcs is clearly marked, and while I can't necessarily blame her, if this results in mood swings, she could suffer all sorts of corollary issues."

"Like making a lot of mistakes during my military career," Kaliya sighs. "I used to hold the rank of Ensign once, but it didn't last long. I fouled it up badly one day."

"Kaliya, if you were to allow me to help you with a few sessions, perhaps we could smooth some of this out for you."

"I don't know…well, maybe. But let's take care of some of this other work first. I think we have a lot of things in front of us that are a little more important right now."

"All right, if you wish, but I'm not going to give up on this entirely, and neither should you."

"Great, another Celestial that doesn't take no for an answer," she chuckles weakly.

"Speaking of our other work," Thaelyn considers. "I think we must again reinforce the importance of our security, as best we can muster it…especially after all this out here," he waves at the canyon and the blast crater. "Once again, we are foreigners in this world, and with enemies on multiple sides. While I would desire to keep a low profile as best I can, that blast out there will likely draw some attention, assuming anyone is close enough to actually take notice of it."

"Aye!" Relissa nods. "I think they probably would. I would imagine it could be seen all the way to Rolsklinde, and probably by the Suuden'kai peeps on the other side of those mountains in the east. Kaliya tells us they probably use some fancy stuff to monitor things from afar. My people have scouts out-and-about, so word will probably filter back on that side, and no doubt the Flame Elves use the same."

"Then this only complicates matters for us, and I will need to be especially careful how I proceed from here. I do not wish to portray any outward aggressive movements which could invoke an immediate retaliation. If they are wise, they will see this explosion and tend to stay away from it. They may instead choose to study us for any openings, and for this, I feel we should use stealth as much as possible until I can find my own advantages to bring this more into my favor."

"Good luck with that," Kaliya winces. "I wouldn't want to be in your hooves right now…figuratively speaking," she smiles.

"Indeed! But this also brings us back to the three of you and your associated factions. We need to maintain a strict level of security. What I have given to you this day accounts for a fair amount of detail. Recall the promise you made when we first began, it still holds. Initially, we should limit ourselves to only the amount that is necessary to gain the support of others, and perhaps, as time goes by, we can build on this later. But information can be stolen just as easily as given, and I do not know who among us is entirely trustworthy."

"Do you think any of us would wish to betray you?"

"I am not saying this of you, but if to whisper the right words in the wrong ears, it can filter down to those who can be dangerous.

I feel you are worthy of my lessons, but you are not the only players in this game."

"Right, well, personally, I doubt any of my people would do anything bad. We're in too much of our own trouble to afford it."

"I think we're all in this basket together," Relissa adds. "We've been fighting this war for so long, we're desperate to see a way out."

"Very well," Thaelyn asserts. "But at the same time, we also have this Sargeras of yours, who seems to be hiding behind all these issues, and directing at least some part of it. This makes me wonder if he has any spies, or other agents we should be aware of."

"Jiggers, you think he might have spies on us? Oh grand, that would be a nasty one!"

"He had to do something to corrupt the High Elves down there, and this suggests a coercive movement. The Calaerea are normally a very noble society. So to corrupt them in any fashion would not only be a high insult to them, but it would also be offensive to every other elf out there."

"Wow, that'll stir things up a bit."

"Therefore, we must be cautious of who we talk to and what we say, in case those ears are attached to someone of lesser virtue."

"Aye, I'm with you."

"And this naturally makes me wonder about Sargeras himself. Who is he, where does he come from, and then how and why would he care to pursue you across such distances, and for such a length of time? Kaliya, perhaps you could go into a bit more detail of his description. For instance, when did he first arrive and what did he do to take control of your people back home?"

"As I said," she recalls. "It was nearly ten millennia ago. Maybe nine and a half to ten, though after a while, who cares, it was half an eternity for most of us."

"Absolutely!"

"The story goes that he arrived on Azgarén, I think seeking help of some kind, and in return he would pay for our...services...with some portion of his great wisdom, which could possibly elevate our society of scientists and scholars to a new level of advancement."

"How typical, so he appealed to the one thing you might find most desirable."

"Yeah, and apparently the Elder Council took it. But then the cu'Nar came to us...that is to our faction, with, um..." she coughs subtly, "...Velen, who was a member of the Council at that time."

"Kaliya," Aerlie interjects. "You seem to have trouble with that word. Can it be related to this trauma of yours, perhaps?"

"Oh, please don't get me started on that one. This runs deep, and it hurts."

"All right, I'll let it pass for now, but again, I'm going to be watching you, and I will strongly urge you to meet with me in a session or two sometime."

"Fine... Anyway, he became their contact, it would seem. They warned him to run away, and so we did. And from time to time, they return with additional information, or instructions, or something, which we often describe as a form of prophetic depictions, for how they appear to us."

"This is rather curious," Thaelyn muses. "How do they deliver this?"

"Telepathically to him. He once studied telepathy on Azgarén, so he understands a thing or two about it."

"How interesting, so your people are capable of telepathy? Are you studied in this, perhaps?"

"No, only he has it in the modern day. We generally regard this as a potential security threat, so it's often restricted knowledge to just the Council. Elder Vankkar, for example, absolutely hates the idea."

"While I can certainly appreciate the fear factor, and if you consider the application of magic, it follows a similar principle. You simply need to educate the people in discipline and respect to perform it responsibly. The dangers can travel in both directions, you know. Amongst us Celestials, this is a common feature, so as a society, we are well-versed in the responsibility aspect."

"We're probably too young for that yet."

"Maybe, but you will not grow if you do not learn how to use such things. But now, what about Sargeras himself? If this has been going on for so long, he must also have a substantial lifespan to see it through, as well as a tremendous amount of patience if he has been simply toying with you during this time. And further, we should ask why he came to you in the first place. You say he came seeking help, but why would he go and chase you halfway across Creation if he was offering a beneficial gift to your people in exchange for a service. This is a contradiction."

"What about the part of the Suuden-Aryku being turned into monsters?" Relissa offers.

"True, this would be a clear indication of an ulterior motive, and not a kind one. It might then suggest the 'help' he was seeking was a servant race of some kind. So, perhaps his ire is that her people ran away rather than stay with the others to be his servants. This might then offer an explanation for the chase, and his desire to play with toys, for lack of a better term, might explain the duration of it."

"And his promise of great knowledge?" Haran muses. "A simple bribe, perhaps?"

"Perhaps."

"I honestly don't know the answer to all that," Kaliya shakes her head. "Other than the cu'Nar claiming he was something really old and really bad."

"Old and bad," Thaelyn frowns deeply. "This is certainly troubling. Did they give any better definition of his origins?"

"Nothing specific, I don't think. But then, who are we to associate anything out of it. They did give some kind of name, although I have no idea what it means."

"Ah, well, what sort of name is it? If these are elementals, they might be an ancient society, perhaps with some unique language components."

"All right, but keeping in mind this was done telepathically, so it's mostly an interpretation, as they don't use words like we do."

"Of course, I can understand this. Telepathic communication is not applied the same as a vocal one. It often tends to be more conceptual in nature."

"Really! Hmm... Anyway, he...that is, Velen...felt this was

as close to the wording as we can get it. For one thing, they said he was a remnant of an ancient race, which is supposed to be dead by now. This actually conflicts with the mention he made for this request for aid.”

“And no doubt part of that ulterior motive. He told you one thing, but the truth is something else entirely.”

“Yeah,” she nods. “And then we have this strange word. We think they described him as a Titan.”

As the depiction makes its way into the conversation, Thaelyn’s eyes suddenly grow wide, and his mouth falls open. Kaliya and the others gazed at him, but before they could say anything else, they were hit by a strong wave of empathic feedback.

“A TITAN?!” Thaelyn shouts! “They called him a TITAN??”

His voice explodes and shakes the air around them. His eyes flash with momentary light. The rumbling causes the full assembly of troops to turn their focus to see what was wrong.

Kaliya falls back a step, startled by the outburst and rattled by the shockwave. Relissa lets out a short yip as she jumps and then cringes. Haran yelps and ducks for cover. Even Aerlie feels the sudden gush of energy as she sways back, fluttering her wings softly to maintain her balance.

“Impossible!” Thaelyn continues, his voice still echoing. “One of the Primordials? This cannot be! The Powers disposed of them an epoch ago! Cast them away into a closed demi-plane, imprisoned for all eternity! There should be no more!”

“Flaming buggers!” Relissa whines. “Easy does it, guy. I can actually feel you right now. Jiggers, is this what happens when you make a Celestial angry?”

“Thaelyn, constraint, my Dear,” Aerlie interjects pleadingly, trying to gain control of the situation. “She’s right, your emotions are seeping out all over the place. Even Aelwyn would be surprised by it, and you know how she is.”

Thaelyn was panting from his shock. He tries to force his temper down and soothe his voice. He looks around to see his troops all staring at him, wondering what happened and if he needed help. He turns and flashes a simple wave to signal all was well.

"My apologies," he resumes, now more in control. "Please excuse me. You are right, Aerlie, now I know how Aelwyn feels whenever she has one of her episodes. But this is truly surprising, as well as disturbing. And these are elementals, so we must recognize the relationship being inferred here."

Haran peeks out from behind Kaliya's back to reenter the conversation.

"It would seem you know something about this being then?" he asks timidly.

Thaelyn takes a deep breath before attempting to explain.

"A Primordial…" he ponders distantly. "The last thing I would ever expect to see, whether in my lifetime or anyone else's in the modern day. The stories we hear about them… Some of you might have your childhood ghost stories at the bedside, but this would be one of ours."

"That's simply scary, and you're half god."

"Indeed! This is a history nearly forgotten, and rightly so. It is barely recalled even by those who live within the Outer Planes themselves. Even the Estelar do not speak of it openly."

"And that sounds even worse."

"The Estelar," Kaliya considers. "So, this race of gods would know who he is?"

"Know who he is? My Dear, they are the reason the Primordials are supposed to be dead."

"Oops!" she blurts with her eyes popping wide open.

"And that sounds even more worse!" Haran moans. "So, what happened that this one isn't actually dead?"

"That, my good man, is a most excellent question to ask," Thaelyn affirms heartily.

"Could it be one of them escaped?" Aerlie asks.

"Unlikely, from what I recall of it. Whatever remnants I ever heard of were supposed to have been imprisoned in a custom-made planar fold, created as a type of tomb, or a prison. There should be no escape possible, as you would need a portal to leave that space, and I must assume none were provided."

"Wow, now that's a tight prison!"

"Yes, and I find it unlikely the Estelar could miss one. But I suppose if he escaped during the heat of battle...and yet, he would have to be hiding somewhere deep to evade them for this long."

"Can you tell us the story?" Haran begs innocently. "I always did want to hear a ghost story on the scale of the gods before," he titters.

"Bloody hell, Haran!" Relissa gripes as she elbows him in the side.

"Something tells me the two of you travel together a little too often," Thaelyn smiles gently. "Very well..."

He pauses to take another breath, now feeling calmer and more under control.

"To understand this story, we must travel back in time to a moment when the Estelar were still investigating the last few pockets of Creation. There is a mention, though indirectly, that they were born in the mists on the far side of it, though the exact nature of it is rather obscure. Furthermore, it would seem they are not the first, as there was a precursor society that came before them, and these were the Primordials. Although this name is not a proper race name, it would seem. Only an interpretation the Estelar used to address them."

"Interesting," Kaliya muses. "Primordial...precursor, something older, and what, more primitive?"

"I cannot be sure how you would interpret that word, but it would seem the Estelar do not use it in a polite form. So this might afford us a hint as to its usage."

"Uh oh...they use bad words up there? Eek!"

"Yes..." he chuckles. "There was no love between the two sides. These beings were seen as criminals for how they so often treated the younger societies. This prompted the Estelar to conduct a campaign of cleansing to purge them from Creation and take over in their stead. And as I understand it, the last of these battles took place in our local space."

"YOUR local space?" Kaliya wonders. "Cu'Nar help us yet again!"

"Yes, as it so happens, the dimensional fold where we have Tae'Eladar was one of the last holdings of these Primordials, therefore, we hold this history. It represented one of their last stands."

"Interesting...and also very convenient, I suppose."

"Convenient?" he muses abruptly. "Yes, and further if you consider the invasion we suffered recently that brought us here."

"Uh oh, now I'm sorry I mentioned it. Maybe it's just coincidence."

"Well, we can mull this at a later time. This dates back a firm epoch ago, although the precise numbers seem to be lost in time by now. The Primordials were once a race of godlike proportions, much like the Estelar. But the history we are most familiar with seems to come out of that last encounter. They apparently ruled as a supreme power in which each held possession of a world. And on that world, they created one or another form of life. But to them, life was not a thing to be admired. It was merely a toy for their amusement."

"Sounds a little familiar already..."

"Jiggers," Relissa winces. "And it doesn't sound nice, either. What did they do to them?"

"As the story goes," Thaelyn continues. "They would breed these lifeforms as challengers in a game of sport, pitting one army against another in what can only be described as a form of gladiatorial contest, a fight very literally to the death to see which of them was more worthy."

"Armies, you say?" Haran grimaces. "Are we speaking of intelligent life, rather than some form of wild beasts?"

"Indeed. Apparently, using sentient forms was more amusing for them, as then you have the possibility for suspense and intrigue."

"Oh, how lovely..."

"Then was the arrival of the Estelar. They discovered this practice and were thoroughly appalled by it, as they hold a very different belief for the value of life."

"Just for the sake of discussion," Kaliya interjects. "What do they believe in?"

"I believe you already had a lecture on the Measure of Balance, at least in summary. All things in Creation must balance, based on the polarities of positive and negative forces, and this includes matter, energy, and also the elements of life and death. Nature will take care of some of this on its own, but the Estelar believe that all living entities must be respected and allowed their fair space. Life is to be nurtured and allowed to grow. That which succeeds may evolve into something higher, and that which fails is simply recycling back into the primordial elements from which it came. Life does not play favorites. You must demonstrate yourselves strong enough to actually survive the challenges of existence."

"Wow! Now there's a philosophy."

"The positive and negative sides each take their roles to motivate life on its path, supporting it as well as testing it on occasion to determine its integrity. Evolution is the result of this path, and if you are determined enough to overcome the challenges of your evolution, you may succeed and develop into something new."

"Fascinating…" she croons. "Is this to say someone like me, or maybe to say my people, or even Relissa and hers, or Haran and his, could one day evolve into something like the Estelar?"

"They can, but it often takes an extreme amount of time for this to occur."

"I think that just blew what was left of my religion," Relissa moans. "Assuming I had any," she giggles softly.

"Anyway," Thaelyn smiles. "The Primordials disrupted this balance, or perhaps they never respected it in the first place. They apparently chose to decide the fate of their creations based on the outcome of these games. According to the story, the loser of these games would be wiped from existence simply for the reason it failed to win the contest. Then, the owner of that world would create a replacement for the next game."

"The entire species?" Kaliya grimaces.

"Yes, all of it, which was another aspect of the Estelar's disdain for these creatures. They did not respect life, or try to nurture it at all, and instead used it as entertainment, giving it only enough to perform as trained animals in a circus."

"Grace of the cu'Nar!" she shouts. "I hope he doesn't get any funny ideas about us."

"The Estelar challenged them to discontinue this practice, but they refused, and so there was a battle, we call it the Celestial War. Although, I am sure this was just one out of many by now, if we are speaking of a broader race. The Estelar won the battle, and the Primordials were either destroyed, or captured and cast into this dimensional pocket I mentioned. This should have been the end of it...permanently. But if we are saying this Sargeras of yours is a survivor, we have a problem."

"Yeah, it would seem that way."

"But not simply for your experiences," he emphasizes with a finger. "First, if we say the Estelar encompass all of Creation by now, how is it he managed to evade them during this time? Where has he been hiding that they could not otherwise see him? Such beings as these have special senses and abilities within the Seas of Creation that resonate throughout the dynamistic flows. If there was a Primordial out there, the Estelar should be able to sense him, and he them, for that matter."

"Um, what are these flows you speak of now?"

"Ah, but of course. They are a type of support layer within that space where such beings as these usually find their residence. As life evolves upwards, it transcends out of environments such as this here," he waves around him, "and into that one. And the body adapts along the way."

"Oh! So that is where gods come from! They evolve into another dimension, and a new environmental layer."

"But the flows can permeate multiple planes, even down to our level. To us, we might describe this as the arcanic energies we use to perform our magical arts."

"Hold on!" she tosses her hands up. "So there actually is a type of power source for it?"

"Indeed. But this is interesting now. A moment ago, you called it a form of mysticism. Is this to say your people have no idea how to use it?"

"Yeah, it doesn't show up in any of our usual sciences."

"Very well, but this is not part of your classic physical science. This is not an empirical form of study like atomic science or electromagnetism. These energies are extradimensional quantities, and they are governed by the power of a focused mind."

"Great cu'Nar!" she gasps and grabs her horns. "Metaphysics?"

"This would certainly give you a better direction for it, yes. That discussion you had earlier, when we restored the land, and again to reference that dream of yours. This is how you might envision it. But it takes practice, and for some, a considerable amount of study, plus an exceptional amount of discipline to show it the respect it deserves."

"Can you teach me a little about how it works, maybe a tiny lesson?"

"Well…" he chuckles. "Perhaps we can find time for this later. But back to the Primordial. Now I am wondering how he evaded them for so long. If we should say you have no idea what these energies are based on a lack of experience, perhaps also a lack of access to them, could it be you live in a universe that is fully devoid of them?"

"Are there such places?"

"There are, if only a few, that I have heard of. We would call them barren folds, where barren is to mean the absence of the flows."

"Barren…as opposed to what? How far do these flows actually travel?"

"To my knowledge, they cover the greater part of Creation, so a barren fold is an exception to the rule, not the rule itself."

"Oh wonderful!" she shouts. "So, we live in the only hole in Creation that doesn't have the good stuff in it."

Thaelyn erupts in a boisterous laugh, followed by Aerlie, and then the rest.

"Now, if we suggest he has been hiding in that universe, it could possibly follow that the others would not see him directly. Therefore, he could evade them, and this actually makes sense to me now, if this was his intention."

"Yeah, it would, actually."

"And if these cu'Nar of yours were possibly following him, they might try to warn you about him, hoping to guard you from his influence. Unfortunately, it would seem most of your people failed to listen."

"Yeah, that too…"

"If this is the case, then we do indeed have a problem, for he will be a most powerful foe for us, even without his armies standing in our way."

"Huh?" Relissa blurts unexpectedly. "Um, excuse me? Are you saying we're going to fight him?"

"He is a creature that should no longer exist. Even the Estelar would agree to this."

"Aye, fine, let them have him."

"It may yet come to that, but first we need to find him, and discover how and why he has remained hidden for so long. Furthermore, why is he coming out of hiding, if as she says, we have this coincidental return with that invasion of my world, which lies in that same place where we had this final battle. This is suspicious to me, as well as intolerable."

"Oh grand, aye, I get it, I think."

"Then, if he is in hiding, I might hazard to guess he would also be watching for them. Therefore, it falls to us to make this search, as he would not as likely expect such small creatures as we to be a bother."

"Bloody hell, suddenly I'm sorry I met you."

"Relissa, this is no longer a simple battle against mortal foes, as he could represent a danger to much more beyond that, and I must rise to meet it."

"But this makes him a god of some kind!" she grumbles. "You'd have to be wacky to go after that."

"Young lady, once again I should remind you that I am no simple mortal. You should place your faith in me, not him, as you will gain more from it. There are secrets amongst the realms you are not privy to, but where those of us in these high places might be more affluent. Entire worlds may fall because of him. Just look at yours and multiply this by whatever number he should care to discover for himself."

"Oh jiggers…aye, again," she lowers her head.

"Therefore, the conclusion is simple. His kind should not be given quarter. But if I make the initial advance, I will not stand out as much as the Estelar would. I will go in search of him, and then take whatever actions are necessary to finish him."

"Even though he's on another world, in another universe," Kaliya smirks tenderly. "And you don't have a star cruiser to carry you there."

"Indeed!" he nods assertively. "And such a fine challenge that would be!"

Thaelyn turns abruptly and marches over to inspect his troops, with Aerlie following close behind after a brief smile and a bow, leaving the three companions in a sweat.

"Buggers to bugaboos!" Relissa mutters softly. "What a day this is turning out to be."

"You got that one right," Haran agrees. "But this does offer a curious note. How do you kill a god?"

Chapter 6

AWAKENING

Thaelyn strolled amongst the troops, column after column, where whole companies had lined up along both sides of a central avenue. As he walked along between them, the regiment commanders would dismiss each unit to move off and set up a temporary campsite to the side, clearing the way for other activities to take place.

Kaliya and the others watched in awe at the precision of movement by the well-trained and highly disciplined army.

"I can tell you one thing, ladies," Haran begins. "While I have no doubt in my mind that this army could easily take on anything else in this world, there will be those who may not be so easily convinced. Some of our own superiors have very hard heads. And with no real experience in mithril, to say nothing of adamantium, or anything else we've seen out here today, they won't know what they're up against."

"Aye, I'm with you on that," Relissa muses. "I don't know much about the metal, but just by looking at it, it gives me the shimmies."

"Kids," Kaliya offers. "My people wouldn't know the first thing about how to interpret any of this. Not the metal, not the magic, and especially not the manners of people who don't even represent anything close to our level, but who would be willing to take on a god with barely a thought."

She continues to observe the scene as her thoughts delve deeper into contemplation.

"But I will tell you this: If he's even half on the mark, we dare not turn him away."

"Aye!" Relissa nods affirmatively. "But how do we bring this up to our supers?"

"Tenderly, I should think," Haran considers. "The Dean won't believe a single word of it, though. I'm fairly sure of that."

Haran started to think about his superior, the Dean Wizard at the Academy. He had been a student there for many years, joining shortly after coming of age once his primary education was complete, and struggling ever since to gain any respect within their ranks. His relationship with the Dean was strenuous at best, bordering between disdainful tolerance and outright harassment.

"The Enforcer will probably accuse me of goofing off again," Relissa relents. "To say nothing of making up stories…"

Relissa now reflects on her post at the Guild of Wardens, where the Enforcer often belittled her for her antics with her furry friends, as well as her underling status.

"How am I going to bring this up to the Council?" Kaliya wonders silently. "Surely, I'm going to need to present this directly to them. I don't think the chain of command will be adequate. There's too much detail, and it's too intimate to our needs."

Kaliya recalled her unappreciated position with the Daanen-Aryku Council of Elders. Her service record spoke for itself, and it wasn't good. As a result, she was barely allowed outside for anything beyond simple recognizance.

"But there's so much more I wish I could learn," she moans. "Especially if the prophecy is involved. And if this could help teach me the principles of metaphysics as it's actually applied, cu'Nar's Grace you two, do you know what this could do for us?"

"Not a clue, really," Relissa shrugs. "I never was one for magic."

"Kaliya," Haran notes. "If we could actually learn anything

useful in our academy, I might hold an opinion. But the trifle we've seen out here…and I'm fairly sure it is just a trifle of what they have back home, makes my studies seem almost nonexistent. So, I simply couldn't offer you an answer."

"Haran," she consoles by patting his shoulder. "I think that's an answer in itself, actually. And maybe you should reconsider your academy studies along the way. But now, where do we go from here? We need a plan on how to bring this in."

"Aye," Relissa affirms. "But this is enough to write a book about, not just a report. Best I can think of is to say we have some new peeps out here who want to join the fight. But if I toss in the bit about the Tel'Quessir, he'll probably toss me out the door," she giggles feebly.

"I'm worried about how to present the issue of my opinions relating to the prophecy. They'll probably balk at it, especially coming from me. And then to say we have a half-god running loose who's ready to take on not only this world, but any other that gets in his way, and they'll surely lock me up in a padded cell."

The day wears on as scores of workers start pouring through the portals to unload and sort out the goods laden on dozens of carts and wagons. Supplies are removed and piled up in an area to the far side of the camp perimeter, which took on the appearance of a large supply yard. Empty carts were relieved and sent back through new portals.

A troupe of dwarves appears, along with another collection of even smaller people none of the three had ever seen before. Relissa studied the quirky little men in overalls and hardhats.

"'Ere now," Relissa gibes. "Just what are they about?"

The small men begin to pull together pieces of a flat wagon on short wheels, easily reachable to their height. They assemble the truck and hook it up to a harness around a set of stunted ponies that came along with them. The ponies are led over to the depot where they begin picking up some of the odd components. At the same time, another group starts assembling a support of scaffolding and a crane. The quickness and apparent ease of their work suggested a practiced routine. Soon, a hefty wagon came up to them carrying a broad, circular slab of concrete with beveled edges.

The dwarves, on the other hand, rounded up several wagons that seemed to be held in reserve. Each of these wagons held a set of larger components resembling white stone blocks. One dwarf, who looked like a foreman, approached Thaelyn.

"Milord!" he announces. "Here be the footstones of the spire. Where do ye want us to start buildin' it?"

Thaelyn makes a quick pass around the region, as if trying to gain his bearings.

"I am told we have hostile forces on three sides of us: East, south, and west."

"Whoa, that nay be a fine place to be sittin', if ye ask me," he chortles.

"Indeed, but at this point, it is probably unavoidable. So, let us position this to the north, where it is at least partially out of the line of fire. Bring it just to the edge of observation from the camp. Hopefully, this will seclude it just enough, in case the camp should come under scrutiny."

"Aye to that!"

Kaliya and her friends observed the interaction, followed by the dwarven team hauling the wagons to the north. She moves in to ask about the delivery.

"Your Lordship? What was that? And why are you sending it up that way," she glances at the wagons leaving the area.

"This is yet another aspect of the teachings in our world, but I find it unlikely you would understand the concepts as readily. However, if you are so daring, we could at least try," he smiles.

"All right, I still have a little curl left in my horns, so we might as well finish it," she grins.

"Curl in your horns…interesting. A colloquialism, is it?"

"Yeah, to say we lose the curl, or maybe to say they sag, is to say we're dazzled by some revelation, maybe overcome by it. To say they fall off completely is to say we're shocked or surprised by something that probably doesn't make any sense to us. We can also pull them out if we are frustrated or agitated by something. And then we have the occasion where they simply go flying. Ouch!"

"Yes, I suppose so!" he chuckles. "I find the culture of others to be both enlightening as well as entertaining. Well, let us see about this gently, so we do not cause injury."

He turns to view the dwarves and their wagons.

"Those fellows heading up there are delivering components to a type of tower we call a Dynamistic Conditioning Spire. This is a part of our native technology based on our magical studies."

"Cu'Nar's Pity!" she shouts. "Yeah, there go my horns. So, you actually can make technology out of this stuff?"

"Indeed, we can, with the right study and a bit of imagination. The native environment of the arcanic energies can be uneven, ebbing and flowing like a slow tide. Once upon a time, there was a member of the Estelar known as Mystra, Goddess of Magic."

"Like that weapon you used..."

"It is named after her, yes, though I doubt she would have approved of it. She was very careful to teach her followers the full and proper respect of her gift, but since she is no longer with us, we are left to tend to it ourselves."

"What happened to her?" Haran asks.

"Intrigue founded by a rival who wanted to steal a creation she was famous for, called the Weave. She once occupied herself, at least within our local fold, to pull these uneven flows into a tight blanket effect, which would then provide for a smooth and predictable layer for mages and scholars to work with. It was fine, at least until this rival, known as Shar, decided to take it for herself. She made a deal with another Power, known as Cyric, and between them, Mystra was assassinated."

"Great gods, and literally," Haran moans. "These Estelar actually do stuff like this?"

"It is not common, but it can happen. They are still people, no matter how high they may have achieved for themselves. We had another example once, known as Helm, the Guardian. He was one of our more prominent examples, but he was slain by a most unfortunate error in judgment, and again as the result of a conspiracy to remove a valued member of our group. Cyric was involved in that, as well."

"That guy doesn't sound at all nice," Relissa winces.

"He received his punishment for it, eventually, but whereas Mystra was involved, we had a disaster on a scale unimaginable even by the gods. The Weave she had been managing snapped back, since it had been pulled so tightly. The whiplash from it hit everything it touched, including Tae'Eladar. Several planes were ripped apart, beginning with her native home, while others were tossed around like marbles on the floor. Our world took some horrific damage, ripping holes in the earth and devastating whole regions. Many people were lost, some simply vanishing in puffs of bluish ash, others twisting and merging with adjacent objects, and this was due largely to them trying to save themselves by applying a magical defense. But since the Weave was erupting with such a catastrophic feedback effect, the spells backfired."

"Ouch!" Haran grimaces. "That sounds horrible, with or without my poor academy studies. How did you survive all that?"

"We survived, but just barely. The magical energies burned themselves out in time, leaving emptiness behind. No mage was able to properly work his craft for years after this until the energies could regenerate. But as they came back, they were unstable, reverting to the more natural flow."

Thaelyn pauses to survey the remainder of the work in the camp before continuing.

"Naturally, I was furious, at least in part for Cyric and his persistent tampering in areas that were clearly not part of the Measure of Balance, and also for the rest of them for not policing their own."

"Gods be blessed, man. Remind me not to get on your bad side if I should ever become a god," he chuckles sarcastically.

Thaelyn smiled briefly as he resumed.

"We had come far before this, but it set us back tremendously. Most of our cities were in ruin, and such as our industry, food production, and other things were reduced to rubble. As a result, I chose to break with my traditions of withholding knowledge and offered my people a few small items to help them rebuild. One was to take control of the arcanic layer to create our own Weave."

"And this is the purpose of that tower?" Kaliya deduces.

"It is. I will not allow my people to suffer at the whims and intrigues of the gods, especially if those gods should hold such manners as to cheat the Measure of Balance. Therefore, I set my people to a task, and this was to investigate the principles of how the dynamistic flows are created, how to control and contain them, and then to harmonize them to create our own Weave. But we would fashion it differently. In our example, they draw in the native flows and emit a modified form on a different harmonic to provide for our layer. We built a network of these towers across the land in order to create a large coverage area. Therefore, if one of these towers should fall somewhere, it would not wreak such havoc, as the harmonics in this case are not as volatile."

"I can only understand part of that, based on my normal science, and here you are speaking of something so outlandish as compared to anything I might otherwise recognize, and doing so as if it was a standardized industry. This is something I simply must see...if you will allow it."

"Very well, we will give them time to build the spire, and perhaps, if you are present at the time, I can call you in to oversee the start-up process."

"I still find it so implausible that gods would do this to each other," Haran shakes his head. "Or even to say one can die by any means."

"Gods can die, this much is evident, though not necessarily by such common means as the mortal races. These are not physical creatures made of flesh, as you and I. Instead, they are composed of an essence, ethereal in nature, that represents a form of energy with properties barely resembling physical mass. This is the substance you will find native to the Fifth Fold, by the way, and largely dependent on the Flows to sustain it."

"But you say they are people," Kaliya muses. "Maybe like us once upon a time, right? How did they get up there, and then, um, I guess evolve into this new form?"

"This is a curious question, but most mortal races might not be fully prepared to know of such things. So, I will simply make a deal with you. I can explain what I know of it, but we should not necessarily spread it around too much. It might spoil a lot of impressions with the younger races."

"All right," she smiles.

"We will start with your average mortal race, like one of you, for example. Within a Prime Material fold, such as this, you might advance by great leaps, learning such extraordinary forms of knowledge as to perhaps boggle the mind. Your bodies will also advance, but again, within that Prime Material fold, you can only go so far, as the physical limitations of this form will begin to hinder you. Therefore, we can say that within such a space as this, there is a cap to how far you can go, and it is not godhood. You could approach that of a Celestial form, however, or at least the threshold of it."

"That already sounds like a nice place to be," Haran notes.

"Perhaps, and here is where the Estelar would also take special notice of you, if not sometime before this to begin conditioning you for later. They would then invite you to join them in what we might describe as a form of apprenticeship. Here is where you might leave your former Prime domain and travel up to the higher folds. From there, and under their tutelage, you become true Celestials, and as servants to the Estelar, they raise and train you as you slowly undergo those final moments of your evolution."

"Jiggers," Relissa croons. "Servants to the gods, to sit right underneath them..."

"Yes, and this can take a while, as most likely you have already achieved a substantial level of development, including your natural longevity. This represents the first of two ascensions, and your original corporeal body becomes vestigial, having moved out of a universe like this composed of primordial matter to evolve it with. Now, it is the mind and spiritual essence that tends to evolve more than anything."

"And here is where they begin to adapt to something new," Kaliya surmises.

"Correct. You will need a certain number of generations to pass by before your final ascension. This can be further complicated as your lifespans can be affected simply by the native energies slowing things down even further. So, we could be speaking of tens or hundreds of millions of years, depending on your normal evolution in corporeal form, and then maybe to double this in that second term."

"Ouch! That's a long time to have to wait for it."

"But it could also be very productive for you along the way. The current generation of beings serving the Estelar seem quite happy to be where they are, so I think it is not as much the destination as it is the path leading up to it."

"Wow," Relissa considers. "Now that really is something to bite into. And I doubt anyone would know what in all the bleedin' hells I'd be going on about if ever I did try sharing it."

Thaelyn smiles again as he looks up at the sky.

"The day is getting late. Soon will be dusk, and still so much to do."

He returns to the three companions.

"All right, listen a moment. As a Celestial, and a Child of the Estelar, I believe in the growth experience, the same as the rest. I know the three of you are truly fascinated by all we have talked about, but this is already more than I might share with strangers in a time of war. So, I need to establish a line here. I must ask you to demonstrate your part that you are worthy of what I have given thus far, and if you should wish to learn more, you must show me you are worthy of receiving it. Knowledge is as much an earning as it is a gift."

"That sounds fair enough to me," Haran nods. "And much more than I get back home."

"Aye, same for me," Relissa affirms.

Kaliya also nods in affirmation.

"Sure, I can do that," she offers. "I just hope you give me clear enough instructions on what you want me to do to actually earn something. Waving my hand so that things go poof is still a little outside my skill range."

"Perhaps so, but now," he glances at the mountains in the north. "Do you plan on returning home tonight? I estimate it would take at least half a day, at a good march, just to reach that line. But I think it will be dark long before that, and I would not wish to send you home without some food and a calm rest after this day's events."

"That is most gracious of you, Your Lordship," Haran declares. "Although, at the same time, our superiors back home will wonder whatever happened to us…if they're not already. But I suppose, if returning home late tonight, we can't do much else until the morning anyway, at this point."

"I could have my mages enchant you with haste spells. They can be rather draining on a person, but this could cut the time down."

"I think we're going to be late no matter how you look at it," Kaliya admits. "His Dean," she thumbs at Haran, "will be in bed by then, and as I understand it, you don't want to disturb him even on a good day in the office. Her Enforcer," she turns to Relissa, "is almost as bad. And then we have me and my people…cu'Nar help us all for what I may have to go through with that. No one is going to believe us for what we have to say about all this. So, whether tonight or in the morning, it's all the same to us, I think…we're going to get our tails chewed regardless."

Thaelyn frowns as he considers the prospect, and he reflexively peers at Kaliya and her tail hanging down behind her.

"Tail being chewed…how quaint. All right, then at the very least, stay with us this night, share a meal, a place to rest, and maybe we might have some time for a fireside chat later. In the morning, we will have another meal to fire up the furnaces, and then you can be on your way."

"That is very kind of you," she bows her head.

"For now, I need to return to my work. Feel free to roam as you desire, but do try to stay out of the way of traffic."

"Of course…"

Thaelyn moves off to supervise the construction. Materials have been brought forward to several work sites by this time, and the assembly of buildings was proceeding quite rapidly. Multiple cranes were now working to lift and drop blocks into place, like pieces of giant puzzles, while workers attached brackets and pounded pins into joints.

The companions wandered around the various construction sites, marveling at the rate at which these people moved. It was a symphony of motion, well-practiced over what they assumed to be many years of repeated occasions.

Relissa studied the curious little men who were busy collecting parts near the large slab of concrete, although she had no idea what it was actually made of. In her mind, it simply appeared as a piece of odd gray stone, and it had been placed on the ground as a platform. The slab had a deep groove running across the middle between two endpoints with small boxlike holes set into the slab. The groove further extended forward on one side to a larger depression in front. There were sets of round sockets, two on either side of those smaller boxlike depressions, along with mounting holes, plus more mounting holes around the depression in front.

She puzzled what it could be for, but her only experience suggested maybe a platform for an altar or a throne. The trouble with this idea was why someone would want to sit on a throne in an outdoor setting like this. Her next thought was that it could be a base for a gazebo or an archway, as is often found in her home city of Solinaia and used for festive decoration, not that anyone does much of anything festive these days. But why put one of those in a military camp?

The workers were placing metal junction boxes into the depressions which seemed to have attachment sockets on top, and they were threading cabling along the grooves, connecting it all together.

A set of two long curved pieces were brought in. They appeared as a metallic frame, but fitted with a kind of stone-like material she didn't recognize. In some ways, it looked a bit like the material used sometimes in dishware from wealthy families. These pieces were broad at the base, but tapered along the length, and each was fitted with brackets on both ends, with the bottom bracket showing round plug-like extensions under it. Along their length, they each had an ornately engraved metal jacket connected between the two end pieces and secured with pins set into fittings. The runic engraving was accompanied by a set of intermittently spaced sockets. Positioned on the ground nearby was a small bridge piece wrapped in a metal coil, and also with brackets capping the ends.

The assembly of components was a mystery to Relissa, and so, unable to think of any other purpose for it, and also developing a slight headache for all the activity, she began to move away. The remainder of the commotion around the construction site caused her to seek a quieter space, as there was nothing else for her to do but wait for Thaelyn to find time again for more talk. She unconsciously found herself drawn to the tree Thaelyn planted earlier. The druids were laying down an outline of wooden stakes in a wide circle around it.

She casually strolled up to the edge of the circle, staring at the tree for many moments, tilting her head this way and that while trying to figure it out. There was something strange here…a sensation of some kind. She could feel it ever so faintly.

✦

Haran was following closely behind Kaliya, this time not letting her out of his sight in case she got into trouble again. They made a circle through the camp observing the activity, and finally arriving at the concrete platform.

"All right, Kaliya," he begins. "Your people are the ones with the science. What do you think this is going to be? It's not a house, a barn, a shop, or anything else I might recognize."

She studies it carefully, passing her eyes along the curved pieces still lying on the side as the small men begin moving a crane over to pick one up. She also carefully examines the platform itself.

"This looks like…"

She tentatively reaches down to touch the surface of the slab to confirm her suspicions.

"Well, well…this is concrete."

"What's that?"

"Your people use stone in your construction, right? Do you use mortar in there? Well, this is a similar product of various materials mixed together to form a stone-like substance you can mold to whatever shape you need. It's often used for construction projects and such."

"Does it surprise you to see it here, with these people?"

"I suppose this isn't too bad, depending on where you are on the scale. If they're Industrial Age, this fits nicely. And knowing him, he probably gave them one of his special assignments or something to develop it. It's a really useful material, and doesn't require too much study. But now, as for the rest of it…"

She again studies the components being maneuvered into place.

"This groove here and the cabling… This thing must be electric, and he did say they were entering an age of electricity, so this must be an example. We probably have a control unit up front, and then these long pieces must fit onto those slots, and also attached with these mounts and connected by the cabling for power. But if I'm interpreting this correctly, I see ceramic insulators on this thing, and that usually indicates a high voltage conductor. Yikes! And that means this framework must be forming some kind of circuit, but for what?"

She pauses to study it some more, then to survey the local area.

"And where are they getting the electricity from?" she muses.

"Maybe it's not ready yet. But then, if you're saying yikes to this, what happens if you touch it?"

"Well, my friend," she chuckles and slaps a hand on his shoulder. "I'll let you be the first to find out! I'll just go over there and stand by that tree…"

Kaliya looks over at the tree in the wide druid circle. Her attention is drawn to Relissa standing there, seemingly in a daze with her arms dangling loosely at her sides and wobbling a bit. Her humor quickly fades.

"What is she doing?" she mutters. "Haran? We'd better check on her, quick!"

"Oh, for crying out loud," he snaps as he jumps to her side. "I babysit one, and the other one gets stuck."

The two of them rushed along to check on the young dark elf.

"Relissa! Are you alright?" Kaliya calls as she comes up to the girl's side.

"Huh?!" the girl yips, as she was clearly startled by the call. "What just happened?"

Relissa looks around trying to gain her bearings, only to realize where she found herself.

"How did I get here?" she murmurs.

"Relissa, what were you doing just before this?" Kaliya asks concernedly.

"I was over there," she directs at the platform, "looking at the little guys, and then I started walking..." she pauses to shake her head. "I must be getting tired. Too much hullabaloo for one day. What say we find a nice place to sit?"

"Sounds like a fine enough plan," Haran remarks while visibly feigning relief.

They start to move away from the circle. Kaliya sees Aerlie sitting off to one side with a group in conversation and interprets it as a rest break.

"Look there," she points. "Maybe we can join with them."

Relissa begins to follow until she hears a slight buzzing pass around her head...or was it through her head? She couldn't be sure at the moment, as the disorientation of her apparent lapse still troubled her. She waves a hand around instinctively in an effort to shoo it away. Her distraction stops her movement.

Haran notices her falling back, apparently waving at something.

"Oh yes... Bugs!" he smirks sarcastically. "Just what we need on top of everything else."

He waits for the elf to start walking again to catch up.

Kaliya was a few steps away by now when she turns to see she's all alone.

"Are you two alright back there?" she wonders.

"Not to worry," Haran returns. "We just seem to have some small visitors pestering us."

Relissa felt better now and started walking again. But with barely two steps into it, she hears what resembles a whispering echo, and feels a faint sensation, like a mild fluttering pass through her. It startles her. She stops suddenly and gasps as she impulsively jerks her hands up over her heart.

Haran takes immediate notice of this, as does Kaliya. They both turn to her, apprehensive of the girl's physical health, though she had never shown any anomalies of illness before.

"Relissa, what's wrong?" Haran demands worriedly.

Relissa stands still for a moment trying to understand what just happened. As the feeling gradually subsides, she relaxes back again.

"I'm alright, peeps. Just nerves…" she replies in a subtly quivering voice. "I really need to sit down, I guess."

She tries taking one more step.

Now, a commanding awareness washes through her full body, accompanied by a prolonged murmuring cry resounding in her mind. She freezes, letting out a droning wail as she clutches hard at herself with both hands. Her knees buckle and she hunches over from an arresting sensation rippling across her muscles.

"Relissa!" Kaliya shouts as she rushes over to her.

The druids in the circle all turn to examine the scene. Aerlie and her group also overheard the cry. She rises up quickly and sends a telepathic shot to Thaelyn, who was presently on the other side of the construction site. This draws his attention as he turns and bolts across the camp.

Relissa's initial rush of fear and shock is slowly displaced by a subtle soothing effect. But the sensation wasn't her own doing. And as she began to realize what was happening, she was confronted with an implausible sense of wonder relating to the cause. Reluctantly, she is forced to recognize an awareness was trying to draw her attention. She feels her perception unconsciously pulled around to the source. But her body was unresponsive so far. She could only stand there gaping at the idea.

Several of the druids moved forward to inspect the girl at a distance, uncertain if she was ill, injured, or with some other symptom. Aerlie rushes up, but halts a few paces away as it would seem the girl is not actually in any real danger. She could see the girl's face, but it was not the face of someone suffering from any recognizable problem. She moved in slowly to observe and is soon joined by the druidic high priestess. Thaelyn arrives a few moments after on the other side, but also halts at a distance to observe.

Kaliya and Haran had both moved alongside the stricken girl, staring into her eyes as she slowly rolls them to the far side of her head. She attempts to straighten herself while still following her senses to turn her attention over her shoulder. Slowly, as her body seemed unwilling to move its muscles, she began to turn a full about-face.

"I don't bloody believe it," she mutters softly. "It can't be, can it? I mean…jiggers! How could this happen! What have those peeps been doing over there in this time?"

She turns fully around towards the circle again.

"It's a tree. It's an actual bloody tree!"

She creeps back the way she came, taking baby steps until she encounters the row of stakes in the ground. There she stops and stares at it some more.

"It's a tree!" she sings innocently and forms a childlike smile.

Haran and Kaliya delicately trace behind her, but unsure what to do. They've never seen Relissa behave this way before. Haran steps up next to the girl to look in her face. She seemed like she was in a dreamland.

Aerlie glances curiously at Thaelyn across the way before slowly creeping in to see what was wrong. The high priestess follows alongside of her. They both step up next to the group. Kaliya sees Aerlie arriving, but can only shrug as Haran tries to interact.

"Relissa?" he asks quietly. "Are you alright?"

"It's…a tree!" she repeats assertively in a more natural voice, but still soft and bedazzled by the sight.

"Yes! It's a tree, a very lovely tree, with a darling little fence around it, too."

She stiffly swivels around to him, grabs his collar with both hands and shrieks in his face.

"It's a TREE!!"

She now begins to sob fiercely and buckles down to her knees. "I am so unworthy..."

"Oh great," Haran sighs painfully. "Here we go again."

Thaelyn decides to join the gathering as Aerlie now tries to investigate the situation.

"Um, Relissa..." she asks softly.

Relissa had collapsed completely to the ground, her face now in the grass, weeping and intermittently calling out phrases of shame and unworthiness in a hushed voice. Both Haran and Kaliya had kneeled down at her side to comfort her.

"What is occurring here?" Thaelyn asks gently.

"Your Lordship," Haran relents. "I really have no idea. This girl is also having mood swings today, it seems. I think it's probably just stress."

"Thaelyn," Aerlie waves him over for a private chat.

The two joined with the high priestess and move away a few steps as Relissa and her friends recover. Kaliya watched, intermittently passing between them and Relissa on the ground. She strained to listen in on what they might say.

"What do we have?" Thaelyn asks, in this case using the Tae'Eladaran tongue.

"Priestess Rumoren tells me Relissa was apparently standing there in some kind of mild trance for an extended period. She was concerned about this, but it didn't look harmful in any way. After all, this is a Tree of Life, so it could be the spirit was attempting to commune with her somehow."

Kaliya could overhear the conversation, and she grimaced at the wild suggestion. She jumped up to join in.

"Excuse me, what do you mean? A tree trying to talk to someone?"

"Kaliya," Aerlie replies. "This tree is special for all elves as a natural part of our heritage. It dates back to our original home where all life tends to be bound by the power of the dryad spirit that lives within the tree. All life shares an intimate bond through this spirit, and this is what ties us together."

"Do you recall what I said earlier?" Thaelyn adds. "How the

people of our world share a bond with nature, and therefore, the necessity to respect all things in our world. This is the bond that holds it together. It is a native part of the elven home world, and when they migrated to Tae'Eladar, they brought it with them. However, over time, and through many plights, their culture degraded, and at least some of them lost their way. When I arrived, and first started building my rule on an official level, I made an agreement with the dryad spirits to bring this back, and not only to the elves, but all the people must be included. This is one element that unified our people as a single society where we are all dedicated to such values that nothing will ever break us apart again."

"Cu'Nar's pity," Kaliya winces. "She was right. What did you people do over there in this time? But can you help me understand what this spirit thing is?"

"This particular tree is not just a stick in the mud as your more common example. It is a curious intermediate form of life that crosses the boundaries between plant and animal kingdoms. It possesses a sentient spirit essence, and when fully grown, it holds some rather remarkable powers over the land and nearby environment. It will also produce a grove of six daughter trees underneath it, and when combined, they hold the power to literally transform the world around them. With these spread throughout our world in the modern day, one can say our world is turning into a utopian paradise."

"Unbelievable! And you can talk to them?"

"Once they are mature enough," the priestess explains. "Which usually occurs around two decades, the spirit can emerge fully from the host tree as an independent body, but only for limited times, and it cannot travel far from its host. They take up a feminine form and can only speak in the ancient Sylvan dialect of Old Elvish. You can also commune with them if you go up to the tree itself and make physical contact."

"Oh, wow," she shakes her head. "Haran will flip when he hears this one, he and his crazy druid talk. But what happened to Relissa? Why did she react to it like this?"

"This is a good question," Thaelyn asserts.

The meeting breaks up and returns to Haran and Relissa on the ground, where Relissa had recovered enough to take a seated position on the grass.

"All right," Haran wonders. "What's the verdict over there? Relissa hasn't said anything yet, so I'm waiting on you now."

Thaelyn circles to one side while Aerlie and the high priestess come along the other side. Kaliya joins in behind Relissa, and they all kneel down.

"Relissa," Aerlie begins soothingly. "Are you alright?"

"Aye," she responds sullenly. "I'm just not right for this. Not when I was so bad with all my lessons back home."

"Oh, don't be silly, Child. The spirit doesn't care about that. But I'm sure we're all very curious as to what happened here. Why did you have this strange reaction?"

"I was surprised to see it. I've never seen one before. My Mum told me about them when I was little, but it's just one more piece of a lost world to us."

"I see. Is this to say you don't have any here?"

"Lady Aerlie," her voice escalates. "We used to have them here… everywhere. But this bloody flippin' war dusted the lot of them in the early days. It was maybe the last thing we still had with us to hold us to the old ways. When they died, a piece of us died with them."

Aerlie retracted from the conversation with Relissa's emotional outburst. She contemplated the situation briefly.

Haran was feeling a little confused by now for the terms being used here.

"Um, can someone explain to me what I'm missing here? A tree with…a spirit? Oh dear gods…"

"Kaliya," Thaelyn directs. "Share with him our conversation for a moment while we try to find an answer here."

She nods and leans in to recall what she learned a moment ago.

"Aerlie," Thaelyn begins again in Tae'Eladar Common. "I must ask myself what effect it would have on the morale of these people if they used to have trees, and then suddenly they were all killed."

"My Lord," the priestess responds. "I can tell you one thing, it would be painful, especially if they had shrines like we do, or like what we had in the early days, and the people all linked into them. Tear that away, and it would tear at your own soul."

"Then how do you suggest we correct this? Relink her through this tree?"

"That would be a fine solution in my mind. It would probably also settle some of her manners."

"All right, so be it. Let us give this young lady a taste of her lost heritage."

Thaelyn now gets up and backs away, along with Aerlie, leaving the high priestess to attend to the work. She begins by tapping Kaliya on the shoulder to draw her attention.

"You speak our language, so it seems. What is your name, Child?"

"Kaliya…"

"All right, Kaliya, does your friend speak Elvish? If her people are so removed from the rest of us…"

"They do, but she's a bad example of this. This war was really hard on her. So, what are you planning on doing here?"

"The one and most important thing that should be done…we must heal her soul by reuniting her with the spirit. This is the healing touch to bring her back to us as part of her natural heritage, one that all elves share…or should be sharing."

"Um, not that I want to argue or anything," she flusters. "But she's a close friend of mine, and all this is very strange to me."

"Do your people hold any sort of religion?"

"No, but I'll tell you, after seeing that nether-wild ritual of yours earlier, I'm almost ready to take one up," she chuckles. "Still, how exactly does this work?"

"We will bring her up to the tree to make contact. The spirit will then commune with her to share its soothing songs and bring her peace. This is simply returning her back to the natural bond with the world around us that we elves are so accustomed to having. Ask her and see what she has to say about it, and if she knows what this is."

Kaliya turns to get Relissa's attention.

"Um, the woman here, I guess she's a priestess…"

"More like a high priestess by the way she looks to me," Relissa notes.

"Well, all right, a high priestess…is suggesting we bring you up to the tree as part of some sort of healing process for your spirit. She says it will bring you peace and reunite you with the natural world, which is apparently where you elves are supposed to be to begin with, or some such…although it's all weird to me, but don't listen to that."

"So, you're actually telling me to go up and talk to a tree, ay?" she attempts a clever smile.

"Relissa, I think I lost my horns for the remainder of the month, so let's not push it," she grins.

"Right, but aye, I know what she means. This is how it used to be before this bloody flaming war hit us blindsided. But I'm afraid the spirit won't be pleased with me."

"Relissa, like Aerlie said, it probably isn't relevant by now, especially if this spirit went to so much trouble to get your attention. That seems like a fairly good indicator to me. It must feel your pain or something."

Relissa looks into Kaliya's eyes as she ponders the notion.

"But I don't really know how to do this."

"Priestess," Kaliya asks. "Is there some special process you use for this?"

"It's actually very simple…" she affirms.

"Do you know how many times I hear people say that?" she smiles.

"Well, all right," she giggles softly. "But listen. The ground is regarded as holy to us, and we must walk upon it with bare feet. I will lead, and along the way, we kneel to offer a gesture of reverence, before continuing to the tree itself. I will help her from there."

Kaliya nods and relays the instructions.

Relissa examines both of her friends before repositioning herself. She fights with her boots, first one and then the other, taking them off and dropping them to one side. She then stands up and looks at the druid expectantly.

The druid takes Relissa's hand and brings her over the small fence. As she steps into the circle, a warming sensation ripples through her, like being wrapped in a snug blanket. She staggers briefly and moans until she can get her balance again.

"Jiggers, my Mum didn't tell me about this part."

They move several steps forward, and the druid stops and kneels. Relissa mimics the motion.

The druid places her hands together in a reverent gesture forming a triangle with her thumbs and first fingers. She moves the gesture first over her heart, then her mouth, and lastly over her forehead, opening them up and passing them away around her head. Relissa follows the same gesture.

They stand up and advance a few steps further, only to kneel again not far from the tree. Uncertain what to do next, Relissa looks to the druid for help.

The druid takes Relissa's hand and pulls her closer to the tree, within easy reach of it. She encourages the girl to place her hand on the trunk of the tree to feel it. As she does, she senses a presence come into her mind. She suddenly feels very sleepy and curls up at the base of the tree.

"All right…" Haran concedes. "I think I've seen everything now. And I don't dare tell this one to the Dean."

"You and me both," Kaliya shakes her head. "Mine to the Elder Council."

◆

Dusk has fallen, and the camp is still a flurry of activity. More people have shown up. A makeshift kitchen had been assembled and food was being served. There was talk, laughter, and even a few songs as the soldiers sat in clusters around campfires and enjoyed the evening break. Thaelyn, Aerlie, Kaliya, and Haran all sat together not far from the large concrete platform sharing their meals and discussing issues concerning the war.

The platform construction was progressing along. The two long curved pieces had been placed into their respective slots with support brackets bolted into the anchoring holes. The smaller bridge piece had been connected across the top using brackets and pins to hold it in place. The full unit resembled a large, nearly circular archway.

The wiring was nearly complete, and a control unit resembling a thick obelisk had been mounted over the forward depression. Sticking up from the top was a curious little U-shaped mounting slot that seemed designed to take some kind of artifact.

As the obelisk-like control unit was being lifted into place, Kaliya edged around to see if she could identify anything. The back side was open at the time, and she could see some basic wiring, coils, and several glowing crystalline components, along with some metallic ones. The full arrangement appeared as some sort of odd power relay, but unlike any form of technology she could recognize. At this time, they had also connected a cable leading off to a large boxlike unit sitting a short distance away. She surmised this had to be the power source.

The empty sockets lining the jackets on the arches were being fitted with glimmering palm-sized metal disks, each with a luminescent glyphic rune inscribed onto it.

"All right, Your Lordship," Kaliya remarks as she observes the final few pieces being put into place. "So, what is it?"

"This is a Gateway. It is similar in design to the ones we use back home, but this one is simplified to make it portable. It is easily broken down for transport, and then reassembled at a new location. The only difference between this and the permanent fixtures we use elsewhere is that those are dynamically addressable, whereas this one is limited to only one destination at a time, based on what rune is inserted."

"Addressable?" Haran asks.

"I think I can answer that one, Haran," Kaliya perks up and turns to him. "But I swear, I probably wouldn't have believed it if I didn't see it. We would call this a conveyor back home, but never on a scale this small. I've heard of such things from our history lessons. We might use them as part of our space exploration, travelling off to distant worlds, establishing outposts, and using these things to make traffic a little more convenient. But they take a lot of power, on the scale of a fusion reactor, and all I see here is that little box over there," she points behind the unit. "And that simply defies any form of understanding I can fathom. Tanjhira, our chief technician back home, would lose her horns over this one."

"Indeed!" Thaelyn smiles.

"Anyway, Haran, what he means is they can be recalibrated to point at different destinations, a bit like the nav system on our old ship used to do…right, Your Lordship?"

"Very good, although I suspect the methods may differ somewhat as our endpoints are fixed whereas yours might have been calculated."

"Yeah, but this really isn't my area of expertise…"

✦✦✦✦

Relissa's eyes slowly open as she wakes up from her deep slumber. She had been asleep for a few hours. As she pulls herself upright, she begins to take note that night is falling. She rubs her eyes in an effort to clear her vision.

"Did you sleep well?" comes a female voice just off to the side. "Do you feel restored now, Child?"

"Yes, thanks. I, uh…" her voice catches.

Relissa's eyes pop open wide as she cranes her head around to the form of the druid priestess sitting next to her, the same one who brought her up to the tree. She had been waiting patiently during this time for Relissa to reawaken.

"Wait a minute, what did you say?" Relissa asks incredulously. "For that matter, what am I saying…we're speaking Elvish here!"

"Yes!" the priestess responds with a smile. "The spirit of the tree has healed you. You are one with us again!"

"And what's more, I understand every word."

"I am not surprised! Her whispers likely filled you with all that you were missing before this. Perhaps even more than that, if she shared with you any part of our history since you became lost. They maintain a kind of racial memory through each generation. But now, come and let us rejoin the others. The time has come to eat and make cheerful merriment and song."

The two of them rise up and move off towards the kitchen to grab a plate of food together.

◆

"By the way," Kaliya wonders. "I've been thinking some more about that thing you used earlier…Mystra's Fury. I'm starting to feel a little nervous about something, and I need to ask you about it."

"And that is?"

"Well, I don't feel sick or anything right now, but I remember some of my old science lessons on the topic. I need to know what was inside that orb. With everything else you did out here, I have no idea what overall effect this might have, but did that thing leave any kind of toxic or radioactive residue behind, like for instance in the fallout?"

"No, not in this case. I believe you mentioned the topic of the atomic sciences, but this would not fall precisely into that category, as it does not involve any of those same materials."

"Oh, good," she sighs in relief. "I didn't think about this immediately, as the science is so old for us by now, and I think we developed clean-up measures to that a long time ago. But then, what was it and how could it make such a huge explosion?"

"For this, I would need to temper myself in case you do not already hold this level of science. Perhaps you would like to take a few guesses? Is there anything else from your science classes that suggest the application of high-level energy production?"

"Wow, I'm not an engineer, but let me see. There's atomic fission, and also fusion, which we tend to use a lot, and these are the two basic forms of energy production you might find in many younger societies. Those of us who move a little farther might try harnessing solar power on a large scale, like with orbital collectors. I've heard of using singularity filaments, but this tends to be a specialized application, and largely theoretical. Um…what about…uh oh…

Oh dear cu'Nar, no, I don't want to think about that one. And that one actually could be weaponized."

"And which one might that be?"

"Yeah, and furthermore, how could you actually do this with magic? That's not possible, is it? Are we speaking of the interaction between positive and negative matter?"

Thaelyn grins and snaps his fingers lightly, then points at her.

"Congratulations, Kaliya! You have just earned my wisdom on this topic."

"Grace of the cu'Nar! How in all the nether-space are you able to do this stuff! But doesn't that send out violent waves of harmful energy?"

"It does, but I sensed that we were far enough from any population center to take the risk. We are surrounded by mountains on all sides, and this can act as a natural barrier."

"Not if you melt them in the process!" she chuckles. "How much did you use, if I may ask?"

"Not a great amount, really. Less than what might cover a fingertip."

"But how did you contain it? You can't just bring something like that into an environment like ours without containment!"

"Um," Haran muses wittily. "And why not?"

Kaliya turns to glare at him for his impish repartee.

"Because it blows up, shorty..."

"Oh! Well, my goodness, I'm sure we wouldn't want that, now would we," he chuckles.

The group shares a round of laughter as they are soon joined by Relissa and the high priestess.

"Mae govannen, mellonea," she beams a bright smile. "Elen sila lumen omentilmo. Sut naa lle sina re?"

"Vedui' Relissa!" Aerlie responds. "Cormamin lindua ele lle! Tula, hama neva i'naur."

Aerlie motions to a space by the campfire.

"Seasamin," Relissa replies cheerfully and sits down between Haran and Kaliya.

Haran looks on in amazement.

"I don't know what in all the hells that was, but it wasn't the 'I… don't…speak…Elvish' we had earlier today!"

Relissa turns to him and simply smiles.

"So, how do you feel now?" Kaliya asks.

"I don't know how to describe it," Relissa responds enthusiastically. "It's like an empty space inside has been filled up with something I never knew was missing. The spirit showed me the ways of my people again. I understand who we are now. The world seems a little brighter, more alive, and I'm more at peace now than I ever was before. It's as if I've been reconnected to something we lost a long time ago."

"I'm very happy for you. Congratulations, Relissa."

Kaliya places a hand on the girl's shoulder and squeezes gently.

"So," Relissa wonders. "What are we talking about that's causing all the ruckus over here?"

"Relissa," Thaelyn begins. "You seem to belong to a fine party of friends here. We were discussing Mystra's Fury just now, and Kaliya was asking how we managed to bring it into play. That orb serves as the container for the substance in question here. It creates a supremely powerful magnetic void at its core, isolated from the outer environment to prevent contamination. Then, when I send it out, it buries itself a short distance underground as a way to partially control the blast effect."

"And the radiation from the blast…" Kaliya wonders. "What about us? We were so close to it."

"The shield…" he responds. "It is called an Infinity Shield, and I suppose under the circumstances, it truly lives up to its name."

"Yes!" Kaliya nods affirmatively. "This much I'll agree to. It also defies several laws of physics I once thought I understood."

"Perhaps, but the magical arts represent a completely different form of science, and as I said before, not part of your more common laws of physics. It is governed by the mind, and the mind can invent its own rules."

"Yeah, but this doesn't help me trying to explain any part of this back home. Surely, someone took notice of it, and they're probably asking what became of me out here."

"I suppose, so we will need to excuse ourselves for some part of this."

"But that thing seemed to represent a solid barrier. Does it also represent a barrier from harmful energy?"

"It does, and it can be attuned to whatever defensive properties we might perceive to be necessary for the purpose."

"Perception…and how it can alter the reality around us. Cu'Nar help us if this doesn't answer that Age-old question."

"You know, despite your lack of understanding of magic, your people must be trying to interpret some aspects of this, nonetheless."

"Yes, but trying and succeeding are two different things. How are you able to create this thing…as if I might actually understand any part of it," she chuckles ironically.

"First, it requires a high-level mage, at least of the Eight Circle, and so far, this is a specialized study for us since it is fairly new and was necessary due to this war. For this point, it is primarily a military application, as we do not have any other purpose for it at this time."

"The Eighth Circle," Haran muses. "Is that some sort of accomplishment level?"

"Yes, out of nine in our study courses back home."

"Do you think you might find other uses for it one day?" Kaliya asks.

"I suppose it might find utility elsewhere, but the applications are probably still some distance away from us. The current application also has a few drawbacks, although nothing especially severe. For instance, it must be maintained by a chant until it is no longer needed. This requires focus from the mage, which could otherwise occupy him away from other activities. So, if one were to apply themselves to this, it is only this, while someone else might be needed to attend further actions."

"Ah, that's interesting. And believe it or not, this is one thing I actually do understand," she smiles cutely.

"Most excellent! But then, just as it protects you from the outside, it also traps you inside the bubble, and you cannot interact with anything else. Although, at this point, I cannot see why you would want to," he grins.

"Aye," Relissa quips. "Especially if all the hells are breaking loose out there."

They share another round of laughter at the thought.

"Can you explain to me a little more about these mage studies?" Haran asks. "You recall what I said about mine, so now I'm wondering..." he glances around the camp. "For what little they teach us in comparison to what I'm seeing out here, mine would seem more like parlor tricks than actual magic."

"Haran," Aerlie begins. "I'm really sorry for your misfortune. In the old days, it is said the old wizards were often very stingy with their lessons, and jealous of their peers and rivals. They might hire apprentices to assist them in their work, but they would often withhold the better studies out of concern those same apprentices might turn against them and take over...which was apparently a very real problem in some cases. This represents a form of power, and as they say, power corrupts."

"Maybe so, but you seem to have so many of them out here, and they all seem to be very powerful," he sighs. "How did you overcome this?"

"With careful culturing and education of our world population on the proper manners and discipline of the Art."

Haran felt his lower jaw fall off with that statement. He gazed at her vacantly as he tried to interpret the full implications of the assertion. He clamps his hands around his head as he feels a pounding rising up.

"Your full...world...population..." he wheezes. "Great gods, does this mean everyone does it?"

"Yes, we tore away that prestige of the elite class holding it as a tool of personal gluttony and gave it to the masses. And our full civilization has found remarkable value in it. Just about every aspect of life has changed for us as we discover new ways to use it in homes, at work, in arts and entertainment, and also in industry."

"Holy jiggers!" Relissa moans. "And here I thought this guy was bad," she thumbs at Haran.

"An entire civilization…" Kaliya reflects. "Dear cu'Nar, what does that do to a society?"

"It allows us to build such things as that device behind you," Aerlie points at the gateway. "As well as to invent things your common laws of physics might otherwise deny you, whether completely, or simply until you work your way through a lot of other prerequisites."

"Unbelievable! And this just makes my report back home even more difficult. They won't believe you can be any kind of threat to the Suuden-Aryku. Not unless you can demonstrate something they can recognize."

"We will work on that as time goes by," Thaelyn admits. "I am sure we can find some form of common ground together. For instance, you mentioned the use of those plasma weapons. Well, the shield should be effective against those, and then our more traditional methods might give us what we need after that."

"Really, so you block them with your shields, and then hack them to pieces with swords, or maybe use those bows you mentioned. Oh, how I'd love to see that."

"But, if we're speaking of your full population," Haran wonders. "How do these courses of yours appear?"

"There are nine Circles of mage craft within our study courses," Aerlie begins. "Each has its own rank for the individual enrolled in study. Starting from the First Circle, you begin as a Neophyte, and then move to the Novice, the Learner, the Apprentice, the Acolyte, and then the Adept. This series takes you up to the standard level of study for a typical person who might seek a career profession, assuming it involves any detailed arcanic elements."

"Interesting…"

"Of course, there are civilian courses, as well as military, and each of these might take slightly different paths."

"How do they differ?" Kaliya asks.

"The military course involves the weaponized forms of the Art. We don't generally give these to common citizens, although I will admit the common lessons could be turned if they simply apply themselves. But we largely treat this on a need-to-know basis, and our civilization is a peaceful one that doesn't experience any infighting."

"What about crime? Don't you still need some kind of law enforcement?"

"Crime is virtually nonexistent in our society, and although the law enforcers do carry a limited selection of weaponized skills, it's very rare to see them use it. In fact, most often they might only apply nonlethal forms to capture and contain those elements that actually do get out of hand."

"Virtually nonexistent..." she winces. "That, in itself, seems an implausible notion. Every society has some form of crime. How do you overcome this?"

"Between the involvement of the dryad spirits harmonizing everything, and Thaelyn's Celestial teachings, along with his positive alignment, they have all generally aligned themselves with a type of quasi-religious dedication to these same principles. No one wants to do anything bad as it would backfire on them so harshly to disrespect the values of our society and the gifts we created together."

"In all the nether-space, now that's a new one. So, you created a paradise, and no one wants to spoil it."

"In essence, yes. We describe the principle as the Sacred Trust, to honor and be honored. Everything we use in our lives, such as the food we eat and the clothes we wear, is a gift from our society. Someone out there made it, and we are each blessed to have it. And we offer our part to others the same. Therefore, we say each of us offers our service up to it, thereby honoring the greater whole for what we made of ourselves. Similarly, we each take out the same, as the greater whole delivers back to us for our individual contribution. And we all benefit as the result."

"That's simply...indescribable! The perfect society. And to think how you actually got them to follow this uniformly."

"Aye!" Relissa nods. "This would fit nicely with that bit of not flubbing things up. Otherwise, you might find yourself getting kicked out."

"A bit absolutist, but I suppose I would have to agree."

"Um…" Haran interjects. "So far, by my count, this is only six out of those nine Circles you mentioned. What about the remaining three? And where do you find those, if not the standard course?"

"The first two are taken in our primary schools by the young children," Aerlie responds.

"Children! Great gods, you're so perfect that you can give this to children?"

"These early lessons are mostly to introduce them to the basic principles of spell craft, and don't really involve anything especially elaborate. It provides a fundamental level of understanding, and a number of simple cantrips and spells that might serve for their age groupings."

"How old are they?"

"Different races mature at different rates. If we speak in terms of humans…which might be easier for you to associate with…the First Circle comes at age twelve, and the Second at age fifteen."

Haran shook his head at the idea, reflecting on his own studies and the difficulty he had getting anything at all out of it.

"Once they complete their primary schools," Aerlie continues. "They typically go to a university for their higher education."

"A…university?" he wonders curiously.

"Haran," Kaliya interjects. "This might better associate with your academy. A larger school for adults with much higher forms of education, and not the sort of thing you put your kids into that barely teaches them to read and write, and count on their fingers… with respect."

"I'm not arguing, Kaliya. I know where that takes me…I was there once. I'll also admit mine didn't teach me much more than that, if I consider the things I've learned from you and Relissa out here."

"Gracious, Haran," Aerlie winces. "What sort of system do you have up there?" she shakes her head. "Well, anyway, if they wish to specialize further, we have technical academies where they can take the advanced course. Seventh is the Practitioner, Eighth is the Master, and Ninth is the Elder rank. But many of these lessons tend to be specialized for either military or highly technical professions. There's nothing that might restrict you from taking these, but most often you would need a reason for it, like if you are seeking a specialized form of career."

"I see…and if to borrow from Kaliya, this would blow my horns off. So, any average guy like me, if I should have so much gumption to do so, could go all the way up and with no one telling me I'm not worthy of their glorious blessings of wisdom, and to kiss their feet for the mere pleasure of it."

Aerlie closes her eyes and shakes her head.

"I feel for you, but yes. However, I suppose I should also mention this. For us, magical authority is a licensed art. No matter your level, you must register your skills and declare your responsibility over them. Power of this sort has been known to be grossly misused in our history, and we do not wish to see this occur again."

"All right, this is fair, as you grant this to the general public, so you need to ensure some level of legal authority over it. It's a strange concept for me, but I think I can see it. And how long does all this actually take to study?"

"Typically, one year per Circle."

"What?!" he wheezes. "One year for a Circle? Great gods… again… I've been in my academy for several years now, and with or without the poor study materials they give us, I can barely light a candle with it. How do you manage all this?"

"Our education system is actually very unique, I think. It's highly compressed and accelerated, so we can deliver a large flow of information in a relatively short period of time. This allows our people to study a huge range of course materials in the time you were simply learning to read and write," she giggles cautiously.

"Oh! But of course…rub it in," he smirks. "But how do you make the classroom study go so quickly?"

"I carry a little bit of history behind me, some of it very strange. Among other things, I've been directed on a path of Fate which brought me to do certain things at certain moments. One of these was to discover an old alchemical formula in my grandfather's library of a potion we call the Elixir of Visions. This accelerates the learning process and memory recall rates."

"An alchemical substance?" Kaliya winces. "Great cu'Nar, so even with your alchemy studies, you do weird things."

"Yes, and this one is especially weird, as we have no idea where it came from."

"Uh oh…what does that mean? You said it was in your grandfather's library. Isn't that a place to come from?"

"Well, yes, the book… But our family was given this strange book, once upon a time, of unknown origin, and calling for what were then unknown ingredients to produce an unknown effect. It's not our own work. And furthermore, the main ingredient is a plant found only in an inhospitable tundra region of an unknown variety that doesn't even look like it belongs on Tae'Eladar!" she chuckles.

"In all the nether-space, where do you people come up with this stuff? So, do we know anything about where all this came from?"

"Our best answer must involve someone amongst the Estelar with some curious connections who might be influencing this path of Fate for us. One member of our founders for our Order is actually responsible for…hinting…at my Fate to go look for it in the first place. And she probably follows direction from someone higher."

"And so, they say the gods work in strange ways," Haran moans.

"Jiggers, Haran," Relissa adds. "You got that one right."

"But now for the big one… Could a guy like me actually sign up for these classes, or is this one of those things limited to your own population, and those rules you mentioned of people growing naturally and such."

"This would tend to fall into a gray area, I think," Thaelyn admits. "I would not personally wish to deny you, but as you said, we do have those rules. Tae'Eladar is special in how it developed, so I cannot say it is your typical example. By comparison, yours is an external society, and we must obey those rules as taught to us by the Estelar. However, there are ways to do this, if you are willing to make a few of your own choices."

"Such as? I'm actually guessing at one, right now."

"And which one might that be?"

"To join your society… It would beat all the hells out of living on this world."

"Indeed, I suppose it would. Amongst the people of Tae'Eladar, and during that time I was still uniting the nations together, those who were among my own would take advantage of my teachings, while those who were outside were…well, outside. But once I brought them into my world unity, they were all included."

"Right, and this gives me a firm idea of where this is going. So, if I wanted to be a part of it, I'd have to be…a part…of it, as would anyone else around here, I guess."

"This would be correct. And while I would certainly welcome your involvement, I do not necessarily hold the authority to simply come in here and do the same as I did on Tae'Eladar. That was also a special case."

"But it wouldn't stop you if we asked for it, would it?" Relissa wonders.

"I, well…" he muses thoughtfully. "If you were to request it, this would certainly change the equation. You are essentially a lost group of travelers, originally from our world. And I would not hesitate to invite you to come back home."

"Jiggers, wait till I tell my Mum that one."

Kaliya watched and listened. She gazed at her two friends and reflected on her people. The Daanen-Aryku were effectively foreigners on this world, and didn't really have any true home anyway. She reflexively hung her head as she found her mind drifting off to her friends finding their origins again…and possibly leaving her behind.

Thaelyn took notice of this, as he could also sense her emotional output at the same time. He studied her face.

"Kaliya, I can feel your pain on this matter. Before you go and, well, lose your horns or however you would describe it on this occasion…"

"Feeling them sag would be one way to put it."

"Very well, and perhaps you can teach me a few of these expressions along the way. But anyway, I would not choose to exclude you and yours if you should also wish to join our unity. As I said before, I do not throw people away. In fact, I hold the opinion that any who can follow our creed may join us as we march forward into a combined future together. If your people are feeling so lonely from your exile, come to me and mine and feel yourselves as part of something bigger."

This suggestion made Kaliya feel better, and she perked up with a soft smile on her face.

"But what would someone like me do in your society? With respect, if you compare what we have and what you have, um…"

"Yes, I suppose that could pose a curious quandary. I must still follow those rules Haran mentioned, even with my own people. Therefore, yours might need to wait a century or two before we find our way up to the stars."

"What?!" she screeches impulsively. "Cu'Nar help us, only a century or two, from an Industrial Age to a Space Age? Oh wow, Tanjhira won't just lose her horns, they'll be labeled as lethal projectiles," she chuckles.

Relissa and Haran both chip in with the laughter, followed soon by Thaelyn and Aerlie.

"Let me see," Thaelyn conjectures. "By this statement, should I interpret that it took you a tad longer?"

"A tad…" she rolls her eyes. "Well, from what I think I recall of our history, we went to space a few hundred millennia ago, and travelled around our local galaxy a lot. But I'm not precisely sure how long it took to get to that point, at least from our own Industrial Age. I am, however, fairly sure it was on the order of millennia, probably tens of millennia, and not centuries."

"Indeed! Then you must take an especially slow path to it. These things tend to go much faster for societies like what you will find on Tae'Eladar and other places I have seen. This is largely a function of their shorter lifespans, and therefore, the inherent drive to seek faster results."

"So, what you're saying here is, because we have such ridiculously long lifespans, we take ridiculously long to get anything done," she smiles.

The group shares another round of laughter at her statement.

"All right, fine," she continues. "But I'm a soldier…or at least that's what I was trying to be during this time. And I fouled things up badly on a lot of occasions. Regardless of Aerlie and her promise of therapy, I always wanted to bring something back to my people to help them survive and get out of this mess we're in. We're just waiting for the end to come, and it hurts."

Thaelyn leans in to consider this notion. He studies her for her posture and demeanor.

"You sound much more assertive than your depiction of the rest. What was this error you made?"

"Assertive…yes. A few of us are like that, especially after so many losses and other bad experiences. I once held the rank of Ensign. I was so proud of it. I was following in the hooves of my brother…"

Thaelyn turns briefly to Aerlie and raised his brow at the wording.

"What do you think of that, my Dear…to follow in the hooves of another?"

"Very unique," she retorts humorously. "And not something you hear every day."

"All right, you two," Kaliya grins softly. "This is part of our linguistic culture, you know. Anyway, I think it went to my head. One day, I went rushing off into combat without proper authorization and almost got myself and my team killed. That's when they busted me to the lowest operable rank in the book."

"I am very sorry for this, Kaliya," Thaelyn nods. "But I would suspect your temper and these old wounds, as you call them, are likely responsible."

"Yes, and probably always will be."

"I do not believe in this, and neither should you. With proper support and conditioning, I think you can do much better. But your circumstances here may not be favorable for this point."

"Uh huh, so are you going to invite me to join your military next?"

"Well, technically speaking, if you can qualify for the testing, why not? At the very least, your elevated vantage point would certainly stand out amongst the ranks," he chuckles.

"Oh! Did you hear that!" she smirks. "Now HE is gnawing on my tail. And do I get my own suit of armor and a sword?"

"Somehow," Haran muses. "I don't think that would suit you. According to my Sis, that armor can be a bit clunky, and with your height towering over everyone else, you'd have to fight on your knees most of the time."

"Yes!" she throws her hands up. "And there he is. Thank you so much."

They shared another round of laughter.

"But Kaliya," Thaelyn resumes. "You do carry many burdens, and Aerlie's therapy would be the first suggestion I would make as a corrective effort. If you can overcome this, I do not see why you could not continue your course. But you must also realize a soldier's life is not about being a hero. It involves a lot of hard work, a well-coordinated team effort, and the skill to get the job done with the least amount of loss. If you were to take these courses, I have no doubt you would carry the resources and the esteem to see your life turn around significantly. I am also reminded how you once said your people were not especially skilled in military affairs."

"Yes, that too. And we're not doing well against those Suuden-Aryku who ARE apparently very military by now."

"What this tells me is you probably do not hold the proper methods available to you. And being in such a diminished position by now simply makes matters worse. But if you were to attend our academy, I think this would change for you."

"Thaelyn," Aerlie interjects. "This might carry a side note."

"Oh? What kind?"

"If her people are largely non-military, what was she doing out there pushing for a fight? That's an offensive combatant, as opposed to a society of people who don't like to fight at all."

"Yes. And so, she was seeking a solution to their tragedies, but unfortunately, it might not have been very well planned."

"Maybe also in the face of that same non-military authority refusing to stand up for itself for any reason. If they don't even offer a plan, she has to invent her own."

"Indeed. So, we might have some oppositional posturing here, as well as a clear lack of support to make it work."

"Interesting," Kaliya wonders. "But wouldn't this also be described as suicidal?"

"As opposed to just sitting there waiting for it to come to you?"

"Uh...yeah, got it. But are you actually serious," she mumbles tenderly. "You would actually hire someone like me?"

"Kaliya, if you continue to play this role, I may actually make it a demand, just like with Relissa over here," he grins. "Recall what I said earlier. I adore challenges."

"Aye, girl!" Relissa yips urgently. "You'd better watch yourself on that one."

"Yeah, all right," she relents cautiously. "I'll be quiet...at least for now. But this would also make me feel bad, like I'm running away from my people."

"Not necessarily," Thaelyn asserts. "Perhaps you simply need a new perspective to fight this war where, so far, you are seeing so few results. For instance, how are you and these others currently engaging your enemies? Perhaps you could use a change of tactics or a new direction."

"Um..." she hesitates. "We don't actually...huh? You mean to fight together? The Governor of Rolsklinde has sometimes allowed us a team of guards to help patrol our fields, but these people don't have the equipment to fight the Suuden-Aryku, and we don't have the manpower to fight anything else. Haran, what do you and the Night Elves do on your side? From what I've heard you say before, you don't go outside for anything at all, just waiting for it to come to you."

"Yeah," he reflects. "According to Marelle, the Guard is forbidden to go out there due to all our supply shortages. As for the Night Elves...Relissa, you never mentioned anything."

"Aye," she infers. "All I have to say is we have a few hits on our outer towers, but we don't go out looking for them, and they don't come to us. And I don't recall any of your Guard coming out to help with anything, either."

"Did your people ever ask for it?"

"I wouldn't know about that. You'd need to talk to the Enforcer, or maybe the Council."

"Just one moment here," Thaelyn pauses with a hand. "You are supposed to be fighting a war, and doing so for a period of time measuring in centuries, and yet none of you are apparently fighting anything, other than perhaps these harassment assaults, and further, you do not join together as a team effort to see an end to it overall?"

"Um," Relissa ducks away bashfully. "I guess that's a wee bit shameful then, ay?"

"Shameful? This goes beyond even that much! And it raises yet more questions as to why you are still present in the first place! They bring you into this condition, oppress you for several centuries, and worse, none of you, who I am guessing to be on friendly terms, join in an alliance to fight back."

"My people tend to be rather reclusive, Your Lordship," Kaliya admits. "I think it comes from being hunted for so long. We don't feel comfortable reaching out to anyone."

"This, in addition to not fighting to begin with. And how do you expect to win anything like that?"

"Technically, we don't. We simply hide from it, or else run away entirely. And this is also one of my long-standing issues with our leadership."

"I see. Then this is a manner we need to break! I will apply myself on your behalf, but I think I must also apply myself to raise you up a bit."

"Um…" Haran raises a finger tentatively. "We also have a few problems in the city back home. A lot of people hold some, uh, rather unpleasant opinions over the rest, especially the elves. So, while we might hold a political truce, the people, um…aren't very eager to go out there and do much of anything on their behalf."

"Why is this? Are you actually so opposed to them?"

"It dates back to the start where four centuries ago the two elven sides went to war, and this caused a lot of havoc in the world. No one was safe from those Flame Elves. This apparently turned the people away from all the elves, as they regard them to be responsible for all the devastation."

"I see, and this would pose a problem. What about her people?" he points at Kaliya.

"Hers are strangers with strange ways, and our people tend to be rather, um…maybe I should say superstitious."

"Oh grand… All right, then we will need to investigate this and see about a solution. But your clear isolation is probably the main reason you are still at war in this world and not accomplishing anything with it."

"So…" Relissa concludes. "What you're really saying here is it's our own bloody fault for not putting it together sooner. Aye, I may have to admit to this. But now I'm wondering how we could do it. We get Night Elves on one side, humans on the other, and her people towering over the rest sticking out like a sore thumb," she snickers. "How do you organize your army?"

"Yeah," Kaliya adds. "What is your military actually like, maybe so I can compare with ours. I might as well learn the differences involved. Like you said, maybe it could offer a new perspective. So, what do you actually teach?"

"Very well," Thaelyn responds. "I suppose this is a fair question. We give extensive training as well as education within our military, which counts as an Order of Knighthood. It does not simply serve to go out and fight wars, as we also serve a number of other roles, some of which are civilian in nature. We serve as disaster aid and recovery, sometimes law enforcement, religious service and support, and health and medical care…which by the way is Aerlie's specialty. We also set a number of standards for other areas, such as education, science and research, and political guidelines."

"Gods be blessed…" Haran blurts. "Is there anything you don't do? That accounts for most of the trouble of living, save for farming and shop keeping."

"Perhaps, but we are the caretakers of our society. So, for those aspects of society that need examples to follow, we will set those examples. And to accomplish all this, we give our military servicemen a high education in a broad area of study. This involves university study as well as mage academies and combat training. We train in a variety of weapons and combat styles, including swords and other hand weapons, whether one-handed or two-handed, depending on the individual, plus bows and other things. We also teach a variety of martial arts combat, which may or may not involve weapons at all."

"I don't even know what that is. My sister is in the Guard, and she only tells me of swords and shields."

"My people mostly use rifles," Kaliya admits. "We might equip small blades, but we prefer not to get close enough to use them. Like I said, we tend to be much more of a peaceful society, and war offends our senses."

"There is nothing wrong with that," Thaelyn accedes. "But if you are fighting for your lives, you cannot simply sit on a log for it… none of you," he passes his gaze among all of them.

"And um…" Haran coughs emphatically. "So, how does one sign up for this training?"

"Haran, you round-eared bugger," Relissa teases. "Do you have something funny bouncing between your ears right now?"

"Who, me? Oh no! I'm, uh…asking for a friend. Yeah!"

"Uh huh, right. And what friend is this?"

"Well, actually, the tall one over there who's probably too afraid to ask in case she should find herself being dragged into conscription."

The group ushers up another laugh.

"I swear," Thaelyn offers merrily. "The three of you are likely to make trouble for me. Again, as I said before, any who can follow our creed may join, but we do have a testing procedure where the application is concerned."

"A testing procedure, oops… What sort?"

"Since we are speaking of so much educational content, there are a number of academic demands you will need to meet. However, I suppose, if any of you should hold such an interest, we could possibly offer some supplemental courses to fill you in before moving on to the official ones. And yet, we still have one very important test that must be met before anything could go forward at all…at least for our military, or any of the very advanced lessons. We call it the Spirit test."

"A Spirit test?" Kaliya wonders. "I've heard of academic requirements before, but testing a spirit?"

"The simplest way to describe this is to say the Spirit test is a measure of your spiritual essence. All creatures emit a type of energy relating to the nature and purity of the soul. As a being from the Celestial Realms, I know of this intimately, and for all that I give to my students, I want to ensure they are worthy, and not take my teachings and abuse them. Therefore, I offer the Spirit test as the primary requirement to admit them into application. If they achieve a favorable score, they may go forward."

"Interesting, but how do you measure the energy of a spirit?"

"I once applied myself with a group of others on a special project to borrow from my Celestial knowledge a technique using a type of energy flow that would interact with a spiritual aura. This creates a color sign to symbolize the polarity of the spirit. Mortals tend not to be inherently pure beings, as their evolutionary standing is still rather, eh...perhaps the best word to use here is unrefined."

"Unrefined..." Haran ponders. "Based on our past discussions, can I assume this to mean we are easily corrupted, or that we might change our loyalties on a whim?"

"Very good, Haran," Thaelyn nods. "Therefore, if you consider the colors of a rainbow, we might look for blue as the minimum requirement for entry. Yellow and green are conditional, if for instance we say the individual is suffering from some sort of anomaly, and I will allow for a special ritual to see if we can correct this. Then we will test again for our result. But I can only allow this once, as I need to draw line. Generally speaking, you are what you are. If we can repair the problem at all, it must be done the first time. Otherwise we may need to fail that person as their issue...whatever it may be...would be deemed irreversible."

"And you don't want any crazy people running around throwing fireballs at each other, I suppose. What about the lower colors, while we're on the topic? Red, orange..."

"These would represent a transition into the negative polarity, and I would not accept those regardless, as they would conflict with my own. They could also represent such mentalities as criminal or deranged behavior."

"I see, and so this makes sense. And what is this ritual you mentioned?"

"It is called the Ritual of Redemption."

"Ouch, that sounds serious. What does it involve?"

"Essentially, it is to have one stripped of all physical burdens and placed into a chamber to contemplate their sins and misgivings. The chamber is devoid of light and all other objects, and strongly enchanted. The applicant enters after spending a period of time meditating in another room with burning incense to enhance the senses."

"Are we talking about a hallucinogen?" Kaliya speculates. "Is this something like a tribal dream quest session? I've seen orcs do this once or twice."

"Indeed, and in some ways, yes. They peer into their deepest thoughts and bring them out. The enchantments of the room allow them to interact with these hidden feelings, enabling them to resolve their issues in a manner that seems physical. This can clear the burden and allow a second Spirit test to pass them."

"And if not, you're out and need to find another job, maybe also another world to live on, as I would imagine staying on your world, with your perfect society, might not work out well."

"I suppose so, in some ways, but it may not be quite as bad as that."

"And speaking in terms of Haran's indirect reference for asking, you can do this for outsiders as well? Wouldn't it be restricted to only your own citizens?"

"Again, I would say the offer is open, but you do call forward a valid point with your mention. The Order is essentially a military organization. Joining it would mean serving me as your new liege, and this also grants automatic citizenship to my realm."

"Yes, of course..." Kaliya concludes.

The conversation, which had been very enlightening for the

three friends, began to settle for the evening. Each of them had seen more than their fill for any single day, or even a full week, and they looked forward to a calm night's rest, even though they had doubts of receiving it with so many thoughts running through their minds. Still, they needed to be ready for the following day when they hoped to report to their respective superiors.

As Relissa settled in, she recalled the voice of the kindred spirit of the tree filling her mind with the soothing graces of her native culture and history. She was anxious to see her mother and father, and tell them what she had learned. Her superior, the Enforcer at the Guild of Wardens, would not be so pleased, however, since she would be a day late in returning from her patrol.

Haran felt as if his life had been wasted in the dingy halls of the academy, where he spent his time struggling to make any progress while his superiors took delight in humiliating him. He dreamed instead of what the academies of Thaelyn's Order might have to offer, a virtual guarantee of a full and proper education in the magical arts, with no ridicule or demeaning regard from his instructors or peers.

Kaliya could only hear the screams of her youth echoing through her mind. It came to her often, but for some reason tonight it was louder. She recalled the many occasions when she would go out on vendettas due to her anger over the suffering of her people, only to come home and find herself the victim of the judgment of her Elders. It was a miracle she still held any rank at all, perhaps yet another indication of how desperate they were, if even to keep someone like her enlisted.

Her thoughts then circled on returning home to report on all this extraordinary detail, most of which she might never be able to explain, and other parts might simply need to be held back, due at least to Thaelyn's security. And then there was the Prophecy. How would she ever convince anyone that she, of all people, might have found the answer. Her first hurdle would simply have to be returning home and explaining why she was still alive, as she felt certain someone would have detected the blast wave out here. But she couldn't help wondering if all she was seeing around her was the hope they had been waiting for, and she wanted to be a part of that hope. And yet, for everything else she ever experienced, it felt like little more than an empty desire.

Chapter 7

THE REPORT

Morning came, and the soldiers began preparing for the new day. Some of the work had continued through the night, but in areas slightly removed from the camp sites so as not to disturb those who were sleeping. The burden of war knows no rest.

The gnomish technicians had begun calibrating the gate. Kaliya woke up early, not that she slept very well anyway, and was observing the curious little men tinkering inside the control box. They spoke to each other in an odd language, and seemed to behave in a very animated manner. One of them pulled out something that looked like a rune stone and placed it in the U-shaped cradle on top. This stone looked different from the ones used by the mages. The other rune stones were oblong whereas this one was round.

She watched a pair of them where one was told to go rummaging through a bag of tools sitting next to him. He picked something out and handed it to the other gnome, only to be scolded and bopped on the head because it was apparently the wrong one, then told to try again. The exchange seemed almost satirical, causing her to smile gently. Their rapid squeaky voices rattled on like some form of rampant gibberish. A waving of hands later, and he's back to rummaging in the bag.

Relissa and Haran, having been disturbed by the rise in activity, rose up and saw the whole camp coming to life. The smell of cooked bacon and eggs, and several other aromas so far unfamiliar to them, catches their attention. People were forming lines near the kitchen to pick up plates of food and moving off to eat. Thaelyn and Aerlie were nowhere to be seen, but Relissa spies Kaliya standing near the gate and strolls up to meet her.

"Anything interesting going on with this thing?" she asks.

"I think they're working on some kind of calibration," Kaliya responds.

"Any ideas on how much longer till they get the bleedin' thing to work?"

"You see there? They put one of those stones of theirs in that mount. Maybe that's some indication."

"I'm hungry," Haran announces as he joins the group. "Is there anything good cooking around here? He did say something about a morning meal, didn't he?"

"Yes, he did!" Kaliya proclaims. "I've been waiting for the two of you to wake up. I browsed the kitchen earlier to see what they have. Some of it looks new to me, but so far no one's died from it, so I'm game to try it."

"So far...?" Haran looks at her worriedly. "You know, your people have some strange dietary perspectives."

"Keeping in mind, Haran, we don't get much of a variety inside the ship. We can't maintain livestock, and our farming...if you can call it that...is a nano-accelerated aeroponics lab, since we can't do anything outside for all the attacks we suffer."

The three of them stroll over and get in line for a plate. They load it up and move off to find a convenient place to sit so they can enjoy their meal.

When they finish eating, Kaliya begins looking for either Thaelyn or Aerlie to find out what to do next. But in the sea of bodies, she can't see anyone with a large set of wings on their back, nor a tall silver-white-haired gentleman, so she steps over to the nearest person she sees to speak with them.

"Excuse me," she asks of a passing soldier. "Where did Thaelyn and Aerlie go this morning?"

"I believe His Lordship is currently inspecting the work on the tower, while the Lady has returned to B.T. in preparation of opening the portal gate."

"B.T...?"

"Ah, forgive me, our home and capital city, Bya'an Tamoranth."

"Oh, and when will they return?"

"Our Lord will likely return soon, but the Lady more often tends to her duties within the city proper."

"All right, and thank you," she finishes.

The construction effort picks up quickly as several new sites are opened up and made ready. They are located some distance off to the side from the first group, and the sites look big. Workers are leveling out dirt to create large foundations on at least five different spots. As the trio watches the rise in activity, a sturdy male voice speaking Elvish ushers up behind Relissa.

"Excuse me, fair lady. May I have a word?"

She turns to see the form of Captain Hagmaert, the guard captain who accompanied Thaelyn and Aerlie when they first arrived. Haran and Kaliya look on as Relissa enters into conversation.

"Aye?" she responds. "You're the man from yesterday, right?"

"I am. My deepest regrets for not coming to you sooner on this matter, but my duties kept me very busy yesterday, and then I did not wish to disturb you last eve in your meeting with my Lord. But now that we have a moment, I wish to offer my most humble apologies for my conduct on our first meeting."

"Huh? What do you mean?" Relissa asks, confused on the subject matter.

"I used an inappropriate word on you when we first met, and now I wish to redeem myself for the error, for my honor and my dignity. I misinterpreted your nature, perhaps due to the heat of war and the unknowing of where I found myself...though I will not use that as an excuse. The term itself is an undignified word to us. I ask your forgiveness," he begs with a gentle bow.

Relissa looks at him, stunned and surprised.

"A word... I'm not sure...oh, wait... You mean the word Drow? It's considered a bad word?"

"Some may deem it that way, largely for the manners and history we share with them."

"Oh, don't worry about it, Captain," she returns in her most polite form of Elvish. "I didn't take any offence by it, mostly because I don't know the word."

"Maybe so, but on my side, it was in bad form. It developed over time within our local culture, and it is regarded by some as impolite to use."

"Captain, it's alright," she waves it off. "It was a hard situation for all of us. Some of the others told me about them, and the story bothers me also, as it hits close to home for my people. Our history doesn't tell us what happened after we left Sein'amar, so we don't actually know about them. For this point, I'm actually glad we didn't stay. But as for you, please think nothing of it."

"I offer my gratitude to you, fair lady," he smiles. "May the Gods walk with you," he finishes and bows again, then turns and moves away.

"What was that about?" Kaliya asks as she watches the man depart.

Relissa stares blankly into Kaliya's eyes.

"Bleedin' jiggers, I don't believe it... He apologized to me. Someone actually took the time to come up and apologize to me for something."

"Must be some of that perfect society they have over there. I'm noticing these people are extremely polite...and very xenophilic. Even to me, and I must surely look alien in their eyes."

"Apologize?" Haran wonders. "For what?"

"Yesterday," Relissa recalls. "You remember he said the word Drow right up to my face? Well, the Drow are what the dark elves call themselves over there. By the sound of it, they are to them a wee bit like the Flame Elves are to us, and maybe worse for the length of time since the early wars we had in the first years."

"Wars?" Kaliya blurts. "Your people got involved in wars? With whom?"

"Our own kind... They were called Crown Wars, and mostly from different clans trying to sort out their proper territories. The Ssri, as we were called back then, had in mind to simply take over everything, but the rest drove them away."

"Where did all this come from?" Haran asks. "I thought you hated your old lessons."

"The dryad shared a lot of things with me, along with those mages and such when we first met. There were five wars in all before things settled and they all found their right places. My people left after the first one, so this is all we remember. But in the end, the others were essentially banished from the lands, and now they simply hate the rest. This is where they started calling themselves Drow, likely out of spite that they couldn't have it their way. Anyway, I look like one, if only by a slight shade, and he wanted to hold up his honor by apologizing. That name is regarded as a bad word to them these days."

"Wow, that sounds bad."

"And this is unusual, Relissa?" Kaliya inquires. "Someone apologizing for something? It certainly sounds like a legitimate cause."

"Bleedin' right it is!" she exclaims. "You know how the Enforcer is. The only thing I ever get out of him is the hard end of a boot. Even my Mum and Dah often give me the cold shoulder for my, um...bad behavior."

"Well, maybe so, but I guess we could also say they have their reasons. This sounds different."

The gnomes begin lining up in front of the gate. One of them is still working behind the control box while another one stands on a block to reach the rune mount on top. A shout issues forth and the glyph-inscribed disks in the archway jacketing flash brightly as a pulse of energy ripples around the circle. This is followed by a bright glow in the rune stone mounted on the pedestal. The gnome on the block pulls out the stone and replaces it with another one.

The disturbance attracts Kaliya and her friends. They turn to watch the affair.

Another shout, another glowing ripple, and another rune is pulled out. A third one is placed in the slot, and the process repeats one more time.

"I'm going to see if I can learn what they're doing," Kaliya states casually.

She steps up to one of the gnomes standing in front of the gate, but she towered over the little man, who barely reached as high as her knee. She kneels down to talk to him.

"Um, excuse me?" she announces.

The little man turns around and lets out a short yip, being startled at the sight of the huge, blue-skinned mountain of a woman kneeling next to him.

"Ooh! Look at you! I was secretly hoping you might come over and talk for a moment," he giggles girlishly.

Another gnome standing nearby overhears the conversation and turns to join in.

"Oh joy! I saw her walking around a little while ago. Oh goodily-ding-dong, this is so exciting!"

"Yes indeedily-do! I wonder what she has to say for herself."

At this moment, Kaliya was wondering if she should stay and talk, or run for her life.

"Um, I don't actually mean to bother you but..."

"But of course you mean to bother me, otherwise you wouldn't have come over to talk! If you didn't want to bother me, you would've stayed where you were. But clearly, since you didn't stay where you were, this is a sure indication that you have the intention to bother someone, and in particular me! Woohoo! Oh, what a joy! And now that you have bothered me, what can I do for you?" he finishes with a curious smile.

"Dear cu'Nar, is this normal for you people? Uh, I had a question..."

"Oh!" he yips excitedly. "Did you hear that? She has a question!"

"Fantabulicious!" the other gnome rejoices. "Oh, the joy of

asking questions. Why, if it weren't for questions, we might never learn anything."

"You're absolutarifically right! And then to ask questions about the questions we were asking the questions about..."

"That's right! Oh, the questions we might ask if only we had the mind to question it."

"Oh please," Kaliya begs. "My horns can't take this much so early in the day."

"In fact," the first gnome continues. "Some of the greatest discoveries in the world came about after someone started asking questions."

"This reminds me of a very important question I had earlier this morning."

"Oh? And here's a good question for you. What was your other question?"

"Where the rest facility was... I had a really urgent need for it," he admits bashfully.

The two of them let out a boisterous barrage of giggles.

Kaliya was now searching for a quick escape route. She gazed longingly at Haran and Relissa, both of whom were glaring at the abnormal form of interaction.

"But anyway," the first gnome begins again. "What sort of question do you want to ask a question about, lovely lady?"

"Lovely lady?" she wonders.

"Ooh, did you see that? She asked a question about my question. How titillating..."

"In all the nether-space, um," she continues urgently. "Let's just get on with it. What are you doing up there with that thing?"

"Ah, of course, and what a fine question that is!"

"And that's a question worthy of an answer!" the other one admits heartily.

"Right-a-roony, and oh ho! An answer I can give, no question about it! Isn't that grand?"

"Oh, my favorite kind!"

Kaliya was at her limit by now. She placed a hand over her

brow, as if trying to hold onto whatever remained of her wits. She wondered if she did the right thing by starting this conversation. Then the gnome returns with his answer.

"We are configuring a set of addressing runes to be distributed for reverse-link coordination of the TDGN routing selectors at a series of previously selected terminal nodes for the trans-positional redirection of resource allocation between our primary production infrastructure and the ultimate consumer endpoint…as well as just to let people move around more easily."

Kaliya gaped at the wordy explanation, unconsciously darting her eyes back and forth as if trying to reread the proclamation from visual memory.

"And now I have a question for you," he continues. "Is there anything else I can help you with?"

"Uh-uh…" she blurts abruptly. "I'm fine, thank you."

"Have a delightful day, dear lady!" he chirps merrily as Kaliya jumps to her feet to make a hasty escape.

She returns to Haran and Relissa, quickly dodging around and ducking behind them, then peering through between their shoulders.

"Right, and how did that go?" Haran asks wittily.

"Word to the wise," Kaliya relates. "Don't talk to them. They're insane."

"Anything like that overconfident Captain?" Relissa wonders.

"Oh no, he was fine. But these people are like little word factories on steroids."

A commotion occurs at the far end of the camp to the northern side, as a series of orders are overheard in a strong voice.

"He's back," Kaliya declares. "Thank the cu'Nar, maybe we can go home for our daily bashing now."

"Ay!" Relissa balks. "Speak for yourself, I'm actually hoping for only a minor foot-stomping."

"I'm more likely to get a moderate tongue-lashing," Haran adds.

"Well, whatever," Kaliya admits. "It's time for us to make our preparations to get back home, but we should give some kind of goodbye to him first."

They trot over to meet with Thaelyn as he works his way into the camp.

"Your Lordship?" she calls out to him. "May we have a word with you?"

"In a moment, please," he responds, moving back in the direction of the gate. "How much longer, Professor?" he asks the lead gnome.

"The diagnostics are complete, and we've processed three addressing runes. The gate is ready to synchronize with the network."

"Proceed."

Kaliya and her friends turn to observe the work on the gate. She takes notice of the lead gnome's more professional mode of conduct with Thaelyn.

"So, they actually do know how to talk normal?" she muses privately.

"Excuse me?" Thaelyn wonders.

"I tried asking him a question a moment ago, and wow! He wore away the fresh new horns I grew this morning."

"Ah, new faces..." he smiles. "Gnomes are a very curious sort. They love making new acquaintances and flirting with the ladies."

"Uh huh...including those who stand as tall as me?"

"The bigger, the better, as they say."

"Cu'Nar give me strength."

A gnome steps up onto the block with a new rune stone. He slides it into the cradle and steps down off the block, which he then pulls away.

He moves around behind the control box and manipulates a small lever into a locking groove. The rune stone begins to glow gently. Energy begins to flow into the tall, curved archway, one-by-one illuminating the metal disks and their glyphs in their sockets along the length, from bottom to top, on both sides. As the top glyph lights up, a crackling of energy sprays across within the circular aperture, congealing into a swirling vortex.

"Fascinating," Kaliya reflects. "That reminds me of our own conveyor units. Or at least what I got out of the lessons in my old school. Where does this one lead?"

"For the moment," Thaelyn replies. "I am confident enough to use a key to our home city of Bya'an Tamoranth. We have a strong enough presence here to secure this region and protect the gate. Should our position ever be compromised, however, it is a simple thing to shut it down and remove the key. We will also provide keys to two other locations and alternate them as necessary to our needs here."

"Keys?" Haran asks.

"Portals need keys to unlock and activate them. We use these rune stones for that purpose, though there are portals to be found in some places amongst the realms that may use other forms of keys."

"Such as?"

"A good example would be a city to which I am quite familiar, named Sigil. It is located in the Outer Planes. I used to frequent there often during the time of my service to my Father. It is sometimes described as the City of Doors, due to the presence of perhaps thousands of portals hidden in the nooks and recesses of its interior. Each will only become visible if the appropriate key is brought to within proximity. The key, in this case, could be many things, not simply an object of any sort. It could be a word, a gesture, an emotion, an action, or some other. Any bound space, framed on its four sides, could hold the potential to contain a portal. It may be a doorway, an arch, even the space under a table framed by two legs and the floor. Bring the right key to it, and it will open."

"How do you know the right key, or where to bring it?"

"Most often, you do not, nor would you know where it might lead. Trial and error, or perhaps some privileged knowledge, may help you to find one, but the true question is whether you would wish to pass through it."

"Um..." Haran cogitates briefly before continuing. "All right, I suppose I can't let that pass without asking."

"I thought not!" Thaelyn declares with a broad grin. "Be aware, that to pass through portals unknown may lead you to places most unpleasant, and with no way of retreat if you are not prepared for it. Most portals are unidirectional, where the flow of energies, and even the image of its origin, will only pass one way. You cannot see through from the side of its source, and you cannot return back from the side of its exit."

"You say most are unidirectional," Kaliya notes. "That suggests there may be some that are bidirectional."

"Whereas many portals may point simply to an open space, as with our stones, there may also be two sister frames that point to each other. In this way, you may pass with less concern of the unknown, for now you can see the other side, and return back again if you wish. Such can be found in our case here, with these gateways. As one is activated for use, it addresses another, which then creates a reverse link back to the first. The links are dynamic, and our network can accommodate a large number of them, negotiating and alternating their routes in a carefully managed affair."

"So, why don't we see anything here?"

"This is because we have yet to return the reverse linking runes to our home. The gnomes made three, of which we will distribute to specific locations of logistical importance to us here. Observe this mage..."

Thaelyn turns to a mage who had been waiting patiently next to him as he gave his oratory. He motions to the gnomes to pass the runes over to him. The mage stows them in one of his pockets and pulls out a rune stone from his belt. He casts the enchantment to open a portal and exits from sight.

"He will return back and pass one of those stones to our technicians currently working on a gate near our guildhall, under the supervision of Aerlie who returned there earlier. The process after that is nearly as simple as dropping the stone into place to activate it. We should see the result momentarily."

They wait several moments, watching the swirling energies move through the glowing archway. Soon, there is a flickering of light within the swirls. A small hole in the center begins to open up, rapidly expanding to fill the circle.

The image of a grand stone fortress appears in the window of the archway, backing up against a curved hillside. Colorful banners waved on flagpoles jutting up from towers along the front walls. In the foreground were a set of ornately clad guards standing at attention in front of a large gate, which was open and looking through to a well-appointed courtyard. To the rear of the courtyard rose a broad stairway of white marble leading up to the front gate of a majestic palace. In the center of the courtyard stood the proud statue of a knight kneeling with his sword in a contemplative repose, and standing over his right shoulder was the form of a winged female, with one hand on his shoulder and the other pointing outward in front of her.

Commonfolk were seen passing in and out of view, as well as the image of Aerlie standing only a short distance away and apparently speaking to a group of gnomes.

"Oh my..." Haran whispers, his voice trembling from the overpowering sight.

"That statue," Kaliya begins. "Is that you and Aerlie? What is she pointing at?"

"The horizon..." Thaelyn answers.

"Any particular reason?"

"It is symbolic. It represents the future. Always look to the future! On the other hand, my image demonstrates vigilance and the protection of what we hold now."

"Um..." Haran mutters while trying to hold back a giddy laugh. "So, where do you go to apply?"

"Through those gates, turn right, pass through a door, left, then down the hall to an administration office."

Haran felt faint as he continued studying the image.

"So simple, so close...but also a world away..."

Thaelyn reaches over to lay a hand on his shoulder.

"Patience, good fellow... We have work that must come first, but if you are so wanting of this, we can find time for it."

"You are simply too kind, Your Lordship."

Haran gazed at the imagery, asking what potential could await him there. Would they even let him through the door? He reflected on his own life, with the experiences of the academy now moldering in his mind. And yet, he still had obligations to attend.

Kaliya looked into the window at the glorious sight. It was a world at peace, prosperous and happy. Its citizens were well-dressed and gave the impression of a sophisticated society, despite its lower technological station. The palace declared itself as the product of a rich culture, and the dominating power of the fortress stood testimony to a righteous cause, a cause she always wished for, but one she could never find in this world. Every attempt she ever made hoping to become a hero to her people only led her back to her Elders for another scolding over her recklessness. The demons of her mind never let her find peace.

Relissa had never seen the face of Sein'amar before. She was captivated. It was only a tiny glimpse of a fabled land once described in the stories of her people, but it inspired her to desire more. She wanted to jump through and run to the far corners, to see it all. But this would have to wait for another day. She still had work to do here in this world.

Her father was a historian and a member of the Elven High Council in Solinaia. He spent much of his time studying in the city library. During her lifetime, she never understood why he struggled so hard to keep the memories alive, but after her communion with the dryad spirit, she finally knew the answer. Her mother, the Matron Priestess at the city's main temple, was also a member of the Council, and in her own way she also tried to maintain the old traditions, as hopeless as it might have seemed during this time of war, which had wrought havoc on this world for centuries.

Thaelyn examined the three of them and understood the looks on each of their faces. But the current business was still at hand, and it had to be completed.

"My friends, we still have much work ahead of us," he admits. "And I believe the time has come for the three of you to be on your way. No doubt, by this time you have more than enough to offer in your reports. But remember we need to keep at least some of our secrets. I realize my entry into this world will bring many concerns, perhaps even a few fears, and I would wish to resolve these before any accidents occur. Therefore, I ask you to deliver only that which is necessary to appease them. From there, I am willing to entertain an audience with whoever is the ruling power, or his assigns, for each of the friendly races here. Have them meet with me at their earliest opportunity, so that we may have time to understand one another."

He turns to look directly at Relissa.

"As for you, be sure to consider my offer. If your superiors are permitting, and you also agree to it, I would ask you to return to share what you can. Even if the friendly races do not wish to give me their intimate details, I should at least be made aware of where not to tread, so as not to step on their toes."

"Sounds fair enough to me," she replies. "I can't be sure what he might have to say about it, but I'll work on it. This is simply too good to pass up."

Thaelyn looks through the clusters of troops, as though searching for something. Kaliya instinctively follows his gaze. Finally, far off to one side, an assemblage of mages breaks up with three of them turning and charging over to Thaelyn's side, promptly saluting on their arrival.

"How...?" she starts to ask. "Actually, scratch that."

"My people are trained to understand my telepathic commands. It tends to save my voice on occasion," he chuckles slightly.

"That one would be obvious, I think," Haran remarks. "If he has this skill at all, he might use it on everyone."

"Are your people trained in telepathy?" Kaliya inquires.

"The people of our world are not as highly evolved to have obtained this power as yet, but I do teach them a few lessons on how to disguise their thoughts to protect themselves from unauthorized intrusions. This reminds me of our conversation last eve."

"Yes, where my people are concerned. I wish I could learn a little of this, but I'm sure our Elder Council would scream at me, especially Elder Vankkar. He's particularly paranoid on the matter."

"Perhaps we can address this, as well, at some moment."

The mages position themselves in front of the three friends.

"These three will enchant you with haste spells, allowing you to move much more quickly overland. That ridge of mountains up there," he points to the row in the north. "It should not take long to reach under these conditions. From there, whatever length of time you might spend on your travels home should become much shorter. The spell has a limited duration of time, however, so do not dally too long," he concludes with a wink.

"How long?" Haran asks.

"About an hour, unless it is canceled prematurely."

Thaelyn gestures to the mages to begin conjuring their spells. Energies wrap around their hands, and then fly forward at each of their intended targets. The companions are momentarily wrapped in an aura of energy as it penetrates into their bodies. Their perceptions seem to intensify as their internal awareness accelerated, and this brought the uncanny sensation that the world around them had slowed down.

"Safe travels to you, my friends. I hope to see you again soon. You are welcome to return at any time."

The mages move off and Thaelyn steps out of the way. Kaliya and the others give a quick wave and dash off to the north at blazing speed.

The wind whistles in their ears and brushes across their faces, and their hair is flung out behind them as they speed along. The camp recedes quickly into the background, while trees and shrubs rush past them. In a few moments, they come up on the construction site for the tower, where the dwarves were picking up slabs of white stone and stacking them atop each other. They barely have enough time to turn their heads to look at it before they pass it by.

Haran was trying to study the odd tower and recalling the things Thaelyn said about its purpose, when he accidentally ran into a stand of trees. He only barely notices his predicament in time to dodge one, but in doing so, angles himself into the path of another. He strikes it and deflects into a third and then a fourth, like a billiard ball bouncing between the pegs.

His momentum finally subsides, and he falls to the ground. He tries shaking his head, but the rapid motions make him dizzy as the world blurs all around him. He picks himself up, carefully aligns himself with a clear path between several trees, and makes an attempt to escape from the glen.

Kaliya and Relissa, both of whom diverted around the glen, waited for him to emerge.

"Pay more attention to where you're going, you bleedin' gawker!" Relissa jests as they rush off again.

The ridgeline of the mountains came into view very quickly. The time it took for them to originally enter the valley and find their hiding space the day before was easily half a day at a trot. Here it took only minutes to return back. As they reach the base of the foothills, they find the trail wending its way up to the peak and over the top.

Coming down on the other side, they moved further along to find a watchtower belonging to the human faction near a roadway crossing. The road continued to the north, while also branching to both sides.

Three human guards standing near the base of the defensive tower were engaged in a bit of idle conversation when a sudden rush of wind struck them. Within that wind appeared three individuals, a human, an elf, and a Daanen'kai trooper. The surprised guards jump to their feet looking for their weapons, but settle a moment later when they realize they were not in any real danger.

"You shouldn't rush up on people like that," chides one guard. "Especially not after what's been seen coming out of that valley down there of late!" he gestures in the direction of the Badlands.

"Sorry about that, good man," Haran offers amusingly. "But we're in a bit of a hurry, you see. We need to get back home to file a very important report, so no time for a chat!"

"Yeah, sure, go file... Hey, where'd they go?" the guard mumbles as the three vanish in a blur.

Relissa takes off to the west, in the direction of her home city of Solinaia. Haran keeps to the road heading north to his home of Rolsklinde, and Kaliya splits off eastward to the citadel of the

Daanen-Aryku, built largely out of the spent hull of the Naarg uy'Sodrad, the former ship that once brought them to this world.

Rolsklinde is a moderately-sized city built within a sturdy framework of walls. Bastions are positioned intermittently along this line to provide an effective, and often overlapping coverage of the surrounding area, in case of attack. There is a large gate, heavily reinforced and carefully guarded, which serves as the southern access. Another one is found on the other side of the city as the northern access. Due to the conditions of war, these gates are often kept closed.

Realizing that the guards around the city are rather edgy at times, Haran tries to temper his running speed to a slow-motion trot as he approaches, which under the circumstances still equates to a quick run as seen by an observer. He waves to the gatekeeper to let him through, and a small access door is opened to allow passage.

Once inside, he moves to the upper center of town where the Academy of Arcana is located, along with the Governor's manor and the headquarters of the Allegiance Guard, the city's main barracks. But before entering the academy building, he considers the situation of his hasted movement and prefers instead to find a comfortable place to sit and wait for the effect to wear off first. Knowing the prejudice he'll find inside the academy; he didn't want to complicate matters by exhibiting such an odd magical enchantment.

✦ ✦ ✦ ✦ ✦

Relissa continues on the road west to Solinaia. The usual travel time from the human city going home is often about half a day for her, but with her accelerated movement speed, it's cut down to a mere fraction of that.

Along the way, she notices a few of her furry friends. She can't help but feel that warm feeling of companionship that so often causes her to become distracted from her duty. But the events of the past day forced her to move onward this time. She has too much on her mind today, and needs to unload some of it. Besides, if Thaelyn can help train her to make better use of her talents, maybe she'll have more time for that later.

Unlike Rolsklinde, a city that stands out of the landscape like a sore thumb, the entire elven city is camouflaged to blend with the local wooded terrain. The entrance is hidden between a fold of trees and other shrubs, such that you need to know exactly where to look, and only then to be positioned at just the right angle to see it leading in. The city is concealed by a carefully cultivated row of trees, and further by an outer wooden wall fashioned to look like an even denser forest within.

Outer watch posts, made similarly obscure, keep the vigil for invaders, offering a hail of arrows from sources unknowable to any who get too close.

As Relissa arrives near the outer perimeter, she stops briefly to give a wave to the watcher in the front line of towers, using a special signal developed by the elves to indicate all is well. She then moves up to the hidden entrance to find her way in.

The interior of the city, typical for elven society, is a horticultural delight. Gardens and shrubs line the streets. Trees tower above homes and shops, which borrow part of their structure from the arboreal scaffolding. The city consists of multiple levels, with the upper ones accessed via stairs and elevated catwalks.

Once inside, Relissa finds herself torn in different directions. She needs to file her report with the Guild of Wardens, but she also wants very much to tell her mother about the tree and the dryad spirit. In addition to this, she must try to make amends with her father and his devotion to the ancient traditions.

As she walks through the lanes, she begins to take notice of the voices and stares of people around her, finally to realize she is still under the enchantment spell and causing a distraction to the local populace who are unaccustomed to such sights. She concludes the only way for her to settle this is to find a pleasant place to sit and wait. She makes her way to a parklike square near the main temple where she finds a small gazebo. There, she will sit and consider her options.

<hr>

Kaliya has the furthest trek of the three, and she wants to make good use of the enchantment before it fades. She picks up her speed and makes long strides. She could easily outrun either Haran or Relissa with her pace, but tends to keep herself in check artificially to stay by their sides when together. Even at a good run, though, she still finds herself coming just short of her target as the sight of the Naarg uy'Sodrad comes into view when the enchantment gives way.

With the ending of the enchantment, she feels a temporary wave of fatigue wash over her, causing her to come to an abrupt halt. But her stamina as a long-distance runner, having spent so much time out in the field, allows her to make a quick recovery, and she briskly trots the rest of the way until she arrives at the gate.

The surrounding terrain, while long since recovered from the damage caused by the crash, still shows the scars of the gorge made when the ship impacted and carved its way through the land. Vegetation has returned, and a few trees lined the area, but the outer boundaries of their territory bore the burns and craters of wartime, as the Suuden-Aryku made their continued raids against them.

Several guards are making their rounds as they patrolled the area. They spot her return and wave her through. She approaches the entrance of the citadel, which was fashioned from the remains of the main hatchway of the ship.

On entering, she worked her way through the corridors and the internal transit system, which still functioned, if only barely, until she arrived in the area that used to be the bridge. This room was a large, almost cavernous space, with control stations to monitor and manage most of the ship's internal systems, including the helm and navigation, engineering and reactor power, stellar cartography and tactical plotting, internal security, and much more.

It was in this room when the last commander piloting the Naarg uy'Sodrad gave the order to engage the ship's drives, even though a band of intruders had been found tampering with critical navigation controls deeper within. On that day, many thousands of refugees huddled in any corner they could find. And on that day, when the vessel arrived in this world, they found themselves in a final struggle for survival.

"And so, Captain," issues the Commander. "The first disturbance gave the impression of a massive explosion?"

"Yes, but Commander, none of the local races has any sort of technology to enable this, so my only…rational…suggestion at this time is along the line of a meteor impact."

The High Commander of the Sentinels was engaged in a review of several disturbing reports at a console deeper in the hall when Kaliya peeked inside. She observed him and his senior officer reviewing the details.

"Not an attack by the Suuden-Aryku?" he responds.

"I suppose it could have been a heavy hit by plasma fire, or maybe an atomic. But why the valley? There's nothing out there."

"Except for those orcs," he muses. "But they're supposed to be on the same side. And yet, if it was a meteor, why wasn't there any sighting of a fire trail? Something like that would be hard to miss, even on this side of the range."

"Maybe, unless we say it had already lost most of its inertia and ablative layers. But this would also contradict such a huge explosion. At least…well, I suppose it might also depend on the content."

"As if to say, something especially volatile?"

"Yes, but this would again demand some level of definition. What could be flying around out there that would ignite on impact, but that didn't otherwise burn up or explode as an air burst?"

"Of course, you're right. It's still a contradiction. And none of this explains that second disturbance, which was simply bizarre."

"A collateral effect, maybe? Like some kind of atmospheric disruption due to the explosion? But then, I've never heard of anything like this before, and certainly not on the scale we observed out there. It sounded like it covered the entire valley with a fierce electrical storm."

"And that would defy any known meteorological anomaly on record. And then we have Kaliya..." he sighs heavily. "Where was she during all this?"

"Commander, I'm sorry, but from our observations of that cloud, I can't help but to think of the condition of that entire valley right now. I would expect it to have been blasted halfway to nether-space."

At this moment, Kaliya decides to step out into view and make her approach, knowing the situation needed answers, and hiding behind corners wasn't helping. The Commander had his eyes on a terminal monitor, but the Captain was facing the direction of her approach. He takes quick notice of the movement and looks up to see her arriving.

"Great cu'Nar!" he wheezes. "Well, all right, we have one answer."

The Commander jerks up and turns abruptly to see Kaliya making her entrance. His first reaction was to lay his hand on his brow and close his eyes as he let out a heavy sigh of relief.

"In all the nether-space, Kaliya, I was worried to death over you."

Kaliya makes her presentation, though feeling uncertain for the outcome. She came to attention as she spoke.

"Sir, I have a report," she announces smoothly.

The Commander glared at her briefly. Although his nerves were already frayed at her absence, and the reports coming from the valley were dire, he was now feeling somewhat perturbed at her apparent bravado to simply arrive like nothing had happened.

"Are we playing this game today? All right, Petty Officer," he responds officially. "While I'm eager to hear your report, I'm also very curious over where you were during this time. We received a report of a disturbance in that valley you were supposed to be investigating. And...Kaliya..." he softens his approach. "Are you actually alright? We saw a cloud over the mountains and thought the worst. Are you injured?"

"No, Kailen, I'm alright," she returns cautiously. "Rattled, perhaps, but physically I'm fine. But I'm expecting a hard debriefing, regardless. Knowing you, I feel this is going to hurt."

"Kaliya, why do you always have to vilify me? I'm your brother, and simply trying my best to look after you when you so often get yourself into trouble."

"I know, Kailen, and I suppose I have to apologize for that. I haven't been easy on you, not since that day."

"All right, so what is this report? And I don't want this to sound wrong, but why are you still alive? If you were on your assignment, you should've been in that valley."

"Yeah, that's a good one. You're going to love what I have to say about it. I just hope you'll allow me to finish before you lock me away," she giggles nervously.

"Uh huh..." he glances over his shoulder at the Captain. "I'm worried over what I'm about to hear now. Did you go off and make more trouble?"

"Oh no, nothing like that, I was in the valley, just like you ordered."

"But wait a moment. That explosion... According to our sightings, it was huge, big enough to blast away the whole valley."

"Oh, it was. You can be sure of that much."

"Then you saw it? But were you in the valley, or just on the edge of it?"

"Oh, I saw it alright. It was a little hard to miss, you know. I was deep in the middle with my two friends, Relissa and Haran. So, we all saw it."

"But that doesn't make sense! According to our forward observations, the blast cloud might suggest either an atomic, or maybe a meteor impact. Whatever it was, it had to be big. We were also thinking of a heavy hit by the Suuden-Aryku, if only there was something out there for them to target."

"Probably not... It was a lot of orcs, and last I heard, they're all supposed to be on the same side."

"Orcs...then let's talk about that for a moment. Hit or no hit, what did you see?"

"All right, but before we begin, I'd like you to know I have a very complicated report to file, and it's not just about orcs."

"Understood. So, that blast might suggest something else?"

"Oh yes, it does. And the Council will need to hear some portion of this after we're done."

"Kaliya, you know the chain of command goes through me first. I'll decide if it's worth bothering the Council."

"Kailen, yes, I know this, and I'm telling you, it will need to go up to them, despite your chain of command. Trust me, you'll know what I mean in a moment."

"Very well. I'll take it into consideration. Now, what do you have? For instance, how many orcs did you see out there? Our reports have been suggesting a nearly nonstop influx in recent times."

"Yeah, and we saw the end result. We saw a lot, and I'm talking about a lot! Relissa was suggesting somewhere around two hundred thousand, and some of our estimates may even go as high as a quarter million. But I suppose when you go that high, the extras don't matter as much, it's still a lot."

"Cu'Nar's eyes! How could they get so many in one place? And where did they suddenly come from?"

"I saw flashes, like from a portal, so they were obviously arriving from somewhere using that. At first, it was rows of warriors, but later we saw a bunch of workers arriving with supplies, so it looked like they were cleaning out an old camp."

"And relocating to our side…and so close to us. But now, as for the explosion, what about that? It should've destroyed them along with the valley. But can you explain what you actually saw?"

"Kailen, that old camp they were cleaning out was from another world, the last of their population after they apparently invaded someone else's home and got chased out."

Kailen's face suddenly went blank. He slowly glanced at his Captain, who by now was stepping forward to join them. Together, they glared at Kaliya for her statement.

"A quarter million of them?"

"They had a full nation over there, now reduced to just this many."

"A full nation!"

"Yes. They must've taken root over there a long time ago, much to the disdain of the people who lived there, at least until recently."

"And the explosion?" he asks tentatively.

"The owners of that world arriving shortly after and finishing the job…by dropping an antimatter device on their heads."

Now both Kailen and the Captain turned aghast at the depiction. Kailen wheezes and stumbles back a step.

"Great cu'Nar! Antimatter!" he shouts. "Whose tail did they crinkle up?! That's a thousand times worse than an atomic! How in all the nether-space did you survive that?"

"I met with them, along with Relissa and Haran. We all hid under a kind of shield bubble that seemed literally impenetrable. It was a conjuration of magic, which these people are much more advanced in than those orcs could ever dream of, and even more so than some of our science. They seem to study this like we do science. Although he said, from our understanding of tech, his society might appear as Industrial Age, but the inclusion of magic changes things. It's a completely different tech ladder and it takes on whatever path you want, depending on the need."

"Fascinating, a society that actually knows how to use it on an official level. Father would surely find this interesting. This was one of his study topics…you know, back on Ruuki uy'Daan."

"I lost my horns so many times out there," she chuckles. "For instance, that shield… I touched it, and it represented a solid frictionless surface that withstood the blast effect, the radiation, the heat…everything. The whole valley was incinerated, but our little circle was neat and clean."

"Unbelievable…and now I understand what you mean by being locked away. Yeah, this would do it."

"But it doesn't stop there."

"Oh no…there's more?"

"Well, there's that second disturbance I heard you speaking about in here," she smirks.

Kailen studies her. She seemed suddenly different. Her mood appeared to have lifted, like she was now enjoying this little game.

"Second disturbance..." he intones warily. "Kaliya, are you actually serious with any of this, or are you just making up a story?"

"You did see one, didn't you? I heard you speak of it just now."

"Well, yes..."

"Kailen, he's here...the Divine Justice, one divided by two. And in his hands, he blasted the place to all the nether-space, and then followed with rebuilding Creation, as he calls it, by rejuvenating the burnt remains back to full life. That place is filled with lush grasslands and wooded glens by now. You should see it, it's wonderful."

Kailen was gaping at her in disbelief, along with the Captain.

"In fact," she continues. "Haran even went on to suggest the prophecy was detailing a sequence of events as they would occur. He arrived in a circle of light...a portal. He explained to us who he was, and by relation to a society of godlike beings, his Father held the role of law and justice. Then he blasted the place and reassembled it again. The coincidence seems a little too convenient to be accidental."

"Yes, it does. Wow. And um, I suppose I should ask how this relates to the Council, although I can probably guess by now."

"Yeah, I carry a political message from him for a meeting."

"You...him...to them? But..." he pants. "Wait, we need to approach this more rationally. Who is he, where does he come from, what relation does he have to anything, and so on, that you can make all these crazy statements."

"All right, but Kailen, I need you and the Captain to promise me something...please. Just give me this one little thing. He has his own need for security in this world, because he doesn't want everyone and their uncle to know about it yet."

"Um, all right, I suppose this is fair if we say he's at war with someone. But I would like to know the reasoning behind it, if only to realize the security demands in play here."

"Right, I understand. But this runs deep, so get ready for it."

Kaliya takes a deep breath as she tries to collect her thoughts.

"His name is Lord Thaelyn, and his wife is Lady Aerlie. They are the King and Queen of another world, which they call Tae'Eladar. This world is apparently in yet another universe, where they once had a population of orcs from an old migration effort…thousands of years ago…and having troubles with them ever since."

"That doesn't sound good."

"Thousands…of years…ago…" she emphasizes.

"Um, all right, so how do you mean this?"

"From places unknown, and by means unknown, but it likely required outside help…by someone who might hold the index for it."

"Uh oh."

"As for the troubles…for the orcs, maybe. Up until recently, they managed to contain them, but those orcs never once made nice with anyone, unlike ours on Ruuki uy'Daan. But Kailen, this also suggests a connection as to how they arrived there in the first place."

"I'm not sure I'm going to like this, because if they had outside help…"

"Sir," the Captain offers. "This conflicts with our own timing."

"It does."

"Then," Kaliya continues. "Something like several decades ago, there was an uprising, probably caused by a new invasion from here," she points figuratively at the ground, "stirring things up and causing his orcs to do things that were really nasty. This was the final knock on the horns for them. He went to war to literally commit genocide on their full population, having had his limit of…" she chuckles briefly, "…limitless divine patience. Wow, that must've really yanked the tail."

"Limitless…divine…patience…" Kailen muses somberly.

"He's related to a society of beings we could literally call gods, Kailen. Beings of such supremely high evolutionary status that it would dwarf everything else, including us."

"Wow! Such things actually do exist?"

"Apparently so, but our idea of evolution wouldn't extend far enough to cover it. And so, here we are with the term Divine Justice, as like I said, his Father was one of them with a professional role of law and justice."

"And this is where we get that term in the Prophecy."

"Likely so, although the relationship is still a little shaky as to how it relates for the part of one divided by two, unless you speak of both of them sharing the same divine father...in spirit, at least, not biological," she grins.

"Uh huh...well, I don't know how to respond to that, so I'll just take your word for it. Maybe we can investigate more on this later."

"Those orcs were refugees trying to escape, but he found their portal leading back here, so he followed. This discovery also led to the disturbing revelation that these orcs, who are supposed to be very poor in their magical skills, are apparently able to open portals, which is regarded as an advanced magical skill. So, he is rather upset over how they may have learned. Furthermore, they could use this in a weaponized form to launch new attacks back on his world. So, he has to continue his war to ensure his world's security, even here, and regardless of any of us."

"I see, and this makes sense. And so, here we have his security issue, I guess, that he doesn't want anyone to know he's here for maybe a tactical advantage?"

"Right, but I'm still not done."

"Sir," the Captain interjects. "The explosion? Cu'Nar's pity, if he's hoping for a quiet entrance, I don't think he succeeded."

"Captain," Kaliya offers. "We already know this. But if he keeps a low profile from this moment, and does not give off any overt indication of what else he's doing out there, maybe we can delay any immediate repercussions. He'll use stealth for now until he can make some progress on all of his fronts. Maybe it could also serve as a deterrence if anyone saw it."

"Well, all right, if he thinks he can do this."

"But now, we get to the hard part. Between the three of us out there, we explained the situation here on this world. We also came to a few conclusions along the way. He's smart, real smart. But he's also angry for what he sees here."

"And what does this mean for all of us, or anyone else?" Kailen wonders.

"He's largely angry for the mess we're all in, and who's behind it. He'll make friends with us, the Night Elves, and the humans, as best he can. He says those Flame Elves, which according to Relissa were once called High Elves, are supposed to be a very noble race. He has more of them on his world. In fact, everyone here is supposed to be from Tae'Eladar…old migrants from some forgotten expedition."

"Really! I sometimes wondered about that, how you had such different races all in one place."

"Yeah, so here's your answer to that. Some of them gathered over there as part of this migration process, and apparently came over here later. But they were clearly corrupted at some point, and this is regarded as a severe insult to elven society. So, he needs to correct this somehow."

"He does? Well, all right, but how?"

"I don't know how yet, but Sargeras, if he's the one responsible, is in trouble for it."

"Uh oh… Did you explain who Sargeras is?"

"Oh yes…" she whistles emphatically. "And here is the big one, Kailen. Hold on to your horns, or they'll go shooting halfway across the plains. He knows who Sargeras is, at least in the context of his society and its origins. And those origins are the same universe he came from, and to which we seem to be aiming at with this last incursion."

Kailen gasped with his eyes bulging, along with the Captain. They glanced at each other briskly as Kaliya continued.

"His society is a dead race of gods the current gods killed at one time. Sargeras, therefore, is a refugee on the run, and likely with spies in this world watching over us, possibly also oppressing us into our respective holes."

"Oppressing!" he winces.

"Yeah. Four centuries, Kailen, they clean out this world and stop with the last few cities. And no one has seen any serious action since. This is now described as a purging effort, followed by a maintenance effort to keep things under control. And we're just toys along the way. This could explain why we were pushed along but never killed outright, even here."

"Kaliya, suddenly I'm getting very angry. This monster would do such things?"

"His whole race did it. They were known to play with lesser beings as entertainment, thus the reason these others, called the Estelar, destroyed them. They were just as angry. And now we have those orcs, which are clearly owned by him, and likely for a long time, if they found their way during that old migration. They're just one more piece of the puzzle."

"Even before Ruuki uy'Daan?" he screeches.

"Thousands of years, he says. That speaks to me. The orcs that recently invaded his world shouldn't even know of his world, to say nothing of having portal access to it…unless they had help. And that help has to be someone or something with personal knowledge. This would also reflect on this world, for that matter."

"In all the nether-space… Then how do we explain our time on Ruuki uy'Daan?"

"I might suggest more maintenance, if they were playing nice with us initially. They never once played this way on his world, so ours had to be a show."

"And the attack?"

"It looks like someone is playing some elaborate games on this world. We're just one piece of it. The sabotage brought us here, probably for a reason, and that being the rest of it is already here. But here is another security catch. Thaelyn is a being called a Celestial, a child of those gods. And these people are seriously iron-horned to get the job done," she rolls her eyes. "He's a powerful being, but he looks generally the same as a human…mostly. On the outside, if you don't know who or what he is, you might not realize it. And he likes to keep it this way as his real tactical advantage. So, if Sargeras has spies here, we don't want them to know, and at this point, I'm under instruction to keep as much of this quiet as possible, to reduce the chances of this falling into the wrong ears."

"Even amongst us?"

"With respect, we can't really know who's walking around at any given moment, and we already know those elves use invisibility magic."

"Oh great!" he huffs. "Kaliya, you have a solid point there. But how about the Council?"

"Only what's needed to gain their support, like for a political union."

"And the prophecy?"

"I've been thinking about this. I don't want to be the one trying to tell anyone, especially them, that I found something as mythical as this. My reputation just isn't good enough," she hangs her head.

"Kaliya, please… I know how you feel, but if you really did find something, we could certainly use the morale boost around here."

"I know," she sighs. "And the events I saw out there sure do look good for it. So, here's what I'm thinking. Without saying it is or is not, we can hint at it, giving our report of what I saw out there, which might offer a clue to a potential relationship. This might butter things up a little."

"All right, got it…that's not a bad idea."

"But Kailen, I think I learned something else out there, and this will blow your next set of horns off."

"Oh no, another one?"

"Yeah, the riddle of Metaphysics… I think I finally figured it out, and it's absolutely amazing!" she croons. "These people are our demonstration. The orcs were amateurs by comparison. These people can not only do magic, but they can also build technology out of it, like a magical version of a conveyor, and at only Industrial Age of the physical sciences!"

"Really! But what kind of power source do they use for it? We need something on the scale of a fusion reactor to make that work."

"I know. This one is personal size, like for an individual to use. I saw them build one in that camp they established out there using what I'm guessing to be a power supply I could carry in my arms. It's probably just enough for the electronics. The real power source is something we don't even have a definition for, all because we were born in a universe that is apparently absent of it. But here…" she emphasizes by pointing at the ground. "This is where the good stuff is. He calls it the Dynamistic Flows, and it's a type of extradimensional energy these gods use as a support layer."

"Extradimensional…" the Captain muses. "That would make things hard on our science labs, I think."

"Yeah! Especially seeing how we like to poke fun at the term nether-space. And other beings, maybe like us, or those orcs, can also use it, if they study it hard enough. And it works on the power of the mind, not empirical numbers. Perception, Kailen…you simply think of something and poof, here it is. Therefore, the riddle of Metaphysics… The mind can alter the substance of reality by applying its own definition to remake existence."

"Cu'Nar help us, Kaliya," Kailen moans. "Do you realize what this actually says?"

"Yeah, godlike powers of creation…therefore these gods. And this is what they call magic. That antimatter device was a conjuration, not a physical object. That shield, and even that storm was conjured up simply because somebody wanted it. If I could learn even a tiny piece of this, it could open a whole new study department for us."

"But would he actually teach you, or any of us?"

"He has schools and universities back home doing this for his whole society…all of them. Think of it, Kailen, a full society of people using magic and inventing new ways to apply it. It boggles the mind. They use portals as a mass transit system. They use magic in virtually every aspect of life, from arts and crafts to industry. And they apparently move forward much faster than we do. He said he expected to be Space Age in only a couple of centuries."

"Centuries?!" he shrieks.

"Yeah, we apparently move extremely slowly, probably due to our ridiculously long lifespans holding us back, which he and his wife think are strange to say the least. And they're both immortal beings."

"Great cu'Nar, what else can they throw at us."

"I don't know, Kailen, but there is one other thing which struck me about the conversation regarding our situation here."

"Oh please, no more…"

"During our meeting, we were talking about the cu'Nar and their original warning about Sargeras. Now, here we are. Kailen, those cu'Nar told us to run away because he was bad, right?"

"Yeah…"

"And they used that famous word on us, which we interpreted as the word Titan, right?"

"Yeah…" he raises his brow in expectation.

"Well, these people say the cu'Nar, by the description I gave, are likely some form of ancient elemental race of energy beings. They even gave a name for them…Positive Primes. This means they know who they are, or at least what form of life they represent."

"Uh huh…and so far, this sounds a little suspicious, I think. This, like all the rest, seems to carry some internal knowledge."

"Right, and that word, Titan… He was asking about Sargeras, and when I used that on him, he hit me so hard with this thunderous divine voice, it blasted my horns off so badly, I don't know if I'll ever grow any back again," she chuckles. "That word holds special meaning, and not simply to the cu'Nar. It's an ancient term used by those beings who once existed back in the day, and who knew these others called Primordials."

"Primordials?"

"Sargeras and his kind… So, if we say the cu'Nar came to us and told us to run, where did they come from? Because according to Thaelyn and Aerlie, beings of this sort are not known to leave their home realms to interact with beings like us. Why are they doing it? And then to see us here, which is essentially back at the starting point where Sargeras and his kind had their final showdown with the Estelar."

"Oh dear…"

✦✦✦✦✦

Haran realized in an instant when the enchantment expired, as he nearly toppled over from a sudden crash of weariness. He had taken up space under a tree in a small park across the plaza from the academy, waiting for the spell to fade so he could enter the academy building without calling any undue attention to himself. He would have a hard enough time trying to give his report, and he didn't need to have a score of his uppers dragging him off into a room to study the strange enchantment he was under.

He now makes his way across the plaza and passes through the entryway into the large study hall of the academy. His thoughts were deeply immersed in how he would present his report, knowing that the Dean would likely balk at most of it, and further ridicule him for what was left. Several students around the hall take casual notice of him as he enters through the doors. Among them was a fair-skinned young woman with long shimmering blonde hair and pleasant features.

"Haran!" she calls out in an acceptably hushed manner, so as not to cause a disturbance.

Still lost in his contemplation, Haran barely notices the young woman's approach, at least until she wraps herself around him.

"Haran, I was so worried," she whispers warmly. "We heard some reports of a huge cloud and a terrible storm over the mountains to the south. I was afraid something dreadful came into the valley. I'm so glad to see you alive and well."

Haran stops his movement as she embraces him. Impulsively, he places his arms around her as his gaze slowly focuses on her face.

"Tristeen, my dearest," he smiles softly. "I'm sorry I didn't see you at first, but I'm severely troubled at the moment. I need to file my report with the Dean, and you know how that usually goes."

"Oh, Haran, why do you go out on these missions, anyway? The only outcome is more intimidation by that man."

"You may be right, but it's the only occupation they allow me. I've submitted requests for other duties, something that doesn't involve so much risk out in the field, but there are times when I think the Dean actually wants me to fall prey to something…he seems to hate me so."

"Surely, you can't believe he would want you dead. I can't imagine he would do that to any student, certainly not by willful intent."

"Tristeen, he doesn't like me, this we all know. You have never been on the receiving end of his ire, maybe due to your noble blood. I, on the other hand, am little more than fodder for his aggressions. But anyway, I need to file this report, and it deeply concerns me. I'm not quite sure how to present it, but I'm fairly sure how it will turn out. Still, it needs to be done. I have important information, and it needs to go straight to the top."

"Is there anything I can do for you?"

"I can't really see any way for you to help. It's a report, after all, on what I saw out there. But the information I hold is critical in this war effort."

"All right, I'll accompany you to his office, but I'll stay outside if you wish it."

Haran nods before continuing through the hall. He passes through a set of doors, turns down a corridor and up a flight of stairs, then down another corridor to the end. He arrives at the door leading to the office of Dean Wizard Malorn, chief administrator of the Academy. Tristeen moves off to the side as Haran opens the door.

As he enters the room, a man in an ornate robe sitting behind a desk speaks out in a distantly condescending voice.

"Haran! You are alive. How...convenient..."

"I have returned from the Badlands, Dean, from the mission you ordered," he replies, knowing the response is superfluous.

"Indeed, and a day late... You should have been back here yesterday, last eve at the latest. Our forward watchmen observed a most disturbing affair sighted over the mountains to the south. I thought I would have to send a replacement to discover what it was. I hope that will not be necessary, hmm?"

"I apologize for the delay but that disturbance, among other things, sort of delayed my return. However, I have everything you need. It's a lot to go over, though, if you will just..."

"Haran!" he interrupts. "Personally, I cannot imagine how you could have anything at all based on the stories I've heard about that disturbance. But I suppose, if you are standing here now, it could not have been nearly as bad as what those guards were letting on, not that I would expect them to know how to report on such a thing to begin with."

"Right, and I'm sure you would know best…unless you were there to see it personally."

"Oh?" he retorts brashly. "And I suppose you can correct for this unfortunate shortfall?"

"Well, I was out there personally, by your request. Therefore, if you will give me enough time to actually report on anything…"

"Haran, I do not care for the local weather in that valley," he declares angrily. "I gave you instructions to find orcs, no more. Well? Did you find any, or not?"

"Technically, yes," he responds curtly.

"Really! Well, technically, your duty is fulfilled. You are dismissed."

"Wow, you certainly seem concerned for the safety of the city. Dean, the report does not end there. Perhaps you would like to know how many there were or what they were doing?"

"Ah, but forgive me," he feigns interest. "I forgot to consider whether or not they were enjoying an afternoon cup of tea. All right, let me ask you this. Are they coming this way?"

"No, at present they are all dead."

The Dean was cut short in his response as he studied Haran for his answer. He frowns deeply and leans forward in his chair.

"Dead… This is interesting. Yes, perhaps I actually should inquire on this. What else did you see out there, and why are they dead…or do you even have an answer for that?"

"I suppose you could associate this with those unfortunate guards who do not know how to report on the weather."

"Haran, do mind yourself in here," he intones sternly.

"Dean, unless you were physically present, I might ask the same of you. You could surely offer a little more respect to those who have their own jobs to fulfill, and not simply demean them as lessers who barely know how to stand upright."

"All right, your argument is duly noted. Then, what is the remainder of your report?"

"Firstly, we found a large gathering settled in the old river valley, about midway into the Badlands. We estimated perhaps as many as a quarter million, but…"

"A quarter million!" the Dean shrieks. "Are you sure? How could they possibly have amassed that many in one place?"

The Dean panned his focus around his desk, then briefly orienting to gaze out the window behind him before continuing.

"But you said they were all dead?" he asks urgently.

"Yes, due to that disturbance…"

"How could a…disturbance…kill a quarter million orcs, hmm?"

"It was a big disturbance," he smiles and shrugs. "It was a kind of bomb launched by the people those orcs offended on another world where these refugees were running from a rather powerful army."

The Dean's expression suddenly drained from rage to shock.

"An army from another world?!"

"Yeah… Would you now like to hear my report, or simply send me away while that army takes over the place?"

"Um…perhaps I should actually hear the rest of it. This sounds like something that might need to go up to the Governor."

"Yes, those were my thoughts as well, because the leader of that other world is asking for a political meeting."

"Why?"

"Well, for one thing, we live here. Therefore, we represent a local authority. Next is he intends to continue his fight, and we, as the local authority, might have something to say about it. And I figure it probably has to do with joining together to fight that very same war out there. We are at war, aren't we? Word on the street tends to suggest this."

"Haran, you are treading on delicate ground here! What else do we have on this…army?"

"Delicate ground? We're boxed inside these walls for a reason, Dean. And the word 'war' is plastered all over that reason."

"Very well! Continue with the rest of it."

"Right. He is the King of a world called Tae'Eladar. He initially arrived through a portal, together with his queen and a small contingent of troops, like an advance guard. They have been at war with the orcs of their world, apparently a branch-off from ours, for some time, and finally beat them back, only to discover the orcs using portals to escape back into our world. He followed to continue his war against them."

"Portals! And a new army from another world…as if we needed such an intruder in our midst."

"He is not hostile towards us, and in fact I had an opportunity to speak with him at length, along with my comrades from the Night Elves and the Daanen-Aryku. He offers his aid against the orcs and perhaps more if we would be willing to accept it. Personally, I think it would be a very valuable offer to consider."

"Haran, do not strain yourself with thinking. This is what I am here to do. But how could a simple man, his woman and, as you say, a small contingent of troops, dispatch an orcish army the size of a quarter million, hmm? Or perhaps you imagined the whole thing by eating some of that weed they grow out there?"

"Oh yes, I…imagined…a disturbance so big, it could be seen all the way up here to the city. First, he is an immensely powerful mage and warrior. That disturbance was a magical conjuration the likes of which completely overwhelmed me."

"Oh, did it now? That doesn't sound too difficult."

"Yes, you are absolutely right, for the lessons they give here in the Academy. Dean, if you could see it from up here, I think that speaks for itself. It was no simple storm, and neither was it a flicker of a candle flame, as we teach in here. And it wasn't the only thing he did down there. In the event the guards reported more than one disturbance, the second one was the complete restoration of the land, after the explosion scorched the place, turning it into a lush valley with grasslands and groves of trees sprouting up."

A moment passes, followed by a sudden eruption of laughter from the Dean. The response forces Haran to realize how his report was progressing. He expected the Dean to react in such a way, but to hear it outright started his blood to boil.

"Haran, there are times when I wonder why I keep you at my

side, but on that rare occasion you do bring up a most amusing bard's tale. Very well, man, I will take your report and file it with all the others, in that little bucket under my desk. You are dismissed."

"I will not!" Haran shouts, much to the Dean's surprise.

Haran steps up to the desk, his temperature now rising. For the first time in his life, he felt the power to stand up for himself against this man. Perhaps it was because he knew he was right, and this report needed to be heard and accepted as fact. Or perhaps he knew that even if his life here collapsed, there might still be hope in the form of an alternate life waiting for him elsewhere. Either way, he was fed up with this treatment.

"For years, I have endured your ridicule and humiliatory regard! I spent the greater part of my days in this hole listening to you and your peers. I struggled and slaved in the libraries and labs, according to my instructors, trying to learn my craft, and all you do is harass me. I was out there and witnessed something that goes far beyond anything we teach in this academy, and certainly more than anything you would ever know about, brought about by a man of such power and nobility that you look like a street urchin by compare. So, if you don't believe what I have to report, then take that flabby backside of yours, walk out there and look at it!"

Haran's face was flushing as he finished.

Tristeen waited outside the door and out of view. She turned at the outburst, aghast that Haran could pronounce himself so boldly at the Dean, one of the most powerful men in the city's directorial authority.

The Dean was in shock. He had never heard such an upsurge, not from any of his students or apprentices, and not even from any of the instructors.

Haran continues, "If you were to send someone else out there, he'll just bring back the same story, but without the explanation of how it happened. And then what, you toss it out with the rest? This man is a KING, and in possession of extraordinary power. If I were the one running this establishment, I'd go out there and make peace with him as fast as my feet could carry me! He's got an army arriving in that valley, and they're equipped with mithril and adamantium!"

"What?!" the Dean shouts as he jumps out of his chair. "Mithril? And adamantium! How would you even know what adamantium is?"

"Well, I suppose if it's anything like the stories go, this stuff might fit the bill. But regardless of that, they use mithril in their swords and shields, and I'm fairly sure of this because I got a good close-up look at it. And it's the same bloody stuff as in your private cabinet over there," he glances off to the side of the room at a tall cupboard. "And there is an army numbering in the thousands wielding the stuff, with more back home. This tells me that even if we might say we don't have it here, they most certainly have it on their world, and they use it in great abundance! That in itself makes them dangerous, at the very least, to anyone who might get in their way, be it orc, or something else."

"And you say they came in and took over the Badlands valley?"

"Yes, and he wants to meet to arrange a treaty on how to fight this war along with the rest of us, so that we might finally be rid of those creeps. As for me, I think this would be a grand idea, despite the fact you like to be the one doing all the thinking. I'm tired of being locked behind these walls, along with the Guard and everyone else. And for this, we should tell the Guard, as well as the Governor."

◆

Relissa was reclining in a gazebo in a small square out in front of the temple when it hit. At first, she simply thought it was fatigue from loss of sleep, but when she found herself rolling off the bench, she began to remember she was under the enchantment and suspected it may have finally passed from her.

She had been contemplating who to speak to first. There were three individuals on her mind that she wanted to report to. First was her superior in the Guild of Wardens about her scouting mission. She was not at all eager to see him with a story like hers to tell.

She also wished to speak with her father and tell him the things she learned about the Tel'Quessir. She suspected he might be excited to hear such news, but getting his attention on these matters might be difficult, as she never showed any interest in the past, and he stopped trying to teach her decades ago.

So, it was down to her mother, the Matron Priestess in the temple just across the way from her. Maybe she could start there.

The square where Relissa had been sitting was once part of a shrine where the old Tree of Life used to stand. This tree was an integral part of the lives of her people. Her mother, when she was much younger, was a priestess caretaker attending to it. That experience, though it was centuries ago by now, should be enough to help Relissa get noticed. She was hoping that being touched by the dryad spirit the day before might get her mother's attention, and with her help, she could accomplish her other tasks.

Relissa got up and started walking over to the temple. It was not a place she visited often, not even to see her mother. The structure was imposing, not so much for its physical stature, but for its meaning. It was one of the few reminders of their old culture, from before the war. Inside were sculptures and paintings left behind by the city's early citizens depicting tales of splendor and better days. Songs passed down through the generations could still be heard echoing in the halls and galleries.

As she entered through the doors, she was greeted by one of the younger priests.

"Greetings, Relissa. Have you come to give praise, or is there some other service you desire?"

"I'm here to see my Mum, Priest Daelis. Where is she?"

"Matron Amariyn is in her study. I believe she will be pleased to see you. We have heard of strange sightings going about this previous day and feared for your well-being."

"I'm sure you did. That bit could probably be seen from a long way off. But I'm fine, Daelis, don't worry about that. I need to speak with my Mum, though, about something very important. Will you excuse me?"

"Of course, Relissa. May the blessings of the Seldarine be upon you."

Relissa continues further in the direction of a series of parlors near the rear of the temple. One of these was where her mother spent many hours studying the ancient tomes and scrolls passed down and rewritten over time to keep a record of the original settlers and their religious worship. The purpose of this during Relissa's lifetime was easily arguable, as she didn't feel the same bond as the rest of her kin. But after her encounter with the dryad spirit, she had a different opinion, and now was the time to test it.

As she entered the study, she found her mother sitting in a large chair in a corner near a table and next to a window, with a small lamp hanging over her. Her mother was an elegant woman in a flowing pale green robe with silver embroidery across its length. She appeared deeply immersed in a book she was reading.

"Mum?" Relissa calls softly. "Can I speak to you for a moment?"

The woman looks up from her book at the figure of her daughter coming in the door.

"Relissa, my child," she answers calmly. "How nice of you to visit. What brings you in here? You hardly ever come to visit me in the temple."

"I know, Mum. I just returned from my mission in the Badlands and need to file my report, but I wanted to see you first. I need your help."

"What possible help could I provide you?" the Matron suggests, her tone becoming flat and indifferent. "You're the scout. It's your duty, not mine, to report to the Guild. You chose this profession. I tried to teach you to admire the bond of our people and all you wanted was to run through the land chasing your dreams."

"Please, Mum, not this time. Besides, you know full well that we need scouts every bit as much as the rest."

"Very well," she relents. "I will admit to this much. But I had higher hopes for my daughter."

"Aye, maybe so. But aside from that, I really need you. It's important and it's special. Something has happened."

"Oh?" the Matron responds as she gets up and walks over to a desk to set the book down.

"Aye, and I don't want to argue with you today. So, can you just give me your ear for a wee bit and be my mum again, not my judge and jury?"

Amariyn glared at Relissa for a long moment. Clearly the girl was disturbed about something, and she seemed to be emitting an unusual glow around her. It was not a visible aura, but her posture and the look on her face was different.

"Relissa, are you well? I heard about something that was sighted out there. I really am happy to see you again, as it worried me for where you were and if it might affect you."

"Aye, that's a fine one. We had a bit of excitement out there. You can be sure of that much."

"Excitement. Is that what you call it?" she smiles delicately.

"Well, as compared to just running around looking at stuff, I suppose so."

"All right, so what is it you want to talk about?"

"Well, first, maybe I need to apologize. I know I've been hard on you, but you know the story, so there's probably no point in going over it again."

"Yes," she sighs reluctantly. "I suppose I have to admit, at least from my side, I hold my own injuries, and mine go much further back. But Relissa, your defiance to accept our traditions is painful in its own way. You know what it means to me, as well as your father, to keep the memories alive."

"Aye, Mum, I do. I'll say it again, blame it on the war, especially as it doesn't ever let up, even though it doesn't make a lot of sense why it seems to be holding back like it is."

"Holding back?"

"Aye! I mean, four hundred years and they burn everything in sight. Why not finish it? We couldn't be that hard, not after what they did to the rest of world out there."

"Um..."

"But anyway," she continues unabated. "I'll try a little harder from this point. I had a little, um…thing that happened to me out there that changed a few bits for me."

"Oh? What sort of…thing?" she muses curiously.

"It has to do with that wee bit you probably heard about over the mountains," she smiles cutely.

Amariyn cocks her head and frowns at the suggestion, and further at Relissa's dismissive behavior relating to it.

"That…bit…was said to be rather frightening. Did you see it? What was it?"

"Oh, I saw it, bright as day, and then some. But Mum, I need to report this to the Enforcer, so maybe rather than repeating myself a bunch of times, you could join me. I have a few things you'll need to hear."

"But Relissa, if this relates to your scouting run, what purpose does it hold for someone like me to listen to it? I don't go out there."

"I know, and that's the other thing. You spend all day shut inside this room with your nose in a book. Do you even remember what it's like to go outside and smell the flowers?"

"I…well…" she sighs again. "It's been a long time, I'll admit, and I lost that habit a while ago."

"Well, then maybe it's time to stretch those legs of yours and go for a little walk with me."

"Relissa, is all this just to convince me to go for a walk outside, or do you have some secret motive here?"

Relissa steps in closer to her mother at the desk. She gazes longingly into the elder woman's face. She could feel her emotions rushing up.

"Mum, I need a hug to let me know everything's alright between us. I'm sorry for hurting you and Dah. This war can really wear on a person, you know? And until recently, I was fully certain I would die in it, so I just figured, what's the point of it all."

"I know, Relissa, and I can't blame you for this, it's been going on for so long."

Amariyn steps around the desk to cradle her daughter. This would account as the first time they shared a tender moment in many years. But as the woman took Relissa in her arms for the gentle embrace, she began to take notice of that strange aura again. She pulled back slightly for a better look, gazing into the girl's face.

"Relissa, are you sure you're alright? I sense something strange here. Something I don't quite, um..."

"You feel it, don't you?" she curls a quirky grin. "I knew you would. You have the Sight."

"Sight?"

"Well, you're a priestess, ay? That ought to mean something. But now, we need Dah."

"Huh?"

Relissa grabs her mother's hand and starts dragging the elder woman out the door. Together they rush out of the temple and back into the square, then across to a lane leading northward. Amariyn found herself being pulled along impulsively.

"Relissa, what exactly are you doing?" she groans. "I'm not as young as I used to be."

They hurried past shops and homes towards the Council district, an area of the city consisting of manor homes used by the Council members and their families, as well as the meeting hall where the Elven High Council gathers periodically to debate the affairs of the city. Also located in this area was a large library used by the scholars and sages to conduct research and to study and record the traditions and history of the elven society. A short distance down another lane, behind the Council building, was the hall of the Guild of Wardens, where Relissa would need to file her report.

They approached the library where her father usually spent most of his time as a historian. On passing through the door, Relissa quickly finds an attendant to help her locate her father. She then wends her way through to a large room on one side. The room, like so many others, is decorated with many bookshelves, some lining the walls, and others extending into the room. Each shelf is filled with a wide variety of historical volumes and artifacts.

Amariyn keeps close behind, her curiosity growing with each

step of her daughter's unusual insistence to involve her audience, as well as that of her father.

As they enter the room, Amariyn, who is much less accustomed to such a quick trot, finds a soft chair and collapses into it. On seeing this, Relissa steps over to give her mother a gentle peck on the cheek before turning to find her father. Amariyn's face goes from surprise to a cautious smile. It's been many years since she last received a kiss from her daughter.

"Dah?" Relissa calls into the room.

"Relissa? Is that you?" ushers a voice from behind one of the bookcases on the far end of the room.

Relissa follows the sound and finds her father in one of the alcoves perusing the shelves of a nearby bookcase.

"Dah, I need to talk to you for a moment, please. It's important."

"Yes, Relissa, I'm sure it is. But as you can see, I'm very busy with my studies. All this so-called paper fuzz, as you say. I'm sure you wouldn't be at all interested in that, now would you?"

"Oh grand, are we doing that again," she mutters. "Look, Dah, this is serious. I'm sorry for all the other times, and I promise I won't call it paper fuzz anymore."

He looks over his shoulder briefly at the young girl standing behind him, checking to make sure it really was his daughter who was speaking to him. When he was satisfied that it was not, in fact, an imposter, he turned back to the shelves to continue his search.

"Very well, Relissa, I'm game, I suppose. What are you up to?"

Relissa struggles to hold back her anxiety, waiting for the right moment and hoping she can make an appropriate impression to attract his attention. This wouldn't be the same as with her mother. Her father was an intellectual, not a holy man with a sense of touch to feel her new energy.

"Maybe if I ask what you're looking for?"

"All right, a thought flashed through me recently about the first arrivals here. This followed with the old stories about the ancient travelers and how they moved about from one world to another."

"Really! That's actually kind of interesting."

"It is?" he turns to study her again, unsure if she was serious or simply trying to humor him.

"Aye, what is it about how they moved around that gets to you?"

"Well, to be honest, it involved the magical conduits they used, which were said to be very powerful. Then we had that disturbance over the mountains…did you happen to see that?"

"Oh, you bet I did. I got a real good look at it."

"Indeed, well this caused me to wonder about those energies again, although I suspect this one has a much different origin."

"Aye, I don't think we're talking about new arrivals in that one. Not with the explosion I saw. It wiped away everything that stood upright, that one."

"An explosion! Are you alright?"

"Oh, I'm fine, don't you worry about that. I can't say as much about all those orcs out there though…" she whistles emphatically.

"Orcs! But just a moment, did they do something to cause that explosion?"

"Nah, they're not bright enough to do anything on a scale that big. They're just orcs, you know."

"Yes, I suppose, but this still doesn't answer the larger question, unless we're speaking of those horrible Suuden-Aryku again."

"Maybe…" she considers. "So, you're looking up the stories about the old travelers again? This is from the time of the Flowering, ay?"

"Yes, this goes way back to those early days. I recall once a story of an ancient artifact, though I'll admit our records don't seem to carry quite as much detail on it. It's a shame, really. I wish we knew more about how it worked."

"The Staff of Ethers, right…" she muses conspicuously.

"The Staff of Ethers?" he retorts uncertainly. "But…"

"That's what it's called, isn't it?"

"Well, um… I think I recall a mention, but it's very obscure."

"Right, but that name sort of stood out once when I heard it."

"Really! I'm impressed, actually."

"Anyway, if we had one of those, then maybe we could find a way to move around a little like those orcs are doing. You know they've been seen to use portals, right?"

"Yes, and good gracious, if only we could rediscover how those work."

"Oh, don't I know it. It would sure make my scouting runs a whole lot easier!"

He turns once again to study the figure standing next to him. He never experienced so much enthusiasm in her before this.

"Relissa, have you really taken so much of an interest in all this? I'm very pleased, of course, but this is rather unexpected."

"Aye, I know, and I've been bad for a long time, too. I know a lot of people around here tend to stick their noses up at me for it, which isn't nice."

"Well, it's not precisely that they dislike you, Relissa. Just that, well…"

"I know, Dah, and I'm sorry for that. It's all because of this war getting on my nerves."

"I understood that a long time ago, Relissa, but unfortunately, you would never let go of it."

"It's not simply to let go of it, it's all around us. It doesn't let go of us!"

"Yes, this is true as well."

"Especially if you look at it like they dusted the whole rest of the world, right up to our doors, and then stopped, simply to hold us in place."

"Um, well, I suppose, if you look at it a certain way, it might appear as such."

"Same as with Rolsklinde, by the way."

"Um…" he frowns and turns more fully at her for the implication. "Is there something you are trying to suggest here, Relissa?"

"Well, simply put, if they wanted us dead, after four centuries, don't you think they could've finished it by now? They did everything else out there. Why not us? But they didn't."

"Oh dear…but you're right. This would suggest something, actually."

"And what bugs me the most is no one was ever paying attention to this. We just kept on saying we're at war, and that's it. We don't even pair up to fight anything. We all just sit here."

"Um…pair up?"

"Yeah. Dah, what do you do if you go to war? What do you do if everyone was at war? Do you just sit in one place and wait for someone else to fight it, or do you join with all the other peeps out there and actually fight?"

"Um, all right, I think I see your point, as well as a failing. No one ever joined forces to drive them back, is that it? Although I have to wonder if it might actually achieve anything, for all their numbers."

"Maybe so, but sitting on a log doesn't do it, either. Anyway, watching that bit out there in the Badlands stirred up a little thing inside of me, and so, now I need to make a few amends."

"Ah, some sort of life-changing experience, perhaps?" he grins softly.

"Oh, buggers, you don't know the half of it," she giggles. "In fact, I even learned a few things along the way."

"Really!" he gazes at her intriguingly. "Although I'm at a loss to imagine what you could learn from a huge explosion…"

"Well, it wasn't the explosion itself, but something on the side."

"Ah, all right, well I suppose I should ask what this was. Because if it was enough to bring you in here like this, I should probably know what happened to my little girl," he smiles.

Relissa beams for her clever maneuvering in the conversation. But this was only the beginning. Now that she had his attention, she had to nail it home. This is where she would put her bonding with the dryad spirit to the test.

"Well, it's about the Flowering. I remember some of our books talk about how the first travelers of the Tel'Quessir migrated from the old Fey world to Sein'amar, right?"

"Yes, they do…um…" he scans the room and points across the way. "In that section over there…"

"Right, and then we have tales of how the different clans made a few dins here and there as they tried settling their borders."

"I wouldn't exactly describe the Crown War as a few dins."

"I know, I'm just teasing a bit," she smiles. "So, let's see…" she clears her throat to make her full presentation. "It was a good many millennia ago, and before the Flowering, when the first of the Tel'Quessir races came to Sein'amar. They were the Syl clan, the Lyc clan, and the Aril clan. The Syl clan, otherwise known in those days as Sylvan, or the Green Elves, was the most successful."

"Very good, so far…"

"The Lyc clan, on the other hand, had a bad time of things, as they went through some kind of transformation. Some think they were infected with something that got twisted by those energies you mentioned."

"Really? Where did you see that?" he scans the room again.

"Oh, I'm sure it's about somewhere," she dismisses the notion casually to continue her presentation. "But because of this, they're not counted as part of the mother race any longer. The Aril also survived, but they suffered badly due to a series of events relating to the Age of Dragons."

"They did?" he emits unexpectedly. "But wait, where did you see that?"

"Well, you know about the Age of Dragons, right?"

"Yes, it is known that there was a group of dragons plaguing the world, and they seemed intent on disrupting our efforts to set down colonies."

"Right, plaguing…that's what some people call it…although I might also ask if anyone ever wondered why they were there, or simply to assume they were plaguing something, rather than there for a reason."

"Um, hmm… I suppose you may have a point, in a certain context."

"But those poor buggers, the Aril, got the worst of it. Some of it was simply for their gift of flight. The dragons might not have appreciated that. But it came to a head during the battle at the Temple of the Protector."

"Huh? What battle? A temple to the Protector?"

"Yeah, the place they were hiding that old staff..."

Relissa was beginning to realize she was now delving into studies that aren't part of their local collection of books, so she needed to hurry before he started arguing.

"But anyway," she resumes. "A second wave came up not long after which included the Ssri, which is our people, and then the Ara, the Teu, and the Alu clans," she pauses to study his face. "It's said that the combined strength of these clans is what really brought the Age of Dragons to its close...or maybe to simply convince them that we're not leaving, as they wanted us to do, so here we are," she smirks.

"Oh! So, they wanted us to leave, but we apparently didn't take the message?"

"This could be the reason they were trying to deny us to set down colonies. They were guarding something we weren't supposed to be invading."

"Um, well, I suppose there is merit in this suggestion, but this also sounds like speculation."

"Maybe, and from where we stand, it might be hard to say. Anyway, this finally gave rise to the Flowering with the establishment of five major civilizations."

"All right, and that part sounds correct, although I'm still wondering about your conclusions for some of these other elements."

"Right, but just hold on a sec... Unfortunately, things didn't stay happy for long as the first of five Crown Wars came about..."

"Stop!" he urges. "Now wait... Five Crown Wars? We only recorded one! What makes you think there were five?"

"Because the other four came sometime after our group left Sein'amar," Relissa replies confidently. "And this is also your answer to that other part. We weren't there to see it."

"Huh?" he blurts. "But how could you possibly know all this?"

"Relissa?" Amariyn calls, having come out of her chair and was now approaching the group. "I have to agree, where did you hear this? What happened to you out there?"

"Amariyn?" the surprised historian gushes. "What are you doing here?"

"Throdeth, something has happened to our daughter. She's glowing. It's like a presence, a spark of some kind, but I don't know what can be causing it."

"Do you remember what I said about that explosion in the valley?" Relissa asks.

"Yes, what about it?"

"There's more to it, but if you want the answers, you need to make a little deal with me."

"Relissa," her father moans. "Is this some kind of game you're playing?"

"Game or no, do you want the answers? Because there's a reason those orcs got blasted to the gods."

"Um…well, all right, if you're going to put it that way…but…"

"I need to report this to the Guild of Wardens," Relissa asserts. "But I want the two of you to be there, because the Council needs to know about it, too. This will change everything for us."

"Change what everything? And how does this relate to those statements of yours?"

"The deal, Dah? Mum? And then you'll know. No one ever cares to listen to me around here, but this time you need to."

The two of them sigh deeply and gaze at each other.

"Throdeth," Amariyn considers. "This might be important. Something did occur out there. We have scouting reports of something big, and likely unnatural. And if she was out there to see it, then to come back with all this, I'd like to know more."

"Yes, Dear. I suppose I cannot argue. But her statements…well, all right, Relissa, let's go. But I hope this is good."

"It will be," she asserts. "I think you'll flip when you hear it, but it'll also be a shocker. Now, let's hurry. I really need to get this off my chest."

Now Relissa leads her parents out of the library and across the plaza to the lane turning around behind the Council building and into another section of the district. There, she finds the main entrance to the guildhall where she'll make her final stop. She was nervous about what might come next, but she reminded herself as she entered the building that she had perhaps the most important news of her life to report.

She works her way to the office where the Enforcer of the Watch presides. He takes notice of her the moment she arrives at the door.

"Ah, Scout Moonshimmer!" he calls out sardonically. "Back so soon after playing with your pets? I don't suppose, during your little outing, you happened to take notice of anything going on in the area of the Badlands, as was your assignment?"

Relissa was still standing in the doorway. She enters fully into the room, followed by her mother and father, neither of whom was pleased by listening through the door at the greeting she received, but who kept silent until they entered. The man instantly stiffens his posture on seeing the two Council members entering, and bows in a show of respect.

"My apologies, Councilman Throdeth, Councilwoman Amariyn, I did not see you there."

"So be it, Enforcer Baeleron," Amariyn accedes. "While I realize Relissa may not be the most esteemed of your recruitments, do kindly try to give her a fair amount of reward for her efforts, even if they do sometimes lead her astray. It might even lead to a form of encouragement to improve herself."

"It's alright, Mum," Relissa submits. "I don't care about it this time, because what I have to say will be more than enough to cover for it."

"Then you have something to report, Relissa?" asks the Enforcer.

"I do, although at the same time, if I may, your attitude at seeing me, if I was in fact out there, and for whatever reports you might have of anything happening, you might try to show a little more concern that I'm not dead."

"Yes," he nods solemnly. "You are actually correct, Relissa, and I will apologize for that. But at the same time, since you are here, and not dead, this might also suggest something else."

"Maybe so. I suppose it's all subjective on what that thing was."

"All right. So, what do you have to say about it?"

"I have something big to give you today. We've been found! And they brought a tree with them!"

"What?! Who! Who found us?" the Enforcer demands, becoming nervously agitated at the prospects. "And what do you mean by a tree? Be more precise, girl! You were out there looking for orcs, not trees!"

"A tree?" Amariyn gasps. "Relissa…you…that glow…"

"Aye, Mum," she admits with a bright smile stretching across her face. "I've been touched. The spirit made me whole again. They're in the valley. You should see it!"

"Relissa," Throdeth announces concernedly. "What do you mean by touched? What spirit?"

"She's talking about a new tree," Amariyn croons. "I felt the glow in her. I barely even remember what it looks like. It's the glow of dawning life."

"Will someone please tell me what's going on here?" shouts the Enforcer. "What about those orcs?!"

"Forget the bleedin' orcs, Enforcer!" Relissa yips excitedly. "They've been blasted to the gods and then some. New people have arrived. The Tel'Quessir, humans, dwarves, they've all come together over there in Sein'amar, and in fact the whole world…which is more than anything we ever did."

"What do you mean, more than what we did?"

"Well, if we say they brought themselves into one big nation, what did we ever do on this side. All we ever did was divide ourselves into independent bodies so we could start wars with each other."

"Oh… That… Um…"

"And we can blame this attitude all the way back to that old Crown War, and whatever came after, until those buggers finally got it in their heads to do it. Now, they're all joined under a new ruler, a King named Thaelyn, and his Queen, Aerlie. They united the world, after all this time, and now found their way here, all thanks to those orcs making trouble for them."

"From Sein'amar…?" he wheezes.

"Aye. Those orcs out there were refugees running away from them. Then they arrived, blasted the rest for the favor of harming their people, and then transformed the charred remains into meadows and woodlands. And they planted a new Tree of Life!"

"Wait a minute. They blasted the orcs..."

"That explosion," Throdeth mutters. "But what could cause such a tremendous disturbance as that? I heard some say they could actually hear it here in the city."

"Aye," Relissa affirms. "They've come forward a wee bit in their wisdom, which I suppose is another of our failings. We're stuck in the mud and not progressing over here. But there's a lot to say about them, although I can't tell it all right now."

"One moment, is this where you got those statements?"

"Aye, they filled me in on some of the history since our people left."

"Incredible!"

"And the spirit also helped me with my bad Elvish, and a few other things. Mum, you need to see it. The tree is only a sapling, but it's as alive as anything I ever set my hands on."

✦✦✦✦✦

"Impossible!" shouts Elder Vankkar. "If you were so close to such an explosion, you would've been vaporized along with the rest of the valley."

"We were all protected under a very powerful shield, Elder," Kaliya replies, trying desperately to hold her stand under the interrogation of the Council. "I touched it with my hand, and it was solid as a rock. It protected us from both the physical blast as well as the radiation. The mages who were maintaining it kept it up even until the fallout stopped. After that, they started spreading ice magic on the ground to cool it and make it safe to walk upon again."

"Can such a shield actually exist?" asks Elder Girhani. "Master Velen, do you recall any such form of science from amongst our old archives?"

Velen had been listening carefully to Kaliya's report and the subsequent rebuttals from the other Council members. He considered the question in his mind as he strained to recall any of the ancient sciences once owned by the Daanen-Aryku, or the Suuden-Aryku, when they were still a civilization back on their home world of Azgarén. As he forms his reply, his voice is weary with age and the burdens of his position.

"I cannot be certain of this precise technology. This would represent a different faction from ours. But a projected shield represented as a solid barrier, this may actually be beyond us."

"This isn't part of any science we might know about," Kaliya submits. "This is more of that magic, but in this case far more advanced than anything those orcs could ever muster. As I was saying to Kailen, these people study it like we study science."

"But still..." Elder Girhani resumes. "How could they possibly produce such a thing to protect from a blast like that, and at such close range?"

"The only way for me to answer that is again with the word magic. This is metaphysics in action here, that old riddle we like to play with about nothing existing until after it is known, and I think I finally understand the meaning of it. The mind must first perceive it and apply its own definitions, and these essentially alter the reality of space to match. And I guess our laws of physics no longer apply if you can simply redefine them."

Velen leans forward in his chair at the mention of this line. His interest is suddenly peaked by the suggestion.

"Do you believe you might understand how this is applied?"

"Well, I saw two very prominent examples out there, neither of which could be defined by the more common sciences. Haran, that human mage friend of mine, tried on a number of occasions to teach me something, but his own studies in his academy are so thin that he simply doesn't have the depth of detail to really demonstrate anything. But what I saw out there showed me how magic is not only a very real thing, but it can also be a very powerful one in the right hands."

"Or the wrong ones..." Elder Vankkar moans.

"Yes, you're right, no different from the atomic sciences or anything else. And this is largely the work of who is using it. That Lord Thaelyn told me they teach their full society how to do this, from children of about middle age and up."

"Children?"

"That's what we said, but it's simply a case of teaching them the proper discipline and respect to do it right. If your entire culture is engineered the right way, I guess this is no longer an issue."

"Maybe…" he grumbles. "Nevertheless, I find this rather difficult to believe. I always had trouble with that…riddle. And then, what about this ludicrous suggestion of turning the charred remains of the aftermath into some kind of spring garden."

"Elder Vankkar, if you have so much trouble with that riddle, I guess there's not much else to say other than it was…magic…" she flutters her fingers. "It's ironic, in a way, as this is supposed to be our factional specialty. But for whatever reason, we can't even resolve our own theories," she chuckles.

"Yes, maybe I have to agree with that part of it."

"And the reason being our habit is to measure things in numbers. But how do you measure the power of ideas in numbers? That is our failure. Anyway, this goes beyond any recognizable science. In this case, this was likely on the scale of a god for what we saw out there. I simply can't describe it any other way."

"You do recall we're not a religious society, right?"

"Yes, but I'll tell you, I'm ready to get down and pray to something after seeing all that, if for no other reason than to ask it doesn't hit me next time. Besides, we seem to refer to Sargeras in such a way… effectively. What's to stop us from suggesting any other society of beings out there of a similar capacity. Whatever happened to our… belief…in evolution? Just ramp it up a few orders of magnitude from where we are. Boom, there you go, gods, especially as seen by little people like us."

"Um…all right, I guess I can't argue with that one, either."

"And if you really don't believe me, the solution is simple. Go see it for yourself. If I'm wrong, I'll dig my own hole this time, rather than make you do it again."

Elder Vankkar sighs heavily.

"Kaliya, this is not my point. You know my position on the Council. It's my job to argue these matters."

"Yeah, but it doesn't make my life any easier," she sighs quietly.

"I must admit," Velen affirms. "She has a point with her suggestion, as well as her arguments. There is one easy way to verify the story, and that is to go see it. If for no other reason, the area was originally a desert, was it not? And if the orc settlements have indeed been eradicated, then that would mean this individual may have enough power to turn the tides of war on this world."

"But is this for better or for worse, Master Velen?" Elder Vankkar proposes. "We cannot withstand a battle on another front!"

"We can't even withstand the battles on the existing fronts," Kaliya chuckles sarcastically.

"Precisely!"

"I do not know the answer at this time," Velen considers. "I have been waiting for the cu'Nar to speak to me again, but it has been so long. Still, if this offer of his is genuine, we should not turn it away."

"If it means anything at all," Kaliya adds. "My impression of him, along with that of my friends, Relissa and Haran, is that he was polite, informative, and helpful. He trusted us with enough knowledge to settle our fears, and though by his statements, he does have his duty to his people and his world, at least some part of that overlaps our own crisis."

"Where orcs are concerned..." Elder Vankkar retorts. "What about the rest of them?"

"It seemed straightforward enough to me. These orcs demonstrated an ability that could pose a serious security risk to his world. He must bring this into alignment. And since they are allied with the rest, he understands and accepts they will likely become involved at some time. By the sound of it, he'll be fighting them by default one day."

"And likely fall to them the same as everything else," he mutters indifferently.

"I wouldn't be so sure, Elder Vankkar. He has some very curious abilities. That shield, for example. If you were to project one of those right in front of you, do you think those Suuden'kai plasma rifles would still be a problem? And then what? I think a simple bow and arrow would be enough to take them down. Those things should still work, even on people like us."

"The Suuden-Aryku aren't exactly like us anymore."

"How do you know that? Simply because they have that weird mutation thing? I doubt it actually matters. We're not militaristic, and our weapons don't blow things up. For all we know, one of Relissa's squirrels might be dangerous to them. But this guy is militaristic, and he's out to protect his world. And he doesn't take no for an answer, not if he can drop mega-bombs on the place. The only reason we can't hurt the Suuden-Aryku is because we never actually tried. You do know what a gun is, right? Or use a simple blade on them. Stick them multiple times if you have to. If they can't shoot you, what difference does it make? For cu'Nar's sake, use a toothpick and jab them a bazillion times," she shrugs frustratingly.

"All right!" Elder Girhani interjects. "Kaliya, Santari, that's enough. This bickering won't get us anywhere."

"My apologies, Opadna," Elder Vankkar relents. "But for all we've seen so far, it sounds too good to be true, and I don't believe in such things anymore."

"Elder Girhani," Kaliya asserts. "I would agree, but I'm also reminded of something he said. We're fighting for our lives here. We might be pacifist, maybe excessively so, and to a fault. But when fighting like this, you don't just sit on a log and let it happen. And I have to agree, as this is the only thing we ever did. He even suggested something to me, which made perfect sense, if also unfortunate."

"And what was that?" Elder Girhani asks.

"All those times I went out and essentially got into trouble. I'm an offensive combatant. I want to take my fight to the enemy. Something none of you are doing, and you don't like it. Well, my apologies, but unless you want to continue sitting here like a lame animal, waiting for it to come to you, a suicide run may be the only way out of it. We're dying anyway, too afraid even to go outside and smell the scorched earth."

"I, well…"

"Build a wall out there, put some turret guns behind it, attach a scanner array and let it blast anything that moves. Build bigger guns for mobile units. Build a huge gun for anything in orbit. They're clearly not trying to finish us, not if they're only using light harassment tactics. We are being oppressed, nothing more. But kill us slow, or kill us fast, they're still killing us. So, at least go down fighting, like animals that hold a little pride."

"All right, Kaliya, I understand…"

"And one more thing," she asserts with a finger. "Some of us are tired of waiting for people like you to make that decision. If such as Elder Vankkar is so jaded that he doesn't believe in miracles anymore, this is why. As for this guy…he goes out and he conquers things. He has the firepower and the determination to get the job done. And with his advanced forms of magic, which might blow the horns off people like us, I think Elder Vankkar should reconsider his opinion of miracles."

"All right wait…" Kailen offers, hoping to ease the tensions. "Kaliya, please. Elders, may I offer a proposal. With your permission, I could lead a small envoy to investigate this matter on behalf of the Council. If it turns out to be legitimate, we could make a more assertive effort for negotiation at a later time. But for now, we should at least try to confirm some of these statements. The reports seem to match the sightings from our long-range patrols, at least as far as the disturbances are concerned. But without a doubt, whatever actually happened out there needs further investigation."

"Indeed, this is true," Elder Girhani admits. "I submit that such a plan may be necessary to ensure the security of our position, and if this Thaelyn is true to his intent, we should discover what he might have to offer us."

"Very well," Elder Vankkar concedes. "But be on your guard, Commander. We can't afford to lose you. If Kaliya is right, and this person has imported such a large military presence, you wouldn't stand a chance out there."

"Elder Vankkar," Kaliya offers. "If he really wanted to attack anything, I don't think anyone would stand a chance out there," she chuckles. "But his attitude with me and the others was very friendly, so I wouldn't worry as much."

"Very well, but I would like to err on the side of caution here. He's still an unknown factor for his newness in this world."

"All right, then I think it would be prudent to ask if I can be involved in this envoy. Lord Thaelyn already knows me, and I can be of value to inform the Commander of what I know as he makes his visit."

The Elders glance at each other and convene privately over the prospect of including Kaliya, or any such low-ranking soldier, in the envoy.

"Kaliya," Elder Girhani considers. "No offence, but a junior officer like you simply doesn't have the representation or training for this level of diplomacy, especially in a wartime scenario with unknowns."

"Unknowns?!" she yips. "Excuse me, but I know them better than you do! I'm the one who made contact, told them about our problems, and I even made a few friends. I spent the night with them, ate meals with them, and once we settled that bit with the language, I even shared a few conversations with them which were truly fascinating!"

"What?!" Elder Vankkar yelps unexpectedly. "Settling the issue of language? Yes, of course. Another world, another language, I suppose. And how could you possibly learn their language in one day? Or they, yours? Better yet, in less than a day?"

"Um..." she hesitates and bites her lip, suddenly realizing her potential error may now cost her. "Well, actually, did I say the local races are originally from that other world?"

"Not precisely, and while this could offer a possibility, my impression is their isolation may have caused some divergence."

"Oh, um... But Relissa's people still seem to hold the same language."

"Uh huh, and do you speak Elvish?"

"Me? Uh..."

"As I thought. I'm waiting, young lady," he intones suspiciously. "To learn a language in a single day, or perhaps less."

"Great, I should've kept my mouth shut on that one. Now I need to explain, and worse, to you, of all people."

"Do you actually hate me so much?"

"It's not that, but you have a...um...reputation."

"Oh, is that so. Well, I'm still waiting for your answer. How is it you came into learning a language virtually overnight?"

"Technically, it wasn't overnight. I can't be sure how long it actually took...I wasn't watching the time, but it was shortly after they arrived and before they blasted the orcs."

"That's even worse! And I'm still waiting for your answer."

"Couldn't we just skip this part? It's really not important. In fact, it can actually be very useful, as I can listen to their conversations and inform Kailen about it."

"While that may be true, I would still like to hear your answer. I'll ask one more time before I pull out the shovel for that hole you mentioned earlier."

"Something tells me you'll be doing that anyway, so I may as well jump in with both hooves now. I'm already halfway there."

She draws in a nervous breath and releases it, but it doesn't help.

"Lord Thaelyn is, um... He's telepathic...very telepathic, apparently. We were having communication difficulties, so he shared his mind with me to teach me his language, and also to learn ours... um, you know, the local one, as well as...oh well, cu'Nar help me now."

"Telepathic?!" he screeches. "And you let him inside your head?! How do we know he didn't steal every little secret you might have up there, or maybe to dominate you and use you as a spy?"

Kaliya huffs at the insinuation. She glares at him for his outburst. Kailen takes notice of her temper rising by her sudden shift in breathing and her virulent gaze, so he decides to intervene.

"Um, Elder Vankkar..."

Kaliya interrupts him by gently slapping a hand to his chest. She closes her eyes and turns her head away, while placing her other hand on her hip. Kailen again tries to speak, but she simply reinforces her position by again patting on his chest.

"Kaliya…" he soothes.

"Kailen, let me handle this. I'm fine, because this time I think I hold enough of a position to actually argue my point."

"All right, if you prefer, but I'm worried about that hole…"

Kailen glances back up at Elder Vankkar, who by now was withdrawing from his outbreak, realizing his own indiscretion.

"Elder Vankkar," Kaliya returns her gaze up to him on the bench. "With respect…and to the rest of you on the Council…that statement is insulting. For as many times as I've been busted, I doubt any of you would give me anything worth stealing by now. Not to mention that we might actually have anything worthy of stealing…not with the Suuden'kai forces burying us in this hole. And yet, here I am giving you a considerable amount of detail on him. So, if I'm such a bad soldier, I must be an even worse puppet."

"My apologies, Kaliya," Elder Vankkar relents. "You are actually correct. I must also admit, I spoke disrespectfully."

"Thank you, I will simply let this pass as the heat of the debate, and perhaps you do also have a point. But I will also say this, and some of this is actually his words on this same subject. First, we had the issue of communication. Drawing pictures in the sand is entirely inadequate for the volume and detail necessary to exchange in order for him to explain what he was preparing to do out there. I suppose, in the absence of this, our only choices might be to run like frightened animals to escape, or maybe to see his guard contingent tackling us and holding us in place while he reinvented the world around us. But still, this would do little or nothing to help us understand who he was, where he came from, or anything else for that matter."

"I would have to agree on this point," Elder Girhani concedes. "For the magnitude of what he did out there, I doubt there could be any other way but to take whatever drastic actions were necessary in order to relay these details. If this involved a telepathic relay, then maybe this is all we had available."

"I suppose I may have to agree," Elder Vankkar admits. "But

I still don't like it, and if this is what she is referring to as my...reputation...then I think it stands to reason I am very uncomfortable with the idea."

"Elder Vankkar," Kaliya continues. "I don't want to argue with you, as I can surely understand your position, but I'm also made aware of something else he said, and this actually makes very good sense to me. His power of telepathy would dwarf any of our own studies. He was playing little vid-com movies inside my head for some of it, which is far beyond anything I've ever heard of on our side. That's how advanced he is."

"Yes, that would speak for itself."

"And despite your prejudice, he comes from a society where telepathy is apparently commonplace, and they know how to use it responsibly. If we're able to do this at all..." she glares at Velen, "... that means we are coming of age as a species where this is becoming a feature in us. Therefore, as he says, we need to evolve and start demonstrating our own responsibility over it. To embrace it, not hide from it out of fear and suspicion. As such, your position is actually the one that should be questioned, not mine. Ignorance and intolerance are not the answer here."

"Kaliya, while I might say your statement is well-made, I can't be so sure we are ready for that yet."

"Maybe, maybe not...but it still stands. As for what he and I did out there, we both knew it had to be done. I gave myself to it willingly, and afterwards, we shared some very informative conversations, and also a bit of laughter. In fact, I had a better time out there in conversation with him in one night than anything I had here for the past century."

"Maybe you'd like to go live with him?"

"Be careful, I might just do that. His world sounds like a utopian paradise as compared to anything we ever had. But I wouldn't want to run out on our people. If I did anything at all, it might be to learn a few things to bring back to us. In the meantime, he seems to trust me, for all our interactions and despite my poor service rank. During our conversation, I asked a lot of questions, and while he shared what he could, he also made it clear that he must maintain his military security. Our position isn't the one in question. His is the issue here."

"Why his, in this case? Although I could possibly suggest a few ideas, but for clarification."

"Right," she nods. "First, and most obviously, he's surrounded on three sides by potential hostiles, and he hasn't a clue what to expect out of them now that he's here. The orcs shouldn't be a bother, from what I've seen. The Flame Elves are a concern for how and why they're called Flame Elves, and the Suuden-Aryku might be a bother if they should turn his way, so he needs to establish himself."

"Why do you say the Flame Elves might be an issue simply for being Flame Elves?"

"According to Relissa, my Night Elf friend, they were once described by a different name. And according to him, those people are not bad people. Sargeras is the reason here, and Thaelyn is upset for the insult to what is otherwise described as a proud and noble race. This would similarly reflect on all the elven races, including those he has back home, who would collectively take offence to it."

"That sounds rather serious," Elder Girhani notes. "And potential reason for a war in and of itself."

"It would be," Elder Vankkar nods. "So, what does he have in mind for this?"

"I don't know yet," Kaliya admits. "But I'm sure he'll want to know how and why it happened in the first place, maybe then to see about a corrective solution. Meanwhile, between them and their magic, we already know they have a form of invisibility cloak. Combine that with who knows what else around here, and he is suggesting all our miseries in this world, as well as our journey up to it, could be Sargeras playing with us like toys."

"Toys!"

"Yeah, and furthermore, we might have spies walking around making matters worse. Those Flame Elves had to be coerced somehow, as I doubt by the description that they would go along willingly. Therefore, he dares not let out too much information that could compromise his position."

"Oh great! All right, I see it now. Spies hiding behind this invisibility thing."

"But we also have another issue he's not happy about, and this represents a failure on our part."

"A failure on our part… All right, what failure?"

"Four centuries, Elder Vankkar. That's how long this world has been under siege, with or without us carving a groove in the canyon outside. This world has been whittled down to the last, and these were then oppressed, not killed outright like all the rest. If they really, really wanted us dead, I don't think I'd be standing here now telling you this."

"Oppressed. But why?"

"I don't know why, but they came up to the walls of the last few cities and then stopped, with no serious attacks since. That's a purging of life, not a war to simply kill things. Then to keep the rest for some hidden purpose."

"Oh dear cu'Nar," Elder Girhani moans. "But she does hold a point."

"Here is where Thaelyn explained something to me. Apparently, our pacifist nature as scientists and scholars is backfiring on us. In this time, four centuries for the rest, and three and a half including us, not once did any of us realize how to join together militarily to actually fight something. Not that it might have amounted to anything overall, but as he says, sitting on a log and waiting for the end to come is not the way to go. Our isolationist manners prevent us from reaching out, the humans don't go outside to solve theirs, and the Night Elves apparently don't bother unless someone comes knocking at their doors. And we call ourselves at war."

Elder Vankkar sighs and lowers his head. Elder Girhani turns away as she reflects on the history they had to suffer in this world. Even Velen turned his eyes down into his lap as he clasped his hands in contemplation.

"And you argue about me going out for any reason," Kaliya huffs.

"He compared my reckless rampages to a lack of support on your part to plan our attacks appropriately, simply to survive, if nothing else. Now, if Thaelyn holds the power and the skill, to say nothing of the motivation to turn this around for us, I think it becomes obvious to make a deal with him. Those orcs that invaded his world were likely under orders by Sargeras for some unknown reason. They had to have help, this much is obvious, and that help had to be someone bigger, and with the knowledge to enable it. This now makes him an enemy to Thaelyn and his people. And he's not at all happy about that. In fact, he dared that if the Suuden-Aryku were to keep up their assaults, he'd steal one of their star cruisers and start hunting them."

Elder Vankkar let out a spontaneous laugh at the suggestion.

"And do you think he might actually succeed at this?"

"Hey, if he can drop an antimatter bomb using just magic, and bring life back from the dead, I don't think I want to underestimate what else he is capable of. He's already fulfilled that full section of the prophecy."

"The prophecy…" he ponders distantly. "While I do not want to question this, I tend to take more of a wait-and-see approach to things."

"A wait-and-see approach. Fine. He arrived in a circle of light, otherwise known as a portal, or a conveyor to us. He described himself to be related to someone, where at least to some societies, they might hold a very lofty title, regardless of our opinions of it. He blasted the place and then rebuilt it…and everything in that same order. Wait-and-see? Yeah, you just got it."

"Hmm…" he frowns at the suggestion.

"He uses portals, apparently quite liberally. If you involve their potential, he can probably pop in right behind you without warning. I think the Suuden-Aryku should be the ones to be afraid, if only they knew."

"She might have a point," Elder Girhani asserts. "We have seen their application on a few occasions, and this does represent a threat potential. But anyway, we must still consider the envoy. I must admit, if she is fluent in their language, we cannot deny this as a potential asset, no matter how it came about. If we were to assign anyone else, he would need to spend some untold amount of time learning it before we could accomplish anything. And considering how this individual is so determined to engage in his war efforts, time is not something we can afford to spend."

"Perhaps if we could offer this," Velen emits intrepidly. "What if she could serve in some capacity as an intermediary?"

"An intermediary?" Elder Girhani considers. "I was actually thinking more like an interpreter. Technically speaking, she doesn't have that sort of training, and there are others that are much more experienced in matters on this level. Lieutenant Lapäli, for instance. He has served in the past with the people of Rolsklinde."

"How hard can it actually be?" Kaliya asks. "This is basically a desk job. How badly can I foul that one up? I take reports and give them to Kailen. I don't need to make any real decisions, as Thaelyn is the one fighting the war. If Kailen has any instructions, I simply pass them along. And as a side benefit, Aerlie is a medical expert and a psychologist, and they already discovered all my trauma issues and offered counseling. How do you like that? Free therapy along with my service position."

"They actually offered this to you?"

"Yeah, they're both extremely supportive. They spent at least as much time trying to rebuild each of our morale failures as they did to answer our questions. Relissa was asked to offer her aid for the local scouting details, and she was also informed about a special course of scout training she might be interested in. Haran might transfer to one of their mage academies on Tae'Eladar, for all the great study materials they offer, and as for me, I actually had to shut my mouth after a while, for all my personal horn-pulling, before I found myself being conscripted into his military just to prove I might hold value if trained properly," she grins.

"In all the nether-space, who is this guy?" she chuckles. "All right, I would recommend, if he seems to hold such confidence in you, that we should take advantage of this. Santari?"

"I may have to agree," he relents. "Maybe it does hold some

amount of promise after all. But I want to leave the final decision to the Commander here. I would ask him to go out there to investigate, and then make his decisions based on what he sees. Commander?"

"This is reasonable," Kailen nods. "I will take her with me, and if the situation warrants it, I will see what possibilities exist for our future relations, and whether she can satisfy those demands."

"Good…" Elder Vankkar pauses in reflection. "And Kaliya, despite my objections and uncertainties, I think I should admit to something on this occasion. You did well during this debriefing today, unlike some of your previous efforts. You stood on your own two hooves and defended your position well. I don't know if it could be that meld, or those conversations you so enjoyed, but it would seem you matured a little bit out there."

"Cu'Nar's Grace, Elder Vankkar," she blushes. "Did you just compliment me? Thank you!"

"Yes, Kaliya, maybe you got a jolt out of that meeting that actually turned your horns around a little. But don't let it overtighten them," he smiles delicately.

"Very well then," Velen concludes. "Kailen, you should make your preparations to leave in the morning. We must not waste any time to understand the situation."

◆◆◆

Tristeen continued to listen to the heated debate inside the Dean's office. The two had been fighting since Haran mentioned the need for his report to reach other elements of the city's authority.

"What do you mean we're not reporting this to the Guard?" Haran argues, shocked at the blatant disregard of protocol. "Last I heard, we hold an agreement with them for the city defense. Not to mention, this army is a powerful force, and the Guard needs to know about it so we can reorganize ourselves in the war effort!"

"Bah!" the Dean charges. "The only thing the Guard needs to worry about is keeping the drunkards off the streets."

"Drunkards?! And what about the war?"

"The Governor makes those decisions, not I, and certainly not you!"

"This is ridiculous! You know, Thaelyn was right, none of you people know how to fight a proper war. You simply hide indoors and leave it to someone else, but there is no one else out there actually fighting anything, and all this for four centuries! We're not even allowed to go outside because of it!"

"Haran!" barks the Dean. "Go study a toad! And leave the dealings of politics to your uppers. If the orcs are gone, then the Guard has nothing else to worry about in our immediate vicinity. As for the Governor, I'll take care of that. Your usefulness is now complete."

"And what about my report on these people and what potential they might offer? I was out there, I saw it, and in my judgment..."

"Your judgment?!" he blasts. "You are nothing more than a simple mid-classman student in this academy! Your entire existence here is to follow the instructions of your Masters, not make judgments!"

"Then what purpose is there for me to go on these assignments if the information I bring back is summarily thrown away? What purpose is there for me even to attend these studies if they serve no functional value?"

"Yes, indeed! What purpose? I'll tell you what purpose. The purpose is to do as you are told and no more. You're not supposed to do any thinking. That's for me to do! I set the rules, and you simply follow."

"Really! And is this why we're told as children in school there's nothing else to learn out there, because you say it's so? Do you like playing God, Dean? I think you do."

"You impudent little..." the Dean's face flushes. "I think I have had as much out of you as I can possibly tolerate. For years, I've questioned myself as to the reasons why I spend my time with you. Now, after this insolent little tirade of yours, I think I can finally say I wish no further involvement of you within my academy. Pack your things and leave. And if I should ever see you again, I'll turn you into a rat and give you over to our alchemist studies!"

Exhausted from the argument, and now broken by the declaration of his dismissal, Haran turned slowly to leave the office. With a scowl on his face, he approaches the door, but before exiting, he turns around one last time.

"Dean," he emits with tenuous restraint. "It doesn't actually matter what you think at all. He's going to fight this war, with or without you. That means the enemies of this world will be wiped away, and then people like you will find yourselves being judged for why you didn't take part. Don't underestimate him, Dean. He's no…simple…man, and all we have here is one paltry city with an even less appealing city guard. He owns a world, and that world is far more organized than anything we have."

He now leaves the room, passing through the door, and closing it behind him. He catches a glimpse of Tristeen waiting off to the side, her posture stiffened by her reaction to the exchange between the two men, but he can't bring his eyes around to meet hers. He simply turns and shambles down the hall, further making his way down the stairs.

At first, Tristeen could say nothing. She waited for him to speak, but as she followed him through the building, she felt the need to start a conversation.

"Haran?" she begins softly. "What will you do now?"

"There is something wrong here, Tristeen," he grumbles. "The Guard needs to know about this, the Governor too. How are we supposed to win this war if no one ever fights in it?"

"Will you go to them yourself? I don't think the Dean would care much for you stepping over his head."

"Stepping over his head? How high do you need to step if you are simply cleaning the streets of drunkards?" he chides. "You heard the report, right? What do you think I should do? We have potential friends with an army tough enough to possibly fight back against all this, and we do nothing about it. That's what the Dean is suggesting. The Guard's only purpose is to arrest drunkards. This is our 'war', not to fight those invaders who have been destroying everything, and pinning us inside these walls."

"Pinning?"

"Yes! Four centuries, they destroy everything else, and then stop at our walls. This is called pinning us down for some reason, and not to kill us."

"Oops!"

He sighs as he continues his thoughts and tries to further calm himself.

"I don't know... Maybe the Governor will take some sort of action. All I know is I don't dare show myself in here again, that much is for sure. I won't bother packing. I don't have that much anyway. I'll just leave and be done with it. I can't stand this place any longer."

Tristeen looks down at the floor as they walk.

"Where will you go?"

"Back to the lower district, I suppose. Thing is, I don't really feel safe here anymore, not anywhere. I don't recall the last time the Dean ever expelled someone from the academy. Sometimes we get funny rumors going around the halls, not that I ever really believe them, but he was certainly angry enough to follow through on his threat."

"And what about us?"

He pauses in his steps and turns to her.

"You know how much I feel for you, but we keep coming back to this, Tristeen. You come from a noble family, and they would never allow you to associate with someone like me. They control your fate as much as my birth controls mine."

"That didn't stop me before," she smirks gently. "And it didn't stop you, either."

Haran let out a cautious smile.

"Nevertheless, right now I need to consider what comes next for me. I can't come back here, and I can't shake off this feeling that the Guard needs to know. Whatever the Dean may tell the Governor, if he says the Guard has no further concerns, what does this say about the war and our friends? I know there's a general feeling of indifference where the elves and Daanen-Aryku are concerned, but I've been out there. You know about my friends, Relissa and Kaliya, right? My interactions with them, and the stories we've shared, do not corroborate with many of the things they teach us in here."

"I don't know, Haran. The Dean is the authority in these affairs, and I need to trust his judgment. Surely, he is only serving the best interests of the city and our people. I've never had contact with the elves or the Daanen-Aryku, and I only know what we hear from our scouting patrols that go out and bring back news to us. We haven't had any direct involvement in the war for years, as far as anyone can recall."

"That doesn't mean it's over, Tristeen. The Daanen-Aryku suffer attacks all the time, and even the Night Elves take an occasional skirmish."

"But it's their war, Haran, not ours. The Daanen-Aryku fight these Suuden-Aryku to our east, and the elves seem occupied with each other and the orcs. We're simply caught in the middle with nowhere to go."

"But you forget, we once had a lot more out there, until the war destroyed most of it."

"That was the work of the Elven war, and then the orcs coming into it as these Suuden-Aryku and their allies joined up. Between those Flame Elves and the orcs, they laid waste to everything. We can't even set up any decent farming outside the walls because the people are too afraid to go out there."

"But Tristeen, we're missing something here. At the very least is the uncanny coincidence of all these others arriving in our world and destroying our civilization right up to our front doors and then stopping. If it was only the Flame Elves, that's one thing. But why did the orcs and Suuden-Aryku show up when they did, and everyone coming together in the end when none of them should hold any true relationship with anything? I'll give you a hint. One word. Sargeras."

"Um, all right. This might pose a curious little paradox."

They continue walking as far as the main hall before pausing again.

"Maybe what I'll do is go speak with my sister about this," Haran considers. "She serves the Guard, so maybe she can offer advice."

"Very well, Haran, do what you think is best."

They exchange a soft kiss and Haran turns to leave the building for the last time. He exits outside and wanders off across the plaza, contemplating his next move.

For the first time in years, he had no occupation. In one sense, it felt liberating to be free of the academy and the torment he suffered on a daily basis. But he felt alone now. That was the only place he could share moments with his lovely Tristeen, even though there could never be any hope for a future between the two of them. Nothing short of a city-wide disaster could offer any possibility for them. Her family was far too ostentatious, like many of the noble families, to allow her the freedom to choose her own path. The two of them would steal moments together from time to time, meeting in secret places to nuzzle and woo each other, but it all began at the academy. He could never venture into the Upper Ward where she lived, and she was often not allowed to wander off into the lower district where he came from.

Haran sorted through his thoughts as he strolled along the streets. He wondered if it would be better for him to simply find a nice quiet chair in a local tavern and sit, maybe to sip a few ales until the bliss of a drunken unconsciousness laid him out on the floor. He recalled his interactions with Thaelyn and what was said the day before, and kept repeating to himself the policies concerning the relationship the academy was supposed to share with the Allegiance Guard. The war affected everyone, not just those currently in the fight. He felt they should have a responsibility to do their part.

The Guard didn't send out scouts due to the constant pressures of resource shortages in the city. Since the city didn't own any mining operations of its own, it was forced to purchase everything from a dwarven enclave in a rocky line of mountains to the north. Due to this, it was decided to use the mage academy for intelligence gathering, as the mages could compensate with magic and potions to offer alternative methods of stealth and surveillance. The information gathered would then be shared with the Guard to help them defend the city, should anything come their way.

Still, the argument he had with the Dean echoed in his mind. The Dean would speak to the Governor, this much he could be sure of. They often spoke on matters concerning the city, but what would the Governor do about it? Would he wish to meet with Thaelyn to make some form of agreement? One thing was certain... Haran could not ignore the implications in those last words regarding the Guard not having any part of this. The way things were currently in the world, the situation was bad and not getting any better by any other means. Thaelyn might be the only hope for progress in this war.

As he walked through the city, he found himself unconsciously moving in the direction of the Allegiance Guard barracks. Marelle, his sister, served there as a lieutenant, and he would sometimes go speak with her when he felt especially dispirited from his experiences in the academy. On this day, however, his feelings were particularly low.

He arrives near the front of the barracks and pauses. The robust building, designed as a fortress within the city, is the main headquarters of the Allegiance Guard. Marelle would likely be found inside attending to her duties as the coordinator of the civic watch patrols.

Haran fought with himself over his perceived responsibility to the city, despite what the Dean said and any threats he might make. Finally, in a moment of determination, he enters the front gate and marches up to the office of the Civil Watch. He crosses the courtyard to a hallway running along one side with doors leading off to administration areas and training facilities. Near the end of the hall, before it turned a corner to run across the rear of the yard, he found his mark. He knocks on the door as he peeks inside.

"Yes?" emits a pleasant female voice from within.

"Marelle? It's me..." Haran beckons as he moves just inside the door.

"Haran!" she replies cheerfully. "What a surprise! How's my little brother today? Is the Big Bad Dean bothering you again?"

"Worse... Marelle, I need your advice, and maybe your help. It's serious, but not here. Can you meet me at the Ten Eagles?"

"Why? What's wrong?" she asks with a look of concern entering her face.

"Just meet me there. How soon can you get away?"

"Well, it's been a bit slow today. The only excitement we had around here came in yesterday. Something about flashes of light and black clouds over the mountains, but my desk is mostly empty."

"Good. I'll go there now. You follow shortly after, all right?"

"Haran, what's this about? Why the cloak and dagger business?"

"Not here…please."

Haran strains a smile, then turns and leaves the room, closing the door behind him.

He leaves the building and moves back out into the streets. His destination was now the lower district of the city where he would find the Ten Eagles Tavern. He felt very self-conscious by now, as he was essentially stepping over the Dean's authority. This imparted a paranoid suspicion that the Dean might actually be watching him, although it seemed unrealistic as the Dean carried such a low opinion of him in the first place. So, he found himself casually passing in and out of the various shops along the way, simply as a way to defray any attention to his activities.

He again reflected on the conversation. Maybe the Dean would inform the Governor and they would share the information with the Guard afterwards. Maybe the Dean was right, and the most immediate concern of the orcish threat was gone, so he could take a more relaxed approach. He did seem very excited when he heard about Thaelyn's army out in the Badlands, especially at the news of the type of armor they were using.

"Mithril and adamantium…" he muses to himself.

He recalled the sea of glimmering metal. How wonderful it was to behold. If only such supplies could be found here. But alas, the only known examples of mithril were held in the archives of the academy. He saw them on display once, during a lecture by one of his instructors. He didn't know where they came from, but they were rumored to have been in the possession of the academy for a few centuries, from a time before the war.

"…And the best we can do is iron and steel from the dwarven mines," he finishes, feeling dejected in knowing how dreary the material was in comparison.

He continued to work his way through the streets until he came upon the Ten Eagles Tavern. It was one of the more popular gathering places in the lower district. The sounds of shouting and laughter echoed out from it, and music could be heard from lutes and pipes. He entered the tavern and soon was greeted by the smell of beer and the perfume of the courtesans. He moved to a table in the rear corner of the room and waited.

Haran sat there waiting for the well-trimmed stature of his older sister for what seemed like a long while. His eyes darted from the table to the doors on the opposite side of the room and back again, nervously wondering who the next person would be to enter, his sister or someone else. After a while, as he was returning his gaze to the table, a hooded figure wearing a monk's robe approached from the side.

"Is this seat taken?" asks the voice from under the hood. It sounded strangely feminine.

Haran looked up into the face of the stranger, at first uneasy over the intrusion, but then to realize who it was that stood before him.

"Marelle!" he yelps in a hushed voice.

The concealed form of his sister, clearly in disguise, took up a seat across the table.

"All right, Haran, so what's this about? I saw you moving around out there in those shops like you were hiding from something. Are you in some kind of trouble?"

"Yes and no, sort of…"

"Well, that's certainly the sort of precise answer I might expect out of you. So, which of the three is it?"

"First, I got into an argument with the Dean, and he finally had enough of me, so he expelled me."

"Oh, Haran, I'm so sorry. I know how much it meant to you to be a part of those studies."

"It's alright, the way they treated me over there, it's for the best. But it doesn't end there. I'm worried about something."

"All right, tell me what's wrong. And why do we have to meet like this?"

"Maybe I'm paranoid, but I learned something recently, and I don't feel comfortable doing this alone. You may have a hard time believing me, but in the end, I'll ask you to take this to the Guard. It may be critically important, or maybe I'm just over-reacting, but if you can check on it for me, it would make me feel a lot better."

"Haran, the terms 'critically important' and 'over-reacting' don't often fit well in the same sentence. What do you mean?"

Haran begins telling his sister the story of the previous day. He starts with the routine scouting patrol, followed by the arrival of Thaelyn and his small troupe, the explosion, the storm, and the arrival of the magnificent army all dressed in the magical metals.

Marelle, being the sister of a mage apprentice, had a bit more respect for the craft than the other officers of the Guard. Her interactions with Haran also allowed her to understand, if only slightly more than the average person, what mithril was about, where the average person would be completely inept on the subject.

"And so, Marelle," he concludes. "He didn't seem at all interested in sharing any part of this with the Guard, even though that's supposed to be our arrangement with them. In fact, he even went as far as to say their only true purpose was to keep the streets clear of drunkards. Now, how does that make you feel?"

"Honestly, Haran, this doesn't really surprise me. No one in the Guard holds much care for how they get the backhand treatment by the wizards at the academy. They seem to be keeping a lot of things to themselves up there, and they barely give us enough to keep the walls safe. I wouldn't be a bit surprised if they should decide to buckle up the gates and let this Thaelyn take care of things to our south."

"But Marelle..." he implores. "What about the elves and the Daanen-Aryku? We can't just abandon them."

"Dear brother, surely you know how things work in our city

politics. The Governor tells us to protect the city and follow orders without question."

"This sounds exactly like what the Dean said earlier…our only purpose is to follow his rules, and not think for ourselves."

"Right, and with the Guard, whenever we had an occasion to help the Daanen-Aryku, we were told only to send a limited force for a few patrols, and presumably to conserve our resources for the local defense."

"All because we don't have enough for anything bigger. But only the Daanen-Aryku, not the elves?"

"Yeah, apparently the elves don't need our help for whatever reason. Don't ask why. But you know, it feels more like they're just yanking our chains. The elves take care of things to the west, the Daanen-Aryku to the east, while we nestle comfortably in the middle. The orders from the top say only to keep on the defensive, not to push outward and drive the bastards away…just keep them from taking the city. But we never get anything coming at the city, so why are we just sitting here."

"Naturally, and how are you supposed to win a war like that? This is what Lord Thaelyn was saying. No one here joins forces to actually fight, so nothing gets done. You know my friend Kaliya, and all the times she got in trouble for actually going out there. Those people are nearly as bad as we are."

"Exactly, it's a war of attrition, and the elves and the Daanen-Aryku seem to be the ones getting hit the hardest while we focus mostly on defense. These orcs you found in the Badlands would be the closest we've ever seen to the city. But now with that Thaelyn fellow of yours down there, they might just ask him to take the south and leave us in a nice little cubby to snooze."

"This is crazy. What about the dwarves? Do they have any kind of army to help?"

"The dwarves don't fight at all. We've never actually seen a dwarven troop movement come out of there, not in living memory, at least. Either they don't have the belly to fight, or they're more interested in profiting off the other races by selling us their wares.

We don't know. As for me, the only thing I can be sure of is the shipments coming through the northern gate."

"All right, what about them?" he wonders.

"Well, they come in regularly enough, but the wagons are small. And we're supposed to share this with the other races? I can't help but to ask, if all they're doing up there is mining and smithing, why are the wagons so small? We've sent requisitions through for more goods, but nothing ever changes. The wagons are exactly the same each time. If the dwarves are making a profit from us, you'd think more metal would put more coin into their pockets, right?"

"Maybe the war has put such a drain on the mines that they're used up?"

"Maybe. But then, why not move somewhere else to find more? Surely there must be more out there."

"Has anyone gone up to check on it?"

"The Governor supposedly has his own people who deal with the dwarves. We usually see the Dean go out that way, but our orders are to stay and keep the city safe…nothing more."

"Do as you're told, that's all, just like at the academy. How much influence does the Guard have with the Governor?"

"Virtually none, it would seem," she sighs. "But your Dean sure seems to have the Governor's ear often enough."

Marelle looks around the tavern and over at the doors.

"Look," she continues. "I need to get back to my desk. I'll pass the word along to my Captain, but quietly. I can't promise anything, but he doesn't have much love for the wizards either. I'll let him know to watch if any word comes down in the next day or two. But to be honest, we're tired of the Governor holding us back in this war. If this Thaelyn is as strong as you say, he could be our best chance to turn things around."

Marelle gets up from the table. She orients herself with a reverent posture, appropriate to her dress, and casually walks out the door.

Haran waits several moments, and then takes his own leave from the tavern. With nowhere else to go, he heads across to the western section of the district to his aunt's house, hoping she might have a place for him to stay for the night.

———◆◆◆◆◆———

"We need to tell the Council!" Amariyn declares anxiously. "And then we need to get an envoy out there immediately! If the Tel'Quessir have found us, we simply cannot delay in making contact. Oh, how I look forward to seeing a blessed tree again! I need my old ceremonial robe. Where did I put it? Oh dear!"

"Let's see," mutters Throdeth as he paces in circles. "I'll need to bring my journals, my notes…oh, which ones to take. Bags! I need bags, lots of bags…maybe I should bring a cart? No, wait, handlers! There are too many for me to carry alone, I should find some handlers."

"Your Excellences, please!" calls the Enforcer in a vain attempt to bring the situation in his office under control.

"Everybody, listen," Relissa interjects. "I have something else I need to say. Thaelyn asked me if I could help him learn the lay of the land so he can find all the baddies out there. He's here to fight the Orcs, at least for now so he can protect his world, but he knows about the others, and needs to get ready for them. The thing of it is he needs someone to show him around, and he's asking me to help, with your permission."

"He wants you to help him?" snarls the Enforcer. "A youngling who can barely find her own feet?"

"Enforcer, he's a very determined guy, and doesn't like people who put down other people, regardless of how much, or how little, they might have accomplished in their lives. He was ragging on me for all my miseries, largely because of my experiences here, and telling me he'll take me simply to demonstrate how useful I can be with the right conditioning, which I apparently do not get around here. So, be careful with this guy," she waves a finger at him gently.

"Oh… I see. All right, I'll take this into consideration."

"But more than that, he says that all my playing with my so-called pets may actually show a gift he can train to use as part of my scouting craft."

"And just how does that help you, girl? Will you be tying colorful ribbons around their necks and dragging them about on little ropes?"

Relissa glares at the Enforcer.

"Probably not. But sending a squirrel up a tree to watch you would be a lot harder to notice than me standing two paces away, now, wouldn't it?!"

"Fine, and then what? Do you have that squirrel write your reports for you, as well?"

"In case you haven't bothered to notice, I can talk to them, and they talk back!"

"Relissa," Amariyn cuts in. "Are you saying you can actually communicate with these animals? Why haven't you ever mentioned this before? I recall a vague mention once in some old journal of something like this."

"It's because no one ever listens to me. Thaelyn says he can train this. It's a scouting profession called a Ranger. He says mostly elves are the ones to sign up, maybe due to our closeness to nature. I could teach any critter I find out there to be my eyes and ears in places I can't go, and no one would be the wiser for it."

"Are you implying that you might go to work for him?" infers the Enforcer. "To do so means you would need to resign from your post here. Are you sure you want to do this?"

"After the way you keep bashing me?" she sighs and pauses to recompose herself. "Sorry... But seriously, to do so means not simply to leave my post, it's also about swearing a new allegiance to His Lordship. It's a military role, but I'd be going back to Sein'amar, which can't be all that bad, and joining up with a powerful Order, which may open a lot of new possibilities for me. There's just one little thing..."

"What is that, Relissa?" Amariyn asks.

"Well, I can't be sure if I'll qualify for it. You see, his Order has some really tough entrance requirements. Before they'll let me in the door, I need to pass some tests."

"What kind of tests?" Throdeth inquires, feeling concern for her chances.

"The worst of it is one called a Spirit test, where they do something to test the purity of my soul, or some such. If I make that one, I can probably do the rest well enough."

"Relissa," Amariyn consoles reassuringly. "If you've been touched by the dryad spirit, then I think you should not worry about that. She'll watch over you."

"Well, for now, I'd just like to take care of the first part…helping him learn the lay of the land so he can carry on his fight. It'll help us a lot in the short and long of it."

"Relissa," the Enforcer advises. "Before I give any authorization for this, I would wish to meet with this man Thaelyn first. Only after that will I give my agreement."

He turns to Throdeth and Amariyn.

"Your Excellences, this sounds rather urgent in my mind, so we should make our plans to leave on the morrow. I'll arrange a carriage and have it waiting in the Council plaza."

✦✦◆✦✦

"Are you sure you can depend on his underling of yours?" demands Governor Dramon.

"His outburst in my office," Dean Malorn responds, "certainly would not have occurred if he were not serious to be heard. He said not only that they had mithril, but also adamantium, which is mentioned only briefly in the lectures. It's regarded as legend, even myth, among the students. He could not know anything else about it."

"If this is the case, then we may have an issue of grave concern. An army so outfitted could pose a serious threat if they should turn against us. We must proceed cautiously."

"My Lord, what about the other races? What if they should side with him? He could reinforce their positions and…"

"We are the closest to his location, so let us be the first to meet him. If we can make an arrangement with him, perhaps we can gain control of this situation before the others intrude. Even if they should make a pact with him, he does not know what waits for him out there, and we should be ready for that."

"Then we should go first thing tomorrow morning," the Dean suggests. "But now, what about the Guard…should we inform them about this new arrival?"

"The Guard doesn't need to know about it so far. There may be a time when word will eventually find its way, but they should know their place by now and not question our judgment. What happens in the valley is not their concern. Their only purpose is to attend to the city's defense, and on that rare occasion to send aid to the others to maintain our…relations," he finishes coldly.

Marelle found her way through the city streets, quickly arriving back inside the Allegiance Guard headquarters. She had removed the monk's robe disguise along the way and held it under her arm. As she returned to her office, she placed it in a cabinet where she kept an assortment of other clothes in storage. She then left her office in search of the Captain. She found him in his office contemplating several reports of odd disturbances handed in the previous day by the guards at some of the forward outposts.

"Sir? Do you have a moment?" she calls as she peers through the door.

"Lieutenant Carronel, come in," he answers, barely glancing up at her.

"Sir, I have something to report, but I wish to make this confidential."

"Oh, and what might that be?"

"It has to do with the events of yesterday, and I have reason to believe the Dean of the Academy may not have an immediate desire to share this with us."

The Captain pulls his gaze from the reports and directs his

attention at the younger officer while she relays the report Haran gave earlier. When she was finished, the Captain held himself for a long moment before replying.

"Lieutenant, you know I don't hold much care for the bunk that comes out of that academy. They just barely give us any word at all on what's going on out there, and even then, the only thing we're told to do is walk the walls looking out for any cross-eared rabbit that gets too close."

He looks at the reports on the table in front of him.

"This Thaelyn character… Who does he think he is, coming in here and setting off the blazes of hell in that valley? These finger-waggling wizards see no end of getting on my nerves."

"With respect, from the sound of it, this particular one actually did us a favor, at least indirectly."

"Maybe so," he acknowledges reluctantly. "But that doesn't soften my regard for them by much. For instance, we have those wizards in the academy and their crazed fetishes. What is this mithril, anyway? It's just a lot of nonsense as far as I can tell! If it's so good, why don't we have any, eh? No, give me a good cold piece of steel and I'll show you who's in command," he waves a finger for emphasis.

"All right, but what should we do about this report? What if the Governor should send an envoy out there without telling us? He could try making a deal behind our backs."

"I'll have the guards at the south gate watch for that and inform me as soon as they see something. If the Governor thinks he's going around me on this one, I'll know about it. I have a few words of my own I want to share with that man."

Chapter 8

MEETINGS

"Kailen?"

"Yes, Kaliya, what is it?"

"I didn't sleep well last night, but then I suppose that's nothing new. This new assignment, for instance, it has me concerned."

"You know as well as I that your service record has been, well, less than satisfactory. You've been serving the Sentinels for…how long? Since you were old enough to carry a weapon…and look at you. Where has it brought you?"

"I want to help our people. I want to make a difference! I want to see an end to this war, once and for all, but we never get a chance for it. Can you blame me for being so frustrated all the time?"

"Kaliya, I can't blame you, but there are rules we need to follow. Simply going out there and recklessly marching around trying to be a hero ultimately won't result in anything."

"Yeah, and this is basically what he said, other than simply trying to make the effort when no one else is… He was trying to counsel me even without the psychology part."

"He sounds like a solid leader, and on multiple levels."

"I suppose so. You should've seen it, Kailen. His people praise him like an icon of inspiration. The way they hold themselves, their dedication and sense of duty, even their attitudes. Cu'Nar's Grace, Kailen, they seem to believe they can move mountains. And I actually have to believe they can do this, if this is how they developed on that world of theirs. I would be truly fascinated to read a little of their history."

"Maybe the idea of actually going there isn't such a bad thing for you, if you should really decide to do this."

"But Kailen, I would feel like I'm abandoning the rest of you, and I couldn't do that."

"I know, Kaliya, but at the same time, you're not getting anywhere around here, and you still have a long way to go in your life."

"Yeah, and yet, even in this short time, I feel something stirring up inside of me. When he first came in, and blasted those orcs, as if the shock of that bomb wasn't bad enough..." she chuckles faintly. "Then I saw them kneeling in some sort of prayer."

"A prayer? So, they do hold some sort of religious belief?"

"Oh, I have no doubt, and it reflects on the teachings of these Estelar of theirs. I got curious, so I walked up to one of their priests and started asking about this. At first, I was confused. After all, these were orcs, and apparently, they committed some really nasty atrocities on their world. So why, in all the nether-space, would you offer any kind of prayer for them."

"Interesting. And the answer?"

"You know how I usually feel about orcs, right? Well, that got shot down so fast that I had to go searching for my horns afterwards."

"Really!" he smiles.

"They hold the belief that life is precious, no matter who it belongs to or what they did. But crime is still crime, and it must be punished just the same. So, while they might punish them for these crimes, they must still respect the essence of life, as it could've served some other role, but it was wasted on this."

"Fascinating..."

"She said that orcs are living beings with just as much right to exist as any other. This thing they call the Measure of Balance is a doctrine to describe the two sides of existence, positive and negative, and how life is simply a contest of survival to find a path down the middle, and it's not a free ride. His people have apparently aligned themselves on what they describe as the positive side of this equation, largely due to his influence on their world. So, now I'm wondering how the negative side appears and how these two create this Balance overall. Then, I wonder about us. Where do we sit on it? He says the cu'Nar are some kind of elemental beings, and likely of positive energy, since he felt a positive glow coming out of me. So, Kailen, does this mean we should also be on that side, and if so, just what sort of role are we supposed to be playing here."

"This is a very curious form of philosophical principle, Kaliya. I'm not sure how to advise you, but if this truly catches your attention, you might want to investigate it further. Maybe you might learn something from it. Then, perhaps, you could share it with the rest of us," he grins.

"One thing is for sure," she reflects dreamily. "When he activated that portal conduit of his, I could see an image of his world. It was beautiful. It seemed so bright and full of potential. It reminded me of our home on Ruuki uy'Daan," she lowers her head.

"I'm sure you miss that, and so do I, for that matter. All I can say is we'll see what happens after we meet him. For now, let's eat and make ourselves ready. You should also gather up a few of your things in case the decision is made for you to stay on with him as our intermediary."

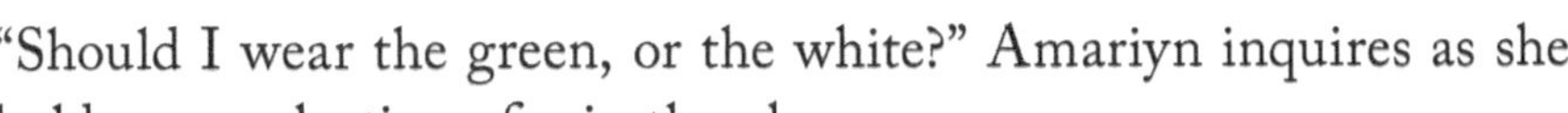

"Should I wear the green, or the white?" Amariyn inquires as she holds up a selection of priestly robes.

"Oh please, my Dear," Throdeth begs while pouring through a stack of old books. "Can't you see I'm trying to decide which of these journals to pack?"

"Will the two of you settle down, please?" Relissa chirps. "They won't be going anywhere any time soon. You have all day, and the rest of the month for it, to be sure."

"Green symbolizes the fertility of life," Amariyn flusters. "But white represents purity. Oh! I want to make the right impression!"

"Mum! Take the green one."

"Are you sure?"

"Why not? You'll be meeting up with a bunch of druids, so they might like it. I saw a lot of them wearing green. But personally, I don't think the spirit will pay much attention to your dress code."

"I absolutely must bring my journals relating to the migration… for reference," Throdeth agitates to himself. "But should I bring any of the books regarding our time here? Would they even be interested in that?"

"Dah, do you have anything simple, a short form, that you could bring? You don't want to bore them on the first day with all your lectures."

"But there is so much to tell! And we've been separated for so long."

"You can come back anytime you want and spend the whole day with them. I'm sure they'll be happy to hear it. Besides, if you ask real nice, maybe Thaelyn will let you visit Tae'Eladar while you're at it. He's probably got a whole library for you to get lost in."

"Really?" he twitters. "Oh, that would be grand!"

Relissa rolls her eyes at her two parents before heading out the door.

"I'm going to check on the carriage," she calls over her shoulder. "Try not to get too carried away. After all, this war will probably be going on for a while yet, and he's not leaving till it's done."

Relissa passes through the house and out the door into the plaza just across from the large Council building. Standing in front of the building was a carriage led by two graceful white horses. Alongside the carriage was Enforcer Baeleron speaking with another Council member who came outside to see him off.

"Scout Moonshimmer!" he beckons. "Are your parents nearly ready? I've been waiting almost an hour for them."

"Well, you know my Mum and Dah. Everything has to be perfect, and they're very excited about today."

"Well, I certainly hope they can hurry themselves. I'd like to see us on our way soon."

Relissa moves up to the horses to see if she can try out her skills on them. She whispers gently into their ears and one of them reacts with a short nicker.

"Enforcer, this one is a bit thirsty. Would you be kind enough to bring it to a trough before we leave?"

"What? How do you..."

Relissa flashes a knowing smile and strolls back to the house.

"Sir, the watchman from the south gate is here to see you," announces a young officer coming in from the yard.

"Very good, Lieutenant, send him in."

"Captain!" reports the husky gate watchman entering the room. "I'm here to report that a carriage left the gate a short while ago heading to the south. They appeared to be in a hurry."

"And so it goes," he reflects. "Did you notice who was inside, and did they give any mention of where they were going?"

"No word on their destination, but we did see Governor Dramon and the Dean of the Academy riding along."

"As I thought... All right, keep watch, and let me know the moment they return."

"Yes Sir!"

The watchman salutes, turns, and leaves to return to his post.

Several moments later, another voice ushers through the door.

"Sir?" Marelle calls.

"Yes, Lieutenant?"

"I couldn't help but notice the watchman coming in. May I ask what your plans are?"

"For now, watch and wait. As soon as they return, I plan on heading out there myself, if there's still enough daylight for it."

"I thought as much. I would like to ask permission to accompany you, as well as to allow my brother Haran to join."

"What? You want to bring that finger-wiggler with us?"

"Roddy, he's my brother. Can you give him a break?"

"Right. Sorry, Marelle," he sighs. "I'm probably just not in good sorts today."

"Anyway, he's already met with this Thaelyn fellow, and could be useful to provide us with information on how to interact with him, rather than to simply rush out there and stampede on volatile turf."

The Captain considers her words for a moment.

"You're a clever one, you know that? I don't really care to have him along, no offence to you, but you may be right. All right then, send word to make ready as soon as those porkers return. We'll be riding out on horseback to make up for time. If he doesn't know how to do that, he'd better learn fast."

"Yes Sir, and thank you."

+ + + ◆ + + +

"Quickly now, driver!" Governor Dramon insists. "We want to be the first to arrive, and then to be back again before any others have a chance to see us."

The carriage raced along the roadway to the south. A short distance ahead was the southern watchtower marking the limit of the Allegiance Guard's territory. Just beyond that were the foothills of the mountain range separating them from the Badlands, with a gradual trail twisting up the slope.

The carriage holding the two men and their driver was sporty and nimble, drawn by two sturdy grey horses. They maintained a hurried pace all the way up the foothills along the trail to the top. As they crested the range, the valley below came into view.

"Driver, stop!" the Governor shouts.

Stretching out before them was an incredible sight. What was once a desert was now a wide expanse of green meadows and forests. A few scattered flocks of birds could be seen flitting through the treetops, and in the distance, the riverbed, dry for centuries, started to show a few enticing trickles of water flowing through it.

"Dear Gods, look at this place!" murmurs the Dean. "What has he done here?"

"What did your underling say about him?"

"Well, I recall he said he was a mage."

"Indeed! But what sort of mage could cause all this? He must be very powerful, or else he holds some unique form of spell-craft. We need to step carefully to ensure our position. If he is new here, he cannot know much about our world, so let us see how far this can take us. Driver, continue. Quickly, please."

They traced their way down into the valley and across the grasslands southward, unsure of exactly how far they must go, but keeping a watchful eye for any signs of activity. They passed groves of trees and fields of flowers, with the sounds of chirping birds occasionally reaching their ears through the pounding of hooves from the horses.

They see the brightly contrasted shape of a tower taking form on the ground ahead of them, still in its early construction, but clear enough to symbolize the beginnings of new occupation for the region. They pass by and continue a short distance further, soon to make out the shape of an encampment with many troops moving about.

They approach a row of guards monitoring the northern line of the outpost. They slow to a stop in front of them, expecting to be examined before being allowed to proceed. As one of the guards moves up to inspect the arrivals, the Governor calls out to him.

"My good man, we are here to meet with your superior."

The guard looks over the carriage and its occupants without speaking.

"Eh… Can you inform us of where we might find him?" the Governor tries again to elicit a response.

The guard raises a hand in pause and turns to speak to the others in a foreign language, instructing them to open a path for the carriage to pass through.

"Dean," the Governor whispers candidly. "That wasn't the common tongue he was using. Could it be they don't speak our language?"

"This is very peculiar," the Dean replies. "Because my apprentice claimed he was speaking to this Thaelyn fellow before."

"Then we must direct ourselves to him, as he might be fluent in both."

The driver leads the carriage through the checkpoint and into the camp. Soldiers are seen assembled in large clusters around the area. Several building sites were very nearly completed, with more under new construction. The two men studied the scene intently.

"Incredible!" the Governor exclaims mutedly. "All this in barely a day? They must have a great many resources at their disposal."

A tall man, ornately dressed, with silver-white shoulder length hair and oddly golden eyes approaches the carriage as it makes a stop in the center of the camp. Following him is a feminine figure with delicate elven features and enormous feathery white wings.

"Greetings, visitors! I am Lord Thaelyn, and this is my wife, Lady Aerlie. Might I know the pleasure of your acquaintance?"

"Ah, yes. I am Governor Dramon from the city of Rolsklinde, and this man next to me is the head of our Academy of Arcana, Dean Wizard Malorn. We have been told of your arrival and came as soon as it was possible for us to arrange ourselves a meeting. Would you perhaps have a few moments to afford us?"

"I do, and I have been expecting your arrival. I trust that my unannounced incursion has not disturbed you too greatly. Such a necessity became imperative during the course of my war against the orcs."

"Surely, your ingress is quite a surprise, as well as to see what has become of this region. When last we had knowledge of this place, it was a slight bit more...desolate."

"When I first arrived, it was as such, but my obligations demanded I repair that which I harmed during the course of my onslaught of the orcish encampment there in the canyon. Nevertheless, my war must also continue, as the orcs represent a threat to my world and to my people, and this cannot be tolerated."

"I am told you arrived from elsewhere, but orcs, you say? How is it they became such a bother to you?"

"We had a preexisting population of them from some earlier migration effort, though we are unsure where they originated, and yet they were never very cooperative with the rest of us. Then, recently, during these past few decades, something new occurred and we began experiencing an uprising of some sort. This became so intolerable that we had no choice but to finally go to war with them and ultimately to eradicate them entirely from our world. But in those last few moments, we discovered they were using portals to escape from us into this valley. And so, we pursued them."

"Truly fascinating, but this simply begs the question of why you would trouble yourselves to come all this way if your world is, well, I suppose the word to use here is to say cleansed of their unfortunate presence."

"The simple fact that they were seen using portals is dangerous, as this same principle could be used again, but to make incursions back into my world, and this cannot be allowed. Therefore, I have no other choice but to continue my campaign until that threat is ultimately resolved."

"And how would you declare this ultimate resolution?"

"In its simplest form, and unless some other possibility presents itself, it is to wipe them completely out of existence, as they have proven themselves to be untrustworthy to coexist peacefully with anyone else, or to possess any such gifts as these. My consultation with your representative earlier tells me this world has similarly been under siege for some number of centuries, and with similar results, in one form or another. This only exasperates the predicament."

"Indeed, I suppose it does, but they are not the only foes we face in this world. Did he inform you of the others?"

"He did. We have a hostile society of elves to the south, and a foreign body called Suuden-Aryku to our east."

"Yes, and those two tend to be rather dangerous, each on their own. You would be well-advised to watch yourself out here. But as I observe this quaint little setting of yours, it becomes apparent that you have brought with you a considerable number of troops, as well as supplies. In fact, it would seem you are making very quick work of settling into this region, which brings me some concern of my own."

"I suppose it might at that. But be assured, I have no untoward intentions to any society that would be friendly to our cause. In fact, it is my understanding that you too are at odds with the orcs, possibly also these Flame Elves, as you call them, and could perhaps use my aid in your own war efforts. Is this not the case?"

"We have had our moments here and there, though with your presence here, I suppose that might change. But my concerns are more along the lines of ownership. You see, this land once belonged to us until that orcish intrusion usurped it away. We regard it as our former territory, and it was quite useful to us to supply our needs once upon a time. Furthermore, you might also be regarded as a foreign body in our world, and now here you are occupying this space. We tend to hold certain policies here where squatters are concerned, that if one such should wish to, ehm, borrow a portion of our land, we might receive a form of compensation from them, hmm?"

Thaelyn frowns slightly as he begins to sense the Governor's direction.

"Sir, while I might not wish to argue your claims of ownership, when I first arrived, this land was occupied by a good quarter million orcs. This is no simple intrusion, and could not have occurred over any brief moment of time. Furthermore, I noticed no on-going battles for ownership, nor did I see any previous remnants of occupation by anything other than that of orcish design."

He gestures his hand out across the land as he continues.

"I took this land from them and set my own men upon it to act as a foothold until I could ascertain my whereabouts and the nature of the enemies I might find here. By some rules of engagement, this could represent the spoils of victory, though I would not necessarily go so far if I found myself intruding on land so obviously belonging to another power. Nevertheless, as for compensation, I think fighting your war would be compensation enough. As we already mentioned, I came all this way to continue mine, but at this point, I am also attending to yours as well. Therefore, to the contrary, if you were to join your army with mine, we could take back the rest of these lands, and then your issue of orcs, Flame Elves, Suuden-Aryku, and land ownership could all be resolved together, and I would be on my way."

"To the contrary, yes," the Governor muses. "But you see, this war has dragged on for so long that we have drained a good many of our resources along the way. Therefore, our army, if you can call it that, must be dedicated elsewhere. This orcish intrusion simply grew too big for us to contend with after a while. Aside from that, there are other races involved in this world, some of which have caused a considerable amount of, shall we say, difficulty for those of us who simply wish to live in peace. These elves, for example... There are actually two societies, neither of which has been particularly kind to the notion of peace around here. They began this war some number of centuries ago, and this has left a wake of utter devastation behind them. As the result, our people are most displeased by this."

Thaelyn turns to glance at Aerlie for the suggestion, and together they reflected on Haran's statement of the apparent bigotry up in the city.

"Governor," he begins again. "Would it not be true that these orcs, perhaps also the Suuden-Aryku, might be just as much the enemy to them as they would be to you? Would it also be correct to say these Flame Elves would carry a similar appearance? Therefore, despite your grievance, you might share a common goal together and could possibly combine forces to resolve this."

"As for the elves, I would leave them to their due for the trouble they caused elsewhere. They, with their questionable religious practices and unholy rites, are unworthy of consideration. I would advise keeping away from them before they set their sights on you as well."

"Unholy rites..." Thaelyn mutters privately.

"Then we have the Suuden-Aryku. They are a most frightening foe, and we tend to stay away from them entirely. It is my understanding they are primarily focused in areas to our east against another disturbing arrival, called the Daanen-Aryku. These people came down to our world with their most hated enemies on their tails and laid waste to the entire region over there. Even worse, these Flame Elves, who were bad enough before this, joined forces with them, along with these horrid orcs, and now the three of them continually harass our people to no end! We care not to get involved in any of that. Let those foreign vagabonds take their punishment as it is properly deserving of them. I cannot see how they could be anything more than undesirable drifters. Therefore, we have these others pursuing them for whatever unpleasantness they once created."

"This is a rather curious depiction. Then is this to say your people hold such an aversion to them, perhaps due to them being foreign, or perhaps as they seem not to have a proper home for themselves, that they should simply be wiped away?"

"I am sure whatever cause they brought down unto themselves was worthy. And since these Suuden-Aryku are also known to carry some, eh, rather elaborate paraphernalia, we want nothing to do with them.

"But Governor, despite your claims of a desire for peace, when you consider this situation overall, you are not going to find such unless you and these others fight for it in an organized manner and against those enemies you can be sure of. I should think learning the true nature of these people would enlighten you of their woes and perhaps also bring you into better alignment of the fundamental need to find common ground together. If these Daanen-Aryku are travelers, for instance, and the Suuden-Aryku are pursuing them for any reason, and this here is essentially a foreign world...to them, that is...one might wonder why the Suuden-Aryku would care to hunt them in this place if it is so far removed from that place they originally came from."

"Because they are criminals, this much I can be certain of! Why else would anyone hunt down such miscreants to the ends of Creation?"

"I see, and your other grievance relating to this second society of elves is simply due to your malcontent that they hold a culture you do not otherwise agree with?"

"Precisely!" he affirms solidly. "Between them and the Flame

Elves, they destroyed the greater part of our world. They are a despicable society of scoundrels that should meet their own end the same as they brought to so many others. But I suppose…" he pauses conspicuously to survey the camp and all the soldiers in their elaborate gear. "If you truly wish to dispose of the villains of this world…oh yes, this would do nicely as a mote of incentive. As I said, we ran short of resources long ago, but you seem to have some very fine accoutrements here on your men. Oh, if we could only get our hands on a trifle or two of this. Then, dare I say, we could join forces and wipe away everything else in this world that is otherwise so undesirable."

Thaelyn and Aerlie again turned and gazed deeply into each other's faces. They shared a number of silent telepathic thoughts over the obvious implications being suggested here.

"Governor," Thaelyn returns. "I suppose at this time I probably need to refer to a few policies of my own. One of these is that I hold a principle where I do not wish to disturb the natural growth and evolution of a foreign society, and yours would certainly count as one of those. While I might grieve for you about your shortages, and perhaps we could negotiate some manner of trade, I am limited to only that which you have previous experience with, not to augment you with that which could alter your prior achievements. This would create a clear imbalance of capacity in this world."

"An imbalance of capacity?!" he yelps.

"Indeed. I am a man of law and justice. I do not take the word of any single man, and instead I investigate the situation. I learn who is out there and what qualities they hold dear, and I judge for myself if they are worthy of my consideration. I am also a man who believes in unity. If one or more of these other societies are actually victims of wrongdoing, I will join at their sides against the villains of the world, including those who otherwise choose not to take the same action. Your prejudice is not welcome in my eyes, as it becomes clear to me you are not even trying to understand your neighbors."

"Neighbors! Bah! And do you think you can actually hold

yourself up against all I just mentioned, with this pittance I see out here and your righteous vows?"

"Governor, I am the king of a full world, a world I united with my own hand out of many nations, most of which did not get along politely. From this, I created a society of highly refined values, and great industrial and economic prestige. This out here is but a tiny fraction of my full military. I doubt there is anything in this world, including your Flame Elves or your Suuden-Aryku that could represent a bother to me. So, if you were truly a wise man, you might take note of the equipment you are so gloating over and multiply that on the scale of millions!"

"Millions!" he wheezes as he recoils from the assertion.

"And the people of my world are wholly and faithfully devoted to my rule. If I should call for it, they will rush forward at the mere mention of the word. Therefore, whatever war you have been so unfortunately suffering from in this world will soon come to a rather abrupt end, all thanks to me squatting on this wasted piece of land. And you can give your thanks to those orcs that apparently invaded my home from this world, and how they called my attention back to it. Furthermore, I will do this if for no other reason than because of those unfortunate victims you find so undesirable. I have conquered entire nations of people with such attitudes as yours. Now they serve me in mine. And when I am finished here, I shall return and teach you the same."

"Indeed!" he scorns. "We shall see about that, Noble Sir! But be aware that there are bodies in this world that can be rather... unpredictable. Driver! Take us home, promptly!"

Thaelyn and Aerlie both watched as the carriage made a hasty departure.

"So, um…that went well," she smirks ironically.

"Indeed, and now I understand Haran's mention of that intolerance. But this goes a little beyond a simple superstition."

"Yes, he seems to like his position of power, and he delights in putting the rest down. One might wonder if he actually has any desire to fight in this war at all."

"True, let the others fight and suffer…this is his message. Further, to buy more power for himself so he could potentially do away with whatever remains."

"While he takes fashion from such luxuries as our prestige," Aerlie muses.

"Perhaps we can speak to Haran more on this, if he should return again."

"Maybe, but I'll also suggest that last statement sounded a bit like a threat."

"He is a typical aristocrat," Thaelyn replies. "I have seen such as this back home, from the early days. We should not expect much help from him, not that we need it."

"Come on, you two!" Relissa urges. "It'll take us a good half a day on the carriage if we press the horses."

Amariyn and Throdeth lumber out of the family home, each of them carrying a large bag.

"Dear," Amariyn wheezes. "Did you honestly need to bring so many books with you? Goodness, there's bound to be time to return another day with this."

"With apologies, my love, but one can never be sure what to expect under such conditions. Besides, some of these are empty journals to scribe my notes of the meeting."

"Empty journals! Just how many notes do you expect to write in one day?" she chuckles softly.

They load up into the carriage and settle themselves on the seat, with Enforcer Baeleron taking up a position on the driver's box. They pull out of the plaza and maneuver through the lanes to the hidden gate leading out of the city. Once on the open road, they press the horses into a quick trot to make up for lost time.

Travelling across the country in such a manner is the lost gift of a pleasant outing. War and troubled times have taken away many of the pleasures of life for elven society, as they are too often forced to huddle within the confines of their concealed homes. But this day held a new meaning, a freshness of life that for so long seemed forgotten.

The carriage sped along the road through the fields that separated the cities of Solinaia and Rolsklinde. They passed by the western watchtower of the Allegiance Guard, marking the outward edge of the territory owned by the human city. Soon, they would come into view of the next one, where they would need to turn south towards the pass and across the mountains into the valley.

Relissa peered out into the distance. She could see the faint blur of a cloud of dust rising up from the lower end of the foothills and moving northward.

"Looks like someone beat us to it today," she offers. "Must be the humans going home. I wonder how things went. They seem to be in a bit of a hurry."

"No doubt they're just investigating the new arrivals," Throdeth suggests. "I hope they didn't scare them away!"

"Buggers to that, I say! Thaelyn's not so easy to push over."

The human carriage passed by the watchtower and continued northward without pause. Neither the Governor nor the Dean paid any attention to the small glimmer from the elven buggy far to the west.

Enforcer Baeleron continued to press the horses around the watchtower and southward to the foothills, where they slowed to make an easy climb after such a long run. The winding trail up the slope brought a new level of anxiety to the passengers, each with their own expectations of what they would see as they crested the top.

✦ ✦ ✦ ✦ ✦

"Kaliya, are you ready?" Kailen asks as he makes the final checks on the hover-shuttle they would be using to travel to the Badlands.

"Yeah, I was just trying to decide on a few things. I guess I'm a little nervous."

"Nervous? About a new position, maybe? Kaliya, serving as

an intermediary is actually a very important job, even if it is a non-combat role. It has its demands, and Elder Girhani is right that you don't really have any experience in it, or training for that matter. But I'll help you along."

"Thanks. But I guess, even with everything else, I'm asking myself where all this will ultimately lead us."

"Maybe so. If this Thaelyn is all you say he is, it could be the salvation we've been waiting for. But I'm not going to be so convinced until I've seen it for myself. I need to remain focused on our own security."

"Ever the High Commander, right?" she smiles.

"It's my job these days, and not an easy one. I don't think I was ready for it when they hit me with the promotion."

The two of them step into the hover-shuttle. The shuttle itself was typical of their technology. It did not use wheels, instead it would glide along the ground hovering on a superconductive cushion of energy. This particular model was configured with an open cab so they could enjoy the fresh air outside.

Kailen made himself comfortable in the driver's seat and powered up. As the vehicle came to life, it began to float effortlessly just a short distance off the ground. He engages the drive system, and they begin to move.

The vehicle hanger where they kept their ground transports was deep inside the ship, which at this point was mostly covered by surface soil…a small mountain of it. In order for them to use it, they first had to dig a tunnel leading out into the open. And as Kailen began driving, he followed the tunnel into the open air and up to a nearby roadway. From there, they followed the road across the local countryside, and eventually onto a main throughway westward in the direction of Rolsklinde.

The speed of the craft exceeded that of even the best horse and carriage team of the other races, allowing them to cover the distance to the first watchtower in only a brief amount of time. From there, and much like the others, they needed to reach the central watchtower, and then turn to glide up the trail and over the mountain.

"I'm still a little concerned about something," Kailen admits.

"What's that?"

"Well, I don't like keeping secrets from the Council, but I did on this one occasion for you since you were such a wreck after your return. The mention of spies is a bad one, and it puts a lot of things into question."

"I know, but until we can find a way around it, I don't know what else to say other than to be careful of what you say."

"Yeah, and this seems like a contradiction."

"But I think we did well on this occasion," Kaliya considers. "We got the information out that was necessary to inform, with enough suggestions of principles to understand the key points. And all without telling them we have a bunch of gods fighting a war over our heads," she grins.

Kailen breaks out in a bold laugh at the thought.

"Kaliya, I think Elder Vankkar is right on one thing, you have changed a bit since before this incident. Your personality has improved."

"Thank you, Kailen," she smiles brightly. "Maybe that meld really did knock my horns back into place a little."

The scenery passes by in a blur, and Kaliya can only think of what waits for her in her new occupation. That is, assuming Kailen agrees and Thaelyn accepts her for the position. Her contemplation is momentarily interrupted as they pass the central watchtower and turn to the south.

She looks up at the mountains, recalling the events of that fateful day, now wondering what the valley may look like after her short absence. It seemed so unreal, she almost expected it to have been a dream, and the valley will be exactly the same as it always has been. But that would most certainly mean a complete end to her career, as no one would ever trust her again.

On the hillside, she thought she could make out a shape, glimmering slightly in the sunlight, working its way up the pass.

"Kailen, do you see that? Is that a carriage?"

"I believe so, and from the gilding, I might suggest it to be elven."

"Relissa?" she whispers to herself.

A gate watch guard rushes through the streets on horseback up to the city barracks. He carries news demanded by the Captain to be brought as quickly as possible. He hurries through the barracks gate where he hops off his mount and dashes across the yard towards the office of Captain Kholgard.

"Sir!" he announces briskly. "I bring news. They've just returned through the south gate."

"Excellent. Thank you, Corporal, that'll be all."

The young officer salutes and leaves.

The Captain gets up from his desk and briskly walks down the hall to Marelle's office.

"Lieutenant? It's time! Get your brother and meet me near the stables by the south gate."

"Yes, Sir!" echoes a shout from within the office.

The Captain turns to cross the yard and leave the barracks, making a quick pace to the southern entrance of the city.

Marelle grabs a small shoulder bag to collect a few items of importance for the journey and dashes off to find Haran. He had been previously instructed to meet her in the lower district in preparation for the trip.

Haran had been sitting in the Ten Eagles Tavern for a good portion of the morning. The sickly smell of the courtesans' perfume was beginning to turn his stomach. He had been approached on several occasions in an effort to entice him to patronize the establishment, but his mind was on far more important matters, or at least far more distracting.

He had learned of the mysterious departure of the carriage earlier in the morning from a note from his sister and wondered what the Governor and the Dean were up to. He was anxious to speak with Thaelyn once more to know what sort of deal he made with them. And so, he sat and waited, occasionally glancing at the door looking for his sister to show up and lead him to the stables. He was unsure about the prospect of riding horseback, however. He has never been on one before.

Marelle surged through the tavern doors and began scanning the room for her brother.

"Haran, it's time!" she shouts across the room as she sees him standing up from a table.

They hurry out the door together and run along the street toward the stables. The Captain was waiting with three horses, saddled up and ready. When they arrive, Marelle helps Haran onto his mount and adjusts the stirrups to fit his legs.

"Take these reigns and hold onto the horn as tight as you can," she advises. "Do as I do. We'll be moving fast, so keep low."

She then jumps onto her own horse and settles in.

"All right you two," the Captain declares. "Stay close and try to keep up."

The three of them leave through the gate and out onto the road. The Captain kicks his horse into a gallop. Marelle helps to encourage Haran's horse to follow, and together they take after the Captain. Haran's knuckles turn white as he grips his saddle horn. The bouncing of the saddle under him makes it difficult for him to find an easy equilibrium of movement and balance. He finally tries using his legs as a sort of shock absorber. It wasn't comfortable, but at least he didn't have as much concern for vaulting right off the back end of the horse.

As they moved along the road out from the city, they could see the shape of the central watchtower in the distance. Further behind that were the foothills of the mountains marking the boundary with the Badlands. And although they couldn't see it yet, somewhere near the summit was a small glimmer of light reflecting back at them.

◆

"Kailen, slow down so we can travel with them," Kaliya bids as she felt a trickle of hope to see a friendly face in the carriage they were approaching.

"I don't think we have much choice. That thing is moving at a crawl and taking up half the road!" he responds with a hint of amusement.

"Well, dear brother," she retorts cheerfully. "That's what you get when you use beasts of burden to do your chores!"

He turns and displays a pleasant grin at her.

"We're coming up on the crest soon," he observes. "Maybe we can try pulling alongside of them there."

Relissa sensed the slight humming sound of something unnatural following behind her. She turned to look over her shoulder through the rear of the carriage.

"Enforcer, there's a Daanen'kai hover-thingy right behind us."

"This pass isn't wide enough for both of us. They'll have to wait."

Relissa sticks her hand out through the rear window flap to catch the attention of the other vehicle. She can see Kailen driving it with Kaliya in the passenger seat.

"Kaliya!" she shouts. "Did they let you out to play again?"

"More like they're putting me behind a desk..." she shouts back.

"What? Why? You didn't do anything wrong!"

"It's not like that. I'm actually happy about it. I finally managed to stand on my own two hooves during that inquisition of a debriefing they put me through. And, in fact, Elder Vankkar actually complemented me for arguing my point successfully this time. Can you believe it?"

"Jiggers, girl, you must've got a good knock out of that meeting."

"Yeah, maybe I did."

"It's not entirely set in stone just yet, though," Kailen offers. "I need to make an evaluation first."

"Aye, that's a good one. But try not to let your horns go flying off in my direction."

The summit comes around as the two vehicles make another twist in the pass. At the top, it flattens out onto a small mesa wide enough to allow both vehicles to pull alongside each other. After that, it's simply a chore of downhill movement before they enter into the valley proper. As they reach the top, they halt to observe the view.

"Cu'Nar's eyes!" Kailen mutters. "What in all the nether-space happened out here?"

"Over there... Do you see it?" Kaliya asserts as she points into the valley. "There in the canyon, the blast center."

From their vantage point, they could make out the form of a large bowl-shaped depression roughly in the middle of the canyon deep into the valley.

"And where were you when that happened?" he asks.

"Just off to the side, over there above the cliff."

"So close?" he screeches. "Baby sister, I thank whatever power it was that kept you safe."

"Grace of the Seldarine," Amariyn's voice trails off as she looks out into the valley.

"How is it possible, Relissa?" Throdeth mumbles.

"Thaelyn's a very powerful being. Don't ask me how he does it, it's all gibber to me!" she jests. "All I know is he had a bunch of druids helping him with this part."

"Is he one of the Tel'Quessir? I've never heard of such a power as this before."

"No, he's something else, something special, but he leads the others, all of them. It's all one big nation back there now. And all part of a special project, by the way, that those dragons were trying to protect. Therefore, they didn't like seeing us arriving."

Relissa moves her eyes across the region until she settles on the river basin.

"Well, I'll be a marsh rat's bumpkin..." she mumbles. "There's water down there!"

"Enforcer," Amariyn instructs. "Take us down there, please, quick as you can."

The Enforcer entices the horses into a carefully hurried step down the slope. Kailen follows patiently behind. They wend their way around the pass leading into the valley and across the fields, picking up their pace as they move along. Trees and grass rush by, and Relissa catches glimpses of birds flying overhead.

"Do you feel that, Throdeth? Do you?" Amariyn declares as her long-dormant senses come back alive again.

"You're the steward, my Dear, not I. I'm clearly not as attuned to it as you."

"You'll feel it as we get closer."

The shape of a partially built white tower comes into view ahead of them.

"Looks like work is coming along nicely on that," Relissa remarks as they pass by it.

"What's that, Kaliya?" Kailen asks on seeing the odd construction.

"It's called a Dynamistic Conditioning Spire. It's a long story, but it has to do with their magical skills, and therefore their technology."

"Fascinating...a form of technology based on something called magic. Now that is a contradiction," he chuckles.

A few moments later, they see the front line of the guard post on the northern edge of the camp. As with the earlier visitation by the Governor and Dean, the two newcomers slow to a stop and allow the guards to make an inspection.

"Guard," Kaliya shouts. "We represent the Daanen-Aryku and Night Elf delegations come to meet with His Lordship. Is he available?"

Kailen gazes at his sister in awe at the ease of her interactions with these strangers, as well as her skill with their language.

"Aye, you'll find him within the camp," the guard replies. "Proceed ahead slowly."

"Thank you."

The guard waves them through as they open a path. Kailen yields again to the slower elven carriage and follows closely behind as they make their way into the camp. They pass by several construction sites, each of which is a flurry of activity, and eventually come to rest not far from the gateway node.

As they unload themselves from their transports, Kaliya notices the portal image has altered from the grand fortress to something new. It now showed a long road leading off from the portal window, lined on both sides with a series of basic industrial buildings and crafting centers. It bore a resemblance to an industrial park, though not nearly as technologically sophisticated as what her people might build. She could see several loading docks where wagons were picking up supplies and building materials.

"Do these people actually have..." her voice trails off.

Kailen follows her attention.

"Looks like a neat little manufacturing center. Early Industrial, just like you said."

"Yeah, but Kailen, they wear medieval armor and use swords!"

"Well, Sis, you can never fully judge something by its outward appearance. Especially if they also have a conveyor," he points at the gateway unit, "which breaks that image even further. You mentioned them taking a different tech ladder, right?"

"Yeah, and I think I'm going to lose my horns a few more times before we're finished here."

In the foreground of the portal window, they saw a series of wagons approaching, where one-by-one they vanished from sight briefly, only to reappear in a brisk flash on this side of it, then to be directed away to the far side of the camp.

"Jiggers, Kaliya," Relissa muses as she joins her friend's side. "What's that now?"

"Fascinating..." Kaliya murmurs as she reflects on the perceived images.

"Kaliya and Relissa!" rings a jovial voice. "I am so pleased to see your faces again."

Thaelyn approaches the delegations from a cluster of workers directing one of the larger construction projects on the far side of the camp.

Aerlie arrives from the other side where she had been attending a campsite in conversation with some of the priests.

"Oh my..." Amariyn declares. "You're one of the Winged Folk, the Aril, aren't you?"

"I am..." Aerlie declares. "And I am very pleased to make the acquaintance of one of the lost Children of the Flowering. Welcome."

"I am Lord Thaelyn, at your service, my friends," he bows politely. "And this is my wife, Lady Aerlie."

Kailen nods to the Enforcer to take the initiative. The elven officer then steps forward to give his greetings.

"I am Enforcer Baeleron of the Guild of Wardens from the city of Solinaia. I offer my greetings to you, Your Excellences. I would also take this moment, if I may, to introduce Councilman Throdeth and Councilwoman Amariyn Moonshimmer as representatives of the Elven High Council."

"Moonshimmer, is it?" Thaelyn eyes Relissa.

"Aye, my parents," she smiles. "They don't get out much, but I managed to convince them to go for a little ride with me."

"But one moment here. This brings up a curious point. According to the traditional role of elven society, members of the Elven Council tend to belong to the noble families. Which would mean..." he raises his brow at the girl.

"Aye, I am. And this was another of my problems as a tyke. I'm just a wee bit rough around the edges."

"Ah! Just a wee bit. How fortunate for us."

Thaelyn and Aerlie both share a bold chuckle as they continue the introduction.

"Indeed, then it is my special pleasure to make the acquaintance. You have a very spirited daughter here."

Kailen steps up next.

"And I am High Commander Kailen Nazég of the Daanen-Aryku Sentinels Force. It is a pleasure to meet with you."

"Whoo!" Aerlie chirps. "Now there's a deep voice."

"Nazég?" Thaelyn muses as he passes his glance between him and Kaliya.

"He's my brother, Your Lordship," Kaliya answers.

"Powers help us, and I thought you were tall," he muses as he studies Kailen's excessive height, which measured nine and a half feet. "Tell me, how do the females of your society manage men of such proportions?" he grins.

"We have our ways," she giggles. "You should see Ankhia, his wife. She keeps him in line well enough."

"Really! Well, nevertheless, it is my special pleasure to meet you too, Commander."

Amariyn's nerves were starting to jump from the strong energies in the surrounding area.

"Your Lordship, forgive me," she pleads. "But I was once a caretaker of a shrine in our fair city, where we used to have a sacred tree. I feel it so strongly here. Could you possibly allow me to look upon it briefly?"

"And, Your Lordship," Throdeth adds. "While I'm sure there are many matters of state we should attend to, I would also hope we may find the time to discuss the affairs of the elven nations since the migration. There is so much I hope to catch up on."

Relissa coughs emphatically.

"You'll have to forgive my Mum and Dah, Your Lordship. Their heads have been spinning ever since I told them about you."

"Indeed, but such exuberance can also be refreshing," he admits. "Aerlie, perhaps you could attend to the needs of our elven associates while I discuss matters with the Daanen-Aryku."

"Of course, my love," she affirms.

"And Relissa, can I distract your attention briefly for a few private words?"

"Private words?" she wonders.

Thaelyn turns to send a quick stare at Aerlie. She briefly rolls her eyes at the Daanen'kai delegates, then returns and smiles with a subtle nod.

Relissa took notice of the interaction. She studied Thaelyn, then Aerlie, and instantly felt a shiver of some kind for the implications.

Kaliya also took notice of the interaction.

"Uh oh…" she whispers silently.

Kailen was not as experienced to take immediate notice of the signal, but he did turn to Kaliya's mutterings.

"Uh oh what?"

"I saw something just now. You speak of Elder Vankkar and telepathy? Well, these two use it often, I think."

"If you will follow me," Aerlie smiles pleasantly at the Night Elf delegation. "We can sit near the tree. I'm sure that would be a delightful place to find our comfort to talk."

As Aerlie moves away with the Night Elves, Relissa turns to Thaelyn.

"What happened?" she asks quietly.

He raises his brow at her to inquire of her thoughts.

"I'm sly enough to catch that look you gave her," she admits. "Something's up, isn't it. Did someone show up earlier? I saw a carriage zipping along the road as we were coming up. It looked like the humans."

"Your scouting skills show good form, Relissa, and your intuition is quite sharp. Yes, something did happen. The Governor of Rolsklinde and Haran's Dean were here earlier, and it did not go well."

"Bloody hell. What did those wonky nits do down here?"

"Let us come to that momentarily. Commander, my apologies for the distraction. Perhaps we can find some pleasant seating for ourselves."

He leads his group to an area of seating for the rest of their conversation.

"Commander," Thaelyn begins. "I am sure you have many questions, and I hope I can satisfy your concerns of my presence here. Is there anything in particular you would wish to engage upon first?"

"There are actually a few things that were in hot debate within our Elder Council, but I think the most imperative is the security of our borders. We have suffered a long string of attacks from our enemies in this world and do not wish to find ourselves subject to another front. Kaliya explained to me her interactions with you, and while it certainly seems positive, I need to take this objectively so I can make my own evaluation."

"Of course, and as a ranking officer, I can fully understand your position. Perhaps we could review some of the details of what Kaliya disclosed to you so I can assess where we stand together."

"Your Lordship," Kaliya notes. "I felt it was necessary to tell him a number of things, since he is the highest-ranking officer in our service, and he does have a need to know, in order to make any decisions. Also, I think we have a few issues of special importance at play here that demand some level of shared knowledge. So, I hope I didn't put myself in a bad light by telling him you're some kind of half-god thing," she grins shyly.

Thaelyn raises his brow at her before continuing.

"Very well, but then we must ask ourselves what sort of reaction he had to it, and how this might affect our relations."

"Reaction..." she muses. "Is that before or after searching for his horns?" she smirks.

"Ah, but of course," he smiles. "We need to remind ourselves of this unfortunate condition."

"We have a few details on our side that I needed to combine into my report, and for this, we can say my decision relating to Kailen's 'need to know' was based on some of our own experiences in recent times with the orcs and Sargeras."

"I see. So, we have something in the background driving us on this occasion."

"Yes. And some of it seems a little too convenient to be accidental. Also, we decided to withhold a few of these details from our Council, due to that issue of potential spies, and chose only to give them a number of rational explanations for things that are clearly evident to the observer. For instance, orcs invading your world, possibly due to Sargeras, therefore, you might be a bit upset."

"Very clever, young lady," he nods. "Did I not say there could be potential, if only you apply yourself?"

Kaliya smiled at the latest compliment as Kailen continued.

"She tells us you had these orcs apparently invading your world, and then you chased them back here, only to find a huge number of them out in this valley. She also explained that bomb you dropped. We detected the explosion, and a few of our forward scouting patrols saw the cloud. It's frightening to think it was an antimatter device, however."

"Perhaps. But I would only use it in cases of dire need, and this was one of those cases. I needed to establish a foothold, time was of the essence, and I did not wish to engage in a long and potentially bloody ground offensive. Therefore..." he shrugs.

"Right, and then all of this..." he surveys the local area for the greenery. "How do we explain this? This goes well beyond anything our science could ever dream of."

"Yes, this application is indeed a very unique one, and also complicated. It involves forces that go beyond physical definition. You would really need to understand the underlying principles before grasping the process, otherwise, as Kaliya says, it would simply blow your horns off."

"Oh, so is she teaching you a few of our expressions now?" he grins.

"Indeed, and it would seem you have some colorful ones."

"Then, let's ask about this. Relating to Kaliya's mention of you being half god, this is a very curious term for us, as we're not a religious society. She tried explaining some of this, but I'm still a little shaky on this relationship between you, these gods, and Sargeras...and I suppose also the cu'Nar. Can you explain this to me a little better?"

"Very well, then we should go into a little history. Once, long ago, and we are speaking of an extreme measure of time here, there was a battle we call the Celestial War. The current gods, whom we describe as the Societies of the Estelar, a conglomeration of races that have combined into one vast society covering the greater part of Creation, where Creation, in this case, represents a great many individual universes and other dimensional bodies, were in conflict with an older precursor society whom we call the Primordials. We take this name from the Estelar, as I suspect it is not a racial name, but rather a symbolic reference to something older than they are."

"Wow, that's already stretching my horns."

"Quite possibly," he smiles. "The Primordials were discovered committing a number of atrocities on younger races, and the Estelar took exception to this. To our knowledge, at least for this final group we know about, these acts involved raising minion races for a competition blood sport. Then, depending on the outcome, the loser society would be wiped from existence, and the owner of that world would create a replacement for the next game."

"Cu'Nar's eyes!" he grimaces. "I could never have imagined any society, godlike or otherwise, could be as cruel as that."

"Indeed! The Estelar were just as offended. Therefore, the battle. The Primordials were defeated and largely destroyed, with the survivors being imprisoned. But here is where we seem to have our upset. If your cu'Nar describe Sargeras as belonging to a dead race, and further to use the word 'titan' to describe him, that says something to me. Elemental societies are often very old. The Estelar, and even the Celestial races, like mine, would be more familiar with them than mortal races like yours, as elementals do not commonly associate with corporeal lifeforms unless there is some special influence."

"Do we know what sort of influence the cu'Nar might have on this occasion?"

"My only guess at this time is they were following him and trying to warn you to stay away. But this also brings a few curiosities, for instance that they know of him, but the rest of the Estelar do not. So, the question becomes why they did not inform the Estelar, as I feel they might hold just as much of an aversion to him as the others would, and as such, I would expect the Estelar to have finished him a long time ago."

"Interesting..." he contemplates. "But now, I heard you say Celestial races. How do we define those? Is this another form of godlike society?"

"This is one of those things I explained to Kaliya. Perhaps we should test her knowledge to see how well she was paying attention," he grins.

"Oh, thank you!" she retorts. "Is this a pop quiz?"

The group shares a quick laugh.

"All right, fine. Here's what I got out of it just before falling asleep," she smiles. "There are two flavors of Celestials, natural and hybrid. The natural ones are an evolved species, like ours or Relissa's, something of that sort, which progress to what could be their highest corporeal position in a material universe like this. Somewhere along the way, these Estelar might take notice of them and send a kind of invitation to join in an apprenticeship under them. Here is where I think we can call them Celestials in a more official sense, as they are now moving beyond the material universe as the result."

"In all the nether-space..." Kailen winces. "And maybe in a literal sense of it."

"The Estelar, like he said, are a combination of many races, and this is where it comes from. After some amount of further evolution, these Celestials might one day ascend the rest of the way to true godhood and become part of the Estelar proper. So, if you ever wondered where the gods actually come from, this is it."

"It seems almost surreal."

"Then we have the other type of Celestial, which is a special case. These would be a hybrid form of life, not an evolved one. The Estelar might take a special interest in one or another of the Child Races, as we're called, where they create a hybridized form between their bodies and ours. Now, I have no tail-flipping idea how an Estelar makes babies," she chuckles. "But in this case, my impression is we're speaking of using artificial means, like genetic engineering, and combining elements of both. Thaelyn and Aerlie are two examples of this. He's based on the human side, and she is a type of winged elf."

"All right, I think you just succeeded in causing my horns to fall off."

"And generally speaking, they might be used as a type of intermediary between the two."

"Good, at least this much makes sense. I would imagine if these Estelar are so unbelievably highly evolved, there might be a few discrepancies in how we might interact with them."

"Very nicely done..." Thaelyn smiles.

"But I'm also noticing, regardless of the Celestial part, you and your wife are different species. Do the people of your world actually interbreed like this?"

"In some cases, they can, most often between humans and elves, as they tend to be the closest desirable match."

"All right, but now, going back to engaging these enemy forces," Kailen muses. "The orcs don't seem to travel to our side, and I don't see those Flame Elves on our turf either, but the Suuden-Aryku are surely a problem. Our experiences with them are that they make occasional skirmish hits on us. Did Kaliya tell you about their capabilities? She mentioned something about a shield you use."

"Yes, we have a magical construct we call the Infinity Shield. Aerlie and I have already considered this and passed some instructions along to our scholars back home to see about modifying it as a portable application, such as to carry it in front of you for personal protection. But a mage handling this would be occupied with only this. Therefore, he would need to be backed up by other soldiers with the offensive capabilities, and in this case, probably ranged. We are also asking ourselves how effective our magic might be against them, if they essentially have no idea what magic is."

"That would be fun to watch. The orcs used fireballs on us on Ruuki uy'Daan, now we use them here on the Suuden-Aryku. What about the Flame Elves? Kaliya told me you think they were some other kind of elf, and then coerced by Sargeras. How would you approach this, and what might be your solution to it?"

"This is a good question, but before I can give a full answer, I must investigate what happened down there. As I mentioned earlier, the Governor of Rolsklinde arrived this morning and made a number of statements. Among these were the elves starting this war four centuries ago. But I am uncertain as to the reasoning here, as well as suspicious of a number of very inconvenient coincidences I am discovering already on this world."

"Jiggers," Relissa moans. "Does this have anything to do with what went on that didn't go well?"

"Not specifically, but give me a moment on that. Let us take these in sequence. You are pursued halfway across Creation by a being that should no longer exist, and further aided by other beings, these cu'Nar of yours, that should not be involved with your society to begin with. The reasoning, so far, is unclear, but I would surely wish to understand it. Then you make this wild jump, as you call it, and I most certainly understand the concept here, and this brings you to Ruuki uy'Daan, where you are able to find some comfort for a time."

"That's right..." Kailen affirms.

"However, this world also seems to be the apparent home world of the orcish population, and here is where one of my coincidences comes in. Many millennia ago, we had a type of migration of orcs arriving on Tae'Eladar. We did not know where they came from, or how, but we long suspected they had help, as they were simply too primitive in many areas of intellectual pursuit to create their own means."

"Yeah..." Kaliya moans. "This is one of those things I was thinking about as I returned home."

"Indeed," Thaelyn nods. "And further is to find us here on this world as the result of yet another invasion, but on this occasion to learn who is behind it, and it is that same being that should no longer exist."

"And I'm sure that would be a very unpleasant coincidence."

"Also is to include you and that wild jump from no less than a completely different universe."

"Yes!" Kailen emphasizes with a finger. "And so happy to find a habitable planet along the way. I never was comfortable with that idea. And with HIM still chasing us..."

"I therefore suspect that jump was not so wild, Commander. And I further suspect that if he was in possession of that world previously, then he was either following, or perhaps driving you to that location. And now, here you are on this world, which I feel holds a focus of some sort."

"Due to all of us?" Kailen ponders. "And the Suuden-Aryku,

the orcs, and maybe also these Flame Elves, which by the way are the ones responsible for sabotaging our ship on Ruuki uy'Daan."

Thaelyn perks up to meet Kailen's face.

"They were on Ruuki uy'Daan?"

"Yeah. We saw them coming out of the engineering section. We think they were using some sort of invisibility cloak to get inside."

"Is there any known way for them to travel to that world from this one?"

"Not that I'm aware of, although I couldn't be sure of anything right now, but I generally suspect there was a covert delivery of some kind."

"Hmm, perhaps, but regardless, I might have to say this simply reinforces the suggestion of their involvement from an earlier moment. That Governor placed the blame for the woes of this world on the elven war. But if it was in fact Sargeras taking possession of the High Elves back then and using them for his deeds, then we have a number of covert operations taking place here."

"Are you saying all the way back to the beginning?" Relissa wonders.

"Quite possibly..."

"Oh grand, my Mum won't like hearing that one, the way she talks."

"How did this war actually begin?"

"Four centuries ago, our holy tree was killed. According to the story, there was a bottle under it with High Elf markings, so we think they did it, which was a big shocker. And it went from there."

"That does not sound very pleasant, and it would surely contradict elven cultural principles. A shocker, you say? In what way?"

"We were all friends before this, and this broke that all to bits."

"Indeed!"

"But now, can we go back to what happened with those peeps we saw?"

"Very well, I believe we can touch upon it now. But my dear young Relissa, I think you will not like it, and neither will the Commander, Kaliya, or any of the rest of you."

"Uh oh… All right, hit me with it."

"At first, his arrival seemed pleasant enough, but I suspect he was simply feeling me out. He asked about how and why we are here, and I explained the part about the orcish invasion and my pursuit. But before we could go into any manner of discussion of how we could join forces to fight this war, he began to complain over how the orcs took this land, which he describes as holding a territorial claim over, and now that I have so conveniently cleared it for him, he wished to charge tax for me squatting on it."

"Bloody hell!" she wheezes. "Now that just ties it."

"Oh, and this is just the beginning. He then went into this long discussion to convince me of all the…villains…of this world, and sign me into an exclusive contract to side with him against all the rest."

"Buggers!" Relissa yips. "What do you mean by that?"

"Do you recall what Haran said about their prejudice up there? Well, I think it runs much deeper than what he was hinting over. The Governor describes your people as conducting unorthodox religious practices and unholy rites. He further blames all the elves for destroying this world and would desire to see the last of you fall as the result."

"And bloody hell again!" she scorns. "Haran didn't say anything about things being that bad up there."

"In addition, he seems to have no interest in fighting alongside you, and neither does he seem to care for fighting the orcs, or anything else around here. He claims his army is occupied elsewhere with supply shortages, but I believe I recall Haran saying the Guard up there does not even go outside."

"Aye, that's the bit I hear, and also they do have supply troubles."

"And then there were the words he shared about the Daanen-Aryku," he frowns at Kaliya and Kailen.

"Uh oh…" Kaliya moans.

"It is with regrets that I must repeat this, but you might want to know. He described you with such words as vagabonds and undesirable drifters being hunted for some crime you most surely committed somewhere, and therefore, he feels you deserve whatever is coming to you."

Kaliya hangs her head at the statement. Kailen sighs deeply and turns away.

"And here I thought we had an ally," Kailen relents.

"My impression is he is much more of an opportunist," Thaelyn suggests. "Along the way, he tried to convince me of this deal to join forces, but only if I handed over some portion of our illustrious military gear to his underprivileged army so he could go out and finish the job."

"Finish the job…of the elves, maybe also us?"

"I am quite sure he is simply a gluttonous aristocrat trying to take advantage of my newness in this land to see if he can gain anything out of me. Unfortunately for him, I am not so naïve."

"And what did you say to this?" Relissa asks.

"Oh…well…" he leans back and casually shifts his position. "I told him I am a man of justice and law, where I tend to investigate things, and then take my actions accordingly. And those actions will target whatever true villains there might be in this land, including they who otherwise falsely blame their neighbors and hold so much prejudice."

"Whoops!" Kaliya yelps. "That doesn't sound good. And how did he respond to that?"

"In your typical manner… He threatened that this land might be more dangerous than it appears."

"Cu'Nar's Pity! He would do that?"

"He doubted that my meager military force out here could do a proper job in this world, at least until I hinted at what I had back home in reserve. That did actually seem to make an impression on his manners somewhat, but in the end, he huffed and drove away at high speed. He was so angry; I could almost see smoke drifting out of his ears."

"I don't believe this! I never met him personally, but I think Padriyl has worked with him in the past. Kailen, did he say anything about these manners?"

"No," he reflects. "So, I have to assume at this point he was hiding his true intentions from us. But then, how do we explain the occasional guard patrols he sends out?"

"If the Governor sends out patrols to your territory," Thaelyn muses. "I might suggest this is a false front, although I cannot be sure of the motivation. If he holds such contempt, I would not expect anything at all, unless he feels a threat of some sort due to your foreign nature and your technological advantage. He certainly seemed concerned for the Suuden-Aryku and their potential."

"All right, this could be a reason, but it doesn't make me feel any better."

"But more than that," Kaliya emits. "What do we do about it?"

"At this moment," Thaelyn asserts. "I would say you should not do anything outside of your normal expectations. Let us not give him cause to suspect I am learning about all his lies. I am going to focus myself on those orcs initially as my most outward intention. I will deal with the rest in a more clandestine manner. If that threat of his holds any true merit, I do not wish to invoke any harsh reactions. I will take this on my terms, not his."

"All right, I suppose I would have to agree," Kailen accedes.

✦ ✦ ✦ ◆ ✦ ✦ ✦

"Oh, it's so young!" Amariyn rejoices. "And so beautiful! It's been so long since I felt such joy. You kept the faith all these years, it's so delightful."

Amariyn was standing near the small wooden fence lining the outer edge of the circle surrounding the tree. She wraps her arms around herself in a personal hug as she soaks in the life-giving energy radiating out from the young sapling.

"...And so, you see," Aerlie explains to the Enforcer and Throdeth, who are the only ones paying attention by now. "Our most critical concern, at the moment, is the safety of our world from these orcs. However, we suspect we may be forced to involve ourselves on the matter of these others in time, especially if they are all tied together.

Thaelyn and I suspect there are hidden activities occurring in this world, both presently, as well as what brings us to where we are now. We are seeing coincidences around us that we simply cannot ignore."

"What sort of coincidences?" the Enforcer asks.

"Ruuki uy'Daan is said to be the home world where these orcs came from. Many thousands of years ago, Tae'Eladar saw a type of migration of orcs arriving from places unknown, and also by means unknown. We suspect they had outside help, as the orcs never demonstrated themselves capable enough to do this on their own. Now, here we are on this world after another invasion of orcs, but this time we see not only where they originally came from, but also who is sending them."

"Uh oh…" Throdeth moans. "And here is where I can see that coincidence. Sargeras, as he is described, is apparently making some sort of trouble for you, it would seem."

"Indeed! But we think it goes even deeper, as we must now involve the Daanen-Aryku. He originally came to their home world a long time ago and corrupted their people, the Suuden-Aryku. Then, Kaliya over there," she points across the camp at Thaelyn's group, "tells us they were pursued across many worlds, and finally to Ruuki uy'Daan, after a highly risky maneuver to escape from him…which didn't work, by the way, as he is still here."

"So it would seem."

"But how strange it is that they arrived on that same world where these orcs came from…and now here we are."

"Yes, I can see how that would certainly peak one's interest."

"This tells us the orcs probably served him from a much earlier moment in time, and further causes us to wonder about a few things on this world, as this is where everything seems to be culminating."

"They are gathering their forces here," the Enforcer considers. "But now, how do you expect to counter any of this? Scout Moonshimmer mentioned that you would wish to use her knowledge to aid you in your initial study of the local area. I would not be opposed to this, but I would like at least some small understanding of the methods you might use."

"This is fair. We hope to use stealth and the element of surprise as much as possible here to confound our opponents as to our activities. We suspect we are probably being watched right now, so anything we do will likely result in a response of some kind. But if we do not give any recognizable indication of our actions, they will not know what we are doing or where we are doing it."

"But I'm still a little bit at a loss here. If you hope to move against the orcs, or anyone else, you must gather and move troops, correct?"

"Yes, but we do not as often simply walk to our destinations," she grins. "We make extensive use of portals, ourselves."

"Oh dear…and I can see where that one is going already. Good gods, I would not want to be on the receiving end of a horde of soldiers appearing out of thin air right on top of you," he chuckles.

"From our earlier talks with her, Relissa said the orcs tend to be grouped to the west of our current location. Is that correct?"

"Generally so, and south of our city… They mostly attack our outer bounds from the south, but on a few occasions, they've tried to circle around to our western flank. They seem mostly to be skirmish attacks, maybe to test our guard. We haven't had any serious engagements for decades, and certainly not on the city itself."

"This sounds like the classic manner of orcs, where we saw this on Tae'Eladar for a long time. They liked testing their younger warriors against our outer patrols. I remember one time when I was in the academy and I was chosen for a field trip," she recalls thoughtfully.

"Interesting…" Throdeth muses. "Does this actually mean you are part of this military?"

"I was trained in the same academy, and although I am a priestess and a healer, I am also a soldier. I simply spend most of my time in more of a civilian role than on the battlefield."

"But you're a Queen, correct?"

"That does not excuse me from playing my role to provide for our people and our lands. Thaelyn and I both take a personal hand in it."

"Amazing… I would be truly fascinated to read some of your history. I suppose you have a library of some sort? Would it be possible for me to visit sometime?"

"Oh, of course, but you should be aware of the difference in language. If you like, we have a course you can take to fill you in."

"Yes, this might be a good course of action."

"Getting back to the orcs, if I may…" the Enforcer smiles politely at the enthusiastic scholar. "I hear Governor Dramon of the humans also claims attacks from their south, likely coming through this valley, sometimes orcs, sometimes Flame Elves. We don't actually see what they send at him, so it's mostly reports we get from the messages he passes along."

"He says this to you?" Aerlie wonders curiously. "This is interesting, because we heard another report that they have not seen anything come at them for quite a long time."

"Oh? Who said this?"

"Relissa has a friend from their mage academy, his name is Haran. He said that within his lifetime, he had not heard of anything coming up against their walls at all."

"Within his lifetime? But…that can't be right. We quite often get messages from them about these occasional attacks."

"Well, I cannot be entirely sure how he is describing himself here, but I'll tell you, from his visitation earlier, that Governor does not seem like a very polite individual."

Throdeth leaned in closer at the mention. Amariyn was returning from the tree and sat down to join the conversation for this part.

"Really!" Throdeth interjects. "How did he seem to you? Because my experience on the Council always gave the impression of a very congenial individual…well, at least from the correspondence."

"Did you ever meet him in person? My guess in those cases might be he was simply putting on a show for you. He visited with us earlier and was most unpleasant, and not only to us, but in reference to the rest of you."

"What do you mean?" Amariyn asks. "I have not personally spoken to the man, but those on the Council who have met with his messengers say he represented himself fairly enough."

"His messengers? He did not show himself personally?"

"Um…" she mulls for a moment. "No, not that I recall… It was always an attendant making the visit."

"Interesting, and how appropriate, as he seems to hold a deep prejudice toward elves…all of you."

"All, meaning what? I can certainly expect this of the Flame Elves…those heathens. But are we also including our people? Why?"

"The 'why' is likely very obvious at this point, if you say this war began four hundred years ago between the two sides. He blames the destruction of this world entirely on you…all of you."

"Oh, well, my deepest apologies for defending our soil," she huffs. "But we are not the ones responsible for destroying so many cities out there. It was those horrid Flame Elves, and later the orcs, and probably the Suuden-Aryku to some extent."

"I'm not the one casting blame here, simply repeating an unfortunate message. He similarly holds deep aversions to the Daanen-Aryku, calling them unwanted drifters and likely some manner of criminals on the run from who knows what."

"Really, and does he know anything about their plight as you just explained it to us?"

"He apparently doesn't care to ask any of you anything. He thinks you, with your so-called questionable religion, are conducting unholy rites. So, this should give you an idea of how willing he is to actually speak to you personally."

"Oh grand! Fine! There goes my last resolve to interact with those people."

"I don't think we should bundle the full population here, and clearly this needs to be addressed. Once we can overcome the issues of war, I think we should overcome a few of these other issues. Segregating ourselves even further will not correct these concerns. Just look at you and the Flame Elves. What actually happened to start this affair?"

"Indeed, what happened," she groans. "My apologies to you, Your Grace, but this one burns. It burned back then, and speaking of it again is simply reigniting it."

"Easy does it, Amariyn. Thaelyn and I think there are hidden dealings in this world, and the High Elves may be as much a victim as anything."

"A victim? Hardly that! They're the ones responsible for killing our sacred tree."

"Killing your tree?" Aerlie winces. "That would seem a contradiction in terms! Why would they do this?"

"We don't know the initial impetus for this devious act. It hit us by surprise. It was four centuries ago, and we were at peace, all of us, our people, the High Elves, and the humans."

"So, this would be before the arrival of the Daanen-Aryku, I suppose."

"Yes, they did not arrive until about half a century later, and that is when these cretins joined with the Suuden-Aryku."

"Um, Amariyn, I already have a contradiction for you on this point."

"Oh? What is that?"

"Well, we Avariel are notorious for our exceptional hearing," she smiles gently. "And I can overhear a few things from Thaelyn's meeting over there. That Commander Nazég tells of those Flame Elves being found on Ruuki uy'Daan sabotaging their ship to crash here. So, this already says they were a part of it from before the official arrival."

"What?" she gapes at her. "But how could they even get over there in the first place?"

"Well, unless they have a portal of some kind, the Commander was suggesting just now a covert delivery, and this means the Suuden-Aryku had to be involved."

"Unbelievable, but this still…um…"

"My Dear," Throdeth interjects. "This would suggest they were also taken much earlier, maybe like those orcs. And like the Enforcer says, this world is becoming a gathering point for multiple forces."

"If the Flame Elves sabotaged the Daanen-Aryku's ship to crash here explicitly," Aerlie explains. "This is also an intentional act of gathering things, in this case his toys to play with. This only exacerbates the situation for what he has in mind overall, especially if he is sending orcs at us on Tae'Eladar. We think Sargeras used to live in that place."

"Uh oh…that sounds bad, although I'm not sure for whom at the moment."

"But anyway, Amariyn, please continue."

"Right, um…" she flusters. "Good gracious, I'm feeling a bit flushed suddenly."

"Perhaps I can get you something to drink?"

"Oh, I think I'll be alright. Anyway, our two societies shared a bond of kinship together. I remember a good friend I used to have… I, uh…"

"Hmm?" Aerlie raises her brow.

"I've been cursing her name ever since."

"You must've had a very hard life in this world."

"Yes…" she sighs. "Then, one night, I awoke to the shrill screams of the spirits in the dryad grove. The trees, all of them, the whole grove was dying. I rushed out to see what I could do to help, but they withered right before my eyes. It was so horrible!"

"What caused it?"

"We found a bottle lying near the mother tree. It was empty, the contents clearly spilt onto the roots of the tree itself. Some foul poison, no doubt. It spread through the roots into the daughter trees and killed everything. And the bottle was of High Elf artisanry."

"Interesting, as well as disturbing… But at the same time, I'm also asking myself what sort of poison could do this to a Tree of Life."

"I have no idea. We took the bottle and were going to use it as proof of their treachery. But when we sent an emissary to speak with them, we found they had changed…their manners, their words. They scorned us harshly, claiming us to be weak, or some such."

"That's your transition, Amariyn," Throdeth nods. "That must be when he arrived. If it was so sudden and dramatic, it had to be the work of a powerful being, and he is certainly being described as powerful here."

"All right, Throdeth, but at the same time, I want to know how, and also why. And I want to know why them, not us or anyone else, or maybe all of us, if as she says, we were purged down to the last for some ulterior motive."

"We will surely investigate this, Amariyn," Aerlie asserts. "Where is that bottle right now? Do you still have it?"

"I haven't thought about that for…well, since that day. I believe we put it into a box and stored it in a room within the temple, for all the good it does now. There's nothing more we can do with it, other than to recall the horror it brought."

"Perhaps, but maybe we can take a look to examine it one day, possibly to learn what was inside. This might hold a clue."

✦✦✦✦✦

"Commander," Thaelyn advises. "It becomes obvious to me that our mutual interaction could bring about a significant corrective influence in this world. And if we can involve the Night Elves… and I believe Aerlie is doing a fine enough job for us over there…this could resolve a number of issues, not the least of which seems to be communication and mutual understanding of all these factions. It would seem this war has harmed more than just people and societies. It has also degraded attitudes and manners. This also brings us back to the human faction."

"Yeah, and this is disappointing, to say the least."

"Indeed, but I am not going to shrug off the entire society for the poor manners of one individual. I would wish to see about the people along the way and whatever rehabilitative measures might be necessary. Aerlie, in her conversation, has been relaying a few details to me as she pulls them out, and one of these we were curious about was the interactions of the races from before this war. It seems they did all hold peaceful relations, perhaps even to say mutually dependent. This is now causing me to become suspicious of that covert element again, and if it could be the cause of this disturbance by breaking apart their relationships. This would be a perfect ploy to isolate them and turn their attitudes."

"And causing them to all go to war with each other? Cu'Nar's pity, someone is playing some nasty tricks around here."

"Absolutely, and I want to find that someone, be it Sargeras or some agent of his. Meanwhile, let me make a proposal to you and yours. We should, at the very least, engage in some level of interaction, perhaps like trade, which could possibly offer you some fresh supplies and other things to supplement your position. Maybe you could reciprocate with some offering of fair value, although I am uncertain of what at the moment, but we can certainly evaluate the choices. It could be goods or services, as is your pleasure."

"That's a very kind offer."

"As for your Suuden-Aryku, I would wish for a bit of time to evaluate them as wartime opponents before making any firm decisions in my actions. Also, if I wish to keep this to a low profile, I need to see about my tactical options in that area...for instance terrain features and such."

"This is reasonable. I can provide you with our maps and other regional details if you like."

"Perfect... And we also need an efficient means in which to communicate."

"Naturally..." Kailen nods. "For this, I would like to establish an intermediary to serve our needs. Kaliya has offered herself for this role, and although she doesn't exactly have the full portfolio of training and experience for the job, she was arguing earlier that her previous interactions here felt good enough to her that she could simply learn on the job anything outside her immediate capacity."

"Most excellent!" he smiles. "I would surely welcome her. As I said once before, I enjoy a good challenge, and I suspect she might afford a most curious one. How do you usually communicate with each other? I suppose you have some form of device, perhaps?"

"Yes, she has a device we call a trans-com, which is used for overland communication."

"This is good. Then, after I have had an opportunity to confer with Aerlie and my own commanders, we will begin making our plans for aiding our friends and assaulting our enemies."

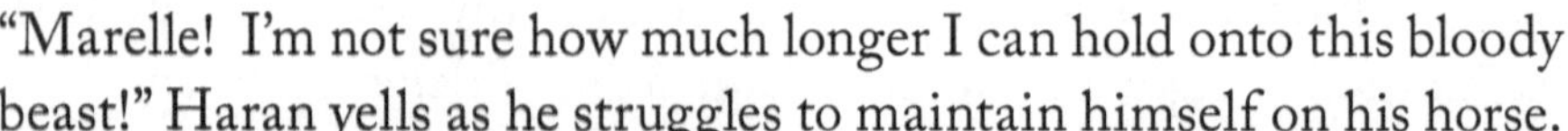

"All right then, I think I'm satisfied with our arrangement," Enforcer Baeleron concludes. "I will return back to the Guild and see what maps I can find for the regions to the west and south, and I'll send a runner back to deliver those to you. In the meantime, Scout Moonshimmer can begin briefing you on the more obvious threats nearby, therefore allowing you to begin making some of your initial plans. I will leave her in your care as our emissary, also to send a few assistants to help her with message deliveries. Would this be to your liking?"

"I'm sure Thaelyn and I will be very grateful for your help," Aerlie admits.

"Now that these matters of state are achieved," Throdeth interjects. "Might there be time for us to indulge ourselves in the intellectual pursuits of a historical nature?"

"I think Thaelyn will want to speak with me about our agreement. But I could certainly introduce you to some of our people here, for example mages and priests. All our people are very highly educated, and this should provide whatever you need to keep you busy for months. I can also send for some of our scholars and historians to visit sometime and enlighten you even further."

"Oh yes, that would be delightful!"

"Marelle! I'm not sure how much longer I can hold onto this bloody beast!" Haran yells as he struggles to maintain himself on his horse.

"Just a little more, Haran, I think I see something up there. Is that some kind of tower they're building?"

The three riders have been making a hard press to reach the camp in the Badlands. By this time, the horses were getting tired, but Captain Kholgard kept up the pressure. In a few more moments, they would see the northern watchmen of the camp.

The line of watchmen, on hearing the fierce gallop of incoming horses, forms up a solid line to block their path. The Captain slows his horse in front of them and signals the group to stop. One of the guards shouts a command to another behind him, sending him running off deeper into the camp.

"My Lord!" the guard calls out. "We have riders on the north side. Your presence is requested."

"Commander," Thaelyn relates. "It would seem we have more visitors. Would you excuse me, please?"

Thaelyn gives a slight bow and moves around in the direction of the north watch. Relissa follows close behind. They arrive to find three people dismounting from horseback; one of them, pale from the harsh ride, was showing a familiar face.

"Haran, I see you brought more guests!" he shouts. "I hope they are a bit more tolerable than the last group that was here," he adds softly.

"Your Lordship? What do you mean?" he asks curiously.

"Well, perhaps I should refrain for the moment. If it involves you in the group, maybe this occasion will be better...I hope. These two appear as military. Who are they?"

"This is my sister, Marelle," he directs to the young lady. "She's a Lieutenant in the Allegiance Guard back home."

"Ah, we are seeing a lot of family making visits, Kaliya and her brother, Relissa and her parents, and now this. Good greetings to you, young lady."

"And this is Captain Kholgard, the head of the Allegiance Guard up in the city."

"Very good, and Captain," he bows his head. "My name is Lord Thaelyn, and a pleasant greeting to you as well. But of course, now I must ask about this visit. Does it involve what your Governor said to me earlier?"

"What he said?" the Captain snaps. "I'm actually here to know what sort of business you're making in this valley. My men told me about the clouds and the noises coming out of here, and then this, um, well, Haran, came in telling us about you."

Thaelyn studies the Captain for a moment before commenting again.

"Haran came to you speaking about me, not your Governor?"

"Yeah, the Governor came down here behind my back. That porker does a lot of things behind my back, and I'm fairly sick of it by now."

"This is interesting. Then may I ask briefly what relation you actually have with your Governor?"

"He tells us to watch the walls, and according to the Lieutenant here, which is according to Haran, and, um..." he coughs briefly, "...well, I suppose this is a very indirect reference, but according to the report I got recently, apparently they expect our only purpose in the city is to, um..." he sighs, "...pick up the drunkards off the streets."

"Indeed!" Thaelyn emits boldly. "And you are supposed to be his army, of a sort, who is assigned somewhere, with all of your resource shortages, trying to fend off the so-called villains of the land he so despises?"

"Huh? Wait, first, let's stick to my original concern. The Lieutenant here tells me that her brother was down here on one of their famous scouting runs over at the academy. Next thing I know, my guards at the outer watch towers are reporting black clouds, booming noises, and right now I'm looking at this place...gods help us all...and I need to know who you are, where you came from, why you're here, and just what in all the blazes you're doing to the place."

"Your Lordship," Haran begs. "You'll need to excuse him a bit. He doesn't like mages."

"Ah, so this is the reason," Thaelyn nods. "Very well, if you will try to calm yourself a bit, I will explain. Although, I would imagine, if you travel with Haran, you ought to know some portion of this already."

He clears his throat in preparation of one more explanation.

"As you can see, I am entertaining some other delegates, so let us see if we can move through this part quickly. First, I come from a world called Tae'Eladar, where I am the King of that world after uniting all the nations together into one world body."

"The whole world?" the Captain winces. "Dear gods…"

"Not to worry, they are all much happier now. No more war, no more crime, and no more of the belligerence you might so often see amongst those types of individuals who care not to get along with their neighbors."

"Roddy," Marelle whispers privately. "That goes a little beyond a simple mage. I would advise you to tread carefully here. I hear a message in that statement."

"Uh huh…and no doubt more of that clever mind of yours."

"Once upon a time, long ago," Thaelyn continues. "We had an infestation of orcs that arrived as part of what we assumed to be a migration effort. We were unsure where they came from or how they arrived. They were a rather unpleasant sort, but we had them reasonably contained, at least until recently when we saw an uprising occur, and this caused me to finally go to war with them. But on this occasion, the atrocities they were committing were so intolerable, I had to decree their final extermination."

"Uh oh… All of them?"

"Down to the last… However, I found a final group using a portal to evacuate some portion of their remainder population. That portal arrived here in this valley," he directs off to the canyon. "The simple fact that they were able to create a portal at all was unacceptable, as it could be used to launch random attacks back at us and cause untold havoc without warning. Therefore, I have to continue my efforts, even though it brings me into your backyard, with respect."

"All right, I catch your meaning. So, um, what was all that noise we heard up there?"

"In short, the result of my arrival… We found an enormous number of them in the valley, and so I had to choose the most efficient means to dispose of them so I could establish myself, and therefore, continue my campaign. I used an explosive device of a rather potent capacity. It follows a form of wisdom we have where I come from that I think would be a bit difficult to explain if you are not as well versed in magic, or any other form of study as what we use there."

"Yeah, I suppose I'm with you on this, but I just hope you don't plan on doing it again."

"Oh, I would not wish to use it at all if it were not for the dire choices I had to make during the course of this war, and the quantity of orcs in my way. That, by itself, made the decision for me. But at the same time, it would seem they are not limited to this valley, and neither to this world."

"Yeah, you got that much right. But then, what about all these trees and such?"

"This is another effort I had to engage upon, as I certainly could not let the charred remains of this land persist. I hold a greater sense of responsibility than that. So, I invoked another process to restore the land to a…reasonably habitable condition," he grins impishly.

"Reasonably habitable?!" Marelle blasts. "Gods be blessed, this place is a garden paradise compared to what it was before. I want to build a house down here now."

Thaelyn offers up a subtle laugh at the outburst.

"But anyway, as for my continued intentions, I was asking Haran, Relissa," he glances at her by his side, "and Kaliya over there," he glances over his shoulder, "to assist me in calling in some political delegations for the local races so I could possibly teach you how to properly join together and actually fight a war, rather than sitting on logs or, as you just now said, cleaning the local refuse from your streets. But while the Night Elves and the Daanen-Aryku seem very happy to comply, your Governor was another thing."

"Right, so let's talk about that," the Captain affirms. "I didn't know of you until the Lieutenant came in after talking to her brother. Maybe you want to ask him what happened first."

"Very well, Haran, how did your report go with your Dean?"

"Badly…" he relents. "He kicked me out of his office, as well as the academy."

Thaelyn frowned sternly for the depiction.

"Why? What did you say to him?"

"First of all, you recall what I said about him before, right? Well, I got a good taste of what he's like even underneath that bad exterior. He's a man with a god complex who likes giving orders, not receiving backtalk. Now I know why Marelle keeps talking about the Guard getting the backhand treatment out of the mage academy, and why the Captain hates us so badly."

"Indeed! But may I ask why the two would interact in the first place?"

"We do all the scouting due to our local supply shortages, using our magic, what little we actually have, rather than them spending those supplies we don't have enough of."

"Interesting. The Governor did mention these shortages, but let us come to that in a moment. Continue with your report."

"All right, so I went in. He was naturally upset that I was late, and barely satisfied that I was still alive, so he would not need to send someone else to finish my job."

"Jiggers, Haran," Relissa moans. "How can you take this? This is worse than my super."

"Yeah, well," he sighs and shrugs. "I started telling him about my run, but he demanded only one thing out of me. Did I or did I not actually see any orcs…nothing more. Not any counts, not what they were doing out here…nothing."

"Oh! Well," Thaelyn muses nonchalantly. "He certainly seems concerned for his surroundings."

"Yeah, this is what I said! It wasn't until I started arguing with him that I was able to get any additional words out, like you being here wiping those orcs out of existence, which would coincide with the cloud they saw up there, coincidentally with him shrugging it off that the guards don't know how to describe the local weather."

"Good gods, Haran," the Captain winces.

"But when I tried going further, he simply chided the notion of a simple man and his woman doing any such thing at all."

"This much I suppose I can understand," Thaelyn nods. "Those examples would surely exceed your normal expectations."

"He laughed at the idea of restoring the land, which I might also understand, but by this time he was only interested in, as he calls it, filing my report with all the rest, which as it turns out is the waste bucket. So, if the Captain doesn't like the backhand treatment, it's not my fault. I did my job, but it apparently doesn't matter, because nothing is reported anyway…at least not unless it's wearing mithril and adamantium."

"Ah! But of course!" Thaelyn praises. "If only for the illustrious accouterments we have to ourselves that the Governor was so drooling over."

The Captain watched and listened, and also felt a mote of pain for Haran's experiences.

"Haran, I'm sorry also. I may hate what comes out of the academy, but maybe I shouldn't blame you people as much, if this is how it is for you in there."

"Thank you, Captain," Haran nods. "Anyway, then I started arguing that it needs to go to the Guard and the Governor, and how we need to reorganize ourselves to actually fight something. His response: It's not our concern, go study a toad. So, it was basically at this point where I had my final fill. I accused him of playing god with our lives, both in the academy and in our schools, denying us to actually learn anything, and so on. Here is where he finally threw me out, not that it mattered by that time."

"That represents a rather serious form of authoritarianism, Haran," Thaelyn suggests. "I recall your mention of your experiences in there, but this goes a bit beyond simple harassment."

"Yes, and this is how it is for us. He controls what we learn, and only if it's of any interest for him to do so. It's this way both in the academy as well as our schools, even as children. His graduate students become our teachers, and he governs all of it."

"How delightful…"

"Yeah, so how does yours compare to this?" he grins cutely.

Thaelyn rolls his eyes and chuckles.

"Afterwards," Haran finishes. "I went to Marelle and told her."

"Very good, at least you got someone's attention. Maybe with this man, we can accomplish something. Now, Captain, you might want to know what your delightful Governor had to say to me."

"Yeah, but after the rest of it, I'm not so sure."

"Captain," Relissa interjects. "If you know what's right, you'll listen up real good. He made enemies of just about everything out here, including us and the Daanen-Aryku."

"Huh, what do you mean?"

"First and foremost," Thaelyn begins. "Does your city claim any sort of ownership rights to this land?"

"No, it's a no-man's land. Our territory ends on the other side of those mountains up there," he angles to the north.

"I see. Well, when they first arrived, the Governor and the Dean…and this already tells me they must hold a relationship…"

"Yeah, this much I can say for certain."

"The Governor tried claiming ownership of this land and how those orcs intruded upon it to the point that your underprivileged army, meaning to say in relation to these shortages, and he also used the word army, not guard…though I suppose I should also note I was assuming he had one to begin with, but that they could not take it back, therefore, they were assigned elsewhere."

"Oh, is that so!"

"However, now that I have so conveniently cleansed this land, he wanted to reclaim it for himself, but my unfortunate 'squatting' was standing in the way."

"Squatting?!" Marelle shouts. "Gods' pity! And here you blasted the whole valley up to them."

"Indeed, but not to fear, for he had a solution to this…I should pay taxes for it."

Marelle covers her head and shrieks in outrage.

"That man!" she growls. "As if I didn't hate him enough before…"

"I tried reasoning with him, using a diplomatic approach, that I was here to fight your war for you, or at least it would certainly work out that way, and that we should join together to see it through. This is where he was complaining of his resource shortages due to such a long engagement. But then…" he waves a finger for emphasis.

"Here we go…" Relissa smirks.

"He began this tirade of how the elves started this war, how they were fully and completely responsible for all the devastation, and therefore, should see the last of their kind fall, if for no other reason than because they are so undesirable to begin with. He continued by blaspheming the Daanen-Aryku and their miseries, and finally… this is the good part…he conjured up this fabulous proposition where he might consider joining forces with me against the villains of the world…if only I would hand over all our grand military hardware for him to gloat over as he made a march to finish them."

Haran, Marelle, and the Captain were speechless, gaping at Thaelyn for the extended rant. They gazed at each other as they tried to recompose themselves.

"Um…" Marelle emits cautiously. "I would like to clarify some of that, but gods' pity, where do I begin. The elves…as undesirable? I know we get a lot of rumors and hearsay going around up there, half of it from the schools, the other half from the temple, but how so in this case?"

"For one thing, he said they conduct unholy rites with their strange religious practice."

"Oh, yeah, I've heard that one plenty of times, and it comes out of the temple. For instance, my aunt is very devout, and she laps it up like crazy."

"What about you?"

"I have a brother who's got a friend who's a Night Elf," she smiles at Relissa. "And he tells me she's a great person to have around. So, I don't buy into any of that bunk."

"How nice," he smiles. "But the Governor seems to hold a different opinion. To him, they are the cause of all your troubles in the world. As for the Daanen-Aryku, he describes them as little more than vagrants on the run from some law that is hunting them for what is surely a crime they must have committed somewhere."

"Well, that's nice. You know, as someone who works in an office where I tend to process law to some degree, I find it fascinating he would conjure up a statement like that without any evidence."

"Indeed, and I as well. Furthermore, that he seems to have no interest in asking questions to find that evidence."

"Well, all I can say is I don't personally know what that's about, but we do have more bunk from the temple priests about strange ways and such."

"I suppose this is reasonable, as they are a strange society, being foreign to this world, and with knowledge and devices that might appear strange to you. But criminals…no…"

"All right, then let me ask this… I know what Haran has said in the past, but if you've learned something new, maybe you'd like to fill us in to help us understand the meaning of it?"

"Excellent, this is a good course for us. Do you know where they originally came from?"

"I heard they came from a world called Ruuki uy'Daan."

"All right, this is a start, but not a complete understanding. What about the Suuden-Aryku?"

"I've heard they come from a world called, um…Azgarén, I think, right Haran?"

Haran turns and nods politely.

"Good," Thaelyn affirms. "But technically, these are one and the same race, and Azgarén is the real home of their kind. Ruuki uy'Daan is only the most recent of a long series of worlds they were chased to by the Suuden-Aryku. Now, do you know the name Sargeras?"

"Yes."

"He is the reason for all this. But here we are discovering a number of issues that I am growing increasingly concerned about. First, Sargeras apparently came to their world, for whatever reason he had in mind, and subsequently corrupted their race. Another body, called the cu'Nar, seems to have followed him, again for unknown reasons, and attempted to warn the Suuden-Aryku not to listen, but they seem to have ignored this. The Daanen-Aryku, as they call themselves during this chase, did listen and, well, ran away."

"And this is the chase they talk about."

"Correct. And Sargeras has pursued them across some rather

grand distances during this time, finally to Ruuki uy'Daan, which as it turns out is the home of these orcs."

"Right..."

"But now, are you aware they were chased off that world to this one, crashing here because their ship was sabotaged?"

"I've heard the one about the ship being sabotaged, so yeah."

"...By the Flame Elves?"

"Huh?" she blurts. "How did Flame Elves get to Ruuki uy'Daan?"

"This is a good question, but so far, all we can suggest is the Suuden-Aryku transporting them. Even if to use a portal, they still need to know where to aim it, and this might still require outside help."

"Bloody hell, then this would mean they were a part of it even before those bastards came here."

"It would, and apparently this information seems a bit lacking amongst some of you, including the Night Elves, which makes me wonder who is keeping it hidden."

"Well, um, including the Night Elves, you say?" she blushes. "Wow, this is starting to look bad for us actually talking to each other."

"It does. According to what we have learned already, before all this began, you were all at peace, and likely friends. Then, something happens, and suddenly you are accusing each other of wrongdoing without probable cause, or the ambition to learn the truth. In addition, if you were made to hide inside your walls during this time, this is a clear attempt to prevent you from actually talking about it."

"To prevent us?"

"Aye," Relissa nods. "We've all been duped by someone, and it probably isn't local. And it probably started way back in the beginning, then filled our heads with a lot of guff along the way."

"Oh grand!" she scorns.

Thaelyn continues, "So, our first objective must be to bring you together and share these critical details. This might also help to resolve some of those rumors you have up there."

"Yeah, probably..."

"But here we come to the most troubling part. For this, we must refer to that earlier arrival of orcs on our world, and the question of where they came from."

"Uh oh...I'm getting visions here."

"Right, and we long suspected it would require outside help, as they did not seem sophisticated enough to do it on their own."

"Oops..."

"Then we have this uprising, which I am going to assume to be a newer arrival corrupting the existing population. And we now know it was by Sargeras. So, we have a rather extraordinary coincidence to see them again on this world and coming from Ruuki uy'Daan."

"Oh dear gods...so the whole thing was planned somehow?"

"And at least some part of it was aimed at Tae'Eladar, although I cannot imagine why, as Sargeras, who we believe originally came from that region, would not be welcome to return."

"Whoa! Wait, he's from Tae'Eladar?"

"I think not Tae'Eladar proper, but that general space, which is bad enough, and this would have been a very long time ago. Therefore, as I look at all this, I suspect you have one or more covert activities occurring in this world. It is said you once had peace in this world between all the races. Now you do not, and I feel this is part of it. Someone came in and started a war, and I suspect it was unjustly."

"How is that...just for the argument of it?" she titters.

"There are multiple elements to this. First, it would seem that the Flame Elves, which used to be called High Elves, turned for some abrupt and inexplicable reason, and it is likely by coercion, if we suggest they currently serve Sargeras. High Elves are a very noble race and would certainly not follow such a creature as he. They have their own pantheon of gods, and he is not part of it."

"Uh oh, that sounds bad."

"Then, somewhere along the way, and according to these Night Elves over here, they went and conducted what I must describe as a completely contradictory act to elven culture and religion. This is the cause of their war with the Night Elves."

"What sort of act?" she wonders.

"Elven culture holds certain things very dear, including a love of nature. On their ancestral home world, all things were bound to each other in a kind of spiritual link through a very unique kind of tree that brought peace and serenity to them. It might be commonplace to see such trees located in elven cities, as they would wish to extend this wherever they go, and it was no different here."

"Um…ancestral home world?"

Thaelyn pauses to study the young woman for her curious inquiry.

"You do not know where you originally came from?"

"Oops, um…but I'm afraid I'm going to now, right?"

"Haran, you also had this problem, correct?"

"Yes," he accedes. "Until Relissa chewed my ear for it."

"Uh huh. Well, now it is your sister's turn. You mentioned something about your schools? Well, maybe some part of your history was simply lost, or perhaps if your Dean is intentionally omitting things, it was excluded. You humans, and the elves, are both originally immigrants from Tae'Eladar. And the elves came from yet another world before that."

"Bloody hell…" she spurns silently. "If that's not the end of it. I do not recall that in any of our lectures in school."

"Yes, and this is unfortunate. Well, anyway, the Night Elves tell us their sacred Tree of Life was killed, apparently by the High Elves, and this would represent a form of sacrilege above any other. I cannot imagine any elf who would wish to harm that tree for any reason."

"I'm still a little unsure on the issue, I mean we're talking about a tree, but I think I'll keep my mouth shut for now. So, this started the war between the two of them because of something unheard of for elves."

"Yes, and this, among everything else, likely carries the name Sargeras."

"Blast! The things you learn when you listen to people you're not supposed to be listening to."

"But now, let us see if there is anything else for us. As you can see, I was in conversation with the Daanen-Aryku, and my wife over there," he turns over his shoulder at Aerlie. "She is with the Night Elves."

Marelle and the Captain both glance at the group by the tree. They wince at the strange figure with the wings.

"That...is your wife?" Marelle mumbles.

"She may appear as an odd one, but she is every bit as much a wife as any could be. She belongs to a race of elves we call Avariel, and they hold the unique quality of having wings."

"Yeah, do they actually fly around?"

"They do! She adores it whenever she gets time away from work."

"All right, if you say so..."

"Now, one thing I would like to ask, on behalf of the Commander over here, is about those patrols your Governor presumably sends out on occasion."

"Yeah, what about them?" the Captain wonders.

"First, I suppose, is how often and for what purpose, if he holds such aversions to them."

"I never heard the one about the aversions, but it's to support them on a few occasions against their enemies. We do suffer from supply shortages, and it has hindered our ability to do a lot of things, but I don't like the idea of, as you say, sitting on logs."

"But his statements gave the impression of fear in the face of the Suuden-Aryku and their dangerous appearance, probably for the weapons they use. Could it be a similar case for the Daanen-Aryku?"

"Um, I don't know. I was always under the impression we were supposed to be supporting them, as well as the Night Elves, although the Night Elves never filed any requests for aid...or at least none that came to my desk."

"According to Relissa here, they might see an occasional assault on their towers, but by the descriptions, these sound more like the orcs playing with their defenses, not hardcore attacks. What about your people?"

"Up in Rolsklinde, we have stories that go around. The Flame

Elves for example, when they first turned hostile, centuries ago, they burned everything in sight; cities, towns, farms, you name it. If it stood in their way, it wasn't standing for long."

"That sounds rather unpleasant."

"It was made worse when those orcs showed up, as far as I know. I recall some of our history lessons about them joining up and finishing the rest."

"And this brings you to where you are now, I suppose, right down to the last of your cities."

"Yeah…"

"And then they apparently stopped, as it would seem they are now simply oppressing you to keep you there."

"Um…oppressing?"

"This is how I would describe it. If the world was fully populated before this, and then it was cleansed of people, for lack of a better term, and if the purpose was to wipe it completely, they did not finish. Instead, they left one city for each of you. This is a purging operation, not a war."

"And another bloody hell," Marelle grumbles. "So, they come in, wipe everything away that's a bother to them, and keep only a few leftovers for later?"

"And this further encourages the notion of a covert intention. Four centuries is a long time for any society to endure a war, especially where no one is apparently fighting, but you still call it a war. What about your city? Haran mentioned something about not in his lifetime."

"Right," the Captain reflects. "And I've never actually seen any of those with my own eyes, either. Not orcs and not Flame Elves… and of course, we're not even allowed to go outside to find any," he chuckles ironically. "But as for the city, we haven't had an attack for as long as I've been in charge, and in fact during my full lifetime, and that's a good long while."

Thaelyn taps a finger to his chin and glances in the direction of Aerlie again. This in turn causes her to interrupt her meeting briefly to turn at him.

"Oh buggers…again," Relissa moans. "Now what?"

Haran stepped over to join her as they studied the scene.

"Relissa, what's going on down here?"

"We're learning a few things, I think, and not nice ones. It probably goes with not talking to anyone."

A moment passes and Thaelyn returns to the conversation.

"Captain, if I may, how old are you?"

"I'm forty-four this year."

"So, in the past four decades and such, you have never seen an attack. What about before this?"

"I recall my father telling me of the same thing during his lifetime. He was also in the Guard, and in fact he held the same office I do now."

"Is he still among us?"

"No, he died a while back. I think he was, um…fifty-one."

"That seems a bit young."

"It's about average for us around here," he lowers his head.

"I am sorry. But if we combine his and your age, we are speaking of the better part of a century without any attacks."

"I suppose so."

"And before that?"

"I can't be sure. All I can say is…for as long as I can remember, we haven't had a direct attack on our walls."

"For as long as you can remember… I see. I am formulating a suspicion here. For as long as you can remember, and with your Dean crippling what you can actually remember…"

"Oh dear gods, I wish you didn't put it into those terms just now."

"My apologies, but I have a tendency to see elements of discussion as arguments to debate for their integrity. It goes with a profession I once held before I came to Tae'Eladar," he smiles.

"Before you came to Tae'Eladar?" Marelle wonders. "Um, and where did you come from, if not this grand achievement you created out of all those rabble-rousing nations?"

"Ah, but my dear young lady, this is a personal item. If you truly wish to learn that one, you will need to earn it," he winks.

"Uh huh…" she eyes him suspiciously. "And how do I 'earn' it?"

"Ask your brother. He already knows."

"Oh please, Your Lordship," Haran begs as he notices Marelle glaring at him. "Do you know how hard she can be on me?"

"These are the challenges of life, my friend," he laughs. "But perhaps, in time, we can share a few more of these details together. Suffice it to say, I am not native to Tae'Eladar, but rather I arrived there with a special mission to…correct things."

"And now you're here," Marelle muses. "To correct things with us, maybe?" she smiles tenderly.

"I suppose this is becoming my new purpose, with one of these involving some new information we gained from those Night Elves. According to Aerlie over there, the Night Elf delegation tells us your Governor, through a series of messengers, sends updates and information to their Council saying you suffer habitual attacks from both orcs and Flame Elves, some of which come through this valley."

"You've got to be kidding me!" Marelle screeches. "Our gates are closed, our walls are silent, and our guards spend most of the time snoozing. We haven't seen anything for as long as we can remember…" she catches her wording and shakes her head angrily. "Blast you, Dean! And not even by any of our watch towers. And the Governor is telling the others we're under attack?"

"This is certainly an interesting twist, and maybe to give an excuse to cover for his prejudice."

"Oh, I'll show him an excuse…" she huffs.

"Could this be perhaps a cover for his allegations of supply shortages? Are you able to monitor these supplies, and what sort of supplies are we speaking of?"

"Iron, from the dwarves up north…"

"Dwarves! You have dwarves in this world? I was not aware of this, perhaps we should speak to them at some moment."

"They don't get out much, from what I hear, and the Governor is supposedly the only one to deal with them…" she begins giggling compulsively. "Yeah, he is the only one to talk to them."

"Yes, I think I would need to agree with you," he smiles. "Very well, I will see about sending a scout to find them. Where are they located?"

"There's a line of mountains north of the city," the Captain replies. "There's a road going out the north gate straight up to it, maybe half a day's travel."

"Very good, I can send a scout to find it, and then maybe prepare a delegation of some kind."

"All right, but in the meantime, what plans do you have down here? Clearly, you're not happy with the Governor, so I guess a deal with him is out...very out."

"Captain, the deal is so far out that once I finish with the so-called villains of the world, I will be coming for him next, and not simply for his mistreatment of his neighbors."

"Wow, all right, just let me know so I can clear the streets."

"Are we speaking of the drunks, or the general citizens this time?" He raises his brow and smiles.

"Cute!" he grins. "Yeah, I think you and I should get along real well."

"Aside from that, I think I would wish to keep a low profile with a narrow focus. The orcs are my most important target for my own world's security. I cannot be sure what the Flame Elves or Suuden-Aryku will do, but if I keep away from them, they might keep away from me, at least for now. However, I will likely use a number of methods, including some of my own covert actions, such as stealth, portals, and so on, to attend to these matters in ways that cannot be so easily detected or tracked."

"Ooh, I like the sound of that," Marelle croons.

"But do you actually think you can stand up to these people?" the Captain asks as he surveys the camp and the soldiers in their armor. "I've heard orcs are tough, and then we have those elves with their magic. The Suuden-Aryku are said to be the worst of it, though. And from what I see here, well, I suppose you might only have some of your people here, especially if you have a full world back home supplying you, right?"

"Yes, my military is rather robust on the numbers, and I feel more than worthy to manage whatever lines I might create here."

"Fine, and I suppose from the equipment I'm looking at over there…which is a little strange… Is it just my eyes, or is that stuff glowing?"

Thaelyn glances over his shoulder at his men and their highly enchanted armor and weapons, all of them made from the magical metals with their own innate glow.

Marelle also studies the arrangement and reflects on Haran's statement back home.

"Is that supposed to be this mithril stuff you people talk about?" she wonders.

"Yes," Thaelyn replies. "The armor is adamantium, and the weapons and shields are mithril."

"How does that stuff stand up to steel?" the Captain asks.

"They are similar to each other in many ways, and they are stronger and lighter than steel, strongly imbued with natural magical energies, and can be further enchanted by other means. This can make the individual very hard to kill and very deadly to their foes, especially if those foes are using only steel."

"Um, hmm…" he flusters. "And do they all use this?"

"All my primary soldiers use it, and we also use it on occasion with our mounts."

"That sounds serious…suddenly. So, against orcs…"

"On Tae'Eladar, they became extinct rather quickly, where the time was largely due to the number we had to cut through. And by the way, some of those were known to be stealing a few of our more common supplies, which might include steel and iron."

"Figures. I think I've heard of them doing this here, at least in the old days. But then, what about these elves?"

"I would first like to see how and why they turned to serve Sargeras, and then see if we can bring them back to our side. They could be victims of wrongdoing here."

"All right, and the Suuden-Aryku?"

"While I might also suggest they could be victims back home on

Azgarén, I do not have ready access to solve that problem. Therefore, I may find myself engaging them to some degree here. This will likely involve magic, as I suspect they may exhibit a weakness to that, and then whatever other methods serve me best."

"Your Lordship," Marelle asserts. "Haran has told me a few things about mithril from some of his studies in the academy. Apparently, they have a couple pieces on display in there. But according to him, we don't seem to have it here in our world, or at least not that anyone knows about. But as I'm looking at all this, you must have a lot."

"Mithril and adamantium both occur naturally in our world, though they are not nearly as abundant as iron. And it takes an especially gifted craftsman to work with these metals. We have dwarves in our world, and their skills are considered second to none. And since its utility is so highly regarded, I do not spare any expense to equip my men with the very best."

"That must cost a fortune, however."

"I suppose it depends on how you look at it. The material is quite valuable, but when you own the entire world..."

"Yeah, I get it. The value simply comes down to mining and smithing it. But as someone who likes to see demonstrations of things, is there any way you could show this stuff in relation to a piece of steel?"

The Captain turns and eyes her carefully.

"Marelle, you're up to something, aren't you?"

"Me? Oh, well, it's just that for all your grumbling about a good cold piece of steel, I want to see what all the hubbub is about."

"Uh huh...sure..."

Thaelyn ponders the request and scans the camp for ideas.

"I am not sure if we have any spare pieces of steel plating lying about..."

"I have an idea," Marelle interjects. "And this will give a good functional demonstration as well."

Marelle begins taking off her armor plate, first by unhooking it from around her girth, then removing her helmet and lifting the chest armor up over her head, leaving only the gambeson behind.

"Let's use this. I just don't want to be inside at the time, thank you."

She hands the piece over to Thaelyn.

"Are you sure of this, Lieutenant?" Thaelyn asks.

"Yeah, I guess so. I never had a use for it, anyway. My job is behind a desk, very boring. Sorry Roddy…"

"That's alright, Marelle, I know your talents are going to waste in that office. We just don't have anything better."

"I know," she smirks. "And this is where my next idea comes in. But I'll wait to see what happens here first."

The Captain simply shakes his head at her amusingly.

Thaelyn examines the armor and the straps holding the front and back sections together. He finds small hooks inside that clip the straps onto rings riveted to the inner surface, allowing for the easy exchange of worn parts. He unhooks the straps and removes the front plate from it, setting the remainder on the ground at his side.

"Now I will need some assistance…" he mumbles.

He passes his gaze among the clusters of soldiers ambling about the camp. He spies one in conversation with a couple of his fellows. The Captain and his troupe follow his gaze. The soldier unexpectedly interrupts his conversation and turns to Thaelyn's attention. Thaelyn pauses briefly, gazing at the man, while Relissa, Haran, and the others watch.

Thaelyn quickly surveys the area near one of the buildings, which drew the man's attention to the same. Together they see a wooden crate, whereby Thaelyn telepathically issues an instruction to bring it over. The man nods and rushes over to collect it.

"How in all the hells did he do that?" Marelle whispers. "He didn't even say anything!"

"Actually, Sis," Haran corrects. "He did. We just didn't hear it."

"Haran! What do you mean we didn't hear it? My ears aren't that bad!"

"Neither are mine," he grins.

Kaliya and her brother were also observing the interactions when she took notice of Thaelyn's summons.

"What is he up to over there?" she wonders. "He just called that guy into action. Did you see it?"

"Yeah, I did," Kailen nods. "Was that telepathy? Wow, not a bad example. Look at that guy go."

"What about, um…um…" she coughs silently.

"You still can't say the word, can you?"

"I'm sorry Kailen, I'll try harder. Aerlie made that offer, so maybe I need to sit down for a few sessions."

"Good idea, but in answer to your question, I've never actually seen him use it."

"All right, but anyway, let's go see. That woman took her chest piece off, and I'm wondering why."

The two of them get up and stroll over to observe the demonstration.

The soldier was arriving with the crate, where he set it down next to Thaelyn.

"What's the plan here, my Lord?" he asks.

"This young lady would like to see what happens when one of our swords meets a piece of steel armor like this."

"Oh dear… Well, I hope she doesn't hold a great deal of love for it," he chuckles.

"Indeed!"

Thaelyn sets the armor on the crate, holding it upright at length in one hand.

"I am thinking of a strong overhand slice down the middle. And do make your aim precise. I would like to keep my hand."

"But of course!"

Kaliya and Kailen both arrive to oversee the demonstration as the soldier turns, marches in front, and pulls out his sword. He holds it in a moment of silent salute, then stretches it out to line up his mark. He then raises it over his head and brings it down hard in a vertical slice, cutting the piece neatly down the middle, along with part of the box. The two halves fall to the ground, and the soldier returns his sword to its scabbard.

"Wow," Kaliya croons. "Now I know why she took it off."

"Aye!" Relissa affirms. "You wouldn't want one of those cutting a new opening."

Thaelyn surveys the result and nods for the soldier to return to his previous activity.

"And that, dear Lieutenant, is what happens when you bring a mithril sword to a battle where you more commonly use steel. Any questions?"

Marelle gazes incredulously at the two halves of her armor. She glances at the Captain, whose face appears vacant. She then bends down to pick up the fallen pieces, holding them up to examine them together.

"Haran," she declares softly. "You lied to me."

"How is that?"

"Well, maybe better to say you never told me just how strong this stuff really was."

"To tell you the truth, Sis, I didn't actually know myself until just now. The samples we have in the academy aren't fashioned as weapons to test against steel. More like sculptures of some kind."

"Ornamental items?" Thaelyn muses. "Sometimes it can be used for that, maybe for special applications, like religious icons."

"I really have no idea, but it's said they predate the war."

"Uh…" the Captain croaks, trying to find his voice.

"Roddy," Marelle interrupts. "It's obvious we're going to need to assign an agent of some kind to interact with him down here so we can coordinate our efforts. I would like to offer myself."

"Huh?" he blurts. "You! Here? Um, but, uh…"

"Roddy, I'm just wasting away in that office, and you know it. Almost anyone can fill out forms, but this will require someone with tact and a bit of imagination."

"Why do I get the idea you planned this from the beginning, Marelle?"

"Probably because you know me better than most," she smiles sweetly.

"Am I getting the impression that the two of you hold a relationship?" Thaelyn notes.

"Um, yeah," she admits shyly. "But it's something of a hidden relationship as we need to maintain a level of professionalism in front of the others, you know."

"Of course…" he smiles.

"But I can't think of a better place to be than out here with all of you. From here, I could coordinate with him up in the city and give my reports of what's happening down here."

"Very well, and Captain, how do you feel about leaving this young mischief-maker of yours on her own out here?" he grins.

"I'm sure you have no idea how much of a mischief-maker she actually is, but you will. My only real concern after this is the Governor and what he might do. We'll need to keep this quiet, I'm sure. He likes holding absolute authority over what we do up there, not that it matters much. I'm the head of the city guard, so if he doesn't like something, who else is he going to call," he chuckles.

"Indeed, but just like I am advising the others, let us not make targets of anything not otherwise necessary to make into a target. We are concerned that these covert actions taking place may involve spies or other agents we are so far unaware of."

"Wonderful… But now, what about us? Do you have anything you want from us, or that you could help us with?"

"I am hoping to open a trade route with the Daanen-Aryku, and I suppose we might do the same with the Night Elves, so why not involve you as well. However, under the circumstances, if your enemies are expecting you to be in such a thoroughly oppressed condition, we should keep it silent with little or no outward activity. I make use of portals quite often, so perhaps we could make an arrangement of some kind to keep it hidden."

"That's a new one. All right, I'm game for it."

Thaelyn turns to Kailen for his opinion.

"I will need to confer with our Council before I can make any decisions," he affirms. "But personally, this seems reasonable to me."

"Excellent," Thaelyn accedes. "And then, any geographical details and reports of known hostile outposts would be useful."

The Captain nods and turns to reclaim his horse, gathering up the reigns from Marelle's horse as he goes.

"Your Lordship," Haran steps forward. "With all that's been said so far, would you permit me to stay on with you for a time here? I can't return to the academy, for obvious reasons, and with the events of today, I'm feeling a bit uncertain if I even want to return back to the city at all."

"I am not opposed to this, but under the circumstances I must ask this question as a matter of political demand. Do you feel this way perhaps because you are disenchanted with your lifestyle in the city, or that you feel unsafe there now?"

"Yes. Both, actually…" he sighs. "The academy was everything for me. But if we are speaking in terms of a political need, then I suppose I am asking for sanctuary. I don't trust either the Dean or the Governor, at this point. I basically went behind both their backs on this occasion. Perhaps I could find some occupation for myself to pay for my needs. And yet, at the same time, I can't help but to think of your own academies," he grins. "Maybe I could immigrate?"

Thaelyn smiles at the mention.

"If you should choose this, there will be a number of demands to fulfill to become a citizen, not the least of which is to learn our language."

"I'm sure that shouldn't be too much of a bother. Let me think on it for a bit to be sure."

"Very good then… You can take up residence here if you like. Perhaps we can find an extra bed in the barracks for you."

✦✦✦✦✦

"Did you see all that armor they were wearing, Governor? Magnificent!" the Dean croons.

"Bring your head back to your shoulders, Dean. That man is going to be a difficult one."

"What will we do about him, my Lord?"

"For now, we'll wait and see. Let us first observe how well he does against the orcs."

"With his men equipped as they are, I doubt the orcs will stand much of a chance."

"Probably, and especially if he has a full world so eager to join the fight. This could be a problem. And then I wonder about the Flame Elves. That army of his could be rather dangerous even to them."

"He sounded mostly interested in orcs for now."

"This is his most immediate threat, yes. But if he should dare move in any other direction..." he mumbles. "Those orcs probably deserve what they brought. As for the rest...well, I suppose the Suuden-Aryku will have something to say about it, but we'll wait and see how it turns out first. I wonder..." he leans back in his chair. "Wouldn't it be a shame if he should find his work becoming more of a challenge, hmm? We should observe and record his proficiency. We will be better able to design our own plans after that."

Chapter 9
PERSPECTIVES

Wandering through the camp, Haran can do little else but watch the activity as it continues to build. It's been three days since Thaelyn and Aerlie met with the delegations from the cities…three days for him to consider his own future and what may wait for him if he were to return back home. Although he was expelled from the academy, he was growing concerned that his general absence from the city might now bring suspicion to the Dean, assuming the Dean was paying any attention to it at all. Perhaps it was paranoia, but he still remembered those final words, the threat the Dean made, and now that Haran had gone around him directly to the Guard, he felt more insecure than ever.

Many of the initial structures had been completed, and the larger sites were coming up fast. They were taking on the appearance of large barracks, suitable for housing the remaining troops still assembled within the camp. A portion of the army had been sent home on leave, giving them a break from the hard battle they fought on Tae'Eladar.

Shipments of supplies were coming through on a regular basis from the portal, including pieces of some sort of wall that was taking shape around the perimeter of the camp. But, unlike a traditional wall, built either as a palisade of wooden pilings or a stone masonry barricade, this one was composed of a circle of intermittently spaced pylons, each one gradually curving inward and supported by a three-pronged buttress on the inside.

The outward edge of each pylon was wrapped by a gleaming panel, similar to the ones lining the interior of the gateway aperture, with sockets along the sides for more disks. Each pylon was equipped with a control box housing another power junction and connected to a network of cabling leading up to a large master controller deeper within the camp. Access gates to the north and south were being installed within the circle to permit the flow of traffic.

Kaliya studied the strange apparatus as it was being installed. It was clearly a wall-like perimeter, but she could not possibly interpret how it might keep anything out...not if it was only a series of pylons sticking out of the ground. She found her answer when it came online with a crackling of energy bolts spraying between the pylons to form a barrier resembling the Infinity Shield used by the mages on that first day.

"Great cu'Nar, and another one," she gasps. "They have a force field! But wouldn't that require something like a fusion reactor to power it?"

She followed the cabling to the master unit, which was connected to an array of large narrow boxes daisy-chained together like a series of oversized power cells. Sitting nearby was a large cylindrical tank with tightly bolted end caps. On one end was a pressure gauge and valve nozzle connected to the piping leading off to the boxes. The other end had a wheel which an operator could turn to manipulate the mechanism inside.

She kneeled down to examine the tank. Along the top was an oblong window she could look through to see rings of curved components pressed together on threaded axles.

"I honestly have no idea what this is," she closes her eyes and shakes her head. "All right, think. This looks like a tank for holding something pressurized. They use magic as a form of technology, and according to the riddle of metaphysics, it can alter the environment in some way. Those disks in there are pressed together, so this must be to activate something, and therefore, produce some kind of fuel for these boxes to turn into electrical energy. Beyond that, if I try any harder to understand it, I think my horns will fall off."

She gets up and starts walking away, still mumbling to herself.

"If this wall doesn't need a fusion reactor to power it, then this arcanic energy stuff he was talking about must be a very potent alternative."

Thaelyn was calling for an assembly of his officers. Relissa and Marelle were included, and word also reached Kaliya's ears to join them. They all convened in one of the structures that would serve as a tactical office.

Their first job was to review the maps and drawings provided by Enforcer Baeleron and Captain Kholgard. In addition, over the course of the last few days, scouting patrols had been sent out in all directions to survey the area and report back on the most recent enemy activity.

The dissemination of the gathered intelligence was painstaking, as language barriers interrupted the free flow of information between the various participants. Thaelyn and Kaliya, being the only two present to interpret, played the role of translators between the native advisors and the Tae'Eladaran officers.

Haran was not involved in these talks as he wasn't assigned a role in the war preparation. He left this to his sister and the others. As such, he was becoming anxious, feeling unused and impotent. He recalled what he had discussed with Thaelyn and Aerlie on that first day, and other conversations they shared since then, and could only come to one conclusion. He did not want to go back to Rolsklinde to face an empty life there and possibly encounter the Dean once more. In fact, the only thing that still held any value to him in that city was Tristeen. She meant the world to him, but it was a vacant dream as she was born into a noble family, and he was not. And such a dream as this could never be realized.

"Tristeen," he mumbles through his grief. "I'm sorry. You know as well as I, it would never happen. Your family would never allow it, and I can't go back there to tell you. I need to survive somehow, and there's only one place for me to go."

He knew Thaelyn was busy in conference and would probably remain this way for quite some time, so he went in search of Aerlie.

Aerlie had been called to the north end of the camp to attend to a group of elves arriving from Solinaia. She led them in and directed an escort of druids to bring them up to the tree. Haran intercepted her as she finished.

"Excuse me, Your Ladyship," he announces. "May I have a word with you?"

"Yes, Haran..."

"I find myself in the middle of a dilemma and I need your advice, possibly your help. I know I cannot simply sit around here indefinitely and need to start earning my keep if I wish to stay. I've been mulling this over, and I can see only one answer. I've come to the conclusion, due to my actions in the city...you know, going around the Dean's authority and telling my story to the Guard...that it might not be wise, or even safe for me to return there," he sighs. "The only place left for me to go now is Tae'Eladar. I will need to find work, but I also wish desperately to continue my studies."

"You would wish to leave this world and join us in ours? Are you saying you would wish to become one of our citizens? To do this, you would need to take an oath of fealty to serve us as your new sovereigns. Would you be willing to do this?"

"I would actually consider it a grand honor to do so. But more than that, I'm also very much interested in your Order, if it might be at all possible for me to apply to it."

"Very well, but to apply for our Order, you must remember what we said about our entrance requirements. Do you recall that?"

"The Spirit test... I remember you said it was the most important. If I can pass that, I'll do whatever is necessary to pass the others, if you would permit me."

"All right, we should go speak with Thaelyn about this."

They walked over to the building where Thaelyn and the others were in discussion. Haran could feel his anxiety building with each step as hope mixed with uncertainty in his mind. They emerged through the doorway to see the others carefully studying a pile of papers on a large table in the center of the room.

"Thaelyn, a word please..." Aerlie begins, speaking Tae'Eladar common out of habit. "First, we have a group of pilgrims from Solinaia come to visit the tree. I suppose we should expect as much, now that word is getting out, and it seems reasonable to assume there will be more."

"While I have no argument with them seeking their spiritual fulfillment," he responds, "this is still a military base. I would not wish them to come into harm's way should we fall under attack, nor would I wish to see our own operations impeded by them."

"Perhaps another option?"

"I suppose it would serve equally as well, perhaps even better, if we could lead them to the grove in B.T. It is a fully mature grove, and they might find greater comfort there. Although, over time, having what may be hundreds, or even thousands of them flowing through here will eventually hinder our own activity."

"Should we ask that they keep their numbers to within a certain limit?"

"Again, I would not wish to deny them their comfort, unless... wait. Of course!" he chuckles and throws his hands up. "What if we were to simply provide them with a new tree of their own? It would serve them for their needs, and solve ours as well."

Thaelyn turns to Relissa, who has been patiently waiting for the two nobles to finish their private discussion.

"Relissa, your mother was a priestess of the tree in your city, correct?"

"She was, but that was a long time ago. Why do you ask?"

"We are getting pilgrims to the tree outside, and although I am not against this, we must remember this is not an appropriate place for civilians. Therefore, I am forming the opinion that it might be of greater value to your people if we could provide your city with a new tree for itself."

"Holy jiggers…" she sighs in exaltation. "Your Lordship, my people would love you forever for a gift like this!"

"Then send word to your mother. I will inform our people in B.T. to arrange for a new life-seed. You will need to allow enough time for one to grow, but when it is ready, we will deliver it to you."

"And on another topic, my dear…" Aerlie continues, now speaking the native tongue. "Haran has made an official request to join us on Tae'Eladar and apply to the Order."

"Haran, you bugger!" Relissa shouts enthusiastically. "You're doing it, aren't you!"

"There's nowhere else for me to go, Relissa," he relents. "And I want to serve a useful purpose."

"Has Aerlie reminded you of the demands for application?" Thaelyn asks.

"Yes, Your Lordship, and I would be willing to take whatever oath you have to make me one of your citizens."

"Very well, Haran. We may need to defer the swearing-in ceremony until later, since we are currently occupied with other important matters. So, what I might suggest for you now is to go to the city and attend the testing. This will give us an indication of your acceptability to the Order. After that, return to me and we shall see to the rest."

"You're not going by yourself, you bleedin' scamper," Relissa scolds. "Your Lordship, you once told me of a kind of training for the Ranger craft. Do you think I could get into that?"

"Do you believe yourself capable enough with animals to train for it? Ultimately, the choice is yours to make."

"I've got a good set of skills with them, to be sure. I just need the right direction to bring them out better."

"And if you are thinking of joining our Order, you would need to follow the same path as Haran, swearing a new allegiance for citizenship. Are you willing?"

Relissa pauses to consider the idea of becoming a citizen of Tae'Eladar. This not only meant to serve in the Order, but also to reconnect with her heritage. She beams a bright smile as she gazes into Thaelyn's eyes.

"No doubt about it. Where do I sign?"

"Aerlie," Thaelyn asserts. "I believe we can release Relissa for a short period of time to attend to this matter. Would you be so kind to assist? Take them to the guildhall and send them through the test, then bring them back once they are done."

"Of course, my dear, it would be a pleasure."

"Relissa and Haran," Thaelyn calls as they begin to leave. "If you are successful, you should know that you will need to attend a series of classes to study such things as our language, our culture, and other necessities to enter you into the academies. This may take some time, but we will see about hurrying you through as best we can."

They both nod in agreement and head out the door.

Aerlie leads the two hopefuls over to the portal and brings them up in front of it. She realigns the runes with the one for Bya'an Tamoranth. The window clears for a moment, to be replaced by the image of the grand fortress again. She turns to Relissa and Haran, both of whom showed signs of awe and trepidation as they looked through the aperture.

"Who wants to go first?" she asks.

Neither of them is able to answer, but Relissa reaches out a hand to push sternly against Haran's back, causing him to make an involuntary step forward. As he regains his balance, he looks back at her in astonishment. She returns with an innocent smile.

"Ah, a volunteer!" Aerlie jests. "Be mindful of that first step. Simply take a deep breath, relax, and jump through, as if it were any other doorway. Understand that the journey to our home from here is technically a long one, and the conduit may play tricks on the senses. But the overall time really isn't that much. And watch your landing."

Haran inches himself forward up to the edge of the portal aperture, peering deep into it as he gets closer. The image was so clear, and seemed so close, like a portrait painted in the air, with the circular window stretching all around him. He turns to look over his shoulder at Relissa, who nods encouragingly for him to make that fateful leap.

He turns back again to the portal, placing his focus on his intended landing site. He gulps one last breath and steps through, vanishing from sight for an instant and reappearing again on the other side, stumbling slightly as he emerges. He could be seen patting his body in an apparent attempt to ensure all his parts were still attached, then turning to peer back through the window at Relissa in amazement.

"Your turn, Relissa," Aerlie encourages.

Relissa turns to look at Aerlie, her face aghast at the sight of Haran's venture. She returns her gaze to the portal and makes a conscious effort to swallow the lump in her throat before taking that first step. Finally, using what few remains of willpower she still had left in her body, she makes a courageous leap forward into the ethereal visage.

Light surrounds her on all sides as the initial image of her destination fades and a long tunnel stretches out in front of her, twisting and snaking through spaces unimaginable. She was being propelled, or so it seemed, though she could not accurately feel the sensation of movement in the traditional sense.

Shapes and distorted images appeared off to the sides outside the tunnel. The universe was unfolding in a perspective entirely alien to her eyes. As the tunnel turned and contorted, she found herself flowing gracefully along a river of light. Time and space seemed to pass in ways unfamiliar until she began to observe, somewhere in the distance, a form that looked like an infinitely broad wall, the filmy membrane of a bubble in a sea of ubiquity.

She passes through the layer only to find her transit now zipping through a tangle of rainbow hues, long streams of light that seemed shattered into its constituent components and then put through a meat grinder. A few moments later, she saw the flash of a massive shell whiz by, followed almost immediately by another glow, and there emerging from the conduit and stumbling across the ground.

Haran was standing nearby and catches her as she nearly topples over. A moment later, Aerlie appears through the portal to join them.

"You get used to it after a few times," she reassures. "Now come with me. We'll go up to the guildhall and take your test. Stay close now."

✦ ✦ ✦ ✦ ✦ ✦ ✦

"Observe this line of outposts," Thaelyn explains as he returns to one of the maps on the table. "This front would be of the greatest concern for the security of Solinaia. The camps appear to be spaced far enough apart that we could take one without being noticed by the others, but I am not content to strike at them individually."

"What then?" Marelle asks. "Do you think you might take more than one?"

"I might take the entire line simultaneously. The initial reports from our scouts show there are four settlements of only moderate size, maybe a few thousand orcs each. We could set up portal entries into areas slightly offset and out of view, delivering several regiments into the field. We would divide the troops to converge on either side of each camp, closing in on them so there can be no hope of anyone escaping to warn others. This would cut the full line in one assault, giving Solinaia some instant breathing room."

"Wouldn't that leave a lot of evidence of your activities? You're trying to be discreet, aren't you? Killing so many at one time, destroying four camps all at once… That'd leave a big mess behind."

"Not if we bury it afterwards. You must understand, Lieutenant, we do not simply kill our foes and leave their bodies to the carrion feeders. We bury the dead, even those of our enemies. And in this particular case, if we also remove the camp facilities, there will be virtually no sign of habitation, bringing confusion to any who might return to the region expecting to find those camps. It will be as though they never existed. But our work must be careful, and it must be complete."

"They'll never know what hit them," Marelle snickers. "And no one will ever know what happened. I'd love to see the looks on their faces when they find out."

"After that, we will convert to a spot tactic for a time," he points at the map, "choosing from this region in the south and southwest of the original line. We shall pick our targets in random order and use the same methods as with the line."

"Um, a thought… You'll be leaving a lot of burial mounds behind. Wouldn't that give some indication as well?"

"It would if those mounds were in a region where someone would find them!" Thaelyn flashes a grin at her.

He looks out the door as he continues.

"This valley has a broad canyon. On the other side, we have a considerable amount of free space. I can issue orders to begin preparing burial sites across the way in anticipation of our assaults. I can also assign areas to act as depositories for the camp materials we remove, at least until such time as we can otherwise dispose of them. You say your city has resource shortages, correct?"

Marelle's eyes light up.

"Yes, Your Lordship, from time to time we could use a little extra."

"Very good. Keeping in mind, the orcs may not have a great deal of high-quality materials, but even small amounts can be useful. I will begin by sending my scouts to mark a series of runes in safe areas. I will also position a few scouts to study the casual comings and goings of orcs in the region, in the event we need to adjust our timing to intervene between their movements."

"Your Lordship," Kaliya asserts. "This may be fine for the west, but do you have any ideas to the east to assist my people?"

"I have considered a few prospects. My most immediate plan on your side would be defensive for the moment. If we can augment your defenses with some of our troops, it could provide you with a bit of freedom from their attacks. But if to also keep a low profile, I think we will need disguises on the field."

"Ooh, disguises…" Marelle coos. "What kind?"

"Your Allegiance Guard is known to lend assistance from time to time. Can you provide some kind of overlay for our troops to cover our own colors?"

"I'm sure we can figure something out. Tabards, at the very least."

"Good. This can give the impression of more of the same as what might be historically recognized, and therefore anticipated. But in our case, we will likely involve some additional ranged fighters, like bowmen and mages. And I think our bowmen will need to use our more advanced elemental bows, rather than the traditional kind. We might find quicker kills this way."

"Elemental bows…" Kaliya wonders. "I recall you mentioning that once. And I'm afraid I'm about to lose my horns again," she chuckles.

"Elemental bows?" Marelle asks. "What are those? I mean, I know what bows are…we have those up in the city, but elemental bows?

"Did Haran teach you anything about the primal elements, like earth, water, air and fire? Well, think of a bow that shoots this instead of an actual arrow."

"Yeow!" she winces. "So, rather than trying to wrap a burning cloth or something to make a flaming arrow, the whole arrow is a flame? I don't think I want to be on the other side of that! Normal armor wouldn't be able to stop something like that, right?"

"Correct," Thaelyn asserts. "And this gives us a distinct advantage with some very certain results."

"Suddenly, I feel for those Suuden-Aryku," Kaliya moans. "This would be as bad, if not worse than fireballs."

"How do these actually play out?" Marelle inquires. "Like an arrow made of water or air or something?"

"The elemental schools of magic," Thaelyn explains, "have a selection of ways to represent the various elements. Water might be represented as ice in this case, as if to freeze the target, and air as lightning to electrocute it. We might use this, as well as fire on many occasions. Elemental earth might be applied as a petrifying or a corroding force, although an earthquake effect can also be created if we are aiming at structures."

"Yeah, and there go my horns again," Kaliya sighs. "You don't need guns. Just throw the forces of nature at them to tear things apart."

"That's right!" Marelle accedes. "And I don't blame you, Kaliya. Let's just hope the Governor doesn't catch wind. I'm sure he wouldn't like his pet Guard going out to play without permission."

"This may be true," Thaelyn considers. "But if your Governor rarely ever shares any useful information with the Guard, I find it unlikely he should know, unless he somehow has eyes out there in the field not his own."

He redirects them to the map again.

"I do not anticipate the orcs to be too much of a bother, except for their numbers. After a while, if we see a similar pattern here as on Tae'Eladar, we could possibly send them running, once they realize who is attacking and how dangerous we are. But along the way, I would expect one or another of their allies to catch wind of it and likely respond in some way. Therefore, I am going to establish some carefully concealed scouting outposts along our lines to the south and east to watch them, as best we can, for any outward movement."

Kaliya nods as she listens.

"And mostly hope they keep their distance long enough for us to take care of business elsewhere, due to that deterrent factor of your bomb."

"Indeed, but I think in time we will need to import more troops to thoroughly inundate the land with a broad line against the orcs. These spot attacks will only go so far. For this, I think we will drive them south away from us. Then we have the Flame Elves."

"Yeah, what do you have in mind for them?" Marelle inquires.

"At some point, I will need to send spies into their territory to investigate how it appears. If they have a city down there, we will likely need to infiltrate it, but this becomes problematic, as their magic could potentially detect and reveal an invisibility cloak. Therefore, I need to see about an alternative, possibly to use some of my own High Elves to sneak inside. But to be inside is a dangerous place if they should find themselves in a tight spot."

"Yeah, be careful on that one."

"And then we come to the orcs and their portals. If your people tell us they are coming from Ruuki uy'Daan, we need to secure those arrival zones, possibly by deploying garrisons around them and simply cutting down anything that shows its face on our side."

"That's not a very nice way to say hello."

"No, it is not, but our options are limited, and we do not want to grant them any new space on this world. Naturally, the deeper concern would be to find the point of origin and shut it down permanently. But for this, we need access, and that means either a portal of our own, or a ship. And this naturally brings us back to the Suuden-Aryku, for which I am uncertain at this point. I think we will need to look for opportunities where that one goes, although I do so hate to depend on luck. But if the only way to find Azgarén is with one of their ships..."

"That'll be a problem on multiple fronts, I think," Kaliya offers. "First, figuring out when and where they are, second to actually reach it, and third to take control."

"Well," he sighs. "I think we will be at this for a while, so let us come to it once we have some experience under our belts."

Aerlie and her two young attendees were arriving back in the camp through the portal. They were now making their way back over to the tactical office to meet with Thaelyn and give him the results of the Spirit test.

"Thaelyn, my love..." she sings. "I'm back with our two young hopefuls. Would you like to hear their results?"

Thaelyn turns to see Relissa and Haran standing inside the doorway. He walks up to examine the badges affixed below the left side of their collars. These indicated the results of their testing.

"Blue, both of you! Congratulations, true spirits, you may apply as you wish."

He offers his hand to both in a gesture of compliment.

Kaliya steps in to take a closer look.

"Very nice! Well done, kids."

Marelle also steps over to examine the badges.

"Blue?" she muses. "It's a color, as opposed to a number or something?"

"Apparently," Kaliya offers. "It's based on a measure of your spiritual polarity, where they envelop you in some kind of horn-pulling energy field, like so many of their other magical things," she smiles. "And it comes out with a color depending on how high you are on the scale. Blue represents a passing grade."

"What kind of scale are we working with? What other colors are there?"

"Just think of a rainbow and you have your answer."

"Ah, all right…so from red, orange…" she mumbles to herself and counts on her fingers the various colors of a rainbow. "There's also violet, isn't there? That's part of the rainbow."

"Yes, but we're speaking of…um…" Kaliya halts as she tenderly glances at Thaelyn.

He senses the direction of her statement and simply nods.

"Basically, this is what they describe as where mortal bodies might be concerned. There's something about mortals where they have these slight flaws, I suppose, that allow them to be corrupted for one thing or another…like certain examples we know about."

"Oh, so this is how it goes! So, my dear little Bro is so pure that he can ride high on the clouds?" she snickers.

"Hey, he's your brother. You should be proud!"

"Yes, I suppose I should be, as well as for Relissa. Nice going, girl…"

"Thanks," she smiles. "But now, Kaliya, when are you going to make the leap?"

"Don't count on it anytime soon. I need to go through a little of that therapy before I dare try any of this."

"Aye, but don't wait too long on it. I know you. Once you get that itch in your tail, you just go running off to find trouble for yourself."

"All right," she relents. "Maybe after we get some of this work done, I can relax a bit and give it a try. I would like to at least show my worth to the Council for a few reports before I go AWOL."

They all share a laugh together.

Aerlie now turns to Relissa and Haran.

"The two of you now need to decide what course you wish to

take for yourselves. The door is open to both of you. How will you proceed? Would you wish to take some time to consider your choice?"

"I already know my decision, Your Ladyship," Haran replies confidently.

"Aye, I'm ready," Relissa adds. "After all, there's no time like the present to get started, and someone needs to keep an eye on this round-ear," she giggles. "Trouble is…how do we work this if you want my help with the emissary bit?"

"Keep in mind," Thaelyn considers. "You will not be able to accomplish much until you have mastered our language, so we should focus on that first. We have a special course organized for the occasions of outsiders who may wish to study with us, although I will admit we have not had much occasion to employ this for a long while. The class runs for six hours of the day during the course of three months."

"Only three months?" Marelle retorts. "Gracious, how is a person able to learn anything in that time?"

"The course is highly compressed, and we use a special elixir to enhance memory function, so the learning process proceeds at a highly accelerated rate and with remarkable retention levels."

"Wow, that sounds like…um…hmm…sounds like something I might want to take part of, actually. Clearly, as we're trying so hard to work together, this language barrier is becoming a bother. Would it be possible for me to join that class?"

"Absolutely, and you are right. If you will be working so closely with us, it becomes a certain benefit to resolve this barrier."

"And if it only takes six hours each day, that still leaves time for me to continue my service here."

"Indeed. Now, as for the two of you," he returns to Relissa and Haran. "You should accomplish this first before trying any of the other courses. Although, I suppose we could begin testing you on some of the primary study requirements for the academies and fill in as we go along to prepare you for the remainder of the prerequisites."

"And the allegiance, Your Lordship?" Haran asks.

"Yes, and then there is the allegiance. Are you both willing at this time to make this commitment?"

"I am!" Haran affirms.

"So am I," Relissa follows.

"Then let it be done. We shall move outside and call for witnesses."

Thaelyn makes a brief detour to a rack where he retrieves his sword. Then the entire entourage within the tactical office files out the door, and Thaelyn calls out to the assembled people to gather around and pay witness to the ceremony. Aerlie steps up next to Thaelyn and prepares herself to act as a translator for the audience. Haran and Relissa are lined up in front of the portal base while Thaelyn steps up on the platform, using it as his dais. They both kneeled before him.

Joining at Thaelyn's side was his senior officer for the war effort, General Gabarleine, who was also accompanying him from the office. The General takes the sword and holds it out for Thaelyn to draw the blade from its sheath. He then holds it up ceremoniously at attention.

"Just be careful where you put that thing," Relissa quips. "I still remember that tree."

"Then you would be wise to hold very still for it."

"Aye! But that tree was holding still for it too!"

Thaelyn chuckles boldly before announcing his declaration.

"Relissa Moonshimmer and Haran Carronel," he begins in a sturdy voice, pausing to allow Aerlie to translate. "You come before us this day to submit yourselves to our cause, to our creed, and to our custom. Do you thusly declare this to be true?"

"I do!" Haran declares loudly for the benefit of the crowd.

"I do!" Relissa mimics in kind.

"Then, by the authority of my rule, and by the Powers I adore, I shall impose upon you this Oath of Fealty. Repeat my words and be true to yourselves in the knowing of them."

He prepares himself to give the oath with Aerlie ready to translate for the crowd.

"By my blood and my honor do I now swear, in the eyes of those Gods above me, that on this day and forevermore shall I serve in due diligence and faith to the homage of my new Lord and King, his Queen, his lands and his people, where only unto my final death shall I seek my rest."

As the words are pronounced, and dutifully translated, the two petitioners repeat them carefully in a bold voice. Thaelyn then steps forward with his sword to tap their shoulders and sanctify their new citizenship.

"Then let it be known, that on this day, we do grant this honor unto you. Rise, Citizen Haran Carronel. Rise, Citizen Relissa Moonshimmer. Be welcome and be friends."

As Thaelyn returns his sword, a rousing cheer gushes forth from the crowd.

Kaliya's eyes well up with tears at the celebration of her two friends receiving a new life and new hope for their future, a future she wished would one day come to her, but that hope still seemed very far away.

Marelle approaches and gives a courteous kiss on both their cheeks, offering up her own cheer to their success, and especially giving a hearty pat on her brother's back.

"You should tender your applications at your earliest opportunity," Thaelyn declares as he steps off the platform. "I would wish to see you beginning your first classes immediately, so that you can engage yourselves in our cause without delay."

"Absolutely…my Lord!" Haran states with a proud emphasis on his new loyalty.

"Kissing up already, are we?" Relissa jests, poking him in the ribs. "My Lord, if we're going to be taking the language classes at only six hours of the day, what should we be doing the rest of the time?"

"You, Relissa, can still be of service here during your time away from your studies. We will have you attend your classes in the morning hours, and then spend your afternoons here with us for a period of tactical review. But my suggestion for Haran, since he does not have any specific duties here, would be to take up some temporary occupation to begin his new life on Tae'Eladar. He is always free to return, of course, but I think his ambitions should be directed primarily on establishing his needs in our world, whereas I will take care of yours here for a time."

"Fine by me, I guess. Then, should we be heading back to the city to give our applications?"

"That would be my recommendation, and then we could rush you into the language courses beginning tomorrow. Bear in mind, the day and night cycles of our world are slightly off from this one, with ours being a nudge ahead. We will provide you with timepieces to help you coordinate your new schedules and lodging within our academy halls to aid you in making your appointed rounds. Aerlie?"

"Right away," she replies.

Aerlie escorts Marelle and the two applicants up to the gate and helps them through. She takes them to the administration office in the guildhall to register Relissa and Haran for the academy, while helping Marelle sign up for the language course. Relissa and Haran are assigned a set of training uniforms for their academy attendance, as well as instructional materials and an identification badge. All three are given dormitory lodging, followed by a brief tour of the compound and the initial class they'll be attending.

"Take note in here," Aerlie begins as she enters the classroom. "This class will begin promptly at eight of the clock in the morning. Be sure you are on schedule. Discipline is very important in the academy. When you first arrive, you will need to imbibe the elixir to prepare yourself for the lesson."

"This is that elixir you mentioned?" Marelle asks.

"Yes, it's called the Elixir of Visions," Aerlie replies as she points at a table on the side of the room. "There are different sizes, depending on race, some being smaller than others. It enhances your ability to learn quickly. There may be three or four instructors at a time in front of the class, often speaking in rapid succession of each other. Without the elixir, you'll become lost very quickly in all that."

"So, I guess we use the big ones, right?" Relissa inquires.

"You will use the larger size, but with a red cap. We don't have any of those out here at the moment, because all our regular students use a standard four-hour formula, and this uses a blue cap. They take one of those in the morning, and another after a midday break."

"Eight hours of schooling?" Marelle winces. "Wow, and I thought my old school back home was bad."

"And worse, Sis," Haran reflects. "This one is accelerated to dump whole volumes of stuff inside your head."

"Ouch!"

"In your case," Aerlie resumes. "You will use bottles with the red caps, which run for six hours each. I will call for a supply to be made ready for you, and we will have them out here in time for your first class."

"You must go through this stuff quickly, under these conditions," Haran muses.

"Yes, the industry to produce it has grown tremendously over the years. It's a hugely profitable production chain by now."

"That would've been a great investment, if you could get into it in those early days."

"Indeed, and I'm sure there were those who made a fair few coins at it," she smiles brightly.

"Uh huh…like a certain winged elf we all know?"

"Well, I did treat myself to a small portion of it. After all, it was my grandfather who found the formula in his library."

"You must have an interesting history behind you," Marelle grins.

When the tour is complete, the group returns through the gate. Marelle goes back to her work in the tactical office while Haran takes up a shady spot to contemplate his first day at a new school.

Relissa recalled her obligations to the Enforcer, where she needed to submit her resignation. She also needed to report to her mother on the prospect of a new tree for the city. She asked Aerlie for assistance in travelling home while there was still daylight. Aerlie calls up a scout to accompany her with a return rune, and they apply another rune to deliver them just outside the city of Solinaia.

Work on the Spire was progressing smoothly. The majority of the outer structure had been assembled by this time, with only a few pieces left to install. A group of gnomes was arriving with components for the internal workings, laying out parts in preparation for the final stage.

Thaelyn had taken yet another stroll to inspect the project. Kaliya, having little else to do at the moment, followed to see for herself how this thing was turning out. She was developing an increased interest in trying to understand their magical arts and the associated technology they use, hoping to compare and interpret it in relation to her own studies.

Scaffolding had been erected around the tower to assist with the upper levels of construction. The tower resembled a gradually tapering pillar, scalloped like an eight-pointed star.

A series of windows were being fitted with hexagonal glass housings, almost like lenses, protruding outward from the walls. There were eight in all, circling the upper portion of the tower on each of the eight sides.

The crown of the tower was composed of a marble cap fitted above a short metal cowl housing a ventilation fan. At the base of the tower were seven silvery busts radiating out from the walls in the shape of dragon heads with their mouths agape. They were spaced all around the tower, except for one side that had a maintenance door.

Standing just outside the door was a gnome examining the inner supports for the mechanics of the facility. A holler resounds from a gnomish worker in one of the windows at the top as a lens slips out of his hands and tumbles to the ground. The gnome by the door, curious as to the ruckus above him, turns lazily to look up at the glass object just as it rings out against his helmet and knocks him comically to the ground.

"Ouch!" Kaliya yips sympathetically.

"They are remarkably sturdy little fellows," Thaelyn states.

Two other gnomes rush over to check the fallen victim and help him back to his feet. After dusting him off, they each pull out little wrenches from their belts and bop the hapless guy on his head, followed by a waving of hands and an energetic lecturing, apparently about observing falling objects from underneath.

"And that is what the hardhats are for…" Thaelyn concludes.

"Um, should I ask why, after he just got hit by the lens?"

"Gnomes are a curious lot. There is no button they will not push, no lever they will not pull, and often they get into a lick of trouble along the way. But their manners are usually good for a laugh or two, as they simply take it all in stride."

"Right, I think I got a taste of that once when I tried talking to one," she smirks.

The gnomes now pick up the fallen lens and lay it on a lift to hoist back up to the window.

"My next question is why that lens didn't break after falling from such a height?" she wonders.

"It is not your everyday form of glass. It is a material called Glassteel, a specialty of the Avariel. Although described as a form of glass, it is better interpreted as a crystalline mineral structure, in some ways similar to quartz, but with some metallic properties and the tensile strength of steel. Once, they used this material to create weapons of a design unique to their race. However, since those days, we have put them to work for us to make other valuable creations, including these lenses, using the same principles."

"Nice! Something like this could find a lot of useful applications, where visibility is desired, but durability is also important. It reminds me of the materials we once had in our old days, when we would build vessels to explore outside our world."

"There may be such a day for our own people, but my work has far to go before then."

◆◆◆◆◆

Nighttime falls, and the camp settles for the evening meal and a bit of revelry. A small band of Halfling entertainers was brought in to add some good cheer to the company of soldiers. The humming of the shield wall gave a subtle glow to the evening landscape, and the activity of the camp began to feel almost inviting, as if it were a recreational camp rather than a military one.

Relissa returned slightly before sunset carrying a bag she packed with an assortment of personal items from home. Her mother was elated over the news of the new tree, and immediately began making preparations for a new shrine. Rumors were now spreading through the city, and plans were being made to decorate the lanes and avenues as the population anxiously anticipated the sacred delivery.

Kaliya and her friends sat around a small campfire with Marelle and the two nobles chatting about the day's events and what to expect on the morrow. The main focus had been on the affairs of the tactical planning to attack the group of orcish camps along the forward line near Solinaia.

Scouts had been dispatched during the day to watch and record any routine travels of supply caravans and troop movement. They would spend the night and continue to observe into the morning hours and through the next day. If all went well, the attack would occur at dawn of the day after.

Kaliya had spent much of the afternoon considering her need to fight her personal demons. She reflected on that first day when Thaelyn and Aerlie arrived, and the various discussions they've had since then. She recalled her brother and the private talks they had where he also tried to help her, and her continued failure to pronounce certain words. Then, she replayed the ceremony where her two best friends found their future, and Relissa's most recent words. Her ambitions were building, and she knew it had to be done, but her pride stood in her way, and she was afraid of exposing herself. But this simply couldn't go on forever.

"Your Lordship," she begins tentatively. "And Ladyship... Um, can we take a moment to talk?" she directs her gaze at Aerlie who returns hers expectantly. "Maybe we can try a little of that therapy you keep pushing at me," she attempts a minor grin.

"Of course, Kaliya," Aerlie replies enthusiastically. "Where do you want to begin?"

"This is hard for me. I don't like opening up that much. I had too many problems in my life, and I guess I made a habit of hiding them.”

“This much I already know. After that meld and watching you during this time…you recall I was going to do that, right?” she smiles tenderly.

“Yeah,” Kaliya returns a soft smile. “And knowing you, you’re not going to let it go that easily. I guess I just need to jump in with both hooves and get it over with, but it’s also embarrassing.”

“Don’t think of it that way. Think of it more like telling a story.”

“A story…all right, that’s an interesting twist. Then I suppose I should go back to Ruuki uy’Daan when I was a little girl. We tried to live in peace, recalling some of our old traditions from Azgarén, hoping to maintain the culture we so loved from the old days and trying to rebuild ourselves. We had hoped to have finally escaped from Sargeras, although our experiences always carried that little dark cloud of uncertainty.”

“I suppose this is to be expected.”

“He chased us across so many worlds back home in our local galaxy, it was crazy.”

“What’s a galaxy?” Marelle wonders as she listens in.

Kaliya lets out a muted chuckle as she realizes she needs to give a lesson of her own.

“Marelle, your people don’t have the ability to travel in space, and you probably don’t pay much attention to what’s up there except to see stars in the night sky. But for those of us who have this experience, we know a little more about what’s out there. Many of those stars you might see up there are part of a large assembly called a galaxy. There could be billions of them circling around as one large body. And then, you may have countless other galaxies out there besides this one.”

“Uh huh…sorry I asked,” she giggles. “Suddenly, I think I’m not so interested in learning about what’s out there. It sounds like more than I could handle in a hundred lifetimes.”

“Easily…” she grins. “But it’s really not all that bad. You just need to grow a little and work your way into it. Anyway, then we made that wild jump to get away from him, and it brought us all the way out to Ruuki uy'Daan. We realized it was nearly impossible to think we could actually find a world after that jump, but our desperation simply led us to thank whatever good fortune graced us on this occasion."

"But as we have already suggested," Thaelyn muses. "By our assumptions at least, that wild jump may not have been so wild after all."

"Yes, but at the same time I'd like to know who was programming the nav computer."

"This is certainly a valid question to ask."

"So, here we are on that world for a long time, trying to repopulate from our last hit, as usual, and then of course one day I'm born. I guess I came along at a very nice, peaceful time in our history, but like you once said, our ridiculously long lifespans probably don't give us the chance to simply live a life and pass on before some major disaster comes along. And so, we have the attack."

"Indeed, but do not blame your ridiculously long lifespans," he grins. "Such things can also be a blessing."

"Maybe. I had a good life, lots of friends in school, a nice home, loving family, but I also had a number of issues bothering me for our situation. I didn't like our history. I didn't like where we lived or who our neighbors were. And I didn't like the outlook so many of us had, especially...my...my..." she closes her eyes and gulps anxiously. "My...father!" she emits with a tremble and begins to weep.

Thaelyn reaches over to lay a hand on her shoulder to comfort her.

"Ah..." Aerlie croons. "So, that's the word you can never choke out. My goodness, Kaliya, what happened with that?"

Kaliya hangs her head and covers her eyes as she tries to collect herself and reflect on her feelings.

"We had an argument once, and I stopped talking to him."

"When was this?"

"During the attack, as we were trying to escape."

"Three and a half centuries ago...the full measure of it?"

"Yeah, the full measure..."

"No wonder you hold such pain. This sort of injury will run deep and affect many other aspects of your life. What was the cause of it?"

"Oh, I suppose a lot of things all tossed together. The chase, always running, losing so many people along the way, and we were never able to fight back. They come, we run, people die… And then there was my mother getting cut down in the street. That was the worst of it, I think. I was so angry and hurt by that time, I blamed it all on him…well, him and the Council, when it really wasn't their fault. Well, not exactly. We never did try to fight back, and people died. What are you supposed to do about that?"

"I suppose you do carry a valid point," Thaelyn accedes. "This would again reflect on the 'sitting on logs' perspective. Pacifism would clearly fail in a case like this. At the same time, however, I might also wonder if you ever had the opportunity to build anything to fight with, as it seems you were being disturbed too often to set down the appropriate roots for it."

"Maybe. Although, how many roots do you need to build a simple gun platform?"

"True."

"And I'm not actually the only one who feels this way. I know a few others amongst us who are just as disgruntled. But the Council is the one to make the rules."

"Kaliya," Aerlie asserts. "This would surely account for some portion of your trauma. And it could easily lead to your aggressiveness and poor judgment where your work in the Sentinels goes. You want revenge, and the reasons are personal. But judgment based on revenge is not only an inappropriate form of retribution; it is also a brash one. It can lead to hasty decisions, inadequate preparation, and a lack of consideration for the repercussions."

"Hasty decisions, I can understand. I made a lot of those. Inadequate preparation, oh yeah, I did that on a few occasions too. But repercussions? These are orcs we're speaking of here."

"Yes, and while we might say they all supported these actions, we must still consider a larger picture. Maybe some were not involved, or objected to the idea, but you attack them anyway. Then, maybe, by doing this, you invoke a response of even greater proportions for which you didn't consider before. Are you familiar with such a concept as the butterfly effect?"

"I don't think I've heard that term before."

"Maybe you use a different name. Or maybe you just never learned this lesson. It follows as part of Chaos Theory."

"Chaos Theory I know of, within reason, I think. At least from the mathematical side."

"All right, but the butterfly effect is a theoretical principle where an alteration within a dynamic process can lead to a cascade of other events, perhaps of larger and more significant proportions. Everything within a dynamic universe is, in some way, great or small, dependent on everything else. If I were to kick a rock down a hill, I might say to myself, it's just a little rock...who cares. But that little rock could tumble into a larger one, which could then strike an even larger one, and so on, until you have an avalanche heading for a nearby town, and poised to ruin countless lives. And all this because you said...it's just a little rock, who cares."

"Oops!" Marelle yips. "Even I can see that one."

"Yeah, she's right," Kaliya nods. "And we do actually have a lesson like this back home...a different name, but the same idea."

"Good," Aerlie smiles softly. "And so, the blind rage that so often accompanies revenge can subsequently deny you to rationalize these actions."

"Like all the bashing she got from her Elders," Relissa offers.

"All right," Kaliya continues. "But this isn't everything yet. There was another thing. It's morbid, to say the least, and relates to my father again. I think the chase we suffered took a heavy toll on him. He's probably the worst for the pacifist side of it. So many people lost along the way, and he probably blamed himself. Now, here we are on Ruuki uy'Daan, thinking we are the last of our kind...the last of our society, last of our history, our culture, everything we held pride in that made us the enlightened society we were. We were in exile...even our very name suggests it, which is another insult to me.

I don't like calling myself some…" she turns partway to Thaelyn, "…vagabond, living on borrowed land owned by such things as orcs."

"And here I think we have another deep form of suffering," he concludes. "For this, I might reflect on that conversation you had once on that first day with that priestess. You certainly had a few things to say about them at that time."

"Yeah, and she shot down every one," she chuckles feebly. "That's one nasty priestess you have there for her talent to debate."

"Perhaps, but then our study courses also provide a large volume of material for them to work with."

"I wasn't expecting that. But as for him, he began this project. It was to create a compendium of all our remaining knowledge into one summary work. It was intended to serve as a type of memorial, a dying reminder of who we were as a people, maybe to be left behind if…and very likely when…we ceased to exist."

"Gracious," Aerlie winces. "Yes, I can certainly see where you would hold such forlorn feelings on this."

"My history lessons in school, what little I got before the attack, tell us our people…the Suuden-Aryku…were a highly regarded society of intellectuals who had accomplished so many fantastic achievements. And here we were on an alien world hiding from a being that wanted us dead, for whatever crazy reason. So, when you combine all this, even though I was born into a good family and had lots of friends, I was still frustrated. Then we had the attack, and I guess that finished it."

"And so, it is. But even though I may already know the answer, based on our previous talks, is there anything in particular about the attack that hit you more than anything else? That is, other than seeing your mother go down, and running for your life."

"Yeah…" her breathing quickens. "It was orcs that did this to us! Filthy, primitive, disgusting things that can barely stand upright."

She closes her eyes and turns away. Her voice degraded to another soft weeping, and she covered her face again.

Relissa was sitting next to her, and she leaned forward to wrap her arms around her friend.

"Kaliya," Thaelyn soothes. "Here is where I am quite sure we have one of your greatest difficulties. You held so much pride in your accomplishments that you apparently could not appreciate what another society might be going through, and clearly these orcs were not as highly evolved as you. This was then compounded by all of your losses along the way, which simply added insult to your injury, as you were being degraded below that threshold of your preferential standard."

"Yes, this is what Kailen and Ankhia told me on many occasions. And then the attack, where our supremely advanced civilization was brought down by beasts and their nether-wild mysticism!"

"Indeed, and this is surely another piece of it. You do not understand magic. Therefore, you cannot accept it as holding any true merit. But for this point, I think we cannot blame you, if you do indeed come from another universe where you simply do not have it to begin with."

"Yeah, and then here you are, doing the same thing, but on a scale not even our science can match. That simply makes things worse. Suddenly, our highly evolved society of scientists and scholars doesn't seem so advanced."

"I would not necessarily say so. For what you had to work with, you seem to have done quite well. We cannot all be so privileged to have everything up front."

Kaliya attempts to drag herself away from her depression to consider his words.

"Yeah, all right, maybe so...and we did have a lot," she emits softly as she wipes away her tears.

"And further," he suggests warmly. "I might also add you did it the hard way. The arcanic energies can just as easily be described as a shortcut method to our answers."

"Really! Then, maybe I'll take that as a compliment. But wow, that's some shortcut! Conveyors and this force field wall of yours, and you're barely into your Industrial Age."

"Necessity was surely the mother of these inventions, but then

I suppose it is for most things. We take our path as it becomes apparent to us."

"So far," Aerlie surmises. "It would seem we have at least a few points of contention to discuss here. One being your dislike of orcs, and in particular how they turned against you and did so much damage. Another is your dislike of being there in the first place, after this long pursuit, and who knows what else contributed along the way. And then there is the element of magic being tossed in, which is so strange to you. Where should we begin? How about your pursuit? You received the warning of the cu'Nar to run, and so you did. How many people were involved?"

"I learned the original expedition involved three hundred thousand."

"Great gods, so many inside one ship?"

"It's a big ship…really big, the size of a small city, and with many levels to add depth for more volume. I'll also admit they pack you in tight, so comfort is something of a luxury."

"Who built it? I recall you said the cu'Nar brought it to you, but I cannot believe the cu'Nar would build something like a spacecraft."

"We have no idea, but I'll tell you something that will twist your horns…assuming you had any," she smiles. "Even though the design layout is totally alien to us, the technology is all familiar and compatible with our own. And even worse, everything is coded in our native language."

"That…simply…doesn't make sense," she places a hand on her head.

"But it does sound premeditated," Thaelyn adds. "Someone planned this, and with enough time to actually build it, with the cu'Nar simply acting as agents to deliver it. And this tells me someone else was watching."

"Oh great!" Kaliya moans. "Who, in this case, and also why?"

"Someone who must know who Sargeras is and was likely following him for some time. Maybe using these cu'Nar as agents on their behalf. Beyond that, I cannot say with what we have to work with."

"All right, let's get back to this pursuit," Aerlie resumes. "You cross many worlds, but then make that wild jump to Ruuki uy'Daan. But you didn't like it, or your neighbors. Is it only due to your neighbors, or was there something with the world itself?"

"As for the world itself," Kaliya responds. "I suppose it wasn't really bad. The local region was a jungle environment, so it was often warm and humid. But my issue was more about the orcs. It was their home, not ours. We were living on borrowed land, and I suppose I didn't like the idea of being a tenant. This was likely compounded with the idea of running away from someone, and also the fear of maybe having to pick up and run again if they should find us. The uncertainty factor was awful. And then my father and his project again, which almost expected that uncertainty factor to come true."

"Yes, I suppose this would serve as a dreary reminder. So, let us move on to the orcs proper now. You clearly didn't like them for their level of sophistication, or lack thereof, but you apparently did take the time to learn a few words of their language. How do you explain that?"

"Yeah, I suppose that does sound a little like a contradiction. We had a class in school to study a few things. It actually became a requisite class to show respect for them, as we were at peace and conducting trade on occasion. Although the trade was limited to only a few basic items they might find of interest."

"What sorts of things? This might be interesting."

"Shiny things, mostly, stuff they could use to ornament themselves, especially their chieftains and shamans. They liked our holo-disks and storage chips, and some of our jewelry and scraps of metal... since they couldn't apparently make their own. They might trade for bits of metal to make blades and other tools."

"What did they trade with?"

"Hides, for one thing, sometimes meat, and a few other things they could either hunt or gather. We didn't have any livestock, so meat and leather were specialty items for us. And then, some minerals, like precious or semiprecious stones that might be desirable for our own use. We tried to find something equitable, since they covered a much larger area and might have easier access to things.”

“How interesting. This sounds like it could’ve been very productive, at least to a certain degree. But now, as a people, we should try to qualify the differences. Surely, Kaliya, you cannot expect every lifeform out there to meet up to the same standards as yours, especially for the length of time you invested in your development. We could just as easily say these orcs represent a much earlier form of life, perhaps in their late Stone Age, if they are not adept at using any kind of metal. Regardless of the fact they might have their magic, which represents an unknown quantity to you, they are a society that would likely symbolize the average for their stage of development.”

“I understand this, and again, Kailen and Ankhia spent long hours counseling me on these same principles. They don’t have metal, they don’t build schools, they don’t have agriculture, or even a proper form of writing. They do draw pictures, a kind of ideographic language, however.”

“This much I believe we have seen on Tae’Eladar, but I think we should also consider our example had interactions with the rest of us, so they did manage to progress a little farther than what you are describing. Not by much, though, as they also seemed to reject a lot of things. And yet, you seem to hold these feelings despite realizing this is simply who they are as a society. This now leaves us with the attack, and your feelings seem centered on how they might do this to you as further insult to your higher station.”

“Yeah, and it hurt. We didn’t do anything to them, and they did this to us.”

“Kaliya, if we look at it in retrospect, the ‘why’ is simple. Sargeras. Although you could not know this at the time, which is unfortunate, and this left an unsettled feeling. You trusted them as friends, and they betrayed you. You had hoped to have escaped from Sargeras, but he was still with you, and likely hidden from view. But again, you could not know any of this. The revelation we have now must itself be the cure for this. As for the orcs, if he owned them from such an early moment in time, everything else was just a show until he gave the word to make it happen. It has nothing to do with their culture, their technological sophistication, their manners, or their lifestyles. They probably worshipped him as a god image, and when your god tells you to do something, you tend to listen."

Kaliya went silent for a moment as she pondered this suggestion. It was clearly evident by now, after learning of so many other details coming out in the recent discussions about Sargeras and their apparent pursuit, which was more of a drive than a chase. They experienced that extended moment of peace only at the whim of that same creature who seemingly wanted them dead, but never actually went so far as to do it. But now, a new question entered her mind, and it was just as demanding as the rest.

"But why..." she mumbles as she turns to look into Aerlie's eyes. "Why would he do this...after fourteen centuries of freedom on that world, which was longer than any other on record, why do it this way and on this occasion?"

"That is a question we may not know the answer to," Thaelyn muses. "Not unless we can find an orc on Ruuki uy'Daan who could possibly provide it to us, assuming there are any by now, or some other reference. And another thing that comes to mind, since we are on the subject, is he had those saboteurs on your ship which caused it to crash here. This represents an alteration to the pattern of that long chase. So, what we seem to have here is something occurring on Ruuki uy'Daan, or perhaps elsewhere, where his attitude changed, and he no longer cared to chase you."

"I'll bet it involves that wild jump," Relissa suggests. "Why a wild jump to a place he previously owned, then to leave them for so long?"

"This is a good point. He wanted them there, and the extended lull might be an indicator. He was there for a reason, and not because of them. Then, he got what he wanted, and now here we are."

"Cu'Nar help us," Kaliya moans. "So, he drops us on that world, maybe for the orcs to simply babysit us, while he goes off looking for something, and then bam! Now he's shedding us off, after all this time! You know, Kailen always said the Suuden-Aryku are probably moving to finish us on this world, although it's taking forever. But here you are saying it started on Ruuki uy'Daan, and he's doing so in this really vulgar manner. Just another insult, but not by orcs, they were simply a tool on this occasion. Dear cu'Nar, give me strength. Then the real reason has to be hidden behind this last attack, maybe also that jump, and why it occurred this way."

"Indeed, but now that you know this…now that you have found this reconciliation, how would this affect your opinion of orcs overall? This is what I would suggest you ponder, if only silently, as part of contemplating your sins."

"All right, fine. But I will admit, there was probably no way for any of us to realize this without outside help. We apparently had too few pieces to add up."

"This is likely correct, and also likely by design, if we say he is intentionally hiding things. Just look at what we see in this world."

"Absolutely! But, hmm. To contemplate sins… Do I need to speak to a priest for this point?"

"Actually, I would recommend exactly that. Aerlie? What do you think?"

"I would agree," she affirms. "Perhaps we could have one of our priests offer some consultation of our principles, and maybe I could also call her into my office back home. I could bring her up to Ilmater's icon for a session."

"Ilmater?" Kaliya wonders. "Is that one of your gods over there?"

"Yes, he is known as the Crying God, and serves to relieve people from torment and psychological suffering. He lifts it out of you and takes it into himself, where he then contends with it in his own way to resolve the matter."

"Wow, someone can actually do that? All right, but this sounds weird. Remember, we're not religious, so trying something like this would be a strange experience for me."

"I understand, but this also reminds me of that final piece, where your society doesn't understand the principles of magic, or anything else that might seem to you as mysticism," she grins. "Maybe we should try to resolve that now and bring you out of this restrictive state of mind where everything has to have an empirical evaluation."

"Oh dear Powers, Aerlie," Thaelyn muses jovially. "Are you suggesting we violate this dear Child's innocence now?"

The group enjoys a moment of laughter as Thaelyn prepares for this next session.

"Very well," he continues. "For this, I would like to refer back to these orcs for a time and build an image using predictable elements. We will move forward from there. Kaliya, are you game for a little… debate?" he raises his brow teasingly.

"Uh oh," Relissa moans. "Girl, if you know what's good for you, you'd better watch yourself. He's getting that look in his eyes."

"Yeah," Kaliya winces. "But I suppose I'll have to, if it involves a lesson."

"We will make a comparison of orcs to your people," Thaelyn suggests, "or perhaps the other local races. Firstly, how do orcs live on Ruuki uy'Daan, meaning to say their homes and living conditions?"

"They had villages with huts made mostly from wooden poles and hides. I didn't see anything like farming, but they would go out on hunts quite often, gather water from local lakes and streams into bowls that I think were woven from plant materials and lined with some kind of gum from trees, and they generally lived off the land in a rather primitive cultural setting."

"All right, good… Let us take their homes first. What can you say about them?"

"The local people as compared to the orcs? Well, the local races use wood and stone in a lot of their construction, from what I've seen at a distance. I've never been inside Rolsklinde or Solinaia, but I've studied it from afar just to see how it looks."

"And so, we can say they live in cities, which could be described as a step up from a village, using more advanced construction techniques involving milled lumber, rather than wooden poles which are probably cut directly from chopped or fallen logs. And rather than hides, you might see stonemasonry, which would provide for a more durable structure against the elements."

"Right. But then, let's talk about food. These people have farming, as opposed to the orcs who were hunter-gatherers."

"Virtually every society would start out this way, at least until they make the association of planting seed to produce crops, perhaps also to involve the seasonal demands for when those crops would grow best. And then we have the domestication of animals for a sustainable food supply."

"All right, this is reasonable, and I can't argue with that. You would also need land to do it on, and a ready supply of water for irrigation."

"Indeed. A stable locale, and a local river or lake, where you can dig ditches or canals to siphon some away, or perhaps a well or a reservoir, if you have the means to draw it out into a plumbing network."

"Good. But now, what about trade? The local races, and even my own people, use a form of currency. Well, actually, my people would use it if we had the freedom to live normal lives. Our condition of simply trying to survive has cut that part out recently, if only because it gets in the way of getting any work done."

"Ah, this is interesting. This is to say, Person A desires payment to perform his duty, say as a farmer, but the rest of your society does not have the luxury of maintaining an active economy. Rather, they need that food more than anything else, so Person A has no other choice, for the good of everyone involved, to do his work regardless, correct?"

"Essentially yes, for all of us."

"This is unfortunate, but I can clearly see the reasoning here."

"These orcs, however, were quite primitive, trying to associate one shiny thing for another, and their valuation often varied from person to person."

"The basic form of trade is known as the barter system, and very often begins this way as a society does not even know of anything they can use as a standardized currency. Such materials as gold, silver, maybe also copper, and perhaps precious stones can be used by some, but these have to be discovered first, and then you must learn how to mint this into coinage, or else divide it into predictable units. Beyond that, trading one item for another may still be used, even in more advanced societies, if only by private contract."

"Wow, all right, you got me there. What about crafting? The locals have workshops, tools, and a form of industry. These orcs might simply hack off a tree limb and call it a club, or maybe wedge a piece of metal into it and call it an axe or a chopping tool for meat. They couldn't figure out how to make their own metal, even though there were mineral deposits nearby, and they often wore hides as clothing, rather than trying to weave something to make cloth. More often, they ran around half-naked."

"In a jungle environment, I might actually say this would be expected, if only for the climate. Clothing might require other inventions first, like the domestication of animals where one could gather wool or other materials to weave into cloth. Certain plant materials can also be used, but I think we should temper ourselves and ask if those are available locally. Like everything else, all forms of crafting must have a starting point to build up to something higher. Metal requires the use of a furnace or a kiln, then to realize methods for producing a fire hot enough to do the work. If your only avenue to make fire is by rubbing two sticks together, this is inadequate. If you do not have the proper infrastructure, you may only be limited to hacking off tree limbs, at least until you can build more advanced tools to do more advanced work. Consider this: If you were to find yourself lost in the wilderness with nothing more than the clothes on your back, how do you think you would survive? You should think on this a moment."

"Yeah, and it's not pleasant, because I'm no good at rubbing two sticks together," she chuckles.

"Indeed, that does require a bit of finesse."

"All right, what about education? You speak of infrastructure, so wouldn't a school be one of these? And maybe also things like, oh, taverns and inns, rather than eating whatever was crawling underneath you, and sleeping on the ground. And temples, for those of us who are religious," she grins as she flashes at Relissa and Marelle.

"Very well...schools first. For this, you also have a prerequisite or two, one of these being an efficient form of writing to record your knowledge. In ancient societies, especially if we speak of nomadic forms, one might see the elder members teaching the younger ones at a fireside. And this might involve storytelling to recall one's history. A school most often represents a stationary cultural building in a city or town where we are establishing a stable center for a civilization to grow. Taverns, inns, and temples can also be described as cultural or social buildings in the same manner."

"Here we go…my next set of horns."

"Group dining and sleeping are a common occurrence in an early tribal society that may gather for feasts and communal living, at least as much for mutual support and protection as for their social interaction. Religion dates back to the earliest moments of sentient thought, as one might try seeking answers to the ways of the natural world around them. Therefore, to invent such notions as spirits, or perhaps later gods, performing the many mysterious acts one might see in nature."

"Cu'Nar help me…" she moans softly. "This is more than my full education during my lifetime."

"Yeah," Marelle exalts. "I could get more out of him at a fireside than I did during all my own schooling back home."

"Aye!" Relissa agrees. "This is a fair bit of learning. It's not anything wildly grand, but it puts it together a new way."

Thaelyn smiles as he continues.

"Now, while a nomadic society might build such things as longhouses that could serve as social centers, in my opinion, the simple fact that they do not settle in one location does not offer the possibility of building a proper civilization around that center. A proper civilization requires population centers with repositories of culture, education, social gatherings, industry, trade, and economics, and do so in a predictable and perpetual environment. Until you achieve this, you are still lacking many of the ingredients of a more advanced age. However, this does not necessarily describe you as uncivilized. You may still possess skills and other inventions worthy of mention, while travelling about seeking more viable habitats, such as following seasonal transitions. The orcs with those bowls you mentioned would be a fine example of an invention for what they had to work with, at least until such time as they might invent pottery, and later, ceramics."

"All right, I think I give up," Kaliya chuckles. "I can't debate with you. Where did you learn all this?"

"I learned many of my skills in the court of my Father, serving as an inquisitor and later an adjudicator for law and justice. I participated in many inquisitions and tribunals, often as the prosecutor, and had to learn to collect and manage my facts in order to create presentations designed to secure a proper verdict. Sometimes, I might also find myself in need to arrange my statements so as to bring out what might be hidden details from those involved, in the event it held any relevance to my cause."

"Your Lordship," Marelle muses. "Remind me never to get into a debate with you. I don't think I'd survive it."

They shared another brief laugh at the girl's misery.

"Another thing," Thaelyn continues. "It would be unfair to classify orcish culture in relation to another, like yours or the local races. How they live, what values they hold, this likely evolved in ways different from yours. For instance, they value strength, as they are largely a warrior society, as compared to yours where you tell us you are scientists and scholars. An orcish chieftain might take his position through a contest of strength over his competitors. You might elect your governors through a civil voting process. There is a significant difference here, but neither can be said to be wrong... at least not within the context of their social culture."

"Context..." Kaliya muses. "That's the key here, right?"

"Yes, it is. To alter this, you would likely need an evolution of culture, or perhaps a forceful takeover, where we might see a movement into a new era of governing philosophies. This could be a transition to a monarchy, where one inherits his position from a predecessor, or it could be the rise of an aristocratic council or a despotic dictatorship. You could also see the development of a democracy, where everyone has a vote in which to choose their leaders. And I might also add, none of these really has anything to do with their technological sophistication."

"No? So, you could have a warrior society even with a high level of technology?"

"You could. Their rate of development might differ from others, as they may suffer a lot of wars along the way, but I would imagine once done, most of it would be oriented at combat and military hardware. In contrast, you could also have a democratic body, but in a much earlier era, like a Bronze or Iron Age, if they are socially enlightened enough to envision it. What about yours? You have your Council, and then you have this body you call the Sentinels. How did this come about?"

"The Council and our modern social environment came as the result of a very famous name in our history, King Saakerav. It's said that he united the nations of our world, way back when we were still a fragmented society, and then established the Council of Elders, orienting us on a new path of enlightenment where we would pursue the discovery of new knowledge and intellectual achievements. It was a turning point for us and marked the beginning of what we now call the Enlightened Era."

"That sounds like a wonderful moment."

"Yeah, and the Sentinels is what we use for law enforcement and security. It's not a true military as some of the others might have. We don't have wars any longer, so there's no need for an actual military."

"I see, but you know, this can also place you in danger of anything that is in fact warlike. As such, you might not hold the technical capacity to fight back, if your combat methods are insufficient against anything truly designed for war."

"Like what's going on right now, I suppose."

"Indeed. Your weapons might not be destructive enough to bring down your enemies efficiently. You might choose to run rather than fight. They might choose to hunt you rather than leave you be. The outcome would be grim either way, and there is no right or wrong way to solve this, other than not to arrive here to begin with. But it would seem it was done outside your control, on this occasion."

"Yeah…" she lowers her head.

"But now, let us move forward to that mysticism aspect of things."

"Ah yes, I've been waiting for this part," she smiles.

"The first thing I would suggest, as far as magic is concerned, is this. A society might find more utility in this than your classic sciences, if only due to the ease at which they can find their answers. Therefore, a society might actually advance faster in magic than anything you could otherwise recognize with science."

"Uh huh…and that already blows my horns off, but I suppose I have to admit this from the things I see around us now," she glances around the camp at the gateway and walls.

"When I first arrived on Tae'Eladar, they had spent many millennia stagnating in a type of medieval-like era. No real science was being investigated at all. They had their magic, and their ambitions were largely satisfied using this alone."

"That doesn't sound good."

"Even worse, magic was often a privileged study for the very astute, or the very mad, because they were the ones with the motivations for power…and this is what it most often represented."

"Yikes!"

"This is like what you were saying on that first day, ay?" Relissa asks.

"It is," Thaelyn nods. "And here is where we had to correct things. By sharing the studies with everyone, we encouraged a form of growth, and this growth brought with it a revolution of new ideas for understanding its utilitarian value. It was no longer regarded as some mysterious force that only a handful of similarly mysterious people could wield. Now we had the opportunity to study it on a more intimate level, and across a broader range of applications."

"And here is where we have your society in the modern day," Kaliya accedes, "inventing things that someone like me would lose their horns over on a regular basis."

"Indeed, but with a bit of education, perhaps you might finally be able to hold on to one or another of those."

"You think?" she grins.

"The orcs were probably just following a natural course, using what was available and producing what they needed from it."

"Like fireballs?"

"Well, fire would certainly be one obvious example, like for instance to start a campfire. After that, it is largely a matter of expanding your perspective for the other applications."

"Yeah, and they sure did that inside the city."

"But if we are saying you come from a universe without these energies, it becomes clear you will need to understand what these energies actually are, and maybe also why you do not have them over there. I may not necessarily be able to answer that here and now, but to answer the first part, try to envision this."

He adjusts his seating as he gets ready to explain this part.

"The dynamistic flows, as we sometimes call them, is a layer of ethereal substance with some qualities of energy and some of matter. It does not follow any classic form of physical science, and they do not necessarily exist in any single dimensional plane, as they have a tenancy to spread across dimensional boundaries to touch other planes. They are created by a rather unique form of life that exists in another layer, and as the result of a type of symbiotic relationship with other forms of life, like our own."

"All right, this is already causing my horns to feel limp."

"Corporeal life, for instance, emits its own biological energies. These tend to radiate outwards. These entities, which some may call arcanids, and for lack of a better term, will feed on this and produce a byproduct as a result."

"And that just caused them to fall off. So, we're drawing on something else's excrement? Ew!"

"Well, not necessarily, if you consider the interaction of plants and animals where the air is concerned. Oxygen in the air, which we need to breathe, is provided by plants. Our breath, which carries away what we might call a waste byproduct, is consumed by the plants, and the result becomes their waste byproduct."

"Yeah, all right, that makes sense, so we have yet another occasion of it. Interesting, but then why is it missing in our home universe?"

"This is a good question, and there are potentially a few answers, not the least of which could be the youth of your universe, if the arcanids have not found their way into it yet."

"Hmm, maybe…"

"I have heard of one or another fold the Estelar cordon off as reserved or maybe sanctuary spaces they might sometimes study for how life evolves in these regions. These areas are generally off-limits for them to enter, if only to keep the results pristine."

"Now there's a concept, gods taking up a study project."

"Indeed!" he smiles. "And then, these flows, after a period of time to accumulate, can ultimately expand to fill an entire dimensional body. The arcanids will tend to cluster around any space where they can detect the bioenergy of corporeal life, no matter how large or small. Of course, the larger and more densely populated areas will draw more arcanids, therefore the more arcanic energies you will find. And this also represents a renewable resource, as it is constantly flowing."

"Nice! And so, we don't really need to do anything to produce it, not even farming."

"Jiggers," Relissa shakes her head. "I'm going to have my hands full trying to study in your academy."

"And being organic in nature," Thaelyn continues. "The mind becomes the catalyst. The more disciplined the mind, the more you can wield, and therefore the more you can accomplish with the craft."

"And here we have that riddle of metaphysics I always hated," Kaliya reflects. "Nothing exists until it is known."

"Kaliya, in the purest sense, you actually have no idea how close you are to a truth that scales well above you. The Celestial races would know this better. The mind can trigger changes in the local environment, creating substance out of what might seem like nothingness. There are societies out there in the Outer Planar regions that can build entire cities in this way, simply by imagining it with their minds and forcing it into Reality."

"Cu'Nar's pity! Wait till I try to explain that one back home."

"The concept is also described in a similar manner. To Know

of a thing, meaning the intellectual perception of its existence. And we are not necessarily speaking of a preexisting object. It can also be created by this Knowing. You must carry a very carefully sculpted concept of the item in your mind, and then overlay your perceptions onto the space around you to alter the reality of existence to match. But admittedly, this is not easily done just anywhere. Some dimensional planes are more malleable than others, and some beings are more potent than others."

"Tanjhira is going to have her horns go ballistic on this stuff," she muses softly.

"Perhaps so, but if your people were to admit to this, finally and completely, just imagine what you could do with it. Observe this small demonstration."

Thaelyn holds out an open hand with the palm up. He then waves his other hand in a circle above the first. Energies pass between the two until a spark forms. He then slowly draws his upper hand further away, stretching the spark into a column of wispy blue energy between his palms. He holds them there while he explains.

"Do you see this?"

"Yes, I do."

"Your science would only represent one side of the coin, while this is the other side. This is an example of arcanic energy made visible to the eye, at least conceptually. We use this demonstration from time to time to educate our children, and believe it or not, there is a science to be learned that explains it very nicely, but it has absolutely nothing to do with empirical evaluation. Instead, it involves mental perceptions and intellectual interpretations of concepts and perspectives to be projected into the space around us. We can teach this to you in our academy, and perhaps one day you could learn to perform this trick yourself."

"Yeah, and I think that also blows the riddle of metaphysics to nether-space. Even though it represents the same concept, your explanation carries it to a whole new level. We would appear as amateurs by comparison."

"I might better say you are simply starting out, but unfortunately with very little resource material in which to experiment."

"If only my instructors at the academy could be so helpful," Haran moans. "Sometimes I think they make it hard intentionally."

"By the sound of it," Thaelyn accedes. "They may not have any intention of teaching you anything at all. I might even go so far as to suggest the whole idea of your academy is simply a ruse to raise hopes for their ulterior motives."

"Probably…"

"Anyway, the arcanic energies around us are being drawn into my body as we speak. My mind channels this through the power of my will. I focus my thoughts and perceive this form. The energy then alters itself within the space just above my hand to produce this effect. Place your own hand in there and try to touch it."

Kaliya reaches her hand into the swirling mist-like cloud. Her movement seems to disturb the swirls within the mist as they redistribute themselves around her hand, but she is unable to accurately perceive any sensation of the cloud itself.

"Fascinating," she whispers.

Thaelyn leans forward for the others to try. Relissa, Haran, and Marelle each lean in to sample the strange phenomenon.

"Now we will try another one," Thaelyn asserts.

He returns to his position as he prepares for another example. This time, he waves his hand above the open palm and a new cloud appears, rapidly coalescing into an undulating liquid form. He brings a hand alongside as the shape settles into a spherical blob, and he snaps his fingers. The substance instantly freezes solid and drops into his hand.

Haran studies his motions.

"Oh, I like that one," he croons.

"Touch that," Thaelyn issues to Kaliya. "In fact, take it and pass it around."

She takes the frozen ball of ice and examines it, holding it out for the others in the group to look at. They each feel the cold texture of the solid body.

"Amazing…" she gasps. "Aside from the metaphysics aspect, this would actually defy my teachings of science. I know there is a science to describe the condensation of matter out of energy, but you can't just wave your hand and poof, it appears."

"This is true, but if we now include metaphysics, and the concept of Knowing, here it is. I focused my will upon the energy to perceive this form, I gave it definition, and this resulted in the formulation of its existence within my mind. From that, I applied myself to bend the reality of this space to bring this out."

"It simply boggles…but here it is. And apparently within reach that I can finally understand how it works…how it feels."

"Just remember, the mind needs to be carefully focused and disciplined to prevent accidents. Furthermore, one must contain one's feelings and not let it go to their head," he smiles.

"Yeah, I'd hate to see anything like that. This would more likely represent a godlike power…to alter Reality."

"Yes, and if we speak of the Estelar, they can do this, and on a gigantic scale. We are small by comparison. So, let us give this a try."

Thaelyn spies a pile of kindling near one of the buildings. He telekinetically retrieves a piece and catches it in his hand.

Marelle observes the floating piece of wood drift in front of her and her eyes grow wide at the thought of whatever ghostly force must be transporting it.

"Haran," she whines. "Did you see that?"

"See what, Sis?" he answers casually as he pretends not to see anything.

She turns and backhands him across the chest.

"You know darn well what!" she scolds.

Haran grunts from the blow, but follows with a playful chuckle. Marelle waves a stern finger at him.

"Haran," Thaelyn inquires. "Have you informed her of any of those…special details…I shared with you during our first meeting?"

"No, Your Lordship. I managed to keep all that quiet during my report and what I gave to her and the Captain."

"Haran!" she snaps. "Are you holding out on me?"

"Sis, there were some things he explained to us on that first day that were very delicate, and he made each of us promise not to tell the others. Please forgive me, but it's a matter of security. We think there may be spies hiding somewhere."

"Spies...yeah..." she grumbles. "And from everything that's been said so far, that's already bad."

"Perhaps we can make an exception in her case," Thaelyn reasons. "After all, she is your sister, so she deserves a special mention. Over time, as we become more familiar with certain individuals, I suppose we will be welcoming more of them inside. And since she will be working so closely with us here, it may be necessary to bring her in, just in case we have need for her support. So, go ahead and explain those points that have been revealed thus far. Marelle, you should know that secrecy is important in this regard. While there may be many things we can share with the others, I feel there might be a few that must be held back if they can represent a tactical advantage on our behalf."

"I understand, and my deepest thanks, Your Lordship. I'll strive to be worthy of your confidence."

She turns to Haran and grabs the edge of his ear, yanking him towards her in a mock gesture of wrath.

"All right, you... Out with it!" she orders.

"And I thought my brother was hard..." Kaliya winces playfully.

"Indeed, elder siblings do have their charm," Thaelyn muses. "But now, take this..." he passes the stick to her. "Using that stick of wood, how might you start a fire?"

"Using just this one? I probably couldn't. Remember, I said I wasn't good at that sort of thing."

"Granted, it takes practice, although I might also admit, we generally do not do it this way to begin with. And if using your science?"

"If using anything from our science, there are lots of ways to start a fire, typically by using a flammable fuel ignited by a sparking mechanism."

"This is reasonable. But now, what would happen if you were to simply snap your fingers next to it?"

"To simply snap, nothing else?"

"Yes, let us begin with this."

"Uh huh…" she grins.

Kaliya brings up her free hand and playfully snaps her fingers in close proximity to the stick. Of course, nothing happens.

"Good, but this did not represent a serious effort. If we now get serious, you need to take all these lessons and apply them to the reality of that stick. You want fire, this much we know. You must then envision how this would appear. It must hold definition in your mind, involving heat, light, and the combustion of the material. We want this on the outer end of the stick, not the whole thing. After all, we do not wish to burn our fingers," he smiles. "But to do this, you must convince yourself it is real in your mind. This is perhaps the hardest stumbling point for some."

"Right…"

"You must reach out with your perceptions to gather up the arcanic energies in your local vicinity. You cannot necessarily see them, but in time, and with a bit of practice and experience, you should develop a form of sensitivity to feel them. Use your mind to draw them in. Think of it in a similar sense to inhaling, but carefully measure yourself for the volume. Early students sometimes bring too much. You will develop a feel for it over time as you progress in your studies. Then, your mind must channel them, causing them to flow like a river through your body. Most often, we might say along your arm, and here into the stick proper. Draw this flow out to the end, and in our case, we often draw a circle with our free hand to gather up these energies into a ring. We might do this twice around, before snapping our fingers next to it. The snapping action serves as a psychological trigger, where our mind transitions the energies to invoke the act of combustion."

"In this case, a little like the sparking mechanism of one of our lighters."

"In some ways, yes… Now, give it a try. Do not be disheartened if you fail the first time. After all, even for those of us who know what it is, it takes a bit of practice to get it right."

"All right, sure…"

Haran leans forward, watching intently to see if she can actually do it. He recalls trying to demonstrate in the past how he performs his craft, but she could never follow his example. This lesson represented a far more liberal form of instruction than he ever got back home.

Kaliya places her focus on the stick and reflects on Thaelyn's words. She further recalls all of her musings on metaphysics. She tries reaching out with her thoughts to feel the local arcanic energies. But, not really knowing what to expect out of it, she is unsure if she is actually interacting with them. Still, she had to try. After all, if she's ever going to understand it, she has to start somewhere.

She places her attention on the stick and tries to imagine fire, hoping to incite a flow of energy through her arm to gather up in place. She makes a tentative double circle with her finger, drawing it around slowly, then moving her hand off to the side and snapping, hoping to spark a flame. But nothing happens.

"Try again," Thaelyn encourages.

She clears her throat and prepares for another try.

"Keep in mind," he instructs softly. "It fills this space, it permeates all things, touching all matter but not hindered by it. Expand your mind into the space around you. Try to feel it. Imagine its form, how densely it flows around you. Then see yourself perhaps like a sponge, soaking it up, consciously drawing it in. Your body is a vessel, a focus to attract this energy."

He makes a gesture by extending his first two fingers.

"Make this gesture with your hand, it may help with your focus. When you feel ready, circle your fingers twice around the end of the stick. As you do, bring your mind to imagine the energies forming a ring trailing from your fingers. Once you have your ring, you will snap and cause your mind to invoke that ring to ignite."

Haran is on edge watching Kaliya try to learn this trick. It was a skill he knew well, although he had to practice it for weeks to get it right, and he could never describe it so fluidly.

Relissa and Marelle look on with enthusiasm. Relissa remembered what he said once about how everybody in his world studies at least a little bit of magic, a common practice for every citizen. She was trying to pay attention to the lesson so she could remember it for later. Marelle never studied magic, but knew a few small details from what Haran shared with her from his lessons. Still, it was mostly a mystery to her, as it was to virtually everyone else outside the academy. She couldn't help but to wonder if she could learn this. It seemed so simple, and yet so useful.

Kaliya gazes at the stick, her face strained in a moment of concentration as she once again attempted to draw a flow of energy. She brings her hand over and makes two circles around the end of the stick, then moves it to the side, pausing briefly before snapping her fingers. Again, nothing happens.

Haran looks down in disappointment, as do the two women.

"Try it again, Kaliya," Thaelyn reassures. "Focus greatly on this. You have a strong mind; I can see this. This should be easy for you. You simply need to believe in it. The energies are a tool, your mind is the driving force, and with it you can alter the space around you using that tool."

As he mentioned these words, she felt a tingle of a memory from somewhere. To alter this space… Will, this is the driving factor. She rededicated herself to her task.

She tried again, placing the thought in her mind that there was a hidden cloud of energy around her, and now it was condensing into her. She imagines this moving through her body and into her hand, then up onto the stick. On this occasion, it seemed like she could almost feel something, like a tingling sensation from her nerves. She continues directing her thoughts as a driving force, and then brings her free hand around to make another set of circles. Her head feels like it's starting to swell from the pressure she's placing on herself. She thinks her eyes are playing tricks on her, seeing an actual ring forming around the end of the stick, but she presses on, bringing her hand to the side and making a solid snap of the fingers.

A small set of sparks shoot out from the air immediately

surrounding the stick, accompanied by the announcement of tiny popping sounds. Kaliya lets out a muted screech as she lurches back from the sudden display. She watches the sparks quickly dissipate into the air. Her instinctive fear reaction temporarily quickens her breathing.

"Gods be blessed, Kaliya," Haran declares. "You almost got it!"

"One more time, Kaliya," Thaelyn directs. "Do not allow yourself to become distracted. Discipline of the mind; you want this, you need this, you will stop at nothing to have it. Your mind must dominate these energies. Keep your focus all the way through, calm and determined."

"I thought I felt something," she relates. "And I thought I could see something from my fingers."

"Exactly! You are starting to feel it now. Bring this again, but better under control. If you can feel it, you know you are doing it right, and if you can see it, you know you are ready. It follows your conscious will. Drive it with your thoughts. Now try again."

Kaliya feels inspired now and tries one more time, following the same routine. She takes a deep breath and recalls the tingling she felt before. She decides to replicate this as a marker for her progress. She imagines the energy condensing into her, building to capacity... circulating...moving. She feels the tingling again. She allows herself to experience this sensation, willing herself to bring it to a fuller intensity. It grows into a surge, and she spends a moment studying this within her mind's eye, trying to interpret its nature. She now directs her thoughts at the stick, channeling this surge along her arm and into the slender piece of wood, envisioning a spiraling tendril running up the length of it.

The others in the group observe with bated breath as her hand begins to glow softly and a thin stream of luminescent particles seems to snake its way up the segment of kindling.

Kaliya watches the movement and readies her free hand. She determinedly swings it over and winds her fingers in a circular path around the top of the stick. As she does, she mentally projects the image of the spiral to gather at her fingertips, forming a well-defined ring, and further intensifying her thoughts to deepen its effect to be sure she has enough. Next would be the trigger, and for this she considers visualizing an implosion effect to collapse the ring and start the fire. She moves her hand to the side and holds the stick at length, then snaps her fingers once more.

Her action invokes the densely packed ring of mystical particles to collapse energetically into the wood, resulting in a harsh crackling and a burst of flame covering the full upper third of the stick. The miniature explosion splits the end of the kindling, sending several flaming shards off to the side, and a small plume lifting into the air. The splintered upper portion now burns vigorously.

The group jerks back uncontrollably from the sudden surge of flame. Relissa pushes herself away while Marelle takes to kicking some of the burning sparks into the fire pit. Haran is breathless at the spectacle.

"Do you have any idea how long it took me to learn that?" he cries.

Thaelyn glances at Aerlie in wonder, and then turns back to the stick and the local area below where the debris had fallen.

"And this is why we teach fire-starting to our Novice class, not the Neophyte," he chuckles. "Well done, Kaliya. You have actually surpassed my expectations. You accomplished in just a few attempts what some might take much longer to study and practice, and you did this without any form of structured education in an academy. I must now wonder what you could accomplish with formal study."

Kaliya sits motionless with a broad grin reaching across her face, while she watches the amazing sight of the fire she started on this piece of wood with little more than the power of her mind and the wave of a hand.

"I did it..." she coos. "I actually did it."

An upwelling of pride flows into her, but she reminds herself to remain calm, so she doesn't create any accidents with this new feeling. She lays the kindling on the edge of the fire pit, adding it to the rest of the campfire.

"Now that you have tasted the element of magic," Thaelyn begins. "You may have an open window to a much larger world. How you use it is another thing, but you should understand the principles thoroughly before you take that step."

"Oh, absolutely! I can easily see where that concept of power corrupting someone can settle itself. This is serious power here. But on the other hand, if to learn more about it, and share it with others, it could change a lot of things for us."

"Um, Your Lordship," Marelle reflects. "Haran has just finished blowing my mind…or horns off, or whatever we're using here," she giggles, "relating to those little secrets of yours. Like that floating stick a few moments ago, the ability to speak with the mind, and then you have some kind of Sight? I know of a few people up in the city who talk about telling fortunes or reading cards and other things they toss on a table, or whatever. I never really believed any of it, myself. But is this actually real, and how does it work?"

"In our case," he responds. "Aerlie and I both have what we refer to as Short Prophecy, as opposed to Long Prophecy. These are not uncommon amongst Celestials, but like with many skills, it also depends on how intensely you work to develop the ability. Ours were a gift from Tyr, as we had the opportunity to actually choose one or another of these for ourselves. Personally, as I am a man of action, I prefer Short Prophecy, as it allows me to see with crystal clarity what is imminent to occur. I may see only moments or minutes ahead, but it is enough to judge my course and the course of others near me to preserve lives and overcome critical errors."

"All right, and the other is…what? To see much farther ahead, I suppose."

"Yes. There have been those on Tae'Eladar, for instance, who possessed this skill. We have a few notable examples in our history and one very special case in our modern day that is well-known for her prophecies. But I hold a habit of not actively pursuing such things, as I prefer to conduct myself with what is readily apparent. Therefore, I tend to say, let others spend their days speculating on the permutations of Long Prophecy, for I care little to chase another man's dreams."

"Wow, now that's a statement," Kaliya winces.

"The reason for this is simple. Long Prophecy allows a man to see far ahead of the current moment…months, years, even centuries, if he has the strength. His visions may give him coverage, but at the expense of accuracy. Often, he will need to make wild interpretations of what he sees in order to make any sense of it. The more distant his vision, the less accurate the interpretation is likely to be."

"Is there some reason for this, like clarity or something?"

"The answer lies mostly in how well educated he is and how much the world might change during this time. Let us say that a man foresees an event one month ahead. The world, as it is in the present day, may offer him enough understanding of its nature to afford him ease of interpretation of his vision. Not much, short of a cataclysm, is likely to alter this in such a short length of time. Then, let us presume he foresees an event from one century ahead. The world may change much in that period, and what he will see may become unrecognizable to his less-enlightened mind. The farther you go, the more change, and the less you would understand of it with your earlier-period education."

"All right, got it… And that actually makes good sense to me. It also reflects on those cu'Nar and their messages to us. They seem to carry something prophetic, but they're also very hard to interpret."

"This would represent an interesting point, by the way. Regardless of the prophetic nature of the cu'Nar and their messages, it might be further complicated by the translation and interpretation of the one receiving it. Consider this for a moment. Firstly, these beings may need to reinterpret themselves to be comprehensible to the recipient. Their capacity to perceive their surroundings may not be compatible with yours. Therefore, the terms they use, the sensations they experience, perhaps even the message itself, if we say they could be no more than messengers for someone higher, might need to transit through multiple layers of interpretation before it arrives with you."

"Yeah, and this sounds like it would be very difficult to get any real meaning out of it."

"It might, and this is often the same problem I see with Long Prophecy. You may have people study this, but until you come upon that moment where some vital clue comes forward, you may have no other choice but to wait and see when the thing actually occurs."

"That's for sure! But you know, after all this talk, I actually feel a lot better for my own problems."

"I'm not letting you off the hook yet, Kaliya," Aerlie smiles. "I would still like to make a few sessions just to be sure we catch everything."

"All right, I won't argue any more. But overall, it feels like a weight has been lifted off me. Maybe I can finally recover from all that trauma."

"Sounds a bit like a firm knock to the head," Relissa jokes. "But in this case from the inside. I'm real happy you put all the pieces back in place though. And it looks like you found a few new ones, to boot."

"A knock to the head..." Aerlie muses curiously. "Such an interesting choice of words... Thaelyn, do you recall that flash during the meld? I wonder if we accidentally broke through a wall, like a mental barrier of that lost child on those ruined streets calling for help."

"Maybe so," he nods. "The meld was a potent form of interaction, and it could have brought out any number of repressed memories."

"You know, you may be right," Kaliya affirms. "I recall my report to the Council, where for the first time I actually stood up for myself and argued my point successfully, rather than crumbling into a heap, like I usually do. Elder Vankkar, who usually grinds my horns for all my mistakes, actually complemented me on this occasion."

"That's wonderful!" Aerlie croons. "And it does certainly suggest you made a turning point here."

"Maybe, although I seriously doubt it'll change anything for my career. It's so badly fouled up by now, I don't think anything can correct that."

"The first thing for you is to continue with this therapy to ensure we have a full containment and corrective influence. After that, we can consider where to go once we reevaluate our condition."

"Yeah, I suppose. But at the same time, I want to be a part of solving the problems we face, not just sit on the side watching the show. This was always one of my big issues. We were constantly under attack, we had little or no chance to rebuild anything, and our lives inside that wreck of a ship were so limited. Even the food gets boring after a while."

"What kind of food do you eat? You don't go outside to do any farming, as I understand it, so how do you make food?"

"Do you know what aeroponics is? Laboratory grown food, which isn't necessarily bad, but it's mostly fruits and vegetables, leafy greens, and roots. There's no actual meat, not unless we can trade with Rolsklinde. So, it's a salad for breakfast, a salad for lunch, and naturally, a salad for dinner. Ugh."

"Yeah, I suppose that can be a bit monotonous."

"It may not be as bad as all that, as we tend to be mostly vegetarian to begin with, but I would happily join you on Tae'Eladar, if only for the new dietary choices," she chuckles. "And then we have your military. I'll admit, this was always my dream, even from before. To be a part of something that actually gets the job done. That little girl running down the street was tired of running."

"I can certainly understand that much. But before we have you apply for anything; I want to be sure we cover all of your ailments. I should also mention this doesn't really offer a guarantee, either. We still need that Spirit test, and all things considered, you're not in the right sorts for it yet."

"I think I should also point something out," Thaelyn adds. "Although I understand your desires to make a difference, your ambitions also tend to stand out that you want something… exceptional…to your credit. There is nothing necessarily wrong with this, but expectations can bring their own consequences, and not always as we would desire. The quality of a hero is neither born nor trained. Most often, it comes about unexpectedly and as the result of dire circumstances. A soldier is simply a part of a larger machine, and in order for this machine to function properly, each of its parts must know its place. Over time, some of those parts may find themselves reorganized to perform a higher level of service, but they are still a part of the machine, and we must honor each one for its tireless duty to serve the whole."

"Yes, I understand," Kaliya nods. "And once again, this reflects on what my brother told me on so many occasions. I'll just have to hold on to my horns a bit longer until I feel myself strong enough to try again, and this time make sure they're turned around the right way to do the job without putting my tail in a vice," she grins.

Thaelyn raises his brow and smiles as he glances at Aerlie and the others in the group.

"Such curious expressions you have. I will surely need to study this. Very well, it is getting late, but there is one last thing I would have you do this eve. Do you know how to meditate?"

"Um, no, this isn't something they teach us over there."

Thaelyn's gaze passes briefly across the camp. A priest jumps up and trots over to his side.

"Yes, my Lord?" he announces.

"Take this young lady and teach her the practice of meditation, so that she may contemplate her sins."

"Of course, my Lord!"

The priest holds out a hand to Kaliya as she rises to her feet.

"And Kaliya," Thaelyn calls after her. "We will have you spend some time in B.T. as part of your rehabilitation. You can arrange your schedule with Aerlie."

She nods as the priest leads her away to a quiet location to begin the lesson.

Chapter 10

FIRST BLOOD

It is the dawning of the second day after the plans were made for the orcish outposts. The scouts returned the night before to report the comings and goings of the orcish troops on the front line near Solinaia. Nerves were tense as the army made its preparations in the pre-dawn hours. The mages were lining up with runes ready to open portals into areas that were deemed safe to enter out-of-sight of the orcish camps. A contingent of soldiers had been assigned to a grave-digging detail, opening up sites for mass graves on the other side of the local canyon. Additional runes had been created to be carried by mages attending the strike force, so the troops could make a rapid egress.

Relissa, Haran, and Marelle had relocated their residency to the dorms in the academy on Tae'Eladar so they could attend their daily language lessons. The three of them would take their classes in the morning hours, but the two women would then return to the camp in the Badlands for their daily review. Haran had arranged for an apprenticeship with a Mage Master in the academy to find employment during the time he was in training. He was excited at the prospect of a new life, where the environment of the academy in Bya'an Tamoranth felt wholly different from his former one. He now looked forward to both his work and his new studies.

Thaelyn was in conference on the last few details of the strike, accompanied by General Gabarleine, who had been in service since before this war began on Tae'Eladar. Captain Hagmaert stood outside watching the horizon for the first dawning rays of light.

"My Lord!" he announces. "First Light is arriving."

Thaelyn rushes outside to observe the sky. He turns to review the troops. Eight regiments of three thousand each had been delivered and organized within the camp.

"Make ready!" he shouts. "Leave nothing standing. Cleanse the land of their stain and return it back for burial. Mages, open the portals and let the flood rush through!"

Scores of mages begin casting portal activations to create the projected forms of the enchantment. Row after row of soldiers began jumping quietly through the apertures, so as not to create a disturbance on the other side. This was a sneak attack, mounted against four camps. The tactic was to attack from both sides of each camp to compress the orcs into a tight space, thus confusing and restricting their ability to fight back.

Soldiers started appearing out of nowhere from portals over the western horizon, just out of view of the orcish camps. As their numbers increased, they moved into gullies and below embankments to keep themselves hidden.

The commanders held their ranks in check, waiting for the last of the portals to close, indicating the final assembly of troops in the field. When all the portals had faded, they gave their commands to launch.

The entire mass of troops jumped up and began charging forward towards the unsuspecting camps, six thousand strong on each of four sites, converging from two directions. Other than for the stampeding of their feet, they kept their silence until almost on top of the camp, when they finally let out their battle cries.

The surprised orcs, still groggy from their night's sleep, never knew what hit them. They dashed to find their weapons, confused and disoriented by the sudden uproar of battle on all sides. Many had removed their armor the evening before and had not yet the time to re-equip it. Others were scrambling to the outer edge of the camp to meet their attackers.

The orcs were equipped with simple steel blades and reinforced clubs, clearly an upgrade from their normal primitive weaponry, and likely stolen from another source. Some wore steel plate chest armor, though also crudely designed. Nevertheless, it was no match for the mithril and adamantium gear used by the Order. The orcish swords chipped and their armor was easily pierced by the harder substance. Bodies fell in quick succession as the soldiers slashed their way through the lines.

Archers rained a hail of arrows onto the camps, many of which were imbued with either ice or lightning enchantments to cause additional injury. Many of the orcish combatants deeper within the camp were brought down by this ranged assault.

Mages and priests formed a rearward line behind the main offensive ready to lend assist, but the orcish defense was no match for the strength of their attackers. No serious injuries were received on the side of the Order, and the mages were instructed not to engage with any magic attacks that could cause fires or raise smoke, either of which could signal trouble to the more distant camps.

The sun was still coming over the horizon when the battle ended. It was over almost as quickly as it began. Now was the time for cleaning up. The mages opened portals for the return back to the outpost. They grouped themselves into clusters, some of them with portals to the burial sites, and others to the dump.

The soldiers stowed their weapons and began hoisting bodies over their shoulders to carry them back. Once the bodies were removed, they started packing up the campsite materials, hacking tents and other structures into smaller bits for ease of transport, and carrying away crates and barrels, no doubt brought in from orcish supply depots located elsewhere.

The land was almost literally swept clean of any evidence of the campsite. Mages conjured up water showers to wash the blood stains into the soil, while others turned over dirt with shovels to bury ash from campfires. When the work was done, the remaining troops departed back to the outpost, leaving nothing but a strangely barren field where once there was an inhabited camp.

"Four down, and I am sure a great many more to go," Thaelyn whispers as the last of his men return safely.

Since the evening of their discussion and Kaliya's cry for help, Aerlie had arranged a schedule of therapy sessions at the temple in the city. She took a personal role in the young girl's recovery, leading her to the ornately festooned halls of the Temple of the Planes, where Aerlie served the ruling position of authority in their religious doctrines and practices as the Matron Pontifex.

The priesthood on Tae'Eladar also provided for the medical arts, and Aerlie served part-time as a physician and scholar, offering services to the public and training for younger clerics. Her Celestial studies further enhanced this with many advanced teachings, granting a level of understanding comparable to Thaelyn's in other areas. Much like her husband, she would use this to teach the people of Tae'Eladar in gradual steps, and it also gave her a rank of authority like that of a Surgeon General.

Kaliya had never visited an actual temple before, as her people were not a religious society. But her visit to this place carried a deeply moving sensation. As she observed the proud statues and icons of their gods, Kaliya felt a soothing calm wash over her. The melodic chanting of the priests in their worship was relaxing to her senses, and the grandeur of the building itself was awe-inspiring.

As she browsed the sights, she recalled the cu'Nar, the pure elemental beings that had aided the Daanen-Aryku since their departure from Azgarén. Although they were not regarded as deities of any kind, the Daanen-Aryku did revere them as a strange, almost supernatural entity. Their regard for the cu'Nar even began to reflect itself in their language after a while.

"Kaliya," Aerlie announces as they approach the altar. "In our world, we have many gods, and each race has their own pantheon. Since you do not belong to any of the local races, you may not feel the same association as we do, but you may still find comfort in their teachings."

"Yeah, and here's the weird part. I need to actually pray to something. But I don't really know how to pray, and which of these do I go to? I recall you mentioned a name…um, Ilmater, right?"

"Yes," she affirms. "I can show you how to pray. There is a special practice to it, where we share our thoughts and passions as a form of living energy we offer up to them. They will then reciprocate with some element of their wisdom, or perhaps a blessing of some kind."

"This sounds like you share a kind of mutual accord, a give-and-take relationship."

"We do. As we offer our energies up to them, this brings them strength. They thank us for this gift by offering something in return."

"Incredible. But now this seems more like a form of trade with a higher form of life that uses this for exchange."

"Very good, Kaliya," she smiles. "The Estelar would not recognize such a thing as gold or silver as an element of value for trade. Instead, what might hold value is that which would bring them support. We describe this as Favor, and for some, it might resemble a form of currency. In return, they offer that which would bring support back to us."

"A barter system, right back down to the primal level, an item for an item, basically. It seems almost ironic. You reach the highest point of your development, and everything reverts back to the most primitive form of exchange."

Aerlie giggles softly at the mention as she turns to find Ilmater's icon.

"I'm a little nervous about this," Kaliya admits. "Well, make that a lot nervous."

"I will help you through it. Come this way. Afterwards, I will show you around for your counseling sessions with the other priests."

They stepped across to a row of sculptures and carvings set into the wall at the rear of the temple hall. Along the base is a series of pedestals embedded with golden plates showing deific icons. Aerlie points to one with an image of bound hands inscribed onto it. She instructs Kaliya to kneel down in front and place her right hand on the icon, while Aerlie begins her lesson.

A small train of wagons had departed from Rolsklinde early in the morning in the direction of the Badlands. The guards at the south gate were under orders to keep it quiet, as were the guards at the three border watchtowers, in case anyone from the upper echelons was to take notice. Captain Kholgard was still holding a grudge for being excluded from the information held by the Dean and the Governor, so he decided that two can play in this game.

The wagon train worked its way through the mountains and into the Badlands, arriving late in the morning at the northern gate of the outpost. After a quick inspection, it was allowed into the camp. Workers unloaded supply crates and cleared each wagon until the last of them was empty and returning home.

Kaliya had returned from her visit to the temple and was catching up on the events of the battle earlier in the day. As the wagons arrived, she and Thaelyn stepped outside to oversee the unloading process. Several soldiers began unpacking the supplies and pulling out the contents. Included were tabards and costume overlays of Allegiance Guard design to be worn over their existing armor.

"This is from our friends up in the city," Thaelyn suggests. "These are the disguises to play our clever little ruse on the eastern front."

"I'll let Kailen know about this so he can expect the aid," Kaliya replies.

She turns to go back inside the tactical office to find her trans-com and make the call. With permission of the Elder Council, Thaelyn had arranged for a rune to be marked near the Naarg uy'Sodrad to allow ease of travel, rather than to march all the way over there. The soldiers will use this to arrive in the local area and begin their work. Multiple duty shifts had been assigned to offer relief for individual patrol groups.

Thaelyn returns to his meeting with the General to plan the next series of strikes. By now, Relissa and Marelle were returning from their study class on Tae'Eladar.

"This cluster here," the General directs as he points to the map, "and this over here. This is where I would suggest we begin, then moving into the further regions as we progress. As time passes, the progressive disappearance of their outposts should create the fear of some mysterious force gobbling up their fellows. This could possibly work to our favor over time."

"Agreed," Thaelyn nods. "But we will need more and deeper scouting in the area, and quickly. Further, we need to know of their supply routes, and if there are any portals in the local region bringing in new troops from off-world."

"Our gryphons may be useful here, but I would first suggest a test run to see what effectiveness they'll have in the local environment. It should also be at a sufficiently high altitude so that they will not be easily noticed."

"I will do this myself. If I keep my senses active, I can detect if anything goes wrong and evacuate immediately."

"Did I miss anything important today?" Marelle jests as she enters the room.

"Ah, Marelle! Our morning raid went along nicely, thank you. And we have some details here for you to look over. By the way, it occurs to me that enough time has passed since our arrival, and yet there is still no sign of a dwarven delegation, if only to show curiosity of our presence. Do you know if they ever received word of us?"

"Personally, no," she responds. "The Governor is the only one who really interacts with them, usually by sending the Dean up there on his behalf. But I'll remind you that they don't tend to get out much, if at all. I've never actually seen them, and the only sign of their activity would be the wagons we receive coming through the north gate of the city."

"Yes, and that brings me to wonder. Dwarves, at least those I am familiar with, are a much bolder sort. They do not tend to hide themselves away inside of a mountain, especially when there is a battle to fight."

"Well, what do you have in mind then?"

"If they will not send a delegation to us, perhaps we could send one to them. They are participants in this world, therefore, should they not be included in its affairs?"

"Are you thinking of sending your own people? Remember, the language difference…"

"While this is true, we have them at home, as well, and they do have their own native language, much like the elves. However, to involve a local representative would be a good idea, just in case we have a failure of some kind to maintain those ancestral traditions, like a certain young elf I know," he flashes a grin at Relissa. "For this point, perhaps you could be of service to us. Would you be willing to make a trip up there, along with Captain Hagmaert, to make our acquaintance? You could serve to introduce us while he represents a figurehead on our behalf."

"Certainly!" Marelle smiles eagerly. "It's a long trip, though. Half a day from here to the city, and a bit more than that to the mountains in the north."

"The scout we sent up there previously made a portal rune for us, just in case. We do this quite often to save ourselves from the long walks. What I will do is send someone up there to make a review of the area, just to ensure there are no surprises waiting for us. Even though we might suggest all is well in that region, I am not one to make assumptions."

"All right, fair enough…"

"We can then make our plans for the morrow."

He returns to the table and the various maps they had strewn about.

"We have a number of ideas circulating around for our quarry out there, but scouting is important to understand their placement. For this, we are thinking of using our gryphons, as they would be our best choice for long-range observation. But we would like to test them first, to ensure all is as expected in this new environment. This would represent the first time to try this on a world outside our local plane. Therefore, I will take one out myself since my skills will allow me to determine the safety of the engagement more readily than some others can."

"Where do you plan on going?" Marelle asks.

"Oh, hither and yon…" he declares casually. "Perhaps a pleasant sojourn out to the coast in the west and follow that south for a trifle before turning back."

"What?" she wheezes. "The coast? That's easily a few hundred miles away!"

"Indeed, so I hear. That should make a fair enough test."

"Excuse me, but when do you expect to be back? Next month?"

Thaelyn simply laughs as he leaves the building.

"Captain! Ready my mount, please."

The captain charges off to the pen to bring out one of the gryphons. He calls out orders to the handlers, who begin harnessing up the saddles and armor plating along the creature's body. A long slender tubular sleeve is attached to the right side of the animal, and into this they insert a long, lance-like gilded staff crowned with a crystal wrapped in a gold spiral frame.

Relissa follows the activity occurring outside. She observes the majesty of the proud creature and the lavish accouterments being applied. But when she notices the staff being put into place, she feels a slight shiver run through her.

"Oh no, not another staff… My Lord, every time you pull one of those out, the bleedin' world turns upside-down on us," she teases.

"Well then, perhaps you would be better to ride with me," he jests in return. "Rather than to simply stand here on the ground."

Relissa jerks her eyes around at him, hoping to see he was just humoring her. But even though he was smiling, he also revealed a serious overtone. She looks back at the gryphon, which was almost ready to ride, and felt a lump forming in her throat.

The captain led the wondrous creature, now fully laden with its gear, over to Thaelyn. As it approaches, it lays down to make an easier climb onto its large form.

"Relissa, come. Another set of eyes could be useful. You will ride in the rearward mount. Step up on these struts and into the forward mount, then hop into the rear one."

"Buggers," she mumbles to herself. "I had to open my flippin' mouth. You know, I've never ridden anything before, like a horse or something."

"It is not so difficult. And you will be thoroughly strapped in here."

Thaelyn gestures to a set of small bars, like a tiny ladder, set into the stirrup assembly on the left side. Relissa hesitantly takes hold of a handle on the saddle mount and steps onto the first strut. She pulls herself up and climbs tenuously into the forward saddle, then lifts herself over a division marked by a metal bar, and into the next one. When she is settled, Thaelyn climbs into his saddle and turns to assist her.

"There is a harness you need to attach so you will not fall out. You are not Avariel, so do not think you can fly on your own," he jokes.

He points to a partial seat back, with a set of thick leather belts attached to it. They wrapped over her shoulders and around her waist, securing themselves into a centralized buckle, and across her thighs to attach to hooks in front.

Thaelyn assists by hooking the belts around her body, securing the buckle snugly. The buckle includes a locking clip that swings over and snaps into place. He proceeds to fit each of the two thigh straps into their respective buckles and locking them in place. He also directed her to a set of specialized stirrups resembling brackets to snap her legs and feet into place.

Relissa's eyes were showing her stress levels as she realized there will be no turning back from this little adventure.

Thaelyn turns to attach his own harness, giving a passing smile to Kaliya and Marelle who are both watching intently as this detailed ritual of preparation unfolds.

"Your Lordship," Kaliya calls as he makes his final checks. "Are you actually thinking of going all the way to the coast, or are you just joking with us?"

Thaelyn passes a mischievous smirk at the inquisitive young Daanen'kai as he gives his order.

"WindTalon, up!" he shouts.

The great beast pulls itself to its feet, stretching its wings slightly to limber up. The sudden jostling rocks Relissa, who is unaccustomed to riding on any sort of mount. She grabs at the bar situated just in front of her on the saddle.

Thaelyn whistles and coos to the creature, coaxing it to move out of the camp. He removes the staff from its sheath and lays it in a hook mounting that juts up on the right side of the collar harness. As the gryphon moves into the open space, he calls to it one more time.

"WindTalon, away! Take to the sky!"

The enormous power of the animal's muscles ripple through its body as it charges off across the ground, spreading its wings as it goes. It begins flapping furiously as it builds up speed from the bold dash. Finally, it reaches a critical velocity to gain lift, and slowly rises off the ground in a gentle ascent.

"I've never seen anything like that before," Kaliya admires.

"It's beautiful," Marelle declares.

"But I still have no idea of how he hopes to travel to the coast and back, unless he's got another one of his little tricks ready to pull out."

Thaelyn guides the gryphon into a spiral ascent, reaching well into the sky, using the staff as a type of steering control. The tip of the staff extended into view beyond the animal's head, and as Thaelyn tilted and turned the staff's orientation, the gryphon would follow that direction.

Relissa can be heard whimpering as she clings desperately to the metal support bar in front of her. She trembles as the ground below moves farther and farther away.

"Relissa," he calls over his shoulder. "We will be climbing to a fair height. You need to settle your nerves and breathe calmly. At the altitude we will be travelling, the air gets just a bit thin, like on a tall mountain. Stay relaxed and all will be well."

"Uh huh…" she mutters nervously. "I just feel a wee bit open up here."

"Granted, the first time can be both exhilarating as well as a bit frightening."

After a while of climbing, they level out and begin orienting towards the west.

"Now remember, keep your head low behind me as we proceed… and again, relax. You will be fine."

He orients the staff straight and level as he now begins a chant.

From the ground, Kaliya, Marelle, and the rest of the camp watched as the tiny dot in the sky began moving gracefully to the west after its long climb. All seemed peaceful and harmonious… until the dot flashes into a streak, darts across the sky, and into the distance. Several seconds later, a clap of thunder hits the ground.

"What in all the nine hells was that?" Marelle exclaims.

"Great cu'Nar!" Kaliya shudders. "He can do that too? Poor Tanjhira, and here I think she just barely grew a new set of horns from the last time."

Relissa shuddered at the thud of the sonic threshold being broken. The world below had nearly turned to a blur, with valleys, hills, more valleys, passing by at a phenomenal rate. She barely had enough time to focus on one sight when it passed from view and was replaced by another.

The gryphon held a stoic posture, with its wings partially withdrawn after being wrapped in an envelope of energy surrounding its body. They observed wispy tendrils of vapor passing by outside, as if blown by a tremendous wind.

For as fast as they were travelling, the envelope served as a kind of airfoil, slicing through the atmosphere with only a slight disruption of the surrounding environment. The sonic shockwave being produced would be only a minor disturbance as felt on the ground. Even at this, they would be out of sight before anyone would have time to notice it.

"My Lord!" Relissa screeches. "Gods' pity, just how fast are we moving?"

"Relissa," he responds calmly. "Since you are now a proper student of mine, I can afford you some of my finer wisdom. There are many studies that can teach you the Ways of Creation, and this is one. Have you ever noticed from afar, an activity to occur, only to hear the sound of it arrive at your ears a brief instant later?"

Relissa ponders the thought for a moment.

"Well, actually, now that you mention it, I think so. Like a loud noise…someone hitting something, but I hear the boom from it just a tad after."

"Very good. Sound is a force in nature, and it travels at a specific rate through the air. That rate may be too quick for the casual observer to measure, but it still has its own speed."

"All right, I'm with you so far, I think. Are we going that fast now?"

"We are actually travelling at three times that speed now."

"That sounds pretty fast. And this shield thingy around us, what is it?"

"We call it a transport sphere. It is an envelope to carry and contain us. While inside, we can survive comfortably during our travel. We do not necessarily feel the force of movement, as the sphere itself is what moves, simply carrying us along for the ride. But it is necessary to envelop us, as the rushing of the air outside is far too hostile for the likes of our kind to withstand alone."

"So, in other words, don't be trying to stick your hand out there, or you might lose it, ay?" she jokes.

"Exactly!"

They continue their westward travel, passing over terrain that would take days to cross any other way. Many minutes later, they catch a glimpse of a coastal shore.

"There it is," Relissa notes. "I can't say I've ever been out this far before, but I've heard of it."

"Here is where we will turn to the south and continue for a bit."

As the shore grows larger in their view, Thaelyn begins angling the staff gently to the left. The steering motion causes the glide path of the envelope to mimic the action, making a smooth turn to a southerly direction. They follow the shoreline for a few additional minutes before he turns again to an easterly heading.

Relissa felt more at ease by now, and was taking better notice of the world from her new vantage point, as she paid more attention to the land formations and the scattered dotting of occasional habitation.

"Looks like they're dug in pretty far out here," she notes. "Lots of camps, maybe more like villages at this point. And I see some on the shoreline, probably taking up fishing. Just how far do you plan to go on this trip?"

"We are nearly done. I simply wanted to examine some of the further reaches of the land that we will need to know about over the coming months. I will send other scouts later to make a more detailed survey and mapping of the area."

"Are you thinking you'll be marching out this far? That's a long trek!"

"Do not forget, we prefer the use of portal runes. We will send scouts to mark the runes, and we will use these to punch a few holes here and there in their lines. But ultimately, we will need to start taking some of this space for ourselves and establish our own forward outposts."

"Aye, and that will be a long march, I think, as now, portals or no, you'll have to move your troops overland. But will you be moving that outpost in the Badlands? What about the tree?"

"I think we will leave our existing camp as-is, to be used as a base headquarters. When using portals, it is not as important to relocate a base camp. The outposts will simply be forward stations to claim territory. We will do here as we did before…push them until there is nowhere else for them to go."

"A wee bit like what the buggers were doing to us once upon a time," Relissa snickers.

A short while passes, and they come upon a clear space in the terrain below. Thaelyn brings the gryphon out of its supersonic flight and back under its natural control.

"Right, so just where do you think we are now?" Relissa asks.

"You can't be that good at figuring out this world after only a few days here, can you?"

"In essence, it does not truly matter. Look here, in this mounting just in front of me."

Relissa peeks around Thaelyn to a fixture in the saddle just in front of him and sees a rune stone set into its own little mount.

"Jiggers! You've got those things everywhere!"

"Indeed! And here we go… WindTalon, swoop for recall!"

On hearing the command, the gryphon pulls in its wings and begins a gliding dive, while Thaelyn casts the incantation on the rune in the saddle. As the incantation nears completion, the gryphon, carefully trained for this process, angles into an upward sweep, ending in a vertical stall just as the portal draws them in.

Kaliya and Marelle were patiently watching for the return of the great winged beast. They had expected to see it returning from the horizon, not reappearing in a flash of light in the sky over their heads. The two of them jerked around at the commotion of the portal exit.

"Those little tail-yankers," Kaliya mutters.

"Yeah…whatever that means," Marelle agrees.

The rune stone used on the gryphon had been marked for an aerial return by the handlers sometime before. Now, the animal was making its descent, twisting and turning to reduce its altitude, then taking a long approach with a final flourish in the form of a corkscrew roll maneuver, before coming in for a landing.

Relissa was not expecting the roll, but she made a squealing cheer of excitement, waving her hand as they leveled out. Cheers erupted on the ground as they made their landing and returned inside the camp.

"Your Lordship," Kaliya shouts as they pull in and begin dismounting. "You never stop amazing me!"

"The day I stop amazing my fellows is the day I should probably return to Mount Celestia."

"So, Relissa," she continues. "How do you like travelling faster than sound?"

"It scared the wiggles out of me at first, but it wasn't so bad after a while."

"See anything interesting?"

"Aye, the whole bleedin' place out there is swarming with orcs. This war's set to go for a long while yet. You'd better hurry up and get your head pulled on straight, girl. We'll be needing you."

"My Lord," squeaks a voice from under the crowd.

"Yes, Professor," Thaelyn responds to the gnomish foreman.

"The tower is ready! We finished the final inspection and diagnostics, and we're waiting for your participation before activating it."

"Excellent, I will be right over."

The handlers take the gryphon back to the pen and remove its gear, giving it a careful grooming and even a little rub down as they go.

Thaelyn and the Professor walked back up to the tower for the final stage of its completion. Kaliya, Relissa, and Marelle all follow behind, curious to see what this thing actually does. When they arrive, they join an audience of gnomes, along with a few dwarves who stayed on hand from the earlier construction stages.

Thaelyn instructs the Professor to proceed with the activation. A gnome near the maintenance door now steps inside and manipulates a series of controls.

Through the windows at the top can be seen sets of crystalline arrays coming into alignment. The arrays are composed of long, narrow gray-white rods with an almost fibrous composition, overlaid with elongated translucent pinkish crystal shards. Each rod assembly is wrapped by a sequence of wire coil rings along its length and extends to a transparent housing with an arrangement of bluish crystals fixed on a circular platform inside. This circle appeared as a wheel centered on a larger pink crystal as a hub, and the housing capped a glass-like columnar enclosure reaching the length of the tower.

As the gnome operates the controls, the first thing Kaliya notices is the ventilation fan up in the crown of the tower coming to life. This much she could understand. The rest of it was a mystery.

"All right," she inquires. "So, what are we looking at? I see a fan up there, so I'm guessing it's to vent heat. What are those rods up there in the windows?"

"The rods gather raw arcanic energy from the local environment. You are familiar with the concept of magnetism, correct? Well, these energies have their attractive qualities, not unlike a magnet, though the application is somewhat different. The rods are composed of synthetic crystals that combine to attract this."

"Synthetic crystals? You're able to make synthetic crystals?"

"It is not so difficult if you have the proper ingredients in a solution and a seed on which to allow the crystal to grow. The principle is very easily observed if you happen to find any underground caverns where natural crystal formations occur. However, due to the Spellplague, I made a few small exceptions to the rules as a way to hasten our rebuilding efforts. I taught our people a few small secrets, if only to give us a chance to restore ourselves."

He steps forward and points to the windows at the top of the tower.

"The gray rods you see grow along a collection of wires stretched through a basin with an electric current flowing through it. The pink and blue crystals grow as seeds in tanks in a heavy solution, then cut and faceted to serve our needs. The pink ones are designed to draw the arcanic energies while the rods channel it. The blue ones divert the energies and function a bit like how the north and south poles on a magnet might attract and repel."

"Interesting..."

Kaliya continued to observe the gnome working the controls and watching a series of gauges. She peered inside the room to see more of those same narrow power cell boxes and a series of tanks similar to the one she studied before with the shield wall. The arrangement was more elaborate, and involved additional tubing that connected to a glass cylinder mounted on a wall with a little ball inside that appeared to be made of a lightweight wood. As she watched, she could see the ball hovering over the tubing entering from the bottom, indicating a flow of some form of gas into the cylinder from the tanks, and further leading to the boxes.

"All right, this here," she points at the boxes and tubing. "I saw this in the camp with that generator thing of yours powering the shield wall. I can only guess by looking at it that you're providing a type of fuel to these boxes from these tanks, and this cylinder must be a flow indicator for some sort of gas passing through the system, right?"

"Very good, your engineering skills are showing good form."

"I'm not actually trained in this. But you know who would be absolutely fascinated by it? Our Chief Technician back home, Tanjhira Lapäli. Oh, I'm sure she'd lose the curl in her horns if she could see this."

Thaelyn and the others let out a hearty laugh at the notion.

Kaliya continues, "So, you have a form of technology that allows you to generate electrical power through the application of…well, magic, for lack of another term," she chuckles. "This is already more than the local races understand."

"As I said, there is a science behind it, but one that operates differently than yours."

"Yeah, but so far this science of yours seems to function more by the will of the mind than by any mathematical equations."

"In our case, this science would be defined by the terms of that will, much like a language, which in its own way is like an equation."

"Really! Cu'Nar's grace, if that doesn't twist my horns."

She continued to follow the action in the strange apparatus, now taking note of the tall column, which resembled a large diameter hollow tube, sealed at both ends. Within the tube she saw two rings of closely aligned fins rising up the length of it, an outer one just inside the glass enclosure with blue crystal shards, and a smaller one set inside the first with pink shards. At the top and bottom end caps, she saw what looked like electrodes protruding inside.

"This tube here looks like something you might find in one of our old vid-com science fiction programs of a mad scientist's lab. It looks like a giant sparking chamber. Is it a vacuum inside?"

"Mostly," he admits. "And filled with an inert gas to a very low pressure."

The gnome had been monitoring the gauges as he brought the power systems online. The indicators were showing nominal readings, so he began to turn several dials and throw a switch. Kaliya watched as the base of the column came to life where a large metallic wheel begins to turn.

The wheel was a donut-shaped enclosure situated around the base of the column, with the column nestled within its center. The mechanism seemed archaic by her standards, but clearly showed some careful workmanship for the engineering design. She could hear the whirring of the machine spinning up and saw the fins inside the cylinder begin to rotate in opposing directions, with the outer blue set turning one way and the inner pink set turning the other. She followed the apparatus up to the chamber at the top with the circle of blue shards following the motion around the central pink crystal hub.

Her attention is next drawn to the rods up in the windows, where she can see a series of lights on the wire coils now flashing in a cyclic pattern along the length of the rods. She then turns to the base again and peers underneath, where she sees a series of channels leading off to the dragon head bust emitters outside. She cautiously steps inside the room to peer down at one to see a long gray-white rod following the channel from the core out to the emitter.

"That looks a little like a control rod," she mutters to herself. "Or maybe a conduit..."

She now takes notice of the reaction occurring inside the cylinder, as the electrodes seem to be charging up a spark flowing from top to bottom. She gazes at it for a long moment, trying to interpret what she sees, and further to follow the conduit to the emitter, then to peer outside to see the end result in a flow of faintly condensed plasma coming out.

"In all the nether-space..." she mumbles.

She then rolls outside the doorway and slides down the wall to the ground.

"This thing, in a completely nether-wild fashion, resembles a reactor. Cu'Nar's grace, you people are barely Early Industrial Age, and you already have a reactor?"

"It is surely a technology unique to fit our needs," Thaelyn affirms. "But in a mild sense of it, I suppose you could describe it that way."

"But help me understand what I'm looking at. Like I said, I'm not trained in engineering, and certainly nothing like this."

"Very well, let us begin with those rods at the top. The coils are powered, and the lights indicate the cycling effect. Can you identify what effect this might have?"

"If the lights are indicators, and the coils are powered, um… right…coils, we're talking about electromagnetism. But I thought you said this doesn't apply in your science."

"Well, perhaps I should elaborate somewhat. There can be applications where one can combine these effects for a rather potent interaction between the two. The crystals interact with the electromagnetic effect of the coils to attune the influence for the arcanic energies, as opposed to simple electricity."

"Fascinating, a type of hybrid technology," she muses. "All right, so this provides a strong draw effect, and if those indicator lights are flashing with the charging of the coils…um, this looks like oscillating electric potentials, and that represents…an accelerator!"

"Excellent, and this drives the energy into the central chamber above you."

"Then we have those blue and pink crystal arrangements. You said they act like opposing forces, so this looks a little like an impeller configuration to me, driving it down into this tall cylinder, where we have more of them on these long fins, which probably serve to contain it while you do something with that spark."

"Not a bad bit of guesswork," he smiles. "The spark harmonizes the energies to a new excitation modulus, such that it would no longer be attracted by the apparatus at the top, but instead can now spread out upon the land in a smooth blanket effect."

"Absolutely incredible! This is an extraordinary example of a form of technology completely alien to us, but representative of a society that seems to know as much about its own environment as we might with ours…within reason at least, for your tech level."

"Indeed, and you can be sure we still have many possibilities ahead of us."

Kaliya studies the machine again, now trying to understand how the fins inside the cylinder are made to turn, as there does not seem to be a direct connection of gears or drive chains.

"What is it that's turning these fins inside here, and then that circular thing on top? I don't see anything attaching them."

"Magnetism… The base is fitted with strong magnets that draw the first wheel around. The same is true at the top as the first wheel has another ring interacting with an opposing set up there. The inner ring rotates by convection from the outer ring."

"Amazing, but wouldn't you have to deal with friction at some point?"

"We do not technically have that concern as the various parts are also floating on opposing magnetic forces to produce a frictionless environment."

"Magnetic levitation and frictionless movement," she considers. "Not bad for such a crazy science," she grins impishly. "You'll be passing us up before we even realize it."

Her thoughts now return to the power cells and how they might function. She recalled the boxes, the tanks, and the glass cylinder and ball with the gas flowing through it.

"All right, help me out with one last thing. How are you producing energy here? I see these boxes and these pressurized gas tanks, or at least they look like tanks that hold gas. What's inside and how is the energy made?"

"The tanks are indeed sealed to retain a pressurized environment, at least low pressure, relative to outside. They are feeder tanks to the boxes, as you have surely noted, and produce the fuel necessary to interact with the components that convert this into energy. Now, to describe this, I think I will need to reflect on our history a bit. Once again, during the time we were recovering from the Spellplague, I gave instructions for a number of research projects to be established.

My rage at the Estelar for their follies made me take a few actions to compensate for our losses. One of these was to reopen an old artifact we found once."

"An artifact?"

"Yes, in our old history, during what we might call my early days as a Duke governing a rapidly growing nation, we conducted a number of studies into our archeological history, trying to understand the origins of life in our world."

"Oh, really! This is interesting. It reminds me of that conversation I had with one of your priests. It was on that first day actually, when she was speaking in terms that sounded more scientific than religious, and it surprised me to hear a religion use such terms."

"Indeed, we do not fall into that same mold where we might suggest a god created this or that, as we know better from our interactions with the Estelar. They prefer to let nature take its course, and then observe the results. They find it much more interesting that way. Only on very rare occasions might they interfere with this for any reason. But in our case, we found something rather unexpected."

"What was that?"

"Well, better to say unexpected by some, as I knew about it, at least in part from my Celestial teachings. But to learn of the rest was intriguing even to me. We discovered that life did not actually evolve in our world, at least not fully. Our world was seeded with life."

"Seeded, but this would come back around to a godlike entity, wouldn't it?"

"It might. Our history tells of something once described in ancient human folklore as a Creator Race. This suggests that life was deposited by that race, and since then may have evolved into what we see today."

"How long ago was this?"

"We are speaking of perhaps thirty to thirty-five millennia ago."

"That's a while, long enough for many things to evolve. What happened with this discovery you mentioned?"

"We learned who they were."

"Really!" she leans forward excitedly in her seated posture. "Who were they?"

"We once found what I can only describe as a time capsule left behind to tell us the story."

"A time capsule!" she gushes. "Ooh!"

"This was a special moment for us, as we found some of their technology, including a portal device they no doubt used once to import specimens from the original source world."

"Wow…"

"We actually used some of the design concepts from this to build our own, by the way."

"Really! So, you borrowed a little of theirs to make your own?"

"A few pieces…not too many, mind you," he smiles. "I still have those rules to follow. We also found computing consoles, some laboratory equipment, and several plaques on the walls with introductions and instructions written in two languages, theirs and Celestial."

"What?" she blurts. "They can speak Celestial?"

"This was indeed surprising, but we have since come to the conclusion that they must be an ancient race, and as such are likely familiar with the Estelar and the Celestial Races. They call themselves the Sarrukh."

Kaliya was deeply entranced by the story, and she listened intently.

Thaelyn continues, "They explained that they were called upon to refurbish our world and reinstate life to it after it had experienced an epoch-long ice age. They described how to use the gateway device, which we now call the Sarrukhan Gate, to find the source world, just in case we might hold any desires to return there and rejoin with our ancient origins."

"Have you ever used it?"

"We did for a period of time, simply to investigate what was on the other side. But the societies we found, while human, were much more primitive than we in their scientific wherewithal. Therefore, I decided we should close the gate until a later time when we might return to see if they have made any improvements. I did not wish to disrupt their society with our influence."

"Right, a superior society to a lesser one…I remember."

"But then, as a result of the Spellplague, I decided to reopen the chamber for another review, this time to see if we could borrow a little of their technology to improve our own."

"'Ere now," Relissa interjects. "Isn't that a wee bit like cheating?" she chuckles.

"I would normally agree with you, but we suffered such terrible devastation from the Spellplague, that this became imperative. One thing I wanted was a more efficient and reliable way for our people to cross our lands, thus the gateway network we have now. Another was to aid our science to begin moving forward in a few areas we needed in order to build these towers, and this included a compact means of producing energy."

"Ah hah!" Kaliya blasts and jabs a finger at him. "The boxes! You learned something that creates electricity using some kind of fuel cell, I'll bet!"

"Nicely done, Kaliya, but the next question is what form of gas is it?" he smirks.

"In a fuel cell?" she wonders. "All right, this fits a little better with my technology."

She peers inside the tower again at the banks of fuel cell boxes and the piping leading up from the tanks.

"It's a clear gas, at least as far as I can tell passing through the flow meter. I don't see anything like a combustion chamber, however."

She gets up and steps inside the room for a closer inspection, this time examining the boxes for any kind of exhaust vent. She eventually finds some tubing connecting each of them in a series and leading outside through the wall. She heads around to find the exit point and kneels down to examine the outlet. It was open and dripping something onto the ground.

"Well, either you aren't too concerned for the environment, or this isn't toxic in any way. And since I already know you have this relationship to protect the environment, this can't be toxic."

She carefully reaches out a hand to test the liquid dripping from the exhaust tube.

"Careful there, girl," Relissa ushers as she comes over for a look.

Kaliya gingerly taps the pipe to test its temperature. When she feels sure it's not too hot, she places her fingers under the tube to catch a few drops. She examines it carefully. It was a clear liquid. She tries bringing it up for a sniff, but there is no discernable odor. She studies it a few moments longer until an idea comes to mind. So, she brings it up to touch it with her tongue.

"Ay!" Relissa blurts. "What are you doing that for? You don't know where that stuff has been."

Kaliya realizes the instant her tongue detects the substance, what was coming out of the fuel cells. A curious smile comes into her face.

"Actually, Relissa, I do know where it comes from, but again this is the last thing I would expect to see from an Early Industrial Age society. It's a hydrogen fuel cell, and this is water…simple water as a byproduct."

"Jiggers…" Relissa moans.

"And now, Kaliya," Thaelyn submits. "Do you see how a society can follow a path different from the one you took? We had necessity take a role in ours, for a number of reasons. We had to virtually skip over steam power as we do not have a ready supply of condensed natural fuels, like coal or natural oils in our world. I believe this is due to the fact of our epoch-long ice age preventing the natural cycles of life during this time. I would also tend to object to their use for the pollution they cause. Therefore, we looked elsewhere and struggled to create this instead, basing our inventions at least as much on our magical studies as they are the physical."

"Magical…" she mutters distantly.

Her mind suddenly flashes back to the pressurized tanks inside. She jumps up and darts back around inside the room to study them again. Like before with the shield wall, these involved crank wheels to turn a mechanism to press a series of plates together inside the tanks.

"These things in here," she states urgently and points.

Thaelyn comes around to observe her direction.

"I see this flow meter here," Kaliya continues. "And with a little ball inside that looks like it's floating to show a flow of gas, right?"

"That is correct."

"Are we saying these tanks are filled with pressurized hydrogen? These don't look so easily interchangeable to replace with fresh ones, and I remember when you said once that you can use your magic to affect changes in your environment. What's actually happening in there? You have wheels to turn something, and I see an assembly of parts in there that I would not normally expect to find in a simple container."

"I think you may be driving yourself to your own conclusion. Those components, when brought together, apply an effect. We can disable this by turning the wheel to disengage the apparatus. But when engaged, it dynamically produces elemental hydrogen to feed into the rest, using the arcanic energies as a catalyst for conversion."

"Grace of the cu'Nar!" she shouts and staggers outside, then plops down on the ground again. "A persistent feed into an energy-producing device! You created what our science would normally describe as impossible, a perpetual motion machine, one that just keeps on going. This represents the dream of engineers everywhere... free and unlimited energy!"

"Indeed!" he grins brightly. "And with a perpetual supply of the arcanic energies, which we might describe as a renewable harvest from our environment, we can continue this way indefinitely. We could also use such devices, or some reasonable facsimile, in other applications of technology."

"I take back everything I ever said about inferior technologies. You just surpassed us, even with your Early Industrial stuff, and with or without our own technology to back us up."

"Jiggers," Relissa groans. "Are you going to make me study all this?"

"It will apply in your classes as you progress along," Thaelyn asserts. "You will need to fill in some of your prerequisites first. After that, the pieces will fall into place in such a manner that they will carry you through nicely."

"And you use these in your world?" Kaliya asks.

"As for the towers, we have them interspaced all across our land area. On the seaside regions, we use a different design to focus the flows outward over the water to aid ships and their occupants. Deep ocean regions tend to be more problematic, but since the flows are covering so nicely anyway, they seem to be resolving themselves. And we designed them to be generally standalone."

"What about your general society? You use this here, but what about homes and industry?"

"I will admit the technology is not especially convenient for the rare materials involved. Instead, we have been experimenting on a number of large-scale applications using a variety of ideas. So far, we use water and wind power, along with a few other proprietary methods, to produce energy for our industrial centers, but the general home user is still a bit ahead of us as we develop our infrastructure."

"So far," she asserts. "But I'll bet my left horn it's not that far off."

"We do have one promising application coming up, which can be scaled large or small, depending on the need. Some of our engineers have been working on a recent experiment involving the use of portal apertures at the base of a dam holding back an artificial lake."

"A dam…this represents hydroelectric, I know of this."

"As with a traditional hydroelectric facility, we have our turbines to harness energy from the moving water. But rather than simply allow that water to run off downstream and into the sea, the portal can recycle it back up to the top. This is where our experiment comes in."

"Cu'Nar's Pity, and I'm already getting visions."

"I suppose you might be, but now imagine this. A reservoir chamber, sealed to prevent evaporation, and with your traditional siphons to move the water through your turbines at the bottom to provide for the hydroelectric action. But here we use our portals underneath to catch the water, sending it back up in what is essentially a closed loop environment, where gravity is the only force needed to perpetuate the flow."

"Yeah, and there go my horns for the next full month. That

really is a great application of perpetual motion. But what about the law of Conservation of Energy, don't you experience any loss along the way?"

"If calibrated properly, the gains exceed the losses. The portals are powered at least as much by the arcanic energies as by electricity, and overall, the power produced is much greater."

"Yeah, and those are renewable natural resources. What about a fusion reactor? You probably don't have it yet, but if you can produce hydrogen so easily for these fuel cells, could you ramp it up for a reactor?"

"We could. And then you would have yet another example to twist your horns," he grins.

"I need to stop teaching you our language..." she chuckles.

Kaliya is now panting from all the extraordinary revelations that magic can perform.

"You know... To the nether-realms with our science, your world looks much more interesting to live in. As I watch you with your peculiar technology and how you've overcome these obstacles, and then think of how my lifespan could carry me across thousands of years, I have to wonder where you'll be in that time."

"A society can work many miracles if it applies itself. I am sure yours did so on at least a few occasions in your history. As I said before, these are two sides of the same coin, and if you combine them, the possibilities are endless."

The dragon head busts outside the tower are now producing a steady flow of a wispy blue-violet plasma mist which seems to be dissipating a short distance away. The humming sounds within the tower are persistent and stable.

"What happens if you put your hand in that stuff?" Relissa asks.

"Try it and find out," he grins, nodding over to it.

Relissa takes a tentative step forward to see if he'll stop her, continuing along until she reaches one of the busts. She puts her hand in front of the flow, observing as it passes around her body.

"I don't really feel anything. A little bit of heat, I guess, but not much else."

"That is probably because you are not a mage. If you were more properly attuned to it, you might feel a slight tingling. Perhaps, after a bit of training in the academy, your senses will improve."

"You'll be teaching me magic? I thought I was going to be a ranger."

"Recall what I said before… Everyone in our world studies at least the First and Second Circle, just for the basic knowledge. What you do after that is your own choice. A ranger does not require a great deal, but it could still be useful if you wish to add it as an elective course. Many of our scouts do, especially if to mark and cast portal runes."

"Aye, that's right. But jiggers," she sighs. "This is starting to look like a lot of work. Right then, so what's next?"

"Professor," Thaelyn calls to the gnomish foreman. "You and your team have done well. I believe we can have you return back to your other projects for now."

"Abso-diddle-lutely, my Lord! And a fine day to you!"

"It is time we get back to the business of war," Thaelyn declares. "There is still much to be done, and time is precious."

Thaelyn offers handshakes to each of the workers as they make a final clean-up of the worksite before returning home. He then leads his group back to the tactical office to plan their next strategy.

Scouting expeditions are organized to occur over the coming days and weeks to carefully map and record the deployment of the orcish movements, with special emphasis on locating any portal activity across the region. Kaliya offered to make this process more efficient by using Daanen'kai photographic technology and processing the images onto hardcopy for a visual review.

The day progresses into early evening, and the scout that was sent to investigate the dwarven enclave returns. He reported no unusual activity in the area, so the outlook was good for Marelle and her envoy to travel there the next day. Relissa will also be assigned to serve as a mediator with the Captain, should he need to interact with the dwarves directly. She could interpret with him in Elvish, and then to the dwarves as necessary.

As the camp settles for the evening meal and the usual light banter, Kaliya recalls the extraordinary revelation that a society can follow a completely different technological path and still find similar solutions to their problems, and perhaps even better ones. She further reflected on her spiritual awakening and psychological therapy with Aerlie and the priests at the temple, and the healing touch at Ilmater's altar. Each step along this path brought her closer to the realization that there may yet be hope for her after all. The path of enlightenment included truth, understanding, and a respect for all forms of life, both great and small, even if they did, on occasion, offend the senses. She would sleep this night knowing that she must come to a decision soon…a decision that could quite possibly change her life forever.

Daybreak rose over the camp, and breakfast was being served among the cooktops of the mess hall kitchen. Kaliya had just barely finished her meal when she found herself being called into the tactical office to review the details of the patrols from the evening before at the Daanen'kai citadel.

"No sightings of any Suuden-Aryku last night," she muses. "While I'm happy for this, it still makes me wonder what they're doing. They tend to make periodic maneuvers just to harass us."

"We will be ready for them on their next visit," Thaelyn affirms. "Our people are disguised in their Allegiance Guard costumes to back up yours, so it is simply a matter of waiting for them to come to us."

"While I'm really happy you're helping us, I suppose I still hold a few concerns over what sort of results we'll have together. I recall some of the occasions where the humans of Rolsklinde sent out their patrols."

"And what happened on those occasions, did you see any losses?"

"Actually, I think we got lucky and didn't see anything at all. The Suuden-Aryku didn't show up on those occasions. Otherwise, well, I'm sure we'd see a lot of bodies lying around."

"Perhaps, but our people have managed to revise the shield spell to make it portable, so this should offer us a curious twist."

"Yeah, but field testing something like this is a little tricky, isn't it?"

"It can be, though we did some of our own testing back home. Nevertheless, we will need to adjust ourselves as we gain experience with this tactic. Still, we need that first encounter to see where we stand."

"And that first encounter is what scares me."

"If we are disguised as Allegiance Guard, I would expect it to be a different scenario than if to go out there as ourselves. This becomes a tactical advantage on our behalf. The Suuden-Aryku may not know our full capacity, especially if to involve our magic, and just like you, they might underestimate us for everything else."

"Oh, that's bad," she moans sarcastically. "They have no idea how much trouble they're getting into."

"Meanwhile, we need to begin preparing a series of long-distance gryphon scouts to survey the region to our west..."

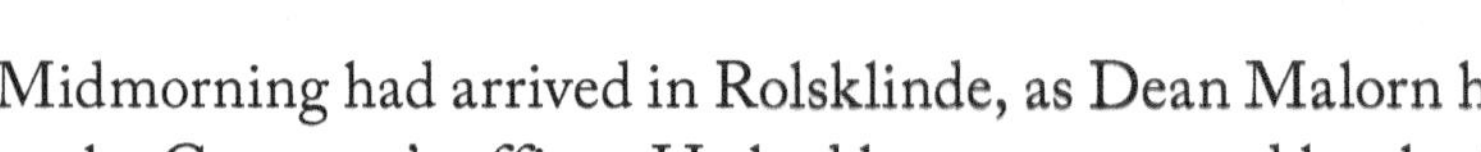

Midmorning had arrived in Rolsklinde, as Dean Malorn hurried up to the Governor's office. He had been summoned by the Governor a short while ago, but without any specific reason mentioned. He rushes up to the door, knocks urgently, and then enters.

"You requested me, my Lord?" he asks upon entering.

"Dean," Governor Dramon replies calmly. "Am I not the governor of this fair city?"

"But of course you are, my Lord."

"And am I not the one who issues the directives of the Guard to carry out their duties?"

"Yes, my Lord. Why do you ask this of me?"

"I am recently in receipt of a report that describes sightings of Allegiance Guard patrols gallivanting about the area of the Daanen-Aryku citadel. However, I do not recall giving any such orders. Can you explain to me why they are out there?"

"Have the Daanen-Aryku delivered another of their requests to the Guard for support?"

"Their requests would come through here first, and I have not received any."

"Then I'm afraid I have no answer for you, my Lord," the Dean replies with a slight tone of worry. "Unless… Could it be the Captain is acting independently?"

"I suppose that may be possible, although he should at least make his announcement through me beforehand, as I believe I am the one who authorizes these things."

"It has been some time since that Thaelyn fellow arrived. Perhaps word has reached the Captain's ears, and now he feels our southern side is safe, so he's making a preemptive effort to aid the others."

The Governor pauses to contemplate the idea.

"Impertinent, to say the least… The Guard is a poor match for the Suuden-Aryku. If the Captain is foolish enough to throw away his troops, then so be it. I have other concerns on my mind. What about this Thaelyn so far? Have your spies discovered anything useful?"

"His troops have been seen coming and going through mage portals, but their destination is unknowable to us. I have tried sending scouts to the forward ranges, but they haven't found any evidence of a battle taking place."

"It is likely he is trying to conceal his efforts, possibly for a tactical advantage. We should continue our observations until we are able to make a more determined analysis of his activities."

"I'll see to it, my Lord. Is there anything else you need from me?"

"No, that should be all."

"What about Captain Kholgard?"

"I'll deal with him. He is supposed to answer to my authority on these matters, and his last orders were to protect the city, not parade around the countryside like some would-be hero."

"Very well, my Lord, then I shall be on my way."

The Dean leaves the office, closing the door behind him.

Governor Dramon reclines in his chair as he mulls the details of his conversation with the Dean. He begins unconsciously speaking to himself.

"What are you doing down there?" he mumbles. "No doubt attacking the orcs, as is supposed to be your duty to your world, but using portals? Such an interesting tactic, but I need to know where they come out."

He turns to peer out the window onto the plaza outside and the barracks across the way.

"And as for you, Captain, you forget who is in charge here. Remember those supply shortages we suffer so often? You really shouldn't be squandering them on those…people…out there. This is simple insubordination. Well, we'll see about that."

He reaches over to his desk and opens a drawer. From inside the drawer, he pulls out an oddly crafted object, seemingly out of place to the level of sophistication of the surrounding office environment. He dials up a code on the numeric keypad displayed on the device's touchscreen.

"Commander Geilv, speaking," ushers a deep monotonal voice from the foreign device.

"Commander, relating to your earlier report, it would seem we have an occasion of disobedience occurring here. That patrol you spotted represents an unauthorized deployment by the Guard to the Naarg uy'Sodrad. It would be such an unfortunate event should they realize how dangerous it is out there."

"Understood, what course of action do you suggest?"

"These little people need a lesson spoken in a language they can understand. Therefore, I will have you prepare that special team we assembled once and give them some exercise. They should be able to attend to this situation well enough, and remind the Guard of the dangers of that warfront."

They end the link, and the Governor places the communicator back in the drawer. He then reclines into his chair to ponder the situation of the occurrences in the Badlands.

The passing of the morning hours saw Relissa and Marelle returning from Tae'Eladar. They were feeling good about their study progress, though they still had much to learn. Haran, for his part, was adjusting to his new residence in Bya'an Tamoranth, and looked forward to his future education in the academy, once the language classes were complete.

Thaelyn was in conversation with some workers in the camp as the two women arrived through the gate.

"Marelle," he announces. "And Relissa, you too... We have work for you."

"Of course," Marelle replies. "What is it?"

"I would like to send you off to your meeting with the dwarves. Let us take care of this before setting ourselves upon the other matters of the day."

"Very well, Your Lordship, if you would just allow me a moment to organize myself, I'll be right out."

"Relissa, you will accompany her to interact with the Captain during your talks. I will also have one of my mages follow to provide transport back."

Marelle sprints into the tactical office to visit her lockbox. She picks out a small mirror and a comb to straighten her hair and check her appearance. A moment later, she returns outside to join Relissa, Captain Hagmaert, and a mage with runes to and from the dwarven enclave.

"Setting ourselves up cute and dandy for the dwarves, are we?" Relissa jests.

"Well, I've never met them before, so I want to make a good first impression."

The mage begins casting the enchantment on the transport rune, forming the classic ring of energy circling around it in his hand. Marelle, Relissa, and the Captain each touch the rune and vanish in a globe of light. The mage follows shortly after.

Far to the north of the outpost, within a rocky line of mountains, four people appear out of a flash of light. Marelle leads the team along a small trail on the side of a gully around an outcropping of rock. The trail climbs a gradual slope up to a roadway that extends across a bridge reaching to the other side of the gully and further winding around the hills to the south.

In front of her, the road passes behind the outcropping of rocks into a large space that seems to have been deliberately quarried as a long, wide boxlike clearing just in front of the entrance to the dwarven enclave. As they approach, they notice the main gate is slightly ajar.

"This doesn't seem very secure," Marelle mentions. "Maybe they're so far north that they don't feel themselves in any danger of attack up here."

She steps up to the gate and knocks, calling inside to see if anyone responds. There is no answer. She cautiously pokes her head inside the door. She can hear noises, like miners hammering at rocks and the squeaking of wheels from carts in motion, but there are no people immediately near the entrance watching for trespassers.

"Dwarves!" she huffs. "What's with these people? They never go outside, and they don't even watch their own doors."

Marelle steps inside and beckons the group to follow. They move along slowly, watching for any abnormal activity, and following a passage leading deeper into the caverns. Eventually, they arrive inside a large junction chamber lined with metal railways passing between side tunnels. They notice a couple of dwarves pushing mining carts along the rails between destinations, and strangely paying no mind to the newcomers.

Marelle tries to catch up with one to speak to him, but he completely ignores her. He simply continues on down the tunnel intent on his work.

"How rude!" Relissa exclaims. "You'd think the least they could do is to say hello to the new faces inside this rock."

Another dwarf comes through on a different rail from the other side of the room, heading around another direction. Marelle tries again, but he simply keeps on moving.

"Is there some kind of main meeting hall in this place, do you think?" Relissa asks.

"Seems like there should be," Marelle responds. "Let's take a look down one of these tunnels. Stay together."

They trot down one of the tunnels following the rail line to an intersection. They try another direction, only to find another intersection.

"This place is like a bleedin' maze!" Relissa mutters.

"How are your ears in here? Can you catch anything?"

"I'm getting lots of echoes. Maybe if we try this one over here," she offers, pointing to yet another side passage.

They follow one of the rail tracks, orienting on the sounds of a loud clamoring in a chamber ahead, this time leading up to a furnace room. Inside, they find an assembly of dwarves shoveling rocky ore from a series of carts into large smelting vats, while others remove empty carts and bring in new ones. The room was abnormally warm, due to the heat of the furnaces, but a set of ventilation shafts had been cut into the ceiling and leading away into the darkness.

"All right, so this must be where they make the iron," Marelle observes. "It looks pretty busy to me, which makes me wonder why the wagons we get in Rolsklinde are so small."

"Let's see if any of these peeps pay attention to us," Relissa suggests.

Marelle tries going up to several people in the room to say hello. None of them respond, instead preferring to keep to their assigned tasks.

"I don't understand this," Marelle declares. "Are they simply being rude, or are they deaf as well as blind?"

"Being inside this mountain with all the clanking," Relissa teases. "I can wager the deaf part, but you can't be doing this sort of work blind, I don't think."

"What about the Captain? His Lordship said dwarves have their own language, so can he try it?"

"I'll ask."

Relissa turns to the Captain and speaks to him in Elvish.

"Captain, we're having some trouble here. Do you speak their language?"

"I do," he admits. "Although I will also admit, if they share common space with you, they should also share a common language, and yet they don't seem to be very cooperative even at that. But I will try Dwarvish on them."

He tries going up to a few dwarves to initiate dialog, but just like with Marelle, he gets no response. He can only shrug.

"You know," he muses. "This is rather peculiar. If I were to try assessing this, I might say they appear in a state of delirium."

Now becoming desperate, Marelle tries some new tactics. First, she tries patting them vigorously on the shoulder. No reaction. She tests to see if they notice her by waving her hand in front of their faces, but again nothing. She even tried interfering with their work by getting into a shoving match on the other side of a cart, only to give up and step out of the way.

"Buggers, I say!" Relissa gripes. "Let's go. These peeps are dead between the ears, and I can't stand this heat anymore."

"Yeah, I agree," Marelle mumbles disconcertedly as she steps away from the activity. "That Governor must have them very tightly wound around his finger. They probably have instructions not to talk to anyone else."

With nothing left to do, they leave the room to find a convenient place where they can open a portal to return back to the outpost.

✦✦◆✦✦

The day passes into late afternoon, and plans are made for the next morning to make a new series of strikes. Scouts had been sent out to create another set of runes for several more entry points just out of sight of a random scattering of orcish camps southwest of the outpost. The tactic would be the same as before, to hit and run, and leave no sign of a camp when finished, removing all the evidence back to the canyon burial and dump sites.

"We need to be vigilant of our southern access," Thaelyn suggests to the assembly. "Keep patrolling the area in a sweeping arc and change the watch posts regularly. You never know when that odd patrol might happen to meander through the valley. I am especially concerned about the Flame Elves. Surely, they must send scouts on occasion."

He returns to the maps and selects several points of interest.

"In addition, these regions west and south are very likely to begin to move once the orcs start catching on to the idea that their brethren are…missing," he smirks. "We will punch a few more holes, but soon we will need to start moving forward. I will send word back home to begin organizing supply stockpiles for our movements and for establishing new forward outposts."

"Just for the sake of talking," Relissa deliberates. "We're pretty sure where the orcs are, and we've got scouts running to the south to check for walkers, but we haven't done much about the Flame Elves or the Suuden-Aryku yet. Should we be worried about them so far?"

"I am hoping our stealth tactics will confound their efforts to track our actions. But no doubt, once someone amongst them begins to take notice of the orcs disappearing, we should expect some sort of response. According to Kaliya, the Suuden-Aryku seem to be primarily focused on the Daanen-Aryku, so I find it unlikely they would divert in our direction immediately, especially as we are keeping a low profile. We have a few scouts hidden on the ridgetop over there to the east, but if to move any closer, I think we may expose ourselves if they use any detection devices."

"And I think it's very likely they might," Kaliya nods, "especially after your rather noticeable arrival."

"This is indeed true, if also unfortunate, but unavoidable. Then we have the Flame Elves, which are likely to be a sly group and far more cunning than the orcs. No doubt they use magic, so cloaked scouts would be at a risk of discovery if we should move too close. Once again, we have a few scouts on station, but at a distance, mostly to spy on the hillsides this side of their city. This could give us a little warning of anything moving this way, assuming it is not cloaked. Elves are also highly adept at long-distance perception. Therefore, we must be careful how we use our gryphon scouts. For now, we will keep ourselves at the maximum range, near enough to see them, but far enough to be outside their offensive range."

A soldier runs up and charges into the room, calling everyone's attention.

"My Lord! Your attention is requested in Barracks One. One of the eastern patrols has returned early with casualties."

Thaelyn follows the soldier as he dashes out of the building and over to the barracks. Kaliya joins along, as well as Relissa and Marelle who were both curious about the sudden rise in tension. On arrival, they see a troop patrol had recalled early inside the building, where the exit point was intended to provide discretion from any outside observers.

Several men were positioned around the room, with a few seated on the floor showing minor injuries and some damaged armor. A group of priests were attending to their wounds.

"What happened here?" Thaelyn demands. "Who did this?"

"We were attacked by a group of Suuden-Aryku, my Lord," recounts one of the men. "They came across the border into Daanen-Aryku territory. A Daanen-Aryku patrol on the front engaged while we were in a rearward position at the time. The invaders seemed to be composed of two distinct parties. One of them occupied the Daanen-Aryku, holding them down, while the other circled around and came straight for us. They seemed to want us specially."

"Any fatalities?"

"Not on our side. This group showed a fair bit of skill with their swords, but not quite the same as what we get back home."

"Swords?" Kaliya blurts impulsively. "Wait, you say they were using swords?"

"Aye! And they were wearing adamantium armor. I got a good close look at it as they hit us. But again, I might say it wasn't as fine a fare as what we have back home."

"One moment," Thaelyn interjects. "Kaliya, do you know if these Suuden-Aryku have ever used adamantium in the past?"

"Until you showed up, I've never even heard of it. They tend to use armor and weapons more like us, only their weapons are nastier…pulse plasma rifles, the kind that you shoot, and the target goes boom."

"Then we have something unique with this group."

"My Lord," the soldier adds. "They seemed intent on us. As I said, the Daanen-Aryku troupe was in front, and the one team took them while the other went around."

"And they came for you specifically? This suggests a directed assault at your position. But if to use adamantium, and also swords, this sounds like a unique operations team, and thus the other team was a decoy."

"Aye, that's my feeling as well. Could it be because we're dressed like Allegiance Guard? Maybe it was a hit to teach them a lesson for pretending to be such noble mates."

"I may have to agree, but then I wonder how this plays out with the Guard's normal procedures. Kaliya, you once said you did not recall any other occasions of attacks during the Guard patrols. Was this the case on every occasion?"

"I don't know if I could answer for every occasion," she reflects.

"But for the appearance of this one…" he muddles.

Thaelyn turns to address Marelle, who was standing behind the group, along with Relissa, observing but unable to understand what happened due again to the language barrier.

"Marelle, I have a question for you…" he addresses in the local tongue.

"Yeah, I'm guessing you might, by the looks of this…" she responds hesitantly. "What happened?"

"My men tell us they were attacked by a rogue group of Suuden-Aryku while another team distracted the local Daanen'kai patrol. This looks like a deliberate hit, perhaps against what they might think to be Allegiance Guard. They were also wearing adamantium armor and using swords. Have you ever heard of such a thing before?"

"Personally, no…" she frowns. "The part about adamantium would be the weirdest one for me, then using swords, as I've heard they don't use swords, only these rifle things."

"Next is you say you occasionally send patrols out there as part of an agreement to give aid, but have you ever heard of such a directed attack to destroy those patrols?"

"Um…" she sighs as she ponders the idea. "I don't recall us sending something out only to have it instantly splattered all over the place. I believe our other patrols, which were few and far between, all made it home alive."

"This is interesting," Kaliya offers. "It also coincides with my experience of no Suuden-Aryku showing up during those patrols. Are we now saying it was pure luck, maybe coincidence that they never showed up at these moments, but on this occasion they did?"

"And on this one occasion using adamantium armor and swords?" Thaelyn muses. "That sort of coincidence is too convenient for my taste. More likely, they did not show themselves for other reasons."

"Other reasons…as if to say, 'Be kind to the little people with their inferior technology?' I don't think I could accept that one either."

"True, and neither would I, especially with such equipment. So, unless we are saying they are changing their manners, this attack was intentional, and I think it was to make a statement."

"Yeah, but then, what kind of statement? The Guard is known to send patrols out on occasion, but on this occasion, the Suuden-Aryku are saying not to get involved. Why on this occasion? Something is different here. And worse, they could do this just as easily with their rifles."

"Indeed, we have a rather curious situation here. Their tactics have changed, as well as their equipment. And this is a most unusual tactic to degrade oneself to a lesser technology just for this one purpose and for this one occasion."

"My Lord," the soldier pipes up again. "One other thing that came to mind…"

"Yes, what is it?"

"I'm sitting here thinking of our little row with the bastards, but you know, I think they were surprised at us."

"Surprised? In what way?"

"Well, I think one easy way is we aren't Allegiance Guard. I get the impression they were expecting easy kills, and we're not so bloody easy," he chuckles.

"Indeed, and thank the Powers for that."

"Aye, but what I mean is our armor. They used adamantium on us, probably hoping to slice us to ribbons, but it didn't work."

"Of course," Thaelyn nods. "And therefore, the surprise, as the Guard only uses steel."

"Aye, but then there's the other side of it."

"Other side?"

"Right. They had a few skills, but not nearly like our training back home, so we got the upper hand well enough, and laid the lot of them to a proper rest. The thing of it is, I hit mine in the flank, not a critical hit mind you...if it were me, I could stand up to it and carry on. But this fellow squealed like a pig and fell over flat."

"As if to say he was particularly susceptible to injury, if only a minor one. What did he do after? Did he get back up?"

"Nay to that, my Lord, he was dead as an old log. In fact, they all went like that."

Thaelyn retracts from the discussion to ponder the implications.

"Kaliya, how would you interpret this? Have you ever had any such experience?"

"We've never had the good fortune to actually kill one before," she admits. "They often hit us by surprise, and we don't have such deadly weapons to play with. This would represent the first time we had a victory of any kind."

"Then we should take advantage of it to see if we can learn something. See if you can have your people recover those bodies for examination. I would like to know how and why they can be killed by a mere scratch."

Early evening was falling on the city of Rolsklinde when a tonal ring sounded out from the drawer in the Governor's desk. He reaches over to pull out the strange communicator.

"Yes, Commander," he answers expectantly. "Do we have a result from today's demonstration?"

"Affirmative…" he responds in his flat monotone.

"Wonderful, the Guard should not be so bold as to try that again anytime soon."

"Negative, this is not our result. Our special ops force was defeated."

"What?!" he shouts. "They were outfitted in that custom gear, were they not? Who killed them? Those miscreant fugitives?"

"Negative, our observation post informs us the Guard members killed them."

"Commander, this is a highly implausible suggestion. The Guard uses inferior materials as compared to…" he halts abruptly. "Wait a moment…but of course, I see it now. Blast! This is worse than I thought. What about the other team?"

"They also suffered losses before retreating."

"By whom, more of the Guard?"

"Affirmative, using ranged weapons resembling bows and arrows."

"Are you telling me those highly trained soldiers, equipped with the finest technological accouterments money can buy, were taken down by simple bows and arrows?"

"Affirmative, although the ammunition seemed strange."

"Strange… Explain strange, in this case."

"Immaterial, not a physical projectile."

"Really! This is a new one. Very well, Commander, I shall investigate on this side how the Guard could come about these most intriguing upgrades to their selection of toys. In the meantime, I will suggest we return to our more traditional methods until I finish my observations of that man down there and decide what may be the best course of action to take."

"Acknowledged."

Chapter 11

HOPEFUL RETURNS

"Dean," the Governor declares. "We still seem to have a bit of a problem with the Guard nowadays, and I am growing concerned over the implications."

"You mean more of the same with the Captain sending troops to help the Daanen-Aryku, as he did a few days ago?"

"Well, yes, there is that. My associates are still reporting sightings, and they seem to be very regular. However, this is another concern, perhaps one of deeper severity, and likely it is related to the first in its own way."

"What is it, my Lord?"

"I am of the opinion, based on a curious report that came across recently, that the Guard may be using something other than their standard equipment."

"I don't understand. What else is there that they could be using?"

"If you will recall, that Thaelyn fellow had some rather luxurious ornamentation on his troops. They were sporting the sort of material that might prove itself more worthy than your typical steel armor."

"Ah, yes, mithril and adamantium," the Dean reminisces. "That was such a delightful show!"

"Yes, well, this report describes a confrontation between some of our Guard members and a group of Suuden-Aryku where the Guard not only survived, but actually defeated the Suuden-Aryku troupe. Now, how do you suppose that could have happened, hmm?"

"Defeated? Our Guard actually killed a group of Suuden-Aryku? But then, wait…are you suggesting that this Thaelyn may be supplying the Guard with new materials?"

"It would certainly explain this report, unless the Suuden-Aryku are becoming lax, which I doubt. Have your spies noticed any odd shipments being made into the city from his camp?"

"No, none of my spies have reported any wagons carrying anything this way. At least not out of his camp. But perhaps I could have them pay closer attention up near the city itself, just in case he's trying to import from another location."

"Good. And while you're at it, I would have you check with our friends up north, just to make sure they are still loyal to us. It has been a while since our last visit."

"Absolutely, my Lord!"

A row of portals opens into the camp as the troops return from yet another raid on a cluster of orcish campsites. Three days have passed since the initial assaults on the front line, and now seven more camps have been destroyed and cleared away, with the evidence removed for dumping and burial. The mass graves on the other side of the canyon are filling up, and the pile of refuse is growing.

An assortment of workers from Rolsklinde have taken to sort and pick through the trash heaps of orcish debris, pulling out anything they can find of value and loading it onto wagons to be sent back into the city. The unwanted portions are now being buried in large landfills for permanent disposal.

Thaelyn had assembled his officers, along with Relissa and Marelle after their return from class.

"Nothing new around the Naarg uy'Sodrad, ay?" Relissa notes.

"Not today," Kaliya replies. "All seems quiet, a little too quiet.

They seem to be holding back. They usually hit us every few days just to make sure we don't forget who controls the region."

"Our victory the other day must have left a bad taste in their mouths," Thaelyn submits. "Perhaps we will see a lessening of their attacks against you, but this does not resolve my concerns for what else they could bring against us."

"We're sitting out here in the open. Anything can happen, and they've been known to use bombardment attacks on us in the past."

"Indeed, then we should see about ways to shield ourselves from that. If we were to revise our shield wall to provide a rooftop..." he continues pondering the topic silently.

"Bombardment?" Marelle wonders.

"Hitting us from above," Kaliya responds. "On several occasions, from what I'm told of our history, they parked a ship in orbit over our heads and blasted us from up there."

"Ouch! How do you defend against something like that?"

"In our case, we couldn't. We just loaded up the ship and left as fast as we could. But a rooftop, a bit like the bubble effect we had when he blasted the orcs that day... Your Lordship, can you do that for such a large area as this outpost?"

"Theoretically, it should be possible," Thaelyn considers. "But technically is another matter. We would need to devise the appropriate apparatus, and then install it. But then, we have the further complication of expanding this base to involve so many additional troop movements. Eventually, the accumulated surface area will become problematic."

"Right. So here we sit, out in the open."

"Thus far, I still feel they might not make a direct assault on our position, if only for the reason that we have not made a direct assault on theirs. Up till now, they should think they are attacking Allegiance Guard in front of your position. And despite their affiliation with the other races, we are not...yet...appearing as an overt hostile force."

"Not yet... All right, so let's hope it holds this way for a bit longer. What's next?"

"I am still pondering the implications of that attack, including how and why they would use adamantium swords and armor. I managed to procure a sample of that armor for our people back home to examine. Perhaps we can learn how it came about."

"Why is that?" Marelle asks.

"Adamantium is said not to exist on this world, and if Kaliya's people are from a world, or rather a universe, without the flows, it cannot be from there either, as you need this in order for the material to form within the rocks. Therefore, where did they find it and how did they forge it into armor, as this knowledge should also be outside their capacity."

"Ah, so if they don't have it locally, they wouldn't know how to use it even if they did find it…I think, right?"

"Yes. I would expect the Suuden-Aryku to be just as ignorant of the magical arts, as well as these materials, as the Daanen-Aryku… with respect, of course."

"Don't look at me," Kaliya refutes. "I fully understand and agree."

"Regardless of this, we will begin by applying some new tactics on that front. No doubt, the survivors of that assault have reported the change on our side, so we should expect some repercussions from it, even if they do seem to be holding back their assaults for now."

"What kind of tactics?"

"First and foremost, we need to secure our backsides as best we can. We cannot allow them to carry information back to their commanders, so we must not allow any survivors to escape from us, nor to allow them communication to their home base. Kaliya, do you use any form of interference equipment on your side to prevent their communications?"

"I don't believe we ever bothered with that before," she muses, "as it can also interfere with ours, and it never really seemed like something to spend time on."

"We must change that. Tell your brother to devise something and deploy it in the vicinity of the Naarg uy'Sodrad to interfere with any and all communications the Suuden-Aryku are likely to use. Then we must employ a series of tactics to ensure no survivors depart the area if they ever do return."

He directs the group's attention to a series of reports and other papers on the table before continuing.

"Their methods seem to prefer the use of ranged weapons, and this might make sense to me if their bodies are so fragile that they dare not engage in melee combat. Kaliya, a question while we are here…"

"Yes?"

"If you will permit me, how sturdy is your body for taking any form of damage? Do you go down so easily?"

"I've been hurt pretty bad a few times, but I don't think I would die from something as minor as that cut your soldier laid on that one Suuden'kai trooper. I honestly don't know how it could kill a man, unless it has to do with this mutation effect we see on them."

"Has your medical examiner mentioned anything as yet?"

"She's still working on it, trying to cross-reference with some of our medical files on what she's looking at. But she did tell me it looks like an artificial lifeform attached to the body."

"Good gracious, that does not sound at all pleasant."

"No, it doesn't. They apparently also use some implanted devices. She noticed something on the right side of the head. It appeared to be an interface of some kind and a couple of chips inside the cranium."

"What has that creature done to those poor people," Thaelyn mourns quietly. "Very well, until we can find a solution to this, assuming there is one, we must press forward. From this moment, we will be using an assortment of battle tactics where the Suuden-Aryku are concerned. There will be three main tactics put into play here."

He now references some of his notes on the matter.

"The first is the Lion tactic. This is a classic head-on attack at full strength, as you would normally expect in a proper battle environment. Next is the Bear, which will employ a decreased attack ratio, and with more emphasis on defense. This will give the impression of a weaker offence to our opponents. We can use this to guard and draw the attention of the attackers. Finally, is the Ram. This also offers a decreased attack, but it uses a ploy of trickery to feign injury or death which, if successful, should cause the attacker to shift his focus onto a new live target."

"Jiggers," Relissa moans. "This beats anything I ever learned about."

"A question, Your Lordship," Marelle asks. "Why would you wish to use a tactic with a weaker attack or a feint?"

"Simple, Marelle…" he responds. "War is like a game, and there are rules to it if you know how to play it right. The first rule, as I would teach in our academies, is to know your enemy. Scouting expeditions, and other information gathering, are very important in times of war. But the next rule, which is also very important, is to not allow your enemy to know you in the same regard. Deception and false information can fool your enemy into thinking you are something that you truly are not. This can work to your tactical advantage."

He demonstrates his notes as he continues.

"For instance, say you use only the Lion technique. Your enemy will see this and know all that you are the first time you meet. Does this work to your advantage on your next encounter? Likely, the answer is no, especially if there are survivors from the first battle to report back. They could then launch an appropriately large assault to counter this, and maybe even defeat it. However, if to use a tactic that gives a false impression of your strength, your next meeting could offer a surprise, thus allowing you to defeat them more easily."

He passes his glance between the attending members to judge their reactions while he references his notes again.

"Using the Bear and Ram techniques can be valuable if you are up against a particularly difficult opponent, for instance one who is himself very clever. I would expect this much from the Suuden-Aryku, if not necessarily from the orcs."

"What about the Flame Elves?" Relissa asks.

"Yes, they as well, though we have not yet encountered them, therefore, I will withhold my opinions as to their capabilities thus far. As for these tactics, if to draw the enemy with the Bear, making your initial power appear weak, then feign some of your troops with the Ram, but continue others with the Bear to pull your opponent further across the line, those who played the Ram can take up behind your aggressors, and together you can squeeze your enemies with the Lion, leaving no one to report on your methods."

"Ooh!" Marelle elates. "Would you adopt me? I love it! Back in the Guard, we train with just one method, to go out and hack away till there's nothing left, though there's never anything to fight. But the intrigue and maneuvering here are brilliant…the kind of thing I might come up with, if I had half a chance to actually do it. Our Governor, bless his soul, simply tells us to sit and stay, like trained hounds. No one in the Guard is happy about that. But with methods like these, we may finally be able to make some progress in this war."

"But, my Lord," Relissa asserts. "While it's fine if we keep tricking the buggers with this, won't they get wise to it after a bit and learn a few tricks of their own?"

"War is a complex set of strategies," he admits. "A game for the thinking mind. The idea here is to kill our foes while preserving our own people. From time to time, we may need to alter our methods, perhaps to add a new twist here and there."

The conversation now shifts its focus with another set of maps and drawings.

"The next order of business is this…" he begins. "We are going to step up our movements against the orcs as best we can, largely due to this incident with the Suuden-Aryku. I want to clear as much breathing room as I can before getting involved on another front."

The initial portion of the meeting had come to a recess as some new reports were arriving. Kaliya was taking this time to call in to her brother to give instructions for a jammer device, while Thaelyn and the others quietly studied the reports.

"Yes, Kailen," Kaliya instructs on her trans-com. "We need full coverage of the area around the Naarg uy'Sodrad. He says we need to up the ante to prevent any reports back to their base."

"All right, Kaliya," issues the voice on her unit. "I'll pass the word to Tanjhira to put something together for us as quick as she can. Is there anything else?"

"That's all for the moment."

"Very good, I'll let you know when we have something ready."

They end the link and Kaliya returns to the discussion. During this time, Thaelyn was taking special notice of the curious little item in her hand.

"Kaliya, would you permit me to take a look at that?"

"Certainly," she smiles and hands the unit over to him. "These are often a standard issue for those of us in the field. Don't leave home without one, as we say in the Force."

"Indeed! And it is so neatly packaged. What sort of range do you have with this?"

"The unit links back to the Naarg uy'Sodrad as a central hub transceiver. I've been able to travel as far as Relissa's home city, and further into the plains region south of that."

"Not a bad example of travel. What about natural landforms impeding your signal?"

"The ship's receiver is very sensitive, although being buried doesn't help much. But we managed to install a few repeater stations along the mountains in the north…that is north of the Naarg uy'Sodrad, Rolsklinde, and so on. I think we also have one on the ridgeline at the upper end of this valley to cover the local area."

"So, we are speaking largely of the other side of our relative safe zones. Can you provide more? For instance, how far away can you extend this network?"

"Technically, it could go all the way around the world if we could find safe locations for the repeater stations. The only issue would be access and maintenance."

"All right, what if we could make an arrangement together. Our usual methods involve the use of portals to send notes, as we do not have our own electromagnetic signaling network…at least, not yet. But if you could provide the units, we can provide the space to install them, as well as your access to maintain them. Would this be reasonable?"

"How far are we speaking of here?"

"Enough to conquer this land away from the orcs."

"Wow, but yes, it would certainly make things easier. Then we could provide trans-coms to your people in comm centers at your outposts. Yes! This would be a perfect way for us to take back this world. I'll pass this along to Kailen the next time I talk to him."

"Excellent."

"Your Lordship," Marelle inquires. "Don't you have anything like that on your world? My impression is you seem so much more advanced than we are."

"In truth, we have not moved into this as yet. I must regulate my teachings to my people very carefully, and this is one that I have not indulged upon thus far. Although, I must admit, as this war progresses, and when considering certain other aspects of our development, this is becoming more and more desirable."

"We should start off with a few units here in this base camp," Kaliya offers. "Since you're going so far with your aid to us, even putting your soldiers' lives on the line, I think the least we can do is help with your communications lines, like for your scouts and such."

"That would be a most delightful offering. But now…"

He returns to the table and a series of new maps on display covering a region extending to the far west towards the coastline.

"General, we need to start stockpiling materials for a new front. First, I want a careful study of the western coastline in the northern corner…discreetly, thus far. The coast itself is around three hundred miles distant from us, and I want to know precisely the uppermost orcish camp in that region, as well as any local resources in the area that we could make use of. We will send scouts to mark runes for a surprise attack and launch a large-scale assault to take and hold that corner, deploying camp facilities immediately thereafter. At the same time, we will organize a second deployment to launch from our location here heading west."

"Your Lordship," Marelle inquires as she examines the map. "Why choose the far northwestern corner?"

"This represents a second front to close the gap between the two sides…let them see us coming from both directions and despair. We have a rather substantial military force to work with. As we begin to move, we will spread at roughly fifty-mile intervals on a weekly basis, closing the gap between east and west, and then branching southward as a long front. Then, as we advance, we will establish new camps at each stage, keeping two rows of outpost lines, and moving the second row forward to the new front as we go along. General, I want our suppliers to have their wagons ready on demand."

"Yes, my Lord!" he responds promptly.

"The Flame Elves and the Suuden-Aryku may be more difficult, so the sooner we can contain the orcs, the sooner we can divert ourselves to the other side."

He pulls back from the table to continue his thoughts.

"We will recall our dormant troops as each new outpost comes into service. I want each forward outpost fortified by a full division of troops. We will take this land and hold it, running those brutes up against the southern sea the same as we did on Tae'Eladar."

"Your Lordship," Marelle considers. "There's a lot of distance to cover going south, from what I hear. Some estimates go about two thousand miles. The east stretches out pretty far too, maybe a thousand and a half. No one has ever been east to see how many Suuden-Aryku are waiting for us, but if we have this many orcs waiting for us out there, we have a long fight ahead of us."

"This is true, although I must also ask why they would keep so many in the first place. I am of the opinion that if their primary purpose is to oppress the local societies, there should not be so many on this world to begin with. And yet, these orcs seem to number in large volumes. If the Suuden-Aryku also number this way, why would they need this. This must surely relate to the reason of this world holding a focus of some sort."

"My Lord," the General inquires. "It would aid us greatly if we could find a way to survey the region."

"I agree, but my concerns are not only for their ability to detect us using whatever sort of technology they might have, but also possibly to shoot us out of the sky with weaponry designed to attack flighted objects, especially at distance."

"Gracious, yes. That would be a rather unpleasant turn for us."

"Perhaps we could conduct a few test runs using cloaks, especially if the Daanen-Aryku can provide us with some sample technology to try ourselves against to improve our methods. Needless to say, we will need to use much harsher tactics with them than the orcs. The orcs are meager strategists by comparison. They are an enemy I know and can defeat easily. But if the Suuden-Aryku are learning to equip adamantium and launching directed assaults, they will be a hard fight. We will likely have to use more ranged and magic attacks on them, perhaps even to include some conjurations, such as elementals, to assist us on occasion."

"Elementals?" Marelle asks.

"Beings from the elemental planes," Relissa offers. "Right, my Lord?"

"Correct, and they can be quite useful in times like these. For instance, a water elemental can envelop an opponent and drown it, while an earth elemental can drag an opponent underground, trapping and perhaps crushing or smothering it. There are also fire and air elementals. But in the end, it all comes down to how well we prepare ourselves for the fight."

"Suddenly, I don't think I want to be on the other side," she chuckles weakly.

"For the moment, let us see about any other weaknesses before taking that action. If they are not otherwise familiar with magic, this could be our hidden card. But we should move forward carefully. Next would be the support infrastructure."

"You mean your supply trains from home?" Kaliya wonders.

"Correct, but we can only move just so much through the gates from Tae'Eladar, and we will need to support many tens of thousands of troops here soon. Therefore, we need to make a few important local supply stores available."

"What kind?"

"Food, most importantly. A local source for it would be easier to manage than to load and unload wagons from Tae'Eladar every day. Therefore, I must ask each of you to send word to your respective superiors about their opinions on our need to expand this outpost. We will need to begin by establishing farming, proper crafting services, and perhaps a full host of other amenities to support our troops over the coming months and years. It is not unreasonable to suggest that this little outpost of ours might very soon become a town. Would any of your societies object to this? Find out and let me know quickly, so I can make my plans accordingly."

"You know, my Lord," Relissa mentions. "Speaking of towns, we used to have a lot of little towns dotting the land all around us, both elves and humans. But this war killed them all off, forcing a lot of refugees to move into the big cities. Even a lot of those got dusted at one time or another. Solinaia and Rolsklinde are the only two big marks out there anymore, and we're both struggling to use any piece of dirt we can find to grow something. We've got the farmers, just no freedom from the buggers out there leaving them to do their work."

"Then this provides us a mutual opportunity. Move your people out into the free areas around you. We will keep the way clear. We also have this land here in the valley, and the tree to watch over it. Use it. If you need seed, let us know and we will provide some to you. We will work this together and share in the bounty."

"Your Lordship," Marelle croons. "That is most generous of you. I'll get a message out to my Captain right away."

"Me too, my Lord, to the Elven Council," Relissa declares.

"We don't actually have any way to do farming," Kaliya sighs. "Not with the Suuden-Aryku outside our doors."

"I recall your mention of an aeroponics lab inside the Naarg uy'Sodrad. This is rather interesting."

"Yes, the ship was apparently designed as a fully self-contained colony ark, with internal food production and a few industrial workshops, making us reasonably self-sufficient no matter where we go, so we could establish a new colony as we land somewhere."

"That sounds like a fine vessel, a well thought out design. Too bad it suffered so badly from the crash. But you and yours are more than welcome to share with us. Just let us know what sort of dietary requirements you have, and we will see what we can do."

"We tend to be mostly vegetarian, with only a small amount of meat involved, assuming we can get any. But something fresh that isn't grown with nano-engineered accelerators would be nice."

The group shares a brief laugh together.

"This also brings my mind back to our friends, the dwarves."

"Don't be wasting your wits on them, my Lord," Relissa snaps. "They were so rude to us up there, ignoring us when we tried talking to them. And according to Marelle, they never go outside anyway. It's like she said before. That Governor must have them wound up tight on his finger."

"While I would not wish to argue, I wonder if we could somehow bring them out with a better offer. After all, what could the Governor possibly be using as trade in a city that is largely locked behind its walls? You say they are supposed to be trading iron, but in exchange for what?"

"Um..." Marelle ponders deeply. "I don't actually know what he trades for. I've heard the Dean goes up there to make these interactions. Sometimes he's seen with a wagon carrying some stuff, but I don't know what."

"Then we should investigate and see if we can do better. What about their behavior overall? I find it strange they would so completely ignore you, even if they were making an exclusive deal with your Governor. After all, you are still a citizen of Rolsklinde. Should you not at least represent your city in some way for this trade agreement?"

"I suppose I should, unless they have orders not to interact with anyone other than the Dean and the Governor."

"But this in itself is still strange. They should still speak to you, if only to say they cannot speak to you, and instead to use an officially authorized agent."

"Then I have no idea," Marelle shrugs.

"You know," Relissa offers. "Now that I think of it, Captain

Hagmaert had a few words for this. He went so far as to say they looked like they were in a…what was it…a delirium."

"A delirium?" Thaelyn leans forward. "Explain."

"Actually, yeah," Marelle interjects. "I tried all sorts of things, talking, shouting, patting them on the shoulder, even pushing and shoving with their carts. And they didn't even look cross-eyed at me."

"This is indeed very odd behavior, and potentially a troubling situation. And if the Captain went so far as to suggest it to be resembling a delirium, I must trust his opinion. These attributes could actually be indicative of a problem of some sort. Could there be an environmental effect, like maybe a gas that causes them to lose their focus."

"That could be a health hazard," Kaliya remarks. "Something noxious, perhaps even toxic?"

"Did they appear ill, their skin discolored, wobbling on their feet?"

"They seemed to be moving around well enough," Marelle recalls. "They were working at a forge…I can't see how you could do that if you're so sick you can't see your hand in front of your face."

"True, this does contradict the notion. Then let us approach it this way for a moment. How long have you known them?"

"Word from my side is we started trade with them sometime early during the war."

"That seems a little too convenient, in my mind. They remain hidden for who knows how long, only to come out for trade during wartime. But then, was there any moment that you are aware of for them to interact on any level other than this trade?"

"Not that I'm aware of."

"So, we have them mysteriously appearing only at the start of this war, and never coming outside for any other form of interaction. Your city is mostly caged inside its walls, which no doubt restricts your ability to supply yourselves, to say nothing of a trade agreement for iron, and they appear as though under an effect that restricts their ability to realize you are standing next to them shouting in their ear. This is not a pleasing scenario. Marelle, I would ask you to see what sorts of goods your Dean is transporting up there in his wagon. We will start with that. It might provide us with a clue as to what sort of trade they are actually conducting."

"All right, I can do that easily enough. The guards at the north gate see him come and go, so I'll ask what they see in the wagon."

"Good. But the fact that they are not responding to anything at all, not even physical interaction, tells me that delirium cannot be a good thing. Maybe it was just this one group you found. Or maybe they are using some sort of addictive substance that alters their manners."

"Like a drug?" Kaliya winces. "A barbiturate or a narcotic? That's not nice."

"No, it is not, but it could possibly answer the question about their behavior. Perhaps I should send a few scouts up there for some casual observation. Maybe the trade materials are these drugs, if you have nothing else of great value inside your walls."

"Wonderful," Marelle moans. "And if we factor in the academy, according to Haran, they have an alchemy lab in their basement. And he told me on many occasions, most of his work was down there."

"This could provide an answer."

The session finalizes and the members are allowed to attend to other matters. General Gabarleine continues his work by dispatching messages to the division commanders to prepare them to return to service.

Relissa, Marelle, and Kaliya each assembled their notes regarding the offer of farming aid and asking for opinions over the need to expand Thaelyn's military occupation in this world.

Marelle's enthusiasm for the turning of this war was beginning to peak, and she found herself with many new thoughts circling through her mind. It represented a moment of progress in an otherwise stagnant tedium, the discovery of Age-old secrets and fresh new ideas to solve problems. She looked forward to being a part of it, if only to having any stories to tell her children and grandchildren. But so far, she was uncertain of her direction for what else lay ahead of her.

Thaelyn went outside to assist in the preparation of a flight of gryphons as they equipped themselves for a scouting run along the western coast. There would be five in this group, and they would examine the landing site for the westernmost launch point in this new campaign. They would need to mark portal runes to the area for the initial invasion, which would then follow with the construction of a forward outpost.

When the briefing was complete, the flight of gryphons loaded up and departed through the north gate of the camp, taking off in a majestic display of power and grace. They reached high into the sky above the camp, forming up in a classic V pattern, where the lead rider directs them onto a westward heading.

He raises his staff and signals to the other riders, instructing them to raise their own and begin chanting to link their staffs into a common control to the lead. They return their staffs to their mounts and the leader begins a chant to initiate a coordinated group engagement.

From the ground, the flight launches forward in a wave of blue energy, streaking across the sky to the horizon, followed by another distant clap of thunder several seconds later.

✦

A new day was dawning, and a special day for the people of Solinaia. During the early morning hours, Aerlie had been overseeing the collection and preparation of the new life-seed for delivery to the Night Elves. A gathering of druids was being assembled in ceremonial dress, and the delegation was preparing to depart the city to the war camp to meet with Thaelyn and the others.

Thaelyn had been in a morning meeting with his officers, including Relissa and Marelle, who had the day off from their classes so they could participate in the ceremony.

It was midmorning in the war camp when Aerlie arrived with the delegation of druids and the life-seed for the Night Elves. Relissa felt a tingling run through her at the thought of her people and the city receiving such a grand gift.

"My Lord," she announces nervously. "Maybe you should know…

My Mum's been sending me notes about whispers going round the city. People are talking about going back to Sein'amar. This tree is making a big buzz too, and that's just making them talk even more."

"You do realize that all of Sein'amar, and in fact the entire world, is combined into our kingdom, correct?"

"Aye, and I've told my Mum about it. They don't mind. In fact, they're just happy to meet back up with the Tel'Quessir again. You know, if you were to ask them real nice, I'd be a bugaboo's pansy if they didn't say yes to join up."

"Are you inferring that all of Solinaia would wish to join into our kingdom?"

"Yes, my Lord, all of them. We'd hand you the keys and call you our new Lord. Also, the city is too crowded, and they'd be looking to spread out a bit. Do you have anything back home to offer?"

"I am sure we could find space, but they will need to demonstrate some patience along the way. Assimilating so many will take time, and a bit of education to bring them up to par with the needs of citizenship."

"Aye, that's right."

"And your city would need to undergo a bit of refreshing to bring some of our native amenities into the local environs, including a gateway to link it with our network."

"Jiggers! You'd build one of those for us?"

"Of course! All our cities and towns are linked together in a large network, for ease of travel amongst our populace. I believe we would likely attach your node to the hub network, at least for now. And later, all things permitting, if our presence here should go forward, we would build a similar network expanding to other cities."

"Other cities? What other cities? We only have the one."

"Perhaps for now, but I fully intend to win this war and purge this world of all those so-called villains. That is the whole point, would you agree? And when we do, there will be open space for future expansion. If you are so overcrowded, some of you could move out into smaller towns and villages to be built when space is secured after the war."

"After the war…" she murmurs distantly. "Gods be blessed, I never thought I would hear those words. I was born in this war, lived my whole life in it, and I fully expected to die in it. Now you're talking about something called peace, a time when the war is finally over. It almost doesn't have any meaning to me."

"Your Lordship," Marelle interjects cautiously. "Would an offer like this be available to the other races here? I remember you saying once that we were all immigrants from Tae'Eladar at one time."

"Indeed. From the very beginning of my reign, I knew that the strength of a people was through their conjoined unity. This is how I brought together my kingdom on Tae'Eladar. If any society would wish to come to our side in friendship and harmony, then I will welcome them at my table. The strength we share together brings benefit to us all."

"That's…incredible!" she wheezes. "I'm not sure how else to describe it, just trying to imagine pulling together a whole world like that."

"Um…" Kaliya raises a finger uncertainly. "Any society? But are we speaking in the context of those in your world, or maybe from your world? Or is it more generalized for…well, anything."

"Kaliya," Thaelyn infers. "The offer would be open to any who might fit with our cultural values. Ours tends to be a very xenophilic society, due to all the experience we have had in our history. We would surely invite your people, if you think you can hold yourselves still long enough. You have played the role of a nomadic society for a long while, but I would welcome you as much as any other. In fact, I might find your contribution to be a most intriguing one."

"Cu'Nar's grace," she emits breathlessly. "I'll admit, my feelings on Ruuki uy'Daan were tainted by my feelings for the orcs, but I've learned my lesson on that by now. Yours, on the other hand, would be a fascinating one to be a part of."

"Perhaps your people could also learn a few lessons on how to perform all this mysticism we strange Early Industrial folks seem so attached to," he grins.

"Now you're just teasing me," she giggles.

"From what I've seen on Tae'Eladar during my visits," Marelle continues. "I wouldn't mind living there. Certainly not in comparison to what we have here. But I need to bring my head down out of the clouds. I don't think this will ever be possible for us with our Governor running the city the way he is. Based on his interaction with your war efforts…or, maybe I should say his lack of interaction, I don't think he cares much for you."

"Yes, this does seem apparent," he admits. "Marelle, understand that I do not wish to suggest anything by this statement, but I should mention that not all of those people on Tae'Eladar saw their leaders turn themselves over as my vassals voluntarily. Some were as gluttonous as your Governor, but the people had other ideas."

"Yeah," she smirks. "I was wondering about that. How long did it take for you to put it all together?"

"Centuries, to say the least… I began small and worked hard to earn the people's trust. As more of them came to me, word spread, and that drew still others. I had numerous difficulties with pompous aristocrats and despots, but in many cases I simply outlasted their longevity. In others, I was forced into conflict, and for the benefit of the people who were left behind, I adopted them as my own."

"I understand. I would like to pass this along to my Captain. I don't know what might come of it, but he should at least hear about this."

"My greatest concern is for the innocent," Thaelyn concludes. "A leader who abuses his charges is no leader by my estimation."

"My dear…" Aerlie beckons as she waits patiently for his attention. "The druids are waiting, and the life-seed isn't getting any closer to planting unless we begin on our way."

"Of course… Do you have the rune to Solinaia?"

"I have it right here. The high priestess has your staff, and we are all ready to depart. Shall I open the portal?"

"Please do. Let us grace the good people of the city with the blessings of their lost heritage."

Aerlie hands the rune over to a nearby mage, who begins casting a chant and orienting it to create a spatial aperture. In a moment, a two-dimensional vortex appears allowing the full assembly of attendees to pass through it.

They arrive outside the hidden entrance to the city of Solinaia. Relissa then guides the entourage into the city and along the lanes up to the temple district.

As they pass through the city, they draw the attention of its citizens. Heads turn and voices echo through shops, inns, and taverns, calling the people outside to witness the arrival of the delegation. A large gathering of people begins following Thaelyn and the others as they work their way through the city. Parents gather up their children and carry them on their shoulders so they can get a better view. People stop their daily chores, putting down their tools and leaving their shops as they step outside to take up a place in the growing procession.

When they finally reach the temple, they are greeted by Relissa's mother, Amariyn, and several other priests of the temple who had been tasked to serve at the new sacred shrine where the tree would find its home. Under her direction, the priests had been spending much of their time to prepare the courtyard area for the new seedling. This courtyard had most recently been used as a small plaza with a gazebo. It was the same one where Relissa took refuge to wait out the haste enchantment she was under on the day she returned from Thaelyn's new camp to file her report with the Guild of Wardens.

The location also held an important historical significance. It was the same site where the original Tree of Life once stood from before the war, therefore it held a religious meaning, but it also held some concern for Amariyn. It was for this reason she and the other priests had been working so hard to prepare the ground, to make sure it was clean from all vestiges of the old tree and the taint that killed it. Amariyn had made special efforts to supervise the cleaning and blessing of the soil to ensure it was ready for the young seedling.

"Welcome, Your Excellences!" Amariyn declares as she approaches the delegation entering the courtyard. "We have been hard at work to prepare the ground for you. I hope all is to your satisfaction."

Thaelyn makes a quick assessment of the wide circular area marked off around the courtyard in preparation of the planting. Just outside the circle, over near the entrance of the temple, was the taskforce of priests waiting nervously for the approval of their meticulous efforts. He knelt down for a close examination of the soil and stretched out his hand to feel the essence of the material through his Celestial senses. He nodded in satisfaction.

"It appears as though you have spent a fair amount of time in this place. I feel the tree will find a good home here. Shall we begin?"

"Is there anything you would wish from me in this ritual?" she asks.

"Since you will be the headmistress of the shrine, I think it is appropriate for you to share a role in the planting. My gift of the dryad blessing will require me to physically place the seed in the soil so I can imbue it with the life-force of Shescellaie's staff, but along the way we can hand it off through you to deliver it into the circle. Perhaps, at a later time, once we establish ourselves here, you and others can continue this to other locations, as they become available."

Amariyn beams a bright smile and moves off to the side where she starts taking off her slippers. She was clearly anxious to walk on the soon-to-be holy ground for the first time in centuries.

The crowd gathers around the courtyard as best they can, with the front rows kneeling or crouching low to allow those in the rear to see. Some of the people climbed on fences and trellises, while others tried peeking through windows and stepping out onto balconies. Even more sought ways to gain a vantage point from the catwalks on the upper levels. So determined were they that they took to stacking themselves, friend onto neighbor, to get more people into the small area.

Relissa, Marelle, and Kaliya took up positions to one side of the temple near the priests since it was the only place with room for them to stand.

Thaelyn stepped to one side to remove his boots. He did not

perform this part of the ritual during the planting of the tree in the Badlands, but on this occasion, he was going to follow the process more intimately. When he was ready, he stepped into the circle, picking up his staff from one of the druids and taking up a position at the center. The druids then formed around the edge of the circle, with the druidic high priestess standing outside at a distance, making ready for her approach. Amariyn found her place at the edge of the circle on the northern side. She felt a nervous anxiety running through her, forcing her to struggle just to maintain her focus.

The druids begin a low rhythmic chant, swaying gently from side to side. This was not going to be the wild dance, like what they did in the Badlands. Instead, it would be an abbreviated form, just to bless the ground and plant the seed.

Thaelyn waited for the chanting to build enough energy within the circle, charging the staff for a simple tapping. When he felt the energy flow was sufficient, he brought the staff up, held it for a few seconds, and then dropped it down for a modest, but firm tap on the ground. A faint echo murmured into the soil under his feet and small sprays of yellow-green energy radiated outward from the staff into the ground. The chanting continued in a low rhythm.

Thaelyn stretches out the staff horizontally in front of him. The staff glows slightly. He holds it over the ground and begins a slow clockwise rotation. As he makes his turn, the staff trickles a rain of dusty luminescence onto the ground under it, blessing the soil with an enriched life-giving power, similar to the effects of the maelstrom in the Badlands, but on a much smaller scale. The land here did not need to be healed, simply kissed with the energy of renewal. He continues the motion around the full circle, and then sets the staff off to one side.

The druidic high priestess now makes her approach. She pulls out the life-seed from the pouch on her belt and holds it reverently as she steps up to Amariyn. She bows her head in deference to the priestess of the local shrine.

Amariyn's nerves tingled as she looked into the cupped hands of the high priestess holding the seed. She had never actually seen a life-seed before. She came into her service in the old shrine of a well-established grove. They never had cause to produce a seed for a new planting during her tenure as all the elven cities had already been fulfilled by that time. Now, she was the one accepting the new seed, and she found it agonizingly difficult to muster enough courage just to hold out her hands.

She cautiously reached out and formed a cradling cup to allow the high priestess to place the seed inside. The priestess laid the seed into her hands and backed away. As Amariyn gazed at the seed, she could feel the softly sleeping spirit inside, like a newborn baby resting in her tender embrace. She turned toward the circle, rotating carefully, and proceeding forward, checking each step as she went along to find steady support in her legs. She walked up to Thaelyn, her eyes still fixed on the seedling, desperately struggling to keep her composure to make those last few steps.

"Relax, Amariyn," he consoles softly, trying to calm her tension. "You are doing very well."

"I'm so nervous…" she responds. "I feel a bit like I did when I held Relissa in my arms for the first time."

"Yes, I can see that. But she came out quite well, and so will this. You are doing all that you can, and the results will reflect the deep compassion you have placed into it."

Thaelyn holds out his hands and forms another cup to receive the seed from Amariyn. She gently lowers her hands into his and opens them to release the seed into his care. She then backs away, feeling a release from her stress, now that the delivery has been made. She takes up a position several steps away, but still inside the circle, and kneels in prayer.

Thaelyn kneels down to scoop out a few handfuls of dirt to make a depression in the soil. He places the seed inside, as he did before, and packs the soil around it to cover the hole. He rises to his feet and picks up the staff again, which had been standing upright by his side during this time under the influence of its powerful enchantments. And just as he did in the Badlands, he waves the staff in small circles above the seedling while a delicate shower of energy pours onto the mound of soil. The druids in the circle continue their chanting while he steps away to allow the seed room to take root.

A few moments pass, and movement begins to stir in the small mound. The soil seems to come to life, as bits of it are pushed away to reveal a small shoot jutting through. The sprout expands into a feisty young sapling, drawing from the enriched soil to give it that initial spurt of growth. It makes a strong reach upward from the ground, just like the sapling in the Badlands, and comes to a stable rest at a height measuring a good arm's length over Thaelyn's head.

"Is that as high as it gets?" Marelle asks.

"Nah," Relissa replies. "It'll get a good bit bigger than that, and even more. This is just the starting point. And then, when this one is grown, you get the daughter trees."

Marelle gazes at the girl, now worried by the meaning.

"I hope you're going to explain that to me one day."

"Aye. But now, Kaliya, what do you think of this new bit of mysticism?"

"Relissa," she replies softly. "I'm not going to use that word anymore. Clearly, there is more to the universe than what my science can explain, and some of it simply can't be explained by science."

"Thank you, Your Grace," Amariyn whispers. "It's so beautiful. And already I can feel it waking up. The spirit is so powerful."

"This tree is a direct descendant of Shescellaie's grove in Bya'an Tamoranth," Thaelyn affirms. "She provided this for you herself, to see you off to a good start in this world."

"Forgive me, but I'm not very familiar with the lineage. Who is Shescellaie?"

"She is the Queen of the dryad spirits found on Tae'Eladar, and she has made her home within our capital city, by a special pact I share with her."

"Dear gods, my Lord!" Relissa yelps. "Is that the one you were talking about before, out in the Badlands, that gives you so much power with this nature stuff?"

"The same... Have you met with her yet?"

"Well, um, no, you've been keeping me rather busy of late, so I haven't had time yet."

"Then you should make the visit sometime. It could be educational, especially since you are soon to be a student at the academy."

Thaelyn makes his way out of the circle, leaving Amariyn to absorb the vibrant energies stirring within the tree. The druids had stopped their chanting and were also on their way out.

"You have a great many onlookers out here, Amariyn," he continues. "I think many of them are waiting to make their offering."

Amariyn looks around at the massive gathering of the crowd around the courtyard, many of their faces showing expectant pleas to visit the new tree. She quickly comes to her feet and summons the other priests to prepare a proper service for the citizens. She calls out to the people, asking them to form up in an orderly manner and to be patient while the priests attend to them in small groups. She knew this would likely take the remainder of the day, and then some, but it was a task that filled her with great joy.

"Relissa," Thaelyn asserts. "I will be returning back to the camp. Do you wish to remain here to assist?"

"I think my Mum could probably use the help, so if you don't mind..."

"Very good, but it is still a long run. Perhaps if Aerlie would like to offer herself, we may find solutions to multiple issues at once."

He turns to Aerlie, who gives a nod in acceptance of her temporary role.

"That would be wonderful," Relissa replies. "Thank you."

He glances at Amariyn again, catching her attention just long enough to signal a farewell before pulling out a rune to send himself and the other members of the delegation back to the outpost.

Kaliya and Marelle returned with Thaelyn and spent the remainder of the afternoon preparing their reports for their superiors. In Marelle's report, she mentioned the ceremony of the new life-tree and the desires of the Night Elves to rejoin the other elven nations on Tae'Eladar. Kaliya also told the story to her brother, trying to explain the spiritual significance of the ritual and how it made her feel for her own healing. They also related the offer Thaelyn made of unity between all the races for their mutual benefit.

Marelle took special care in her wording with Captain Kholgard where the Governor's animosity was concerned, even though she knew he didn't care for the man any more than the rest. But she also knew the general consensus of the people was more often entwined with public gossip and hearsay, much of which held no true value where real-world events were concerned. She hinted that the people may find themselves one day pressed to consider which is better, to stay with their Governor and his slipshod management practice, or to join Thaelyn and realize a new era of peace and prosperity.

Evening arrived and dinner was well underway when Aerlie and Relissa returned to the camp.

"My Lord," Relissa shouts as she approaches the campsite.

"You return late," he calls back to her. "I trust all is well in Solinaia? And did you have an opportunity to speak with your mother about our offer?"

"Aye, it took a wee bit longer than expected. The whole city wanted to see the tree. The streets were packed side to side."

Relissa makes a quick detour by the chef's table to pick up a plate of food before sitting near Thaelyn and his group.

"The Council is a mite overwhelmed with the tree," she continues. "So, they won't be able to make any big decisions for a while till they've had time to settle themselves and think things through. I told them about your offer. They'll probably want to talk about it for a good stretch, like they always do on the heavy political chatter."

She pauses to take several bites of her dinner.

"Knowing how the Council works, I'd say you should give them the better part of a month, maybe more, to make this kind of decision. Mainly just to get their heads put on straight. I'll let you know what I hear as it comes in. They did confirm one thing, however. They'll gladly help in any way on the farming side of it, and whatever else you do here in the valley."

She finishes her meal as the conversation turns to lighter subjects. Eventually, she and Marelle both need to return to their dorm rooms in the city so they can attend to their schedules the next morning.

Chapter 12

A VENTUROUS JOURNEY

The morning activity picked up as usual with a review of the reports from the previous evening. No unusual sightings had occurred around the Naarg uy'Sodrad on this occasion, and the troops, along with their supply trains, were organizing for the large-scale campaign they had planned against the orcs.

Kaliya's work in the tactical office finished early, giving her time to think. Her efforts at resolving her emotional difficulties had resulted in a release of many of her tensions, but she felt as if one stubborn little shadow still haunted her. She desired to be a part of Thaelyn's military Order, this much was certain by now. To live on Tae'Eladar, to experience their cultural teachings, to study in their academies, it all seemed like a dream, and by now it was nearly within reach. But that one last shadow could spoil everything for her.

She knew she would never know the answer unless she tried, but Thaelyn's words about the Spirit test being a one-shot deal frightened her. And yet, she couldn't hold it back forever. For this, she needed to hear a supportive voice, so she found a secluded spot and pulled out her trans-com to call her brother.

"This is Commander Nazég," answers the voice.

"Kailen, it's me."

"Kaliya! How are things going on your side of the mountain?"

"Smoothly… It's fairly calm today, so far."

"Good to hear. What is it you need?"

"I needed to hear your voice, mostly. I've been considering something and I'm a little scared of the results I might get."

"Oh? What is that?"

"Well, I told you I was doing these counseling sessions with Thaelyn, Aerlie, and their priests, and I'm sure it's helped. I've finally been able to realize my errors, and I feel pretty foolish after all these years, but I'm more at ease now, I think."

"I'm glad to hear it. I know we tried to teach you these things for a much longer time than that."

"Yeah, and you were right. I had to hear it from another source to realize it's true. I suppose I also had to meet with people who might hold the other side of these mysteries we've been fighting with. This has certainly answered some of it, and helped me find a little peace of mind. I just wish I could've listened to you a long time ago."

"So, is this what you wanted to talk about? You mentioned something about being scared."

"Yes, and I needed to hear you before I do this. You see, I have this, I guess you might call it a longing to join Thaelyn's Order. I don't know how else to explain it. It's like a craving, like what you get for a certain food you really enjoy. My dreams seem to have cleared up from all my nightmares, and now I hear something new. It's peaceful, maybe even inspiring. Like a little voice in there telling me it's good for me."

"That sounds a little strange, actually."

"Yeah, but it's better than that lost girl on a ruined street. Anyway, I feel like this would be such a positive step forward for me, a chance to start over and maybe do it right this time. The way they live, the things they teach… Cu'Nar's Grace, Kailen, watching him and his people has been filling me with all sorts of new ideas and motivations, but I'm afraid I might not qualify."

"For his military? You know your history with the Sentinels.

Do you feel so much more confident in yourself that you could do better in his Order?"

"I feel better, this much I know. I'm also reminded of that first day. I'm an offensive combatant, not defensive. But ours doesn't teach this, and therefore, I felt stifled. I didn't do so well because no one amongst us has the horns to actually do anything."

"Right, I get it."

"And yet, there's still a little bit of doubt, and it scares me. It makes me wonder if I'll be able to qualify for it…just to get a hoof in the door."

"What do you need for that?"

"There's a test I need to take…well, probably several tests, but most of them are academic and I doubt they'll be a problem for me. But one in particular involves some kind of evaluation of my spirit. I'm not really sure how they do this, but if the spirit is pure, you're in. If not, you might be able to take some kind of ritual to redeem yourself and try again. The problem is, I feel like there's still one little thing inside of me, and I can't seem to get it out. I may fail the test, but maybe the ritual will help. If not, well, it's over for me."

"I see. But I'm still not sure how I can be of any help to you in this. I don't know how to purify your spirit…if such a thing is possible."

"Just tell me you love me and hope for the best. It would boost my feelings a lot."

"All right, Sis, you got it. You know I've always tried to help you, even if I was hard on you on occasion. If this is what you want, may the cu'Nar watch over you, and guide you safely. And I'll keep you in my thoughts with my highest regards."

"Thanks, Kailen," she sighs heavily. "You know, there's something that's been on my mind a lot lately."

"What's that?"

"I've been thinking back on everything I did, all my old feelings, all the way to Ruuki uy'Daan, which is where I'm sure a lot of this got started."

"I'm quite sure of that, as well. You had a good life back there, and then it all went kaboom."

"Yeah, one big explosion of shock and horror," she chuckles ironically. "I'm thinking of our old home, and Mother. I never had a chance to tell her I loved her before all this madness occurred. Now it's too late. Maybe this is what hurts so much?"

"Could be, Sis, she loved you very much. And do you know who else loved you?"

"Yes, Kailen, and that hurts too now. I'm ashamed and embarrassed. I had so many problems since that day. Everything just fell to pieces on me."

"Do you think you can put those pieces back together now? You know I'll stand by you if you need a hand to hold you up."

"Thank you, I'll try. So far, I'm still trying to build up my strength after all these revelations. But anyway, thanks again, and I'll let you know how it turns out."

"I'll be waiting. Good luck, Sis."

Kaliya puts the trans-com away in her holster and returns to the tactical office to look for Thaelyn.

"Your Lordship," she announces into the room. "May I have a moment, please?"

"Yes, Kaliya, what do you need?"

Kaliya approaches Thaelyn with an uncertain look in her eyes. She realizes she needs this if she ever hopes to find her answer, but she is nervous over the potential outcome.

"I have something I need to ask you. I'm unsure of the result I'll get, but if I never try, I'll never know if there's any real purpose waiting for me."

"Very well, you have my ear. What is it you desire? Is this related to our previous discussions?"

"Yes, I wish to try out for your military, please."

"Do you feel yourself ready for this? This is a serious step, not one to be made lightly."

"Your Lordship," she sighs pensively. "The only way I can answer is like this… I've listened to your priests, and I've opened myself up and realized all my past errors. I feel better, I really do. That time when I visited your temple and the altar for Ilmater…it felt like a hand came down and lifted me up again."

"This is how I have heard many people describe it. You felt the touch of Ilmater carrying away your woes."

"And what I've been learning since that time has made me realize these gods are actual living entities of some sort, and you people seem to share a truly fascinating relationship with them."

"Indeed, and this is good."

"I'm also realizing how many people I hurt along the way, and when I get the chance for it, I'll go back and try and heal over some of those old wounds. And then we had all those revelations that answered so many old questions. It gives closure to a lot of things, and explains how and why it all happened. This may not help me feel better simply by knowing it, but it does give me better understanding, and that provides a clearer direction to take. And so, I would like to ask you to allow me to take your test."

"You are referring to the Spirit test?"

"Yes. I feel as though I have come as far as I can, but there is still something inside, and confession isn't resolving it completely. So, my only hope now is that the ritual will help. With everything else you've taught me, maybe some small bit of this magic of yours can finally show me the way."

"You only get one chance at this. If you succeed, it will allow you to pass, but I can only permit this once. I must do this to draw a line to ensure the integrity of our membership."

"I understand. I'm nervous, but at this moment I'm willing to try anything. What I feel inside is like…well, there are actually two things I feel right now, and they seem to be tugging at me."

"Two things. Such as?"

"The first one, which I suppose is expected, is like an empty space, something torn away from me that I need to put back. Simply talking about it doesn't help. I need to fill it with something, and this is where I hope the ritual can come in."

"Do you have any ideas on what could be causing it?"

"Some thoughts have crossed my mind, but it may be impossible to repair in a physical sense, at least not where we are now. This is a piece of my past, I think, one of those injuries of that little girl running through those ruined streets. If this ritual of yours works as I think it does, taking me into a kind of dream realm where I can confront this within my thoughts, that's probably the only way. I recall a concept we describe as lucid dreaming, where a person can control what happens inside their dreams. It's one of those things we sometimes taught in our metaphysics faction, although it's a little obscure, like everything else," she chuckles.

"Indeed, I am familiar with this process, although it can also take some time and practice to get it right."

"The other thing is a little strange. I'm almost afraid to say something, or else you might think I'm losing my horns again," she chuckles softly.

"Uh huh. Perhaps we should touch on it, just to be sure."

"I was speaking to Kailen a moment ago about this. I feel more at peace now, and all those bad dreams seem to be clearing up, if only because we understand more of what is causing it. That little girl running through the ruined streets isn't running any more. But now I hear something new. I'm sure it must be my imagination, maybe something from all this counseling, but I feel a kind of motivational drive telling me to do this. It's almost like a voice, but not necessarily in words, saying I need this."

"A voice, but not in words, driving you. This is interesting. You did share that moment with Ilmater, and if he lifted you up from your miseries, perhaps there is a lingering effect. How does this voice sound? It is masculine, like what He uses?"

"No, not in this case. More feminine, and it feels mature, like a parental voice."

"But not in words. Maybe a sensation? Hmm..." he pauses in contemplation. "I wonder if you are drawing attention from someone. These cu'Nar of yours brought you here. Perhaps they are delivering something behind our backs."

"Oh, great!" she shrugs. "I wonder what sort of trouble I'm aiming for on this occasion. So, we have this test, but I'm a little unsure if

I can make it the first time. Do you allow that ritual before taking the test?"

"The general philosophy is that you can succeed or fail in the ritual, but it only occurs once. If the pain is so deep that you cannot reach it, or simply falter when trying to correct it, subsequent attempts may not change this. So, we perform the test first, and only if it becomes necessary will we do the ritual, followed again by another test to determine our results."

Kaliya sighs deeply to gather her resolve.

"This is frightening," she admits tenuously. "But I don't think I can do anything else at this point except to jump in with both hooves. And if there's something driving me…I don't know. Does it think I'm actually ready for it? Is there anything else you can tell me about this ritual to help prepare me, maybe some words of encouragement to see me through?"

"Come with me and I will give you a few words as we move along. I will take you there myself and see you on your way."

Thaelyn and Kaliya leave the room and walk up to the gate. Kaliya's nerves were virtually standing on end as she forced herself to contain them. The gate was already set for Bya'an Tamoranth, as was testified by the magnificent grandeur of the image in the window. He motions for her to step through first, and he follows close behind.

They arrive in a plaza dominated by a large circular structure accompanied by a complex switching apparatus on one side. Kaliya turns around to observe the strange device.

"This is amazing!" she declares. "You know, this looks very similar to some of the structures we used to have, based on our old technology. We call them conveyors."

"Yet another application of wisdom bringing about a similar result," he asserts.

"Where does it lead? Is this used for transport around your world?"

"This here is one of many we use for local routing within the city. We have another one, located elsewhere, which acts as a hub for travel between cities and around the world."

It was after midday on Tae'Eladar. The sun was shining, the air was sweet, and only a few light clouds hung in the sky. It was a pleasant autumn day, and Kaliya noticed decorations were being placed around the area.

"What is this for?" she asks. "Are you preparing for something?"

"We have a seasonal event approaching soon for the autumn equinox called High Harvestide. It is a celebration of the bounty of the land, and one of our more important holidays for the year."

"A holiday... I can't remember our people ever having a holiday."

They travelled up to the guildhall and through the front gates. She paused briefly to study the large, sculpted statue of Thaelyn and Aerlie in the courtyard before turning off to the side and passing through a door. They proceeded down a hall to the left, around another corner and partway down another hall to a room where the Spirit test was performed. Along the way, he signaled for Mage Master Sagrid to oversee the service. Master Sagrid then called his assistant, Adept Howald, to aid him. They entered the testing room and Thaelyn began to explain how it works.

"This chair is the focus of the test. Here on the chair's arms, you have pads where you place your hands, and then your feet..."

He looks down at Kaliya's hooves.

"Hmm... This may be interesting to see if it works properly. Normally, we have people with fleshy feet, but I suppose any exposed part of the body ought to suffice in this case, so long as the energies are able to circulate through you. Your feet should be placed on those pads on the floor just in front."

"I have a kind of thick padding under there. Perhaps that'll work."

"You would make an interesting study for our anatomy courses, Kaliya."

"So long as you don't try dissecting me," she chuckles.

He grins and moves around the chair, directing her attention to a ring-like hood suspended on a metal arm hanging over the top.

"This is called the Veneration Crown. It collects the energies that swirl around you from the chair and forms an orb just above of the appropriate color to your level of purity."

"And for this," she replies with a soft tremor in her voice, "I want blue to pass, right?"

"That is correct. If you should get green or yellow, you may take the Ritual of Redemption in an attempt to cleanse yourself, and then try one more time in the chair."

"Is there anything I should do to prepare myself for this?"

"You are what you are. Preparation, other than what you have done already, is largely irrelevant."

"Well, I guess there's no time like the present. Let's do this."

Kaliya steps up to the chair and sits down. Thaelyn helps to position her hands and hoofed feet into their proper locations. He then pulled the crown over her head as best he could, considering it was designed for those applicants without horns projecting out from their temples. He moves away and gives instructions to Master Sagrid to begin the process. Master Sagrid makes a brief survey and signals the Adept handling the control.

The Adept turned a knob on a control box sitting across from the chair. The pads under Kaliya's feet and hands started to glow softly, and a swirl of energy began forming around the base of the chair, spiraling up like a graceful vortex and condensing into the crown. It channeled through the crown and into a glowing orb overhead. As the swirls coalesced, the color of the orb altered, attuning itself to her unique spiritual alignment and purity. When the orb had fully formed, the true color was revealed.

"A late green, my Lord," the Mage Master announces. "She qualifies for the ritual, if she desires it."

The Adept deactivates the control and Kaliya is helped out of the chair.

"Not bad, actually," Thaelyn declares. "Now, although I already know the answer, it is procedure for us to ask this question. Do you wish to take the ritual?"

"I do," she responds.

"Master Sagrid, do be so kind as to prepare her for the ritual."

"Yes, my Lord, right away," he replies.

"Your Lordship," Kaliya begs. "About this ritual... Is there anything else you can say to help ease my nerves and maybe give me some advice on what to expect? I want to do this right, especially since I only get one chance at it."

"This color should give a bit of its own encouragement, as you have clearly come a long way already. But still, I will have you reflect back on all the things we have discussed since that day you opened up to us. The ritual is performed within a chamber that has some rather unique properties to it. These properties allow the mind to free itself and present its deepest feelings in open space."

"What about this hallucinogen you mentioned once?"

"A type of incense, yes. You will first go to a room where you will meditate. We have found that people often benefit from this as the smoke tends to relax the mind greatly, thus allowing the ritual to be more effective."

"Sounds like fun," she chuckles.

"I have seen the power of your mind, so I would expect you to have a rather profound experience in there. Remain calm and use your finest wisdom to understand your goal. You may find yourself drawn, perhaps unconsciously, to memories of a place or a moment in time within your past. Follow this and allow it to bring you to your solution. We do not generally place a time limit on the duration, so do not think you must rush yourself."

As Thaelyn finishes, he motions to the Mage Master to take over. Thaelyn then leaves the room, stepping outside again and working his way back to the front gate and towards the portal in the plaza.

"Dear lady," Master Sagrid asks. "May I know your full name?"

"My name is Kaliya Nazég."

"Very good, Kaliya, please follow me. We will first go to a meditation room where you can prepare yourself. Adept Howald, fetch the lady a robe. Kindly make it large enough to accommodate her features."

The Master leads Kaliya out of the testing room and further down the hall.

"A robe?" Kaliya wonders.

"When you enter the meditation room, you will remove your clothing and don the robe instead. You will then be left alone for a time, often an hour, to contemplate yourself. We will fetch you when it is time to proceed. The ritual itself is performed devoid of all physical affects in a darkened and empty room, where you will seek out your innermost thoughts and contend with them as best you can."

"All of my clothing?"

"Yes, you must be completely devoid of any article placed upon your body. This also includes jewelry if you wear any. Think of it as a return to your primal form, a moment of birthing as you will be passing through the trials of renewal the same as you once came through your mother's womb."

"Um, I'm a bit more developed now than I was when I first came from there," she jokes weakly.

"Granted that, and you would not be the first," he chuckles. "We understand that there are some cultures that may find nudity offensive or inappropriate, but we are not one of those. To us, the body is a natural creation and not a thing to be ashamed of. Within the right context, nudity is perfectly acceptable and respected. For instance, if you are applying to our guild, you must know that this is not the only place you will find yourself exposed to the world around you."

"What do you mean?"

"For one, the bathhouses… We make it into a social affair. While we do offer private bathing within individual homes and apartments, people will also gather in these public venues to bathe and talk about topics of concern and interest to life and to each other, celebrating the joy of society without the burdens of shame that some might possess in this form. It may take an adjustment of your mindset to accept it, but you may also find it liberating after a while."

They enter a small room, dimly lit by sconces on the walls, and with a large, cushioned mat in the center of the floor. Just in front of the mat are a set of racks with candles and sticks of incense.

The Adept rushes to catch up to them while carrying a large white robe. He gives the robe to Kaliya as she begins removing pieces of her uniform and setting them on the floor next to her.

As she works her way through the undressing process, she notices Master Sagrid lighting the rows of candles by waving a set of fingers in loops around each, then snapping to ignite the full set. He performs this on two racks of candles, positioned on either side, finally moving to a third rack in the middle which holds a row of incense. As she watches, she is reminded of her lesson to ignite the piece of kindling back in the camp.

The Adept assists in collecting Kaliya's things into a sack, ensuring she is now fully undressed, checking one last time for anything forgotten, such as rings, necklaces, and other jewelry.

She puts on the robe and closes it around her. The length falls short on her, but under the circumstances, she doesn't concern herself with that. Master Sagrid then directs her to sit on the mat in front of the candles and incense and meditate while he and the Adept both leave the room and close the door.

Time passes as she sits on the mat with the candles slowly diminishing. The incense burns its way through, and the smoke fills the room, curling into shapes that seemed almost familiar, like faces or images of animals. She feels herself becoming light-headed as she breathes in the pungent vapors. She tries to recall her lessons on meditation from the priests, first to let go the body, and then the mind. She felt her arms and legs becoming very relaxed, almost numb from sitting so long. Her body felt like it could be floating, and her mind drifted around the room as with the many puffs of smoke from the incense. Her thoughts meandered like a lazy river across a quiet valley. All was calm in the room.

After about an hour, although Kaliya had no way to measure its passing, a gentle knock came at the door as Adept Howald opened it and called to her.

"Your time is here, Kaliya. Please come with me."

She pulls herself back into focus to move her sleepy body, lifting herself up onto her feet and turning to follow the Adept out the door.

She felt heavy, and the room seemed to be moving. She staggered slightly, and reached out to find a wall to lean against as she walked.

He leads her down the hall to another door not far from the meditation room. As she passes through, she finds herself in an antechamber with several doors set into a curved wall on the opposite side.

"Please remove your robe here and choose a door," Master Sagrid instructs. "It makes no difference which one. Pass through and seek yourself. Be cautious of your judgment and proceed thoughtfully."

"What will I find inside?"

"The answer is different for each applicant. The rooms are enchanted. Most describe it as living a waking dream, where you may find your fears, your anger, or whatever it is that troubles you, and confront it in some manner. Beyond that, I cannot answer you."

Kaliya takes off her robe and sets it on a table next to her. She walks slowly into the room, examining the doors in front of her. They all look identical. She continues forward and selects a door just off to her left. She steps up to it, reaching out to the wall for stability, and opens the door carefully. She makes a final quick glance over her shoulder at the Master and the Adept standing at the table, and then moves inside. The door closes behind her. The room is pitch black.

She steps further into the blackness. She cannot see where she is going, or if there is anything in her way, like another wall. The incense from the meditation chamber combined with the enchantments of this room worked deep into her mind. She thought she saw flickers of light, but was unsure if it was real or just tricks being played in her vision. Her mind was recalling sounds, like voices, echoes of memories, and faint cries of chaos. She was feeling sleepy.

"What was in that stuff?" she wonders out loud. "I'm so dizzy, I feel like everything is moving around me, even though I can't see it. What I need is a light to see by. Something shining down to spotlight the place…"

As she ponders her statement, she unconsciously tries to envision a directional light from above to illuminate her position. The local environment was impossibly dark, and the more she strained to see through it, the more she wished for that light. Then, almost as if by command, a focused beam begins to shine down on her. She impulsively looks up at it."

"Well, that was nice. Now, if only I had a place to sit down… before I fall down. A nice comfortable recliner…yeah, like what we have in the lounge area back home, so soft and luxurious that you just sink right into it."

She recalls vividly one of the chairs back in the Naarg uy'Sodrad where she would sometimes find a place to rest after her patrols, often further to lose herself in quiet contemplation. She allows herself to indulge in the memory of reclining in the soft cushions, the feel of the cool simulated leather upholstery, the wrapped armrests, and a pillow for the head. As her memories drift to the ship's lounge area and its furnishings, she finds herself getting lost in this new vision, being distracted by her wooziness, even though she realized she had work to do in here. But her wobbling interrupted her focus since she was so unaccustomed to this sensation.

Suddenly, to one side, she caught a glimpse of a vision. It took on the form of a chair, and it seemed strangely familiar to her. She turned to focus on it, somehow realizing it was supposed to be that same chair from the lounge, and her dreamlike delirium caused her to play into the vision.

"Come on you, I know you're out there," she croons playfully. "You're teasing me…yeah. Come out of hiding."

She glares at the blurry image forming out of the local haze, mindlessly willing it to come into better focus. And as she places greater attention into it, the object seems to grow out of nothingness, taking on substance and form.

"Perception…definition…" she mumbles indistinctly. "Substance…reality… Just like the riddle," she giggles incoherently.

Her focus seemed to pull the item into the reality of her local space, until it took on a solid form. She then examined the result.

"Ah, there we are," she coos. "Yes, that'll do nicely."

She steps over to it and sits down, where she reclines deeply.

"I love these chairs. So soft, so comfortable, I could just…"

She closes her eyes and relaxes, hoping for just a moment of rest to collect her strength. Deep down, she still recalled her purpose, but at this moment, she felt as if she needed to enter a dream state for it. And so, she passes quietly into unconsciousness.

The room is silent. Kaliya is resting peacefully in the chair. But she feels her mind is still active, and soon she begins to stir, with her dreamlike form tenderly lifting itself forward from her soothing recline. She no longer feels tired and pulls herself out of the chair to her feet, taking a few small steps forward. But then she stops abruptly, sensing something is amiss. She turns to see what it could be, and there she sees the nude form of her body sitting in a very comfortable chair that remarkably resembles one of those from the recreational lounge at the Naarg uy'Sodrad.

"That's me! But how is this possible? And where did that chair come from?"

She halts to examine the figure, reminding herself to remain calm.

"Right, I think I made that; it's part of my dream. Good, let's leave it there. At least my head has stopped spinning, so maybe I can find what I'm looking for in here."

As she observes her form in the chair, she tries to recall Thaelyn's last instructions.

"He said I might find myself drawn to something," she muses. "Everyone's experience is different, and I'm likely to have something big. Just relax and let it come."

She pans her gaze around the scene, but everything was black.

"I still find it interesting I would see myself sleeping in a chair," she chuckles. "Hmm, you know, this seems a little familiar suddenly. What was it…?" her voice trails off.

She can almost recall a distant memory that seemed locked away in a remote corner of her mind. But she needed to focus herself on her primary purpose.

"I'm in here to solve something. An emptiness, yeah… And cu'Nar help me, if I think I know what it is, but how do I do this? That was so long ago, and so far away."

She allows her mind to drift back to her childhood. This is

where she held her deepest pain. A feeling begins gushing up, and this led to the one and only conclusion she could muster.

"I have to go back there."

She turns to survey the room, but it was simply too dark to see anything. There were no clear images appearing, no apparitions forming, and her body still seemed to be happily resting on the chair behind her.

"To go back there..." she reflects privately. "Across nether-space and across time, to those streets again..."

She begins to reimagine her old visions. And as she directs her mind into these distant thoughts, something catches her attention from the corner of her eye. She turns to see a tiny dot of light passing by, followed by another one.

"Movement..." she mutters absentmindedly.

She turns around to see more dots chasing along, some on paths high over her head and others low beneath her feet. She follows the spectacle around her form. The blackness was being replaced by a menagerie of dots, some moving fast and others slow, seemingly appearing out of nowhere.

"Something is there," she whispers. "That's where I need to go, I know it!"

She continues to peer into the void when a thought begins to solidify.

"Movement!" she asserts determinedly. "The mind defines Reality. Move!"

She turns fully away from her body into the blackness and reaches out an arm. There she begins projecting her thoughts into a sensation of movement. Much like she once tried projecting the magical energies moving through her, now she was the body in motion. And ahead of her, she envisions her target destination.

The scene around her changes abruptly. As she stretches out a hand to guide the way, her body in the chair whisks away into the background, along with the room she was in, along the guildhall around that room, along with the city around that, and the remainder of the world around that. A sudden wave of rainbow hues rushes past, accelerating into a rapid blur, followed briskly by what seemed like a barrier. Ahead of her was a dot, a focal point on which to latch onto. Strange shapes and wispy curls danced around her as her mind drove her forward through what seemed like a tunnel.

"In all the nether-space," she wheezes. "This actually does look like nether-space!"

She struggles to maintain her focus of mind, just like she was taught during that magic trick. She was travelling through what seemed like a sea of light. Around her, at great distance, she saw the vague forms of rounded bodies, with one of them coming into view along her path. She saw another barrier, like a wall, or perhaps the membrane of an unimaginably immense bubble. The dot appeared to be planted on its surface, or maybe it was a hole burrowing within. She pressed on harder, willing herself to move faster and more determinedly. The sights blended together as a curtain of light surrounding her on all sides and increasing in velocity. She plunged fiercely towards the wall, defying it to hold her back, and still the dot seemed distant to her.

"This thing is far away, but I'm not letting up. I want it...I need it...I must have it."

She penetrates the wall and now finds herself immersed in another sea, this time of distant lights. She could see shapes, some of them nebulous, others spiraling. Spheres of light streaked past in yellows, blue-whites, and dim reds, followed by ribbons of their own afterimages. Her focal point now grew stronger, and her determination was only encouraging her to press harder. She could almost see where she wanted to be.

Her body was leaning forward steeply, almost horizontal. She felt as if she could be floating, gliding through space and pulled by her deepest desires to find what waits for her on the other side. A tiny image becomes visible within the glowing object, gradually enlarging as she sees faint color, shapes, and texture. And around it was a rapidly approaching spiral shape.

"What in all the nether-space is that thing?" she muses. "It looks like a galaxy!"

She continues driving herself to get closer, now reaching out with both arms, straining as if to grab hold of it.

"Come on girl," she urges. "It's coming, just a little more!"

The image grows larger in her vision, and her body begins to transform as her distant memories take over her perceptions. Finally, the arrival rushes up to her. The space around her alters with a melding of light and color, of substance, and of strange definition. In a moment, her vision clears, and she can see her new surroundings.

She is standing on a street. It is pitted and aged. She blinks her eyes several times trying to focus. There are buildings around her. They appear dilapidated and worn with age, covered by vegetation.

"That was weird," she mumbles softly. "But now, where in all the nether-space am I?"

She looks around at the sights. Everything seems so…big. She looks down at the ground in front of her, which seems abnormally near. Her attention is quickly drawn to her body. She was clothed in pale blue leggings and a patterned dress. She was a young girl.

"Huh?" she blurts unexpectedly.

She pats her hands on her body, checking to see if it was real. It felt solid to her, as far as she could tell. She turned to examine herself from all sides. She brought her hands up to her face, feeling around her temples where she found the tiny nubs of prepubescent horns.

"I'm a child! Why? Where am I? This place…it looks so old. But I thought…"

She studies some of the nearby buildings. The structures are decayed and broken, but still show a resemblance to civic buildings. It begins to dawn on her.

"Cu'Nar's pity, this is Ruuki uy'Daan!" she exclaims. "I mean, yeah, but…I mean…huh?"

Kaliya cannot help but find herself walking along the broken roadway. The buildings near her looked familiar, but the overgrowth and erosion made them look alien.

"Welcome to your nightmare, girl," she muses tenderly. "You might ask why you came back here, but I think it's obvious. This is where it all began."

She moved in closer to examine a few buildings. Many of them were in ruins, possibly destroyed by fire or explosion. Some distance away, she could see the remnants of a tall skyscraper, toppled over and crushing other structures underneath, and blocking a section of the street.

"This isn't right! This isn't how I remember it, not even during the attack. Not even in my nightmares. Why would I dream of it looking like this?"

She starts to run down the street, turning around a corner and continuing to another intersection, only to find more sights mimicking those she saw before.

"This vegetation looks well-established, like it's been here a long time. Why would I choose to see it like this? This stuff simply looks wild."

She continues along, following once-familiar paths through streets and alleys until she comes to one with a dead-end. In front of her stands a wall. Though worn, it still seems sturdy, where its crown reached well over her head.

A driving sensation tells her she wants to follow this course, not to go around another way. She curiously studies the wall and unwittingly recalls a lost memory.

She compulsively steps up to it, turns and begins pacing off a measured distance, then turns to examine it again. She pauses a moment to collect herself, studying the distance and her angle to the top. She launches forward making a series of bounds, followed by a small leap to gather her energy, and then coiling down on her haunches to release it in a powerful vault. As she springs upward, she hooks her hands on the crown to assist, and makes a smooth somersault over the top. She comes back down on the other side, firmly landing on her hoofed feet and throwing her arms up in a classic gymnastic exhibition.

She turns over her shoulder to look back at the obstacle with a contented smile forming across her face, until another lost memory comes forward and she catches herself in the moment.

"That wall… I remember it. What am I doing, reliving an old experience?"

Her instincts draw upon her again. She leaves the alley and starts running along the street, but stops short when she hears voices coming from around the next corner. They bore a distinctive tone.

"Orcs… I'm in no position to fight, and I don't think I'm supposed to right now."

She ducks for cover behind a building and under some rubble, watching and waiting for the sounds to pass.

"Which brings to mind another thing…why am I imagining orcs to be patrolling the streets? Girl, you've got some weird dreams going on here. Let's just hope you don't start talking to yourself," she giggles softly.

A group of four orcs walk by, passing the alley without taking notice of the small child huddling behind a pile of debris. Kaliya pauses a bit longer before cautiously moving out from the rubble and back into the street. She observes the passage of the orcish patrol as it turns around another corner and out of sight.

"Good, but where am I going with all this? I can barely recognize the place."

She starts running again, first along one street, then turning and sprinting up another one, winding her way through the remains of the city. She passes along rows of buildings, some of which have collapsed either from decay or damage. She was moving into a residential district, finally arriving at an intersection with a cross street. On the opposite side was a large manor house. She rushes up to it.

"Cu'Nar's pity, look at that!"

Foliage and vines covered the house. It was dirty and dilapidated. The double-door entrance looked like it had been kicked in at one time, and the pieces were simply leaning against the frame. She steps forward to peek inside through the slit of the opening. The interior appeared dusty and cluttered with debris. She squeezed through the space between the two doors and stepped inside.

"This place is a wreck!" she mutters softly. "It looks like it's been ransacked, and then some. This is not how I remember it, this house, the city, everything. It's like a nightmare image of my old home. Could this be some kind of horn-twisting interpretation caused by the shock and horror from the attack?"

She works her way into a large gathering room, her thoughts becoming entangled in the disjointed visions of her former home. Broken bits of furniture are piled up against the walls. Shards of pottery and splinters of wood are scattered across the floor. The air appears dusty as it wafts around and becomes highlighted within rays of sunlight passing through the cracked windows.

She sees a table in one corner, the only thing still intact, illuminated under a broad ray of light coming in from a nearby window. She walks up to it. On the surface, she sees several small statuettes and some portraits. The table and its contents are neatly arranged and seem eerily out-of-place in the ramshackle array of debris cluttering the rest of the room. She picks up one of the figurines. It looks like a model of a dancer, crudely shaped as if created by a child's hand. One arm was broken off and the base was chipped.

"I know this…" she whispers to herself. "I was in school…in my art class. Mother really liked this one."

She felt a sudden chill run through her. She sets the figure back down and glances over the other objects on the table, grabbing one of the portraits and brushing away a layer of dust from its surface. The image was of a young girl in a party dress, a birthday.

"That's me!" she cries, now with her voice escalating. "What is this, some sort of eerie shrine of my life's history?"

Her elevated voice rang out through the empty room. A moment later, a thud is heard from the hallway behind her, followed by the sound of heavy hoofed footsteps.

Kaliya's motions come to a halt, and her gaze rises up as a fearful stare at the wall ahead of her. She listens to the approaching sounds, still holding the portrait in her hands. The footsteps stop, seemingly across the room from her. She slowly places the portrait back on the table and struggles to turn her body around, bringing her gaze upon the form of a large, disfigured hulk standing in the hallway on the other side of the room.

Her breath seems to catch in her throat as her voice fails her. Her feet felt like they were glued to the floor, her muscles were petrified and unresponsive. In this brief instant she knows, finally to realize, this is what drew her to this place. This was her goal.

"Mother?" she whispers impulsively.

The simple uttering of that word broke her unyielding form, allowing her to move again. She slowly stepped in closer to examine the figure in greater detail.

The creature standing before her was huge and unsightly. It had been grotesquely altered in disproportionate manners among its arms and legs. The skin was dingy and mottled, and covered with grime. Its clothing was little more than tattered rags.

Kaliya looked even closer, around its neck, where she saw a pendant, partially encrusted with filth, but still holding the mark of her family crest.

"Mother!" she shouts apprehensively. "Mother, it's me! Kali, do you remember?"

The creature leaned out of the archway to take a clearer look at the small child standing in the room. It began making groaning noises, as if trying to remember how to speak after a long absence of its voice.

"Kali..." it mutters hoarsely, slow and deep, but distinctly feminine. "Kali...daughter?"

"Yes, it's me, Mother! I know you must remember. You must! Try, mother! I know you're inside there somewhere."

"Daughter...yes...Kali, daughter...here?"

"Yes, Mother, do you remember me? I needed to speak with you. It's been so long, and I missed you so much," she emits with a soft tremor.

"Kali... Yes. Me remember... Long time, Kali not here. Where Kali go?"

"We were going to the Naarg uy'Sodrad, remember? The orcs

were attacking, and we were all trying to get to the ship. We were running. But then something horrible happened."

"Run… Yes, me remember run. Orcs come, hurt people, people run. Kali run. Me run. Me hurt. Kali run more. Kali not hurt?"

"No, Mother, I'm fine, I got away. I made it to the ship safely, but then we had more trouble. Our ship was sabotaged, and we crashed on another world. But why am I standing here explaining this?" she ponders.

"Orcs hurt ship?"

"No, the orcs couldn't hurt the ship, it's too strong for them, but we had someone else inside. They were new and surprised us…and I still don't understand how this topic relates…"

"New people hurt ship?"

"Yes, they're called Flame Elves. They come from another world, the one we crashed on, and now we're fighting for our lives."

"People fight?" she moans. "More fight…more hurt."

"Yes, Mother. I'm sorry to tell you this, but the ship was, well, badly damaged this time. It won't fly again. There's nothing else for us now. Sargeras found us and now he's trying to finish us."

"Sarg-us! Sarg-us find people? Here? Oh no… Now Sarg-us hurt people. Me sad."

"Well, maybe not completely," Kaliya encourages. "It might not be the end. We met someone new…friends! We're hoping they can help us. They're led by a very powerful being, and he's offering to help us fight Sargeras."

"Friend people help? Good. Help fight Sarg-us. Stop hurt more people."

Kaliya pauses to catch her breath, but now she feels a wave of emotion taking over.

"Mother, I'm sorry," she sobs. "I'm sorry I left you. I was frightened, very frightened. We were running, and then you were hit by that orcish magic. Everything was exploding around us, people were screaming…"

"Kali, daughter… Kali run. Kali not hurt. Kali good daughter."

"No, Mother, I haven't been a good daughter. I've been very

bad, and I'm sorry for that too. I was angry, I was frustrated, I was scared, and I was also very hard on Father. It's been three and a half centuries, Mother, and I haven't spoken to him since."

"Kali not talk Father? Why?"

"I was angry...you know me, but this time it went too far."

"Not good. Kali go talk Father. Say Father, Kali sorry."

"I will, Mother, I promise. Just as soon as I get back, I'll go talk to him."

"Where Father?" she looks around lazily.

"Mother, like I said, we're on another world. Me, Father, and Kailen too. Do you remember Kailen?"

"Kailen... Yes! Kailen, me remember. Kailen not hurt?"

"He's fine. He's a High Commander now. And I'm still wondering why I'm explaining all of this," she puzzles. "What purpose does it serve here?"

"Kailen good," the woman muses pleasantly. "Me happy."

The brutish form of Kaliya's mother begins to shift, shambling forward out of the hallway entrance and across the room to the table, its apparent focus leaving Kaliya and drifting into the distance. Kaliya steps out of the way for the large body to pass by. She notices the disfigured shape and uneven posture.

"Mother, are you alright?" she asks unconsciously.

Her mother stops to look at the statues and portraits sitting on the table, picking up one of the portraits to study it. Kaliya moves alongside to examine the image. It shows her brother, Kailen, as a young officer, with Kaliya as a small child standing next to him, and her mother standing on the other side. Kaliya looks up at her mother to see a tear rolling down her cheek. She watches her, perplexed by the odd conversation and the peculiar behavior, as if her mother seems lost in her own memories, not even fully realizing her surroundings.

"Mother, answer me, are you alright?" she asks again softly.

"Me remember old time," she responds. "Long time, Kali not here, Kailen not here, Father not here."

"You're all alone. Mother, I don't know what to say."

"Me alone, yes. Many people alone...hurt-people."

"Huh? What do you mean by many people…and hurt-people?"

"Orcs come, people run. Orcs hurt people. Kali remember. Kali go ship, ship go. Hurt-people stay. Orcs make more hurt."

"Mother, I'm confused. I thought I understood why I came here, but now I don't know what you're saying. You're saying there are other people here?"

"Yes, Kali, more people. We hide. Orcs come, we hide. Orcs come more, we hide more."

"Who? Who are these other people? Here in the city?"

"Yes, hurt-people. Kali look, me hurt…"

The woman angles to peer over her shoulder at her back where the mutation seemed to erupt out of her body. Kaliya follows her motion, grimacing at the sight of it and further reflecting on the old memory of what happened that day.

"I remember that. It was awful, and I was so young at the time."

"Yes, not good, Kali see."

"You're telling me? Cu'Nar's pity, Mother, I was traumatized for centuries after that. And then to see all those other people chasing the rest of us. What did those horrible orcs do to create all this?"

"Orcs make magic, hurt people, make more hurt. People run, yell, make big scare."

"Huh?!" she screeches. "Wait a minute! What do you mean to yell and make a big scare?"

"Kali remember…" the woman turns away from the portrait to explain. "Orcs come, make hurt, yes?"

"Yes, this much I remember, and then you went down."

"Yes. What Kali remember…people run, people yell, big scare, all people, yes?"

"The panic, yes… It was crazy, as everyone was screaming and running in all directions trying to get away from the orcs. But then we had those mutants chasing us, which only made things worse."

"Yes. Orcs make this. Orcs hurt more, make people run, yell, make big scare, people run more."

Kaliya gazed at the woman in astonishment, such that she had to go searching for her voice again to respond.

"The panic was engineered? In all the nether-space!" she shrieks. "Are you telling me the orcs forced the people to get up and run around like that?"

"Yes, orcs bad. Now people hide."

"Wait! People hiding…where? And for that matter, why am I even asking the question?" she shakes her head perplexedly.

"People hide, big houses, little houses, all houses."

"How many?"

"Me not know."

"And the orcs? What are they doing now?"

"Orcs come, hurt more. Hurt bad. People hide. Me hide here."

"How often do they come? Cu'Nar's grace…" Kaliya yelps. "Why am I asking these questions? I feel like I'm in a debriefing session."

"Orcs come not all time. Long time, orcs not come…orcs come little…long time, orcs not come again."

"They only come sometimes, but not often? And they come to hurt you more? Well, isn't that just typical!" she huffs and crosses her arms. "Measure of Balance, my crinkled tail! This is yet another example of their criminal acts."

"Me think, orcs not many. Orcs go, not know where."

"I'll tell you where! They're using some kind of portal thing and arriving on Therinë to harass us."

"What thing? Where?"

"A portal…um, do you remember a conveyor? Like that. And Therinë is the name of the world we're on now."

"Conv-yor," she muddles. "Orcs have conv-yor?"

"Yeah, and between them and the Suuden-Aryku, we've been fighting hard for three and a half centuries."

"Suuden'kai…they come now?" she growls. "Not more Suuden'kai. And orcs fight people. People hurt more?"

"Not with orcs, not in our area. Mostly the Suuden-Aryku for us. We take a few hits here and there, but we lost of lot of people on this attack."

"Friend people help?"

"We just met them recently. They're new, but now they're helping. Oh! And they understand magic."

"Magic! Oh, this good. Kali learn?"

"I did a little. I actually learned how to make fire using magic. But I need to go to school to learn more."

"Kali go school, learn magic? Oh... Me want learn now. Me head not good. Me sad."

"But we lost a lot of our knowledge in this crash," Kaliya recalls. "All our science, our libraries...they were all here."

The woman had returned to her portrait, weaving left to right while partially in a dreamlike state as she listened. But then she turned to Kaliya again at her statement.

"Smart... Huh?" she ponders. "Kali say people not have...erm..."

"The holo-disks, Mother. They were all relocated to the libraries after a while as we felt we were safe from Sargeras. But then we had the attack, and they were left behind."

"Wait... Ship not...erm...people not have more on ship?"

"Oh, that," she throws her hands up. "Yeah, let me tell you about that one. There were saboteurs on the ship. We figure the Suuden-Aryku probably brought someone here unknown to us. They tampered with the computers, and this killed a lot of the backups on the ship."

"Ugh! Suuden'kai bad! Why they hurt ship? Old times, not hurt ship."

"I know. We figure they're moving to finish things. But without those old records, we can't rebuild anything to fight back now. All we still have are the medical files."

"Kali say, friend people help?"

"Yes, but it's not the same as our science. They think they can help. Still, I wish we had our old science to help too. And of course, here I am, once again asking why I'm going through this long interview. How does any of this relate to solving my childhood trauma and getting me through this crazy ritual thing?"

Kaliya sets her hands on her hips as she pauses to scan the room. It seemed strangely quiet except for the two of them in their conversation. The lull was broken only by the creaking of the floorboards under her mother as she continued to rock sideways while studying the portrait.

"So, um…" Kaliya wonders cordially. "What do you do all day around here?"

"Me hide."

"Yeah, but do you just sit around all day?"

"No go out. Maybe orcs come."

"Yeah, I suppose."

"What Kali do?"

"Me? Oh, I'm just pulling my horns out trying to figure out why I'm having this imaginary conversation with my mother about things going on back home on Ruuki uy'Daan. But I don't dare tell anyone. Oh no! They'll lock me away for sure if they hear this one!" she giggles compulsively.

Her mother is silent for a moment, still rocking sideways on her feet as she continues to study the portrait. But then she comes to an abrupt halt and her posture stiffens. Her eyes refocus ahead of her, and she frowns softly, as if beginning to realize something she previously took for granted as fantasy. She cautiously rolls her eyes to the side, as if unsure what she might find there.

She gasps suddenly as she unexpectedly jerks around to face the young figure standing next to her, dropping the portrait on the ground, and falling back a step in the process. The motion startles Kaliya, and she reflexively jumps back, letting out a short yip.

"What?! Mother, what happened?"

"Kali?!" she yelps. "Kali…here?"

"Huh?"

"Kali go ship. Ship go. Ship hurt. Kali come here. How Kali come here?"

"Um…" she emits uncertainly as she glances around the room. "Well, I think I was moving somehow. I saw a lot of weird stuff along the way. You know, flashing lights, strange shapes. It reminded me of the old school lessons of travelling through nether-space," she titters.

Her mother gingerly reaches out a hand at the image of the

young girl. Kaliya is hesitant to allow the contact, but holds fast. Her mother's hand gently taps on the girl's shoulder. She brings over the other hand to touch Kaliya's other shoulder, and slowly traces around the girl's head and face.

"Kali go new place? Now Kali come back here?"

"Mother, I wish I knew half of what was happening right now. First, I don't know why I look like this," she briefly examines herself. "I'm grown up now, not a little girl. And second, I don't understand why the city looks like this outside," she points at a window.

The elder woman glances out the nearby window.

"Plants come back. Long time, plants come back."

"The jungle… Well, all right, I suppose that makes sense, but how and why would I imagine this in the first place? My last memories of this place are when we were running through the streets, and everything was burning. Now it looks like a city lost to the ages."

"Kali not come back? Where Kali now?"

"Mother, once again, we crashed on another world. I'm currently sitting in a chair, although I actually have no idea where that chair came from either, but I'm in a room and I thought I was supposed to be dreaming something. But this is one nether-wild dream."

"Dream…" she whispers.

The woman pulls herself upright and glances around the room, then again at the young girl standing in front of her.

"Dream?" her mother recites anxiously. "Kali say dream? Kali sleep?"

She again reaches out to touch the girl just to reconfirm the shape was solid.

"Kali here…" she mumbles. "Kali here! Kali not more bad head think!"

"Mother, you're losing me. What are you talking about?"

"Kali here!" she repeats as she starts laughing hysterically and jumping in excitement.

"Mother?" Kaliya intones warily.

The woman now becomes animated, hopping about in a dimwitted prance around the room. The pounding of her hoofed feet reverberates through the floor and walls, shaking away years of accumulated dust.

"Kali walk! Kali walk! Long time, Kali walk. Me remember!"

"Mother…" Kaliya whimpers as she looks around the room. "It's probably not such a good idea to do that in here. This house doesn't look very stable. What are you talking about?"

"Wait, me think," her mother orders. "Me head not good. Kali wait, me think."

"I don't understand. What do you mean with all that, um, the bad head think thing?"

"Kali, me head not good. Orcs hurt people, now head not good."

"All right, I get that part. But why are you acting so funny now?"

"Me think bad. Me see not here," she grumbles briefly trying to form her words. "Me alone, see not here, see Kali, see Kailen, see Father, not here."

"Oh! Right, I think I understand…but once again, I have no idea why I'm dreaming this. You say you're seeing things that aren't real, maybe because you're all alone and your head is all mixed up, right? Isolation sickness?"

"Yes. Good. Now me see Kali. Me feel Kali. Kali here! Not more bad head think."

"Uh huh, and here is where you're making me worried. What are you talking about?"

"Kali walk! Kali…Kali not remember?" she intones curiously. "Kali, little Kali… Little Kali sleep, little Kali walk…" she pauses briefly, only to smack her hand against her temple. "Argh, Kali not know!" she grumbles more intently and stomps a foot. "Wait, me think," she rests again. "Father! Yes, Kali talk Father. Father tell Kali. Little Kali not know."

"Yeah, this will be a fun story to tell him about," she muses ironically.

"How Kali look? Kali not little now?"

"Me? Yeah, I'm full grown now. Don't ask me why I look this way here, I'm still trying to figure out that last part."

"Kali pretty?"

"Pretty?" Kaliya giggles. "Well, I never really looked at myself like that. Things back home aren't good, and I don't dress up to go out much. And there aren't any men around my age to say something."

"Kali not have man-friend?" she frowns.

"Mother, there's not that many of us anymore. Most have already paired up, and it's not looking good that I'll ever have someone for myself. Not with what's left of our people."

"Me sorry. Kali say friend people help…help fight Sarg-us!"

"Yes, and so far, we had one good victory. I don't know if we can do it again, but we're in a bad place without our technology. Even without the Suuden-Aryku attacking us, we can't rebuild anything without all our libraries. This was always one of my biggest problems, even before all this. I was so proud of who we were as a people. We had such a nice city here. And now with the crash destroying everything…"

"People hurt ship. Ship have no more. Yes, me remember. People here smart. Me remember, Father make…"

Her voice comes to an abrupt halt and her eyes roll off to the side. She stands there motionless, hunched slightly from her disproportionate posture.

"Mother?" Kaliya inquires. "Now what?"

"Me think…Kali wait. Me try think."

"Don't hurt yourself…" she smirks, trying to display an obvious grin.

"Kali laugh me? Ha ha… Kali not good, laugh mother."

"I'm only joking, Mother."

"Yes, me remember, Kali like laugh. Long time… Little Kali…" her voice trails off in deep thought.

Her mother begins shifting around, examining the room, passing a glance at the hallway entrance, then to the table, and finally the portrait on the floor.

"…Dream…walk," she finishes. "Kali, pick up," she orders, pointing at the portrait on the floor.

"Sure…" she responds, bending down to pick up the object. "Here…"

Kaliya offers the portrait while holding it in both hands, but her mother does not take it immediately. Instead, the woman bends down to examine it closely.

"Yes..." she mutters distantly. "Kali hold it..."

"I am holding it. Do you want it?"

"No, me say Kali hold it. Kali look, Kali hold it."

"Um, yeah, so is this unusual?"

"Put in hand here..." she points to Kaliya's left hand.

Kaliya shifts the object to her left hand and continues to hold it out to her mother.

"Now, put in hand here," she points at her right hand.

Kaliya is unsure of the purpose of this new twist in her bizarre dream, but complies.

"Yes!" the woman laughs heartily. "Now, put here..." she points at the table. "And pick up new."

"Why do I feel like a laboratory specimen?" Kaliya muses uneasily.

She puts down the first picture and picks up another one from the table. The woman now examines this latest example.

"Kali, walk here..." she directs to a location across the room.

Kaliya and her mother both stroll several paces away from the table. The woman carefully studies the girl for her performance, almost as if she were in an audition.

"Good," she nods. "Now go back."

"Mother, can you explain to me what you're doing?"

Kaliya turns and strolls back to the table, where her mother points to return the picture.

"Kali make good, Kali hold this..." she points at the picture. "Kali dream, Kali walk, Kali hold things!" she begins clapping her hands. "Me remember! Me make good head think!" she bellows and begins prancing around again, and once more laughing wildly.

Kaliya is stunned by the strange behavior, and once again taking note of the dust and loud echoes crashing through the room.

"And I thought I was going to get locked away..." she proclaims softly as she examines her mother. "Um, Mother, I think we covered this once already...the house?"

"Kali!" her mother declares imperatively as she comes to a rest. "Kali say people not smart. Ship hurt, people not smart. Yes?"

"Yes, when we crashed…"

"Kali say Sarg-us come, Suuden'kai fight people?"

"Yes, I…"

"Kali say friend people help? Kali people, friend people…erm…" she grumbles and slaps her head again. "…Want help with smart things."

"Well, I…"

"Kali wait. Wait here! Kali not go, Kali wait!"

"Sure…" she nods hesitantly. "Like I have someplace to go right now…or would even know how to get there."

The lumbering hulk of Kaliya's mother ambles quickly across the room and through the hallway, disappearing into a room at the far end. She hears the crashing of furniture and breaking of glass. Another loud crash issues forth followed by the sound of something heavy falling over. The woman then comes plodding out of the doorway and back over to Kaliya.

"Take!" she emits firmly.

She hands over a rectangular hard-shell case. A dusty window on top reveals a transparent circular object inside with a small hole in its center. She places it firmly in Kaliya's hands.

"Kali take. Go talk Father!" she commands.

Kaliya stares at the unimaginable sight resting in her hands.

"This isn't that thing he was making, is it?"

"Yes, Father make. Now, Kali take, go help people."

"In all the nether-space, now there's a twist," she yelps. "The bane of my existence is going to be the salvation of our people. Cu'Nar give me strength. But this is a dream, isn't it?" she grimaces at the bewildering notion. "I can't carry physical objects outside of a dream, can I? I'm in a dark room…a dark and empty room, dreaming."

"No, Kali… Not dream. Kali sleep, Kali walk! Little Kali walk, me not tell. Me scared hurt Kali."

"Cu'Nar's pity!" she wheezes. "You know something, but you didn't tell me because you were afraid you might hurt me somehow?

Oh great! Yeah, Father will probably lose what's left of his horns after this one. So, how do I use it?"

"Me head not good. Me try tell. Kali pull. Kali think, where Kali sleep. Kali pull back."

"Motion…movement… Oh dear…" she gasps as she begins to recall her earlier journey to this place. "Now I know what it was. I actually was travelling. I saw it all, nether-space, the local galaxy… from the outside! Great cu'Nar, I was travelling through nether-space to come here."

"Kali, pull home now. Go talk Father. Ask Father. Father tell Kali more."

Kaliya looks once more at the object in her hand and draws it up to her body to secure it tightly. She looks up again at the unfortunate hulk of her mother and throws herself at the figure, wrapping her free arm around her mother's body for a generous hug.

"Mother, I love you! Before I go, I want you to know this. I came all this way to tell you I love you! Although, in all honesty, I thought it was a dream, but this is much better!"

"Me love Kali," she bends down to give a hug. "Now, Kali go. Say Kailen me love. Say Father me love. Say Father, me not forget!"

Kaliya pulls herself away and steps back.

"I'll tell them, don't worry. I'll tell them everything I heard here…although they'll probably lock me away in a small, padded room afterwards," she chuckles uncertainly.

Kaliya closes her eyes and grips the box tightly in her small hands. She struggles to collect her thoughts, recalling the room, the chair, and her body.

"The chamber was supposed to be enchanted," she mutters to herself. "Allowing the mind to bring out its perceptions physically. But if I'm not actually dreaming, what am I doing?"

She reflects on Thaelyn's last words to her before the ritual.

"Powerful mind, indeed!" she muses. "Profound experience? Yeah, wait till he hears this one. If he thought I was trouble before…"

She recounts what was said to her during the magic lesson.

"The riddle of metaphysics: Nothing unknown exists; it only exists after it is known. To Know a thing, the intellectual perception of its existence. Cu'Nar help us, what am I creating here. This goes beyond even their magic!"

She recalled how she was able to focus her mind to create fire on that stick. She envisioned what she wanted, and the space around her changed to follow her will. She reflected on Thaelyn's strange technology that seemed to produce an effect out of almost nothingness.

"Nothingness…" she mumbles. "That chair. I made it out of nothingness…inside that room. I remember now, I was thinking of it so strongly, I literally willed it to exist. Mother, can you even imagine such a thing, to create something just by thinking of it?"

As she gazes into her mother's eyes one more time, her mind unexpectedly diverges as she connects the meaning, and one final old memory returns to her.

"In this space I have will, and my will can alter this space."

The meaning finally becomes clear. It was a memory from another dream, spoken in a loving voice. She looks up at her mother.

"That was you!"

Her mother offers a gentle smile as the words barely registered on her restricted memories.

"Mother," she emits determinedly. "I'll learn what this is, and I'll come back one day. You wait for me…please!"

"Me wait, Kali."

Kaliya begins to concentrate her thoughts. She once again imagines the sensation of travelling, of folding space much like she did the first time. She placed the image in her mind of where her body was sleeping, using this as an anchor, and directed herself at moving towards it…and her form begins to blur.

In the lost memory of an old manor house on Ruuki uy'Daan, one that once stood as a home and a symbol of life and love, the image of a small child turns to mist and fades away.

Kaliya's mother looks around the room. It is empty again. She hangs her head low and slowly turns back down the hall.

"Kali good daughter," she mumbles. "Kali remember. Kali come back. Not wait long time, come back more. Me wait."

◆

"Well, Adept," Master Sagrid teases. "That's another ten gold you owe me. When will you learn how to guess these things right?"

"All right," Adept Howald replies. "But it's only because she's from another world and a different race. That makes it hard to guess how long she might take. After all, she looked more like the warrior type to me at first, so I figured it would take less time."

"I've heard tell that her race is actually very highly developed, much more than we are! I can't help but to wonder what marvels they must've achieved in their day."

"All I know right now is she's achieved four hours on the clock so far in the chamber."

"I'm getting a bit hungry. Adept, do you think you could run out to the kitchen and pick up a few of those muffins I saw earlier? This may take a while longer yet!"

"Certainly! Do you like the apple or the blueberry best?"

"Oh, those blueberry ones are so good, although they never last very long. But if you happen to see any..."

"Of course, right away."

The Adept gets up from the table and begins moving across to the door. As he reaches for the handle, a sound is heard from across the room...the sound of a latch turning.

"Adept, wait... She's out! Go help her while I get her robe from the closet."

"Yes, Master!"

The Adept rushes over to aid Kaliya as she stumbles through the door of the ritual chamber. Her face appears pale, and she seems groggy. She falls back against the wall with her legs barely stiff enough to hold her up.

"Easy does it..." the Adept advises. "You look like you had quite a run in there."

"Is this the real world again?" she mumbles incoherently.

"Yes, it is. But you don't seem to be in very good sorts for it. Maybe you should sit down. Here, give me your hand and I'll…"

The Adept reaches out to take Kaliya's hand, only to see some kind of object inside.

"What in the… Master!" he shouts. "She's got an artifact!"

Master Sagrid rushes over while carrying the robe over his arm.

"What do you mean an artifact? How is that possible?"

"Look here, in her hand."

"Did she carry anything into the chamber?"

"No, Master, I checked as she made her way to it. She was completely empty."

"Kaliya," Master Sagrid asks. "Did you find this lying about inside the room?"

Kaliya looks down at the object in her hand, still shocked to see something physical clutched within her grip.

"Uh-uh…not from the room," she begins to feel giddy. "This is actually…well, you probably wouldn't believe me if I told you."

Now she starts giggling uncontrollably.

"In fact, I doubt anyone would believe this one!"

Kaliya is soon overtaken by an upwelling of emotions, where she descends into a full breakdown, and her giggling turns into a blend of weeping laughter. She covers her eyes as she continues trying to explain.

"It's from my Mother…on Ruuki uy'Daan…" she blurts between her outbursts. "She gave it to me… To give… To my Father…" she pauses as her feelings overwhelm her. "She knew something about me," she pants between statements. "But she didn't tell me because I was too little to understand."

"Knew what? Can you explain it to us?"

"I barely understand it myself! She wasn't able to explain it to me due to that orcish magic doing things to her. So, she said I should talk to my Father."

"Incredible! But is this to say you actually visited your old home and spoke to her in some way?"

"Yeah," she nods. "I think I travelled there somehow, but don't ask me how."

"This is amazing. Adept, we need His Lordship to see this, promptly."

"Yeah, he'll love this one," Kaliya relents. "He was saying he expected something big out of me. Well, here we go," she giggles some more.

The Adept jumps at the order and dashes out the door into the hall.

"Kaliya, are you well?" Master Sagrid asks. "You look very weary for your affair, and well…um…"

"I think I'll recover. I just need a moment to rest. After all…" she begins another round of giggling. "I just travelled halfway across Creation to visit my nightmares, and then bring back the one thing I never wanted to see again in my life!"

She now erupts with hysterical laughter and slides down to the floor covering her face. Master Sagrid tries to wrap the robe around her to keep her warm.

Adept Howald runs outside into the courtyard. Not sure where to go next, he looks for someone to give assistance.

"You there, Guard! Where did His Lordship go earlier?"

A watch guard standing at the fortress gate turns at the sound of the call.

"I saw him travel down to the portal gate there in the plaza. I think he may have returned back to the war camp."

The Adept runs down the lane to the portal. He checks the addressing index to make sure it's pointing to the right destination, and then jumps hurriedly through the gate.

Thaelyn and General Gabarleine were in conference again in the tactical office, along with Relissa and Marelle who had returned recently from their classes.

Adept Howald makes an abrupt appearance through the portal and stumbles off the platform base, catching himself before colliding with a passing soldier. He scans the surroundings to locate the most likely building to serve as the tactical office, and sees Captain

Hagmaert sitting outside one such candidate. He runs over to check his guess.

"Captain," he shouts, trying to catch his breath. "Is His Lordship inside?"

"Yes, he is. Is there a problem, Adept?"

The Adept nods his head as he steps around to the door.

"My Lord!" he calls into the room. "Your presence is urgently needed in the ritual chamber."

"What is it, Adept?" Thaelyn responds calmly. "Is our new applicant ready?"

"My Lord, you're not going to believe this! She came out of the chamber carrying an artifact!"

"A what?! An artifact, you say? Where did she get it?"

"She claims it came from her mother in her vision."

"Such a thing is not possible, not with any mortal creature I have ever encountered. The chamber may permit visions to seem virtual, but they cannot pass through to the outside."

Thaelyn turns to follow behind the Adept.

"My Lord," Relissa inquires in response to the heightened level of tension. "What's happening? I'm only getting a wee bit of this. Is this something about Kaliya? Is she alright?"

"Our tall blue friend may have just done the impossible," he calls back as he proceeds across to the portal.

"Aye," Relissa mumbles. "She always was good at getting her foot caught in the wrong craw."

As Thaelyn and the Adept emerge through the gate, Aerlie senses her husband's arrival. She was in the temple at the time giving a service. Her telepathic link with him made a fresh connection once he reentered the local space.

"*Thaelyn,*" she communes in her mind. "*I sense your feelings. Is there something amiss?*"

"*I cannot be sure what it is, but I need to investigate something. I will share it with you after I learn of it myself.*"

"*Very well, I will wait. I hope it is not too unpleasant.*"

Thaelyn and Adept Howald charged back up to the guildhall

and across the courtyard, hastily marching through the halls and into the ritual room.

"Master Sagrid, what is going on here?" he demands. "The Adept mentioned something about an artifact."

"Here, my Lord," he asserts. "See for yourself. She says she received this from a vision of her mother."

Thaelyn kneels next to Kaliya and looks down at the strange rectangular box in her hand. By this time, she had managed to bring herself back under control.

"Kaliya, what is this?" he asks.

"You're seriously not going to believe this," she responds softly. "You'll probably lock me away for the rest of my years…and centuries… and maybe even a few millennia."

"All right, gently now, one thing at a time…"

"My Lord," the Master interjects. "This young lady is in a rather sensitive emotional condition. When she first came out, she experienced a breakdown where she couldn't decide whether to laugh or cry."

"I see, but do we have an explanation for this, and how might it reflect on our success for the ritual?"

"Your Lordship," Kaliya emits delicately. "Before I go into hysterics again, maybe I could try explaining what happened."

"Absolutely, if you desire… I do not wish to pry into anything personal, but if it brought you into such a condition as this, and further with an artifact, I would surely like to hear your story."

"All right, try this out for your Celestial ears. I went inside and made a chair for myself to sit in."

"A chair, very well, I suppose that is not too outlandish, as the chamber is enchanted to allow the mind some flexibility to create things. Although I will also temper myself as these are more like apparitions, not necessarily physical objects to recline into."

"Maybe, and this was just like those we have in the Naarg uy'Sodrad rec center. Of course, this was after I apparently created a light shining down on me so I could see something."

"Um, well, hmm... That would be a rather interesting sequence. And then what?"

"I apparently sat down and fell asleep. Then I got up, turned around, and I looked at myself sitting in the chair and figured: All right, so now I must be in my dream thing."

"Powers behold," he winces. "You were able to actually see your own body?"

"This sounds much more like an out-of-body experience," Master Sagrid muses.

"Indeed."

"Yeah," Kaliya accedes. "And I looked very comfortable in it. So, then I start asking myself what to do next. I wanted to find my inner pain and resolve it, but where do I go for it? Well, it has to be back on Ruuki uy'Daan. But I don't see anything that looks like a vision of it, so I figure I need to travel there somehow. Then I see these little flickering things floating by, and I get the idea of movement. Here is where I come back to that nether-wild riddle of metaphysics. The mind defines Reality. Next thing I know, I'm putting my attention into moving through space."

"Moving through space. As if to say, folding space."

"I briefly recall a flash of departing the room, then the city, and then the world around us. Then I see this rainbow soup buzzing past me, and next is a wall of some kind, and after that is a lot of stuff like they teach us for travel through nether-space."

"Indeed!" he croons.

"I could see things out there, like big bubbles of some kind."

"Powers behold..." he whispers. "You were able to perceive of whole universes, but from the outside."

"Next, I'm diving down into one, passing through another wall, and now with a barrage of suns and galaxies zipping by, finally to spiral down on one in particular and bam, here I am on a ruined street, overgrown with three and a half centuries of jungle encroachment, and with an occasional orcish patrol walking by."

Thaelyn and the others gaped at her lengthy account. They all glared at each other as Kaliya continued.

"I was in the form of a young girl, like I was last time I was there."

"You altered your form, as well?" Master Sagrid asks.

"I would imagine, at this point," Thaelyn considers. "If she is somehow projecting her consciousness over there, shape does not matter as much, as she may be attempting to relive an old memory."

"It was weird, anyway you look at it," Kaliya sighs. "So, I find myself running through the streets, trying to work my way up to our old house, which was nearly falling down by now. There, I find the place was a shamble, probably due to being ransacked by orcs, and who knows what else happened to the place. There's a lone table in a corner with some of my old art class sculptures and some family photos, and I guess I made enough noise by this time to wake up my mother, who was hiding in a back room."

"Your mother?" Thaelyn wonders.

"Yeah, deformity and all, she's apparently still alive, if just barely. We had this delightful conversation, where neither of us had any idea who or what we were actually talking to. She, being alone, is probably suffering from isolation sickness by now, and having hallucinations."

"Yes, this much I can probably understand. And I am sure Aerlie would concur."

"Then there's me, thinking this is just a dream. So, we start talking about how the family is, and the ship crashing, and then Sargeras and his cronies attacking us. She was telling me about how she and some number of other survivors on Ruuki uy'Daan, all mutation victims of that orcish magic, were still alive and hiding around the city, and also where the orcs apparently came back from time to time to abuse them."

"Abuse! Is it not enough that those heathens once conducted their vile antics on these people that now they should return and abuse them, on top of things?"

"Yeah, that's just about what I had to say, and further it's not the first time. This is what caused at least half of the panic during the attack. Do you remember when I explained about that magic they used to mutate our people, turning them into monsters to chase the rest of us? Well, it wasn't turning them into monsters, it was to add further insult to injury by forcing them to get up and run around screaming at the top of their lungs to panic us even more."

"Great gods, those beasts!" the Master winces. "So, it was to incite even greater panic in an already troubled scenario!"

"Yeah. Beyond that, they're probably no different from my Mother, if only debilitated for the mutation."

"This is a disturbing situation," Thaelyn notes. "And made worse for the fact of being located on another world entirely, and out of our reach. What else happened, and how does this relate to this artifact of yours."

"Well, I'm standing there asking myself why I'm going through this nether-wild experience. The whole thing seemed more like a debriefing interview than a family reunion, or anything else I could otherwise describe."

"Yes! This much I can also understand."

"So, without anything else to do, I started up some idle small talk. Here is where we had our revelation. I think she finally made the connection that I wasn't a ghost. Of course, this doesn't help ME in any way, because the next thing she does is start jumping around the room cackling like a madman, and then ordering me to pick up this, walk over there with it, go back, exchange it with another one, and so on."

"Indeed!" he smiles. "This is a curious one. Was there some purpose to this?"

"Apparently, yes. She said I wasn't dreaming, but instead walking in some crazy fashion. Her speaking skills are also debilitated by this mutation. It would seem, when I was little, I must've been doing something, but I don't personally recall this, and she knew about it. And knowing her, as a psychologist in our old university, she was probably studying it, therefore, these instructions. She was testing me."

She takes a moment to catch her breath and gazes longingly at the box in her hand again.

"This is that thing I told you about, what my Father was making, that compendium of our science, our history, and everything else. I explained to her we lost virtually everything in this attack, as it was all in libraries and archives on Ruuki uy'Daan, and the saboteurs wiped most of it from the shipboard computers. This is her gift to us to help us rebuild, maybe also to fight Sargeras."

"Incredible!" Thaelyn mutters. "That woman must have a strong spirit to survive all this time and still maintain her resolve."

"This thing is a holo-disk," Kaliya continues. "It's a recording device, a holographic form of medium. If I'm right, it should contain all or most of whatever knowledge we carried with us up to that moment. I'm supposed to give this to my Father, which will need to be my next stop after this, although I truly have no idea how I'm going to approach him, or anyone else with a story like this."

"I fully understand. But Kaliya, if it means anything to you, there is a practice we sometimes speak of called astral travelling. Typically, this is to send the spirit to another dimensional realm outside our own. It also tends to behave in a dreamlike manner. But by your description, you did this in the material world, and furthermore, if you were able to transport a material object, this excels well beyond any reasonable definition I can imagine for a mortal creature. In fact, I would not expect to see a skill like this in anything outside of a Celestial being!"

"Wonderful, I didn't actually need to hear you say that just now. So, what does this mean for me?"

"I cannot say, and I think it might be premature to suggest something at this time without further analysis."

He leans back to consider the conversation for a moment.

"Very well," he muses. "So, how do you feel about your experience, overall?"

"Shocked, confused, and like the Master said, I had a breakdown where I couldn't stop laughing or crying, due probably to realizing, not only did I see my mother, but I learned about things I never knew existed. You talked about an extraordinary experience. Well, does this live up to your expectations?" she grins tenderly.

"Indeed, I think this is worthy of a mention or two," he smiles.

"I did what I wanted to do. I found her and told her I loved her, although I was expecting a dream version of her, not the real one. On top of that, learning of what's happening on Ruuki uy'Daan, answering a number of those old questions about the attack, and finally this piece of nether-bilge," she chuckles ironically. "Never would I have thought this thing, which brought me so much grief, could actually be our salvation."

"It would certainly offer a very strange twist of Fate. Then, I think we have nothing else ahead of us but to run the test again and find our result. I think I would also like to learn more about this gift of yours. You say you had this once as a child?"

"I suppose so, and this must be some gift. But if I had this as a child, I clearly forgot what it was, and this would certainly amount to a huge discovery...um..." her eyes lose their focus as she drifts off. "A Child...finding...a gift... Oh dear cu'Nar..."

A shudder suddenly flashes through her, and her eyes bulge as she reflects on her words. Thaelyn studies her as he senses a rapid shift in her emotional state.

"Kaliya," he urges. "What is it? I felt a flutter shoot out from your mind."

"The Child will find its Gift..." she reminisces tenuously. "Oh no, it can't be, not another one... And why me? Have I found another piece of the prophecy?"

"A prophecy? What do you mean?"

"We have a prophecy. It's those cu'Nar again. You remember what I said about them before, right?"

"Yes, so this is a part of their message?"

"This is the last one we got out of them, not long after we arrived on Therinë. We think it was a form of positive encouragement to hold on..." she turns to meet his eyes. "...until YOU arrived."

"Me!" he draws back unexpectedly. "Oh wonderful. Who is doing what to us on this occasion? Perhaps I should inquire on this now. What does it say?"

"Several parts have already come true, so I'm fairly sure it has to be you. It starts out like this. From a circle of light, he shall come, the Divine Justice, one divided by two. In his hands he carries the power of infernal destruction, and the power of blessed life. So far, this explains the first day of your arrival, and in that same sequence, as Haran once mentioned."

"Indeed, I may need to agree on this part, although the references seem to be using metaphors. Perhaps this is part of that interpretation element between the races."

"Maybe. Then it says evil will crumble under the weight of his majesty. I suppose you can interpret that any way you want, but ultimately, it seems to work that way with you," she smiles.

"Yes, I suppose this is also reasonable."

"Then we have this part. The child will find its gift. This is followed by the lost will be found, and the sundered will be restored, as vengeance arrives on silver wings."

"Most interesting... Do we have any interpretations to go along with these things?"

"None," she shakes her head solemnly. "It's a complete mystery to us, especially that last part."

"Very well, let us see here. We have a Child and its Gift. Yours would certainly qualify, especially if it represents something profound enough to incur a special mention."

"Maybe, but how do we use it?"

"I cannot say for sure right now, but maybe your Father might offer some ideas. Then we have the next part, the lost being found. The term seems to imply a plural form, so there may be multiple items involved here. For instance, could this disk be a part of it? Are there others, perhaps a set of them?"

"No, just this one as far as I can recall, unless we speak of all those libraries. But I hesitate to suggest if this could be something profound enough to mention in a prophecy."

"Possibly. Then perhaps this is for later. But this disk would certainly be a remarkable find, even at that. And then, something sundered being restored. This is the worst example of all for ambiguity. It seems the concepts are becoming more blurred as we progress. Sundered can imply anything that is damaged. It could be a city, a land, or even a world. It could also be something as small as an individual item in your hand. There is no true way to know what it entails unless you already have it in your sight.”

“And that final piece about the silver wings?”

“Again, with a metaphor, so we are referencing something playing a role of some kind, and it seems to portray a final solution, perhaps a form of comeuppance. But this would surely be ahead of us.”

“Yeah, then I guess we still have a long way to go.”

“If it involves the war, then I might suggest this as well. For now, we should get you back into the testing room so we can see what your final result is.”

“And I also need to take this to my father. He needs to see it. And I need him to explain to me what, in all the nether-space, is going on here.”

“Indeed! And if you would permit me, I would like to listen in.”

“Fine by me...”

“We will go as soon as you finish your testing. I will take you there myself to ensure your safe passage.”

Thaelyn gets back to his feet and helps Kaliya up to hers. Master Sagrid assists Kaliya more appropriately don her robe again, and then leads her back to the testing room. Thaelyn marches out into the main hall of the guild to wait.

As he paces around the hall, he begins to wonder what was on that disk to make it so important that her mother would have her bring it all the way back here. If it contained anything to help them rebuild, it must therefore be the missing portions of their technology they so cherished. But, as much as this might be useful to rebuild some semblance of civilization for them on Therinë, it could also be useful in the war effort against their combined enemies.

Nevertheless, he would have to wait and hope he could learn something about it from her father. After all, it was his property, and so it would be his decision to reveal it or not.

Some moments later, Kaliya returns with Master Sagrid. She was fully dressed again, and the two of them were approaching hurriedly from a corridor on the side of the hall.

“My Lord!” Master Sagrid shouts while appearing noticeably

flustered. "We have the results of her test. I am at a complete loss here!"

"Why? What happened this time?"

Master Sagrid gestures at the badge being worn on Kaliya's uniform, hanging by a stylish ribbon over her coat.

"Violet?!" Thaelyn roars. "She got violet? From redemption? Are you sure about this, Master Sagrid?"

"I ran the test twice, my Lord. The results were the same. It's extraordinary, a strong violet on both occasions…bold and deep!"

"Incredible! There was only one other time we ever got a violet, and I married the girl!"

"Cu'Nar help us…" Kaliya moans. "So, does this mean I need to marry you now?" she giggles softly.

The others shared a subtle laugh as Thaelyn shakes his head incredulously while trying to collect himself.

"Dear Child," Thaelyn admits. "You have just earned yourself the distinguished honor of becoming one of the very few beings I have ever met who actually brought surprise to me."

"Thaelyn!" Aerlie urgently communes again. *"What is going on up there? Are you alright? I just felt a tremendous shot from you."*

Thaelyn holds the conversation and turns towards the door. He raises a hand to his temple as an indication of his telepathic conversation.

"My dearest Aerlie, you are not going to believe this. You might want to come up here. I will explain on the way."

The Mage Master and Kaliya both wait as Thaelyn begins relaying the details of the test to Aerlie, while she rushes out of the temple and takes flight up to the guildhall courtyard, then rushes inside to meet them. As she arrives, she takes a moment to study Kaliya's badge.

"Unbelievable!" she emits, astonished at the sight. "You have done the impossible twice over, Child! And it might appear as though I have some competition now," she giggles.

"Yeah," Kaliya smiles shyly. "And I'm not even officially enrolled yet."

"Competition…" Thaelyn muses. "This reminds me of a conversation we shared before she got started."

"And what was that?" Aerlie asks.

"She mentioned some kind of inner voice delivering motivational sensations to do this at this time. Now we have this discovery, which seems to coincide with their cu'Nar and a prophecy they gave once. This makes it appear as though we have an element of Fate guiding us for the occasion."

"Oh no, not another one of those. Very well. But now, Thaelyn, what do you have planned next? This talent needs to be researched, even developed, if we can muster it."

"Yes," he nods. "Although, I would like to see her acclimate first, to settle into a routine before we send her through any strange new studies. We should also consider how to train something like this, as I have never seen such as this before…certainly not in a mortal-child."

"Perhaps we could find a private tutor. But it would have to be a Celestial, in this case. Do we know of anyone up in Sigil? What about Aelwyn?"

"She would be a good choice, if we could convince her to actually come down here," he smiles. "She can be rather stubborn, you know."

"Oh, I think she simply spends her time in that guild of hers as an excuse not to get out," she chuckles.

"Very well, but let us come to this after we settle ourselves a bit. I am sure we will have a fair number of requisite courses to condition and prepare her for such a thing as this. Her experience on this occasion was more likely accidental. I want to be sure we can contain it properly, if to go official with it."

"Yes, I think I would need to agree. But now what?"

"Now, she needs to make a visit with her father, at least as much to turn in this artifact, as to receive a more official explanation of what this is."

The group was arriving through the gateway into the war camp.

Thaelyn led them across to the tactical office where the General, Relissa, and Marelle were still in their meeting. On seeing the royal pair arriving at the door, the assembly all turned and offered their greetings.

"Jiggers, girl," Relissa moans. "You must've got your tail in a nasty tangle if it's got both of these peeps dragging you out."

"Relissa," Kaliya replies meekly. "You would've been impressed by just how tangled my tail got on this occasion. Take a look at this," she points at her badge.

Both Relissa and Marelle step in closer to see the test results on her badge.

"Criminy, girl, you got the violet? How the bloody hell did you manage that?"

"Don't ask me, Relissa, my horns are still recoiling from that ritual they put me through. I got green before this, and apparently, getting violet, for any reason, is supposed to be outside mortal values."

"Jiggers, and that just makes it worse."

"Oh, not quite…I can do one better. I also brought this back…" she pulls the box out of her pocket to show off to the room.

Relissa and Marelle both stare at the curious item in her hand.

"Brought back?" Marelle wonders. "From where?"

"From my house on Ruuki uy'Daan," she responds casually. "My mother gave it to me. It's supposed to go to my father."

"Uh huh…and did I hear it said they use some kind of drug or something during this ritual?"

"Yeah, and wow, was my head spinning…at least until I apparently projected my spirit, or whatever you might call it, outside my body into the room. Then I didn't feel anything. After that, I decided to take a little trip down memory lane, all the way back home to that wreck of a city we used to own."

Relissa and Marelle gape at each other as they glare at Kaliya for her assertion.

"And before you ask," Kaliya continues. "I don't know how I did it, but apparently, my mother tells me I did this as a girl, but she never told me for fear it could cause trouble."

"Aye it would!" Relissa yips. "Jiggers, I don't know if I want to be around you after this. That would scare the flippin' wiggles out of me."

"Meanwhile," Thaelyn asserts. "We need a rune to the Naarg uy'Sodrad. I would like to make this visit personally to escort her, and maybe to hear her father's explanation for this most unusual gift. The potential it holds is already swirling in my mind. This might actually give us access to that world, despite any space travel, or lack thereof."

"How do you mean?" Marelle asks.

"If she holds the potential to project her consciousness outside her body, and apparently to make it tangible enough to grasp and carry material objects, and further to reach such extraordinary lengths as another world and another universe, as she did on this occasion, this is a truly phenomenal skill. She could possibly carry an item to that location, perhaps to allow others to follow."

"Now there's a new way to travel," Kaliya winces. "Interplanetary exploration without the need for spacecraft..."

"And then we have this artifact of hers. She says this is that same item her father was creating at one time with the summary of their knowledge. If her mother believes it can help, it might contain more than just a few historical notes. It could also provide some of their technology, and if her people are permitting, we might be able to use this to resolve some portion of our other woes where Sargeras and the Suuden-Aryku are concerned."

"Thaelyn," Aerlie interjects. "I have the rune here. Perhaps we should go together? I am very curious to know who her father is, based at least in part on her speech difficulties," she smiles mischievously.

"You know," Kaliya admits. "I could just come right out and tell you."

"Oh no! I would find this a most delightful surprise."

"Your Lordship, has she ever been trouble for you in the past?"

"Yes! She has. And not just once..." he chuckles.

They step outside to find a mage, passing the rune to him, where he enchants it for the others to pass through.

Within a small gully, not far from the Naarg uy'Sodrad, and reasonably hidden from view of the larger overland scene, Thaelyn and his group flash into sight from their portal travel. Kaliya then leads them in the direction of the citadel's main entrance. In the distance, they can see the routine patrols of Daanen-Aryku guards surveying the area, as well as a team of cleverly disguised Order troops in colors resembling that of the Allegiance Guard of Rolsklinde.

"All seems well out here," Aerlie muses. "I don't sense anything coming over the horizon, so we must have picked a good day for a stroll."

"According to Kailen," Kaliya offers. "The attacks have lessened considerably since that first day. Now that we have a fighting force out here worth being afraid of, the Suuden-Aryku don't seem as eager to spend their people."

"And this is the Naarg uy'Sodrad," Thaelyn observes. "That ship you once mentioned."

"What's left of it…it's been refashioned into a citadel now, and just barely holding up after everything that's happened to us."

"Still, it is an impressive sight."

"A massive one, to say the least," Aerlie adds. "And that's just the portion I can actually see."

Thaelyn surveys the local terrain and the condition of the land while Aerlie tries to fathom the immense scale of the structure in front of them.

"It's the size of a small mountain," she surmises. "This would've taken a huge volume of materials and labor to build. And they just gave it over to you?"

"You mean, whoever built it?" Kaliya wonders. "Yeah, apparently so. All I can say is they must be rich beyond measure."

"And this large ditch," Thaelyn directs. "If you can call it that…"

"I would better describe it as a gouge the size of that river canyon," Aerlie notes.

"Indeed, but to imagine anything the size of this vessel carving such a feature as this…" he shakes his head. "Anyway, this is where you came in?"

"Yeah," Kaliya affirms. "And the blast from the spatial rupture we created on entry flattened almost everything in sight, and burned the rest. It's just barely recovering, even now."

They proceed through the entrance of the citadel and course their way through the corridors and hallways, taking a little tour along the way, until they arrive in what used to be the bridge. Kailen notices their arrival and steps up to greet them.

"Your Lordship, such an unexpected surprise! Welcome to the Naarg uy'Sodrad!"

Kailen turns next to Aerlie.

"I don't believe we had the opportunity to meet properly. You would be Lady Aerlie, I believe, correct?"

"I am," she smiles and bows her head.

"Then it is a special honor to meet you, but this is even more of a surprise to see the two of you making a visit. What's the special occasion?"

Thaelyn briefly gestures at Kaliya.

"Do you recall once how you said this young sister of yours would make trouble?"

"Uh oh…"

"Indeed, and as Relissa said earlier, she has managed to get her tail in a tangle on a rather impressive scale," he chuckles.

"Oh really! Yeah, I know about Relissa's manners. But, um…" he examines Kaliya and quickly takes note of her pallor. "Kaliya, you look a little pale. So, what sort of trouble is she causing this time?"

"No doubt such that it could turn this war on end for us," Thaelyn responds pleasantly. "We have a need to speak to her father. Is he available?"

"Father? He should be. He doesn't do much outside of the occasional Council meeting. Wow, Kaliya, after all this time, you're finally coming back to us?"

"She went through a considerable amount of soul-searching," Aerlie admits. "I helped her through some of it, but she also found several of her own answers along the way."

"That sounds great."

"But Kailen," Kaliya submits. "It's not simply about reuniting. I have something else on my mind, and I think only Father can answer it for me."

"Like what?"

"That's the problem. I don't know what it is, but he does."

"You lost me…"

"Join the club. But before you fall into that same hole I just crawled out of, let's go see him. Is he in his usual place?"

"Yeah, he spends most of his time there these days, just staring at the walls."

"Then let's go. We shouldn't waste any time on this."

Kailen offers a quick nod and begins leading them out of the room. They travelled along several corridors, turning corners into new ones where they passed conference rooms and executive lounge areas. He leads them down one more hallway, finally to arrive at a room at the end. He presses an announcement button on the wall before opening the door to step inside.

They enter a study room to find several bookcases lining the walls, mostly empty except for a few stacks of papers with handwritten notes and some hastily bound journals. Several tables were scattered around the room displaying small figurines and statuaries, most of which appeared to be of amateurish quality, resembling city buildings and monuments of a lost age. A set of plush chairs is arranged at one end of the room, positioned around a small casual table. One of the chairs had been turned to face the far wall.

"Father?" Kailen announces as they enter. "Excuse me for the disturbance, but you have visitors."

"Yes, Kailen? Who is it?" ushers a weary and forlorn voice from within the chair.

"It's His Lordship, Thaelyn, and the Lady Aerlie, both of whom are making a very pleasant visit, along with, um…Kaliya."

The aged male moans as he slowly rises up out of his chair to turn and face his callers. On the way, he takes hold of a long, gilded staff set with a glowing crystal on top. He moves around the chair and takes several stiff steps forward to meet the two guests.

"I have not had the pleasure to meet with you personally," he proclaims with his placidly rolling voice. "But Kailen has told me of the aid you have provided thus far, and I am very grateful for it. I am Master Velen of the Daanen-Aryku Council of Elders. To what do I owe the favor of this visit, Your Lord and Ladyship?"

"Master Velen?" Thaelyn mutters in surprise. "You are her father?"

"Well now," Aerlie smiles cutely. "Why doesn't that surprise me? And you too, my Dear."

"Well, I, um…actually, I suppose you are right," he chuckles softly. "After all, she had at least as much difficulty speaking that name as she did the word 'Father'."

"Yes," Velen responds. "And no doubt this is from that awful childhood trauma she once endured. I am so deeply sorry for it."

"I would hardly believe you could claim any responsibility for that. From the way it sounds, that entire episode was largely outside your control. And it would seem your journey was fraught with such moments. But still, it is an honor to meet you. I have had the occasion to encounter many curious examples of beings from amongst the planes, but yours is certainly a noteworthy one. Your interaction with these cu'Nar, for instance, leaves a number of interesting questions as to how and why it began."

"All I can say is the cu'Nar first came to us to give a warning relating to the arrival of Sargeras on our old home world, Azgarén. We did not know specifically why, but they related to me, in their most unusual manner of address, that he was a being we would not want to come into contact with."

"Indeed, but we have been speculating on a few matters over there, one of these is how and why a race such as this would find its way to you in the first place. My understanding of such beings is that it is a rather uncommon form of behavior for them to come out of their native homes and interact with corporeal lifeforms like yours. And then, we figure they must be serving someone even higher, perhaps as scouts or messengers, watching Sargeras and his movements."

"Oh? And how would you suggest this?"

"First is that they even know who and what he is to begin with. This word they gave you, Titan, is an archaic term to identify an ancient race once known as the Primordials. Sargeras must be a remnant of that society, and someone knows this, further that they must be following him, and dare I say the cu'Nar must be spies. Next, we have all this…" he waves around him at the vessel. "We were admiring this from the outside just now, and Aerlie mentioned what should be the extreme cost, both in resources and manpower to build something like this. It would also take time, and someone with enough drive to actually do it. And then to have the cu'Nar deliver it into your hands suggests a premeditated effort to evacuate you."

"Oh dear…but of course, you must be right. I will admit I did not place as much thought into the cause, other than to think the cu'Nar were responsible. They are a strange enough race of beings, so I could not be sure what they were capable of."

"I doubt they would build ships like this," Aerlie offers. "They sound more like elemental beings, and this one in particular would not likely require material vessels to transport them. If they are composed of energy, they probably have their own internal means of travel."

"Yes, perhaps, although I think I would not be as familiar with such details, as this would transcend beyond my own studies. But this does indeed propose a few additional questions."

"Anyway, this young lady has a few words to share," she directs at Kaliya.

Kaliya was feeling another upsurge of emotion as the others shared their conversation. It only prolonged the inevitable, and while she had been trying to use the time to build her strength, it was quickly collapsing now that her turn was at hand.

Aerlie studied her and could not only see, but also feel the girl's emotions taking over. She stepped over to wrap an arm around her and pat her on the back.

"You can do this," she whispers. "You're already most of the way there. It's just a small step to cross over now."

Kaliya nods and takes a deep breath. She tentatively clasps her hands, and folding them together, she brings them up to rest her forehead on. This is a moment she never expected would come during all the years after their arrival, but it is a moment she knew was necessary now, to finalize her spiritual healing. She takes a few cautious steps forward to stand before Velen.

She looks up into his eyes as he returns a puzzled gaze back at her. Tears begin to well up, and she loses her composure, falling softly into him and placing her hands around his sides.

"Father!" she cries, sobbing loudly.

Velen's face wrinkles with confusion as he passes his glance around the room at the other attendees, and back down to his daughter, her head buried in his robe and weeping.

"Kali?" he whispers in disbelief. "Kali, what has happened? You haven't come to me since…well, since the day of our departure from Ruuki uy'Daan!"

"I'm sorry, Father! I'm sorry for wasting so many years, and centuries of our time together. Please forgive me…"

"Oh Kali…" he soothes. "A mere few centuries will not drive us that far apart."

Velen puts a hand around her to comfort her as she continues to bury her head into his robe. She weeps for many long moments, spending her lengthy three and a half centuries of stress in one cumulative event.

Kailen turns discreetly towards Thaelyn.

"Your Lordship…" he whispers inquisitively.

Thaelyn glances back and waves his hand calmingly.

"At ease, Commander, all is well. She is simply having an emotional release…and not the first one, I will admit."

Velen caresses Kaliya's head softly to console her until she is finally able to bring her composure back into alignment.

"Kali, what happened?" he asks.

"A lot of things combined, and finally something broke and I knew what I did wrong."

"Are you alright?"

"I had a lot of ups and downs, lost my horns on numerous

occasions, and as my friend Relissa is so fond of saying, got my tail in a tangle a few times."

"Yes..." he chuckles softly. "Kailen told me a few stories about your friends. She is that Night Elf, correct? She sounds like she has a very ambitious personality."

"Oh, you don't know the half of it. She's a real horn-twister. But anyway, Lady Aerlie was helping me with some counseling and therapy...she has a very interesting way of doing things. I learned a lot about my errors, and from people I didn't otherwise expect to hear it from."

"People? What kind?"

"Priests, for one thing... They have a religion over there with some really fascinating perspectives on things."

"You know, even though ours may not be a religious society, I believe there are certain truths out there that can be understood if only you have the right teachings."

"Yeah, like the riddle of metaphysics. I've finally understood how it works, and I even went so far as to prove it."

Velen suddenly frowns and pulls back to examine his daughter's face.

"You were able to prove it? But how?"

Kaliya sighs and glances around the room, hoping to find a way to explain her exceptional experiences with Thaelyn and his teachings. She spies a cup on one of the tables with several decorative sticks arranged inside. She steps over to examine it more closely.

"Do you mind if I take one of these and, well, basically trash it?"

"Trash it? How do you mean?"

She takes one of the slender wooden strips and holds it in her hand. She glances tentatively at Thaelyn and Aerlie as she turns around.

"Be mindful of the carpet in here," Thaelyn cautions wittily.

"I've been practicing a few times privately since then," she smiles coyly. "I was speaking to one of your mages, and he helped refine my technique, and even to show me another little trick. So, I think I have a better handle on it now."

She holds the stick at length in her hand and begins concentrating, just like she did at the camp site with her first magic lesson. Both Velen and Kailen watch intently, wondering what sort of trick she has in mind to pull.

She focuses her mind to draw in the arcanic energies around her, this time more determinedly and with greater precision. The flows gather within her and travel along her arm into the stick, wrapping around it as she draws the double circle around the tip.

Kailen leans in to study the display. He could actually see the strange mystical particles snaking their way along the strip of wood.

"Father, do you see that?"

Velen could only nod silently.

Kaliya finally brings her hand alongside, and snaps her fingers.

A robust flame bursts out of the stick with a gentle poof as the stick ignites. Both Velen and Kailen lurch back as she holds it up for display.

"Cu'Nar's eyes," Kailen wheezes. "She did it!"

"And that effectively proves the theory," she asserts proudly. "At least within this context. This is what they call magic. The same stuff the orcs were using, but these people are much more advanced, as well as much more liberal in their lessons," she chuckles. "That famous riddle of metaphysics, where nothing unknown exists. It only exists after it is known. Perception enables recognition… My mind perceives what I want, in this case as fire applied to the stick. Existence demands definition… My mind defines the principle of fire as a form of heat combustion, and from this, substance becomes our reality. My mind imposes its redefinition of existence on the reality of the stick to invoke this alteration."

"That is a very creative application of thought, Kaliya," Thaelyn muses. "You are taking your own and merging it with ours. Nicely done."

"But Kali," Velen gasps. "We've been trying to study and prove this for…well, technically, since I first presented our faction to the Council. Although this particular theory came during our voyage.

How is it you managed to achieve what we could not, and in almost no time at all in proper study?"

"Because I had a good teacher," she gazes at Thaelyn. "They know what it is, and they can do it. Also, it requires a little help from the natural energies found in this universe…which we seem to be absent of back home," she shrugs.

"Natural energies? I recall our attempts to study the orcs, but we could never gain any observable result from it."

"That's because we were trying to apply our empirical science to it, but it doesn't belong to any of those sciences. This is a completely different side of the coin, as he likes to say. The energies are extradimensional, and mostly governed by the mind, not any of our regular science. First, you need to know what they are and how to apply them, not simply trying to measure them with numbers. And it takes practice to work it."

She pauses to redirect herself at the stick again, where the fire was still burning. She brings up her free hand and draws a long squiggle downward from above, terminating near the end of the stick where she makes a single circle and casually waves her hand as if shooing away the flame. The effect caused the fire to abruptly extinguish.

"Touch this, I dare you."

"That would still be hot, wouldn't it?" Kailen asks.

"Try…"

Kailen reaches out a hand and cautiously touches the burnt end of the stick, tapping it until he could be certain it would not burn his fingers. But as he begins to realize it's not hot, he also takes notice of something different.

"It's cold…ice cold!"

Velen then reaches up to touch the stick, placing his fingers on the charred end, only to feel the sensation of unnatural cold.

"And how did you do that?" he asks.

"There are basically three components to make fire," she explains. "Heat, oxygen, and a fuel source. I took away the heat component and replaced it with deep cold. Poof, no more fire."

"Incredible."

"Now, just imagine if I could learn more of this in his academy. They have official courses over there, and this could revolutionize a lot of things for us. But we need to take it slow to fully understand the implications. As he says, this is a potent natural force and demands just as much respect."

"Oh, most certainly... I wonder what our technicians would think about this."

"For one thing, I think poor Tanjhira would lose her horns a few times, just like I did," she chuckles.

She sets the stick on the table and returns back into the room.

"Anyway," she sighs as she prepares for her next step. "I wanted to patch up all our old broken family ties. A lot of bad things happened on Ruuki uy'Daan, and I was just too young to deal with it."

"Yes, Kali, I know this. It's a burden I've been carrying ever since we left Azgarén."

"Personally, I think it's an unjustified burden. You were told to leave, and you did."

"Well, yes, this is true."

"And it's simply not your fault those creeps started chasing us."

"Yes, I suppose..."

"And of course, we never knew what happened to cause all this, or why. Especially after that wild jump. It just didn't seem rational after that."

"This is also true. I had so hoped we were free of their pursuit."

"We all did, I'm sure. And then this last attack," she sets her hands on her hips. "And those orcs using their magic on us, doing all those bad things to the people..."

"That was a truly horrific scene. I heard stories from some of the survivors of what happened out there."

"Yeah, that mutation thing is what really got to me. I wish I knew what it was they were using."

"I cannot even begin to imagine."

Thaelyn and Aerlie watched the scene unfold. Aerlie moved closer and took his arm gently, as she could sense the scenario building up. Thaelyn turned to gaze at her, but as he did, he took note of that telltale glint in her eyes that spoke of something playful brewing.

"Why do I suddenly feel as if you gave her more than just a few simple counseling sessions?"

"Me? I did no such thing. She probably had it in her from the beginning."

"Powers help us, and she will be entering the academy soon."

Kaliya continues, "And it was made even worse when they were forced to get up and stomp around like madmen, screaming like wild animals and further frightening the people who were already in a panic."

"I…huh?" Velen gushes unexpectedly. "What do you mean forced to get up…and so on?"

"And even more," she waves a finger while bypassing the question. "Those brutes were abusing them!" she crosses her arms and pouts conspicuously.

Velen studied his daughter for her sudden shift of abnormal behavior. Kailen also glared at her, suspecting something had happened and she held a new secret.

"But at least they're hiding now," she relents contentedly. "So, hopefully the orcs won't find them anytime soon. Especially if they're so focused on harassing us on this side."

"Kali, what are you talking about?" Velen wonders worriedly.

"Oh, and I saw Mother today," she smiles sweetly. "She says Hi."

"Yeah, and I think that explains it," Kailen nods. "She's lost it now. I think that riddle of metaphysics blew her horns right out the window."

"Oh, Kailen," she chides playfully. "You should know me better than that. Besides, she says Hi to you too, and that she loves you both, and she hasn't forgotten…although I'm not entirely sure what it is she hasn't forgotten, but she was very happy for the visit."

"What visit?"

By this time, Thaelyn was covering his eyes at the scene unfolding in front of him. He had no idea how she planned on delivering the punch line, but he was dreading the final result. Aerlie watched with a bright smile stretching across her face.

"What visit?" Kaliya explains more seriously. "Oh, the one I made today…completely unexpected and without any tail-flipping idea of what I was doing. So, here I am," she gestures figuratively, "standing there in the remains of our old house, talking to her. Neither of us realizes the other one is actually a real person present in the room. We're each giving reports of what happened, both here with us and there in the city, until finally she comes to what few senses she still has available after living alone for so long, and takes notice that I'm actually standing there next to her. But this doesn't help me by much, except to think I'm having some crazy dream or something. Then she starts quizzing me on stuff like, oh, pick this up, move it over there, walk this way…yeah, like that makes sense to me," she giggles.

The two men are baffled at the strangely animated depictions, as both of them stare at her in bewilderment.

"The next thing you know," Kaliya continues. "She goes running off to a back room, probably your old office. I hear a lot of noises, like she's trying to unbury something, and then she comes back out to the family room with the one thing in the universe I hated the most…sorry Father…"

"What thing?" he asks hesitantly.

Kaliya now reaches into her uniform pocket and pulls out the box she received from her mother. She holds it up to him and sets a hand on her hip, then begins tapping a hoof on the floor as she waits for him to react.

Velen gazes reflexively at the strange object, at first barely recognizing what it was or that it could even exist, to say nothing that she was actually holding it. A moment passes as he begins to realize the identity of the item his daughter was offering him, as well as finally realizing the basis of her story. His eyes grow wide, and he draws in a wheezing gasp.

On noticing the object, Kailen steps in closer to look at it. He also feels a wave of shock wash over him as the implications of the artifact settle into his mind.

"Kaliya," he intones warily. "Where did you get that?"

"Kailen, if I understood any part of what I did, I could probably answer that. But Mother, with that mutation effect, was unable to fully articulate herself enough to explain it to me. Instead, she said to ask Father. Apparently, I did this once as a child, and I suspect they both knew about it."

"Kali, my precious daughter!" Velen exalts. "Praise be to the cu'Nar, yes! Oh, how I hoped this day would come, though I could never expect it to come like this! How did it happen? Can you tell me? What were you doing at the time?"

"Um, do you really want to know?" she chuckles bashfully. "Well, I was applying to his military academy, and they have this strange test you need to take to check the purity of your spirit. Mine wasn't quite right for it initially, and I expected this for all those little traumas I had, though most of them were gone by this time. So, I had to take this ritual. They put you in a room, fill your head with this hallucinogenic incense, then take you to another room where you're supposed to have something like a dream session to bring out your dark feelings so you can deal with them somehow. Mine didn't quite turn out that way, however," she titters.

"Oh? How did it turn out for you?"

"Oh, yeah, you'll love this one. First, I made a chair for myself, like the ones we have in the lounge area. It just popped into existence as I was thinking about it."

Velen's eyes bulge as he tries to envision the scenario.

"So, I sat down, and I guess it was so comfy, I fell asleep. Next thing I know, I'm standing up. I turn around and see my body in the chair. And if that's not wild enough, I'm asking myself, where do I go from here? I figure I need to have a vision relating to Ruuki uy'Daan. After all, that's where it all started, right? But in the clear and obvious absence of any visions simply appearing out of nowhere, I decided I need to go there intentionally. Now, keeping in mind, I think I'm dreaming. So, I try to imagine travelling to Ruuki uy'Daan.

Here's where 'wild' turns to 'crazy'. I actually see myself travelling through nether-space, just like in the textbooks, all the way from Tae'Eladar, which is in another universe, across dimensional bounds into the universe with Ruuki uy'Daan, plunging down into the local galaxy, and boom! I'm standing on the street downtown."

"Cu'Nar's pity," Kailen moans. "But you were in a dream of some kind?"

"Probably not a real dream… I ran across town to the house, dodging orcish patrols along the way, went inside to see the place was a wreck, and here is where I eventually found Mother, hiding in a back room. She's apparently still alive, as are some number of other survivors hiding throughout the city from orcs who occasionally come back to abuse them, probably just for fun at this point."

"Oh really!" he blasts. "As if the initial attack wasn't enough?"

"Yeah, but there's not a lot we can do about it from here. Anyway, after a bit of conversation, and with her finally realizing she wasn't hallucinating, she gave me this and told me to come back here and ask you, Father," she sneers playfully at him, "what I was actually doing as a child that you didn't tell me about. Although, she did explain it was for my own good not to know, since I was so young."

"Incredible!" Velen wheezes. "And you carried this back to us. This might finally confirm our old theories, at least up to a point."

"So, what was it if not a dream?"

Velen gazes at the box again and takes a deep breath as he tries to compose himself.

"This reflects on an old study we once had on Azgarén. A very few children were being discovered with a most amazing feature, but we could never fully understand what it was. I was part of the study project, as were several of the senior members within our faction. Unfortunately, the studies were interrupted before we could find any definitive results, but we did manage to gain enough observational data for me to draw a few fascinating conclusions. None of the other factions, like the medical or biology factions, could come to any rational interpretations because the phenomena simply didn't carry any recognizable parameters."

"What were they looking for?" Thaelyn inquires.

"The medical faction, naturally, was trying to interpret this as a physiological cause and effect. The child was seen in bed, presumably asleep. The monitors all showed it was perfectly healthy and resting as usual, albeit with elevated neural activity along certain wavelengths. But this was simply interpreted as a dream state. And at the same time, there was an apparition-like projection of that same child standing in the room, interacting with people and objects as if it were simply playing with its toys and carrying conversations."

"Most interesting."

"It felt tangible to the touch, within reason, and therefore, if you were to give it something to carry in its hand, the child could do this. It could pick up a pen and write its name, interact with a variety of devices, and so on. As for the biology faction, they were at least as baffled as any other, because this apparition simply did not register as a physical object to study in any way. There was no apparent mass, and not even a heat signature. It was a complete mystery to us."

"I would imagine such a thing might invoke a bit of trepidation after a while."

"Oh, it did. There was an initial news sensation over the discoveries that I recall. There was a myriad of questions, but no true answers. We had a few of these occasions occur, and with increasing desire to find our results. But then, of course, was the arrival of Sargeras, and then the cu'Nar, and we departed. We have not seen it since, until that day on Ruuki uy'Daan when Kali was first discovered with it. My wife, Tyanna, was a psychologist at the old university, and she opened a secret research program to study it. We decided on this occasion to keep it completely under wraps. Not even Kailen was told about it," he glances at the young officer and lays a hand on his shoulder.

"Was there a special reason for this?" Kailen asks. "Is it dangerous in some way?"

"The other cases were interrupted for inexplicable reasons. We were concerned about her health, as well as the social stigmas that might follow, at least as much this time hoping to actually learn something about it, as to contain, maybe also to control it. And while Tyanna did manage to confirm some of those early reports and observations, and even to reinforce some of our ideas, ultimately, we had the attack, and that interrupted us yet again. Since then, poor little Kali was simply too troubled, and she apparently no longer exhibited the condition."

"I wonder if this is another part of that hard knock she took with that meld," Aerlie muses. "We broke through something, and here it is. What were some of these theories and ideas of yours?"

"Although it was regarded as a very rare occurrence, I was developing the idea that this could be a most wonderful development coming to light in a few precious examples. I took to naming it the Prodigy Gift, and these were Prodigy Children who found it. I thought perhaps it could be a sign of some sort that we, as a race, might be entering a new era, a new evolutionary transition, and this might be a precursor trait of some sort."

"That is a truly fascinating account. And surely, we would be just as interested to know more about this. We were thinking of trying to train this further. Have you ever attempted this before?"

"To train it? My goodness, we barely had time even to test their abilities, to say nothing of trying to teach anything. Do you actually think you could train something like this?"

"Master Velen, um…" Aerlie pauses as she glances first at Thaelyn, then at Kailen. "Commander, how much did you actually tell your Elder Council about us?"

"How much?" Kailen responds gingerly.

Aerlie flashes a quick telepathic image into his head of her meaning. Kailen was initially surprised, but quickly realized her direction.

"Oh, right," he nods. "Well, we only really touched on the… visible aspects of your arrival, what happened in the valley, and so on. Did you have something else in mind?"

"Master Velen," Aerlie resumes. "I would wish to ask you to keep this classified just between us for now. We suspect there could be spies about, and who knows what they might try peeking in on.

This might also include Sargeras, in case he has such a desire, as he might also try fishing for information. If he likes playing with you as toys, who knows what other interests he actually holds."

"I am aware of this mention from our meeting once," he responds.

"Good. Thaelyn and I are not your typical example of people. We are known as Celestials. We are essentially a hybrid form of life between mortal bodies, perhaps like yours and the other races here, and a race of gods known as the Estelar."

"Gods?" he wonders.

"The counterpart to such beings as Sargeras. These are beings of such extreme evolutionary development that one might as well call them gods since they can very easily fulfill all or most of the characteristics you might normally ascribe to that term."

"Fascinating."

"As such, this grants us not only a rather prestigious range of abilities, but also knowledge. Therefore, this thing you might think of as some wildly advanced skill representing an exceptional evolutionary trait, would likely be known to us already from our experiences with other beings that are already there. In fact, from our perspective, to find it in yours would be extraordinary, to be sure. And yet, as Celestial beings, we would be far more qualified to understand it, even to teach how to use it. For this, I would say, if she can do it at all, we would most certainly wish to see how far she can go with it, and offer our assistance to see it through."

"That would surely be a most generous offer. But how would you do this? I can only begin to theorize how it might play out."

"Yes, I'm sure of that," she smiles. "We know of people who might be able to offer tutoring, and in fact we have a friend who may be of value for us here."

"I see. Well, if you think you can help, I will not stand in your way. I only hope you can provide us with some of your results when they are ready."

"Oh, absolutely! After all, she is your daughter, and I'm sure you would like to keep abreast of things."

"But Father," Kaliya interjects. "Does this have anything to do with the prophecy?"

Velen gazes into her eyes and sighs heavily.

"Yes, Kali, it does. When the cu'Nar gave me that vision, it included a rather clear image of you. But you were so very angry with me at the time that I did not dare to mention it openly."

"Yeah, I was afraid you were going to say that. Why me…" she hangs her head, "…as if I don't have enough burdens to hold up already."

"Kali, my dearest daughter," he caresses her head. "You need to be strong. I feel you have many great accomplishments ahead of you, and I feel confident that we may have indeed found our hope. You could be the forerunner of a new generation."

"Oh please, Father, you don't really need to rub it in," she chuckles weakly.

"Master Velen," Thaelyn submits. "I take it you are the one who received this prophecy? Kaliya told me about this vision, but do you have any more precise detail on the latter portions of it?"

"Unfortunately," he relents. "The vision became blurred as I was trying to scribe it in my notes. This happens often, much to my sorrow. By this time, I can only hold a few fragments of what they gave to me."

"Yes, this can be a problem in such cases. Then, I suppose we must proceed as we usually do, with what we know of for the present. And this naturally brings us to this disk of yours. Would you allow me to inquire as to what it contains? Your wife seemed to hold the opinion it could be of service to us."

"I, uh…of service? How?"

"Father," Kaliya begins. "She gave it to me after I told her we lost virtually everything in this attack. All our old libraries and archives were on Ruuki uy'Daan, and our ship's computers were wiped. Now, I know I always complained about this project of yours, and twist my horns if I'm about to say this, but it could be the one thing to save us now."

"Really! So, you are referring to the compilation of knowledge I recorded inside."

"Yeah, and I think it can do more than simply help us build a new city for ourselves. It could also help us fight Sargeras."

"But Kali, we do not carry any real military knowledge. Science, yes, and I suppose some of it could be manipulated in some way, but…"

"Father, we do not, but they do," she points assertively at Thaelyn and Aerlie. "If we share it with them, we could create something really unique, and I doubt the Suuden-Aryku would know how to deal with it. I've already seen their arcanic technology, and it blows my horns away. Fabricating stuff out of nothingness, perpetual energy production, solving problems before they should even know what they are…you can't judge it by our standards, because it doesn't follow those standards."

"But Kaliya," Kailen notes. "It's one thing to develop something to help us fight here, but are you suggesting we take this all the way back to Azgarén and fight Sargeras directly?"

"That's what he needs to do. Sargeras is a leftover from an ancient battle with the Estelar, and he needs to be destroyed at any cost. It's not just about us."

"But if this is true," Velen muses. "Why would they not take this, themselves?"

"More than likely, they need to hold back for now. If he sees them coming, he might run. It's quite obvious he's hiding from them. So, we will make the advance to find him, and then…well, whatever comes after that."

Kailen and Velen exchanged their uncertain stares before returning to study the disk, which Velen finally took from Kaliya's hand.

"My first suggestion," Kailen offers, "is to see if we can still read the thing."

"Do we have any readers still in operation?" Kaliya asks.

"I believe there's one in the engineering lab."

"Oh, naturally…why didn't I think of that," she chuckles. "And you should call Tanjhira. She'll love this one."

Kailen begins leading the group out of the room at a hurried pace through the ship. They arrived at a transport chute to call a car that would take them to another section of the immense vessel where they would find the research labs. The bullet-shaped car zipped along through a network of subway-like tunnels, until it came to a stop at another station.

"Such a delightfully curious mode of transport," Thaelyn mumbles. "And so appropriate."

They hurried again along the corridors until they came to a large double-door entrance for the engineering research lab. On entering, the resident technicians take quick notice of the arriving visitors and stand to offer a respectful bow to Master Velen as he enters.

"Master Velen," ushers a pleasant female voice. "What do you have for us today?"

Kaliya steps forward to interact.

"Tanjhira, you'd better grab hold of your horns. I think your life is about to go ballistic. We have the salvation of our people in our hands."

"Let's try not to get too excited, Kaliya," Kailen cautions. "We still need to be able to read it."

"Kailen, I think the cu'Nar know more than they're letting on. If the prophecy means anything, this is just the beginning for us. I was also getting some kind of voice or something inside my head during this time telling me to do this. So, I think someone, or something, is driving the occasion."

"All right, but for now, I would prefer to take a more cautious approach."

The room is equipped with numerous scientific instruments and analytical devices. Several workstations in the center of the room contain measuring equipment, precision tools, and cabinets with spare parts and components. Along the walls are rows of consoles, replicators, and nano-fabrication assembly engines. One console was fitted with a large monitor and a holographic reader.

Velen steps up to the reader unit, with the rest of the group gathering around to observe. He opens the box to reveal the round holo-disk inside. Tanjhira glares at the unexpected sight.

"Where did that come from?"

"This is Father's project from Ruuki uy'Daan," Kaliya infers.

"Oh, really!" she snaps. "And how did it find its way here?"

"I brought it back from Mother in our old house."

The middle-aged technician turned in astonishment at Kaliya's smug grin. Kaliya simply shrugged as she returned to see Velen gently removing the disk from the box and setting it on the reader tray. The activity draws the attention of the other workers in the room, and whispers begin to pass around as they see the disk being set into place.

Kailen presses a button on the console and the device closes, drawing the disk inside to begin accessing the data. An image begins to form on the monitor.

The likeness of Velen appears in a well-appointed office. Running along the edges of the screen are symbols, representing the written form of their language as a translation lexicon for the unknowing to use in order to learn how to decipher the data. He begins to speak.

> *"Greetings to you who have found this lost artifact. My name is Velen Nazég, formerly of the Council of Elders for the people who once called themselves the Suuden-Aryku. There was a time when our civilization held such great esteem, that we felt we could accomplish anything. But as times have turned against us, a portion of our populace has had to go into hiding. We are all that remains now.*
>
> *On this medium, I have recorded the last vestiges of our history, our culture, our wisdom, and our lives. If you have found this, here in what may be the final resting place of our society, then I offer you my sincerest hopes that you might find a place within your own memory to recall our names and our prestige, so that we may not pass from existence forever..."*

"Good gracious!" Aerlie winces. "No wonder you felt so much despair, Kaliya."

"Yeah, it didn't give much of a positive outlook for us."

"Well, we shall see about that! Master Velen, perhaps we could skip ahead a bit. I doubt we need to review such a dreary prologue."

"Of course," he accedes. "My apologies, but this is how I felt on so many occasions."

"Well, there is one very easy solution to that. Stand near enough to us and you will see a few changes occurring!"

"Cu'Nar's pity," Tanjhira moans. "Is this what kind of people you have out there?"

"It most certainly is," Aerlie asserts. "And with good reason."

Velen presses another button on the console and a list of chapters appears on the screen. He scrolls through the list and selects one positioned several lines down, pressing another button to skip ahead and begin playing that portion.

> *"In this chapter, I will discuss the mechanics of dimensional warping and the nether-space generator used in our vessels during our exploration of our local galactic body. The field induction energies are drawn from the interaction of anti-particles within a containment sphere built into the main reactor core. These are siphoned through to the lateral nacelles, which then wrap the ship in an envelope of nether-space, subverting its mass into a non-physical state relative to real-space..."*

"Such a quaint manner of definition..." Thaelyn smiles as he pulls back from the monitor. "Very good, I think this might give us our answer as to the readability of this data. But now, what to do with it..."

"What do you mean, what to do with it?" Tanjhira wonders.

"What he means is," Kaliya offers. "To reinvent everything, and finally finish this war."

"Kaliya, how do we fight something like the Suuden-Aryku?"

"First, by actually fighting. Second, I think with a hybrid form of technology."

"A hybrid form…huh?"

"Just ask them," she thumbs at Thaelyn and Aerlie. "They already use it. And it'll blow your horns off."

"But we're not a military society."

"Tanjhira! We're dying here! Military or not, how long do you have to go before your horns get so twisted up that you finally realize, if you want to live, you're going to have to change that attitude of non-military to something that actually does fight."

"All right, I see your point, and I suppose I have to admit, I do have enough of my own reasons for it."

"And there's more to it than just us, it seems. Sargeras isn't even supposed to be alive right now, and everything you see around us is the reason why. And they know this, as they know who he is, and why he isn't supposed to be alive. Now they have to fight him to the ends of Creation if they must. Just look at this one world. Now multiply by whatever number he has in mind to destroy next, or already has. That's your answer."

"Oh dear cu'Nar, you must be joking."

"It's probably no accident we found Ruuki uy'Daan. Those orcs probably worked for him long before we ever arrived. This tells us he's got his fingers in a lot of places, with or without us. He's a godlike creature that shouldn't even exist, left over from a battle that killed off the rest of them for exactly this reason."

"Wonderful…" she sighs deeply. "So, our misery is only a small piece of something bigger, and now we need to straighten our tails and own up to the responsibility of trying to save whatever is left of the place? But how do we reinvent everything, and then create this hybrid technology out of it?"

"This is a good question," Thaelyn admits. "Here is where I think we have a rather remarkable opportunity, as well as a number of decisions to make. And I would further say time is of the essence to make these decisions if we are to have anything ready before he makes his next move ahead of us."

"A next move? Wait, you lost me. What exactly are we talking about with movements?"

"We believe you are here for a reason. The first element of this is your so-called wild jump that so conveniently brought you to a habitable world that also contains those very same creatures that once invaded our world many millennia ago. Coincidence? I think not. If this most recent invasion that brought me here is due to those orcs belonging to Sargeras, this says he owned that world from well before you arrived…and further that your arrival was planned."

"Cu'Nar's pity! That doesn't sound at all nice."

"Indeed. Then, you are aided by these cu'Nar, who by their nature as elemental beings would not as likely interact with such like yourselves due to the extreme differences you share, and neither would they normally leave their native homes to begin with, unless someone told them to do so."

"Like who?"

"My guess is the same person or persons who built this ship, which is so conveniently designed to be compatible with your species."

"Oh, thank you, but I suppose I have to admit to this much."

"And then we have Sargeras chasing you, or better to say driving you as playthings while he makes some unknown plan that seems oriented at my home. Not only is this intolerable, but it is also the last place I would expect to see a Primordial return to, as they once occupied that space."

"Oh great! And what about those others who kicked them in the tail?"

"This is a most curious question, but one I do not have an answer to at this time, other than to say he has some form of subversive designs on them. Nevertheless, I would not wish to see that answer occurring in front of me."

"Yeah, I suppose I would have to agree. So, you're saying we need to go chasing after him now. But if he's on Azgarén, and our ship is basically dead with no navigation logs, how do we do this?"

"This is another good question, but again one without an answer. However, I will remain optimistic that we might find an opportunity for us if we look hard enough. Meanwhile, we need to build ourselves up in preparation of this."

He turns and begins his classic pacing as he continues.

"Master Velen, I would wish to offer you a very important proposal. I realize our relationship is still rather fresh, but this is a situation that speaks for itself. Sargeras must be brought down, there can be no argument to this. At the very least, we must seek him out and target him for destruction by whatever forces may actually take the action. He will not likely expect such…small things…as we to be a bother. His kind holds a reputation, from the stories we are told, of being exceptionally arrogant. Therefore, if we make this advance, we could undermine his position in preparation for his final downfall."

He now turns and paces the other way.

"As I once said to Kaliya and her friends, you do not win wars by sitting on logs, and this is essentially what you have been doing ever since your arrival on this world. You are making a last stand, and doing so very poorly. Now, I can understand if you choose not to fight as a way of life. There is nothing wrong with a pacifist mentality. But even pacifists need to defend themselves on occasion, and especially if faced with extinction, and this is essentially what we have here."

The room suddenly erupts in a rush of murmurs amongst the technicians and others who have found their way through the corridors to listen in. Thaelyn observed their reactions, knowing he hit something tender inside.

"Yeah, you got that much right," Tanjhira sighs. "I still recall Ruuki uy'Daan…and my dearest husband. He made one such last stand for us…for all the good it did."

"Tanjhira," Velen murmurs. "I feel for this as well, but they told me he held a purpose of some kind."

"Master Velen, with respect to you and the cu'Nar, I can't see what purpose there is to stay behind on a hostile world while the rest of us run."

"This does indeed sound strange," Thaelyn notes. "But overall, while we may weep for those who are lost, it is just as offensive to allow their loss to be in vain as it is to do nothing in one's own defense. But at the same time, we must expand our visions for what capacity this one particular foe is capable of. If we hold the power to do anything at all, we simply must do it, and not for ourselves, but all those who could be future victims. Our extinction does nothing to help them, but our efforts to fight could very well make a difference, if we are wise about it."

"All right, you've got my attention…pacifist or otherwise, I'm tired of sitting on logs."

Thaelyn could sense the emotions circulating around the room by now and knew they needed this sort of inspiration, so he pressed forward to make his conclusion.

"Good, but this will likely need to go up to your governing body. The information on this disk, if it involves any technical detail we could employ to this purpose, might represent a turning point in your long chase. It could help you the same as it could help others. But here is where I feel I need to make a few small stipulations."

He pauses in his steps to tap a finger on his chin.

"Sargeras is an ancient being, described as godlike for all practical terms. This could imply many qualities, most of which are undesirable for our purposes. He is likely capable of telepathy and other such talents, and so this discovery of ours must be held in the tightest security. Next is to say that any work we conduct must also be kept secret, and isolated from his reach. For instance, if he knows you are here, it cannot be done here. Furthermore, it will require time, effort, and resources to research and develop anything, and from what I understand of your situation here, you are sorely lacking on most of these."

"Yes, that much is for sure," Tanjhira admits.

"But I am the king of an entire world, with all the resources of that world at my disposal. Ours may not be as technologically advanced as your society, but our people are very clever for what we have available. As for me and Aerlie, we were explaining to Master Velen and the Commander a few moments ago that we come from much higher backgrounds than what you will find on Tae'Eladar. We can only teach the people of our world in small increments, thereby elevating them gradually. Our background carries certain rules of conduct, and this is one of them. However, due to our situation of war, and this one particular adversary, we might need to make a few exceptions to this rule, if only to keep them as secrets, maybe within our combined military ventures, and only for this one purpose, where afterwards we would need to revert to a more natural rhythm of growth. Here is where the proposal comes in."

He clears his throat as he prepares his thoughts.

"If your Elder Council would permit this, we should enter into a more formal partnership agreement to develop this technology as a joint effort. But as Kaliya mentioned, this is not simply to reinvent your old ways. We will share our magical studies as you share your physical ones. What we create together will represent a rather curious and unique blend that should thoroughly stifle the Suuden-Aryku, as well as many of you, I should think," he chuckles. "And provide us with capabilities to solve our problems our way. This places the tactical advantage more to our side of the game field. And I will dedicate my people and our world's resources to see it through until our objective is met."

"So, let me see if I have this..." Tanjhira surmises. "I think I heard yours is an Industrial Age world, right?"

"Yes, we are still in the early stages of it."

"Uh huh... So, you want us to join together and design a new form of technology, using magic, of all things, as part of the theory of operation, and do so to chase a godlike thing all the way back to Azgarén, which by the way, we don't have jump coordinates to, and from there, you and these other godlike things will finish the job they apparently started who knows how long ago, and all of this while probably fighting our way through the Suuden-Aryku, as I think they might have something to say about it."

"Generally yes... Are you up for a little challenge?" he grins impishly.

"A little one?!" she blasts. "Cu'Nar help us…and where will we set up our research facilities, if not here?"

"I think the only other choice for us is on Tae'Eladar, which would surely be an unexpected location for him. I could give instructions for a dedicated research lab and industrial park to be built in a remote location, to ensure our security, and we could import you and your team to join with ours."

"Yeah, that's what I was afraid of," she relents.

"We will also need to attend to the issue of language. I think this should be an easy component to decide upon for your Council. If you and some number of others would wish to join us in an exchange of languages, we could at least establish a common means of communication. We can teach you ours, and then you could assist in developing a similar course in yours."

"This sounds interesting. Yes, I'm sure we could agree on this much, at least. And this could offer us time for them to decide on the rest as we progress through these courses. How long does your language course take?"

"Three months."

Tanjhira gapes at him for the outlandishly small figure.

"Did you say three months?!" she wheezes. "It takes me longer than that just to decide what to have for dinner!"

"Oh, surely, we can convince you to do better than that. After all, I think your dinner would grow cold long before you could find time to eat it," he grins.

"Uh huh…yeah," she emits feebly. "Kaliya, you mentioned something about horns flying off?"

"Yeah," she smiles. "How do they feel so far?"

"Soft. Very soft."

"Well, this is just the beginning. Wait until you meet the gnomes!"

"Gnomes? What's a gnome?"

Relissa and Marelle were still in the meeting with the General in the tactical office when Thaelyn and his envoy returned. They all reconvene inside for a quick review.

"My Lord!" the General announces. "I trust your meeting went well?"

"Indeed, General," he replies. "And I feel as if we will have a considerable amount of work ahead of us. For one thing, we should expect some new arrivals to sign up for language classes, at the very least, as we will need to increase our interactions with the Daanen-Aryku considerably."

"What are we planning this time?" Relissa asks.

"That disk Kaliya brought back contains some invaluable scientific knowledge for their society. We will be negotiating to share this and develop some new technologies out of it for our mutual benefit. But before we can progress on this, first we need to solve the issue of language, and we also need their Council to agree to the proposal."

"He also gave them a heavy dose of moral encouragement," Aerlie grins. "They needed to be made aware of the imperative nature of pursuing this all the way back to Azgarén."

"Jiggers," Relissa rolls her eyes. "So, I guess that means things are going to start jumping around here."

"We certainly hope so. But it needs to be done very carefully, and out of reach of anyone who might try spying on us."

"Aye, I'm with you on that! But how does this relate to those Suuden-Aryku out there, and then the orcs and such?"

"As for the enemies of this world," Thaelyn muses. "We will need to continue in a very clandestine manner for these studies. I will need to give instructions for a new research facility to be built on Tae'Eladar, to keep it out of sight to anyone here. We will dedicate ourselves to these efforts quietly. Meanwhile, I would wish to make a quick review in here before attending to an important task outside. General, did anything occur during our absence?"

"Nothing of special importance," he responds. "We still have not seen anything from those Flame Elves, no sightings of Suuden-Aryku during this time, and the orcs are showing signs of a disturbance from our attacks. I think at least a few of them are beginning to take notice of the absence of their forward camps."

"Yes, I am sure by now some of them would."

"Also, I've been thinking some more of that odd attack. I think you are right to say it was a demonstration of some sort, but I am at odds with myself for the timing. I must ask myself, could it be due to our arrival in some fashion? Although this does not play out fairly in my mind, as we have not had any obvious interactions with anyone, other than those political meetings. So, perhaps that may be a cause, which is to say the Suuden-Aryku took notice of our arrival and subsequent meetings, and are reacting to it in such a manner where we may be responsible for an alteration of their local behaviors."

"This is an interesting thought. They had containment before our arrival. Then we arrive, clear the local area, securing the human city up north, and now they feel confident to offer more support to their neighbors to the east."

"But the thing I do not understand is their choice of equipment. Not simply that they would use something so non-native to their own, but also on this one special occasion. If we borrow from Kaliya's mention of being nice to the little people, meaning to say the Guard up north, we might offer the suggestion that they were only interested in the Daanen-Aryku, and for whatever reason were holding back for those occasions of Guard members patrolling the fields."

"Perhaps," Thaelyn considers. "But if we reflect on the population of this world before the start of this long siege..."

"Yes, and then we have that, which resembles a purging operation. This can only bring me back to the aspect of this being a demonstration. Adamantium versus steel would leave a rather gruesome display on the field, do you think?"

"It would, and that would amount to quite a demonstration...a little like overkill, if you were to ask me."

"Yes! Overkill, as a way of demonstrating to the little people, perhaps in terms they might easily associate with, meaning to use swords instead of these rifles, that they should not overstep their bounds beyond what is otherwise granted to them."

"How interesting…" he muses deeply. "They had containment, and allowed the humans to make these forays, if only to permit them this luxury of thinking they held the capacity to do so. So, the containment aspect must be one of these covert procedures, and part of this oppression effect. And here, the humans appear to be sending patrols out in excess of their usual practice. But still, to use adamantium swords and armor?"

"Maybe as further demonstration, more on their level, that no matter how you slice it," he chuckles quietly for the obvious pun. "They are still superior."

"My goodness, General," Aerlie giggles. "So, this is to say they used this method of a direct assault as a way of saying, we know who you are and where you come from, and we allowed you this before, but not on this occasion? That would be a cruel eye-opener."

"It would," Thaelyn nods. "And this simply tells us that we have someone's attention out there, regardless of who is actually on the field. General, we need to be sure our people are ready for any and all new attacks. If this is how they wish to play it, we will show them who they are playing with, at least within reason for the disguises we are using."

"Yes, my Lord," he affirms. "But this further brings me to that situation of our victory and how easily they went down. They do not seem very worthy as battlefield opponents, at least not against our people."

"Indeed. Kaliya, do we have any word on this yet?"

"That sounds so strange to hear," she shakes her head, "when you consider our long history with them, and how long we suffered. Although, I suppose I need to go back to the same statement. We're not military, and never once even tried, it seems. But unfortunately, Ankhia is still trying to figure this one out. One thing I heard is that she thinks none of the sword injuries you inflicted should be the cause of it. They didn't look like they ought to be fatal wounds by themselves. She did see a lot of necrotized tissue, but she's uncertain where it came from. You say your weapons are enchanted in some way, so could this be a reason?"

"It is certainly reasonable to suggest they can cause additional injury, but on the scale of killing an opponent entirely by itself? Unless they are particularly susceptible to it, I cannot be sure."

"Well, she's still working on several ideas and cross-referencing her notes."

"Very well, we will need to give her the time for it. Meanwhile, we have matters outside to attend."

He waves for the group to join as he assembles another gathering of witnesses in front of the gateway platform. He takes up his position with Kaliya kneeling just in front and brings out his sword to conduct the swearing-in service once again. When the oath was complete, Kaliya stood up a newly welcomed citizen of Tae'Eladar, followed by another rousing cheer from the assembled crowd.

"Now that's what I'm talking about!" Relissa shouts. "Welcome to the family, girl!"

Kaliya gets a long series of handshakes and pats on her back from a growing line of fans. Gossip had been spreading throughout the camp since her return about her extraordinary test results and the artifact she brought back from her ritual experience.

"Kaliya," Thaelyn proclaims. "You have a lot of work to do. I will send you back with one of my people to assist in submitting your application, but you still need to qualify for the other requisite testing. I have no doubt, with your enlightened education, you will more than adequately pass most of it. As for the rest, I think we will see about cutting a few corners, and fill you in with additional classes during your first year or two of formal training, just to get you involved more quickly. I want you into full training as soon as possible."

"Yes, Your Lord…uh…" she catches herself on the new wording. "That is…yes, my Lord!"

"We will consider this Prodigy Gift of yours as time permits, but for now I am sure you will have more than enough on your mind."

Thaelyn summons a nearby soldier to assist Kaliya, and together the two of them jump through the gate back to Bya'an Tamoranth. Thaelyn then sets himself back to work in the tactical office.

Chapter 13
INVASION!

"I need way-lines!" Thaelyn shouts to the assembly of mages. "We must move the troops quickly and efficiently. The time of war is upon us! Let us show them the strength of the Order!"

It is early morning, and a large gathering of mages has assembled in the field outside the war camp. Two full divisions of troops, ten thousand strong each, had been imported in the wee hours from Tae'Eladar. It was still dark on Therinë when they had been assembling in preparation for their deployment.

Several rows of portal way-lines began opening up, twenty-wide each. The field commanders organized themselves into unit gatherings, forming whole brigades of troops. Each soldier was fully geared for hardline battle. This represented the initial launch of the main assault on the orcish positions.

The first of these begins marching through the portals to take their positions as a sneak attack on the orcish encampment on the western shoreline. Once they had been delivered, the mages opened up a second set of portals for the next division to launch against the nearest orcish camp west of the base. These two launch points would further expand with additional deployments to close the gap between them and form a full line advancing south.

Many caravans of supplies and building materials were being gathered up on Tae'Eladar in preparation to send forward and establish the new outposts once the area was secured. In addition, crews of craftsmen and laborers were beginning to arrive within the camp to survey the region and begin construction of the expanded support facilities. Crates of tools and wagonloads of raw materials were brought in and dropped at a local supply depot. The camp is buzzing with new activity as scores of workers begin construction on the foundations for a modest settlement.

A series of wagons had arrived carrying bags of seed and other materials for the farming activities underway by the local human and elven societies. Construction plans for the new farming communities, including homes, barns and animal pens, and storage silos were being organized and supplied.

It was midmorning when a set of Daanen'kai hover-coaches arrived at the north entrance of the camp. These vehicles were like small buses, larger than what was used by Kailen and Kaliya, and capable of seating many more occupants. The guards make the obligatory check and direct them off to the side where they could park and offload. The arrivals drew the attention of many of the people in the camp, as a large delegation entered through the gate. A guard was sent to inform Thaelyn in the tactical office, and he was now strolling outside to meet them.

"Greetings, friends," he announces. "Do I have the pleasure of meeting our exchange students?"

A male junior officer steps up to make his acquaintance, followed by Tanjhira from their earlier meeting in the Naarg uy'Sodrad.

"Good day to you, Your Lordship," he begins. "I am Lieutenant Padriyl Lapäli, here as a replacement intermediary to Petty Officer Nazég. Accompanying me are some of our technicians and researchers, including my mother, Chief Technician Tanjhira Lapäli. I believe the two of you have already met. She is the head of our research department."

"Indeed!" Thaelyn responds. "And I am pleased to make your

renewed acquaintance. It seems we are discovering a number of family relations in these interactions."

"I recall the mention of your magical technology from our earlier meeting," Tanjhira reflects. "And as I look at this unit over here," she glances at the gateway device, "I am wondering how many sets of horns I'll be going through before we're done."

"Yes, and I would advise taking care of the breakable items around you when they go flying off," he smiles. "But I think we may need to ease our way into it, perhaps with Kaliya's help, as she has already made a few very important connections. That way, you can bring yourself up to speed on how we do things back home."

"The Elder Council was still debating when I left, but I carry a bit of clout where the technology side is concerned. If I could make a brief review of what we have to work with, I'm sure I could push them a little towards a decision."

"Most excellent. My suggestion is to confer with Kaliya and what she has learned thus far. She would make for a good starting point to help you associate with your own studies. Then, once the issue of language is resolved, we can proceed in a more assertive manner."

"Regarding this issue of language," Padriyl continues. "We understand time is of the essence here, and my mother mentioned this thing only runs three months, but cu'Nar's grace, how do you manage that?"

"Our education system is rather unique," Thaelyn admits. "This is due in part to an elixir we found once that greatly enhances memory function, allowing one to learn at a much-accelerated rate. As such, the course schedules are highly compressed."

"Dear cu'Nar," Tanjhira moans. "I think I already feel my horns sagging."

"And this is only the beginning," he smiles. "If you should wish to engage in any of the other courses in our academies, you may find additional studies to further cause your horns to crumble away."

"Thank you, as if I actually needed that," she chuckles. "I recall Kaliya explaining how this class runs for only six hours a day. This leaves us with a lot of free time, and that pep talk you gave us in the engineering lab got a lot of us thinking. If we need to make our move before Sargeras does whatever else is on his mind, I think we should expedite the process as much as possible. Is there any way to use up more of the day for better efficiency? We're all professionals here, so we would like to go as far as we can while our tails are still twitching from your motivational rally."

"Really! Very well, our normal class schedules in the academies run as two four-hour sessions. We limit ourselves to this for the sake of our students as well as our instructors to prevent any overexertion."

"All right, this is reasonable. Can you create such a course for these language studies?"

Thaelyn makes a quick survey of the gathering for their numbers.

"It would seem you brought along a fair number of people on this occasion. Yes, I believe this would make for a very efficient example. What I believe I can offer would be a custom class schedule exclusively for this study, maybe also to involve the weekend periods, which normally serve as rest days, if you think you would be willing to sacrifice those to further expedite our efforts."

"Perfect..."

"As for me," Padriyl resumes. "I will be serving part of my time here, so the six-hour course might work better for me."

"Very good, but I should mention we already have one such course running with a few of the other agents working with us, so yours would be out of sync with that. Perhaps what we could do is to put you into this new schedule until you catch up on your lessons, and then transfer you, giving you more time in the day for your work. It should not take too long for that, I think."

"That would be acceptable."

"Your Lordship," Tanjhira adds. "As I'm looking around here, two thoughts come to mind immediately. The first relates to our transit options. I'm looking at this conveyor unit over here, or whatever you call it...I believe Kaliya used a different name...and it brings to mind a delicate issue of security. At the risk of sounding like a laboratory bore who never goes outside, I'm actually regarded by the Council as a high-value representative for my skills and technical expertise. They don't normally allow me the freedom to enjoy the outdoors for the risk of attack."

"I fully understand, and therefore, sending you out here is regarded as risky for your potential loss. Very well, how would you suggest we correct this?"

"Kaliya once mentioned these units of yours, and a thought came to mind. Would it be possible to install one of these somewhere in or around the Naarg uy'Sodrad? Perhaps in a concealed area, especially if we hope to be working so closely together for this conjoined research."

"Do you have a location in mind? I should think it may need to be indoors, or some location out of view from any observers."

"Yes, actually, and I think I can push this through the Council to ensure their cooperation. We have a vehicle hanger deeper inside the ship. When we crashed, it was buried under the hill we plowed up, so we had to dig it out in order to use our ground vehicles. However, it should provide plenty of room for a unit like this, and we could access it from indoors. Do you require any special power demands for it?"

"We have our own designs, actually, so the installation should not be too difficult. Then we need to think of how to link it with the rest...let me see..." he pauses to consider the issue. "I would desire to keep this one here as it is for our own needs, but perhaps we could create a new link for yours..." he surveys the camp for a possible solution. "No, wait, I think I have a better idea. If security is an issue, especially with you and perhaps others we do not wish to be seen passing through here at all, we should establish a dedicated link to Tae'Eladar. That way, you may come and go as you please and no one will be the wiser. And if you should wish to visit us here, you may use the standard routing."

"That sounds very agreeable. My next thought is this defensive wall of yours. Kaliya mentioned it uses a similar technique as that bubble effect you presumably used when you dropped that bomb here in the valley. I'm asking myself how effective it might be against a pulse plasma weapon."

"We currently have some of our people out in the field with a portable form of the shield, although your friends, the Suuden-Aryku, seem a bit reluctant to try us lately."

"So I hear," she smiles. "But still, I was wondering if we could try a few field tests just to make sure. We picked up some of their weapons from that last fight, and I've been studying them in the lab. But if we could set something up, we could try it out to see if this could aid us in our future engagements."

"Excellent, we have a few training and testing fields we could use, at least for now. And I have people looking for a good location to establish a new facility for us."

"All right," she nods. "As for the Suuden-Aryku, I wouldn't expect them to be absent for long. I was speaking to Commander Nazég about this, and we both agree they will likely try a stronger approach next time."

"Then we must be ready for them. I will pass the word to our people to be on the lookout and make ready to provide a sturdy defense on our side."

"I just hope it works."

＋ ＋ ◆ ◆ ◆ ＋ ＋

"Governor Dramon, I have news!"

Dean Malorn charges into the Governor's office with a look of determination on his face.

"Do take care, Dean! Although I may anxiously await your report, there is still the matter of the appropriate protocol when entering my office."

"My apologies, Governor, but I have a report from one of my spies. It would seem Thaelyn has been busy of late…quite busy from the sound of it."

"Ah, it is about time," he leans back in his chair. "What has he been up to these past weeks?"

"It would seem as though he has been laying into the orcs rather heavily. You may recall that our spies out on the western frontier have not been able to report anything of significance in his war activities. I believe I now understand his methods."

The Dean steadies himself on the opposite side of the desk as he prepares his thoughts.

"For instance," he continues. "We know already that Thaelyn delights in the use of portals. This, combined with the apparent lack of any visible troop movement in or out of his camp, makes me believe he is using portals to make quick jabbing attacks on the orcish outposts."

"While this is certainly reasonable, do we have any actual evidence of these attacks?"

"In an indirect manner of speaking, I think the answer must be yes. A team of my spies have returned after following a series of wagons leaving the city, going down to the valley, and then diverting off to the other side of that canyon out there. They apparently got curious as to why so many of these wagon trains are coming and going lately."

"Coming and going is one thing, but to the other side, you say? For what reason?"

"They reported the appearance of a large stockpile of, well," he coughs. "For lack of a better word, orcish rubbish building up in the canyon. These wagon trains are people from the city apparently, um…scavenging whatever might be of value within these heaps and bringing it back to the city as scrap to be reused locally."

"Ugh…" he winces. "So far, your report sounds suitably revolting, but I am unsure how this might sate my cravings to fathom what that man has been doing with himself! What has become of the orcs this rubbish formerly belonged to?"

"My Lord, further investigation of the canyon has revealed the development of what seems to be a large burial ground. Estimates are that we could be looking at mass graves holding many thousands of bodies."

"Indeed…" the Governor considers deeply. "This might explain a few reports I am also receiving from my own contacts. These reports suggest the disappearance of several complete orcish camps along the northern line near the elven city of Solinaia, along with a dotting of other camps in the near vicinity."

"My Lord, I must admit one thing. I am at a bit of a loss to understand the purpose of this strategy. Why clean up the mess after killing off the orcs?"

"Confusion, my dear Dean. It actually makes very good sense, from a military standpoint. If you leave the bodies behind, you leave evidence of your activities. But if you clean it up, it is as though nothing was ever there. A devious plan, if I must say, but it cannot hold out forever. Even the orcs will grow wise to it eventually."

"Very well, so Thaelyn is cutting through the orcs," the Dean concludes. "Considering how his troops are equipped, I would expect the orcs will be in for a hard time of it."

"Yes, Dean, and it may be just a matter of time for him on that front. We should watch him carefully."

"What about these wagons carrying the scavenged goods?" the Dean asks. "It could fully reverse the perceived supply shortages we have been creating for the city. The other races might even start to demand more once they realize we have more to offer. This could change the balance of the war!"

"Calm yourself, Dean. Orcish materials are hardly a cause for concern. It might placate the desires of the people if they wish to wallow in such filth, but I would hardly believe it could alter the conditions we have so carefully worked to create. This war is far from over. We will not see this Thaelyn do as well once he realizes his betters in the Flame Elves and the Suuden-Aryku."

In this third week since their initial arrival, Thaelyn began pressing hard on his advantage against the orcs. The war would likely grind on for years, especially considering where it might ultimately take them.

Meanwhile, the patrols around the Naarg uy'Sodrad were augmented with mages to reinforce their position. The testing of the Infinity Shield against a pulse plasma rifle proved very effective, as the shield simply absorbed the energies harmlessly. Now, shield mages were on patrol as forward guards to offer a defensive line against any new incursions. To further augment this new defensive line, the Daanen-Aryku deployed electronic countermeasures in the area to scramble the Suuden-Aryku communications, thus adding to the disruption of their troop movement and coordination.

After a while, the Suuden-Aryku were seen again making their advance. This time, the shield mages and Daanen-Aryku militia took the front, and carefully fell back to lure the Suuden-Aryku into an ambush with the other Order troops lying in wait. This gave the impression of further upgrades to the Allegiance Guard forces in the area, as the Order troops were still using their disguises. And even though the Suuden-Aryku were taking further losses, they seemed determined to make continued advances.

As the current week wore on to the next, the Order began sending additional mages to supplement their forces by using elemental and conjuration magic to further confound the Suuden-Aryku troopers, as they were demonstrating a severe weakness to magical attack.

The recent string of victories made a clear impression on the Daanen-Aryku, invoking many to begin exchanging gossip and whispers among the halls and corridors of the Naarg uy'Sodrad. Talk of the developments with the alliance and the inspirational speech to stand up and fight back dominated the discussions. And these echoes did not pass by unnoticed to the Elder Council, as they were still debating some of the suggestions given to them weeks before, and found they were becoming swayed by the public enthusiasm.

"I must admit," Elder Vankkar begins. "I am feeling a sense of encouragement over the recent events outside, even though my position is to argue the implications. We allowed the installation of their conveyor device in our vehicle hanger, and I suppose this was a good choice to allow the efficient travel of our people to and from without the risk of discovery outside. Then, according to Chief Tech Lapäli, she believes there is a sizable potential for us to learn from them what their magic is about. Further, we have seen this demonstrated outside with these troops providing a very effective defensive line."

"Santari," Elder Girhani considers. "In all I have ever learned of our past experiences with the Suuden-Aryku, we've never had such an effective defense that could so completely block their attacks. I would say this alone is worth seeking to further our relationship."

"I might have to agree with you on that. But my role here is to try to argue, not to agree so easily," he smiles. "We have a long way to go yet."

"A long way to go, yes, but at least now we can hold the ground we stand on. What I find interesting is that these people are able to bring down the Suuden-Aryku so easily whereas ours could not."

"You mean with these weapons of theirs?"

"Yes, the Suuden-Aryku have apparently made a number of very potent advances in their technology during our absence from Azgarén. Our weapons have very little effect on their armor. But to see a simple bow and arrow do more than our own pulse weapons is a bit humbling."

"I agree, although I hear those arrows aren't normal by any recognizable measure. And then to use swords, of all things," he chuckles. "But then, we never could've expected they would be so vulnerable to injury."

"Therefore, they prefer to use ranged weapons, and mainly on a scale to match their other high-end technologies."

"I believe I heard it said once that these people use some sort of enchantment on their equipment, whatever that means. Apparently, it's some sort of augmentation to further increase their potential."

"More of their magic," she nods, "which I think we should certainly investigate for ourselves. The orcs of Ruuki uy'Daan were nowhere near this advanced, and did not seem as interested in teaching us anyway. But His Lordship is offering this exchange, and I think we should take it without any further hesitation."

"Master Velen," Elder Vankkar directs. "Do you have any opinions on this?"

"Santari," he responds. "You know me and how I feel about

warfare. But this has to be regarded as moot, by now, as his explanation of our predicament must take precedence. I have reflected on His Lordship's words on many occasions, as well as the visions I received from the cu'Nar in that last prophecy we received. I feel quite confident, at this time, that we are watching the prophecy unfold before our eyes...slowly, piece by piece. Where it will take us, I cannot say, but I am quite sure the cu'Nar have been trying to help us since we departed from Azgarén, and that last prophecy did make it sound as though we are aiming at a form of reconciliation."

"So, you're saying we should move forward with these relations? I could argue this by reminding the Council of the promises our people once listened to on Azgarén when Sargeras arrived."

"Yes, but as I recall it, he came with the initial claim that he was running from someone and seeking sanctuary, and further to ask for our aid, and our payment would be these promises of great wisdom. Now, we can see where the others found themselves. But you should also remember, I was part of that same Council, and they were rather drunk on their authority. It becomes very apparent to me that it would not take a great effort on his part to persuade them to follow him."

"I may have to agree, Master Velen," Elder Girhani confirms. "We who are still of our own free will are wiser for the wear, so I do not believe we would be so easily led astray. Lord Thaelyn has demonstrated every word he has promised and saved many lives along the way. Not even Sargeras did that much."

"And I should also point out," Velen adds. "Many of our people were enthralled by that speech he gave in the research hall. Even though I had always considered us a peaceful society, it would seem there are those who recognize the value of their own survival, even if to go to war for it."

"At this moment, Master Velen," Elder Vankkar offers. "I wouldn't call that a bad thing. Each and every one of us has lost something dear...Opadna and her son, me with my daughter, as well as our respective spouses. And then we have Med-tech Tad'vaal losing the rest of her family, including her younger sister, which was probably the most painful. So, I'm ready to go to war for what's left, no different from the rest."

<hr>

A chirping ring comes from a trans-com in Thaelyn's holster. This was one of the units donated by Kaliya and her connection to provide a few to the higher-ranking officers, and other local agents. He takes it out to answer the call.

"This is Thaelyn."

"Your Lordship, this is Commander Nazég. How are you today?"

"Doing well, Commander. Do you have any interesting news on your front?"

"Mostly a status report on the results of the recent attacks here. As you know, we've been at war for as long as any of us care to remember, mostly on the defense with virtually no sign of victory."

"Indeed, they are relentless in their pursuit. And now they feel they have you cornered like an injured animal."

"Yes, but this time, and largely with your help, that injured animal has some teeth to it. We're making some good progress here, and not only with our battles. The recent victories outside have provided us with some additional material to study relating to our enemies. The bodies left behind are being brought in, and we're starting to learn a few things on what may have occurred with the Suuden-Aryku that causes them to appear, and maybe even to behave the way they do."

"Anything useful, so far?"

"Let me transfer you over to our chief med-tech. One moment…"

Thaelyn waits while the link is transferred to the Naarg uy'Sodrad medical ward. Soon, a pleasant female voice arrives on the line.

"Your Lordship? This is Med-tech Ankhia Tad'vaal, how are you today?"

"I do well, Med-tech. And I believe I have heard your name mentioned on occasion. The Commander said you might have some information for us on the Suuden-Aryku."

"Yes. The information I have is still preliminary, but I'm

beginning to understand more about what I'm looking at. I hope you understand, my experience with Suuden'kai technology, or at least whatever they've been inventing during this time, is virtually nil, so I've had to return to the old books and catalogs for a refresher course."

"Absolutely," he grins. "And what did you learn?"

"For one thing, we're noticing a couple of cranial implants which seem to be positioned in locations known to effect behavior, emotions, and perhaps some of the higher thought processes."

"That does not sound at all pleasant. By this description, they were turned into some sort of machine hybrid."

"Maybe not to such an extreme, but certainly governed by something. The rest of their natural body appears normal. Although, what these things do is still questionable because the units are nonfunctional at the moment. I think when the body died, the units shut down automatically."

"Very well, perhaps we can pursue this at a later date, should we find such an opportunity for ourselves."

"Next is this lifeform. At first, it appeared as a sort of parasitic entity, but I believe this is actually a bioengineered augmentation. I did some research in our old archives with what we call a biotech seed. This is an artifact of an ancient research project our people once made in the hopes of formulating an artificial lifeform to enhance the body. It was supposed to provide us with innate capabilities allowing us to colonize hostile environments."

"How curious, even fascinating, but also a bit disturbing for the implications. With respect, Med-tech, I think I would not wish to have my body modified in such a way."

"My feelings exactly. According to our records, the project was abandoned at some point for these same ethical reasons."

"But it would seem someone reopened it."

"Yes, it does. But my autopsies of these bodies are revealing something disturbing."

"Oh? Relating to these entities?"

"Yes, they are the primary cause of death here, not the injuries."

"Excuse me?" he frowns sharply. "In what way?"

"The injuries I saw on the bodies were not what I might call life-threatening, and many were not on the host body to begin with, but instead on these entities, since they seem to cover such a large surface area. On further study, I was noticing large regions of necrotized tissue in the host body near the point of injury on the entity, as if the injury reflected a harmful response to the host."

"Dear Powers, so this entity is the one responsible, creating a condition of extreme vulnerability to the host underneath."

"I don't know if this is intentional or incidental to the design of the entity, but it certainly offers a few complications if we should ever want to remove one."

"Indeed! But in relation to engaging them in warfare, as unpleasant as this may sound, it does provide us with a convenient method to oppose them."

"Yes, I suppose it does, even though it's disturbing to my senses as a medical professional."

"I understand. Is there anything else?"

"Nothing on my side, I just wanted to share these results with you."

"Very good. Oh, by the way, on the topic of medical results, it occurs to me that it might be valuable for us to exchange a few of our own."

"Oh? What kind?"

"As we move forward in our combined efforts, it becomes apparent that medical knowledge could be useful if any of our people should be called upon to give aid to yours. Our healers can mend wounds using their divine gifts much faster than another race with surgical or medicinal methods. But to do so would require some prior knowledge of the body they are trying to heal. Would you happen to have anything you could share with us to help us teach our healers about the anatomical design of your people?"

"I'm sure we can put something together for you. Our medical database contains a full set of studies that we can assemble for your people to examine."

"Excellent. This will benefit all of us in the long term."

"All right, I'm giving you back to Kailen. I think he had something else for you."

Thaelyn once again waits for the link to transfer.

"This is Commander Nazég."

"Yes, Commander, that charming young lady of yours said you have more?"

"Yes, actually. We're picking up a lot of equipment from the bodies outside, including weapons, armor, and other items. Some of this can be useful to help resupply our own needs, but I'm also reminded of your proposal for our combined research. I believe the Council is near to making their decision, and it's looking good for us, so I'm holding this aside as part of our initial studies."

"Ah, this is very pleasing to hear. Our people are mobilizing to break ground on that new research facility soon. This should allow us the seclusion we need to build and test whatever is necessary to see this war come into our favor."

"I'm very interested to see how this plays out. Also, the Council is talking about your magic and whether we might one day learn something about it. Can you suggest anything?"

"Are we speaking of outside our wartime ventures? We have both civilian and military courses available back home, although we should remind ourselves of the language issue. But if any of your people would like to take up lessons, all I ask is for you to take the time to understand the delicacies involved. We do not want any accidents."

"Absolutely, I'll pass this along. I've been hearing a lot of people whispering in the common areas about what's going on outside and rumors relating to your mages. Now they're becoming interested to learn more."

"I am pleased to hear it, Commander. Is there anything else?"

"That's all for now. And I'll pass along the Council's final response as soon as it's in."

Relissa, Marelle, and Haran have just finished their daily session in the language class at the academy in Bya'an Tamoranth. The two women had become good friends, since working and studying so closely together gave them a sense of fellowship. As they were leaving the classroom, they bid goodbye to Haran, who diverted to his part-time apprenticeship service. It provided occupation, and a bit of income, to pay for his needs. Relissa also looked forward to the day when she could begin her full training. The prospect of using her natural talents with animals excited her.

Marelle, on the other hand, felt torn between two worlds. She would often find herself daydreaming about what life might be like living and working in such a grand setting. No wars, at least not any in which you are told to sit on the side and wait for your first gray hairs to appear. And if there ever was a crisis, you jumped at the chance to serve. Furthermore, your contribution actually mattered. But her mind would inevitably snap back into focus as she remembered Rolsklinde and her duties to the Allegiance Guard.

As vain as it might seem, she continued to struggle with her sense of responsibility to the city and its people. It was her home. She held a strong sense of duty, but this duty seemed lost in a city that had no real use for her, where all her efforts, and those of all the other Guard members, did so little to change the quality of life.

The two women were on their way out of the guildhall to return to their work, crossing the main courtyard heading towards the front gate, when Marelle's thoughts began circling irresistibly. This had been going on long enough. She needed to know if there was any truth to it. The questions in her mind demanded answers, and even if there was no future in it, she needed final confirmation. She had to make a stand for herself.

"Relissa," she announces, suddenly stopping in her tracks. "You go on ahead. I'll catch up with you in a bit. There's something I'd like to check on before going back."

"Do you need any help with it?"

"No, thank you. This is just a simple little matter I need to tidy up. I'll be along quickly."

Marelle gives a brief wave before returning through the doors into the academy.

Relissa smiles and returns the wave, then exits through the main gate on her way to the portal.

Marelle peers through a crack in the doorway waiting for Relissa to depart out of view. When the way is clear, she exits the academy and crosses the courtyard to the administration entrance.

General Gabarleine was addressing the assembly in the tactical office on the latest troop movements. Two weeks have gone by, and the deployment is on schedule. The march to take control of the western theater of operations is proceeding well.

"Our first assault wave is complete, my Lord," he declares. "The troops have moved into position on the two fronts, and we have wagons ready to relocate their posts when the time is right. The second and third outposts have narrowed the gap between the two flanks, and our gryphons report there is nary an orc to be seen above the line to the north."

"Good, General," Thaelyn muses. "What about the activity to the south of the line? Have the orcs launched any counter attacks?"

"A few skirmishes have been reported, but once the orcs realized our overall strength, most of them pulled back. It could be that the initial precision strikes we made, combined by the sudden rush of our new forces, have put a sizable chunk of fear into their hearts. For the present time, they appear uncertain of us."

Thaelyn pulls himself back from the table to consider the General's words.

"This may offer us a valuable opportunity to make some rapid movements. If they are in such a state of confusion and fear, perhaps we can exploit this, even to exaggerate it. We can use that same ploy as what they did on Ruuki uy'Daan and cause a true panic. We should attempt to maintain this vision of overwhelming power in their eyes. In doing so, we could send them running. Orcs respond to a show of strength. It is what keeps them in line."

"True enough," the General agrees. "Would you wish to accelerate the original plan? If the orcs can be sent running, we could reduce the overall time to take this front."

"Let us make an experiment in this regard. Rush the closing of the gap and send additional deployments southwards beginning from the two outermost camps, closing in on their flanks. We will create a bowl formation and compress the orcs into it. Then, we will rain fire down upon their heads from gryphon-mounted mages, bombarding them from the sky. Orcs are not very keen on ranged attacks, especially upwards, and such a display will certainly offer an impressive show of force."

"Very good, my Lord, I will see to it at once!"

"Am I missing anything important, my Lord?" Relissa quips as she enters the structure.

"Only a carefully organized invasion of your world by a foreign power..." Thaelyn retorts. "Where is Marelle? She needs to hear the latest briefing so she can make her report to Captain Kholgard."

"She'll be along shortly. She told me she had some little tidbit to take care of before coming back. How is the attack going?"

"We are pushing in from the two sides along our front and will be closing in on their flanks to see how they respond to our advance. So far, they seem frightened and confused. We want to maintain this."

"Are we still hauling back all that trash? It gives me a few wiggles thinking of people rummaging through that stuff."

"This is true, but at the same time, I would rather not leave it to sit out in the open. I do still feel my responsibility to keep the place clean."

"Aye, I'm with you there...I suppose."

"It is somewhat curious, however, now that you mention it."

"How's that?"

"We set up an auditing desk out there to tally up our spoils, simply to see what the orcs have in their possession that we might need to consider in our future engagements. And we are seeing a lot of steel and iron tools and weapons, as well as portions of armor in that lot."

"Is it normal for orcs to use this?"

"Not unless it is stolen. On Tae'Eladar, the orcs were not known to conduct mining, instead to steal their materials from other races. I wonder if the same is occurring here."

"It's a good bet they are. Like I said, a lot of towns got dusted in those early days, so I'll bet they picked up a lot of goods."

"I am quite sure they did, as we saw this on Tae'Eladar quite often. But iron and steel, if not maintained properly, can wear out over time, especially if left to rust and corrode. And if these orcs are not the ones to mine or otherwise maintain these materials to keep them in a functional condition, eventually they will give out completely."

"Really! So, what are you actually seeing with the goods we're bringing back?"

"Our people have noticed what appears to be a fair number of new items, not just recycled bits from lost habitation."

"Jiggers, which means they must have a supplier somewhere, if they don't do this themselves."

"Indeed, and likely through their relationship with the Suuden-Aryku."

Marelle was finally returning to the camp as the discussion came to a close.

"Ah, Marelle," Thaelyn announces. "We have some reports for you to go over."

"Give me just one moment and I'm all yours."

"Actually, I will have the General and Relissa attend to this, as I need to leave for a time. I have a few matters that need my attention back in B.T."

Marelle nods as Thaelyn leaves the building and heads over to the portal. As he passes through, his image can be seen on the other side moving up to the guildhall and disappearing beyond the main gates.

Marelle steps up to her lockbox in the rear of the room. Relissa found herself distracted momentarily by Marelle's arrival, and follows the young officer with her eyes. As Marelle opens her box, Relissa observes her removing a small silver-trimmed medallion-like object from her vest pocket, brightly colored on one side and attached to a uniquely ornate ribbon, then discreetly placing it into her box and closing the lid.

"'Ere now! What was that?" Relissa asks as she moves closer.

"What was what, Relissa?" Marelle responds coyly.

"Don't you be trying to bamboozle me, girl. I caught enough of a look at that to know it wasn't some mite of a trinket. That was a badge! I should know enough since I have one of my own. You were out getting the test, weren't you?"

Marelle is silent for a moment, softly biting her lip, not wanting to lie to her friend, but not yet willing to admit her deepest feelings.

"All right, but only between you and me," she replies in a hushed voice. "Yes, I did get the test. I needed to settle a little personal question I had."

"What color did you get?" Relissa inquires with a hopeful tone.

"I got blue," Marelle answers with a cautious smile.

"Nicely done, Marelle!" Relissa applauds, trying to maintain a discreet posture. "But now what? Are you going to join up?"

"I don't know. I need to think about it. I still feel there's a lot for me to do here. Relissa, I'm a soldier in the Allegiance Guard, and as such I have a strong sense of duty to my home and our people. I can't just leave all that on a whim like you and Haran did. I know you had your reasons, but I need to see this through, at least until I can relieve myself of some of these burdens."

"You know, Marelle, with this war going on, even if you join up, you'll still probably be standing here serving up for Rolsklinde."

"You may be right, but eventually I'll have to go away for whatever training they put me through. I know the Order offers a lot, and I'm captivated by the possibilities. It's just that I joined the Guard for a reason…" she reflects on her words briefly and lets out a soft chuckle. "And not simply to pick up drunks off the street. I wanted to make a difference for our people, and right now I feel it still needs me."

"All right, Marelle, but when the time comes, rest easy in the knowing that you'll be siding up with good people who'll take care of you."

Relissa places a comforting hand on Marelle's shoulder as they return to the table for the daily review.

✦

"Professor Cogswoggle! I trust your crew is enjoying themselves with all their wonderful little projects?"

Thaelyn sat behind his desk in his personal office as he greeted the gnomish professor entering the room. The Professor was serving as the head of a new scientific research project studying some of the lighter elements of the data on the Daanen-Aryku holo-disk. This early progress represented a few pilot concessions with the Elder Council and served as an entry-level cooperative effort between the visiting Daanen'kai technicians and the gnomish scientists of Tae'Eladar.

"And a blessed greeting to you too, my Lord! Such a fine jing-dingling day it is today!"

"Yes, it is, Professor. I have called you here to relay some new instructions and to outline some future plans I have been considering of late. Please take a seat and bring out your notebook for me."

The gnome promptly jumps into the chair on the opposite side of the desk, anxiously whipping out his notebook and a pen, and waits intently for Thaelyn to begin.

"First and foremost," Thaelyn announces. "In our war efforts, our preliminary interactions on the primary front show promise. Though it might be early, I am of the recent opinion that we may be able to accelerate our progress in the initial stages of this new campaign. In so doing, we may find ourselves engaging the more difficult opponents earlier than was first expected. To this end, it is prudent for us to make our best progress in these new research projects without delay."

"Abso-double-lutely, my Lord! I fully agree! Never a moment

to lose! Leave no stone unturned, no theory unproven, and no paper un-scribbled upon!"

"Precisely," Thaelyn grins pleasantly. "In any case, as we have discussed earlier when we first made these arrangements with the Daanen-Aryku, I have consulted with my advisors, and we will be apportioning a substantial quantity of funds for the construction of that new military research center we were speaking of recently."

"Oh, yes! How fantastarifically wondabulous! I'm so excited!"

"And I am sure it will get even better! The center will be located outside the city in a remote area, thus affording you a secure environment to conduct all your research away from prying eyes. Everything we bring back from Therinë is to be classified under the heading of Military Intelligence. It will be carefully researched, perhaps even reverse-engineered if necessary, and the knowledge used to augment our combined forces as we press forward in this war effort."

"One quick question, if I may most graciously interrupt for a brief moment… You have in mind to augment the needs of the Daanen-Aryku, but what of the other races in that world?"

"The Night Elf and Human populations are not as technologically advanced as the Daanen'kai body, and therefore do not use such innovations as these. As you recall, it is our policy not to artificially boost a society too quickly. Giving out details such as these, whether to those two races, as well as to our own people, would violate that practice. All things must come at the proper time. The people will learn, but only when they are culturally prepared for it."

"Indeed, my Lord, so then we'll be keeping all these new discoveries under tight security until you can determine the right time to let them out?"

"Yes. The Daanen-Aryku are already familiar with most of these technologies, if only to apply them in a different form, and theirs represents a more imperative need whereas Sargeras is concerned, as theirs is the world he is occupying. And I will have you oversee the project as it transfers into these new facilities."

"Wonderful, my Lord! I can barely contain my anticipation of all the delightful bangs, blams, whizzles and pops we can expect to see in the coming years."

"Of this, I am sure. Let us now move on to the next topic, one that I have been considering in recent times, especially in light of our interactions with the Daanen-Aryku, and the prospect of this war extending across new frontiers, and perhaps even to new worlds."

"I am putty in your hands, my Lord, eagerly awaiting the caressing fingers of your most exalted wisdom and direction!"

"Good, then turn your notebook to a new page and begin taking down these principles. You will begin a new project, effective immediately. This project will translate into a new technological advance for our people in the coming years. You should bring together whatever resources you have available that are not otherwise dedicated to other important tasks."

"Astoundamazing!" the Professor roars as he searches for a clear space in his book.

Thaelyn pulls out the trans-com he was carrying and shows it to the professor as part of his demonstration.

"If you will observe this device, it is the product of Daanen-Aryku technology. Now, this particular example is rather advanced for where we will travel, but it occurs to me that this war will demand we investigate the underlying principles of its functioning. However, we must follow this in our own traditions, not simply to copy theirs."

"Naturally, I understand. We study what it is and…invent…our own. What does it do?"

"This is a ranged communications device. It allows them to speak to one another at a distance, using a centralized hub to route their signals, perhaps also to use repeater stations to further extend their reach. It is a very useful device, and given our war is demanding us to spread over such distances, our own methods are showing their age."

"I fully agree and concur with this predicament. In fact, a few years back, I have to admit I thought about this and got a few people together to run some experiments. But we didn't actually finish since we ran into one or another conundruminium fouling up some of our ideas."

"Indeed. Well, I will give you a few principles for how this particular project will proceed, and have you follow them to create this new technology for us. These principles should not give you as much difficulty."

The professor holds his notepad and pen at the ready while Thaelyn prepares his lecture.

"Sound carries force in nature, this much is evident. We experience it in a storm by the flashes of lightning followed by the crashing of the thunder. Similarly, you have already studied the phenomenon that occurs when one of our gryphons engages its transport sphere and the booming shock that is heard on the ground by it."

Thaelyn sits back in his chair as he continues.

"This has created curiosity in some of you to study the progression of sound through space. However, sound is not the only force in nature that travels. Light also travels. From its source, your eyes can perceive a distant object by the light it emits, whether by reflection or as a source emission. Your eyes receive this across the distance of space and your mind interprets it in such a fashion that it makes sense to you. The same is true of your ears to receive and interpret sound, such as my own words being spoken now."

Thaelyn gestures over to a nearby stained-glass window. The afternoon sun shines through it casting an image on the floor.

"Consider the colors of a rainbow when you think of light, and how they appear through a glass prism. But it does not stop there, for there can be much more beyond that which cannot otherwise be perceived with our eyes and ears."

He returns to his desk and the anxious little gnome on the other side.

"Professor, the first of your objectives here will be to make the preliminary research of the specific physical principles of how this works. You may wish to start with sound, as it might be an easier subject matter for study, but you will soon need to move on to light as it shares many of these same properties. The flows of these forces vibrate with certain harmonics, and these harmonics come in a wide range of frequencies."

He pauses briefly to allow the Professor time for his notetaking.

"The second of your objectives will be to discover ways in which to use this. Sound is easy…we speak, others listen. A bird may chirp its song while others interpret its meaning. Light, on the other hand, or perhaps some derivative, can be used in a constructive manner as a simple signal, but it could possibly go deeper than that with a little creativity. Light also bears an additional quality, as it can travel far and very quickly."

He leans forward on his desk as he wraps up.

"The harmonics of these energies can carry further benefits. And so, just as the sound of my voice can relay these instructions to your ears, or the drums of an orcish war party may communicate a message to others, so too can other forms of energies be used to convey information to distant reaches…and not simply as a series of primal codes, but in a much more complex fashion, as language does. Seek it out."

"Marvelous, my Lord!" the Professor sings. "I love it! Such delightful intrigue and carefully laid clues. I'll get my people working on this at once!"

The excited little gnome bounces out of the chair as he speaks. He gives a courteous bow and dashes out of the room.

A rhythmic tonal announcement sounds out a series of beeps and twitters from a drawer in Governor Dramon's desk. The Governor pulls open the drawer and picks up the odd device making the disturbance. A visual display shows an iconic button flashing below a line of foreign symbols. The Governor presses the button and speaks into the device.

"Yes, Commander?"

"I have a report."

The voice carried the usual deep monotonal ambiance.

"Very well, Commander, what is it?"

"Confirmation, the invaders have engaged the orcs. They have established a forward line and appear to be southward bound."

"And the orcs? What is their reaction?"

"Frightened and disorganized, I do not expect them to survive long."

"Indeed, and I might expect as much. But I will not shed any tears for them. Those filthy animals served their purpose on Ruuki uy'Daan, and further they showed us the path to the Wheel. I would consider that to be quite sufficient for their degree of usefulness. So, we shall leave them to their fate. Has he made any movements on anyone else?"

"None reported on our lines. I have also been in contact with the Priestess, and she reports no sightings. Only the human Guard at the Nazég vessel, but they do not fight as expected. We now suffer losses in that area. You must discover the reason."

"So far, we have suspected Thaelyn to be supplying them, but we have not discovered the source yet. I will continue the investigation and do what I must to put an end to it."

"They do not simply fight with improved supplies. They now use techniques and abilities not seen before."

"What sort of abilities?" the Governor inquires cautiously.

"We have observed them producing effects of an abnormal design."

"Are you speaking of magic here, Commander?"

"Affirmative…"

"But this doesn't make sense," he muses quietly. "The Guard doesn't even study magic, and those undereducated students at the academy can barely even ignite a barbeque, let alone fight a war with it. All right, I will have you tend to your business, and I'll tend to mine. We will maintain our tactics as a means of dissuading any special interest. I will see about the Guard and their actions, but as far as Thaelyn is concerned, I do not want him becoming overly ambitious if his primary focus is with the orcs. We will bide our time so far."

"Acknowledged, Geilv out…"

The Governor sets the device back into the drawer and closes it. He calls in one of his attendants and gives him instructions to fetch Dean Malorn. A few minutes later, the Dean makes his entrance.

"Yes, Governor, you summoned me?"

"Dean, we have some serious developments occurring around us, some of which are deeply disturbing, and I wish to understand why."

"My Lord, which ones are you referring to?"

"I just received another report of the Guard out there by the Naarg uy'Sodrad. It would seem they are using a few new tactics, and this makes we wonder about the issue of loyalty in this city."

"What?" the Dean winces. "Whose loyalty? I thought we already settled the one with the Guard."

"I'm actually referring to the mage academy now," the Governor glares at the Dean and raises his brow.

The Dean studies the Governor's face and recognizes the determination in his eyes.

"My Lord, you should know, you have my loyalty. What is it that troubles you?"

"Yes, I suppose your loyalty is well-enough evident, but let me ask about your students. Where are they at this time?"

"As far as I know, they are all attending classes. Why?"

"Have you seen any absences recently?"

"I will admit I don't tally the attendance personally. I usually leave that to the instructors. But I haven't been informed of any large lapses in attendance."

"Then can you explain to me why the Guard has been spotted out by the Naarg uy'Sodrad now using magical attacks on the Suuden-Aryku?"

"Ah! So that's what this is about. Actually, I think I can, if you will indulge me for a moment."

"Very well, this should be interesting," the Governor relaxes back in his chair.

"Let me carry you through my full report, while I'm here."

The Dean pulls out a paper he had tucked away in this vest pocket.

"First, my spies are telling me he seems to be involved in a large-scale assault on the orcs. They've seen large numbers of troops moving through portals in his camp."

"Yes, my information confirms this as well, and he may even have them on the run soon."

"Good, but then, if you will recall last week when I reported sightings of new construction efforts occurring near Thaelyn's camp... Well, it has grown even further, spreading out across a broad area. It would seem he is making himself quite comfortable down there. Some estimates suggest he'll have a large settlement established soon."

"This is most troubling," the Governor relents. "This little invasion of his is becoming quite a bother. Is there anything else?"

"Yes. In addition to this, we're seeing new farming activities, and not just in the northern part of the valley, but also in the countryside around the city proper. They appear to be our own people! Furthermore, I've heard of similar activities near Solinaia."

"What?!" cries the Governor. "How dare they go outside the walls! We had these peasants confined inside the city where we could control them, and now they dare go outside and build new farms and outlying communities again? This is intolerable!"

The Governor pushes his chair away from the desk towards a window to look outside.

"Four centuries, Dean... That's how long this war has been waging, beginning with the conversion of the Flame Elves, and later with the arrival of the Suuden-Aryku and the orcs. A systematic reduction of the world's population down to a manageable content, that's what is occurring here. And in just one month, an outsider comes in and turns it all around. We had these people restricted in their movements as well as their contact with anything outside. Now they have hope. Enough, that is, to go out there and start building again."

"That's not all, Governor," the Dean states gravely. "I've heard rumors that the citizens of Solinaia have been offered a political union with Thaelyn's kingdom. I don't know if they've agreed to this yet, but the rumors are suggesting they might. Also, I've heard a few echoes of the same desire running through the streets here. Not much, mind you, but in certain districts at least."

The Governor turns away suddenly from the window to face the Dean with a pained look on his face.

"This could be the foundation of a revolt! Do you realize what this could do to us, Dean?"

He makes a quick glance around the room, then turns back to the Dean.

"What about the Guard in all this, and this report of using magic, on top of everything else."

"Right, the good part..." he clears his throat for emphasis. "My spies have not seen any unusual supply trains coming in from Thaelyn's camp, or anywhere else for that matter, to reinforce the Guard. The only so-called supplies showing up are those civilians I mentioned before rummaging through the orcish refuse in the valley, which is still ongoing, by the way," he shudders.

"Yes, how amusing."

"However, in light of this, I decided to test a theory."

"And what might that be?"

"At the same time as my spies haven't seen any supplies coming in, they also haven't seen any Allegiance Guard troops going out, except for the usual watchtower patrols. So, I sent my people around the city to conduct a careful tally. Would you like to know my results?"

The Governor turns a derisive stare at the Dean.

"As I expected," the Dean continues confidently. "All the Guard members are present and accounted for within the city."

The room goes silent for a moment.

"But if it's not... Blast him!" the Governor shouts as he jumps to his feet. "They're his own troops, and further disguised as our men to throw off the enemy! They must be, especially if they're using magic! And this would also explain that attack and the equipment they're using out there. Enchanted weapons and armor, and also some rather extravagant bows with what I'm guessing now to be elemental arrows."

"That goes a little beyond what we have here."

"It does! And the Suuden-Aryku are apparently taking heavy losses from it."

"That doesn't sound especially good for them. If it were me, I might stay away from that."

"You may be right, Dean. I will need to pay closer attention to this to see how it develops."

"But all this tells me the Guard has not only been in contact with Thaelyn, but they are also in league with him. They probably provided those costumes and informed him of their methods so he could put on this charade for the Suuden-Aryku."

"Yes, Dean, and this also suggests the Guard may be as much a threat to our position as Thaelyn himself."

"Is there anything you would have me do, my Lord?"

"Yes, I will have you send spies to Thaelyn's camp and watch him carefully. I want to know his precise movements in and out. We may need to make...special arrangements...to deal with this pest and his unwelcome intrusion."

Chapter 14
SUBTERFUGE

Another two weeks pass, and the Order progresses well in a hurried assault on the orcish lines. The orcs were reeling from the sudden vigorous movements of Thaelyn's army, being confronted on multiple sides and with no escape. Bombardments from the air only served to further shock and confound the orcs as they have no proper defense against such attacks. Several front-line camps began pulling back as the orcs learned of the pattern being used by the Order. Smaller camps formed up with larger ones to add numbers into their defense, but it only served to provide a bigger target to hit from above.

The Order further incorporated summoned elementals into the fray. These beings are virtually immune to attacks by common weapons. They rampaged through the orcish camps wreaking havoc and disturbing the orcs from settling into a coherent fighting force. The fear tactics were working.

The morning assembly with Thaelyn and his officers gathers in the tactical office.

"General, have we seen anything on our southern watch?"

"Not as yet, my Lord, and this actually disturbs me greatly. If these orcs are in league with the other members of their alliance, those others should be well aware by now of the peril facing the orcs, and at least some of them should come to their aid. Yet, we have seen no activity approaching us from the south or east, nor have we seen any movement to reinforce the orcish positions."

"Indeed, and I find it hard to believe the others would not have noticed us by now. This gives the impression they are letting the orcs fall intentionally, but for what reason...to study our methods? Or do they simply care so little for the orcs to begin with. With the Suuden-Aryku described to us as they are, they might see the orcs as no more than fodder, an expendable ground force."

"That was my thought as well, my Lord, and although I may feel some comfort in knowing our campaign against the orcs may go unchallenged by the others, I am increasingly concerned over what we may face once the orcs are no more. The Suuden-Aryku, in particular, may be the most difficult, as I would expect their advanced nature to demonstrate some rather peculiar strategic designs."

"If they keep at bay long enough, perhaps we will have time to research some of their technology and bring it into our cause, but I would not wish to depend on this. Our interactions with them out near the Naarg uy'Sodrad have taught us enough to know how to defeat them if they should ever march in this direction. Of greatest importance is to maintain shield mages on-hand at all times, and plenty of archers, especially with elemental bows. They seem to be particularly effective on that armor of theirs."

"Agreed, and we should augment the shield wall, as well, to offer more defense to the newly developing settlement. It cannot defend against an aerial attack, but ground forces can be routed around it and into bottleneck spaces where they have less of an advantage."

"Good. Make it so, General."

As the morning briefing continues in the tactical office, a different conversation is taking place miles away to the north in the city of Rolsklinde inside the Governor's office.

"Commander Geilv, speaking..."

The voice on the alien communicator makes its announcement in a typically cold manner.

"Commander, I believe we have enough information by now on Thaelyn's movements that we can confidently suggest a few of our own. Here is what I have in mind..."

◆

Early afternoon arrives, and with it are Relissa and Marelle from their daily language lessons. As they come through the portal, they find Thaelyn meeting with a group of merchants from Bya'an Tamoranth. Their visit is designed to help coordinate efforts to establish a centralized marketplace in the soon-to-be settlement here in the valley.

"If we are to become the hub distribution center for the region," declares one of the merchants. "We will need to establish a large stockyard. The other outposts you're creating across the land will need to have a dependable supply depot in order to maintain themselves."

"Agreed..." Thaelyn nods. "For a time, however, it will have to be an open yard, rather than an enclosed structure. Most of our resources are being used to build housing for the farming communities and other laborers. At present, we must give this a higher priority. The marketplaces where you will conduct your work will come shortly thereafter once the families settle themselves."

"Very good, my Lord! Then we shall return home and begin making arrangements to organize and prepare our shipments. Oh, and by the way, have you given any thought on what name you will give to this fair little village?"

"As it so happens, I have. Aerlie and I have given this some thought, and we have decided to call it Firstfall, in memoriam of those who perished during our initial arrival."

"You mean the orcs you encountered here?"

"Yes. They may have been orcs, and enemies of our kin, but they were living creatures and deserve an epitaph."

"I understand, my Lord. We shall make the appropriate recordings on our return home. Good day to you."

The merchants give a polite bow and turn to leave through the portal.

"Firstfall, ay?" Relissa quips. "Sounds dandy enough! So, when do I get a house here?"

"You may have one at such fair time as you can afford it," Thaelyn chuckles.

"All right, fine enough…"

"Marelle, you should make your attendance with General Gabarleine on today's meeting. Our efforts with the orcs are progressing well, but concerns are generating on the other factions in this game."

"Yes, Your Lordship, and I've been thinking about this. It's almost as if it's going along too smoothly for us."

"This is our conclusion, as well. We will be making some new efforts to affect our local security by moving the wall and posting shield mages along various points to offer a quick response should we encounter any hostile actions from the Suuden-Aryku."

"Jiggers," Relissa intones warily. "But you say they're doing a fine enough job out by the Naarg uy'Sodrad, right?"

"They are, so we must borrow from this example."

"And what about the Flame Elves?" Marelle asks. "Shouldn't we be equally concerned about them?"

"Although the Flame Elves are more advanced than the orcs, they are not as likely to show the same level of sophistication as the Suuden-Aryku, even though they might be in league with them. We have not seen any evidence within the orcish camps of Suuden-Aryku technology, not that it surprises me as I doubt the orcs would be able to comprehend such items. Therefore, I am holding an opinion that they may not share any of this with the lesser races, thus leaving the Flame Elves to their own devices."

"My Lord," Relissa interjects. "On the downside of this, the Flame Elves are known to use a good bit of magic."

"Yes, Your Lordship," Marelle continues. "We've heard of this, as well. Even though it's been a long time since we've seen anything, in earlier times, they attacked the smaller towns and villages that used to exist out here, often burning them to the ground using magical fire, so the story goes. Finally, there was nothing left for them, and for whatever reason, they stopped their advance before approaching our city walls. Or, at least, that is to say as an advancing army trying to attack us. Most of us believe this is because Rolsklinde is too strong in its defense."

"But could it actually be for this precise reason?" Thaelyn muses. "Or could there be another one. Recall what we said once, they purge this world down to the last, and then oppress whatever is left."

"Yeah, that's right, so whatever the reason, they must be holding us in reserve for something, right?"

"This may or may not necessarily be, but there must certainly be a reason to it. Let us recall a few details briefly. Regarding that odd attack by the Naarg uy'Sodrad, they take to unconventional…for them…methods to attack our patrol. This was in contrast to their classic behavior, and as we have already suggested, that behavior involves this oppressive mentality to keep you confined. Until my arrival, they had containment, but I have upset that for them. Now, the Guard seems to be making additional patrols out there, and they do not like it, therefore the attack. It was a message saying you are not welcome out there without their permission."

"Without their permission. Real nice…"

"The demonstration may also be to suggest they do not need their rifles to do so. Simple swords, but in this case made of adamantium, are all that is needed to literally cut you to ribbons."

"And again, real nice…"

"Now, you say to your knowledge you never suffered an attack on your walls."

"Right, not in my lifetime, or Roddy's… And just for reference, I'm thirty-two, and he's forty-four."

"And I believe he also mentioned that of his father as well. So then, we should probably ask, when was the last time you actually did take a hit?"

"Good question, but I don't think I could offer an answer. Relissa, what about you? You also had smaller towns and villages once upon a time. How do you fare from your side now that they are gone?"

"As I remember it," she offers. "I think the last of them got kicked about half a century ago, and we haven't had any major hits near Solinaia since that time. The orcs have come close on a few occasions, but never further than our outer watch posts."

"As you remember it?" Marelle asks tentatively. "Are we speaking of historically or..."

"In my lifetime, Marelle... I'm eighty-seven."

"Egads! How did you manage that?"

"Keep in mind, we elves have much longer lifespans than you humans. That's still considered young for us. In fact, I wouldn't say I'm fully of age till my first century."

"Gods' pity, I think I hate you now," she laughs teasingly.

Thaelyn offers a minor chuckle at the exchange before continuing.

"What if it was longer than you might expect?"

"Uh oh...what do you mean?"

"The current Governor does not seem to care much about fighting this war. Could there be a reason? Is it simply due to his gluttony and prejudice for the others, or is there a hidden motive here? And then, what about his predecessor, was he the same? How do you go about selecting your authority figures?"

"We don't. The Dean, as far as I know, is selected by the Governor. As for the Governor himself...I don't actually know how it changes from one to another."

"Excuse me, but you, who should know at least as much about where your authority comes from, do not actually know where it comes from?"

"Um...all right," she emits bashfully. "That's making it look bad. We generally assume it follows from one to another privately."

"You do not have anything like a vote, or a public rally to appoint a new one?"

"Not that I've ever seen."

"Then this sounds much more like an autocracy than a proper political appointment. If it follows from one to another privately, you have yourselves a form of despotism. It is no wonder he cares not to involve himself politely with the others. This further invites me to conjecture on the other elements of your troubles up there."

"Oh wonderful, which ones?"

"For one, your supply shortages… You say it involves iron from the dwarves. My scouts have reported very little activity up there, that is to say of shipments coming out to your city, but there are stockpiles of iron building up in a storage area near that one furnace room…lots of it…more than enough to cover for your shortages."

"Gods above!" she shouts. "So where is the rest of it going?"

"This is a fair enough question to ask, and I will wager it involves our recent tallies out in the refuse mounds captured from the orcs. There are plentiful supplies of what appears to be fresh milled iron and steel in that lot."

"Oh grand!" she blasts. "So, he's selling our iron to the enemy, and this is why he doesn't want to go to war with them. He's probably pocketing all the coin from it."

"This could possibly also answer the question of that rogue attack."

"How, as we don't have adamantium to sell anyone…I don't think."

"Perhaps not, if you say you are not aware of it locally, but one thing that does stand out is all your other…sanctioned…Guard patrols went out and came home without incident. Now, what is the difference in ours by comparison?"

"Uh oh…sanctioned…and yours wasn't sanctioned…by HIM!" she screeches. "So, what you're saying is he's in cahoots with the bloody Suuden-Aryku somehow, and only on his order are we told to go out to play hero, and the Suuden-Aryku were probably also told to stay at home so our people could come back safe and sound, with stories of how brave they were walking in circles out there."

"And ours, who are in disguise as yours, were unsanctioned by him. Now we have a potential link, if only to answer the one about the adamantium. If he is in league with the Suuden-Aryku, then it could be he who is watching us, and maybe through them."

"This could further explain why we're expected only to pick up drunks. He doesn't want us doing anything else, shortages or otherwise."

"This could represent a problem, Your Lordship," Padriyl ushers from behind the group.

They turn to see the tall Daanen'kai officer strolling up to join the conversation.

"Very well," Thaelyn notes. "And just for the sake of debate, how would you describe this?"

"The adamantium armor, your magic, your enchanted weapons… Marelle, do your people use any of this?"

"Nope!" she asserts. "Haran was constantly complaining about the lack of teachings they give in that academy, and the Guard doesn't study it at all. Then our steel armor and weapons, nothing enchanted. His people would represent a significant improvement over us, especially if you count the magic."

"And those mages would outclass whatever your academy puts out. So, I think this would be a very clear indication to anyone with a little background detail, like your Governor. The Suuden-Aryku might not know the difference, but he would."

"Very nicely deduced, Lieutenant," Thaelyn nods. "And for this, I think our little ruse is likely exposed by now. So be it, we learned some vital details on our enemies, and this is enough to allow us our advantage."

"But it doesn't necessarily help us if they want to bomb us," Marelle mumbles.

"Well, no, this is still a problem. But I am going to hope they keep to their side, as we have not made that direct advance on them yet. In these past weeks, they seem to be determinedly making their advances out there, and fairly routinely after recovering from that initial setback. This is strange, but at the same time, it might also stand out as a tactic of a sort."

"How so?"

"Playing as if nothing has changed… If the Governor is receiving reports, he might be playing his own game against us. He could be planning something, and the Suuden-Aryku are under advisement to play business-as-usual, a show for us until this other plan is ready."

"I don't think I like the sound of that."

"Yes, but ultimately, the worst scenario that I can see out of this so far is they stop attacking the Naarg uy'Sodrad. If they are shedding off the orcs, and we do not represent ourselves as an immediate danger to them, this simply leaves us wondering what they will do next. Clearly, they must desire to resolve my invasion and subsequent disruption of their affairs, but if they are not making an overt movement, it has to be..." his voice trails off suddenly.

Thaelyn's gaze drifts off their faces into a blank stare ahead of him. Relissa felt a quick shiver rush through her, as her senses were starting to learn of his manners. She instantly goes on the offensive. She darts her eyes around the camp, then sets them on Captain Hagmaert over by the tactical office, contentedly sitting in his chair.

"Captain?" she calls anxiously. "Your attention, please?"

The Captain jerked around abruptly to find Thaelyn. His posture instantly stiffened, and he jumped to his feet.

"To arms! To arms!" he resounds. "Take your stance and know your awares!"

The whole camp bursts into action. Soldiers jump to their feet and draw their weapons. Mages begin casting defensive spells around themselves and others. The troops form up into tight circles, ready to attack in any direction.

Relissa steps back and draws her daggers, not knowing what to expect or where it might be coming from. She scans around the camp and its perimeter looking for anything that shouldn't be there.

Lieutenant Lapäli, being so well conditioned from his own background, picked up on the signals instinctively. He pulls out his sidearm and stands at the ready, waiting to catch sight of whatever was about to appear.

Marelle is taken fully by surprise at the near instantaneous elevation of tension around the camp. She can only watch as the scene unfolds. She didn't often carry a weapon with her, as most of her duties placed her behind a desk, and today was one such day.

"Gods above, Relissa," she wheezes. "What's happening?"

"Look at him, see his eyes?" she directs at Thaelyn. "That's a clue I've been hearing about recently. He's picking up something with his Celestial senses."

"That's simply scary."

"Indeed, ladies…" Thaelyn emits soberly.

Thaelyn's unnatural pause breaks. His arms swoop downwards, returning up again in a series of small spirals. A glow forms around him, rapidly intensifying. His hands elevate to eye level and make a final set of circles. A myriad of small electrical sparks begins radiating all around him as his body becomes charged with a powerful flow of energy.

Marelle steps back away from him, exhibiting confusion, fear, and worry. Such a powerful display of magical energy, so close to her, made her feel uncomfortable.

Relissa also stepped back and crouched slightly. Her previous experience told her that whatever Thaelyn was doing, it is not to be judged lightly.

Time seems to stop as the whole camp waits, their motion frozen in anticipation of Thaelyn's next move.

As the energies come to full power, arcing their way through his body, his eyes begin to glow brightly with divine light.

"Jiggers, what's that now," Relissa whispers.

He clenches his right hand and turns to the side, swiveling his gaze and swinging his arm around to aim directly behind him. He uncoils his fist, and the energy is released in a fierce bolt of lightning sent flying across the camp.

The shot rockets away toward the southern wall, slightly offset from the access gate, streaking before rows of soldiers, each of whom tries in vain to follow its swift movement. Finally, at a position a short distance inside the gate, it strikes against something unseen.

The powerful impact produces a cloud of plasma and steam as an object is revealed bursting forth from an invisibility cloak. A body, charred and limp, hurls itself out of the cloud and onto the ground.

"Cu'Nar's Grace!" Padriyl wheezes.

"Son of a..." Marelle gasps. "How did you know that was there?"

Thaelyn glances around the area briskly before relaxing from his stance to respond. As he does, his eyes return to normal.

"In this case," he responds. "It was a form of sensory perception to detect the presence of a malicious intent aimed directly at me."

"Bleedin' head-knockers!" Relissa gripes. "That bugger's an assassin?"

"How were you able to see it?" Padriyl wonders. "It was invisible... at least to the rest of us...I think."

"Yes," Thaelyn accedes. "But as a Celestial, I can see through such things. My senses pinpointed where it was, but I needed to engage my divine sight to reveal it fully in order to target it with my lightning strike. We can provide similar enchantments as augmentations to our soldiers if we should ever expect to engage such foes. Though I will admit, this is not necessarily a standard adornment, except with certain elite operatives and our scouts."

"Uh huh..." Marelle grimaces. "Remind me to never get in the way of that. But I think this does answer one question. They definitely know you're here. They know who you are, and they're not happy about it."

"Yes, this might represent what I was just about to suggest...a secret plan. Captain, what do we have out there?"

Captain Hagmaert walks over to examine the body.

"My Lord! It looks like an elf, female with light skin and dark blonde hair."

"That's a Flame Elf, my Lord," Relissa observes.

"As I suspected," Thaelyn nods. "I doubt the Suuden-Aryku would be directly responsible for an assassination attempt using a cloak, although they could certainly arrange it if they are in league with the Flame Elves. But this sounds more like a plot to eliminate me personally as an unwanted guest. If the Suuden-Aryku are capable of so much more sophisticated means of destruction, it seems beneath them to try a simple trick like this."

"So, you're thinking of the Governor on this occasion?" Marelle asks.

"To send an assassin against the head of an opposing authority is a common tactic from one leader to another, and I am already known to be intruding in his backyard. This could relate to his threat to me."

"Buggers!" Relissa scorns. "That ties it for sure!"

"My Lord," the Captain continues. "The body is badly burned, but I might say the armor stood up to it rather well. It looks to be adamantium! A chain-weave coat and legs…"

"More of it?" Marelle blurts. "Where are they getting this stuff?"

"Captain," Thaelyn asserts. "Stand down the alert. I sense no more threats in our immediate area. And collect that armor for further study, as well as the body. I want to know how these elves differ from our own for compare. This presents us with an opportunity to see if there are any outward clues to their nature and reasoning to side with our enemies."

"Curious," Marelle muses. "She was wearing this super armor of hers, but it didn't seem to help her against your magic. Is this a weakness of some sort?"

"Magic is a powerful force, particularly when wielded by a highly proficient mage, and my time in practice makes me especially dangerous. Regardless of this, it can often bypass many forms of defense, including even the finest armors, unless those armors are carefully enchanted to offer resistance. Many of ours are, but if we are suggesting hers was made by the same people, it could be as simple as the Suuden-Aryku examples."

"All right, but this just brings us back to who did it and where the stuff came from."

"If we are suggesting the Suuden-Aryku are not aware of the principles of magic, it also follows they should not know how to use such materials as these. Elves are not known to conduct mining operations, at least not on a serious level, but they have been known in some cases to produce items from it. But again, if done by elves, they would most likely enchant it somehow. This leaves us with a mystery. So, unless this piece offers a clue, we may be dealing with an unknown element here."

Thaelyn turns to see General Gabarleine peeking out of the tactical office.

"General," he shouts. "We need to take immediate action to increase our security here against further incursions. I need Truesight towers ordered and installed at once!"

"Truesight towers, Your Lordship?" Marelle asks.

"As you have surely noticed by now, some of our own technology involves the combination of physical science as well as a form of science developed by our arcane studies. There is a mage spell called Truesight, which causes hidden and magically cloaked bodies to become visible again. It is a counter-spell to the invisibility cloak. Based on this, we created a tower device to serve the same purpose."

"Why weren't you using this before now?"

"Granted, I suppose we should have installed one or two a while ago. The towers were invented in the early years of the war, but our experience with the orcs told us they are not prone to engage in the art of espionage, and certainly not like this. So, we had little need for them during our previous encounters. Now, with these Flame Elves in our midst, and especially launching cloaked invasions, that will change."

A cart is wheeled around to the body of the former spy, which is then carefully placed inside. A pair of soldiers begins pulling the cart up to the portal. They step through, dragging the cart behind them. On the other side of the aperture, they are seen pulling the cart out of view to the side, in the direction where one would find the city's main temple. Marelle and Relissa watch.

"They will take that body to the temple," Thaelyn advises. "Our priests are the primary caregivers of health and anatomy. They will make a study to see if there are any outward signs to help us understand them better."

"Good luck with that," Marelle winces.

Later in the day, a call comes into the office of Governor Dramon.

"Yes, Commander, is it done?"

"Negative, the mission has failed. An observation scout reported that the spy was slain shortly after infiltrating the camp. Thaelyn still lives."

"Was the idiot spy simply walking around? Why wasn't it cloaked?"

"It was cloaked."

"Well then, how could it be so easily slain if it were cloaked?" he huffs. "Blast, it must've been detected by someone."

"The scout reported a disturbance just before the spy was killed. It would seem as if it triggered the event somehow, although I cannot explain how."

"Yes, Commander, those mages probably detected it. There is a way to do that, and they must be rather touchy down there, but it doesn't matter now. No doubt, they'll be on the alert for anything new."

The Governor relaxed back in his chair as he pondered this undesirable outcome.

"What's the situation down there right now?" he asks.

"The situation appears as normal operating procedure as compared to before."

"Confident little mongrels, aren't they? Clearly, he's a tougher mark than we first expected. We will need to separate him from his support troops…to isolate him. He should be easier to take down after that. I'll consider this and keep you posted."

"Why do we not attack his camp? A large assault would crush them quickly."

"Firstly, Commander, because every soldier over there uses mithril and adamantium. Simply recall what happened to that special unit of yours. They won't be so easily defeated by a frontal assault. Next, by your own admission, they're using magic, and this is bad for a number of reasons, not the least of which is you have no proper defense against it. Third, you are taking so many losses near that ship. Attacking their main camp will likely produce a great many more, and perhaps also to invoke his own reaction. And finally, I recall my initial meeting with that man, and he claimed to have a lot more where this came from. The implications are rather unfavorable."

"What about an orbital strike?"

"While that might be an interesting solution, I think in the end it would not serve us, as they have these portals to deliver more people. If we were to draw that sort of attention, we will have a mess on our hands, and at this moment, I really do not care for that."

"Understood."

"Remember the elves, Commander. Everyone has a weakness. If we can take him out separately, we can disrupt his rule and perhaps weaken the rest of his people. He might be clever enough to survive the first attempt, but he is no god."

The Governor ends the link and drops the communicator back into the drawer. He summons an attendant to bring Dean Malorn to his office right away. Moments later, the Dean enters.

"Yes, my Lord, you wanted to speak with me?"

"The first attempt to remove Thaelyn has failed. We need to think of something else, something that can isolate him, and then confront him with a danger he cannot fend off. As long as he is among his troops, he may be untouchable."

"Then, my Lord, may I offer an alternative. It's a little something that has intrigued me for a while. But, well, you know, without something to try it on..." he grins softly.

"Uh huh, and what might this be?" he asks uncertainly.

"If you'll give me a moment, I'll explain. But to make this work, I'll also need your blessing of enough time to prepare for it..."

Several days pass, while parts are brought in for the construction of the new towers. They were to be interspaced around the camp to offer careful coverage from all sides. The wall segments, originally placed around the perimeter of the initial camp, have also been moved to expand their defense of the new areas under development.

Patrols of mages have been circling the outpost all week,

periodically casting Truesight spells as they go along in their efforts to catch any new intruders. The overall level of heightened tension within the camp is keeping everyone on edge.

During this time, a report came back from Aerlie, who took a personal interest in the research of the body delivered days earlier. Another report came through from the Forgemaster in the Order's smithing works. Thaelyn was now convening a meeting in the tactical office to review the details of these two reports and their implications.

"The information we have in these two reports leaves us with only a few avenues on which to draw conclusions, and yet more opening up that need resolving. The first of these is the study of the Flame Elf spy. The body appears to match that of a High Elf, with no significant differences from our own on Tae'Eladar. At most, we might see a few minor deviations due to your long isolation here on this world, but there is nothing to suggest any sort of alteration in their physique like what we see on the Suuden-Aryku and their mutation effect."

"And so…" Marelle considers. "What you're saying is they don't bear any physical signs of his influence. Then, what is it that drives them? I've heard you say High Elves are a very noble and decent people. They wouldn't just get up and turn themselves over to him, would they? Could it be something else, if not the body, then maybe the mind?"

"This is one of those questions we need to answer, but unfortunately, we cannot do so with a corpse."

"Ah, I think I see where this is going! We need to capture one alive."

"My Lord," Relissa intervenes. "They're a dangerous lot, at least by the telling of it. They won't be an easy snag. They've got sharp senses and quick moves."

"I have no doubt," he affirms. "And this incident may place them on alert, since I am sure they will realize their error very quickly. Nevertheless, we also have a few tricks to play. We will have our samples, and they will be rendered down to their least threatening potential. But my greater concern, at this point, is not in the manner of how we will contain them, but rather how to keep Sargeras from knowing we have them."

"I'm not sure if I follow you, Your Lordship," Marelle ensues again. "If you capture them and take them away somewhere, isn't that enough to keep them isolated from anyone who can report back on it?"

"This would certainly answer part of it, but I suspect there is more to the issue at hand here. If we reflect on Lady Amariyn's report that their behavior had changed when they last tried contacting them on the death of their tree, this tells me something got inside there. And if we are suggesting an alteration of behavior, and further involving such a being as Sargeras, this can point to a very serious form of violation."

"Oops, I'm not sure if I like the sound of that, especially coming from you."

"Indeed, but I think, to demonstrate my point, a small example might prove useful here. What if we have you accompany Captain Hagmaert outside. Bring along a scrap of paper and a pen. While outside, write down a series of instructions for him to carry out. Be creative, then give it to him and return back here. I will simply stay here and wait."

Marelle is intrigued by the proposal, although she is not sure what purpose it serves. With a curious grin, she takes up a piece of paper and a nearby pen from the table while Thaelyn calls the captain inside to relay his instructions. At the same time, he also engages in an extended gaze with the man, who begins showing a quirky grin on his face.

Relissa notices this exchange and begins to suspect what is about to occur. Her past experience with Thaelyn and his mentalist abilities has afforded her clues to see into his extraordinary talents. But she knows well enough to keep silent during his experiments.

Marelle and the Captain step outside where she writes down a series of actions for him to take. After a few moments, she returns to the table. She is beaming from ear to ear.

"All right, Your Lordship, impress me! You're in here, he's out there. I don't know what it is you have to pull this time, but I'm anxious to hear it!"

"Aye, Marelle," Relissa smiles. "I think we're in for a wee bit of a show."

Thaelyn collects his focus, draws a breath, and closes his eyes. A curious smile stretches across his face as he forms the visions in his mind.

"I must feel for the poor Captain right now. He is currently skipping across the camp with a yellow flower clenched in his teeth, as a young girl on a spring day."

Thaelyn continues to focus his thoughts, watching a sequence of events unfold outside his field of view and relaying them to an audience of snickering listeners.

"Now, he has taken that flower and stuck it behind the ear of a young auburn-haired priestess… He is next attempting, very poorly I might add, to perform a series of forward cartwheels… And now he has taken a male soldier and is dancing with him while singing a popular tavern tune… Ah, and I believe this is his last maneuver. Oh dear Powers… Marelle, I think I need to pay closer attention to you. Yes, naturally, he is undressing, much to the surprise of everyone outside. Uh huh…now dashing around the camp…why not, after all, it is a bright sunny day. And finally, here he comes, prancing along back into the building."

At that moment, the captain jumps through the door, proudly displaying his manliness to the room. He takes a gracious bow to the assembled officers inside the building, then turns and does likewise to the audience outside, before jumping out again to retrieve his clothing.

Relissa blushes at the sight, not sure if she should cover her eyes, or her mouth, as a rush of laughter wells up inside of her.

Marelle's jaw fell nearly to the table as Thaelyn gave the oratory, only to snap it shut again at the sight of the naked man standing just a few paces away from her, a grand smile on his face for his performance.

Roars of laughter could be heard outside as the whole camp took up in the display. While not knowing exactly why, the diversion was a welcome relief from the recent stresses.

Thaelyn relaxes his breath and opens his eyes again.

"I must actually thank you, Marelle. The troops loved your little display. Now, do you wish to understand the true nature of what just occurred?"

"Uh huh..." Marelle grunts, unable to find her voice.

"Clairvoyance: The ability to project one's mind into places unseen or through the eyes of another. But there is a catch to it. If one would project to a location, one must either have sight of it at a distance, or prior knowledge of it from a previous visit."

"This reminds me," Relissa recalls. "Back on that first day, when you and Aerlie were gawping up at the moon, was this it?"

"Yes, we projected ourselves to your local moon for a better view of where we found ourselves, only to discover we were in a completely different universe from our own."

"Jiggers, that's a good one to have."

"As for seeing through the eyes of another, one must be previously familiar with that person to recognize their mind. In addition, one must also have the cooperation of that individual. Every soldier in my command knows me and grants me their allegiance, thereby allowing me to use them in this regard, should there ever be a cause for it."

"And you are able to see everything he sees?" Marelle asks.

"I can see what he sees, hear what he hears, and smell what he smells. I can absorb all the senses. I only need his permission to enter his mind for it. Some might say this can make him something like a puppet under my control, although I would never take it quite that far unless there was dire need."

"Right...and do you use this often?" she mutters hesitantly.

"No. Mostly on special occasions of scouting where I need to see something for myself, but where I may not be able to participate personally for some reason. Aerlie and I use this occasionally on each other, both for important matters, as well as a form of recreational activity."

"Recreational activity...?" she grins impishly.

"Indeed! As with so many other talents, it does not always need to be work-related. But do bring your mind out of the gutter for a moment, as there are other uses for it besides bedroom antics," he smiles.

"Um, right," she titters. "Anyway, I've never heard of anything like this before."

"But criminy!" Relissa moans. "What you're saying here is these bleedin' elves could be doing it, and Sargeras is the one pulling their strings?"

"This is certainly a suspicion I must consider," he nods. "Sargeras is very likely in possession of these skills, and I would not be at all surprised if he uses them on his minions. Therefore, if we were to capture any Flame Elves, we must deny them…and by association him…the knowledge of who has abducted them and where they are being held."

"That sounds bloody tricky. If he's able to feel them, wouldn't he just be able to follow them to wherever their bodies are being held? You'd need to cut them off from him completely. The thing of it is, how do you manage that on a mental link?"

"This does pose a problem, but for those of us who are more experienced in the ways of such skills, we also know of ways to defeat them. For example, there are methods to boggle and deter such a link. There are also locations amongst the planes that may block such emanations of the mind from passing through. Aerlie and I will often share a permanent link with one another, but our experiences tell us it can be broken if one of us travels across a dimensional bound."

"Right then… So, if you take a Flame Elf and portal the bugger out of here, you might cut him off from his bleedin' master?"

"Perhaps, but I think I would not choose to remove him to just any location. Keep in mind, the Daanen-Aryku tell of Sargeras coming to Azgarén, so I might suggest him to still be there, and that is already another universe. While Aerlie and I may lose touch with each other if she is on Tae'Eladar and I am here, Sargeras might have a longer reach than that. Therefore, I would need to take the captive somewhere…special."

"And I suppose you're not going to tell us where this someplace special is, ay?"

"You learn quickly, Relissa. With apologies, but we must remember the condition of security during this time of war. I will disclose only this much: There is a place I know of that is special to me. I have maintained it for nearly a thousand years. It is the result of a challenge my Father once made to me, and I am pleased to say I was successful."

"All right, Your Lordship," Marelle relents. "So, the idea is to capture some Flame Elves. But after this little show of theirs out here, I think they'll be watching for us to make some kind of move by now."

"Indeed, therefore we need information. I will order some of our scouts to survey the region to our south, far from here, to put some distance between us and our quarry. We will look for a small patrol and study their movements. At such a distance, if they should go missing, it might not be as immediately apparent that we were involved, and thus affording us enough time to secure them."

"And just for the asking," Relissa wonders. "How do you hope to catch them before the big guy notices you?"

"We have an assortment of techniques and non-lethal forms of magical attack to confound and deaden the senses. Use this, combined with a quick method to put the victim into a deep slumber, and there you have your prisoner."

"Well, that sounds just ducky!" she quips. "Then what's next on the list?"

"Next might be the armor the spy was wearing. Adamantium is a difficult material to work with if you do not know of its nature. By definition, I find it improbable that the Suuden-Aryku, not being a magically gifted society, would understand it well enough to work with it. But our only two…reasonable…choices at the moment, relating to those who are occupying this world, are the Suuden-Aryku and the Flame Elves. The orcs would be entirely unrealistic for this point."

"Especially if they can't even work iron," Marelle muses.

"But the elves, not being naturally inclined to conduct mining, may not be a desirable choice either. So what is left? Look here…"

Thaelyn pulls out two separate reports and sets them down side by side.

"The first of these is for a sample of armor from the Suuden-Aryku attack. The other is the chainmail from the elf spy. They both tell me the craftsmanship was of very fine quality, meaning to say whoever made them knew what he was doing. However, there were no maker's marks, which is unusual of anyone who does this sort of work for a living."

"Curious…" Marelle intones. "Is this to say he wished to remain anonymous? Is this normal?"

"If to work such a rare and precious material as adamantium, no, not in my opinion."

He glances at the papers again.

"He also states there were no enchantments on the armor, which confirms our earlier hypothesis that the craftsman did not engage in any magical augmentations. This further confounds the statement that anyone who works this for a living would be responsible, because if you are going to such lengths as to craft something using either mithril or adamantium, you go all the way."

"I suppose so. Then, whoever did this didn't finish it, or maybe he was sloppy for the final result."

"Yes, perhaps he did it in a hurry as a rush order to fill a need. But we still have a hole in the theory for where it originally came from. Perhaps someone did actually find it in this world, or maybe it came from some other world, and if this is the case, we might have a third party conducting the work outside our view."

"Oh wonderful… But now, who?"

"My Forgemaster offered the opinion that this might be the work of dwarven hands, but the only dwarves we know of, in this world at least, are your friends up north."

"Oh blast!" she scorns. "Those same ones with the exclusive deal for iron we never see? And then our Governor, the only one to deal with them, and his backroom dealings with our enemies while keeping us in the dark. Now it makes sense! We might have a potential source and potential smiths doing the work."

"And we again have a number of curious conditions. They first appeared at the beginning of this war with this trade agreement. Where were they hiding before this? And we also have Captain Hagmaert describing them as in a delirium of some sort."

"What about your scouts since that time?"

"They report the dwarves appear to be unnaturally dedicated to their work, such that they do not even carry casual conversation with each other."

"I can't say I know anything about dwarves, but that doesn't sound right to me."

"Aye, me too," Relissa adds.

"And neither I," Thaelyn offers. "Therefore, the idea of that drug effect, which is becoming ever more disturbing."

"I'm not sure if I can offer anything to answer that," Marelle considers. "The guards at the north gate tell us the Dean usually goes up there with a couple bundles of straw and occasionally some medium sized barrels of some kind."

"Straw...and barrels? What could they be using straw for... bedding perhaps? But then, if this is a replenishing effort, I wonder if it could reflect upon animals. We were once asking about their food supply. Maybe, if they tend not to go outside, they have some form of livestock in there with them."

"That'd be an odd one," Relissa muses.

"I wonder what else they have in there. Dwarves adore meat, but they might also use vegetables and other things, if it is available. Hmm, barrels. I wonder if this is relevant. If they have a farming plot in there, perhaps they need nutrients for it from time to time. But being underground would not be a desirable location for most plants."

"My Lord," the General offers. "If they are actually in league with the Suuden-Aryku, therefore the materials supply going off to the enemy forces here, could they also be using some manner of artificial setting, possibly with illumination and regulated growing conditions?"

"This is entirely possible, General," he admits. "Marelle, how did those barrels appear?"

"The guards said they looked weird," she affirms. "Not like anything we might otherwise have in the city."

"This would be interesting to investigate. Perhaps we can send some of our people in there to carefully scout the rest of it and see if we can confirm any of this. General, have a few of them go in under a cloak. We will keep out of sight just in case those dwarves do actually pay attention to unwanted visitors. Have them map the tunnels and see about living quarters, including a kitchen and where the food comes from. And if they actually are making adamantium, let us see how that appears as well."

"Of course, my Lord," he nods.

◆◆◆

A few more days pass before the towers are ready for activation. As the towers were going up, energy conduits were laid out to connect them with the same power array that the shield wall was using, now expanded by a few additional cells. By the end of the week, the gnomish engineers were ready to give the word for Thaelyn and his officers to witness the first of them go online.

Relissa and Marelle both watched as the gnomes made the final adjustments to the controls near the base of the tower at the northern end of the camp. They had been observing the construction phase with more than a passing interest. These towers had a different appearance than the Spire standing to the north. They were slender, with four metallic prongs projecting out from different sides and at different stages of the column, then running upward parallel to it, almost like a mechanical tree. Each prong was capped with a spherical white orb. The central spire also had such an orb, but on a larger scale.

"I can only imagine how many more horns Kaliya would go through if she saw this," Relissa snickers.

The patrols of mages that had been circling around the camp for almost two weeks were given new instructions this morning to move the patrol outside the southern wall in a broad line across the terrain. This would effectively bar anyone from making the attempt to cross into the camp from that direction. Thaelyn had also been engaging himself to actively scan the area for any new sensations of a malicious presence, such as what he felt before when the Flame Elf entered his range. Beyond this, the day had been fairly calm.

"My Lord," ushers a call from the lead gnome. "Tower One is ready for activation!"

"Proceed."

The gnome throws a small switch inside the control box and the tower begins drawing power through the conduit. Initially, there is little sign of activity, until the orbs at the top start to glow. As the energy builds up, the orbs begin emitting swirling wisps of plasma circling around them.

Some distance away, standing near the tactical office, behind the row of officers watching the display, the form of a man appears. He is dressed in an ornate robe with the hood pulled over his head and appears to be watching the display very curiously.

Several soldiers standing around the area catch notice of the new addition and turned to look at him. As whispers begin to spread, more soldiers turn to gaze at the revealing of the unexpected visitor. The whispers eventually attract the attention of Thaelyn and the other officers.

The man, seemingly content in believing his activities were insofar unheeded, suddenly takes notice that many eyes are turning in his direction. Cautiously, he arcs his head around to look at the other participants. The entire camp has now focused on him.

He tentatively glances down at his body, and realizing he is no longer hidden, he slowly brings his hands up to pull back his hood, forcing a friendly greeting into his face. He turns to display the introduction to the assembly, waving a hand in a vain attempt to divert any suspicions, while at the same time searching for a quick exit. The northern gate is a fair trot away from him, but with no other option, he abruptly turns and makes a mad dash for it.

"Get him!" rings out a shout from one of the officers, resulting in a score of soldiers charging after the spy.

"Block the gate!" cries another, calling more soldiers to rush up and close off the exit.

Confused and with nowhere else to go, the man searches desperately for a safe haven, but he will have no such luck on this day. The stampede of troops collides into him, knocking him harshly to the ground, and then dogpiling on top of him.

"Look there! Another one!"

The shout is heard coming from one of the guards at the gate. Outside the camp, up near a cluster of trees, another man had been spotted in a similar robe. But before anyone could reach him, he appeared to imbibe some form of potion and darted away at lightning speed to the north.

Realizing that the second spy is likely a lost cause, Thaelyn hurries over to the pile-up of men.

"Clear the way!" he orders.

The soldiers slowly pull themselves off the pile, revealing the bottom layer to be tightly constraining the intruder.

"My Lord," declares one of the soldiers. "He appears to be human and dressed in mage apparel."

"Lieutenant Carronel, front and center!" Thaelyn commands.

Marelle briskly marches into view.

"Do you know this man?"

"Not personally, Your Lordship, but I can tell you who he works for. That's an acolyte's robe from the mage academy. He must be one of Dean Malorn's spies."

Thaelyn looks into the face of the spy, who by this time has been pulled off the ground to his feet, but still under careful restraint by soldiers on either side of him.

"You there... Who are you and why do you spy on us?"

The spy is silent.

"We know who you work for," Thaelyn continues. "The question is why would the Dean of the mage academy in Rolsklinde be so interested in our affairs when neither he nor your Governor has demonstrated any interest in participating in them."

"The Dean is curious," the man states calmly, but with muted contempt. "You are a foreign entity, and he is uncertain of you."

"Uncertain? He and your Governor made a visit on that first day after my arrival to meet with me. I explained who I am, where I come from, why I am here, and even invited them to join me, but they refused. If this is not enough to placate them as to my intentions, I cannot be sure what else they might want. And after fighting off half of your enemies in this world, I might expect a little more consideration for my efforts. By this time, I feel quite certain they should know well enough what my intentions are."

"I'm aware of your fight against the orcs. I don't know about the rest. I'm not the one who makes the rules."

"No, of course not..." Marelle blasts. "If you're anything like the rest, you're just another trained dog licking the Dean's boots."

"And how would you know what we do in there?"

"Don't even dare..." she growls. "Your dean thinks the Guard is only good for local pest control."

"What?"

Marelle glares at him, and then feels a strange compulsion to laugh.

"You don't even know!" she sputters. "Now that is funny... From the argument my brother had with your precious Dean, I would think the whole academy should know by now."

"Your brother?"

Marelle shakes her head and turns away.

"You are an acolyte?" Thaelyn resumes. "Is this your academic title?"

"Yes, that's what we use up there," he affirms. "My name is Willit Sarens."

"Ah, very good, Acolyte Sarens, and thank you for giving us a name. But as for your dean, I would not otherwise wish to hide my intentions since there is a clear and evident correlation between us for who our enemies are. Therefore, if he should wish to know, he can come down here personally and ask me, perhaps even sit and share a cup of tea with me for the favor of it. But spying on my attempts to solve your world's dilemmas can be interpreted as you actually desiring them in the first place."

"I honestly have no idea what you're talking about," he retorts.

"Then let us approach it this way. Are you or are you not aware there are orcs in this world?"

"Yes, I am."

"And Flame Elves, and Suuden-Aryku?"

"Yes."

"And are you or are you not friendly with any of these?"

The spy turns a curious gaze at him.

"Friendly? What kind of question is that? Of course not!"

"Then why are you not fighting them, as I am?"

"I, well, we have shortages in our city, as far as I know, and this restricts our efforts."

"Very well, but here I am, and with what might appear to be far more resources than what your lone city might have available, and doing a rather fine job at fighting your war. Why do you not join my efforts, even with what meager supplies you do have? Even a token effort could persuade me to consider you an ally."

"I don't know the answer to that. Like I said, I'm not the one to make decisions."

"This is a fair response. However, they who do make the decisions already did so on that first day. And those decisions were to demand taxes from me for occupying this space, and also to hand over all of my precious artifacts to their personal delight. How amusing, for people who claim there to be so many villains in this world. I wonder if any of those include their own reflections."

"What?" he wheezes.

Thaelyn passes a disturbed glance at Marelle, who simply returns a shrug.

"Yes," he adds reluctantly. "I must admit your assessment is likely the most correct. He only knows what the Dean tells him, and nothing more. And he apparently does not tell him much, including the one about his secret run down here with your Governor to investigate what schemes they could hatch against me."

"A secret run?" he glares at Thaelyn, and briefly passing to Marelle. "But what does this have to do with her here? Isn't that indication enough of his interest in fighting your war?"

"Ah, an interest you are told to spy on for those who presumably should already know?"

"Acolyte," Marelle interjects. "I'm not here because the Governor ordered it. I'm here because that bastard didn't even bother telling Captain Kholgard about his secret visit. The Captain is a little peeved right now for the Governor going behind his back when it's supposed to be our job to protect the city. But according to your dean, our real purpose is to simply pick up the drunks from the street, not fight anything. And once the Dean and the Governor returned home, that agreement we're supposed to have for sharing scouting details stopped cold, as if it ever did anything to begin with."

"What do you mean, stopped?" Willit snaps. "He's not doing it anymore?"

"The better question is: Was he ever doing it? The Captain sincerely hates you people for your arrogance in not doing as you're supposed to be doing. Furthermore, whenever my brother went in with his reports, they were filed in the waste bucket, and sometimes before the door closed behind his back on his way out. This tells me the Dean doesn't do anything unless it benefits him somehow."

"I, uh...wait... Your brother... What was your name again?"

"My brother is Haran Carronel, do you know him? He's the one who brought us this fabulous information of a man who could save our world, and your dean refused to tell us...the Allegiance Guard... who are supposed to be responsible for keeping our people safe and fighting all the bad things out here trying to destroy us. Now, how do you like that for your illustrious Dean and his rules?"

"But...are you saying..." he mumbles. "Haran...he did this? And he was kicked out..."

"It is a most unfortunate situation," Thaelyn muses. "This level of authoritarianism is very disturbing."

"It's the same as what we get in school," she moans. "This is all you need, there is nothing else, and stop asking about it."

"And you know what else," Relissa adds as she joins the conversation. "It just makes things worse for what he and that bleedin' Governor had to say about the rest of us. They made good and proper enemies of us that day, with all their moaning about unholy this and improper that."

Willit glared at the young dark elf for her statement.

"And just what are YOU talking about now?" he scowls.

"Oh, don't you give me that look, Mister Holier Than the Rest. What I'm talking about is your bloody Governor griping about us doing this and that when the rest of you don't even know your own history. We were friends before someone came along and started this war on us. Then he came up with all his bleedin' tripe about us being responsible for it. We were under the impression you were our friends up until that time. His messengers to our Council back home painted such a lovely picture of how nice you peeps were. Not anymore, though. But what you buggers don't know is where all your iron is going off to, because those dwarves up there seem to be making up a fine bundle of it. I wonder why you're not getting any."

"Iron?" he whispers.

"Aye! But we're seeing a lot of it on those orcs out there, and most of it looks new. And as far as we know, orcs aren't that good at making it."

"What?!" he shouts.

"And here you are, sitting nice and cozy with nary a thing to worry about outside your walls. Your Guard is told to stay put, and the rest of you told to keep your noses in whatever business keeps you from asking a lot of nasty questions. And doing it…for as long as you can remember…as you peeps like to say it. You're also told to blame the rest of us for all our unholy nonsense you don't want to get involved with. And here we are, four centuries later, with our world torn apart and no one actually fighting anything to put it back together again."

"But...but..." he whimpers. "Gods above..."

"Anyway," Marelle continues. "Like Haran, you're expected to behave like a trained dog wrapped around the Dean's finger."

"Excuse me, Lieutenant. I'm not quite the trained dog like some of the others. Yes, I do know how to kiss his bum whenever he asks for it. The alternative is to listen to him blasting my ears out the door, just like he did Haran."

"All right, fine, but this doesn't seem to help if you don't ever pay attention to what you're looking at when you come out here spying on stuff. I remember when I was a girl in school, and one of you was my teacher. I didn't learn diddlysquat about the world around me. Now that I'm out here, I'm seeing it for how it really is. And gods' pity, is there a lot to learn!"

"Maybe so, but while you might be working with these people, I'm not. I just have one thing to do," he asserts with a finger. "To look at something and report back. I don't speak the language out here, so most of it is lost on me. I see troops moving around, construction projects, new farming up north, people rummaging through refuse heaps... How in all the hells am I supposed to interpret anything out of that other than someone doing strange things, and for reasons I don't understand?"

"Strangers doing strange things... Where have I heard that one before?" she huffs. "Maybe, instead of lurking around under a cloak, you could pop into this office over here and ask a few questions. His Lordship speaks our language in case you haven't noticed."

"Yes, now I can see this..." he sighs wearily.

"Only now? After all this time he's been consulting with so many others? Wow, some spy you are!" she chuckles ironically.

"Very well, that is enough for now," Thaelyn interjects. "Guards, take him back to B.T. and place him in detention until further notice. I will meet with him at a later time."

"I would like to be a part of that, if I may," Marelle asserts.

"Of course, I will call on you when the time comes," he looks off to the north. "That other one will surely report back. Maybe, with the new towers in operation, the Dean will think twice before sending any more this way."

It is mid-afternoon when a feeble knock comes at Dean Malorn's door.

"Enter…" he calls.

A man in a robe, panting heavily, stumbles into the room, dizzy from the aftereffects of the speed potion he drank earlier.

"M-Master, I h-have news…"

He topples over, barely catching himself on the chair opposite of the Dean's desk.

"Dear Gods, man! Pull yourself together! I would think by now you apprentices would be a bit more accustomed to the effects of that potion so you could hold up better than this."

The Dean grumbles in the direction of the young mage as the man tries to stand up again.

"You're back early. Should I assume this unexpected return brings something of great import?"

The mage tries to catch his breath long enough to make conversation.

"Thaelyn, his camp…" he puffs. "We were finally able to get close enough…this morning. As you know, his mages…blocked us before. They had been using detection magic since the day the elf spy was killed. The first of the towers is complete and functioning."

The mage pauses to catch another deep breath.

"And so?" demands the Dean. "What does it do?"

"Master, it's a detection tower. It unmasks the invisibility cloak at range. Acolyte Sarens was inside the camp when it went active. He was revealed instantly, same as I while outside near some trees. The soldiers captured him, but I managed to escape using the potion."

"Blast it!" screams the Dean. "With these towers in place, there may be no further point in attempting any intelligence operations in that region."

"It is clearly a response to that elf spy, I would think. These people seem to have some very interesting devices in their possession."

"Indeed, they do, so unfortunately for us."

The Dean turns in his chair to look out the window behind him.

"Thaelyn will surely attempt to interrogate the prisoner," he reflects. "Hmm... Thankfully, we don't give any of you enough information to make you useful to the enemy. The most he might get out of him should be that the Acolyte studies at the Academy and how much he adores his instructors. Very well, Acolyte Galwen, you may go now."

The Acolyte makes a bow, even though the Dean still has his attention peering through the window. He turns and exits the room, closing the door behind him.

"The Governor is not going to be pleased about this," the Dean mumbles to himself. "Not pleased at all."

Acolyte Galwen makes his way through the corridors out to the main study hall near the front of the academy. Several of the students pause from their study to notice him coming back into the room after rushing through the first time to make his report. Among them is Tristeen.

"Jared!" she calls out to him. "Are you alright? I saw you run past here, or at least something that looked like you through that blur. What happened?"

"I just came back from that camp down there in the valley. The Dean had me and Willit watching that guy Thaelyn again today. We finally got close enough to see something, and then they activated some kind of tower that broke our invisibility cloaks. I just barely got away."

"What about Willit?"

"Captured. He was inside the camp, and they blocked his exit."

"Oh wonderful, what do we do now?"

"I doubt there's much we can do. The Dean wasn't happy about it, as you can guess."

"Is he going to try to get him back? He must! He would never leave a student out there like that, would he?"

Jared looks around the room at the other students sitting at tables and browsing shelves. He makes a determined gesture to take Tristeen by the arm and lead her outside through the main door.

"Jared!" she protests. "Where are we going?"

"Shush…" he replies, exiting the building and closing the door behind them.

He looks around the plaza and diverts the two of them around the side of the building to a secluded area.

"All right, Jared," Tristeen declares. "You got me out here. Now, what is it?"

"Tristeen, there is something wrong here. I don't think the Dean has any intention to help Willit, not that it would make any difference. I'm sure Thaelyn will be taking him to his home world anyway, and out of reach. But there's more, and I'm not sure how much you actually know. You never go out there. What do you know of the things they're doing down there, or anything else for that matter?"

"Jared, all I really know is what you and the others bring back, especially Haran, when he was still here, and then hopefully share it with me. I remember when Haran came in with his report and the Dean balked at it so harshly. It cost him his scholarship. And with all that you and Willit, and the others, brought back since then, it sounds like the Dean is treating Thaelyn like a criminal, when in fact he's winning this damnable war for us. Who is our real enemy here, Jared? I can't even be sure of it now. I have to trust the Dean because he's one of the leading authorities of the city. And if you can't trust that; who else is there?"

"Yes, so it is said so many times. And at the same time, the Dean does describe that savior of a man as an enemy, like as if he doesn't want him winning this damnable war for us."

"But that's ridiculous, isn't it?"

"Let me tell you a little secret, Tristeen. Do you remember when I told you about that Flame Elf spy that was killed?"

"Yeah, you saw it from outside the northern gate while under your cloak."

"Right. When I came back later that day to report, the Dean didn't seem to care. He treated it as old news, but I was the only one out there to see it. Now, I wonder where he might have heard about this before me. Or is he just so indifferent that it doesn't matter to him if the one and only hero in this world might have an assassin chasing after him. Either way, it's not very kind, to say the least."

"All right, fine. You and I both know how the Dean can be on occasion, so this behavior might not be so unusual. Haran got it very hard all the time. Maybe it's a male thing, some overinflated bravado, I don't know."

"What about some of these whispers I'm hearing lately about Thaelyn, his recent proposals to the Night Elves, and something I heard a few times going around the back alleys here in our own city? How do you feel on that side of it?"

"I don't know…confused, maybe. We have the opinions of the people here on the Night Elves and the Daanen-Aryku, which often isn't very considerate, and Haran and his stories from his friends, which completely contradicted the other things. And then, we have the reports I'm hearing in the academy about this coalition of people down there in Thaelyn's camp. I really wish I could find Haran again and talk to him about all this. Even if the Dean didn't like him, he had a lot of good ideas, and he made me feel so happy inside. Have you seen him anywhere?"

"I'm sorry, Tristeen, I haven't seen him for a long time. I remember he used to visit the Ten Eagles down in the lower district, but I haven't seen him there either."

"Maybe I could go there sometime and check."

"I wouldn't recommend it, Tristeen. It can be a rough place."

"You don't think I can handle myself in that putrid beer hall?" she smirks.

"Well, you probably can, knowing you like I do, but I'm just saying I wouldn't want to see you get into trouble to start."

"Very well, I don't think I have the stomach for it anyway. I remember his sister is supposed to work at the barracks. Maybe she knows something."

"I suppose it's worth a try. I don't know her, personally."

"All right, thank you, Jared. I think I've had my fill of the academy for one day. I'll just stop by the barracks, and then go home to relax."

He nods and returns back inside the academy while Tristeen makes her way through the plaza in the direction of the barracks. She passes through the front gate and across the yard to the office of Captain Kholgard. As she approaches the door, she knocks politely.

"Yes, come in," sounds a voice from inside.

She steps inside the room to meet the Captain behind his desk.

"Well, isn't this interesting…" he declares coarsely. "Is the Dean finally catching up on his backlog of duty? I don't think I've ever seen you before. A new recruit, maybe?"

"Excuse me, did I do something wrong?" she asks. "All I did was knock and enter. I haven't even had a chance to speak, and you're already berating me."

"I don't like mages, especially your Dean. All right, I'll tone it back a bit. What's your name, little lady?"

"Tristeen Macaid."

"Oh great!" he moans. "And one of those, to boot!"

"Now what? You don't like nobles either? I think I came into the wrong office. I'm looking for the man who is supposed to serve and protect our people and our fair city. Is this the right place?"

"That all depends on who's pulling the strings, because it isn't me."

"What?" she responds disbelievingly. "You are the Captain of the Allegiance Guard, right? Doesn't that give you the authority to serve our city?"

"The only authority I have is what your beloved Dean and the Governor give me, and that is to chase cutpurses and break up barroom brawls. And in fact, I heard recently, and this is from your dean, that he expects us to do no more than pick up drunks. And that, dear little lady, of the extent of my…authority."

"Drunks…" she muses in reflection. "And what about the war?"

"What war? We're not even allowed to go outside, not that it matters much, as we haven't had an attack during my full service here, and your dean stopped giving us details on what's happening out there since the valley got taken over by those people to the south. The highlight of my day is watching alley cats catching the rats crawling up from the sewers."

"That…isn't the story I've been hearing."

"That doesn't surprise me, knowing the Dean like I do."

"Uh huh, and do you now have a complaint about him personally?"

"Yes! I'm told by what I'm going to describe as a reputable source that he has a god complex. Does that suggest anything to you, young miss mage student who doesn't know diddly about the world around her? And further, that none of you know the better for all the bootlicking you go through over there."

Tristeen suddenly went silent at the statement. She stared at him blankly as she paused briefly to reflect on her conversation with Jared, and further on her interactions with Haran in the past. She glanced around the room as she tried to recompose her thoughts.

"All right, look," she tries again, but under restraint of her feelings. "I'm not looking for a fight. There are a lot of strange things going on lately, and I'm a bit lost. I'm here looking for a friend of mine. You speak of not knowing things? This is my attempt at trying to learn, as he had some interesting ideas. So, I was hoping one of your officers might be able to help me."

"Which one?"

"I think her name is Marelle Carronel. I was told she works here. Is she available?"

"Nope… Sorry, but she's been reassigned to another office."

"Can you tell me which one? It's important, and I need her help."

"You know, regardless of what you need, you people certainly don't give us much help when we need it…no disrespect to your noble blood, dear lady. And I would consider our needs to be rather important."

"And here we are with another reference to my family. Why do you hate me so? What did I do to you? I've never gone around and harassed the Guard like so many of the other families! I've always tried to show better respect than that. And as for being a mage, the only reason I wear this robe is to get away from my family, to meet people and play a more productive role in our city. The academy is simply the only outlet for me to do this."

"Is that so. All right, fine. Maybe you are different. I'll admit, I've never met you before. But I know a few others I would like to see go the same way as those sewer rats outside."

"Granted, and I don't feel any better for it, as it taints my own image."

The Captain takes a brief moment to sigh as he considers his response.

"Still, you should know that I don't trust your dean, whatever you might say about yourself. And you work for him. That's bad enough. Lieutenant Carronel has been reassigned to another post due to…security issues regarding, um…a series of domestic outbreaks in the lower district."

"That is a very poor example of an excuse, Captain."

"Maybe it is, but as far as your dean is concerned, that's where she is."

"All right, listen," she sets her hands on her hips. "I do not work for him such as to reveal outside information, like some of the others who run his scouting missions. And according to some of the statements I've heard recently, half of it seems to be tossed away, anyway. I simply work in the classrooms and lab studies. So, kindly do not place me in that same mix."

"Fine, Miss Macaid. But your dean had an agreement with us to share information, not that he ever lived up to it, especially if that same information was being dropped in a waste bucket. Then he broke it completely. Now, I'm giving it right back to him. So, if you really care about this city, more so than your dean, then I'll tell you this much. I hold the opinion that both he and the Governor don't care much for the affairs outside these walls. They keep us boxed up in here, and feed us a lot of rubbish simply to keep our mouths shut. Therefore, if you really want to serve the city, don't give them any information about what we're doing over here. Because we are trying to save our world, even if they aren't."

"Really..." she muses softly. "So much for that saying, if you can't trust them..."

"...Who can you trust? Oh, yes! I'm sure that's one of their favorite sayings to bribe us into compliance."

"Compliance. It's that bad? Very well, Captain, I will keep your secrets. This is my vow. Now, can you tell me about Marelle?"

The Captain shuffles behind his desk, running a hand through his hair before coming to a decision on his reply. He leans over his desk and lowers his voice. Tristeen impulsively steps in closer to meet him.

"Miss Macaid, this is all I can tell you for now. Marelle is working as an agent for us to Lord Thaelyn's camp down there in the valley. She serves my office here to give me reports on what he's doing, and so far, the only thing I can tell you is he's fighting a war, a war we're supposed to be fighting, but the Governor doesn't want to."

"Doesn't want to? Why?"

"We're still debating the reasons, but he made a secret visit down there behind my back shortly after that guy arrived, and he made a lot of trouble for a lot of people."

"Trouble? For whom? What people, ours or his?"

"Those people out there we're supposed to be friends with and fighting alongside in this damnable war...the Night Elves and Daanen-Aryku."

Tristeen recoiled from the statement in shock.

"But what about all those rumors we hear about...you know, unholy rites and so on..."

"Bunk. All of it. And probably due to the Governor as all his prejudices. We think this might be nothing more than propaganda to turn us away from them, and reinforced by hiding inside these walls. Communication, Miss Macaid. Does this say anything to you? The lack of it turned a good thing into a bad one. We're not allowed to go outside, and stopped talking to people to share information about our friends and allies."

"Oh grand! And so, the rumors. Further incentive to turn people's noses up at them."

"Exactly. The Governor owns the Dean, and therefore, everything you hear in school and everywhere else. I wouldn't be surprised if those priests over there also worked for him, for all the rubbish they keep spewing out."

"Naturally! That's where half of it comes from, as I hear it."

"From what I heard once, he wants to see everything out there finished off, while keeping us nice and neat behind these walls."

"But then, what do we say about this war? Some people don't even think we should be involved in the first place."

"It's our world as much as any other," he asserts. "Not only are we supposed to be involved, but we should be teaming up with the rest to actually fight it. But we're not. More of that propaganda to foul things up. And not only on the inside, as the others out there get a load of it from their side saying we can't for whatever reason. For instance, those Night Elves get continual reports that we're under attack on a daily basis. And this comes from the guy in that office across the way..." he points in the general direction of the Governor's Manor.

"Oh, how convenient," she scorns.

"But we've generally come to the opinion that this war isn't really a true and proper war at all, more like a purging operation."

"Wait! A purging operation...how do you mean?"

"Four hundred years, Miss Macaid. They blast away everything out there and leave only the last few cities. Then the fighting stops, except maybe for a few skirmishes here and there just to remind us there's people out there holding us behind these walls. If they wanted us dead, we'd be dead already, but we're not. Therefore, this isn't a war to destroy everything. It was a purging operation to destroy everything except us. Now, here we are, pinned down just like they want us."

"Oh grand! And you say the Governor doesn't even want to fight?"

"Not in the least. He must feel nice and comfy in that office over there, gloating over his position of authority of a city that can't go outside the walls. And no one talks to anyone out there to learn what's happening, so we have these rumors instead. Then, he goes out for this secret meeting, and tries swindling that guy for squatter's tax and contributions to his personal treasury. A few of us are putting together some nasty ideas about what he's really doing out there that he doesn't want to fight, but I think I should keep this quiet for now. We need proof first, before going out pointing fingers."

"Unbelievable!" she fumes. "All right, I understand. You know, my father and some of the others have occasional debates on this issue. None of them like the Governor being in that office. They say he's got to be illegal somehow, to say the least."

"Really! That's interesting."

"But I've also heard of supply shortages holding us back. Isn't this much true?"

"Yes, we have that, but His Lordship has been helping us with a few new stockpiles."

"Um...His Lordship?" she raises her brow. "Who is he that we're using a title?"

"He's the king of a world called Tae'Eladar. So, the Governor and the Dean really flubbed up big time making enemies of him."

"Uh oh..." she moans. "Gods' pity, then where does that leave us? Is he actually hostile towards us?"

"Not necessarily the people, but the Governor and the Dean are another matter. That man over there apparently used such words as to purge the world of its villains, when in fact he's probably one of them. So, at this point, I wouldn't be surprised if Thaelyn were to haul both of them out and throw them in the stockade."

"When you say villains..."

"Those friends we're supposed to be siding up with," the Captain affirms. "The Night Elves with all their unholy rubbish, when ours is probably more unholy than anything else. And the Daanen-Aryku, with their strange ways, when they are simply victims of abuse looking for refuge."

"Unbelievable," she shakes her head. "You know, my Dad would love to hear that one."

"Well, try not to spread it around too much. We can't let either of those porkers know we're catching on to them."

"All right, fine. But, in the end, I suppose there is no way to get help from Marelle to locate my friend right now. Not unless I want to go all the way down there and ask her, which may not be very safe for me. And then I'd need to listen to my family ranting for a week for travelling outside the Upper Ward again."

"Sounds to me like you have a few of your own problems. Look, I'm sorry if I was rough on you before. We've had a lot of hard times over here, and many of those have been dumped on us by the academy and the noble families."

"I understand, and I thank you for your help. Maybe I can return later, and we can talk some more."

Tristeen leaves the office and trudges across the yard out of the barracks. She angles off to the upper part of the district, passing a quaint little park, and into the Ward where the noble families have their large estate homes. She strolls along a tiled avenue to a regal house with a manicured garden enclosed within a wrought-iron fence. She passes through a gate in the fence and up to the door.

"Mom, I'm home," she calls as she enters.

"Tristeen!" her mother hushes as she strides into the foyer to meet her daughter. "We have guests. Kindly do not shout your announcement as a common laborer returning from the local mill!"

"Guests? I should've known, actually. So which of these young bucktoothed nut-chiselers are you trying to push me into this time? It isn't that Timon again, is it? Ugh, I hate that one worst of all."

"For your information, Timon is a very fine young man from one of the most noteworthy families in the Ward. He may have a slight overbite, but..."

"A slight overbite? I could draw a portrait on it and sell it at the local bazaar!"

"That will be enough out of you! Our guests are in the parlor, and I want..."

"Oh yes!" she extols flamboyantly. "Heaven forbid they be anywhere else but the parlor. And let me guess... You want me to run upstairs, put on my finest tea dress and come back down to play cutie-doll for your little party. Mom, I hate tea. And those dresses are so restrictive, I feel like I'm suffocating. And right now, I want to relax with something intellectual, like a good wholesome debate with the fathers. I learned something today that I think they might want to hear."

"I simply cannot understand you at times! You are a young lady, Tristeen."

"Yes, I'm a young lady with a mind that prefers to think, not dress up as a plaything for the boys. Mom, it's not me, it's you and your inability to understand things, because you do not choose to think for yourself. It's just as the Captain said. You listen to those creeps under the Dean's thumb, and that's all you care about."

"Huh? What are you saying here?"

"He owns the schools. He owns our education, and it's all engineered so that people like you stop thinking. That's the point, Mom, and you bought it. We're locked inside these walls with dictators telling us what to say, and when to keep silent. I learned the city is in trouble, and by those very same people we're forced to respect as our authority figures. So, if you like Timon so much, you marry him, because I am not. Excuse me... I need to tell Dad about this. But first, I need to change clothes."

"Tristeen..." her mother calls as the girl begins towards the stairs. "I honestly don't know what you're saying with all that, but at some moment in your life, you will need to consider marriage. Our family must continue on, and I am too old to have another to follow after you."

Tristeen pauses to look back at her mother in contemplation.

"Yes, Mom, but not today," she concedes. "I'm simply not in the mood. I have other interests on my mind which are a little more imperative than marrying, raising children, and like so many others, pretending the world is rainbows and flowers...because it isn't. There's a war out there, and we're supposed to be fighting it. But we're not, because those same people we're told to trust refuse to do so, feeling so much power of control that they don't want to spoil it, and telling the rest of us it's good for the city."

Tristeen continues up the stairs to her room to change clothes. When she returns back down, she proceeds outside to the terrace to join the elder men.

They often gathered there for debates on city issues, like politics, economic matters, and other topics of the day. Tristeen enjoyed sitting in on the discussions, but she enjoyed it even more when they would involve her. Over the years, she had become quite adept at holding her own amongst the deliberations. But today, she was feeling a bit frisky after her conversation with the captain.

"I simply cannot accept that he can still be in that office after so long," argues one of the fathers.

"Josef, surely there is an explanation that we can all agree on. After all, the man cannot be immortal. There must be something we missed during this time."

"Such as what, Abraim? That he passed on to a new heir without the city noticing? The man isn't even of noble blood. How dare he pretend to the Governor's chair, much less pass it along to his bastard children?"

"Are we talking about this again?" Tristeen asks as she sits down on one of the recliners.

"Ah, my dear," Josef declares. "Are you returning early from your studies today?"

"Yes, Dad, I've had about as much as I can take out of that place for today, so I'm looking to relax a little. Are you talking about the Governor again? How many times do we need to stomp around this issue?"

"Dear, this debate may never be at an end for as long as he sits in that chair."

"Well, be that as it may, I heard a little bird whisper something in my ear today, but I dare not tell where it came from."

"Oh? And why is that?" he smiles.

"Because neither the Governor nor the Dean would be happy to hear about it."

The three men all stopped and glared at her, then studied each other for their reactions.

"Um," Josef gazes at her cautiously. "And why would that be? What is it you heard?"

"Let's talk a little about your side first. Where are we today?"

"Well, um…" Abraim begins. "Tristeen, the man that occupies the Governor's Manor has been there for as long as any of us can remember."

"Yes," Josef continues. "And even my own father once described this same man to me when I was a young lad. It seems as if this man never dies. So, we have been considering, once again I must add, that there is something amiss in how the Governor's seat has changed over the years."

"And worse," adds another man in the circle. "He doesn't come from a noble bloodline, which irritates us to no end. We've never seen any outward signs of a transition, either as a public election, or from father to son."

"Indeed, Seth," Josef affirms. "That would be the greatest offence of all if this charlatan would dare to suggest his rightful decree to rule our city by his illegitimate lineage. In fact, as far as any of us know, he doesn't even seem to have a history."

"All right, let's consider this," Tristeen offers. "Does anyone here know if he has a family of any kind, whether as any form of ancestry or current children?"

"None of us knows of any ancestry," Abraim insists. "And as your father was suggesting, this man may have pre-existed even before our own generation, and this is simply unreasonable to assume with the plague taking our lives as it does."

"Could he be immune to the plague?"

"If he was, he would need to be exceedingly old by now, and this still troubles us, as we recall from the history passed down to us in our family lines that our kind cannot live as long as what this man seems to have accomplished."

"Very well, so this doesn't seem to be a proper argument. What about this… For the transitions, we have not seen anything made publicly. Maybe they keep it private."

"This is another issue that I have been very troubled with," Seth asserts. "We've managed, over the years, to infiltrate a few spies into the Manor as attendants to the Governor. He seems to live alone, with no family at all; no wife, no children, nothing."

"Maybe he keeps them locked in the basement," Josef chuckles. "No one is ever allowed down there, and to our knowledge, the only person who has ever been seen with access to it is the Dean on occasion."

"Yes, and we all know what sort of spineless worm he is," Abraim concludes.

"Spineless worm…" Tristeen muses quietly. "He doesn't behave that way in the academy. In there, he holds a hard line of authority."

"Tristeen," Josef contends. "The Dean may hold a position of power, but he is no more a nobleman than the Governor himself. He was taken from the lower quarters and elevated to a position of authority under the Governor's office. This alone has swollen his ego to such proportions that he can barely stand upright."

"Right, a god complex. Now it makes sense."

"And so," Seth considers. "This essentially leads us back to where we started with the Governor. We have never seen a public transition to install a replacement, and there is apparently no family, either before or after him, to prescribe an heir."

"Well then, what about this," Tristeen perks up. "At this point, it has to be private. And if he's not a…recognized…nobleman, what if they're not located within the Manor at all? All the noble families we know of tend to keep to their homes up here in the Ward as dynasties. I don't know about the common families as much, but could he be descendant from a line that doesn't normally associate with the other noble houses, and with the remainder of his family located elsewhere?"

"This is fair enough, Tristeen," Josef offers. "But then we need to ask where he comes from. We are fairly certain this man is not a noble, or else we would know more about his bloodline. Any noble house worthy of their name would not mix themselves with the common folk, and those of us up here are well familiar with each other. This leaves us with only one other possibility, and again the reason for our primary discontent."

"That he's a commoner, or maybe someone who pretends to a higher station?"

"Yes, this is all we have left, unless you have another explanation. The only source to draw from is here in the city."

"Right, and I wonder how this might fit in with what I heard today."

"Why is that? What is it you heard?"

"Apparently, as it goes, we are supposed to be involved in this war, according to Captain Kholgard at the barracks. After all, it's our world as much as any other, as he says. But no one is allowed to go outside. The reason? Publicly, our supply shortages, to say nothing of all the bad things out there."

"Right," he nods. "I've heard this much often enough."

"But privately, it's to keep us boxed in and under someone's information quarantine."

"An information quarantine?"

"And worse, this isn't being described as a proper war anymore. It's now being described as a purging effort, down to the last of us here, and apparently just like the Night Elves. And this is probably intentional to keep us boxed inside our walls…with our information quarantine. We're not allowed to go outside, not allowed to talk to people, and so, not allowed to share details of any kind, which only leaves us with rumors and hearsay turning our noses up at what used to be friends and allies."

"What?" he jerks forward in his chair. "And for what purpose?"

"In a word, I might say isolation. The Governor, for all his illegal occupation in that chair, apparently hates everything outside our walls. All those trashy rumors about the Night Elves and Daanen-Aryku are apparently a form of propaganda. We're actually supposed to be friends and allies fighting this war together, but we're not. We don't even go out to speak with them to learn anything."

"This speaks of oppression to me," Seth intones.

"Indeed!" Abraim affirms. "And this would be criminal! Slander, at the very least."

Tristeen continues, "The schools are effectively owned by him, through the Dean. The temple may also be involved. Therefore, everything they teach. As such, what he says is what you have to swallow. And the Dean works for him to make sure you actually swallow it. So much for that spineless worm."

"Grand! Just grand!"

"According to the Captain, it's been four hundred years. That's a long time for no one to figure it out. No one is apparently fighting any real wars out there, just occasional skirmishes to remind us to stay put. It seems very neat, when you piece it together, assuming you actually had all the pieces to put together to begin with. But looking at it from inside these walls, I doubt you would see it that way."

"Why would you say this?" Josef asks. "Not that I would argue, but…"

"All things considered, and when you include our debates, there's something backhanded occurring here. The Captain tells me he's got a deal going with those people in the valley. The Governor apparently made a secret visit, which is to say behind the Captain's back, to those people down there and made trouble for us."

"Uh oh! And what sort of trouble are we speaking of here?"

"From what I hear, some of it from my friends in the academy who go out on these spy runs, that guy down there, his name is Lord Thaelyn, is fighting the war we're supposed to be fighting. But the Dean has been sending spies at him, as if he doesn't like the idea of him winning all those battles we never fight."

"Oh, how tragic!" Seth intones sarcastically.

"Then we have the Governor, bless his poisoned soul, and that secret trip out there. According to the Captain, he tried charging squatter's tax just for occupying space, and then to demand tribute of some kind. By the sound of it, when he didn't get this, he played out all these prejudices, and I guess the final result was to make enemies of the one guy in our world with the power, and maybe also the gumption to actually fight something."

"Unbelievable!" Abraim roars. "And that truly is criminal!"

"This might also be leading us in a new direction here," Seth urges. "No self-respecting man, not a noble or even a commoner, would behave this way. But a criminal…"

"Blast! You're right. And further that he could transition to someone else behind our backs. It's a bloody conspiracy!"

"Dear Gods, Abraim!" Josef snaps. "But by whom?"

"No doubt by some hidden party who usurped the Governor's seat for themselves."

"Now, just a moment," Seth offers. "I think we need to consider when this originally occurred. Recall that the Governor's seat only came into being after the Manor was converted from the old Council building where our ancestors once held power. Now, let us consider when the Governor's seat was first taken. How long ago was that?"

Chapter 15

ACQUISITION

"**M**y Lord, the prisoner is here, by your request."

A prison guard, summoned a short while earlier, was bringing the mage academy spy to a conference room in the detention block on the lower level of the guildhall. Thaelyn and Marelle were both sitting at a table in the room, along with Haran who had been called in as a consultant. As a former student at the academy in Rolsklinde, they thought he might be familiar with the man and could offer assistance in interrogating him.

"Bring him in, Guard," Thaelyn orders. "Set him down in the chair here."

The guard ushers in the spy and sits him in a chair on the opposite side of the table. Willit found himself gazing at the three of them, but settles on Haran.

"Hello, Haran," he offers softly. "Some of us thought the Dean may have locked you in a closet after that noise you made upstairs."

"Yes…" Haran responds coolly. "I'm sure if I had stayed around long enough, he might have done just that. He threatened to turn me into a rat and stick me in the alchemy lab."

"Well," Willit chuckles weakly. "I doubt he might be able to do that, but I know the feeling."

"Haran," Thaelyn interjects briefly. "Do you know this man?"

"Yes, my Lord. He and I go back to our childhood. We're friends, actually, part of a small group within the academy."

"Did you just call him 'my Lord'?" Willit winces.

"Yes, I'm a citizen of this world now, and attending classes in his academy," he thumbs at Thaelyn. "Which is a far sight better than the one we have back home."

"Really, so you left us to come over here?"

"I had nothing left for me in Rolsklinde, except maybe Tristeen. But you and I both know, she's a noble and I'm not. And I had to survive."

"Yes, of course."

"So, Willit, what brings you to us?"

"Haran, you should probably know better than to ask that question. The Dean sent me out there to observe what these people are doing."

"That's fine, but does this mean the Dean actually cares enough about the war to offer assistance with it? When I was talking to him, he said the Guard doesn't need to know, and told me to stuff my opinions in the outward hole."

"Haran, you and I both know how he is. Though I will admit, his attitude tells how he doesn't care much for these people."

"Yes, and I certainly got a good taste of it up there, even that part he might not normally show to the rest. But then, I brought this to my sister and her Captain, and they were a little upset when he and the Governor made their unannounced visit to the camp. By the time I arrived with the two of them, both the Night Elves and the Daanen-Aryku were fuming with the reports of what those two had to say about them."

"All right, wait. Before we get involved in another argument, I don't personally know what was said out there. As you can probably already guess, by what your sister laid upon me, the Dean doesn't tell us anything outside what he wants to tell us."

"Fair enough. Then, let me clue you in on the highlights of that conversation. Although I wasn't present at the time they arrived, and I heard this secondhand from His Lordship, I would tend to trust his words far more eagerly than anyone else's around here."

"Why is that, just for reference?"

"Let's just say he impressed upon me that he holds a much higher background of authority and trustworthiness than anyone we have back home."

"Well, all right, and I suppose you should know what you're looking at as much as anyone else. So, what is it those two had to say that made everyone around here so uppity?"

"First, the Governor tried making a claim of ownership of that land down there and to charge squatter's fees for occupying it."

"Ownership?!" he shouts. "Haran, even I know that place is a barren waste. Why would he try doing this?"

"Probably to fool the new guy... When that didn't work, he tried bargaining a deal of exclusive allegiance against what he called the villains of the world, meaning to say the Night Elves and the Daanen-Aryku, to say nothing of the real enemies we face, but only on the condition that Thaelyn supply him with all his fine military goods as a gift to shore up our most unfortunate supply issues."

"Well, that certainly sounds nice of him. But Haran, how am I really supposed to interpret that statement. You know the stories we hear about those people."

"Yes, but Willit, you know the stories of my two friends, Relissa and Kaliya, right?"

"Yes, and this has often confused me, thinking maybe you found a couple exceptions to the rules out there."

"No, Willit, the exceptions are the Governor and his rhetoric over his apparent prejudice over them. He feeds this to the Dean, who then feeds it to the rest of us, whether we like it or not. The Night Elves, for instance, worship a legitimate group of gods and for legitimate reasons. There's nothing unholy about it. In fact, if I were to suggest anything unholy, it would be our own priests for not worshiping those same or similar gods. These gods are also found on this world among these people, which, by the way, is our ancestral home before all of us travelled to Therinë."

"Huh? Where did you hear that?"

"Willit, hear or not hear, look around you. How likely do you think it to be to find another world out there with humans on it, to say nothing of elves."

"Um…well, all right, you got me on that one."

"The Night Elves carry some of this history with them, but we apparently forgot, and I say no thanks to the Dean and his teaching practice. And you'll notice all the people on Therinë are also represented here. This is our point of origin. Then we have the Daanen-Aryku. For whatever the people might say about them, they are not even religious. They're intellectuals; scientists and scholars. So, if they're doing anything…strange…it's simply because we're too primitive to understand it."

"We are primitive…" he muses.

"Willit, compare us to the orcs. Now compare the orcs to us, in reverse. Then multiply that several times over, and you have us versus the Daanen-Aryku. Their civilization is two million years old, Willit, and they are able to travel the stars above. What does that suggest?"

"Wow…" he croons. "All right, so the Governor tried making a backroom deal that didn't work. And it would seem he revealed a few things along the way. Then how does this relate to the Dean sending us out to spy on them, and this idea we're supposed to be fighting the war together? What about the elves and the row they started up?"

"Acolyte," Marelle begins. "The orcs and the Suuden-Aryku are the only true enemies to our people, as they're the real invaders in our world. Everything else is likely collateral. And Sargeras is behind the whole thing, with some kind of ulterior motive we're not sure of yet."

"Uh huh, and those elves?"

"Victims, including the Flame Elves, we think…"

"Just a moment," he pauses with a finger. "How do you describe those Flame Elves as victims?"

"Those Flame Elves are supposed to be called High Elves, and High Elves, as a race, are probably better than we are. Something got inside there and seriously messed things up. They were found once on Ruuki uy'Daan sabotaging the Daanen-Aryku's ship, and this is why they crashed here. Therefore, if Flame Elves were found on another world before they were officially declared to be following Sargeras here in our world, this says they were secretly following him before any of the rest of us knew what was happening. This now tells us Sargeras was here long before we ever knew of it."

"Oh grand…"

"Next is to ask how the elven war really got started, which none of us ever did. Not that we might understand, or even listen to it, even if we did ask. The Night Elves tell us the High Elves did something no elf would do in their right mind, and I mean that almost literally. This is now suggesting Sargeras took them from the beginning of the war, and he is the one responsible for everything that happened here."

"So, you're saying, the elves didn't start anything. Instead, someone came along and broke up a nice little pact we must've had once upon a time, ay?"

"Worse, those orcs come from Ruuki uy'Daan, right?"

"That's what I hear…"

"But they made a recent invasion of Tae'Eladar, and this is why His Lordship is on Therinë, fighting to protect his world, despite any of us and our objections to it."

"How wonderful… The Dean apparently neglected to mention that part."

"I'm not surprised, but it doesn't stop there. Those orcs preexisted on Tae'Eladar from a much earlier invasion…thousands of years ago from places unknown…or at least unknown to them at the time. Now, he arrives on Therinë and finds more orcs, but this time he discovers who owns them. Now, what do you think of that for a most remarkable coincidence?"

Willit grimaces at the inference. He gazes at Thaelyn to see his expression, and then returns back to Haran and Marelle.

"Bloody hell! Are we saying by all this that he owned those orcs thousands of years ago? You know, this whole bloody thing sounds like some sort of a ruse. But why in all the hells would he do this in the first place?"

"This is part of the puzzle we don't know yet, but one thing we do know. He is a leftover from an ancient battle that apparently started somewhere far away from us, and with those same gods we're all supposed to be worshipping."

Willit wailed and drew back in his chair. He gaped at Marelle as he tried to put it together.

"Gods' pity, ma'am! And are we just toys for him along the way?"

"Basically, yes. But now, for the really interesting part...our shortages...and as it turns out, another fascinating coincidence..."

"I'm not so sure I like all these bloody coincidences of yours."

"Neither do we, but here we are...the iron from the dwarves."

"Aye, and you mentioned this before."

"Those dwarves are behaving really strangely. I went up there to see about a political talk on behalf of His Lordship, and they didn't even look at me, not even after pounding on their shoulders and screaming in their ears hoping to draw their attention. We think they might be under a drug effect, and in some kind of delirium as the result. This means, someone owns them too."

"Uh oh...that doesn't sound good. And that one sounds nasty."

"One thought we had, if the Governor and Dean have anything to do with it, is if the academy with your alchemy lab could be making something the Dean takes up there. Do you know of anything?"

"We don't make anything like drugs to put people into a tizzy. Speed potions, aye. Invisibility ones, too. Also, there are a few labs outside the academy. I've heard they make medicines and such, so maybe one of those is it."

"All right, we can check on that later. Anyway, we have scouts up there checking on their iron production, and they seem to be making plenty of it. So, if our wonderful Governor, with his exclusive trade deal, is supposed to be supplying us, we're not getting nearly our fair share of it."

"Oh dear, and here is where that Night Elf and her words come in, I'll bet."

"Right. We're cleaning up after ourselves out there on the battlefield with those orcs, and they seem to have a lot of what looks like fresh iron and steel. But orcs aren't known to make this themselves. So, where do you think they're getting it?"

"Blast! So, the dwarves are double-dealing us? Or is it something else?"

"Let's also involve our city, with virtually no attacks coming at us in living memory, maybe even longer. Then let's include the Guard patrols we sometimes send out to assist the Daanen-Aryku, where each one came home with nary a sighting on the horizon. It's a little too convenient, when both the Night Elves and the Daanen-Aryku take hits on regular occasions."

"Aye, that does sound a bit wonky."

"Furthermore, His Lordship is supporting the Daanen-Aryku out there with his troops, but my Captain gave him some disguises to make them look like us, at least in the beginning, to fool the Suuden-Aryku, since we have this history of going out there."

"But why would you do this at all if it's his people? Don't they know about you by now?"

"They probably do, but this is a tactical play to keep a low profile and not draw attention directly to him so far. The trouble is, those Suuden-Aryku made this really crazy run at his troops using armor and weapons more like ours, rather than their rifles. It was clearly a message to keep out, and the first time a Guard patrol ever came under attack. But the material wasn't steel, like ours. It was adamantium."

"What?" he shrieks. "Gods' pity…again. You mean to say that stuff is real?"

"It's not just real, his full army uses it," she glances at Thaelyn. "Every soldier out there."

"Great gods, so all that stuff I've been studying on your men is adamantium?"

"That, and mithril for shields and weapons," Thaelyn offers. "We have a good amount of it in our world, though I will admit it is regarded as a rare material. Still, we do not skimp on the details here."

"I'm aware of mithril. The Dean has some old artifacts of some kind made from it, but it's not supposed to be found in our world."

"Then we might suggest this could date back before your arrival."

"Maybe, but if we're saying the Suuden-Aryku came at you like this, what does that mean for the result?"

"Our people are far more proficient with swords, so we dispatched their assault. But the curious aspect is they seemed intent on us, and since ours is not a sanctioned deployment by your Governor, and when combined with the rest, we think his real reason for not wanting to fight is because he is taking benefit from it behind your backs."

Willit slumped and sighed despondently.

"He's selling us out to the enemies whom we're told destroyed our world and who keep us boxed inside our walls. How bloody charming of him. But this must've been going on for a long time now. My Dad told me stories of the Governor that came before, and he sounded like the same sort."

"Then we could be looking at some manner of conspiracy to keep you oppressed, just like the others are being oppressed by their respective foes out there."

"Aye, that's a fine one. And now with you out there fighting, and no doubt shaking things up for his neat little tryst. No wonder the Dean wants to know what you're up to, and speaks of you like yet another invader out to make trouble."

"Perhaps, but the trouble I am more likely to make is for people like him who keep people like you boxed inside cities like yours. As I said to your Governor, once I finish with the real villains of the world, I am coming for him next."

"Well, that's fine by me, after all is said and done here!" he shakes his head as he tries to pull himself together. "Oppressed, aye! That's a good way of putting it, including those Flame Elves…keeping us on edge like they do with that bleedin' curse of theirs. No doubt that's another part of it, just one more reminder in case we forget something new."

"A what? A curse, you say?"

Willit perks up at the mention. He studies the three of them, focusing on Haran and Marelle.

"Um, have either of you told him about the Plague?"

"Oh, actually no…" Marelle replies. "That one hasn't come up yet. Although, I suppose I should've mentioned something by now. My Mom has it."

"Dear gods, I'm sorry to hear that."

"So am I."

"A plague?" Thaelyn intones curiously. "Explain…"

"The city may not have come under physical attack," Willit reflects. "But if the Governor is making deals to keep us under his thumb, those Flame Elves must be a part of it. We have this plague that's said to be a curse by them."

"What does it do?"

"It's awful, and it's been with us since the beginning, I think. Our people take ill sometime around fifty years, maybe a little after. They get sick with bad headaches and then memory loss. Once it hits, they're dead in less than a month."

Marelle lowers her head as she reflects on her own miseries.

"Marelle," Thaelyn observes. "You say your mother currently has this?"

"Yes, so this hits a little close to home for me. My dad died from it a few years ago."

"My sympathies to you, and at the same time, this is most peculiar. You say it is described as a curse by the Flame Elves?"

"Aye," Willit admits. "I'm not sure of the history, but it's a story that goes way back, so they say."

"Have you made any attempts to reverse this?"

"It's been said the priests of the temple and the mages of the academy have tried, but to no avail. They just keep pressing it against us."

"I see. Very well, we must look into this somehow."

The meeting slows as they each take a momentary break, until Willit speaks up again.

"May I know what you'll be doing with me after this?" he asks. "I didn't do anything especially harmful, just peeking in on you to keep us…well, the Dean, informed of things."

"Acolyte," Thaelyn infers. "While I recognize your duty as a scout, and I shall use that word rather than to say spy, your actions are nonetheless as much like those of a spy informing on foreign matters to aid a potential enemy. If your Governor held any interest in participating with us, I might simply say this is your way of keeping abreast of things. Although, with Marelle here, I should think this would be unnecessary."

"Aye, maybe…assuming you were sharing it to begin with, which I guess you're not for all his other grousing."

"Indeed. But this is a time of war, and it carries its own rules, to which I suspect some of you are not as familiar, since you apparently do not participate in any true wartime activities. Some might say you are performing espionage to inform those I am currently fighting of my actions during the fight. This could potentially explain that rogue Suuden-Aryku attack or a recent assassination attempt by a Flame Elf spy."

"Um, I'll actually have to admit to that one. The Dean had us watch you real close. He didn't actually say why, just that he wanted to know when you come and go around here."

"Indeed! Then, this is clear enough indication that he and your Governor are likely the ones responsible for organizing the attack."

"Bloody Hell!" Marelle screeches. "That bastard would go so far? Threatening you is one thing, but actually doing it? That just makes me want to march in there and drag his flabby backside out onto the street for a public flogging."

"Gently, Marelle…" Thaelyn smiles tenderly. "His time will come. We will simply add this to the list for now. But two can play this game, and if this is how he likes it, I will oblige him. We will start by sending a few of our own spies up to the city. But we will need to prepare them, first."

Marelle huffs as she leans back in her chair. Then she looks at Willit and gets an idea.

"What about him? Could we use him as a spy under the Dean's nose, like the Dean was doing to us?"

"I wouldn't recommend that," Haran muses. "Not inside the academy, at least. You said someone else was spotted out there running home? No doubt, if the Dean were to see him returning after a clear capture, there will be a few hells to pay for it."

"He's right," Willit affirms. "Gods' pity, I wouldn't want to hear that one."

"Willit, who else was out there?"

"Jared. The Dean has been sending the two of us down here a lot recently."

"Haran," Thaelyn interjects. "Would you be familiar with this other one?"

"Yes, my Lord, another of our little group."

"Most interesting, I wonder if we could use this."

"Give him to me," Marelle smirks mischievously. "You need a spy? I'll whip him into shape. After all, I did that with my little brother enough times."

"Hmm," he eyes her suspiciously. "What do you think, Haran? Would you trust your sister to this man?"

"More like would I trust him to her," he chuckles.

"Dear gods," Willit moans. "I think I'm in serious trouble now. To all the bleedin' hells with being a spy, if she wants to get her hooks into me now."

"But then…" Thaelyn wonders. "How would you suggest we use him, if not to insert him back into the academy?"

"Oh, I can think of a few ideas," Haran grins. "Willit, how often do you visit the Ten Eagles?"

◆

Two days have passed since the activation of the towers. All is quiet in the camp. Tensions have soothed now that the towers are keeping a watchful stance over the camp's security. No new sightings have been discovered.

It is late in the day, and Thaelyn shares a conversation in the tactical office with several of his personal advisors who are visiting from Bya'an Tamoranth about the next day's events. The Night Elves have sent a reply on their decision relating to his offer to join the kingdom. Councilwoman Amariyn is expected to arrive in the morning with the official word.

"My Lord," announces an officer entering the room. "I believe we have found a suitable target."

"Yes, Lieutenant, what do you have?" Thaelyn responds.

"We found a patrol of three Flame Elf scouts making a routine circuit around a woodland area approximately one hundred miles to our south. They make this route every morning, the same path."

"Interesting… What about the terrain? Are there any clearings we can use to ambush them?"

"Yes, my Lord! Our scouts report there is a clearing in the area that the elves pass through. The elves also seem to make a pause in the center of it to rest."

"How convenient! Our people can surround the clearing, hit them from multiple sides, and incapacitate them before they know which way to turn. Excellent! Begin assembling your team, Lieutenant. I want you stationed in the area ready for their next patrol."

"Yes, my Lord. Their patrol sets out in the mid-morn. I'll have my people in place by first light."

The Lieutenant turns to leave the building. As he does, he calls up several other soldiers who were standing in wait, and rattles off a list of orders.

Thaelyn turns to look at Relissa, who had been attending the discussion with Thaelyn's advisors. She looks up at him with mild apprehension.

"My Lord," she mutters softly. "All I can say is we have stories about them. I'll admit it's a wee bit scary to think of. Not the sort of thing I would care much for."

"Not to worry, Relissa, our people are very well trained. Maybe one day, your time will come, and you will stand just as tall as the rest," he smiles.

The dawning of the next morning breaks over the budding settlement of Firstfall. Many of the soldiers are collecting at the kitchen for their morning meal. One group, however, with its members already fed and geared up for an early excursion, is opening a portal for transport.

"Good luck, Lieutenant," Thaelyn offers. "Be swift as the eastward wind and silent as the night."

The Lieutenant nods as he and several others heft large packs over their shoulders before vanishing through the portal.

The morning progresses and Thaelyn convenes the meeting in the tactical office. The war moves forward. The front line is steadily advancing, and there is still no sign of reinforcement from either the Flame Elves or the Suuden-Aryku in the defense of the orcs.

Scouts have been carefully surveying the eastern and southern frontiers for any signs of activity by the latter two factions, but neither seemed to be advancing as yet. However, there were indications of reinforcement being conducted along the common borders with Thaelyn's territory, giving rise to suspicions that they were preparing for some future operation.

Around midday, a carriage arrives at the north gate. It was Councilwoman Amariyn. The guards pass her through, and she drives up into a small village square that had been recently laid out. As she steps out of the carriage, Thaelyn walks up to meet her.

"Lady Amariyn, such a fine pleasure to see you again."

"Truly, it is more my pleasure, Your Grace. I trust you are in receipt of the note I sent to Relissa?"

"Indeed I am, and we are all very excited. Is it my understanding that your visit today is to carry the official word from the Council?"

"That it is, and the word is that the Council has deliberated on this carefully and solicited the opinion of our people. The voices of Solinaia are unanimous. We wish to submit ourselves to your most gracious rule, and rejoin our brothers and sisters back in Sein'amar."

"Excellent," he smiles pleasantly. "I have been in council with my own advisors to make plans for your reunification with our people. Of course, there will need to be an official ceremony to swear in the city and its population, but we will make all efforts to see this transition go smoothly and efficiently."

"My thanks to you, Your Grace," she bows modestly. "Is Relissa around? I was hoping to spend a few moments with her. It's not as common of her to be away for so long. Although I realize she has her duties, as her mother, I still worry for her."

"At this time, she would still be in her class in B.T., but I expect she will be finishing up soon and returning here for the review with our officers. You are welcome to wait for her if you like. It should not be too long."

"Very well, I think I will. It's a rather long drive back home, and I wouldn't want to miss seeing her again."

"Naturally. Then feel free to wander about as you please. I hope you will excuse me for a time as I still have a few details to attend in the meeting here."

"Of course, Your Grace."

Thaelyn returns back to the tactical office to continue with a review of several recent scouting reports, while Amariyn decides to make a brief visit to the tree to offer her piety. When she is done, she engages herself in a slow stroll around the young settlement observing the vigorous bustle.

✦✦✦✦✦

"And around we go again..." moans the young female mage. "This pathetic routine bores me! We simply go round in circles through the wood and back again. There's nothing out here better than birds, squirrels, and gnats!"

"Be silent, Adept!" demands the priestess. "We're given this patrol to watch for any intruders. You heard the reports from up north. They could stretch their arm this way at any moment! And we need to know about it the instant they arrive!"

"Right, and in that instant, what are the three of us supposed to do about it? Count it, three of us in this little patrol that is supposed to accomplish so much. I may be skilled in the Art, but I don't like being sent out on a fool's errand with nothing more than a stick-thrower behind me!"

"Excuse me, Adept, I'm an archer!" corrects the male following up the rear. "And if it weren't for me, you might not even know if there was anything out here! In fact, for all the complaining you do, if there were intruders, they would need nothing more than to follow the sound of your wailing to find us. Now be silent in case there is someone watching."

"Watching, watching! Yesterday, there was nothing. The day before, there was nothing. The week before that, nothing! The outlanders are fighting the orcs, and until those filthy heaps are wiped clean from this world, that is all they care about."

"Adept Mynae!" shouts the priestess. "If you'll recall, the early stages of their campaign began with surprise strikes against the orcs, wiping their camps clean from the land."

"Yes! And that's just it, Eilihel. They were surprise hits. Do you think the orcs to be so incredibly stupid that they might not notice an army of thousands rushing their way? If such a thing were to occur here, the three of us would hardly be in a position to do anything about it. I would much rather be on the lines with soldiers fighting an enemy I can see rather than out here getting my backside stung by pests."

"Be silent! Both of you!" the archer shouts.

"Or what, Kethron? We get ourselves pecked upon by the birds of the trees for disturbing their nests, or have squirrels run up our britches looking for breadcrumbs?"

"All right, Mynae..." Eilihel demands. "That's enough, from all of us. We have a job to do, and do it we shall. He needs our eyes to survey the land, and our ears to listen to the sounds coming up from around us. As pointless as it may seem to be out here, it is our purpose to serve him. Now, let us continue, and do so quietly."

The three quarrelsome Flame Elves trudge through the wood on their patrol, a circle they have made many times before. They step around brambles and over logs, taking care to watch themselves for dried twigs and downed tree limbs. From the treetops comes the singing of the occasional bird and a rustling of leaves from a jumping squirrel.

The route would normally take about two hours to complete, but today Adept Mynae was feeling abnormally sluggish. Her boredom was getting the better of her, while dreams of battle wafted in her head. She had only recently completed her training as a mage and was eager to test herself against the enemies of her people, meaning the humans, Night Elves, and more recently, Thaelyn's troops. But much to her frustration, she had been positioned in a remote outpost far behind the lines where there is often nothing more to do than to fight off the local insect population.

Curate Eilihel was a ranking member of the outpost and an ardent follower of Sargeras, as were all the clergy. The songs of his mind rang out most potently in their thoughts as he drew part of his strength from them. They, in turn, used this association to help contain the others.

Kethron was the only male in the group. As an archer and woodsman, he drew upon the inherent qualities of the elves to find his way through wooded regions and overland, leaving little notice to follow behind him. His keen perceptions allowed him to see and hear the faintest of murmurs and shifting of leaves on the ground.

The first leg of the hike lasted through to the late part of the morning. Just after midday, they see the small clearing that would mark the midpoint of their tour. They made a habit of stopping there, resting a short while to eat and drink before continuing the remainder of the way around. As was the usual practice, Kethron made a sweep of the area before they entered the clearing to settle down.

They sat in a circle, facing inward towards each other so they could carry on a conversation, confident that the area was clear of any dangers. They brought out their packs and flasks of water and tried to find something of value to talk about.

"I wonder if there are any rabbits out today," Kethron remarks. "If I see one, I'm taking it home with me. It's been a long time since I had a good rabbit roast."

"I could cook it for you…" Mynae responds. "Just point the way and I'll flame the entire area!"

"Yes, I'm sure you'd like that, and half the wood along with it. That would also solve your pest control problem quite nicely."

"Do the two of you ever stop bickering?" Eilihel complains. "Why must I bring such argumentative attendants on patrols like this, I'll never know. But it is the will of Sargeras that young partisans like yourselves bear the weight of discipline to make you strong. Unfortunately, all you ever do is complain. Do you wish to draw his wrath?"

Kethron and Mynae both hush their whining and drop their heads.

"That's what I thought. Now eat. We still have a long walk ahead, and our progress has been rather slow today," she glares sternly at Mynae.

Off in the distance, somewhere in the trees surrounding the clearing, the chirping of a bird sounds off. The song is a curiously musical assemblage of notes, first at midrange, then dipping low and up high. The strange call draws the casual attention of Kethron.

"Interesting. I don't think I've ever heard that particular call before. I wonder what sort of bird has found its way into the wood."

The announcement repeats itself once more, followed by three rising chirps and a two-tone yoo-hoo call. This new sequence repeats again and stops.

"Clearly, it's looking for a mate. It must be quite lost, however. I have never heard a song like that in this region."

"Maybe you could shoot it down and take it home as a wall mount," Mynae quips.

In the distance comes a firm thumping sound, as though something heavy fell to the ground. The origin of the sound seems to have come from somewhere in the direction Kethron was facing, and behind the two women.

Kethron jerks his head up and looks intently into the wood. His heightened alertness draws the attention of the two women, who turn sideways over their shoulders to see where he is looking.

Another chirping from the bird issues forth. First, a single rising chirp followed by a downward chirp, then a double rising chirp and another downward chirp.

"What is going on over there?" Kethron demands. "I heard a sound in the wood, but that damnable bird isn't shutting up!"

With their attention focused on the apparent disturbance on the far side of the wood, they didn't even notice the gentle whistling sound of two softly glowing orbs approaching at opposite angles from behind the archer. They impact directly adjacent to the two women.

A blinding flash of light permeates the area, accompanied by a shockingly loud bang! Each of the two orbs explodes in a fury of torment for both eyes and ears, leaving neither able to focus on the surrounding environment.

Before the trio is able to get to their feet, a second wave comes in, further blasting the senses and disorienting the group. Finally, one last orb is cast into the circle, this one a sickly green color. As it impacts within the circle, it detonates, releasing a cloud of fetid gas to befoul the nostrils and induce an uncontrollable choking.

The three elves struggle to stand up, fighting against a world they can neither see nor hear, and now unable to breathe. They find themselves quickly losing consciousness and fall to the ground.

A dozen darkly clad forms rush forward out of the woods from all sides. Their bodies were covered in black featureless garments, and their heads concealed under thick hoods. The only openings are tiny slits for their eyes to see through.

As they approach the greenish cloud of stink-gas, one of them weaves a divine chant to clear the air so they can enter the area without falling victim to the same effect.

The three Flame Elves are motionless on the ground, unconscious as their attackers hurry into place. Several of them set down a collection of large packs, pulling out ropes and black hoods. One pack also produces a set of three oddly glimmering silver circlets, adorned with small gems and runic carvings. The elves are bound hand and foot, and the circlets are placed around their necks and secured with locking clasps.

One of the figures gestures his hand over the face of one of the elves. With two fingers, he draws a clockwise circle around the elf's face, starting at the top, wrapping around, and finishing with an open hand sliding down above the face. He repeats the same gesture on the other two elves, placing each into an enforced sleep.

The hoods are placed over their heads and shoulders. Securing ropes are then laced through holes in the bottom of each, under the arms and around the torso.

The bodies of the hapless victims are hefted up, while one figure pulls out a small oblong stone. Holding it in one hand, he makes several circling gestures over it, causing it to glow. Each of the figures then touches the stone and vanishes in a ball of light.

✦✦✦✦✦

Once again, Relissa and Marelle made their way back to Firstfall from their classes in the academy. They were almost two-thirds of the way through and able to carry on a proficient level of conversation by now.

Relissa was anxiously waiting to see this next month through so she could get started on her proper academy training. She had been away from home longer than ever before and missed her furry little friends.

Marelle still fought with herself over her obligations to Rolsklinde and the Guard, versus serving the Order and maybe finding a more valuable service for herself. The discovery of Acolyte Sarens spying on them only served to intensify her anxiety over the Dean and the Governor, but she struggled to temper herself. As such, she was diverting her anguish by spending time in session with Willit to condition him as her own spy.

The two women emerged through the gateway into the burgeoning settlement to find a group of people gathered around in a circle nearby. Curious as to what was happening, they approach to find a number of soldiers dressed in plain black, along with an assortment of others from around the camp. Also present are Thaelyn and his officers, Lieutenant Lapäli, and Lady Amariyn. The mass was standing over three bodies tightly bound with black hoods covering their heads.

"I'll bet those are the Flame Elves they caught," Relissa whispers to Marelle. "Jiggers! It looks like they got them blindsided and slack-jawed!"

Marelle casts a proud grin at Relissa as she responds.

"I guess this should teach you never to underestimate the power of a well-organized military."

"Your Grace," Amariyn declares. "While I recall that first day when you suggested these…" she pauses to clear her throat, "…people…to possibly have been taken by that monster sometime early on, I will not so easily submit to forgiving them their sins against the rest of us."

"Lady Amariyn," he offers. "I understand your pain. There can be many reasons why this war first came to this world, and who is ultimately responsible for any one crime. But we must hold certain standards for ourselves, and we cannot allow our prejudices to dictate our actions. These, in particular, appear as younger members, so we surely cannot blame them specifically for anything. Clearly, it would be wrong for us to place blame on someone simply for belonging to a race of people, where someone, at some moment in time, did something wrong to someone else."

"Yes, of course, you are right. Forgive me. I simply carry a long memory of this. I was present at the time all this began, and that is a long time to watch the demise of our world."

"Indeed, I am sure it must have been very painful. At the same time, I feel it is important to reiterate, due to the involvement of Sargeras, a being that I believe has many powers of the mind, that these elves may not be wholly responsible for their actions. That one example we collected before showed no physical markings of corruption, and this leaves few other choices for us."

"Then you still think they did this not of their own free will?"

"This is what we hope to discover once I find time to interrogate them. There must be a clue hidden in their past."

"I see. You are an exceptionally noble man, Your Grace. All right then, do as you must. I think I would not care to participate in this interrogation, as I doubt it would hold much promise for me. But I do wish you luck in learning something of value from them."

Amariyn moves away from the crowd and over to Relissa, who was standing patiently on the side waiting for her.

"Captain Hagmaert," Thaelyn instructs. "These prisoners are to be removed from here to the sanctuary. Aerlie has the key and will let you inside. They must be rendered completely ineffectual, Captain. See to it."

The Captain salutes and orders the soldiers to carry the prisoners through the portal back to the city.

Thaelyn calls the other officers to return inside the tactical office. Marelle follows along, as much to hear what they have to say as to review the other morning's events.

"Mum!" Relissa shouts as Amariyn approaches. "I'm so excited about the news from Solinaia. What's happening over there right now?"

"Many of the people are preparing for a celebration. I'm hearing of food and drink being made ready, decorations are going up, and you can even hear the music in the people's voices again. It's so delightful! It reminds me of the old days, before this horrid war took away the people's spirits."

"What about the tree? How is it doing?"

"Oh, the tree! If I didn't know better, I'd say it's nearly doubled its girth, for all the attention it's getting!"

✦✦✦

"Lady Aerlie, your presence is requested up at the guildhall immediately. A message is sent that you must bring the key."

A page that was sent just moments before from the guildhall was delivering the announcement to the temple's main hall, where Aerlie had been conducting her service along with several other priests.

She interrupts her practice and moves off to a private room on the side. There, she casts an enchantment on a sealed metal box with no latches or handles. The box opens by itself. Inside, she finds an especially ornate and curiously shaped rune stone, along with a small satchel and a silver icon in the form of an aging male face. She pulls open a nearby drawer and removes a set of white silk gloves, neatly pulling them over her hands. She then removes the silver medallion, studies it carefully, and bows her head in reverence. She places the medallion back into the box and takes the satchel and rune stone. She waves her hand, and the box closes again.

Aerlie turns to leave the temple. Once outside, she spreads her wings and lifts into the air, flapping vigorously to gain altitude and hurry herself over to the guildhall. When she arrives, she lands inside the courtyard to meet with Captain Hagmaert. Standing next to him are a half dozen soldiers arranged into pairs and carrying the three Flame Elf prisoners, still under their magical sleep spell.

Aerlie brings up the rune and casts the magic to open a portal aperture within the courtyard. The Captain, followed by the soldiers, moved sequentially through the portal. Aerlie then follows by transporting herself.

They arrive in a broad and desolate expanse of land. For as far as the eye can see in all directions, it is as featureless as it is flat, save for one enormous column of rock jutting up next to them and out of sight above.

Aerlie steps up to the Great Spire and places her hand against it. The rock ripples and then parts to form an opening. She motions the soldiers to move inside to a spiral stair leading down. As she enters through the opening, she turns to seal it again.

They progress down the stairs into a small chamber. The chamber is empty except for a single arched frame. Aerlie pulls out the satchel and opens it. She takes out a powdery white leaf of an unknown variety, brings it up to her mouth and bites into it. The taste is bitter.

As the unpleasant flavor swirls in her mouth, a haze begins to form in the archway, intensifying into a glowing vortex. While still holding the leaf in her mouth, she waves the soldiers to pass through. She follows close behind them, and the portal closes.

Time passes, and the portal opens again from the other side. Aerlie and Captain Hagmaert are the only ones to come through; the others have stayed behind to attend to the prisoners. After passing through the portal, Aerlie brings out another rune from her belt and transports both of them back to Bya'an Tamoranth.

"I wish to call the room to attention."

Thaelyn speaks out to the gathering in the tactical office. The officers, along with Padriyl and Marelle, though excited over the success of the mission to capture the elves, all come to order to hear his plan. Now that they had the elves, they had a new matter of security to contend with. Not necessarily with the prisoners, but what repercussions might come due to their disappearance.

"The Flame Elf prisoners should be secure enough in E.D. Of this, we should not be overly concerned. However, they will eventually be missed, and with no other potential reason for this other than ourselves, we can expect some form of retaliation. In doing this, we may have proverbially unbuttoned our drawers. We should therefore make the most of our situation while it lasts. I will lead an interrogation team into E.D. and begin examining the possibilities of what we can obtain from them."

"My Lord," the General inquires. "May I ask what methods you might use under these circumstances?"

"The Flame Elves are an unknown factor to us. If they hold an association with Sargeras, a creature from times long forgotten, there is little to know of what to expect from them, other than perhaps a stream of obscenities. My first goal will be to study them. I will need to scan their minds to know if there are any psionic links present. If our plan does not meet with expectations, and Sargeras still has his thoughts within their minds, we may need to abort the process, put them back to sleep, and think of something else."

"And as for the interrogation…assuming all goes well otherwise?"

"We will begin simple, and work our way from there. I would resist using telepathic intrusion, in this case, unless there is no other choice."

"Your Lordship," Marelle inquires. "Although you may say no to this, it is my duty to make this request as a representative of the city of Rolsklinde and a partner in these proceedings. I wish to make a formal request to attend this interrogation."

"Under any other circumstances, I would likely agree to that request. But considering our opponent in this war, and my concern to maintain a certain level of security for the location of where these prisoners are being held, I feel I must decline."

"What if I said…please?" she asks with a sweet smile and soft hazel eyes.

"Marelle," he smiles tenderly. "Your Captain was right, you are trouble. But you do not have the right training and discipline of the mind to accompany us to every corner of the realms. I would worry that your thoughts could betray you and others if they are not properly constrained."

Marelle lowers her head to think.

"Well, that's easy to fix! So, what if I put it to you this way… What if I start following you around like a little puppy until you relent and start teaching me some of these amazing tricks of yours? If you can teach others, surely you can teach me."

A pause ensues, followed by soft laughter. Thaelyn couldn't help but offer up a momentary chuckle before returning his answer.

"Indeed, I suppose I can, at that. And I do owe you a piece of this, for everything else you have done for us," he sighs heavily. "All right, if you do exactly as I tell you and stay precisely by my side, I may tag you with a silver chain and draw you along with me."

"My Lord!" Relissa calls aloud as she enters the room. "May I ask to come along? It would be a good bit of learning for me, and maybe I can think of something along the way to make myself useful. Besides, you already got me on a chain."

"Oh dear Powers, the two of you are developing a few habits together. Well, I suppose we should permit a representative from your people, if we also allow it for hers. Just remember to guard your thoughts over this situation."

"Aye!"

The meeting adjourns, and Thaelyn leaves the camp in the care of the General. He returns home with Marelle and Relissa in tow, there to walk over to the temple and meet with Aerlie, who had been preparing a selection of priests for this occasion to join the interrogation.

"This group here, Thaelyn," she motions to a gathering of four people in ornate robes. "These will serve as witnesses in your tribunal. I've been working with them these last few days to meld and share the local language with them. I couldn't do much more than this, as it was already a bit of a strain."

"It is quite sufficient, my dear, and thank you."

Thaelyn diverts into the side room to retrieve the items out of the plain metal box. He studies the medallion, as Aerlie did before, then takes the satchel and rune before closing the box again.

When he returns, Aerlie reaches out to draw him close for a gentle kiss on the cheek. He then prepares the rune in his hand. Relissa and Marelle look on, noticing the odd design of the stone.

"That doesn't look like one of your usual runes, my Lord," Relissa observes.

"It is not," he replies. "It is much older, from my time in the service of my Father. And this one is specially made for this purpose."

He casts an enchantment on it to activate the portal energies within the stone. As the glow comes to full prominence, he instructs everyone to place their hand on it to be whisked away.

The group arrives in the flat, barren land that Aerlie passed through once before. Relissa and Marelle notice a warm dry breeze blowing past. They look around at the empty landscape, turning to inspect the entire scene, until they notice the huge rocky spire extending out of sight into the sky above.

"All right, I'll bite," Relissa asks. "Where in all the bleedin' hells are we?"

"We are not in any of the Hells, Relissa. They are in that direction..."

Thaelyn points a finger across the vacant expanse to the horizon. Relissa's eyes follow his gesture as she gulps at the implications.

"I didn't mean for you to interpret that literally, my Lord."

"Perhaps not, but it is. This place has been known by many names, most commonly as the Outlands by the local inhabitants. It is a colloquial term we use here. More formally, it is known as the Plane of Concordant Opposition. On Tae'Eladar, it is known as Cynosure."

Relissa feels a shiver come over her, even though the ambient temperature is moderate.

"What does that actually mean? Especially the part when you said it's a term 'we' use?"

"This plane we are standing in now is a part of the Outer Planar region of the multiverse. It is a place well known to me. You asked about the Hells... Many of the other planes are accessible here through special portals to be found within what we call border towns. The Lower Planes have their associated border towns in that direction, while the Upper Planes...what you mortals call the Heavens...are found on the opposite side of us."

"The Outer Planar region, Your Lordship?" Marelle exclaims. "But... Isn't this where the Gods are supposed to live?"

"It is and they do. Scattered all around us, in the other planes, both Upper and Lower, are the homes of the Estelar."

"Gods above, literally... And I actually asked to come out here."

"Aye," Relissa mumbles. "And you're not the only one."

Marelle feels faint and nearly doubles over. Relissa helps by catching her, and the two use each other as support.

"But just think of the stories you can tell your children one day," Thaelyn smiles.

"Right, but is that before or after they lock me away for it."

Thaelyn shrugs as he surveys the region.

"It was here amongst these planes where I spent the first millennium of my life. It is where I was taught, trained, and served in the court of my Father, until my tenure of contract was complete. I hold many memories of this place."

"And this big rock?" Relissa asks.

"The Spire... At one time, this plane was the center of a planar conglomeration, and the Spire represented its axis. At the top, or so it was said, though its exact location came into debate on many occasions, was the city of Sigil."

"I'm almost afraid to ask this," Marelle states. "But what is this city you mention?"

"It is a city, like many others, filled with people of many races.

Some of them are mortal beings, much like you, and often the result of the hybridization of races from around the planes, as I am. The city is an artificial construct, a closed space, with no doors or windows looking out. It is curved inward unto itself, as a torus, a hollow tube enclosed in a circle. To the natives, it is sometimes called the Cage, and at other times called the City of Doors for all the hidden portals located within its recesses."

"And why are we here?"

"We are here because this is where I placed the access portal to my special place. Behold..."

Thaelyn places his hand against the rock on the side of the Spire. The rock ripples and forms an opening, revealing a stairway leading downward. He motions for the group to enter, and he follows after. As he passes through, the entrance seals up behind him. They descend the stairs into the small room with the single portal archway. Thaelyn takes up the satchel, opens it, and removes a white powdery leaf, as Aerlie did once before, and bites into it.

Relissa studies him carefully, recalling some of the stories he gave during those first days after he and his army arrived through the portals into the Badlands.

"The key..." she whispers to herself.

A portal opens within the archway and Thaelyn directs the group to pass through it. As he follows behind, the portal closes again.

They find themselves in a seemingly infinite black space, devoid of sights except for a modest segment of floor they were standing on, and a path leading away to a massive rectangular cuboid shaped object in the distance. There are lights shining down on them, as well as the path and the object, but no visible source for them.

"Um, my Lord..." Relissa mumbles meekly. "I'd like to ask you where we are this time, but I'm not sure if I want to know."

"Welcome to my personal creation," Thaelyn announces. "This place is called Enduring Domain, my own demi-planar construct."

"You have the power to make your own?" Relissa asks, her voice fluttering.

"I did just this once, as a challenge from my Father to test me.

It is not as glamorous as what the Powers themselves may create, but I am proud of it nonetheless."

"Aye! That's a fine one!"

"And what's that big boxlike shape over there?" Marelle inquires softly.

"It is a hastily gathered prison for our elven guests," Thaelyn accedes. "They are being held within separate chambers, isolated from each other. A small contingent of my guards should also be in there attending to their needs."

Marelle slowly gathers up her will again and tries to pull herself straight to judge her surroundings.

"So, we will be doing the interrogation inside there, I guess, right?"

"Not exactly…"

"Um, all right, so where do you have in mind for this? The rest of it looks a bit vacant."

"Indeed, so we must create a tribunal court. We will keep the design of it simple, as there is no need for any grand ornamentation at this time."

"And how do we do that?"

"For this, I will ask you to hold onto yourself. You wanted to learn something? Well, here is your first lesson. Observe, as I bring this into the reality of our space."

"Bring…into…the reality…?" Marelle stammers, but halts the words in her throat as she watches the scene unfold.

Thaelyn steps forward on the small platform that serves as the entrance from the portal archway standing just behind the group. He looks out into the blackness of the void ahead of him and raises a hand up to it. A swirling mist forms in the distance, coalescing into a shape. A large platform forms out of the wispy ethers. He continues his focus, forming walls around three sides of it, the rearward wall being curved into a semi-circle as a backdrop to the court.

Marelle feels her knees growing weak again. She decides, for her safety, to bring herself to a seated position, since the platform was of only a limited dimension, and with nothing but inky blackness all around it. Relissa, still clinging to her friend, is pulled down reflexively along with her.

The court continues to form, with a series of sconces on the walls and a semi-circle of braziers arcing around the rear edge of a dais lifted up out of the center flooring. In the center of the dais is a rack. The rack appeared as a cross piece set on top of a square pole, with another smaller cross piece at the bottom. There were shackles at either end of the top piece, and again on the bottom. At two positions on the floor in front of the dais were pedestals capped by brilliant torches.

Thaelyn next moved his focus to the boxlike structure. He created a new path from the small doorway opening in its side over to the court, ultimately to curve back around to the entrance platform where the group was standing.

"Unbelievable!" Marelle wheezes. "When Haran said you were half-god, which half are we speaking of?"

"In essence, a Celestial carries a number of rather prominent qualities. These can be made even more potent with a bit of training, no different from you teaching yourself a new skill. And my time out here has taught me many such skills. If you know how it is done, it may not seem so godly after all, but I think this example would surely reach well above what most people might ordinarily experience."

"Is this anything like Kaliya was saying with her metaphysics bit?" Relissa asks.

"Indeed, it would be. In fact, if she could see this, no doubt she would lose yet another set of her horns, perhaps violently on this occasion," he laughs.

"Aye! I'm with you there! Just wait till I tell her about this one."

"But the Outer Planes are not the same as the universe you occupy. The mind is a powerful force here. If one is well-trained and properly disciplined, they can alter the reality of what they perceive. They can create objects, transform space, and perform other deeds that mortals like you would probably describe as miracles."

"Absolutely amazing," Marelle muses dreamily.

"Indeed, young lady," infers one of the priests. "We know much more about his abilities, and even at that, I would still say this is an extraordinary example."

"And, as a matter of fact," Thaelyn continues. "There are societies out here who make their homes out of nothing more than the wisps of ether and their pureness of thought to shape entire cities. Even one such as you, if you could bring yourself into a pure state of mind, could potentially affect some small aspect of your environment. All you must do is believe in it to such detail as it can become real to you, physically. However, this is not so easily done without a great amount of practice and conditioning."

"Oh, absolutely!" Marelle nods. "I can be sure of that much."

Thaelyn leads the group across the newly formed walkway over to the edge of the court. The priests move around to the sides and form up along the walls to serve as a panel of witnesses to oversee the inquisition process. One of them steps in front of the dais to serve the function of a bailiff.

"I will ask the two of you to stand here and be silent during these proceedings," Thaelyn directs to the two women. "If there should be anything of great importance you wish to provide, we will see about it after my initial questioning."

They each nod and take up a position near the outer edge of the court beside the walkway.

"Summon the first prisoner," Thaelyn orders. "We have two females, take the younger. She may be more malleable for our initial test."

The priest-bailiff rushes off to the prison. A few moments later, he and two guards drag out a young female elf. She had been stripped down and dressed in a simple loincloth and a cropped cotton top to offer her some covering. Her hands were bound behind her back with shackles, and around her neck, she still wore the glimmering silver circlet with the three rune-carved segments attached.

They bring her up on the dais, where they remove the shackles, but only to lock her hands in the new shackles on the cross piece. They then proceed to secure her ankles in the shackles at the bottom.

Marelle, on seeing this unusual procedure, feels a strong urge to ask Thaelyn about the need for it. She steps up cautiously and taps him on the arm.

Thaelyn turns to look at her and casts a brief glance at the prisoner before he speaks.

"Yes, Marelle, what is it?"

"I'm sorry to interrupt. A question or two before you begin, please?"

Thaelyn nods.

"First, why is she naked...or nearly so?"

"Elves are often powerful magical creatures. As I mentioned before, they typically wear mostly enchanted clothing, and also jewelry. In order to reduce them to their least harmful condition, you need to bring them quite literally down to their skin. And even at that, they can still be dangerous if not properly restrained to prevent them from casting spells."

"All right, that answers my first question, and also my second one about this rack thing here. But why not simply replace her old clothes with something plain?"

"Technically, we did, as you can see..." he motions at her scant attire. "But as a prisoner, and particularly as a minion of Sargeras, she might wish to find ways of escape, not that she can escape from this plane, but she could attempt to attack her guards using those same clothes as a form of weapon. For instance, she could tear them into strips, fashion a rope and use it to strangle someone, or even in an attempt to commit suicide, foiling us from gaining anything useful out of her."

"Wow! I never actually thought of that before. I guess we don't get too many of those back home..." she pauses as she forms a grin on her face. "They're all too drunk for it," she chuckles. "But you really think of everything, don't you! All right, thank you."

Marelle moves back to join Relissa. She gazes at the prisoner again, who is now carefully held by her bonds. There is no hood on her head this time, only the circlet around her neck, yet she bears the appearance of someone who is clueless as to her surroundings. She attempts to pull at her bindings, but they are tightly secured. When she realizes she'll get nowhere from this, she settles herself and waits.

"Remove the muting and deafness symbols," Thaelyn instructs.

The priest steps over and unfastens two of the rune-carved segments from the circlet.

Marelle and Relissa exchange glances in wonder of the odd neckpiece.

As the priest moves away, the elf realizes she can hear again. She attempts to speak, at first a moan, and as she feels the vocalizations rising up from within her throat, she begins a tirade of abuse.

"You pustulent curs!" she screeches. "Release me this instant! I'll ravage this whole prison and burn it to the ground! How dare you assault me! Do you have any idea who I serve? He'll rip the flesh from your bones and leave you drowning in your own blood!"

Thaelyn steps in close to the elf, ignoring her insults. He remains quiet as he examines her manners. During a brief pause in her outbreak, she notices the sound of his footsteps moving in. She turns her head in an attempt to orient in his direction.

"What do you want? Are you going to torture me? Do you think you can make me talk by beating me? There is nothing you can do to make me betray my Lord."

Thaelyn raises a hand in front of her head, making a passive telepathic scan of her mind to sense anything other than her own thoughts inside.

"Why don't you speak?" she growls. "I can feel you standing over me. What are you doing?"

Then her demeanor suddenly changes as she feels a surge of confidence pass into her. Her voice calms to portray a sultry derision.

"Ah, that! Yes, I should've guessed. I know what you're doing. You stripped off my clothes so you can look at me. You want to gloat over my body, don't you. Do you like what you see? Does it please you?"

Once satisfied that her mind is clear from Sargeras's immediate influence, Thaelyn begins to move away.

"I can tell you're a man by the sound of your footsteps. I wonder...

where is your hand right now, hmm? Did you slip it within your trousers?"

"You would do well to tame that tongue of yours, young lady."

"Or what? What will you do to me? Beat me? Bend me over and have your way with me? Maybe I would actually enjoy that."

"Perhaps if I were to do this…"

Thaelyn turns and waves a hand at her, reaching out with partially clenched fingers.

The girl suddenly lets out a bold wail as she experiences a vision of panic and dread. The images Thaelyn was forcing into her mind caused her to wrench from side-to-side screeching.

"No! Get it away! Get it away!"

She shakes her head violently and squirms within her bindings, still shrieking from the visions in her mind, until Thaelyn finally let go. She sags under her cuffs as she tries to catch her breath.

"Speak not such blasphemy to me, Child!" he shouts. "Actions carry consequences in this place. You speak of burning? You speak of your Lord and Master? In this place, I am Lord and Master, and yours cannot enter."

She tries to speak again.

"What…what are you? What manner of creature are you…that you can do this to me?"

"One that demands more respect than that tongue of yours may be capable of, but I will offer you to make the attempt."

"Fine! But you're wasting your time. You may be able to cause me pain, but you cannot compare to my Lord. He is all-powerful. The torment he can lay down is far worse than what you just did. I would rather die than risk betraying him."

"Do not think to underestimate my potential. I simply need you with at least a few of your wits intact if we should hope to conduct any sort of conversation. As for your Master, I seriously doubt he even knows you are alive at this moment. So, spare me your idle threats."

"How is such a thing possible? He is a god! He knows all things!"

"He is not the only one, and I am personally familiar with several.

Therefore, unless you would wish for me to call a few of them in here, you should step down from your podium for a time."

The elf goes silent and turns her head away as she realizes the potential of this statement.

"Now," Thaelyn continues. "If you think you can stay your insolence for the remainder of this inquest, we will begin. First, what is your name?"

The elf does not answer.

"I say again. What is your name?"

"Come a little closer and I'll spit it in your face!"

"How quaint... Do we capitalize that, or place it all in bold lettering?"

"A joke? You're actually making a joke?"

"It is such a simple thing, and yet you cannot seem to provide a valid answer. Very well, perhaps we can ask about what role you play amongst your people."

"Remove me from these bonds and I'll show you."

"All things considered, I think your statement of burning was sufficient for this point, but a simple designation would not kill you to speak aloud. How about this... We already know the Flame Elves are aligned with the orcs and the Suuden-Aryku. What we are curious about is this. Apparently, between yours and the others, much of the population of your world has been obliterated, up to the last remaining city each for the humans and the Night Elves. Why?"

"I don't really pay much attention to politics."

"Indeed, but you live so close...you could be considered neighbors. Perhaps you would like to exchange love notes or share home-baked goods on occasion."

"Are you trying to interrogate me, or ridicule me with these absurd statements?"

"You are not cooperating with proper answers. What sort of response do you expect out of that?"

"All right, I suppose that speaks for itself."

"Good, but do you have an answer to that last question?"

She is silent again.

"Very well, perhaps another one… Do you know anything about the death of the Night Elf Tree of Life?"

"Maybe they're just bad gardeners?"

Thaelyn glares at her briefly before attempting to clarify the statement.

"Do you even know what a Tree of Life is?"

"Why, am I supposed to?"

"A simple yes or no will suffice."

"No, I do not know what a Tree of Life is. Is it actually so important? Why care so much about a simple piece of firewood?"

Thaelyn glances at Relissa for an opinion. She frowns and shrugs.

"Very well," he continues. "I suppose this provides us with at least a reasonable response. Clearly, if the only trees you are familiar with are those to be used for construction or fuel, this reference might be lost to you. This particular one is more often kept within a city for religious reasons. But next… We have seen evidence of adamantium used on some of the forces here. Are you familiar with this material?"

"Ada-what-ium? I'm sorry…I don't understand Fool-speak."

"Such a lovely attitude… Should I remind you of where you are at the moment?"

"Oh, I'm sure I remember that, but should I remind you that you're wasting your time?"

"How you define wasting my time, and how I might define it are likely to be quite different. Do you recall that vision I planted in your mind?"

"Yes."

"Planting thoughts into a mind is not the full limit of my talents."

"Well then, why are you…wasting…your time by talking to me?"

"Because I would prefer to carry a little voluntary interaction with you, rather than, as you said it, bending you over and having my way with you."

"You'll probably end up doing that anyway," she chuckles mischievously.

"Young lady, I will kindly ask you to stay your rampant harlotry.

You may play this role amongst your own, but you will find no such satisfaction here."

"A role?!" she screeches. "You would dare suggest I'm a harlot?"

"Well, without any indication of your true profession, and your manners being such as they are, it certainly gives that impression."

"I am NOT a harlot!" she shrieks.

"But you most certainly are belligerent and overly salacious. Let us try one more. We understand that the orcs are a part of this military body occupying your world. But thus far, they are doing rather poorly in this campaign, and yet we do not see them receiving any form of reinforcement by the other members. Can you at least give me an answer to this one?"

"All right, this one I might answer. We just don't like them."

"Well now, at least that one makes sense. But then, why did you side with them in the first place?"

"They were entertaining at first, but watching the same head-bashing every week became tiresome."

Thaelyn turns away and shakes his head at the inanity of her response.

"Perhaps if we change to a topic you seem so clearly eager to throw in my face. Why did your people turn to serve such a creature as Sargeras?"

The elf pauses and turns her head in the direction of Thaelyn's voice.

"If you had any idea of the power he wields, you would choose to serve him as well! He is a god! He speaks to us, and we must obey or face his punishment."

"As I said, he is not the only one, and I know of several. I hold numbers on my side, so you may wish to reconsider his potential in the face of that. Furthermore, I am such a creature that would never serve such a monstrosity as that."

"A monstrosity??" she roars. "You will burn for that!"

"By who's hand, yours? You are not the only one capable of magic in this place, and I have a considerable amount of practice."

"By him, fool! He will sear the flesh from your bones."

"More likely, if he knew who I was, and who my friends are, he would continue to hide under that rock he has been using for so long."

"Hide?!" she shrieks.

"Yes!" he shouts. "As what he has been doing ever since my gods destroyed the rest of his kind an epoch ago. That is who we are!"

The elf suddenly goes silent. Even though her vision was blacked out by the runic magic of the circlet, her face still twisted in fear over the implications of his statement. She continued to hold her attention in his direction, even though she could not see him.

"You must be lying," she mutters weakly. "What do you mean by that?"

"They were once known as Primordials, an ancient and now defunct race of godlike beings that held the misfortune of being discovered by mine. They no longer exist, except for this one who somehow escaped and has been hiding from us ever since."

"You lie! You must be! You're just saying this to try to break me! I know it! I know he's real, and I know he's all-powerful!"

"Oh, I will credit you that he exists, and surely, by comparison to such a small creature like you, he might represent himself to be quite powerful. But he is not a ruling Power. He may feel real to you back home, but is he here with you in this room?"

"I...actually, no...but I'm sure he's just distracted by other things."

"Oh, how incredibly unfortunate!" he retorts acerbically. "And right when you need him most."

"How dare you!"

"How dare I? All I did was point out the blatantly obvious. You say he is a god, and yet he is not here to save you, nor is he here to smite me. I am still standing, the sky has not come down around my head, and neither has the earth opened up at my feet. How is that for your all-powerful Master?"

"You would be so brazen as to tempt a god?"

"Ha! I would do more than that! Show me his face and I will leave my mark upon it!"

"You must be insane!"

"Is it insanity, or is it confidence that I know I am right. I have a history of wisdom behind me. What do you have, but the word of a mysterious figure you know nothing about!"

She pauses as she tries to analyze his words, finally shaking her head briskly at the notion.

"No! It's all lies! Curse you!" she blasts contemptuously. "You blow more smoke than a meat house."

"Very well, let us peruse your perception. You say he is all-powerful and that he speaks to you. In what manner?"

"Why would you actually care about that?"

"Call it curiosity. You deny mine, so tell me about yours."

"We hear him. That is enough. He makes his thoughts known to us."

"Was it anything like what I did earlier?"

"That… Well, no, not like that."

"All right, then how does it play out for you?"

"Are you actually serious with these questions?"

"Yes, as a matter of fact. It is quite simple. You are making claims to something, so explain to me what they represent. Otherwise, they are as empty as you argue mine to be."

"All right, fine. We hear his songs. Does that say anything to you?"

"Songs… This is an interesting statement, but also incomplete. Is this to say he sings a collection of soothing lullabies to you at bedtime?"

"Oh please, you must be jesting with that one."

"Then kindly elaborate for me. What are these songs? How do they convince you that he is such an all-powerful being? For instance, I might hear the songs of a tavern bard, so am I now expected to kneel before him and offer worship?"

"You are amazing! Can you actually be so ignorant?"

"Ignorance, is it? The gods I know of do not sing to their worshipers. They represent scholars and parental figures, offering wisdom and guidance…something useful for us to grow and learn by."

"Oh really! Well, ours does also…" she halts as she considers her words. "Well, to our priests, he does…not to me, I'm not a priest."

"And do these priests share this beloved wisdom with the rest of you?"

"Of course! Um…well, it's more like instructions, not…um… Why am I telling you this!" she huffs and turns away.

"But in your case, you simply hear songs. And these songs are apparently enough to convince you he is an all-powerful being capable of smiting me and anything else that might otherwise offend such as you, correct?"

"Exactly! Are you happy now? Just what are you trying to do here?"

"Get answers as to why you would follow such a creature as he. Is it not obvious?"

"He's a GOD…is that not obvious?"

"This is a subjective statement, no more. Any being that can be rated so high as to appear as a god to a lesser being might qualify for this, and yet it may not be a true god as we would normally apply that term. There is a difference here, as there are many forms of life out there, and of many scales of complexity and potential. Consider an insect. By comparison to that, you might be a god. But do you fall into those same depictions that someone like you would use for such as your own? The simple answer is no. But to that insect, it might not matter."

"Huh? That is…um, well…all right, I suppose I can see your point, but mine is completely different."

"Different in such manner that you think your perception is more accurate than that insect?"

"Well, I would certainly think myself to be a little more intelligent to make the determination."

"Perhaps, and yet, how can you prove to me your determination is so much more accurate than that insect and what it might produce. You speak of causing pain. You could do the same to that insect. You speak of punishment. You could do the same to that insect. You can control the prospect of life and death where that insect is concerned, the destruction of homes, of land, and all things that insect might regard to exist around it. Now consider such as the Suuden-Aryku.

How familiar are you with what they might possess. The weapons they use, their ships, the places they can travel, and whatnot. This must surely seem at least a little godlike to one such as you. And they may have even more capacity beyond this. Can you agree to this?"

"Um, agree to it…" she pauses a moment. "Well, all right, for what I've heard of them, I suppose I must. But they also follow him, as far as I know. Doesn't that say something?"

"The only thing it says is this god of yours must be especially high on the ladder if it can also exceed their position. But a god? As if to say a true god? I hold a specific definition in my mind for that station, and it is truly high on that ladder, such that if yours were to qualify for it, I think we would not be here speaking so casually about him."

Relissa and Marelle turn to glare at each other, shaking their heads.

"Jiggers," Relissa whispers in Marelle's ear. "That's a tough one to argue."

Thaelyn continues, "And that ladder can extend for a long distance. Especially if you truly want to describe yourself as a god above any and all other forms of life. And I will point out, if you can include such as the Suuden-Aryku, this must include anything else that might be out there we are not even aware of. This station would need to be higher still. How would you respond to this, if only in principle."

"In principle?" the girl wavers. "Wow, but um… Well, still, I would stand my ground that this one must be a real god. I mean, he feels like it. We hear his thoughts. Only a true god could do this, right? And, um…" she appears to grow nervous.

"And still," Thaelyn asserts. "I would say your statement is insufficient. Do you, young lady, actually know who your real gods are supposed to be, Little Miss High Elf Turned Flame Elf?"

"What? I don't even know what you're saying with that line."

"Your kind describes themselves as Flame Elves, correct? Do you not know who you were before your precious god interrupted your lives and turned you into the horrors you are today?"

"Horrors?!"

"Yes, it is said you burned everything in sight once, leveling the world to ashes. By most accounts, that would define you as horrors, as I seriously doubt any of those innocent people were warranting of your god telling you to destroy so many lives without proper cause. This is called murder by most societies, and NO ONE would grant you such privilege to perform this, not unless you can tell me they committed something so heinous that they were thusly deserving of it. And do not think that the simple command of a god is sufficient, as not even he should hold such authority as to demand the death of those he does not govern. Neither should he hold such authority to simply declare whole societies to be destroyed for the simple fact of their existence."

"Oh?" she retorts defiantly.

"Yes, dear young lady, as life is precious, and no one, not even a god, should declare it otherwise."

The girl retracts from the argument, uncertain on how she should respond.

"Furthermore," Thaelyn continues. "The other gods out there, those who might take an interest in this, would also take offence to it."

"Then why aren't they doing something about it, if you claim them to be so powerful?"

"Ah, this is actually a very good question…" Thaelyn considers.

At this moment, Marelle has a thought flash in her mind. She begins mulling it through as Thaelyn responds to the young elf's last statement.

"Had your god not run away and hid under that rock, we might already have done so. But he did very successfully hide from us… until recently."

The prisoner suddenly went silent after this statement, and held her attention in his direction. The statement did carry merit, especially when combined with the others, although it was also up to interpretation if one simply chose not to accept it.

"That must be another lie…and a very clever one. If they're gods, shouldn't they be all-seeing?"

"This is a term very often used by younger societies. But if you understand such a term as a universe, meaning that space you see in your nighttime sky, the Suuden-Aryku come from a completely different one, and my home is in yet another. This might confound the notion somewhat. Think of it as if you are standing outside a collection of houses, and you can only turn your attention to one window at a time to see what is inside. It is no different for them."

"Really!" she relents softly. "That's interesting."

Marelle now waves at Thaelyn to draw his attention. He turns to her, and she points at her head, as if asking him to look into her mind while she tries to visualize her thoughts for him.

Relissa studies her, offering up a subtle smirk at her friend's bold ambition to pass a telepathic suggestion.

Thaelyn directs his attention at Marelle, peeking in to listen as she tries to speak using her inner voice, explaining to him the idea she was formulating. He then smiles and nods as he returns to the elf.

Relissa watches, and as the message is passed, she nudges Marelle's shoulder playfully before returning to the scene.

The priests who were overseeing the inquiry all observed the interaction, and several of them passed their glances around the room, smiling at Marelle's attempt to offer her contribution.

"We might also suggest this," Thaelyn begins, glancing at Marelle as he goes. "Have you ever heard such a statement as the gods working in strange ways?"

"Huh?" she blurts. "The gods...we only have the one. And, um...well, all right," she relents softly. "I suppose I might have to admit, the way our priests talk, he does tell us to do things that don't always make a lot of sense."

"Yes, this is likely due to them keeping some portion of the reasoning to themselves. Surely, you might receive instruction from someone, like a superior, and he simply tells you to perform some function, whereby he might know the ultimate outcome, but perhaps your station is not so privileged. Is this true?"

"Yes, actually. My...station...doesn't always get a full explanation for what I'm told to do."

"And the gods would be no different for what they have in mind. Therefore, the statement of them seemingly doing strange things. Strange to us, perhaps, if we do not receive a full explanation of it."

"And how does this relate to anything?"

"It could relate to them taking that long overdue action against yours with my arrival."

"Oh! Yes! I would love to hear this fable. And how do we explain you to be their solution to us ravaging the world in the name of our god?"

"By taking it back...away from your god."

"Um..." she falters.

"You are aware of my war against the orcs, correct?"

"Yes..." she replies softly.

"Are you aware of my success in that war?"

"I've heard a few things."

"Further, neither yours nor the Suuden-Aryku are coming to their aid, correct?"

"Um..."

"And neither are you coming at me directly to challenge my arrival and occupation in that valley, correct?"

"Uh...I, um..."

"So, the clear and obvious question is why? Am I not perceived as so undesirable that you would want me removed from your world? And if not by yours, then surely the Suuden-Aryku, along with all their superior capacity?"

"But... They're not doing this?" she asks timidly.

"Not as yet, and I am fairly sure they should know of me by now, perhaps even to know I am reinforcing the Daanen-Aryku out by their home, and the Suuden-Aryku are taking consistent losses out there by now."

"They are?" she emits worriedly.

"And if your god is so all-knowing, he should know this, therefore, he should make stronger efforts to purge me and mine, but he is not. I wonder why, unless he truly is hiding, and rather determinedly from my gods. And this could be further compounded by those orcs, who made the error of encroaching on my home world, thus drawing me back here, and perhaps rather unexpectedly, with all my military that is so far causing such despair in your world. I am therefore your answer to the horror you caused, as I am correcting it."

"But wait. Is this to say you are some sort of gift from your gods, or simply lucky? Those orcs aren't much to speak of. Surely, you can admit to this. Even my people could cut through them."

"I will grant you this much. Yes, I think your people, if given enough time and opportunity, could do as much. I simply have a lot of resources to throw into it."

"And those Suuden-Aryku…maybe they're holding back for some secret movement."

"This could also be true, though they are taking their time with it, and losing people along the way."

"That's not very smart, actually."

"I am also attempting to organize the survivors of that world such that they can return to normal lives again. Whereas they were trapped behind their walls, now they can go out and conduct farming and other common activities. With those orcs out of the way, they have the freedom to move around again. And while we could possibly say this is due to the good fortune of my arrival, my simple existence is no accident. This is simply what I do for people, and those same gods are the reason for it."

"Oh really! Wow, your world must be a paradise for all you claim yourself to be," she huffs sarcastically.

"Indeed!" he grins proudly, even though she can't see it. "And therefore my success, as all those resources I have to throw into your war are as plentiful as my full world can provide for me. And my people serve me well to do exactly this. So, you might want to stifle that attitude of yours, as your world seems a bit paltry by comparison. Most of what you once had…as a world society…is left in ruin, no thanks to you and yours. Now explain to me the power of your god. He is the god of a ruined world."

This hit the elf hard, and she turned away from him, puckering her face and lips.

Relissa and Marelle both grimaced at the hard knock.

Thaelyn continues, "The Night Elves still worship their original gods, and granted, one might suggest those gods should have done something earlier. But if we reflect on them doing strange deeds, it could be they had to wait for your orcs to make that wrong turn into my garden before bringing about that correction."

"That ruined world happened a long time ago, well before my time," she relents. "Why it's still ruined, I don't know. So maybe, my god, with his…strange ways…just hasn't gotten around to fixing it yet."

"Very well, but it still does not satisfy my earlier statement of why you would do it to begin with. One could possibly suggest a full world, one that is undamaged by war, would be more desirable than a ruined one, for all the additional people he could attract. Instead, what we see is a world laid waste down to the last surviving cities for both the Night Elves and the humans, and neither of which seems to be attracting his interest. Even worse, no one is moving to finish it, if he does not want them at all."

"Not moving to finish it? How do you mean?"

"Four hundred years of war simply to bring these populations down to their last cities, then to stop. This is not a war to destroy everything. It is a purging operation to destroy everything that is unwanted. But to what end, if he does not finish it with something? This is one of our questions, but I suspect you might not know this answer, especially if your station does not give you everything you need to know."

"That much is for sure, and this one especially."

"Perhaps you are simply too young to know of it. And further, to know your kind used to carry a different name, and higher ethical principles. Then he came along and changed everything for you, but not for the better, as he robbed you away from your true gods. You speak of being bent over. Look no further than your beloved Master, as he keeps you there every day."

Thaelyn now turns and walks away several steps for emphasis.

The elf falls silent again as she listens to his footsteps.

"Now what are you talking about?" she asks mildly.

"Let us assemble a few pieces from all this. You ravage a full world population. Why? Could it be your god simply wanted to see the land stained with so much blood, or could it be none of them would likely follow him, with or without these songs in their ears. We may not know this answer, but if any of them worshipped the gods we hold dear, he might not care for them to begin with. Then again, maybe he does not care for such large quantities of people he cannot otherwise control. And he is most certainly controlling you and yours. Does the name High Elf hold any meaning to you?"

"No, it does not. What is it?"

"It is that thing you see in your reflection, or at least it would be if not for your Master."

"I don't hold any knowledge of this, so it must be another lie!"

"Carefully, Child, as I have a full population of them back home, and yours were once a part of it. There is a history that dates back countless thousands of years, so you would do well not to blaspheme it."

"I don't care! And even if it is true, they must be more of those weaklings, like those Night Elves!"

"Weaklings… An entire race that arose from their primal origins, grew to a powerful civilization, covered a full world, learned great wisdom, and overcame so many trials that once held them back. And this is weak. I think not! Yours, on the other hand, has defiled everything they ever stood for."

"Still lies! All of it!"

"This might also carry weight if we consider your world, a world full of people he did not want to see challenge his takeover. He took you, and made you destroy the rest, along with the orcs and Suuden-Aryku, and likely through a lot of deceit and backhanded intrigue. This is not strength, Child. Not on your part. This is simple villainy. And worse. This sort of villainy is very underhanded, brought out mostly by those who are indeed so weak that they cannot take a head-on approach to it."

"And more lies!"

"Lies? Your world is destroyed, is it not? How many people, who likely never saw it coming, and for what reason, if, as we mentioned before, they could serve greater value if alive and serving him! No. You speak of being bent over, but it is he who did it, and you committed mass murder on his behalf. And here you are gloating over it."

"I'm not gloating! Um…" she shakes her head from the confusing suggestions. "I mean, well, I don't know the reason for it. But surely, all your other statements are lies. They simply have to be. Nothing like that could ever possibly exist."

"Oh, do you truly believe this?" he asserts strongly. "Take care, young one, or I will personally take you by the hand, bring you out into the streets of my home city, and rub your face in what we have built there. The evidence is very apparent!"

She stifles her response and turns away.

"I am the king of a full world," Thaelyn continues. "Assembled from the masses and united in purpose. What we accomplished together is nothing short of miraculous, if for no other reason than we do not have wars tearing it apart on us. And you dare suggest, from your own paltry experience in a ruined world, that such a thing is impossible?"

The elf is silent and seemingly despairing for the obvious implications.

"Furthermore, the elven societies of our world, to which yours were once a part, and others besides those, have a full pantheon of gods who watch over them. It has been this way since the beginning of their kind, and at least partially due to this, they arose to such fame. You have but one, and who is regarded as the enemy to everything else. But let us take this objectively for a moment. Why do you describe them as weak?"

"Because they are!" she moans gently.

"That is a rather immature response, like that of a child without the proper reasoning to give credit to the statement. What is it that makes them weak?"

"Fine! They are weak because they are empty. They are weak

because all they ever feel is pain. They are weak because they don't feel the fulfillment of our Lord to make them strong."

"You know, one could easily suggest this to be no more than hearsay. Are you personally walking in their shoes to experience this? Or is it simply words filling your ears to give cause to something? Emptiness, pain, and fulfillment..." he muses. "This is interesting. What sort of pain is this you speak of?"

"I simply don't understand why you care!"

"I care because we have a destroyed world in front of us. Is this not enough to invoke a few questions as to the reason why, or do you simply not care enough for all the lives lost? Be careful how you answer that, young lady, as it could label you quite profoundly."

"As if I'm not already labeled by you? All right, but I'm unsure what you're getting at here."

"I am trying to interpret your statement with rational definition, not emotional outbursts and baseless accusations. I do not give myself to something unless it can provide a functional explanation of why I should give myself to it. And this includes a god of any kind, as even they need to offer an explanation on occasion."

"You must be joking!" she shakes her head. "Why does a god need to explain himself to anyone?"

"Oh please. If I came up to you on the street with a bag in my hand and told you it contained a magical dust that could make you rich, would you buy it? The concept is very similar."

Relissa and Marelle both clamped their hands over their mouths as they felt a sudden giggle coming out. Many of the priests did the same, and the assembled rumbling was drawing the girl's attention that she and Thaelyn were not alone in the room.

Thaelyn continues, "Reflect on what we said earlier. How do you define a god in relation to yourself, or any other creature, on that ladder which may be exceedingly tall to measure by. Such a small thing as you might see many things as gods. How would you know one from another if all they need to do is impress you with something that appears...godly. For all we know, he is simply a being of some curious potential trying to impersonate something he is not."

"Impersonate?!" she screams. "I... That... Aargh! Not that again!"

"And here you are denying my interpretation of the gods, when in fact I actually do know my gods rather intimately. And they do impress upon me that they are worthy of this definition for how they behave, what they offer, and even for how they arrived there in the first place. But you assert yours is better, simply because he sings to you. You claim he is godly because he gave some manner of fulfillment, and took away some sort of pain. You know, a healer can take away pain, and an alchemist, with the right concoction, could probably make you feel very...happy."

"How do you mean that?" she pants. "An alchemist? Happy?"

"With a drug or something to make you feel a kind of euphoria."

"Oh. Um, well, I'm not personally familiar with anything like that, and I did take an alchemy class in my school. And, well, yes, I do know of some odd plants that can do something," she reflects timidly. "But this isn't the same thing."

"Maybe so, but perhaps it could relate in some fashion. He may hold a form of wisdom that exceeds yours. And therefore, the logical question to ask is what sort of pain you had, and what sort of fulfillment he replaced it with. Is there anything so extraordinary about this?"

"All right, fine. I can see your point. But personally, I think you're just trying to yank my chain."

"I am seeking answers I can accept as reasonable explanations for why we are standing here now."

"Uh huh... All I can say is it's the pain of being weak. It comes when all you cling to is lost. But Sargeras showed us that we can never be lost, so long as we have his songs to guide us."

"This seems a bit thin, but perhaps we can work with it. Are we speaking of something emotional, perhaps? Psychological? Or is it a physical sensation?"

"I...barely even know what you're trying to ask with that. I don't think I would call it physical. Emotional, maybe this might work. Psycho...whatever...I don't know what to say on that."

"I am tempted to suggest it might be involved, especially if you think the emotional component is included. It has to do with the condition of the mind."

"Yes! I think this would be a part of it."

"Very good, this is at least a step forward to help me understand why you might hold him so high. And so, this is the virtue of these songs, possibly to replace something, or to bolster your strength in the face of this pain, which was brought about by some form of loss. And how long have you heard these songs?"

"Me personally?"

"You personally, perhaps, or perhaps your kind as a whole."

"Well, me personally...um..." she pauses to think. "I don't know, all my life...well no, I didn't hear them when I was very young, but later they came to me."

"This is rather interesting. You did not hear them as a young child, but later in life at about what age?"

"I wasn't counting...a few decades, maybe."

"So, you were still rather young, but we might say old enough to interpret these songs."

"Yes, I think that's it."

"This causes me to wonder if this pain was involved in those early years, or is it simply for the maturity factor. What about the rest of you? How long as a whole for your people...which is to say, when did these songs first come to you?"

"Are you actually so interested?"

"Why must we return to this question? I find it interesting to know how long your god existed in your mind that makes you so sure he is real and lives up to your expectations. Furthermore, the reason for that world of yours, and what you did to it. It is said to be the result of a war. So, was it a war due to something local, like a political dispute, or did he command the whole thing."

"Well, fine... Um, I think it was...um...oh, yes, I remember now. The stories we hear say we were lifted up by his songs about four centuries ago, after we all started to feel this horrible pain of loss."

"But this once again begs us to ask what caused this pain. Where did it come from? Do we know?"

"I don't know…it was just there."

"This seems to carry a missing element. I recall you mentioned a form of emptiness, as you claim for the others. And likely psychological, or emotional."

"Yes, and then he brought us out of it, but the others are still weak."

"Still weak… Meaning to say, they are still missing something, which you also suffered, and this would thereby suggest something large-scale occurring to cause all of this."

"To cause it?"

"Young lady, pain does not simply come about by spontaneous action. It demands a cause. And if it was affecting a full population, it must be a rather significant cause. Further, if you are also involving the Night Elves in this, it is not limited to your own, which only magnifies the cause further. And there are not many rational explanations to justify this. A natural event might do it, but we may be speaking of people from across a wide expanse, and any natural event on that scale would likely bring a lot more than simple pain to you. It might destroy all life in the area, including yours. So, it must be something targeted, such that the general population would not be destroyed outright, leaving it to…well, to you to do the deed instead."

"Uh huh, and therefore, you describe us as horrors."

"Again, the magnitude of death and destruction, no matter who ordered it and for what reason, is inexcusable. Any creature who would demand it, unless you can give me a justifiable reason, must himself be destroyed. The greater good must be acknowledged, and your reason is inadequate. But let us continue. Referring back to the Night Elves, who are also described as weak. Is this to say he might want to bring them out as well? Could this be part of that reason why the war stopped at their doorsteps?"

"I don't know. That's not my role to say."

"Not your role… You appear young, so your role, whatever it is, might not be high enough to make decisions, am I right?"

"Yes, actually. I'm only recently accomplished in my training, so I'm new in the field."

"Very well, there is nothing wrong with this. We all need to start somewhere. But is it simply for this reason, or do you need a specific role, like that of a priest?"

"Yes, a priest might hold that role. But one of the higher-ranking ones."

"Of course, naturally."

Thaelyn paces in a circle as he thinks of a new approach.

"Here is a curious thought… What might he want from you?"

"Huh? What do you mean he wants something from us?"

"I must reflect on our previous discussion. If one were to give oneself to a god, they should have good reason for it. Maybe you do with this fulfillment of yours. But a god might also hold a reason for doing this in the first place. Therefore, it occurs to me that your god must have some motivation here. He came to you and aided you by lifting you up from this pain, so he must have a desire of some sort. What could it be?"

"Why would he need a desire? He did this because…um…he did it because…um…"

"You are not a priest, so perhaps you do not know?"

"Yes, I'm sure that's it."

"How would you respond if I were to say to you this," he clears his throat in preparation. "The gods I know of may pick and choose amongst the mortal races those who might hold interest and those who do not. And among those who hold this interest, they may offer their teachings and guidance. And this may be irrespective of anything that mortal race has or does not have unto itself. Furthermore, it may also be irrespective to what that mortal race wants, or does not want, perhaps even what it needs, or does not need, as these are not typically the criteria for how they make these choices."

"That's simply strange. But I would probably say that your gods are worthless that they don't give you these great gifts simply for being there. Isn't that what gods are for?"

"Ah, but this is where we find our misunderstanding, as it is not their job to do so."

"Not their job?!" she shouts.

"Indeed! Should it be my job to give you a mountain of gold simply because I am standing here, and you are standing there? Why should I? Are you worthy of it? Am I supposed to empty my pockets every time you ask for it? Why should it be the job of a being of any sort, god or otherwise, to give something to one such as you simply because you feel this is the only thing they are made to do? It is not."

"But...but..." she wheezes.

"They are people, not unlike us in many ways, who make choices of who to interact with, or whether they would wish to interact at all. Therefore, if one should wish to do something, there ought to be a reason for it, as simple pity for your pain might not necessarily qualify. Generally speaking, you are beneath their concern. That world was full of life at one time. I am quite sure there were plenty of other people who might be described as sick, infirm, or otherwise. But rather than blessing them to ease their pain, this...god...of yours told you to kill everything indiscriminately. So, why are you so special that you are gifted by this fulfillment, when the rest of the world was destroyed by it? This suggests an ulterior motive, and not a kind one. The gods do not owe such beings as you anything. They are a society with their own lives and their own rules. But if a potent enough being wanted something from you, he might surely perform enough godly acts, and fill your head with enough nonsense, that you may hold no proper rationality afterwards."

The girl's tolerance was now at her limit. She screams fiercely.

"A world destroyed," he continues. "And for no rational reason. People killed, who did nothing wrong, other than to exist in a place he did not want them existing. He took you, but not the remainder of those he kept alive. Four centuries, and we find ourselves in a stalemate of activity. Oh, yes, he wants something...something specific, and from specific people. The rest might be nothing more than playthings, or perhaps a reserve population in case you should fail."

"Fail?" she shrieks.

"Therefore, I put it to you again. He is here because he wants something from you, and this fulfillment was simply an excuse to bribe your favor."

"You bastard!" she sobs.

"That man with the bag of magical dust, and you did buy it! You serve him because he took this pain away, meaning to say you lost something by some unknown means, which resulted in this pain, and so conveniently he arrived to ease this very same pain. Something large-scale which affected not only you, but the Night Elves as well. Something targeted, that could be taken away, but not destroy you outright, leaving you in what we must describe as a vulnerable condition that he, with his songs, could cover up with false strength. And here we again have our question. What does he want that he would do this for you, but no one else."

"Because he loves us. That is why!"

"Oh, he loves YOU, but not the millions of others he killed? He must be very selective, for a god who is supposed to care for all things in Creation, as the rest do. Just one more count against him. Those other gods might truly feel ire for this, as those you killed would be their children. And one more reason why I might be here now."

"Yeah, and a bit late in coming."

"Until your orcs arrived in my world, I did not even know of yours. Neither did I have the means to travel there, as it required a portal to do so, and I did not have one at the time leading to your world."

"And what. They couldn't give one to you?"

"The gods do not give out free gifts, young lady. We are their children, all of us, and we are expected to grow and learn these mysteries ourselves, as any children should."

"Bah! Children learning. Ours is clearly much more generous."

"Young lady, be mindful of that statement. The gods I follow are THE gods out there, and they have one very important rule. Life is precious...all life. It is a part of their principle of law. And yes, they do have laws. It is a ruleset called the Measure of Balance. And all gods, no matter who they are, where they come from, how they arrived there, or what they represent, are expected to follow this rule. Failure to do so might result in extermination. It is that simple. And there are historical examples to demonstrate this."

"Then I'll say it again, why is this one still out there?"

"I might simply answer that with my recent arrival. It is a prelude to just that. But I am an investigator, and your world has a lot of twists in it I want to unravel. And Sargeras, as far as I understand, is not likely to be found physically located on your world. More likely, he is on Azgarén."

"I don't know that name. What is it?"

"It is the home world of the Suuden-Aryku. It is said he arrived there some while back and began all this."

"Huh? On their world? As if to say… Wait. You mean to say he came to their world…he's standing on it, or whatever he is doing there?"

"It is. And this clearly marks him as a physical being, with physical parameters one can measure, and physically located in a physical domain. This now brings that notion of a 'god' much more down to our level. The Daanen-Aryku tell of his arrival before they departed, and in the absence of seeing him on your world, and therefore, exposing himself so openly to the Estelar… My gods… He is likely still there and keeping a low profile."

"Hiding…" she whispers softly. "Is this also the reason they don't go there themselves? They're gods, after all. Can't they go to that place, and as you say, finish it?"

"This is actually a very good question. There could be a number of ways to answer it, one of which is the Estelar are known to mark some locations as off-limits to travel for one reason or another. If he is using this for himself, taking advantage of an opportunity, it could offer an explanation. I am not so limited, however, and this could be yet another reason why I find myself here, if such a thing as Fate could lead me this way."

"Fate? Not the gods working in strange ways?"

"This is sometimes one of those ways, if they see it coming ahead of time."

"Ugh. This is getting confusing. I hate confusing things."

He takes several steps to consider his next approach, as well as to offer a small break.

"We still need to understand where this pain originated that he found it so desirable to come here in the first place. You said to me, four centuries ago, you felt this horrible pain of loss. Then Sargeras came in with these songs and…fulfilled you…with this newfound strength. Therefore, we should narrow our focus to this loss. What was it and what was the cause of it? Especially if it came to so many of you over such a wide area that we might suggest your entire population."

Her face now contorted with confusion.

"Why would any of this actually matter? Whatever it was, it happened centuries ago!"

"Centuries ago? But excuse me, you cannot be that old, and yet you still claim he gave this to you for the same reason. You cannot be subject to whatever brought this pain to those original people. More than likely, he came to you when he did only after you were old enough to make it worth his time."

"Worth his time!" she yelps.

"Indeed! Did you feel any sort of pain when you were young? And then what? Did he come to lift it out of you simply due to this reason? You were already a few decades old, which is enough to realize a few things about life."

"Um…"

"In fact, this represents a rather significant event in your history. Do you never ask such questions as to where this or that may have come from? Or are you so content that he, or maybe your priests, tell you everything you ever needed to know about everything that ever existed? Knowledge, my dear young lady, is value, and there is a considerable amount out there, if only you look for it. But you may have a lack of ambition to do so. I have seen a number of examples in this world so far where people either do not have access to it, or do not bother to ask about it. I, on the other hand, do not choose to be so ignorant. So, let us see about this."

"Ignorant, now…" she huffs silently. "Fine, ignorant. I studied hard in my academy, and thought I was done."

He paces around some more, not necessarily for his own purpose, but for the footsteps to sound out.

"Could it be the loss of some precious item?" he continues. "Could it be the loss of a family member, a dear friend…?"

"You must be joking again."

"Why is that? Have you ever lost a loved one and felt pain from it? Most people would, you know. No, I am actually quite serious, as there could be many possibilities. The loss of a loved one can hit very deep for most of us. And this had to hit deep. People can survive the loss of many things without the need for a god, of all things, to come in and console them. So, what was this loss about, and where did it come from? Why was this one so severe. All things have a beginning. What was this one?"

"And I still question the need to know."

"Young lady, your people must be older than a mere four centuries. What were you doing during the full length of your existence over there if not suffering from a pain of loss where your Master only arrived when he did to correct it? Your civilization in that world grew and prospered to cover the greater part of it, and over thousands of years, according to the history the Night Elves carry. You do not accomplish this if you are so weak that you can barely hold yourselves up."

"Um…well… Whatever. You're probably talking to the wrong person for this."

"Is this because you are not a priest who might hold the answer?"

"It was four centuries ago! As you said, I'm not that old!"

"Admittedly, you are right. And there is not much we can do about that. Nevertheless, old enough, or not, you should record your history better than that to teach your children. And yes, you must teach your children all that you are, and all that you once were. Otherwise, you become as ignorant as those orcs out there you so hate for their primitive nature. They may be lesser developed than you, but even they teach their children whatever they have to pass on important knowledge. And you do not? For shame!"

"All right!" she shouts. "I'm sorry! But that isn't my role back home. I just barely got OUT of my school. I don't have enough in me to go back in as an academy Master."

"Very well, so be it. But even what you did get in school had to come from someone recording your knowledge. But this knowledge does not include what happened even as little as four centuries prior? The world must surely be older than that, and so must your people."

"I don't have an answer to that. As far as I know, this is all they gave me."

"I see. Then we seem to have yet another occasion of missing information, and in your case, I would hazard to guess it is intentional, to completely delude you and distance you from your past."

"I, um… Oh, the blazes with it. Maybe you're right. If it's gone, and there must surely be more to the world than what I got, it's lost to us now. And what? Is this to say someone erased it on us?"

"Likely so, at this point. And I would further suggest this is part of that fulfillment, causing you to forget everything else, so you stop feeling the pain from its loss."

"Uh huh…sure. And here we go with that again."

"His songs are absent at present, are they not?"

"Yes…" she admits wearily.

"And by your own admission, you are beginning to realize a few things out of this discussion, are you not?"

"I will only admit to this for those parts that I can't otherwise argue against, because the reasons are kind of obvious by now."

"Good enough. But does this also cause you to feel this weakness you were describing?"

"It's starting to," she relents. "But don't think you will break me that easy!" she surges again. "His songs will return, and then you'll see."

"Young lady, songs or no songs, the realization of any or all of this should be enough to make you fight for more. And then his songs should not matter, as it would become moot."

"Moot?" she gripes.

"Yes. Put it together, young one. Your history has been erased. By whom? You? Your academy masters? Your priests? It was apparently four centuries ago, so we might not know who did it. But it came about at the same time HE arrived. He with all his songs and false promises. You do not need songs. You need an education! Otherwise, you are simply lost. Lost to your history, lost to your prestige, and also lost to your original gods."

"I am not lost!" she shouts. "And if those same original gods were so all-powerful, why would they let us get lost in the first place?"

"This is a fine one to ask, unless we say he came in behind everyone's back. Like I said, the Estelar may be many things, but they are still people, and if he is a being of sufficient potential, he might have just enough capacity to sneak around under them. Much like you and I, if my focus is on one thing, it is not on any other. And gods may, in fact, place their focus on only a selection of things, despite that statement of being all-seeing. I might also suggest, if your loss was something important, like a focus of your worship, this could disconnect you from them."

"Huh? Disconnect? Don't they just know who we are simply for being here?"

"Not necessarily. Do you know every neighbor in your city by name simply because they live in your city? Do you visit your temple on a regular basis? Do you announce yourself to your god every day, saying such as, 'Here I am, for my daily reminder that I am still here.' They might not take such notice if you fall off a cliff or drown in the sea. You, among so many thousands, or perhaps millions, who might get lost in a crowd. You need to make those announcements with active worship if you want to keep their attention on you for any reason."

"Isn't that the job of a priest?"

"It is the job of anyone who wants to receive the attention of their god personally. Otherwise, you are only hearing of it indirectly, if you listen to another, like a priest."

"Hmm..." she turns away to mull the idea.

Thaelyn studies her, and realizes he hit a small note. Nevertheless, he must continue.

"And therefore, I say you are lost, and you were lost the moment you first heard his songs. You probably had more of your right mind at ten than you did at forty."

"You would dare suggest..." she scowls.

"I will dare a great many things, young lady, especially after all we have spoken about. Your god is as false as this bravado of yours."

"My bravado is not false!"

"You do not hear his songs, yet you claim he is all-powerful. These two notions contradict each other. You claim your people were weak before this due to some loss, but you do not know what caused this loss in the first place. We have already admitted to the loss of your history, and who knows what else along the way, distancing you from everything you once were. Someone came in and took it away. A loss? Yes! And this leads us in a very clear direction. Maybe he caused it simply to dominate you."

"WHAT???" she screams. "Impossible!!"

"Why? He is a god. Domination is certainly one thing a god can do. And if you were so weak, it would surely place you in such a vulnerable condition for him to do exactly that. You are a High Elf. I know what a High Elf is supposed to be like, and one of those, you are not. Remember his motivation. Gods do not give free gifts to mortals. Maybe he wanted slaves, and you were conveniently located. How would you know? You were not alive back then, and apparently you are not educated on this well enough, not being a priest or anyone else with license to know, assuming he would grant this to you in the first place."

Now she screams in anguish and begins sobbing.

Thaelyn relaxes from the interrogation. He considers the results of his findings and displays a visual cue to the priest, waving his hand over his ear and mouth. The priest moves in to reattach the two runic symbols onto the circlet. Thaelyn then returns to Relissa and Marelle to consult with them.

"Great gods!" Marelle gasps. "I really don't want to get into an argument with you. That bit with Kaliya was nothing by comparison to this."

He reaches out to lay a hand on her shoulder, squeezing gently to soothe her.

"These are some interesting methods you use," she relents. "Is this how you conduct interrogations back home?"

"It stems from my time in the court of my Father. My first duty was as an inquisitor. Later, I earned the position of adjudicator. The Measure of Balance is quite strict. The powers of Good cannot be slack where Evil is concerned," he pauses to glance at the elf, which seemed to be calming down a little by now. "But now I am considering there may be more at work here than previously thought."

"Oh? Does that mean you learned something? I did pick up on a few bits here and there…"

"Yes, this, at the very least. First, she is quite difficult and uncooperative, but then I might expect this."

"Yes, this much even I can see," she chuckles faintly. "Though I saw her softening up on a few occasions."

"Indeed, we did hit a few tender spots. Aside from that, to gain any useful information out of her, I had to work on her devotion to her religion, attempting to crack it open just enough to peer inside, then to learn how and why her people might fall to Sargeras."

"Right, I think I saw that, and in your usual manner, you twisted her own statements against her."

Thaelyn smiles at his achievement.

"It is a carefully crafted skill. It would seem they did, in fact, convert four centuries ago, so we were right about that. Further, it was apparently due to some sort of loss or sensation of pain that they could not bear up against, and as such, Sargeras came in and conveniently filled it with some manner of substitute. Now they feel strength from these songs of his which persuade them to follow him."

"And it would seem some part of this included erasing their own history, so they don't even know better. Talk about us and the Dean. This sounds as bad, if not worse."

"It does, and so unfortunate. But I suspect this alone cannot be the whole answer. Losing a library full of books could not be the sole reason for this level of pain, and certainly not if it involves so many people across such an expanse, and if also to include the Night Elves for something similar. Relissa, you still have much of your history, correct?"

"Aye, we do, a big library of it."

"So, this cannot be the one. It may only be collateral, maybe as the result of the takeover to cleanse anything that could contradict his songs."

"That might make sense."

"Then, how would you interpret this," Marelle wonders. "Or do you have any interpretation at all?"

"As for the songs, I would interpret them as a form of persuasive mind control. She said she did not hear them as a young child, but they came later when she was old enough to interpret them. So, as young children, they are probably of no particular value to him. Then, at some moment in time, he might deem them worthy, and thus he fills their heads with these songs which drive them to follow him unerringly."

"And this sounds like they didn't convert willingly…another of our suspicions. But it also contradicts this as a pain that lingers from one generation to another. The first ones, sure, if something was stolen or destroyed. But new generations? I don't think I could buy that."

"Very nicely stated, Marelle. So, he simply applies this mind control until they buckle under the pressure. Then we should ask ourselves about that first generation. Those who were present at the time to feel the initial hit. It might be related to something stolen or destroyed, and more, by the sound of it, when including the Night Elves, it had to be universal to both, but only one of you was taken. So, what happened four hundred years ago that we know of, and for this, we know it might include the Night Elves."

"Four hundred years ago?" Relissa considers. "Something stolen? I can't think of anything stolen, not from us. I would probably have to ask my Mum if she knew of anything. Destroyed? Let me see. Our city didn't see any direct hits in all this time. Like we said before, the orcs might play with the towers, but nothing on, or even in the city proper."

"It might not be physical, Relissa," Marelle reflects. "It was emotional, maybe psychological. Something hitting you personally, on the inside."

"Jiggers, that cuts it down a wee bit. Up close and personal, hmm…oh wait. Buggers…" she whispers urgently. "But, um, let me think…yes! And what did that druid priestess say about it?"

"Druid priestess?" Thaelyn mumbles. "Who?"

"Your high priestess. Um, sorry, I forgot the name. She was out there on that first day…still is, for that matter."

"You mean Priestess Rumoren Summersong?"

"Aye, her, on that first day when I had my little, um, episode with the tree. Ours was killed back then. And as I understand it, every elven city should've had those, both sides. This could be your universal thing."

"Something targeted…" Marelle whispers. "Yes, and didn't I hear it said once that no elf would do such a thing?"

"Aye! That's for bloody sure! That priestess once said that it could rip away at your soul if you did it. This way, no elf would do it. So, if the bugger is erasing stuff, did he erase this one too?"

Thaelyn gazes into Relissa's eyes as he makes a connection with a curious memory, resulting in a minor revelation.

"By the Powers! Yes! The tree! And your reaction to it in the camp."

He cups Relissa's head in his hands and draws her up unexpectedly, planting a firm parental kiss on her forehead. As he lets her back down, she tries to steady herself from the remarkable reward.

"That must be it!" he asserts. "What if something happened to their Tree of Life? If we say the early elves of your world were following their usual traditions, they should have had one. But she did not even recognize the reference, which could mean she had never encountered one before. Therefore, they would feel the same sense of loss as you did."

"Aye, and wow…is that what happens when you do something right?" she chuckles. "Jiggers, I need to remember that one. But anyhow, in their case, then Sargeras got inside and fouled things up for them."

"Indeed, and this may be the answer. Now we need to make a test."

He begins moving off towards the archway.

"Everyone stay as you are. I shall return shortly."

Relissa observes him as he moves away. He places his hand up against his forehead in a quiet moment of concentration. The portal opens and he steps through. Relissa looks on as he vanishes from sight, taking notice of how the portal simply appeared for him without any obvious sign of how he opened it. But the gesture of his hand made her wonder if it was mental in nature.

Almost an hour passes. Relissa and Marelle wait patiently, as do the other members in the room. The elf prisoner seems to be becoming impatient, as she shuffles about on occasion, still apparently disturbed from her previous session, and likely uncomfortable in her bindings. Finally, a shimmer forms in the archway as the portal opens into the room from the outside.

The form of a woman emerges, her nearly nude figure wrapped partially in a vine-like draping with patches of tree bark and leaves. Where a mane of hair should be was instead a dense foliage of leaves that seemed to wave and ripple in rhythmic patterns. Embedded in the center of her chest was a large nutlike object that appeared almost to be growing out of her.

Following her through the portal was Thaelyn, who walked alongside her as she placidly strolled over to the group. Her motion seemed as fluid as a gentle breeze.

On seeing the woman approaching, Relissa gasps in shock. She draws up her hands to her mouth, barely touching her fingers to her lips.

"Dear Gods be blessed! It's a..." she mutters faintly.

Her knees buckle and she crumples to the floor in a penitent kneel.

Marelle studies her friend. Not knowing what to do, she simply steps out of the way as the woman appears to move toward the humble form of the young devotee. She watches as the woman places a hand on Relissa's head and strokes her gently. Relissa takes the woman's hand, brings it around and kisses it reverently before returning to her feet.

"Relissa?" Marelle whispers. "Who...and also what, is this?"

"She's one of the spirits. She's a dryad!"

"Do you mean to say that she...that is, in your religion...but does this mean that she is a... Relissa, am I supposed to do something right now?"

"It's alright, Marelle. You're not elven, so it's not the same for you."

"Well, yeah, maybe, but I don't want to offend her."

Marelle gazes at the dryad. Her face is a vision of beauty, and her form was a symbol of feminine perfection. She feels an urge to show some manner of respect.

"Eh...my apologies," she begins, drawing the dryad's attention. "I'm not familiar with the practice, please forgive my disrespect."

Marelle follows with a deep bow.

"She wouldn't understand your words, Marelle. They only speak one language, the ancient Sylvan tongue of our ancestors."

"Well, maybe the gesture would hold some meaning," Marelle appeals nervously. "Or perhaps you could translate for me."

The dryad smiles and speaks several soft words in her native form, then brings a hand up and places it on Marelle's cheek. As she makes contact, Marelle draws in a sudden breath. A flush of warmth flows through her and she feels a strange sensation of emotional contentment.

"Look at that..." she mumbles dreamily. "It's so beautiful. So perfect..."

The dryad holds her hand for several moments as she relates a vision into Marelle's mind.

"She's singing to me…" Marelle continues smoothly. "It's like springtime, baby animals, cool breezes, the trickling of water…and everything is alive, all part of one big body where all of its parts feel each other."

The dryad now takes her hand away, allowing Marelle to return to her own senses. She blinks as she tries to refocus herself.

"Relissa, that was amazing," she ushers softly. "I think I understand now. Do all your people feel this?"

"Aye, Marelle, this is what holds us together. It's like a bond we share with the Great Mother. She watches over all of us, even if we don't always know it. The elves simply have a deeper feel for it than humans."

"And now," Thaelyn submits. "To see about this theory in our example over here, I have brought Shescellaie to assist me."

"Shescellaie…" Relissa wheezes. "She's the one you spoke of before, the Queen of the dryads."

"Oh wow…" Marelle whimpers. "Yeah, her… And she's here now."

"Relax, Marelle, she's not quite the same as the Gods. She won't smite you for anything. They're spirit creatures of nature."

Marelle studies the woman for her curious features. She finds herself focusing on the nut in her chest.

"Um, not that I want to stare at anything inappropriate, but, um, is this a nut she's got sticking out of her?"

"Sure looks like one," Relissa smiles softly.

"It is necessary, in her case," Thaelyn admits. "The dryad spirits may come out of their trees for brief periods and move around in close proximity for a time, but never too far away. If they should have such a desire for longer journeys, they need to imbue themselves with additional strength, and this is how they do it, by embedding a life-seed into their body. This will allow them to travel to such places as where we are now, so far from home."

"Interesting," Marelle muses.

Relissa turns to Thaelyn to continue her thought.

"My Lord, we're saying the High Elves got hit somehow. But if that's the case, then why did Sargeras take them and not us? It seems there is still a piece or two missing."

"Relissa," Marelle considers. "I recall she mentioned something about the Night Elves in all that. How he might hold an interest in them for this weakness of theirs."

"Aye, you're right. Buggers, now I'm sorry I asked."

"For the moment," Thaelyn asserts. "Let us see what happens when we bring these two together."

Thaelyn moves towards the dais and instructs the priest to remove the two runic symbols again. The elf quickly realizes the sensation of hearing and speech has returned and tries talking again.

"Are we back for more?" she muses bitterly. "We can keep this up forever, but you won't get anything useful out of me."

"Actually, I beg to differ. That last conversation did, in fact, provide some useful information, if only to help me understand a few details about this being you call a god, and what he did to your people."

"A being?" she shouts. "A simple being? He is a god!"

"Once again, young one, what you call a god, and what I call one are clearly different. And he is not a god by my definition. And neither would any of the races I know of call him such either. And I know of quite a few from all my travels."

"Uh huh…sure."

"Furthermore, I think we were able to paint a clear enough picture, from all those pieces, that we can surmise a possible motivation, as well as the cause of that pain."

"Oh! Really! Um…" she pauses tentatively. "Well, some of it, sure. But I wouldn't say it's enough to call the full fare."

"From those statements alone, perhaps. But I suspect you probably realize we are not alone in here, and those who are remaining silent are suggesting a few ideas based on their observations."

"Ah, suggestions! I simply love those! Anything juicy?"

"You have a rather curious temperament, you know? Actually,

one did come forward that invoked a bit of consideration. First and foremost, he probably caused it by taking away something both you and the Night Elves cherished as holy. And doing so would surely cause pain."

"He did this… Uh huh. Didn't you say he was on some other world, and intentionally keeping away from here for all those other gods taking notice?"

"You are actually right. Nicely done. But he could also have agents doing some of his work. After all, he has you, the orcs, and also those Suuden-Aryku."

"Well, all right, I suppose we can say as much."

"Next, in your case at least, he replaced this loss with these songs, thereby turning you from a sweet and lovable High Elf into a monster that destroys countless innocent lives."

"And here we are with that word horrors again, right?"

"Well, he would certainly be a horror, if he dominated you to do his work for him. And his kind, from the history my kind carries, would most assuredly hold this definition."

"And this sounds like more of that storytelling you were giving earlier."

"Yes, it probably would. And since I have hard evidence on my side, you might want to stifle that insolent tongue of yours again until you visit our library and read a few books on the subject. The stories are not mine."

"I don't actually care whose stories they are, he helped us with our pain, and we gave ourselves to him for the favor of it."

"Yes, and wiping out your history which would otherwise teach you who you actually are, not that it matters anymore with this mind control affect he forces onto you at your third decade. No, whatever interpretation you might suggest, if he is still filling you with these songs, that, young lady, is not a simple gift of healing. It is an ongoing barrage of influence to constrain and control you. The entire purpose of dominating one's mind is to prohibit the original consciousness from regaining control. Or, at the very least, if not the full consciousness, the awareness of rational thought. It is not a one-time application, as it must be continually applied for the life of the individual…that is, from whatever moment that individual might hold enough value to the one doing it, like you as a child."

"Now wait just a moment…" she blasts.

"Therefore," he interrupts. "You become a puppet, possibly to serve as his eyes and ears, as well as his hands and feet."

"You must have lost your mind. I'm not…um…eyes and ears?" she hesitates as she recalls Eilihel's words from their outing.

"You recognize this reference…I can see it in you. And surely this also applies for the devastation you caused out there. High Elves would never cause the mass murder of innocents. But if to be made subject under someone else's will, who knows. But one thing is for certain, it would be a grave insult to all elves to see you out there doing it."

"No! I mean…wait. We have to serve him as his eyes and ears. After all, we're at war."

"Oh! A war, is it? When was the last time you actually attacked someone? And do be careful of your wording, for I have heard more than my share of such statements as, 'for as long as I can remember…' such and such. It seems that beast is corrupting more than just you and your history. The others are made to think they are at war, but no one is actually fighting anything. And it all goes as…for as long as they can remember…"

"They aren't? But I thought I heard…"

"A few odd skirmishes, but that is all. And this is not what I call a war. The Night Elves might speak of a few hits by the orcs, but it is simply the manner of orcs to toy with things. The only one who can really say they are fighting anything would be the Daanen-Aryku with their foes making repeated skirmishes to pin them down, but no more."

"But…well…um…"

"I might further suggest this. If to borrow from this statement, you are at war, but where is HE? Remember, he is a god, and I doubt he would need you to fight his wars. Such small mortal creatures as you would be incapable of fighting a war on the scale of a god. And a god would not waste his time on a war down on your level."

"And how would you know this?"

"Oh spare me, young lady, I think this carries its own definition. Even you can see it. Whatever capacity he should have, as a god, would scale up much larger than anything you could even comprehend."

"All right, fine, but he needs us for other things, I'm sure of it."

"Other things? This is curious. Let us not forget, he is a god. What other things would he possibly require you for?"

"I...I don't know, and I don't think I would tell you even if I did. Why should I?"

"I suppose one of these could be to sabotage a ship on another world. I doubt he would care to bother himself with such a menial task as that."

"A what?"

"The Daanen-Aryku. Their ship was sabotaged...by your people. So, how did you manage to cross from your world to theirs, then miraculously figure out how to tamper with a form of knowledge you have absolutely no idea how to use?"

"You must be kidding me!"

"Ask the Daanen-Aryku. They found your agents inside their ship on Ruuki uy'Daan, their former home, as they were forced to evacuate after your...god...ordered his orcish minions to slaughter most of their civilian population simply for fun."

"Huh?" she whispers.

"This is your god for you...a murderer. I can only imagine how many other worlds came before this."

"That simply must be a lie."

"You are amazing. The evidence is right in front of you, and yet you refuse to see it. Well, I suppose that sort of response is to be expected, for someone who does not have their right mind to think with. But a curious thought came forward a short while ago for something that might be lost and needed to be found again. This also relates to a kind of pain when it goes missing. And it applies to all elves, whether yours or the others."

"And now, what are you talking about? You know, you sure like to speak in riddles."

"Indeed, and it is quite fascinating to see the people around me try to decipher these abstract notations. Would you like to indulge me in one?"

"Oh, are we going to play a game now? This should be fun. Does it have anything to do with bending me over?"

"Young lady, I should probably inform you that I am a happily married man, and I prefer to keep it that way. No, my thoughts are more on straightening you out."

She feels a sudden compulsion to laugh at his suggestion.

"And how do you think straightening me out will make any difference?"

"It may actually be simpler than you think. Something was taken away from you, leaving a form of emptiness. It was targeted, and universal for its coverage. It applies to all elves, both yours and the Night Elves. It causes a pain of loss. And if you are too young to remember anything, it clearly predates you. But due to this, those songs can take over your mind, even without the direct influence of the original cause of that loss."

"Oh! So, for my youth, and not dating back that far, I'm simply being taken over, irrespective of any actual pain?"

"I will say it again. Were you in pain during your early youth? Would you even know what I am talking about if you do not even know what sort of pain we are speaking of, or what might cause it in the first place? It predates you. Therefore, you were born into a world already absent of it."

"Oh! You!" she spurns.

"Furthermore, as we have seen elsewhere, your history is being so badly muddled that even if you did have your right mind to think about it, the knowledge was more likely erased, causing you to forget anyway. And there is only one direction to point a finger…that being who so conveniently arrived and drove you to follow a god image your kind would never follow willingly."

He now waves at Shescellaie to make her advance, and the matron dryad gracefully saunters over towards the dais.

"What are you doing?" the elf shouts. "What's that sound? It sounds like...rustling leaves! Huh? Wait... What...what is happening?"

The dryad's aura flows around her body, radiating a nurturing glow of harmony and life. As she closes in on the prisoner, the outer edges of this glow make contact.

"I...I feel something," the young elf hesitates. "What are you doing to me?!"

"Giving you back what was apparently stolen from you four centuries ago by Sargeras."

"No! You lie... I can't...I..."

Her voice softens as her body becomes enveloped by the energies. As a result, her mind loses focus, and she becomes incoherent.

"Singing..." she mumbles deliriously. "It's singing to me. A voice...a little voice...growing..."

As the dryad arrives at the dais, she steps up onto it with her aura now swirling around the platform and the elf. The elf instinctively looks up, somehow sensing where the dryad's face is to gaze into it.

"It's alive..." she whispers remotely.

The dryad now stands directly in front of the bewildered elf. She raises a hand and gently lays it on the young woman's forehead. The elf's voice fades to silence as she falls into a recuperative sleep.

The dryad holds her hand on the elf's head for several long moments. The elf's body has gone limp, sagging into her bindings. In time, the dryad pulls away and returns to the group with Relissa and Marelle.

Thaelyn moves in to examine the elf's mind while she slumbers. He passes his hand around her head briefly to study the emanations, nodding as if to suggest they seem normal now. Once satisfied, he again returns to the group and together they wait for the girl to regain consciousness.

The court is silent for a long time. Relissa and Marelle, so far impressed by the day's presentation, can only wait to see what comes next. Thaelyn glances at the two women from time to time to see if they have any needs, but neither is able to suggest anything, until Relissa recalls a thought in her mind.

"By the way," she begins.

"Yes, Relissa?"

"This is just a little thing. When you opened that portal over there, what kind of key did you use? I saw you doing the bit with the odd leafy thing out on the other side, but you didn't have anything in your hand this time."

"The key for this one is very personal. It is the memory of an image I must recall in my mind. Before we came here, I spent a moment examining a small medallion I keep in the box with the rune and the Bitterbalm leaves. It is the image of my Father. He is the key, and that makes the gate here very secure, as you need to know his face to open it."

"You miss him, don't you," Relissa offers sorrowfully.

"I had a millennium and a half," he looks down and sighs. "Some might call it an eternity. For me, it seemed like barely a flicker of time."

Relissa places her hand on his arm to comfort him. He responds with a gentle pat on her shoulder.

"How do you manage living among all us mortals then?" she asks.

"It is difficult, at times. I have known a great many during my stay on Tae'Eladar, and still more from Sigil. I take delight at their birth, but must also weep at their death. Needless to say, I realize it is a cycle of life, as it must be for all living things. Immortality may bless upon a person many great offerings, but it also has its drawbacks. Many immortals may prefer to stay among the Outer Planes with their own kind for this reason."

"Do you have any friends who are immortal?"

"Actually, I do. There is a group of us. Some of them live in Sigil. One of these is just slightly older than I am, a dear and lovely woman by the name of Aelwyn. She is Aasimar, as I am, and she works as a revered member of the Guild of Sensations, a Cardinal Sensate."

"Guild of Sensations?" Marelle wonders. "What's that?"

"In the city, you have a collection of guilds. Each one proposes its own philosophy for a goal one must achieve in order to attain true enlightenment, and therefore fulfillment in life leading you to ascension. The Guild of Sensations is one where the aspirant should seek to experience as many varied sensations as possible, whether emotional or psychological, to understand the great diversity of the triumphs and tragedies of life. The broad accumulation of these experiences may grant a person with a higher form of awareness."

"That sounds a bit odd to me. So, to do this, do they have to create situations where they can experience these emotions?"

"While that may occur from time to time, they also have a sort of library within the guild. Emotions and other memories can be stored in special orbs we call sensory stones. By touching one of these, you can relive a moment in the life of the person who recorded the memory. This allows another person to share the experience and understand its influence."

"And I thought the first part was weird…" she snickers. "I should keep my mouth shut."

"The Outer Planes is an odd place when you compare it to your Prime worlds."

"Can anyone go in and try these stones?" Relissa asks.

"They have a public area as well as a private one for guild members. I should probably also mention there is a professional establishment for young aspirants to ply their trade to the general public outside the guild."

Thaelyn stretches a wide grin across his face as he continues his thought.

"It is called a brothel."

"'Ere now!" Relissa snaps. "What's that look you got plastered all over you there? Don't you be telling me you went spending any time in a place like that?!"

He lets out a prominent laugh at her reaction before continuing.

"It is not that sort of brothel, Child, so remove your mind from the sewers. This one is a place to experience such delights as argument, debate with perpetual victory or defeat, a release from your emotional tension, as well as simple abuse. This actually reminds me of a few special people I once knew in there. One of them was a young tiefling named Kimasxi."

"What's a tiefling?"

"It is one of those hybridized forms I mentioned before, part humanoid and part fiend, though the tiefling itself might take on any number of characteristics, not simply follow the negative path of its fiendish parent. One thing is common, however, and that is they often have a quick temper."

"I can see I've got a lot to learn in your academy. Why was this one so special?"

"Her specialty was abuse. If you ever wanted to experience someone laying into you with insults, harassment, and verbal molestation, she was the one to see. It is where I first learned to swear. She taught me how to use language as a weapon, and to her benefit, I have created a course for it at the academy."

"Aye, I could give up a few good ones if I wanted, but how does this play into training as a soldier?"

"One might describe it as an art form, as you can unbalance your opponent with the right combination of words to throw off his concentration and cause him to behave in an unwise manner. This might invoke him to take a certain course of action or diminish his defense to give you an advantage for a brief moment. Think of those orcs on that first day, the group that came up from the valley. I threw a statement at them belittling their mettle to actually attack. This would count as an insult, which invoked them to charge ahead brashly, rather than turning around to warn others."

"Your Lordship," Marelle reflects. "More and more, as I listen to the lessons you give, I'm amazed at the depth of knowledge you have to offer us. And you teach these things in your academy, which makes me wonder what sort of results you get in the end."

"Yes, the Brothers and Sisters of our Order are highly educated and skillfully adept at a wide variety of talents. This gives them the benefit of meeting virtually any challenge with little or no additional special exercise."

"It almost seems too good to be true. But considering where it's coming from, I guess that's the point. You're making an army of what…super soldiers?"

"As far as mortal bodies can be pressed to achieve their maximum effectiveness, then I suppose you might describe it that way. In the early days, it was not as such, as we often had to pick and choose the best lessons for our people. But with Aerlie's gift of the Elixir of Visions, we were able to speed their training and involve more lessons in less time."

"So, our most noble Lord spent time in a brothel," Relissa jests. "That's a good one. Anyone else special in there we should know about?"

Thaelyn pauses in thought for a moment. Relissa notices his face turn to deep contemplation, as if a long-lost memory had resurfaced.

"My Lord, I didn't mean to bring up anything bad…" she infers.

"It is alright, Relissa, I was just thinking of a special moment in my life…my early life. I was barely a few centuries old. There was this one young lady in there that held my special interest. But due to my commitment to my Father and his court, we could never indulge ourselves in anything more than a few precious moments of social interaction."

"Who was she?" Marelle inquires tenderly.

"Her name was Ecco. She served as a confidant, listening to the woes of others. But my relationship with her was different. She took special delight in the experiences I would bring back with me from my travels across the planes. She also helped me in another way."

"How's that?"

"She suffered from a most unfortunate affair with a powerful mage once. He confided in her some great misery. She was young at this moment, and somewhat inexperienced. The burden proved to be too heavy for her to bear alone, so she shared it with another. In time, the mage learned of the indiscretion and was outraged. He returned to her while in this fury and magically removed her ability to speak. She was mute for a long while after that."

"Ouch!" Marelle yips. "That sounds harsh."

"Indeed, I felt this was too high a price for her to pay, so I sought ways to help restore her. In the meantime, I had recently received one of my divine gifts from my Father, my telepathic skill. It was new to me, so I needed ways to develop it, and Ecco had no other means to communicate, other than writing. Therefore, she and I practiced together."

"That's a terrible thing to have happen to a person, but it's also an incredibly sweet story for the two of you. Did you ever find a way to help her?"

"I did. It was through a sequence of odd events that I found a way to reinstate her proper speech, though I will admit I did so by following the aid of another individual who also contributed. His offer helped to return the ability to speak, but the results were, shall we say, somewhat crude. I then offered an agent to help settle the effect."

"And what about the two of you?" Relissa asks. "Did you ever get anything more out of this together?"

"In her lifetime, no... I continued to make my visits, we would sit and chat, share a few meals and other pleasantries, and finally that tender embrace as the time came for me to depart. But in the end, I could only watch as she aged through the years until one day, I returned to find she was no longer there."

"Jiggers, my Lord," Relissa mourns. "I'm terribly sorry."

"I wept for her, and questioned my own intentions for even making the initial contact with a mortal being in this way."

He looks up at Relissa and begins forming a soft but curious grin.

"But fear not, young one, for this girl was no fool, nor was she simple of mind. It turns out she played a little trick on me that gave us a second chance."

"What do you mean by that?"

"I will reveal only that she did have a small amount of help, but beyond that, rather than simply giving the answer, I will challenge you to find the rest on your own. Go to the city library and ask to see the books on the Prophecies of Adalon the Silver. There, if you are wise, you may learn the rest."

"My Lord, you're a hard one," she chuckles. "Right then, I'll do it when I can get some free time away from all these other chores."

It is almost two hours passing. Motion is detected in the body of the elf as she slowly begins to stir. She pulls her head up groggily, turning it side to side and blinking her eyes firmly in an effort to elicit some response from them. She soon realizes her hands and feet seem to be bound, and tries jerking them loose, but to no avail.

"Hello?" she calls out tenuously.

She tries her bindings again, apparently becoming nervously agitated at her predicament.

"Hello! Is anyone there?"

Thaelyn walks up slowly. The elf, on hearing his footsteps, turns instinctively in his direction.

"Who's there? Please, what's going on here? Why am I tied up? Where am I? Please, say something!"

Marelle gazes at Relissa in a moment of disbelief. She whispers gently into her ear.

"And to think, this scamp was spewing curses and obscenities a short while ago. Now she's saying please!"

"You are here in a court under interrogation," Thaelyn states calmly. "You are restrained due to the belief that you may be harmful if let free. There is a charm around your neck that currently denies you your sight, with additional slots for denying hearing and speech."

"Why?" she retorts. "Did I do something wrong? How did I get here? I don't even remember it. Everything is going around in circles inside my head."

"Let us remain calm, if we can, and proceed in a rational manner. You passed into unconsciousness a short while ago due to what I might describe as a form of shock, and this may leave you feeling a bit dazed still. Perhaps a little conversation will help. I will ask you a series of questions, and I will bid you to answer them to the best of your capacity. Understood?"

"Well, yes, but… Who are you, and why am I here? Dangerous? Me?"

"Gently now…" he soothes. "Let us approach this gradually. Perhaps if we begin with your name, this should be simple enough and easy for you to recall."

"My name? My name…wait… My name…ugh…my head. I feel like something big and heavy hit me. Um, right, Mynae… Eh, Mynae…Silverwind."

"Very good, Mynae, and what sort of occupation do you perform?"

"Occupation? I, uh…" she sighs heavily. "It's all so fuzzy. Lessons, right, I was in study…just finished recently… Oh, of course! I remember, I was studying arcane teachings. I'm a mage…a mage newly accomplished."

"Very good. And did you do well in your studies?"

"I…yes, I think so. Why? Does it matter?"

"I am simply trying to soften the moment with a bit of idle conversation."

"Oh, well, yes, I think I did quite well, thank you. My instructors certainly seemed to praise me enough."

Marelle glared at the girl with her brow prominently raised at the radically altered manner of the elf's behavior. She turned to look at Relissa, who was similarly amused.

"Now, Mynae," Thaelyn continues. "In your condition of confusion, you may need to apply yourself to recall a number of things. For instance, there is currently a war ongoing. Do you recall this?"

"A war! Oh no! Who is fighting?"

"Your people, along with a number of others… We found you out there, which is how you came to be in here."

"But wait, does that mean I was out there…" she hesitates as her memories begin to clear. "Wait, yes, I was out there! This can't be right! It feels like I must've died and I'm looking at my life as if it were a dream! How is it possible?"

"Again, try to remain calm. We will step our way through this together."

"But I don't know what's happening! It's like I'm waking up from a deep slumber and realizing I was living a life that wasn't mine."

"Then let us try to analyze this. Although I could possibly offer a few ideas of my own, I think it would be best to understand this in a more procedural manner. At what moment in your life, if you can recall it, were you living your life as yourself? This is to say, if you feel you were living an alternate life most recently, when did this begin?"

"I, uh…wow, that's a big question, and my head is still spinning a little. I remember something. Yes, something like a song, or a voice, going through my head. It was constantly inside there, telling me things, making me feel like I had everything I needed in life."

"So, in a manner of speaking, we might say it made you feel confident, perhaps if to say it gave you a sense of strength or fulfillment."

"Yes, I think that would do it."

"And when did you first hear this voice?"

"I think I was very young, only a few or so decades, maybe a little more."

"This represents a long time, if to look at you now. How old are you at this moment?"

"I'm, um…seventy-two."

"This is a fair enough age, if also a bit young for an elf. And from that moment forward, you heard this voice as a constant murmuring, perhaps?"

"Yes. And this is where I'm so upset. It told me to do things it wanted me to do, and I…well, I suppose I wanted this as well."

"To want this as well. Can we say this is because of these whispers imposing a form of influence, like suggesting a purpose to follow?"

"Yes! Right. Exactly. I was slowly being convinced to do this for all the nagging inside my head. Finally, I couldn't take it anymore. And this is also why it feels like I was living a life not my own… like a dream."

"Jiggers," Relissa whispers in Marelle's ear. "That bugger had them wrapped up tight."

"Do you know where these voices came from?" Thaelyn inquires.

"I can't be sure, but I recall a name, and an image of something big, something powerful," she pauses as her face contorts with mild revulsion. "It was something trying to get inside of me!" she screeches and turns away.

The girl begins moaning and shaking her head, as if trying to toss away the visions she was recalling.

"Mynae," Thaelyn asserts, trying to redirect her attention. "We must try to understand this. You mentioned a name. What name?"

The girl was visibly disturbed and panting from fright.

"Name… Yes, I remember a name…Sargeras. And he put these things inside my head, even though I didn't really want them there, but he put them in there anyway. I feel so dirty now," she begins to sob.

"Mynae, once again, let us try to restrain ourselves. You are here now and apparently in possession of enough faculties to recognize these matters. It is now a process of trying to understand how this came about and for what purpose."

"What purpose?" she shouts. "You mean he might have a purpose for raping my mind?"

"Well, under the circumstances, I feel there might be, although we also have the question of whether you would personally know of it. But let us continue. It would appear that all or most of your people are like this, can you confirm this for me?"

"Yes, actually, now that I'm starting to remember things better, they all talk about him, as well as his songs and other things. I'm sure he's been doing this to all of us."

"That would represent a great many people."

"Yes, but he's apparently something like a god, or so it seems…"

"I see. Then let us see about a summarization to this part. Some manner of godlike being, from some unknown point of origin, comes in and begins filling the minds of your people with these songs, or voices, whatever we may call them, and this essentially drives you to behave as he commands. Does this seem appropriate?"

"Yes! I would agree to this."

"Most excellent, this gives us a good picture of what is going on over there. But then, we must ask ourselves when this initially occurred. Do you happen to know when he first arrived?"

"First arrived," she muses. "All right, let me think, I seem to remember stories of our history, such as it is. Four centuries ago, I think. There was something about pain and weakness because of a sense of loss."

"Do we know what sort of loss we are speaking of?"

"I...um... No, I can't think of anything. I don't think anyone ever really talks about it. Only to say that it's a weakness that came from some loss of something you need, and we were all suffering without it."

"This brings a very curious mention to us. Could it be there was something preexisting but taken away, thus you felt the loss from it?"

"Well, I suppose that's possible, but the way people talk, it was something absent and unmentionable, like it didn't matter. Only Sargeras and what he offered mattered."

"Of course," Thaelyn nods. "And this represents to me a form of control of information. If you did not know what came before, and in fact tended to downplay it anyway, you would not know if it was worthy to maintain over what he offered you. Therefore, you take his word since it is the only word you are allowed to have."

"I think you may be right, the way I'm starting to remember it."

"It also suggests this moment of loss occurred sometime before he arrived, and he so conveniently offered what we might describe as his service to fulfill it."

"Maybe, but I wouldn't call it a service I would choose...if I had such an opportunity."

"Indeed. Very well then, I think we made a fair amount of progress on this, so let us move on to other matters."

"Again, I'd like to know if I'm in some sort of trouble. I remember now I was involved in something, although I don't think I actually did anything bad. I recently finished my studies, and my last memories were that I was wandering around out in the woods on a patrol."

"This is true, and I cannot necessarily fault you for simply being out there. But for the moment, I have a need to follow a rather precise procedure, so kindly bear with me."

"All right, but in the end, I hope you'll tell me what's going to happen to me."

"We shall see about that once these questions are satisfied. Now let me ask you about a few things of importance to our war. You may or may not know these details, so we will try to pass through them briskly. Do you know what a Tree of Life is?"

"A Tree of Life? I've never heard of such a thing before. What is it?"

"It is a special type of tree that some regard as a sacred item in a form of worship."

"Worshipping a tree?" she intones curiously. "People do that?"

"Indeed, there are those who regard the blessings of nature very highly, such things as the unity of life, the harmony of the natural world around us, and a bond that all things may share."

"I've never heard of such a thing as that, sorry."

"Very well, not to worry… You are young, and likely this never came up while under the influence of Sargeras. More than likely, he would disallow any other form of worship, anyway."

"Right."

"On a more serious note, are you aware of a form of alliance between your people and a society of orcs and the Suuden-Aryku?"

"Yes. And worse is that we all serve Sargeras," she looks away and hangs her head dejectedly.

"Stay with me, Mynae. Perhaps we can find a way to help the rest of your people, maybe even more beyond that, but for now we need information. We have observed on a couple of occasions when certain members of this body were wearing a most unusual form of armor, composed of a material we call adamantium. Are you familiar with this?"

"I have heard the name mentioned a few times, but I've never actually seen any, myself."

"Have you heard anything about where it can be found? Do any of these other members speak of a mining operation or some other source for it?"

"No, I haven't heard anything. And that sounds like something I probably wouldn't be told about anyway. My position didn't give me much."

"What sort of position did you hold, precisely?"

"I was a mage in an outpost scouting a region south of our home city, although as I recall now, I was angry that it was a futile role to play."

"Oh? For what reason? Do you not like scouting?"

"Actually, no I don't. I understand it can be necessary on occasion, but it was boring for me. I trained to be part of a war, not chase rabbits and be bitten by bugs."

Thaelyn chuckles humorously at the mention.

"Yes, young ambition at work. It seems to prevail, no matter the circumstance."

"Besides, if you're who I think you are, I didn't see a point in patrolling anything when the stories we got about the orcs told us you were a lot more dangerous than bugs."

"Ah, but of course. Our tactics played a little role on you, did they?"

"Yes! The surprise attacks you made on the orcs didn't even let them see you coming…and neither did we, it seems," she chuckles ironically.

"The trials of warfare. A professional military must indulge itself in a number of curious tactics, if it wishes to win anything. But rest easy, young lady. At this time, my opinion of you is notably different from when you first came in here."

"It is?" she wonders optimistically.

"Let us continue briefly. You mentioned orcs, and this is one thing on my mind. Our campaign against them is moving forward rather nicely, but we are surprised that no one, not you nor anyone else around us, is coming to their rescue. Do we know why?"

"Word from my side is they aren't worth saving, not that I can actually blame anyone for this opinion."

"If your opinion of them is so low, why involve them in the first place?"

"It's not my opinion, specifically, but a general consensus. For one, they're not something we might normally find appealing to work with."

"Yes, I can understand this easily enough…with you being who you are, and they being who they are as a race."

"And this probably dates back to well before me. When I came into it, they were already here. But we mostly kept to ourselves, each of us. As for them, I think it's all because of you, actually. They brought you here, and now you're making trouble for all of us."

"Making trouble…this is how you see it?"

"Well, this is how it's described."

"Perhaps, and I suppose it makes sense. But this is also a subjective term. They made trouble for me on my home world, so I am simply returning the favor."

"Oops!"

"By the way, we are seeing a fair amount of such like iron and steel tools in their hands, and my experience with them tells me they do not normally produce these themselves. Can you provide anything on this point?"

"We have a supplier. I'm not sure who it is, but the Suuden-Aryku deliver it to us. Where it actually comes from, I don't know, but we get it in Kynesoth, and I think the orcs get some also."

Marelle glares sternly at Relissa at the implication as the two of them continue to listen.

"All right, we are getting near to the end now," Thaelyn reassures. "During the time of this war, which has apparently lasted for four centuries, we have seen a number of players involved. One is the Daanen-Aryku. Do you know of any history between your two peoples?"

"I know of the Daanen-Aryku…never seen one myself…and I don't recall any talk about us doing anything with them."

"Are you aware they are not native to the world you live in?"

"I am aware of this, yes."

"Are you aware of how they arrived there?"

"It was said they crashed in some big ship of some kind, right? And then…" she frowns softly.

"This is correct," he issues. "But I am actually aiming at something in particular here. Perhaps again, in your position, you might not know, but this ship was sabotaged to crash there."

"I remembered some words just now," she looks up in his direction. "We were talking about this already."

"Are you recalling our earlier conversation now?"

"Yes, although I remember I had so many of those awful thoughts going around inside my head still."

"Very well, but are you aware it was your people who sabotaged their ship to crash there intentionally?"

"I do not know of this personally. I don't even know how we could do it, unless it involves more of that…monster…filling our heads with stuff."

"Maybe so, although it could also be the Suuden-Aryku offering aid. You would need transportation, so they are likely involved. Unless you have other means. For instance, do your people use portal magic?"

"No, we don't study that in our academy."

"Interesting. This is something I might expect for an elven society to develop and study."

"Sorry, not in our schools."

"Very well, perhaps this study was either lost, or something else occurred. Your people are not native to Therinë, which means someone had to use a portal to bring you there."

"Not native? Where did we come from then?"

"My world. I have the rest of your people back home."

"Oh great!" she shouts. "That's so lovely! So, we are told you are invaders we need to fight, assuming someone would actually let us go out and fight something, when in fact you're our own people from some forgotten home?"

Thaelyn chuckles again at the poor girl's distress.

"Let us move on. What about the other races, the humans and the Night Elves."

"Again, I know of them…it's a little hard not to. But again, I never actually met one. I don't get out much," she sighs.

"You are young, so you probably spent most of your time in training thus far. But as far as these two are concerned, we have a rather curious scenario that needs to be explained. The world is said to have been well-populated by all the local races. Today, it is but a shadow of this, with just one city each for those two societies."

"One for us, too, for that matter…"

"You are down to only one city?"

"Yes, my home of Kynesoth."

"Interesting. But do we have an explanation for this?"

"It's said we lost a lot in the war, and then consolidated into the one remaining city. As for the others, well, I can only guess it's the same thing."

"Yes, but curiously, for as long as this war has been waging, and for all the destruction, these remaining cities are standing virtually untouched in modern times."

"Oh, that…yes, I get the direction now. Our instructions are not to attack those last two…and another reason why I was angry to be put so far behind the lines. I was born and raised to think we're at war with someone, and I wanted to be a part of it."

Relissa and Marelle exchanged glances again at her mention, and further reflected on the earlier statements of a future interest by Sargeras.

"I can understand your perspective," Thaelyn affirms. "But under the circumstances, we must bring this war to an end if it is truly Sargeras that holds this interest. Because of him, an entire world population has been nearly destroyed, and for some insofar unknown reason. Do you know of any such reason for not attacking?"

"For not attacking, not personally."

"I am also recently advised of some manner of plague circulating around the city of Rolsklinde. Do you know anything about this?"

"A plague? No, why do you ask? Do you think we might be suffering it also?"

Thaelyn pauses briefly and turns to look at Marelle. She frowns at the irreconcilable response. He returns to the prisoner.

"Do you actually have one in your city?" Thaelyn asks.

"No, not that I'm aware of. What is it?"

"This one is said to be afflicting the human population only after they reach age fifty or thereabouts, and causes symptoms of headache, followed by memory loss, and finally death."

She responds to this suggestion with a grimace.

"Ew, that sounds awful, actually. Fifty years? Help me out here. I don't know much about their age ranges. What is that in relation to their lifetimes?"

"It would represent upper middle age for them. Typical human lifespans are well less than a century."

"All right, but where did it come from? Do they know?"

"It is said to be coming from you."

"What?!" she shouts. "Wait a minute here! Those people are saying we started this plague?"

"They say you are pressing it continuously as a form of curse, and have been doing so for an extended measure of time, possibly since the beginning."

"That's...well, I would tend to say ridiculous, but in my position, I don't know anything about this, and never heard anyone say anything. This doesn't sound like something to go around in our mage academies. Curses might be more of a temple thing."

"Perhaps."

"But even at that...well, I don't visit the temple much, so who am I to say something."

"Maybe."

"But this sounds like one of those things Sargeras would make us do, or maybe the Suuden-Aryku..." she pauses to think. "You might have to go to the city for this. If this is something we're doing, only they would know. I don't think they would tell someone like me."

"I see, and I suppose this is reasonable, all things considered."

Thaelyn holds the discussion to consider where they had brought themselves during this time. He glances around the courtroom at the various attendees before returning to the prisoner.

"Very well. I feel that I am satisfied, within reason, with what you have to offer to explain how these events have been unfolding. And I will thank you most graciously for your cooperation."

He motions to the priest-bailiff to remove the last runic charm on the girl's circlet. As it comes off, her eyes begin to refocus, and her sight returns. She blinks several times to adjust her vision while looking around at the strange courtroom and the deep murky blackness stretching off into the distance.

"That's a very powerful enchantment you have on this thing," she looks down at her circlet. "What is this place?"

"It is simply a secure location that I felt might be necessary to use, where we could ensure your isolation from the influence of Sargeras."

"So, you knew I was under his influence?"

"I strongly suspected it. You may have been born into a society that calls itself Flame Elves, but this is not your native name. You are actually a race known as Cala'Quessir, otherwise known as High Elves. This is a member clan of a parent race called Tel'Quessir. You have your own dedicated pantheon of true gods, and your natural manners are substantially different from how you behave under Sargeras's influence."

"So, you're actually being so nice to me because you're giving me a chance to prove who I am underneath all that. Is that what you're saying?"

"Indeed. I also believe I know what this loss is about, although I cannot be sure how it came into being. Do you see that curious creature over there?" he points at Shescellaie.

"Yes, that's a new one. What is it?"

"She is what we call a dryad, and the reason you are restored to normal. Prior to this, you were spewing every blasphemy your tender mind could generate," he smiles. "Do you recall my mention of a Tree of Life? Well, that is her home, and an intricate element of elven heritage and culture. You elves hold a natural bond with nature, and a very close one at that. The Tree of Life is a sort of link that binds you together. To lose it is to lose a part of yourself, and thus I believe the cause of your loss and subsequent pain."

"Really!" she asserts emphatically. "And so, what you're saying is something took our Tree of Life away and gave us this pain, and then…" she halts and frowns morosely. "…Sargeras came in, with that convenient service, as you called it."

"Yes. Our next concern must be to understand the timeline of what actually occurred four centuries ago. But I suspect you would not hold this information. So, perhaps we need to find someone else, someone in a higher position or with the longevity to recall those moments."

"Are you asking me, or simply mentioning this need?"

"Well, unless you happen to know of someone. Do you have any instructors, mentors, elder members of any kind?"

"Um, wait, let me think…" she ponders for a moment. "I'm thinking of elders right now. The rest of us probably wouldn't know much. The Suuden-Aryku seem to pass their instructions through the priesthood. The priests sometimes talk about Sargeras giving instruction, but I never heard anything personally, only his songs."

"This is curious. So, your instruction is mostly passed along through a chain of command?"

"Yes, that's the best way to say it, I think. And this would have to go up to someone who would remember those days personally."

"This is reasonable. But four centuries, even for an elf, and especially in a time of war, can be problematic."

"We normally live longer than that."

"Yes, I am aware of this, in peacetime, but how many of your elders might have survived in this time for all the troubles you describe?"

"True, so it would have to be someone native to Kynesoth, I think. That city didn't see as much action as the others."

Relissa and Marelle both decided to make an approach while she was able to see, and the main portion of the interview seemed to be complete. Mynae looked up to see the two of them coming closer.

"You're a Night Elf, right?" she asks Relissa. "At least by the description, you look like one."

"Aye, I am," Relissa affirms.

"And a…human?"

"Yes," Marelle admits.

"Are you one of his, or from Rolsklinde?"

"Rolsklinde… I serve the Allegiance Guard up there."

"Wonderful. So, how much trouble am I in with your people. I thought he said my outlook was looking good for realizing myself in all this."

"In truth," Marelle asserts. "When we first captured you, even though he suggested this possible influence, and then to see how you were behaving in those first moments, I expected to be talking to a blonde-haired demon. We have a lot of stories up there, both of us," she glances at Relissa. "None of them good."

"A blonde-haired demon…" she muses and bites her lip. "And now, what do you think?"

"I'm surprised, maybe better to say shocked, by this turnaround. I know what this dryad over here can do. She touched me a little while ago to share this feeling of bonding, and it was amazing. Now I'm looking at you and thinking the effect here was even better."

"So, you think I've been healed in some way?"

"We humans don't hold this natural bonding. This is something I'll need to learn more about. But yes, I think so. The next thing is whether we can do this for the rest of you. In the meantime, I think we're both wondering a few things…" she casts off first to Relissa, then looks up at Thaelyn and raises her brow.

"Very well, Marelle," he accedes. "Do you wish to offer something?"

Marelle glances at Relissa for her opinion.

"Did you want to say something? Your history goes back a little longer."

"The only thing bouncing between my ears is our tree," she considers.

"Your tree?" Mynae wonders. "Are we speaking about another of these Trees of Life?"

"Aye, your people killed the one we had once."

"I don't know anything about that."

"Aye, I suppose so. Like he said, you're too young, and if no one tells you anything, I doubt you'll hold any answers. But we were friends before this, all of us."

"Do you know if we were under Sargeras's influence at the time?"

"I, um…well, actually… We think you were when we tried asking you about it, or at least it sure looked that way."

"And just for the sake of argument, what makes you think we did it?"

"We found a bottle with your markings on it. It must've held some kind of poison."

"Oh, all right, that probably would make a good enough indication."

"I'm still a little curious as to why you don't attack us," Marelle asks. "You say you have orders, but the question is why. There was a mention in a previous session about this weakness and pain, and the Night Elves may still have this, which suggests there might be an interest for Sargeras somewhere along the way. Does this apply to both of us? If we're speaking in terms of these trees, how would this apply to Rolsklinde, as we never had one?"

"I think I understand what you're asking, but I doubt I would have the answer to this. You would need to speak to someone much higher than me and likely a priest," she resumes her contemplation. "OH! Wait, I know of someone. She's easily old enough for this, and she's a senior-ranking priestess in our temple. Her name is Sehnisavain…the High Priestess Sehnisavain Deepglade. If anyone could answer these last few questions, it would be her."

"All right then," Thaelyn resumes. "From this moment, I think we have a new direction for ourselves. Mynae, I am going to have my people return you back to your cell for now. You were travelling with two others, and although you provided us with some valuable information, I must be thorough and interrogate them as well, just to see if they hold anything else."

"You probably won't get much out of Kethron. He's not much higher ranking than I am. Eilihel is a Curate, not especially high ranking, but she might know something. The trouble is, we were all stationed in a little outpost, too far outside the central workings, so I think none of us would be of much help, especially for the questions you gave."

"Very well, I will take that under advisement."

"And now, finally, can you tell me what you'll do with us, after all is said and done."

"I feel confident that we have a favorable end result here with your redemption. If your only true failing, that which caused you to turn over to Sargeras, is due to this loss you felt, and this loss is related to your tree, then we have a potential solution to correct this situation and redeem you back to our side. But four centuries, Mynae, is a long time. I would imagine most of you do not know of your true heritage, and as such, you will need to undergo a considerable amount of counseling and rehabilitation."

"Meaning, you're going to help us?"

"I will most certainly try. But let us take this in steps. I will need to introduce you to a number of people, priests to be sure, and other High Elves, who can refresh you on your proper manners."

"Other High Elves..." she contemplates. "We're speaking of your people now, right?"

"Indeed, we are the original source of your society, all of you on Therinë. Although, it is also a mystery to us how you did it."

"Uh huh. Well, for what it's worth..." she emits sarcastically. "How nice to meet you! I wish someone could've told us about this on that first day!" she huffs ironically.

"Yes," Thaelyn smiles. "It would seem we have a lack of communication occurring around us."

"All right, so I need to go back to school," she sighs. "Fine, at least this time I hope I'll learn who I really am."

Chapter 16

REVELATION

The end of the Order's second month of occupation in the Badlands is near at hand. Over the course of the last few days following the interrogation of the Flame Elf prisoners, scouting runs have been underway in the direction of the city of Kynesoth. This was proving to be a difficult operation, however. The city was their center of operations. Therefore, safety would take the priority to prevent the capture and potential torture of the spies for information.

General Gabarleine was advising the morning committee in the tactical office.

"Our early reports tell us of the local guard patrols and city defenses. This one is tough. The Flame Elves, being the magically gifted sort, seem to be periodically engaging in detection magic at random intervals within the city walls, leaving it nearly impossible for a cloaked spy to enter and maneuver about safely."

He directs the attention of the other members to a series of photos and a rough map.

"These were taken by a high-altitude gryphon scout using the Daanen-Aryku cameras. The drawing here is an interpretation of what we're seeing based on our own understanding of elven architecture. We can see here the placement of the gates, along with several buildings of strategic value, such as the barracks and a mage academy, as well as what appears to be a main temple structure."

He stands up from the table to continue his presentation.

"We know from our observations that the patrols are many and frequent. Sending a scout inside will likely be especially difficult, if not impossible, without detection. One possibility might be to use a disguise. If we employ some of our own High Elves, dress them in clothing like that of the Flame Elf captives, and send them in, it is much more likely they could pass by many of the patrols unnoticed, so long as they keep at a distance."

"This is good, General," Thaelyn remarks. "But our ultimate goal is to pull out one of their higher-ranking elders. This is not something that will likely go unnoticed. Judging from the security they maintain; it seems improbable that we could simply send someone in to drag them out by the heels or tossed over a shoulder. More than likely, we would need to infiltrate, and then escape by means of a rune. How does the security compare at nighttime?"

"At night, as you may expect, there is less civilian activity on the streets, but the guard patrols still seem to circulate on a regular basis. An intruder would not likely make it far without being noticed. I think if an unknown individual were to be seen walking along the street, it might actually stand out more if the general populace is supposed to be in bed."

"True. This situation is problematic. We need this information, assuming Sehnisavain has it, but how do we bring her out of there? This is our primary concern; she is too deep. Even if to simply abduct her, her disappearance becomes another issue. We need better access to her without the high security around her. I wonder if she ever goes outside."

"Unfortunately, my Lord, it may be impossible to tell. We do not know specifically which one she is, so as to follow her movements, and I feel she would not engage in any activities outside the city anyway. More likely, she directs others to do her bidding."

"Granted. Then we may have hit an impasse unless we can send a spy in under cover. But I would not wish that spy to remain long, if only to prevent discovery."

"My Lord, what if you could apply a meld with someone to teach the local tongue. We could then instruct them on the local manners so that they would not stand out as much. Then, with a bit of luck, they should be able to pass by any guards inside the city."

"This is an interesting thought. Let us consider this for a moment. We would wish to reduce the prospect of interaction as much as possible. Their priests are often very highly regarded, and seldom questioned. Eilihel was a priestess, so if we borrow from her gown and hood design, and have someone enter under a guise..."

"Yes, and they could go directly up to the temple with little question about it."

"Indeed, this would be a natural destination in their case."

"But then what?" the General muses. "They are inside, but as you said, they cannot simply abduct a well-known high priestess and carry her out, rune or otherwise, as the simple absence would stand out by itself. We will need an alibi, or a distraction to defer attention to ourselves."

"Yes. And perhaps if we affix ourselves with a means of entry, as well. Find a secluded room, like a storage room or a closet... somewhere they do not pass through regularly, and mark a rune for easier returns, in case we need to make multiple visits to find our mark and plan our movements."

"Very good, but this may require some time to investigate."

"Then this will be our plan. Select perhaps two High Elves, a mage and a priest of suitable rank. We will pair them up as a team and dress them in disguises. I think two priests would present themselves better than one lone individual wandering along the roadways. We can fashion some costumes for them, and Aerlie and I will conduct the melds. Although, I think one of the priests we had with us during the inquiry was a High Elf. Perhaps I could simply call on him again."

"Perfect, and then we need a means of infiltrating them into the local region. I think this should not be too difficult if we can find a secluded location and use a portal to drop them in position out in the woods. They can walk in from there."

"And they should carry a story of returning home for some special duty or service," Thaelyn adds. "Maybe we can consult with Eilihel for ideas on this. Then have them head for the temple and find a suitable location for a rune with all due haste."

"Excellent, my Lord, this sounds like a workable plan."

The morning review moves on to other topics until finally the meeting is dismissed. As Thaelyn leaves the building, he is greeted by a junior officer accompanying the three newly reformed High Elf internees.

"My Lord, the prisoners have arrived, by your request."

"Thank you, Lieutenant. I will see to them now."

Eilihel, Mynae, and Kethron each step up to Thaelyn to present themselves for his judgment. The three had been relocated to a detention facility in Bya'an Tamoranth, as much for the sake of convenience of access, as for the improved confidence over their security.

During this time, they had been spending many long hours in counsel in the city temple. This included debriefing them of any additional recollections they had, as well as their interactions with the Suuden-Aryku and orcs. A large part of their rehabilitation was simply to unload their emotional burdens and the fury they felt about their treatment by Sargeras, as well as to reconnect with their native traditions.

"Lord Thaelyn," Eilihel announces as she steps ahead of the group. "We offer ourselves, most humbly, to your distinguished appraisal. We have made all attempts to cooperate with your counselors and officers, providing whatever knowledge we have to share. Your priests have helped us find our true gods again, and they have allowed us to repent for our sins. Now, we simply await your final sanction so that we might know what future lays in store for us."

"How do you feel on this day, the three of you?"

"I think I can safely speak for all of us in this matter when I say we feel much more at peace with ourselves. Albeit we still hold a deep grudge against that fiend who caused us so much humiliation and suffering. Perhaps, with time and the guidance of our gods, we can eventually overcome this."

"If I may pardon myself to intrude," Mynae interrupts. "Eilihel is right in this, but she is also modest in her words, Your Lordship. I tend to be more outspoken and would like to make my own statement, if I may."

Thaelyn nods.

"While I know we still need time to heal, I would also very much like to have my honor restored. If there's one thing I've learned about your people on Tae'Eladar, it's the social manners you use, so I don't want this to be misinterpreted…but personally, I want revenge. Not just for myself, but for each of us here and all the others who have ever been violated by that monster."

"Mynae, I understand your grief, but we should take care to direct ourselves in the right form. Retribution, taken out of fury, is an improper form of retaliation. If taken by the rules of Justice, however, it can restore your honor while at the same time retaining the pureness of your spirit. Do you understand?"

"Yes, Your Lordship. And it's for this reason I wish I had a way of fulfilling this cause. But unfortunately, I feel stifled. I have the desire to serve, but there is no army for me to join in this war. And somehow, I doubt you would grant me to join in yours."

"There are steep requirements for joining my military, Mynae. I cannot be sure if you would qualify at this time. My first suggestion would be to take your time and heal. This war is far from over, and there will be time enough later for you to make your return."

"It will be hard, but I will try. Thank you."

"Lord Thaelyn," Eilihel continues. "May I ask what will become of us?"

"From this moment forward, and until further notice, depending on your progress within my keep, you shall become my wards. You will have the freedom to move about within the city of Bya'an Tamoranth, and you will be given fair access to its amenities and teachings. I would also encourage you to find some reasonable occupation for yourselves while you stay with us. Do you have any preferences?"

"I am at a loss to suggest what I would do," Eilihel admits. "I was described as a priestess before this, but now…"

"You can still study the priesthood if you like, although mine are also members of my Order. Perhaps, if you take up with my wife, Aerlie, she could help you find a place for yourself on a trial basis. As this war progresses, it may become possible for you to find your place once again amongst your own people, if we are able to liberate any more of them. The lessons you learn here could be useful to them."

Thaelyn turns next to Mynae. She is clearly showing signs of depression for her loss of self-respect.

"Mynae, relax. You will find yourself again and all will be brighter for you. Do you have any ideas for how you will proceed from here?"

"Your Lordship, I'm a mage. It was intended for warfare, but without a target to practice on, I'm not sure what good I'll serve to anyone."

"There are other uses for the arcane studies, Mynae. We use them not simply as a wartime tool, but to even greater purpose within our common society."

"Your common society? Meaning everyone?"

"It is a common study for all our citizens, at least to some degree or another depending on their choice of career."

"That sounds interesting, but also even more disparaging. In ours, the mage study is only for those of us who would specialize for the inherent value the Art provides in combat."

"This is how it was in our society once, long ago. But then I realized the value it could provide for the masses, and it has indeed provided those masses with tremendous value."

"Really! Maybe I should take a closer look at this. In the meantime, I also took some courses on herbal remedies and potions. Since I was thinking I'd be sent out to war, I thought it might be useful to be able to put something together out on the field."

"This is good! To be an herbalist is a useful profession. There is always a need for potions, both in civilian life as well as in times of war. You could serve well to that end, at least until you can find yourself an opportune moment to restore your honor. And now for you, Kethron," he continues with the pondering archer. "What are your thoughts?"

"As an archer, I was bred for war duty. As a woodsman, I was trained for scouting. Under the circumstances, I find that I may not be able to perform either of these services living and working within the city. So, I must fall to the one remaining skill I can be sure of. As one who would spend much of his time outdoors in the wood, I developed a fine play with a fletching knife. Mostly for my own use, mind you, creating arrows and such. Perhaps I could take up an apprenticeship in a workshop."

"Very nice, and we also tend to enchant many of ours, so perhaps you may find opportunity to learn a few additional skills along the way to meet the higher professional needs."

"Is this to say my craft might not be sufficient in your market?"

"Oh, do not feel that way. Your skills will surely find a good market. We have civilian sports and military training, both of which go through a large number of these."

"A sport? People use bows as a sport in your society?"

"Indeed, the sporting activities of archery are quite popular for many people. If you were to involve yourself with that, perhaps as a supplier, I think you will find yourself quite busy."

"Interesting...yes, this might give me a direction to focus on."

"Then I shall bid each of you to follow these goals for yourselves," Thaelyn asserts. "From time to time, I will monitor your progress. I would also have you report to your counselors on occasion for a periodic review."

"Thank you, Your Lordship," Eilihel replies with a bow. "I trust we will not disappoint you. Good day to you."

The three wards pay their respects, and then depart through the portal back to the city. Thaelyn sends the Lieutenant along to help them orient, communicating with them in the Elvish tongue until they can acclimate to the local culture.

As midday passes into early afternoon, Relissa and Marelle make their return to Firstfall and the tactical office to catch up on the daily events. Thaelyn reviews with them the map of Kynesoth and the delicate hopes of infiltrating a spy into the city, to say nothing of making a successful raid to kidnap Sehnisavain.

"Drat it all!" Relissa laments as she studies the diagram. "Sending a spy in there might be a fine one, and pulling her out with a rune might be good too, but how do you keep her quiet while you grab her and open it up?"

"This would present a cautious concern," Thaelyn relents. "We would need to incapacitate her somehow."

"That's a tricky one, my Lord. You might have been able to knock those three scouts flat on their backs out in the bush, but this here is dead center in the city, and I don't think you can use those pop crackers without someone noticing. Then, how do you keep them from noticing she's gone. I think someone will wonder where she ran off to if she was last seen in her office."

"This is another of our concerns. We will need a story of some kind to cover for ourselves. Do you have any suggestions? So far, our thoughts are to mark a rune inside somewhere for ease of access until we can find our target."

"That's fine by me. Quick in, quick out. But if it were me, I wouldn't want anyone to see me, even if I was in disguise. The fewer people to point fingers at, the better, in my book."

She peers down at the map of the city and considers the general area surrounding it.

"If only there could be a way to get the old girl out of there on her own. A bit like whistling for a dog, you know?" she lets out a slight giggle.

"Yes," Thaelyn admits. "But unfortunately, she already has a master. We need something else to attract her."

"Aye, but the thought hits me that if she is at least seen going for a walk, this can offer an excuse for where she disappeared to, rather than vanishing into a hole inside a building."

"Indeed, I must admit, this would offer a much more reasonable cause."

"Then, who knows what happens out there. Maybe she was abducted, but we don't want anyone pointing fingers at us."

Thaelyn frowns and pulls back from the table as he listens to this curious depiction.

"This is interesting, but then who is abducting her?"

Relissa turns her gaze up to him, initially stifled for her reaction, until her trademark quirky grin begins to form. Thaelyn studies her.

"Uh oh... General, do you see this? Her true colors are showing. We may need to watch this one."

"Indeed, my Lord," he grins. "And good gracious, just look at her. This must be her Morier side coming through," he chuckles.

"All right, Relissa, what do you have rumbling along?"

"Oh..." she muses innocently. "Nothing those peeps didn't play on us once or twice. We'll just turn things around on them. Let's break up their neat little alliance the same as they did us once. We'll say, oh, the orcs did it."

"Fascinating..." he muses. "And quite genius, actually. Our attacks on the orcs...yes!" he jerks forward again. "This is actually a fine example. They are not coming to the rescue of the orcs, so the orcs are turning coat on them out of spite for their isolation."

"Brilliant!" the General applauds. "But we still need the means to pull her out."

"Aye," Relissa considers. "This is the hard bit. What she needs is something to get inside her and bug her just enough to get up off her bum and start walking. It reminds me a bit like when I was over here and..."

Relissa halts her statement as a memory emerges into view. She then ponders the situation momentarily, with her eyes darting around as a thought materializes.

"Jiggers," she mumbles. "That would do it, if only... But it's too far away, I think. Blast! If the tree were older, maybe, but not like it is."

"What do you mean, Relissa?" Thaelyn inquires. "What are you thinking?"

"I...well, this one probably wouldn't work. It'd be great, maybe if the tree were older..."

"The tree?" he glances out the door. "How do you mean? Do not be afraid of telling me. Even if it does seem futile, we are open to ideas here, and perhaps those ideas can lead to others of a more practical nature."

"Well, if you say so. I was thinking of that day I heard the tree calling to me. It got so deep inside of me that I couldn't ignore it. The thing of it is the tree is too young to reach that far. I don't think it'd work."

Thaelyn ponders the thought for a moment before responding to it.

"Relissa, it may be that you have just given us yet another of your gems of wisdom."

Thaelyn turns around to the door and calls for Captain Hagmaert. As the Captain enters, he is given instructions to summon the druidic high priestess to the meeting. A few moments later, the priestess enters the room.

"Priestess Rumoren," Thaelyn begins. "A thought has been presented into our discussion that could use your perspective. Our goal is to somehow attract a temple priestess from the Flame Elf city of Kynesoth, which is a good two-and-a-half-day march to the south of us. We are hoping to cause her to simply walk out of the city as an excuse for her disappearance, later to blame this on orcs abducting her outside their walls."

"Oh!" she smiles. "Are we playing a little game of espionage now?"

"Absolutely! And naturally, we must apply the credit to the inventor of this scheme..." he points at Relissa.

"Yes, I should've expected as much from a Morier," she smiles.

"Ay!" Relissa yips. "It takes talent to come up with these things."

"Furthermore," Thaelyn continues. "We must also divert attention away from us. But it is unlikely for her to come out of her own free will. Therefore, she must be driven out forcefully. Relissa has reminded us of her experience with the tree on that day of our arrival, and how it called to her."

"Yes, I remember this. That was quite a reaction, too."

"Good, but now, can such a thing be made possible from this distance with our quarry?"

"My first thoughts are the tree is still quite young. If it were fully grown and mature, I would say it might be possible, maybe with a little help."

"That's what I was afraid of," Relissa acquiesces.

"Wait, let me think a moment. It would need...but as it is..."

The priestess considers the prospect a bit longer, and then raises a finger to draw the attention.

"Maybe... Yes, I think we could actually do this, but it would require the aid of a large circle of druids empowering the tree to extend its reach. The call would not be strong, but it might be enough, if made over the course of days, to drive one to follow it."

"How long do you need to prepare for this?" Thaelyn inquires urgently.

"Give me the remainder of this day to gather my people. It will be difficult, and we will need to perform this chant day and night to see it through to the end. I will also need to assemble a lot of replacements to relieve those who become weary."

"Make it so, priestess! This may be our best chance."

"My Lord, in order to find our mark, I will need the name of the one we are calling."

"Her name is Sehnisavain Deepglade."

The priestess makes a bow and leaves the room, hurriedly rushing across to the tree to consult with the other priests. A flurry of activity ensues within the group. One of them returns back to the city to call out more members, bringing another dozen shortly thereafter, with even more appearing as the day progressed. By the end of the day, the area around the tree was swarming with druids.

The mass divided itself into sections, with part of it moving off into a reserve pool. These would be used to fill in for others as they come out to rest. Those who stayed within the circle would make up the first shift. They aligned themselves and took up seating around the tree to begin a steady harmonious chant.

Relissa was excited about the contribution she made, so she added the news to the general report she sent off to her mother on the activity to summon the Flame Elf priestess for interrogation. The prospects of drawing her in to the camp were exhilarating, but also a bit unsettling. It was one thing to capture and detain a group of lesser-ranking recruits, but one of their elders, one who might hold a high rank and close relationship to Sargeras, could be dangerous.

To prepare for this, they made plans to augment their scouting patrols to the south. They would also establish several watch points at fixed locations to offer an early warning system if they should see anything coming out of Kynesoth.

Night falls and the next day dawns, and the chanting in the circle continues. Life in Firstfall goes on as usual. As people arrived to occupy the new construction, the settlement had become rather busy. What was once a military camp had now grown to resemble a small, heavily garrisoned village. Merchants conducted their trades with the occupying soldiers, as well as other townspeople who were managing the new taverns and workshops.

The farmers from the northern fields, mostly settlers from Rolsklinde, would make occasional visits to purchase tools and supplies for building their new homes, as well as to patron some of the local establishments. Their relationship with the people of Tae'Eladar, which began on a trial basis out of necessity for food and materials, was steadily improving.

The morning meeting convened and adjourned without incident. The war with the orcs was progressing well, with the front having advanced another two hundred miles during the previous month. The cautious pace against what was becoming an increasingly frightened and skittish opponent was a primary focus of attention for the officers in the tactical office. The successes against the orcs, combined with the lack of support they were receiving from their alleged allies, had them on the run.

Relissa's note from the previous day had been delivered early in the morning to Solinaia. She, along with Marelle, were just arriving in Firstfall when a carriage was sighted racing down from the north.

The carriage, which was led by two graceful white horses, charged across the valley, and came to an abrupt halt at the north gate by the guard post. As the guards were preparing to let it through, an excessively agitated Elvish noblewoman jumps out and commands the guards to step out of her way as she scurries through the gate and into the camp.

"Your Grace!" she hollers. "Where are you? I must speak with you immediately!"

Thaelyn had been inside the tactical office with Relissa and Marelle at the time of Amariyn's arrival. When her shouts rang out across the camp, he hurried outside to see about the commotion.

"Your Grace! Do you have any idea what you're doing?"

"Excuse me, Lady Amariyn, you have me at a disadvantage. At the moment, I thought I was conducting a war."

"That's not what I'm talking about! It's that heretic, Sehnisavain! You're trying to summon her here...to this camp of yours!"

"Do you know this woman?"

"Indeed, yes!" she shrieks. "She's the one..."

Amariyn ceases her outburst sharply to take note of her manners and withdraws. She struggles to recompose herself before continuing.

"My apologies... Old feelings are hard to resolve. We both go back to a time before the war. Those of us who are of age remember those times, you see."

"I fully understand, but did you forget our earlier meeting about those scouts we picked up?"

"I did not," she takes a deep breath to settle herself. "But this one predates the war, and I am quite sure she holds relevance in it. The younger ones may be innocent of any immediate wrongdoing, but this example is another thing. I do not trust her. I don't care when, where, or how Sargeras came into it, something had to open the door, and if she's still around, that lends enough suspicion to ask what role she actually played. Remember, someone had to kill our tree, and it carried the High Elf signature to it. Even if every other person in that city down there is dead and buried, and replaced by a younger generation, SHE still remains. So, I hope you will have a sufficient amount of security here waiting for her arrival."

"Do not concern yourself, Lady Amariyn, I have the situation well in-hand. We have scouts lining the path all the way up here serving as watch posts. If anything other than this one woman is seen moving this way, we will be ready for it. We will also have a full contingent of troops lining the camp."

"All right, I will try to settle myself, and I will apologize again for my outburst."

"It is quite alright as I am sure the stresses of these past centuries were great."

"Um, Your Grace, under the circumstances, I would very much desire to be a part of this occasion. I would wish to oversee her arrival myself. With our related history together, I would find it most interesting to hear what she has to say for herself."

"Very well, I will see to it that you are notified before she is set to arrive here. As I said, we have scouts lined up from here to the southern highlands where the city of Kynesoth can be seen. As we follow her approach, I will send updates to you on her progress."

"Thank you, Your Grace, and please excuse my interruption. It was just such a shock to see that name mentioned in Relissa's note. I should take my leave now. I shall await your word on her arrival with some amount of...pessimism."

Amariyn gives a polite bow and returns back to her carriage. She takes another deep breath and closes her eyes briefly, then gives the instruction to return home.

Thaelyn looks at Relissa, who can only shrug.

"Don't look at me, my Lord," she comments. "I've never seen her so upset like that before."

"This suggests a previous association of some sort," he muses. "Was it not said the two elven societies were partners at one time?"

"Aye, but bloody hell if I know what crawled up her skirt."

"Perhaps we will learn more when they meet."

Thaelyn directs the group back inside to continue the review of the day's reports. The remainder of the day passes with no further interruptions.

Another day has passed, and a third one is dawning. The chanting has not stopped since that first evening. On occasion, priests from the circle will rotate out to be replaced by fresh members from the reserve pool. The chanting has remained at a constant pace and amplitude.

The morning meeting is midway through when a scout arrives through a portal from the furthermost position to the south.

"My Lord! News from the far reach, Watch-Point Four! A sighting! We have spotted what appear to be three figures coming out from the city. They are moving to the north, in our direction."

"Three? We are only expecting one. What are these three about?"

"Best estimates make it as three women. At range, using scopes, they look to be wearing priestly attire, where one of them seems rather ornamental."

"I hope that one is our goal, but as for the other two... How long before they arrive?"

"At the rate they're travelling, I would put it at two days from now, unless they continue through the night."

"Good, that gives us time to prepare. Return to your post and keep watch for anything else to come out of that city."

The scout makes a salute and leaves through another portal.

"My Lord," the General considers. "If my understanding is correct in this matter, the tree should be calling to only one of those women. I must wonder why the other two are involved, and whether they may also be under the spell of the tree. Could it be that they are simply following along under the suspicion of foul play that draws the first one out?"

"A good point, General. We should ask the druids about this. Is the high priestess available out there?"

The General looks out the door at the assembly of druids. He directs Captain Hagmaert to fetch the high priestess, who is currently sitting in a group, resting. Thaelyn calls to her as she enters the room.

"Priestess Rumoren, a sighting has been made by the first watch-point outside the city. Three women are coming this way. We believe one of them may be our mark, but the other two are a surprise to us. Can you explain this?"

"No, my Lord, this is a surprise to me as well, unless they are somehow bound to the first one. Perhaps the spirit saw they could not be easily separated and is spreading its call to all three."

"We need to ensure our position of security here. One was a sizable risk, but three is excessive. I need you to make sure the other two are under the spell of the spirit call. In addition, you should see about intensifying the call as they get closer, to completely overwhelm them. By the time they enter the valley, I want their full focus of mind on reaching the tree for purification, shutting out any of these so-called songs of Sargeras."

"Yes, my Lord, I'll see to it."

The priestess hurries off to conduct her work while Thaelyn and the others continue their morning report. As midday arrives, Relissa and Marelle return from their study to receive their own instruction. Relissa is advised to send word to her mother in Solinaia on the sighting, and the estimation of time it may take for the women to arrive.

By late afternoon, a second scout comes in with an update on the priestesses' progress. They appear to be moving at a steady, albeit sluggish rate, and have passed Watch-Point Three along the path to Kynesoth, progressing into the hills on the other side of the valley. Captain Hagmaert begins organizing troops to station themselves within the settlement, ready to deploy when Sehnisavain arrives. And the druids increased their chanting slightly to enforce their command over the inbound women's minds.

As the day comes to a close, the support troops settle themselves for the evening. Thaelyn and his officers, along with Relissa and Marelle, sit around their traditional campsite, which had recently been updated and set under a tent with proper seating and a large andiron. The evening meal was complete, and now they were engaged in some light conversation. The sun had set, and the stars were shining brightly.

"My Lord!" shouts a cry from yet another scout arriving through a portal. "I bring word from Watch-Point Two. Three females in priest's cladding have passed our waypoint moving north. They do not appear to be stopping for the eve, and we expect them to enter the valley proper before first light."

"They seem determined, which may be to our advantage. If they do not stop to rest, they will be quite weary by the morrow. How do they appear out there?"

"They were moving along slowly, stumbling over rocks and gullies in the hills."

"The two extras, do they appear to be following the call, or simply following the first to watch over her?"

"All I can say with certainty is the three are clinging to each other for support, and they bear the appearance of weakness and fatigue. They seem to be moving along with a stubborn purpose."

"This is actually pleasing to hear. Their motivation may be externally driven, and weakness suggests they will be less of a threat when they arrive. Very good, you may return to your post."

"Your Lordship," Marelle submits. "Although I'm unsure how I feel about them personally, I hope they manage to arrive safely without falling somewhere along the way. That would not serve us well for their information."

"Agreed, fatigue might serve us on the issue of security, but it can also cause accidents. Fortunately, the terrain between us is not especially dangerous. We will see what the morning brings."

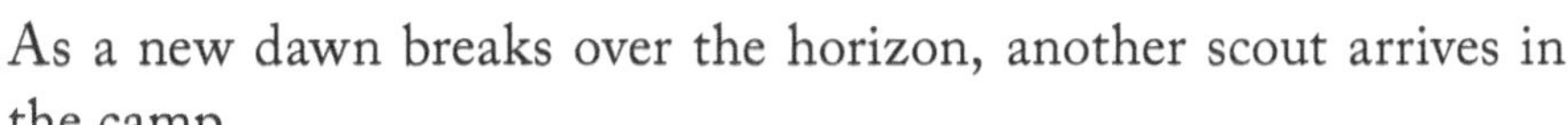

As a new dawn breaks over the horizon, another scout arrives in the camp.

"My Lord, I come with a report from Watch-Point One."

Thaelyn was just finishing his breakfast at the time of the interruption.

"What do we have?"

"The three women are inside the valley, but they've stopped and are seemingly going in circles at the far end. We can also hear what sounds like bickering, although we can't be sure of the words from such a distance."

"Uh oh, he is fighting us! Quickly, I want you to return to your watch post. Bring additional support with you from the camp. I want fresh reports every half-hour from your station."

The scout salutes and moves to collect more men to take back with him.

Thaelyn puts down the remains of his meal and rushes out to find Priestess Rumoren.

"Priestess! We have a problem. He is fighting our call. They are at the far end of the valley turning to-and-fro. We need more emphasis in the song. Raise them up, Child! We cannot let him take them back!"

She nods vigorously and goes over to encourage more energy in the chant. The choir elevates their voices and begins a swaying motion, raising their hands to the tree and around in circles over the ground.

Thaelyn observes the activity for a short while. When he is satisfied that there is nothing more he can do for now, he returns to his meal before setting to his duties.

The morning routine begins with sending a message out to Amariyn on the expected arrival of the trio of priestesses later in the day. The meeting in the tactical office progressed in its usual manner, with the exception of the intermittent arrivals of scouts from the first watch post. With each update, Thaelyn issued modified instructions to the druids in the circle. The women were on their way again, but it was becoming a game of tug-of-war with Sehnisavain and the other two in the middle.

Amariyn arrived in the camp shortly after the noontime hour. The druids in the circle were now a boisterous chorale, side-stepping and swinging their arms in wide circles. The scouts were reporting

Sehnisavain and her attendants to be roughly three miles away and plodding along slowly. The guards at the south gate kept a watchful eye for the first sighting from across the fields and wooded glens.

Another hour passes. Aerlie had been summoned from the city to join Thaelyn and await the arrival. A short time later, Relissa and Marelle entered through the portal. They were greeted by a cacophony of chanting rising up from the circle and echoing around the settlement.

"My Lord!" Relissa shouts to be heard over the commotion. "What's the news here?"

"They are close!" he answers back. "Just over a mile away…"

"But what's with all the bleedin' ruckus?"

"He is fighting our call. We need to make our song louder than his."

"Gods be blessed, does this mean he knows what we're doing?"

"He may not know exactly what is occurring, but he surely knows Sehnisavain is not where she is supposed to be. He has been trying to call her back all day."

"Can you see anything out there yet?" Marelle asks.

"Not as yet. There are too many trees in our line of sight. Perhaps another several minutes and we may have a sighting at range."

The druids in the circle had grown in number. Many of the reserve members had joined in to add additional power to the chant. The circle around the tree was a crowded mass of waving hands and prancing bodies. Finally, a call comes out from the south gate.

"A sighting, my Lord!" shouts a guard. "Three of them! They're coming through a yon grove of trees and into the clear."

"Aerlie, can you see them?" Thaelyn asks anxiously.

Aerlie positions herself for a better view.

"Yes, I see them. Goodness, they look like zombies!"

"Show me what you see."

"Certainly, share my eyes with me."

Thaelyn projects himself into Aerlie's mind to share her sight. Marelle looks on, recalling that day with the little demonstration by Captain Hagmaert.

"Powers pay pity," he moans. "They look as though they have not rested for many days."

"Thaelyn," Aerlie calls back to him. "See how they move, lurching and shuddering along. He must still be trying to call them back."

Thaelyn pulls himself back to his own mind. He goes up to the circle and begins an inspirational lead to heighten the vigor of the chant.

"Sing, my Children! Pour your hearts into it! Raise your voices to the sky and let the Almighty themselves dance to your music!"

Those who were still sitting on the side had moved over to the circle to add their voices into the song. By this time, there were nearly a hundred druids crowding around the tree.

Sehnisavain could be seen clearly now. She was slogging her way across a field in open view of the settlement, along with her two cohorts. Their motion seemed mechanical, unconscious and deliberate. Their bodies jerked, their joints being pulled first to one side, then to another. Their heads turned and twisted at odd angles while their eyes remained fixed on one solitary point ahead of them. They were like marionettes being directed by a warped puppet master.

The guards within the camp take up their positions, forming a solid wall on either side of a narrow corridor leading from the south gate up to the edge of the tree circle. They lined up in full tactical formation, with soldiers in front and mages behind them, and with their weapons held in a ceremonial salute.

Gradually, Sehnisavain and her companions came closer, soon to be within proximity of the gate entrance. Thaelyn continues his supportive arousal of the song, with the druids shouting their words in the direction of the arriving guests. The dance sways in a rhythmic pattern to the lyrics.

> *Valmaer a tulit mensina (Lost one come this way)*
> *Tel' fëa yalarë na, a hlara a'he (The Spirit is calling,*
> *hear her)*
> *A tulit a'he, a vilit a'he (Come to her, fly to her)*
> *A tulit a'he, a vilit a'he (Come to her, fly to her)*

A estit ar nauva envinyanta (Rest yourself and be healed)
Na lindauvárë tulyatas tel'menta (Let her song lead the
way)

The druids in the dance open their hands to the sky, swinging them down around the form of the tree, then over in the direction of the inbound priestesses, making a come-hither motion, bouncing forward on their knees. They finish with a fluttering of their hands inward to the circle, rising up into the tree again.

Amariyn was fascinated by the power of the chant and strained to catch a glimpse of the approaching elves. She tried moving to peer around the rows of soldiers as the three women passed through the gate, settling into a convenient place near the edge of the circle looking straight down the corridor. There she witnessed an elder pale-skinned elf, her face was a macabre mask of spellbound agony. Her fair skin was made paler from the stress and loss of sleep, with prominent bags under her eyes. Her lips were dry, and her long locks of ash blonde hair were matted and ragged.

"Oh, dear Sehnisavain," Amariyn mutters somberly. "What have the years done to you?"

The two other women appeared younger, with a similarly pale and ragged appearance, and matted ash blonde hair. Both of them are clutching the elder in the center, supporting her as they move along, and dragging their feet on the ground with stiff joints and pained steps.

They cross the settlement grounds, coursing their way through the corridor of soldiers, oblivious to their surroundings. Their eyes continue to focus on the object of their purpose, the tree. All other sensations are vacant to them. The song of the druids has completely obliterated their cognitive awareness.

With only a few more steps, they cross the threshold of the tree's fenced-off circle, where a section of the fencing had been removed for their ease of passage. The powerful aura of the circle, further amplified through the duration of the chant, penetrated the soles of their shoes, and blasted into their bodies, sending a wrenching wave of holy energies pulsing through them. All three crumble to the ground, letting out a ghastly wail.

Amariyn reels back from the grim display, gasping and covering her mouth. She shakes her head reflexively in disbelief that this woman she once knew had fallen so far.

The druids press on with the song. Sehnisavain and the others begin to claw their way forward, dragging themselves along the ground, digging their fingernails into the soil and heaving ahead. A partition forms in the chorus as the druids make way for the elves to pass through. Slowly, the elves encroach upon the base of the tree, each movement showing as a monumental struggle for the three exhausted women.

The tree is coming barely within their reach. They make one more desperate lurch upward and stretch their arms out towards it. Their hands tremble as they extend to their fullest length, barely allowing the tips of their fingers to curl around the trunk. With their mouths agape and their eyes bulging, they take one last gasping breath, freeze their motion, and then collapse into a deep unconsciousness. With this, the chanting stops, and the druids come to rest.

Thaelyn lets out a sigh as he collects his thoughts.

"Beware the strength of the Order, Sargeras," he whispers with a contented grin. "We are a force unlike any you would have ever encountered before. You had better start looking over your shoulder, for I will one day be there behind you."

+ + + ◆ + + +

"General," Thaelyn begins as he convenes a special afternoon meeting in the tactical office. "Regardless of whether or not the Flame Elves would respond to the disappearance of the scouting patrol, they will most surely take notice of this action and have something to say about it. So far, there is nothing coming out of the city, much to our benefit. Therefore, we will need to put a lid on this quickly using our own spies."

"I agree, my Lord. I would also suggest increasing our patrols to the south, as well as to the east, in case they elicit aid from the Suuden-Aryku, assuming the Suuden-Aryku would come to their aid at all in this matter."

"Yes, but I would propose one alteration to our usual methods," Thaelyn suggests. "If it turns out that we can consistently drive out Sargeras's influence from their minds, thus turning them back to our side…in a manner of speaking, to redeem them…then I would wish to give this a priority over the classic methods of wartime conquest. We should use non-lethal methods whenever possible and bring them back here to the tree for purification. Perhaps this could serve to our own benefit later, either for intelligence gathering or otherwise."

"Of course, my Lord, I would agree."

"Your Grace," Amariyn begs. "My apologies, but this issue of language can be a bit troublesome."

"Of course, Lady Amariyn, I wish we could offer a more convenient solution, but so far, our options are limited. What do you need?"

"Yes… I am wondering what you have in mind for those three out there, now that you have them, and apparently in such a state."

"Naturally, we will need to interrogate them, as we have a number of concerns that need to be addressed. And so far, our information suggests this one may be our best hope to find our answers."

"I…cannot be so sure, but you should know that I have a few of my own that need to be fulfilled. At the very least, we need an explanation of their actions where our tree is concerned."

"I fully understand this. When I asked this of those scouts, none of them knew what a Tree of Life was, much less that any were killed."

"Not even know what it is?" she urges. "How can that possibly be?"

"I must assume they were born into a world without one in their immediate vicinity."

"That's preposterous! They have one in their city! How could they…" she halts her statement as the realization comes to her. "No tree?"

"Yes, we learned some rather interesting details during our interview. We believe they did not go willingly. Furthermore, they apparently lost a good portion of their history, and likely due to it simply being erased…destroyed…to deny them anything to otherwise contradict Sargeras and his songs.”

“That sounds despicable!”

“Despicable, yes, but it does make sense if you want to take control of them. You remove their existing identity and replace it with your own. For instance, Mynae described Sargeras and these songs of his entering her mind perhaps at her third decade or so, forcefully and persistently. They essentially took over, a form of mind control.”

“Mind control…” she winces. “And is this why they joined the others?”

“Yes, but this occurred the full four centuries ago, not the three and a half with the official arrival of the Suuden-Aryku.”

“So, it was back in the beginning, like you suggested. But was this before or after our tree was killed? That’s the one I would like to know. If he was already inside there,” she pauses solemnly. “Then, I suppose I may have to excuse it. But if SHE was the one who opened this up…”

“We will see about it, but I would wish to proceed in an orderly manner. So far, we seem to be pointing at some sort of covert operation that corrupted the peace you once had. According to Mynae, this apparently invoked a sensation of loss and pain for them, and this likely paved the way for Sargeras to take his possessions. I was able to finally redeem them by bringing a dryad into the room for a healing touch. They were completely different people afterwards.”

“Such a thing can be done? I know the power of the Spirits can be strong, but…”

“In my tenure on Tae’Eladar, they have likely become even stronger, as we have embellished their presence, and thus allowed them to grow somewhat.”

“Amazing… But then, how do we explain our tree? We found a High Elf bottle next to it. And then, we have these past four centuries of so much death and destruction! How do we account for all of this if there is truly no one to blame here?”

“I fully understand, and I am no less appalled by it. My personal belief is that Sargeras was in control from the beginning, and they were little more than puppets being driven by these songs of his telling them what to do. This follows as a classic example of what he represents, according to the old stories we have of the Primordials. Small creatures like we are simple playthings to them."

"Unbelievable!" she wheezes. "And so incredibly intolerable! That such a creature can feel himself so capable to come in and simply have his way with anything he pleases."

Amariyn finds herself in a tizzy as she tries to reconcile four hundred years of rage and misery all misplaced to the wrong culprits. Relissa steps over to comfort her, putting an arm around her and offering a firm hug.

"He's right, Mum," she affirms. "I was there, I saw it. That girl was a flaming witch when we first let her open her mouth. Then the dryad came in and she was tame as a kitten."

"Relissa, I'm sorry. We had such a long history together, all these years and with so much deep suffering. Very well, I will contain myself and make a more objective review when she comes back around."

"Your Lordship," Marelle wonders. "Two things... First, what about those other two who are with her, do we know anything about them?"

"Unfortunately, no," he responds. "Although I have a suspicion based on their appearance and what Priestess Rumoren said that they may be bound to Sehnisavain. They appear young, so it could be they are related."

"All right, I suppose that's reasonable. Next... What do you suggest doing with them after all this is over? I know you put those other three to work in the city, but Sehnisavain, on the other hand, is probably more like a high-ranking official to them. I doubt you'd want to put her to work in an alchemist's lab."

"No, surely not, but she would certainly find good use in a number of other areas. Helping us to redeem others, perhaps to find ways into that city down there for additional covert operations, maybe to inform us on the Suuden-Aryku, or even...hmm, yes. If we are hoping to plant spies down there, I wonder if we can use her to assist with some of our own misinformation."

"Oh, that's simply nasty…and I love it," she smiles.

"My Lord," Relissa interjects. "With all this talk about mind control, how can we be sure they stay with us and not go back to Sargeras again?"

"This is a curious one, but for now, if we are right and it is related to the loss of their trees, this offers its own solution. Simply reconnect them and ensure it stays that way."

"Aye, sure enough…and keep them away from anything else he touches."

"Indeed! And for this, I might further wish to simply remove them from his potential reach, maybe to take them to Tae'Eladar for safe keeping until we can find some other solution for them."

The day moves into its late hours. Dusk is approaching. The three women had been sleeping most of the afternoon. A watchful assembly of druids had been tending to them during this time, observing and waiting for the first sign of movement. Then, one of the younger priestesses begins to stir. Her motion is accompanied by a gentle moaning. The disturbance spreads to the others and they too begin to wake up.

The first girl pushes herself up groggily into a sidelong recline, while the other one props herself onto her knees, trying to brush the hair out of her face. Neither of them is fully able to open their eyes to see the world around them at first.

Sehnisavain rolls over and pulls herself to a seated posture. She tries shaking her head to dislodge the debris from her hair and face, and then lifts a hand up to brush it away, only to see her hand is covered in grime. As she rubs her hands to remove the dirt, she takes notice of the many people standing around her. The two girls, now able to see through the haze, also observe the large crowd of strange people gathered nearby.

A soldier charges up to Thaelyn, who had been resting in the officers' tent with some of the others from the meeting they had earlier.

"My Lord, they're awake!" he reports urgently.

"Excellent. That took a bit longer than expected, but maybe it was due to their exhaustion."

Thaelyn makes a quick assessment of his objectives before continuing.

"All right, listen up. I wish to make an initial survey of their minds and cognitive status before we launch into any serious questioning. In order to spare them any excessive shock and confusion with too many sights at one time, I will have most of you stand behind some of the soldiers to conceal you. We shall reveal ourselves in a cautious sequence as we bring them forward in our discussions."

The others in the room all nod as they leave the tent.

The reclining girl looks up at the camp full of people. She turns her gaze over her shoulder to see a group of oddly dressed men and women in tribal attire. Their skin was noticeably darker than hers, and their clothes included tree bark, vines, and feathers. Many also had tattoo drawings on their faces and arms. Frightened and unsure what to make of this, she instinctively moves closer to Sehnisavain.

"Mother," she mumbles with an alarmed tremor. "Who are all these people? And where are we?"

The other girl cautiously passes her glance around the gathering, feeling similarly vulnerable. But with nowhere to go, she stays on her knees trying to pull the last few strands of hair out of her face while keeping a careful eye on the group.

Sehnisavain looks around her, finally able to see through the mats of hair. She observes a large number of humans amongst the rows of soldiers in brightly shining armor. She studies the tan-skinned elves, and a host of others of various colors, many of whom were dressed in either mage or priestly robes.

To her left, through the crowd, comes a deep, authoritative voice.

"Do I have the pleasure of speaking with Sehnisavain Deepglade?"

She turns to follow the sound of the address. The two younger ladies also turn to see who is speaking. They notice a tall man with flowing silvery-white hair and golden eyes.

"I am she, the High Priestess Sehnisavain Deepglade," she returns calmly. "To whom do I have the pleasure of speaking?"

"For the present moment, and for reasons of security, I must restrict myself on certain topics. This is a military camp, and we are in a state of war. Therefore, we must maintain a cautious approach."

"Are you saying we wandered into this camp and offended you somehow? I don't even recall how I could be here in the first place."

She looks around the area, trying to gain her bearings, then stands up for a better look over the heads of the troops. She catches a glimpse of the settlement and a lush valley around her, but the sight is entirely alien to her.

"Where are we? I don't even recognize this place."

"This region is known locally as the Badlands."

"The Badlands?!" she yelps. "This cannot be the Badlands, that region is a desolate waste. How could this be the Badlands? Where did this village come from, and all these trees..." she looks down at her feet, "...and this grass...and the soft soil...and...and..."

Her voice trails off as she begins to notice a very distinct and nearly forgotten sensation ushering up from below. She puzzles at the point of origin, but then finds herself being drawn around in an about-face towards the tree. She stares at it for a long moment, trying to interpret the significance, and then it hits her.

"Blessings of the Seldarine! A sapling!" she exclaims in a hushed tone. "A blessed sapling...and so young! Where did this come from? I thought they were all gone!"

Thaelyn glances over his shoulder at a row of soldiers behind him, and behind them were Amariyn and Aerlie, both of whom were in hiding and appearing very bemused by the reaction. He returns to their guests.

"I am sure there are many things we must discuss, Priestess, but for now if you could just come this way and step outside the circle..."

"Oh, but of course. My deepest apologies, but I'll tell you, I truly have no memory of how I came to this place. To be honest, I have not travelled through here for nearly as long as I can recall."

"Then this would be something of a surprise to you, to see it this way?"

"A surprise?" she yips. "Dear Sir, this is more than any simple surprise. We have heard a few stories in recent times..." her voice suddenly cuts off as a memory resurfaces causing her to halt in her steps. "Oh dear...you're those invaders, aren't you?"

"Indeed, we are," he smiles gently. "This way, please," he gestures for emphasis to a position outside the circle in front of him.

Sehnisavain makes her way forward towards the small fence.

"Come, my daughters," she instructs. "We should move..."

She again halts as another memory resurfaces. She turns to each of the younger women.

"Daughters..." she mumbles distantly. "I have two daughters."

"Mother, what are you talking about?" responds one girl. "You don't remember us now?"

"My apologies, Tyshalis, perhaps it is simply the confusion of waking up in this place. Everything inside is spinning, and my entire body aches for some reason. I think I might be ill or something."

"We were walking a long distance," the other one submits. "I remember something about walking."

"Rhyvanith, if we found ourselves up here in the Badlands, I would dare say you may be right. But gracious me, that would be a long walk, especially for one of my years."

Thaelyn offers a helping hand as they continued over the fence to present themselves.

"Again, my humblest apologies," Sehnisavain emits. "But can you tell us what happened, and how we came to be here? And furthermore, as I'm beginning to remember a few things now, what do you have in mind for us? If you're those invaders I recall hearing about, by your manners so far, you seem to be acting unexpectedly polite."

"Why thank you," he smiles. "I do so enjoy surprising my guests. These moments are a precious commodity for me. Perhaps if we could begin with an introduction of these two young ladies of yours?"

"Oh, yes. These are my two daughters. The eldest is Tyshalis, and the younger is Rhyvanith."

"A pleasant greeting to you…" he bows his head.

"But now, as to what happened that brought us here?" she begs.

"Of course, but I will ask you to contain yourself during this time as we move forward. You may not necessarily like some of what we have to say."

"Very well, at least you are affording me this caution."

"First, it is important to know we have essentially, ehm, kidnapped you from your home, with apologies."

"Oh, you are apologizing for kidnapping us," she chuckles faintly. "That is certainly a new perspective. And why did you kidnap us?"

"Well, other than for the pleasure of this meeting, which I must admit is indeed a fine occasion, it is quite simply because you are a high-ranking official within your city, and we need information. It is believed you might hold this, and for this reason we needed to carry a little conversation with you. But your city is a difficult one to gain access to, therefore…" he gestures to the tree and the assembly of druids.

Sehnisavain turned to survey the tree again, along with the gathering of people, both inside and outside the circle.

"But how did we actually arrive here?"

"You walked, as this young lady mentioned. These druids, along with our tree, sent a call to draw you to us."

"A call…by such a young tree and at such distance… But why?"

Her memories were now coming more fully into focus, recalling who she is, her position of authority, and the reasoning behind the earlier mention of a war. A strong upwelling of emotions begins to stir within her.

"Oh dear Protector!" she moans tensely. "What have we done?!"

Her voice trembles as she begins to weep. She covers her face and doubles over sobbing.

"Mother?" Tyshalis stoops to observe the elder woman.

Rhyvanith also comes to inspect their mother as the woman wails openly.

"Four hundred years!" she howls. "The greater portion of my life! How dare he! Such a waste…so many years lost."

Tyshalis and Rhyvanith gazed vacantly at each other, unaware of the meaning as they were both born into it.

"Mother," Tyshalis begs. "What is it? What are you talking about?"

"I'm talking about HIM, Child!" she screeches at the girl. "That scourge that robbed us away from our true gods! Oh, such a pity that you do not even know the meaning of it."

Thaelyn once again glanced around at Amariyn for her impression. He could see her face as she was clearly affected by the display.

"Priestess," he continues. "We must try to contain ourselves…"

"Contain, nothing!" she screams. "That monster stole our very lives away from us! Can you even begin to imagine the indignity of this? And so many of our people!"

"In fact, I believe I can. I have learned a few things during my time here. This is why you are in this camp as part of our investigation, so we can understand how deep it travels and find a way to correct it."

"Correct it?! Do you honestly know what you're talking about? How can you possibly hope to correct for four centuries of his domination. Most of our people do not even know what really occurred, like these two," she gestures at the two younger women. "All they understand is what he delivered into them during this time. We were not even permitted to carry any of our traditional history or culture!"

"This might be expected. But I must still ask for containment so we can discover how these events came to pass in the first place, and then see about some form of redemption."

"Redemption?!" she screeches. "For us? Are you mad? I would imagine every other member of this world would want us dead by this time, not that I would actually blame them," her voice trails off and she turns away.

"Priestess," he offers calmingly. "If you would kindly slow

yourself, we will discuss these issues, and I will explain what I have in mind."

"Explain…" she mutters wistfully. "I am sorry, but what can you possibly offer. You are a stranger in this world, and now it seems you have inherited some part of its woes."

"Perhaps, but I accept these woes willingly, and hold the intention of correcting them."

"So, you think you can correct for this somehow. Very well, let us suppose that you can. How do you think you can correct for this?"

"First, I will direct you to a rather obvious demonstration."

"An obvious demonstration? My apologies, but I think I am lost in your meaning."

"The one you just now woke up from."

"Huh?" she puzzles as she examines herself and recalls the tree behind her. "Wait, just how do you mean that?"

"Perhaps your mind is still a bit muddled. You, personally, have been redeemed, as are these two who are standing next to you. And we are responsible, along with our tree."

Sehnisavain blinks emphatically and draws back from the assertion, now realizing she was apparently no longer under the dominating effect of Sargeras, as was also the case with her two daughters. She studies them carefully.

"How is it possible?" she asks. "His songs were insidious, persisting day and night until even the strongest among us could no longer resist. Then, finally, the last of us fell."

"I would describe this as a form of telepathic domination. But in order for him to do so, he would have to break you in some way in order to weaken your resolve."

"Right, I remember it now. We were in a terrible state after the death of our tree," she pauses to recall her memories and gazes once again at the sapling. "Yes, we used to have a tree like this in our fair city. It was actually a fully mature grove…are you familiar with such a thing? But then again…" she ponders briefly. "If you know of these trees at all, then I must assume you are aware of the ancient elven traditions."

"Indeed, they are an integral part of our modern-day culture on Tae'Eladar."

"Tae'Eladar? Is that the name of the place you come from?"

"You do not recognize the name?"

"I…well, um, with apologies, am I supposed to?"

"Perhaps you are not as familiar with the name of the world, but rather one particular continent…Sein'amar."

Sehnisavain studied him for only a short moment before the memory of that word returned to her.

"Grace of the Gods! Are you part of the Tel'Quessir? But wait, no…you do not look elven…more like a human."

"Indeed, we are many people on Tae'Eladar in the modern day, and the Tel'Quessir are an important part of it."

"An important part? Only part? Who are the others? You have humans, of course," she reviews the rows of soldiers for reference. "I recall that much."

"Humans, dwarves, gnomes, and also halflings…"

"Gnomes! I recall that name from our ancient history. And in the modern day, you have come together in some way?"

"We are a large nation on that world now, all of us."

"Gracious! Times do change. I only wish ours could be as promising."

"Yes, we seem to have found you in a rather poor state over here, but let us proceed to how we can help. I have a need to ask a series of questions."

"Very well, I recall you mentioned this was supposed to be some kind of investigation. But if I may, I would like to know what you will do with us afterward."

"My thoughts are to give you rehabilitation and allow you to reacquaint yourselves with your proper gods. But this is simply a starting point. Perhaps you can also help us help more of you."

"So, you would actually wish to assist us return to our gods? That is a rather extraordinary gesture, especially if you consider our history in this world. Are you actually familiar with our history, and what my people have done during this time?"

"I am familiar with many stories, but I am also discovering a number of inconsistencies in a few of them. Let us begin, and see what we can uncover together."

"Inconsistencies! All right, I will try as best as I can to help, if the reward is to help my people return to our old gods. What do you wish from me?"

"First, we have several important concerns relating to our war effort. Although I am sure some of us may have a few personal issues, my first duty must be to this war."

"Right, you look like a military leader, so this much I would expect."

"You are probably aware of our campaign against the orcs by now, correct?"

"Oh, yes, we are," she rolls her eyes. "We were informed of your arrival almost as soon as you set all the blazes of the abyss down in this valley."

"I see…" he chuckles. "Very well, I suppose I should be expecting that, considering the circumstances. Who was it that informed you, the Suuden-Aryku?"

"That, and also our own scouts who saw, and in some cases heard, the commotion. But amongst the Suuden'kai forces, our contact is one named High Commander Geilv. He is the leader of their military force. He may contact us occasionally through a device he calls a trans-com, or else send one of his officers to deliver instructions and materials."

"Interesting… Suuden'kai? Do you speak their language?"

"I do, as part of my…participation…in their efforts."

"Of course. And thank you for the name, in case I should come into contact with him."

"He is a very cold-mannered individual. Not at all charming."

"I will remember that. And I suppose you speak to him in their language?"

"Yes. I was made to learn their language, as were a couple of my close attendants to aid me."

"Very good. Now, relating to the orcs, we are asking why you and the others do not seem to be coming to their aid. My armies are laying into them rather heavily, but there is no apparent response from the rest of the forces here."

"My instructions say the Suuden-Aryku are shedding them off. They apparently served their value and are no longer necessary. I think I also heard mention once by one of his officers something about punishing them for drawing your attention to us."

"Oh, how unfortunate..." he chortles. "They invade my world, make trouble for my citizens, and YOU are upset for the commotion left behind that brought me here."

"Yes, I understand your meaning. I was not the one to send them there, but your pursuit of them here to our world has a few people concerned for your interference in our local affairs."

"Ah, interference...this is interesting. What am I interfering with? I am fighting a war against orcs, who are said to be enemies with at least some of the residents of this world, and I am interfering with something?"

"Yes, I suppose the suggestion carries a certain level of contradiction, but you should also know those orcs did not arrive there by accident. They were sent there on a mission."

Thaelyn glares at the woman and subtly cocks his head. He glances around casually to find Relissa and Marelle in the rows behind him, along with Aerlie and others, before returning to the conversation.

"I suspected they were sent for a purpose, but a mission?" he intones warily. "What mission?"

"I don't know the specific details, as the Suuden-Aryku tend to be very tightlipped, only revealing what we need to know at any given moment. What I do know is they were sent to find something, some sort of path he is following."

"A path that leads to Tae'Eladar? Are they planning on invading us?"

"Specifically that? I think not, actually. They were sent to look for something, and we received word a while back that they apparently found it. We were then called upon to deliver some manner of device into an ancient portal structure."

"A device…into an ancient portal… Hmm, what manner of device? Did they give you a name, or can you offer a description?"

"I can tell you it was given to us by the Suuden-Aryku. I think it was said they would use this to help them find where this portal leads."

"That sounds like some manner of tracking device…" he muses.

Thaelyn briskly turns to scan the assemblage of people for help.

"Lieutenant Lapäli, come forward please."

The tall officer steps out of the ranks into view. Sehnisavain gazes at him as he approaches.

"Interesting," she mumbles quietly. "You look like more of the same…except for that unsightly growth."

Thaelyn glances at the woman briefly before returning to the Daanen'kai officer.

"Do you know what she might be referring to, in this case?" he asks.

"It sounds like she is describing some form of beacon transmitter," he responds. "This would then allow them to locate the exit point and send a ship to investigate."

"But if this is not Tae'Eladar, where could it be, as there cannot be too many options after that."

He pauses to consider this a moment before continuing.

"Clearly, we will need to investigate this more, maybe to try to locate that portal and see for ourselves. How long ago was this?"

"I cannot be precisely sure by now," Sehnisavain responds. "But I think it was several decades ago."

"That gives them a fair amount of time to conduct themselves," he muses gravely. "And this would coincide with the beginnings of our troubles on Tae'Eladar. Very well, we have one correlation to add into the puzzle. Onto the next matter… The orcs seem to be in possession of substantial quantities of iron and materials I would not normally expect them to hold. We have a suspicion they are receiving this from the Suuden-Aryku, but worse is where the actual source may be. Are you aware of anything?"

"I am aware we also receive occasional supplies of iron, delivered to us by the Suuden-Aryku in our city. My impression is they have a local operation somewhere. Generally speaking, it's not our place to question such matters. They supply us, and this is all we should concern ourselves about."

"All right, another instance of the control of information. We are seeing several examples of this here. Since we are speaking of resources, we should also touch on the issue of adamantium. We saw this on a rogue Suuden'kai patrol and also with one of your spies that came through here."

"Yes, I know of the spy, and although I was the one to send it, I hope you will also understand, I was under his influence at the time, and with instruction by the Suuden-Aryku. I did not truly have my own right mind until I woke up here under this tree just now."

"I understand your misery, and I will not hold this against you, as I know a few things about telepathic domination. On a side note, however, this also confirms an unfortunate suspicion we have up here with a few of our other dilemmas."

"Which ones are those?"

"This one relates to who may have initially ordered it."

"You don't think it was the Suuden-Aryku proper?"

"Actually, no. If to use adamantium armor, this should run outside their personal knowledge for any sort of application. Also, if to consider the alternative choices they ought to have, a simple assassin should be beneath them."

"How interesting…to describe an assassin as something simple."

"With respect, in this case, it does not fit with their historical manners. Their native weaponry would be more than sufficient."

"I see. So, they spend one of us on some folly instead of using their own."

"Indeed. But as for the adamantium, the troubling part here is where it comes from. I do not feel the Suuden-Aryku would normally be in possession of this material as it would not likely be found on their home world. Can you offer anything?"

"I have heard they have a supply somewhere, but the question of where is apparently kept a secret. Although, this also makes me wonder why you would think they should not have their own."

"It is my understanding, based on my talks with the Daanen-Aryku, who are part of the same race, that they should not have it on their home world, and not know how to use it at all. They seem to be completely ignorant of the principles of magic, and you need this much to understand any part of it."

"Ah, all right, I understand."

"But all things considered, having a secret supplier does not actually surprise me now. Next, do you know who it may have been to craft those items? Was it you, perhaps?"

"I think none of our people hold these skills. This material is not known to exist in this world, at least not to my understanding, the same as another metal to which I'm familiar, called mithril. Neither of these was ever found by us here."

"Elves are not normally known to hold such tendencies as to conduct any extensive mining."

"No, we do not. And as I recall it, the human population was never adept enough in this art to learn anything, either."

"Very well, then neither of you ever found any, if only due to the reason you do not hold the proper skills for it."

"I think this would be a fair reasoning."

"This is a bit disturbing, as we also know of a band of dwarves to the north that seems to be offering trade to Rolsklinde for iron. I wonder if they hold any connection."

"Dwarves? Here?"

Thaelyn pauses to stare at her again. He then turns to Marelle for her impression. She simply furrows her brow inquisitively.

"Is this to say, you are not aware of these dwarves?" he resumes.

"This is the first I ever heard of them here."

"Here…" he raises his brow. "Did you know of them elsewhere?"

"Yes, I know of them mostly by reference. Right about the

beginning of this horrid affair with Sargeras, we were given instructions to assist with an invasion of a world said to be occupied by dwarves. This was apparently a follow-up to an earlier invasion where they tried using orcs."

"Great cu'Nar..." Padriyl moans. "I didn't need to hear that."

"Did I hear him address you as a Lieutenant?"

"Yes Ma'am, my name is Lieutenant Padriyl Lapäli of the Daanen-Aryku Sentinels."

"Very good, Lieutenant, but I regret to inform you he had those orcs for a much longer period than your attack on Ruuki uy'Daan. My impression is those orcs were sent perhaps five centuries ago to try taking that world, but it would seem they failed. Then he used us, after he apparently found this world."

"Priestess, I thank you for this, but we also have some information on those orcs from our side. Apparently, many thousands of years ago, someone sent a migration of them to his world," he points at Thaelyn. "So, this tells us he owned them for a very long time."

"Indeed!" she yips. "Well now, isn't that something. It would seem that monster has been busy in this time."

"And with a lot of it spent chasing us all over the place," he sighs.

"Easy now, Lieutenant," Thaelyn soothes. "Dear Powers, for all the tensions we are unraveling during this interview. Priestess, how long was this new assault of yours?"

"The campaign with our people lasted for several years before it came to a close."

"What was the reason for the invasion, and then what was the result?"

"The reason, I believe, is the Suuden-Aryku had an interest in that world. They helped by transporting our people on large vessels that lifted away to the sky. But we never saw them returned to us. It was said the war was a bloody one and we were called again and again to send more of our people. Between that, and the losses we suffered here from all we did, we are now down to the last of us in Kynesoth."

"Fascinating...and also disturbing. And as for the result?"

"I don't know. They stopped calling on us after a while. I never received word on their result."

"But this offers a potential link, as dwarves are regarded as masters over such metals as mithril and adamantium. Surely, if you found such a world, I might suspect these metals to be found there as well."

"And you say you found some of them here?"

"Yes, in an enclave in the mountains north of Rolsklinde. It is said they opened up trade relations four centuries ago at the start of the war, selling iron to Rolsklinde."

"They sound like a very enterprising group, but my first knowledge of dwarves was this mention of the invasion. If we are seeing them here, I must ask how they arrived. To my knowledge, we have been here for thousands of years, and there were never any dwarves before this."

"This does offer us a few intriguing new mysteries. Especially if you consider the iron Rolsklinde is supposed to be getting, but it is not, and rather you and the orcs seem to be getting more of it. And then, those dwarves do not seem to behave in a normal manner, instead as if they are under a control effect of some kind."

"Oh, no! You can't mean another like what he did to us!"

"It might be using a different method, but ultimately, it could be related."

"Protector, help us all."

"I suppose this now carries us to the next part. Why do you not actually attack the city of Rolsklinde? It is said you are supposed to be enemies, and between you and the others, you laid waste to virtually everything else out there, both human and Night Elf. Why leave these last two cities untouched?"

"As to Rolsklinde, our orders were to leave them be. They are apparently being supervised by someone, and we are not to attack them."

"What?!" shouts a voice behind the lines.

Marelle jumps into view of the interrogation.

"What do you mean by supervised?" she screeches.

"Gently now, Marelle," Thaelyn cautions.

"I'm sorry, Your Lordship, but this suddenly steams my cooker to a boil. It's bad enough for all the Governor and the Dean are doing to us, and then listening to the part about the dwarves got me simmering, but now this here…"

Sehnisavain studies the irate young woman standing in front of her.

"Are you part of their Allegiance Guard?" she asks calmly. "I believe I recognize the uniform, if only barely."

"Yes, and my apologies, as I know you're also suffering from a lot of bunk, but this demands an answer. Someone is watching us and ordering you NOT to attack us? For how long?"

"This seems to be the case, and for as long as I can recall it."

"For as long as you can recall…bloody hell, I hate that term. But how long is that, actually?"

"Well, actually, I believe this has been our instruction since the beginning. It would need to date back to when he first took us and began issuing his directions."

"Blast! That bastard!" she fumes.

"Take ease, Marelle," Thaelyn asserts. "Let us follow our procedure here. We will find our answers, do not worry about that."

"Right, and again, I'm sorry. But our dear beloved Governor is representing himself as a crook for a lot of things he's doing out here. Now to hear we're being managed by someone just puts the cap on the stein for me."

"I would agree, and all the more reason to pay close attention to him in the future."

"And what about us?" Relissa shouts as she also comes into view.

Sehnisavain takes one look at the young dark elf and instantly spurns the presentation.

"Yes, as for you…" she replies with a distinct loathing. "We might have suffered with four centuries of his tortuous domination, but YOU…I would actually adore watching your kind behold a taste of it. He's keeping you on the side for something special, I'm fairly sure of that!"

"Jiggers and more jiggers," Relissa retorts. "First because he wants us to join up in his bleedin' army, and second because I haven't seen so much flaming hate coming out of a person in all my life. What did we do to you?"

"Indeed! And furthermore, such manners, coming from a youngling like you. Where did you learn this, I wonder?"

"All right, you don't need to rub it in. I got this from enough of my own, and all because of YOU peeps flaming the place for four centuries. It makes a person ask why we bother with anything."

Sehnisavain pauses to study the girl before relenting from the debate.

"Very well, I will retract my argument for this topic, as I have my own miseries where these two are concerned," she directs at her two daughters. "But you ask what you did to us?" she begins to shout. "Would you like to know what your blasphemous people did to us, young Morier? Then I'll tell you! You killed our tree!" she screams.

Relissa's jaw instantly dropped, and her eyes popped wide open. Thaelyn also turned a stern glare at the statement. He jerked around to find Aerlie just as Amariyn was marching out.

Sehnisavain's view quickly turned to see the elder Night Elf make her approach, and before Amariyn had a chance to speak, the infuriated priestess was launching another volley.

"And here she is!" she spews with turbulent disdain. "The one and only, Amariyn… I should've known she would be lurking nearby in the shadows. It goes so nicely with her skin!"

"Sehnisavain!" she barks. "What in the names of our gods are you talking about? Just when I was about to invite you to my home for tea, you go and assault my daughter for some blasphemy?!"

"Oh! Blasphemy, is it? And in the name of YOUR gods, no less. Those gods you claim to adore so much would see you burn for those words!"

Aerlie had joined at Thaelyn's side by this time to examine the situation.

"Priestess Sehnisavain," she interjects. "Calm yourself, please! Rather than make all these accusations and heretical statements, perhaps you could tell us what actually happened?"

"And who are you?" she scorns as she examines the unusual figure. "You look like one of the Winged Folk."

"Indeed, I am. Do you have an issue with that?"

"Um, well, not personally. That is, if you come from Sein'amar…"

"Right. I'm called Lady Aerlie, and I am the Matron Pontifex of our temple network back home."

"A Matron Pontifex?" she ponders curiously. "I'm not even sure what that title means."

"Granted, we had to invent the position. It's an office that presides over the entire religious authority of our world."

"Everything?" she hesitates more guardedly.

"Yes. I also happen to be his wife and Queen," she asserts with a sturdy thumb-point at Thaelyn.

Sehnisavain's demeanor suddenly falters as she attempts to assess the meaning. She looks up tentatively into Thaelyn's golden eyes.

"You're married to him…a human?"

"Humans and elves sometimes do this in our world, although the two of us are special in a few ways."

"Uh huh, and you said queen… Meaning to say, he is a king?" she asks cautiously.

"Yes. We rule over the entire world of Tae'Eladar."

"The entire world?" she raises her brow beguilingly.

"All of it! We did what no one else in our world ever bothered to do…unite the whole thing into one body. This was actually the original purpose of Tae'Eledar, according to the goddess who owns it, at least until we elves, and the others, accidentally intruded in places we were previously unwelcome to be. It was a human world before that."

"Uh oh… So, the Tel'Quessir, by entering into that space, violated something? Oops! And now, here you are. But that would be a rather daunting effort, would it not?"

"It was! He spent three-quarters of a millennium on it. I came somewhat later."

"Three-quarters of a millennium?!" she gasps disbelievingly. "But how is that possible?" she turns to Thaelyn. "You look human, and I was not aware they lived that long."

"My similarities are only skin deep," he affirms. "I am actually something of a hybrid form with a much greater longevity, and part of that same plan by that same goddess to resolve those same woes we had once."

"Oh dear! She must have been very determined with this project of hers!"

"Indeed. Now, what is this about your tree, because from what I am observing here, I suspect whatever it is you are thinking is NOT what actually occurred."

"And why would you suspect that? Were you present at the time?"

"While I cannot say I was present at the time your tree was killed, I am aware that she..." he thumbs at Amariyn, "...was present at the time THEIR tree was killed. Now the question becomes, who killed that one."

Sehnisavain rolls her eyes to follow his direction. She frowns again in contemplation of the suggestion.

"Are you now trying to say we killed your tree?"

"We found a High Elf bottle in our grove, Sehnisavain," Amariyn states smoothly. "Who in this world makes those?"

Now Sehnisavain's mouth falls open as she begins to connect the dots.

Amariyn continues, "And this simply begs the question of why you think we did it to yours."

"We found a Night Elf bottle in ours," she replies subtly.

"Powers pay pity!" Thaelyn blasts. "How contemptuous! And this occurred four centuries ago? No wonder you went to war, and when neither of you is truly responsible for anything."

"But why..." Sehnisavain responds meekly. "How could this happen to us."

"Can you explain your experience?" Aerlie asks.

"I was a young priestess attending to the shrine in our city. One night I heard these horrible screams coming up from the grove. I went out to see what was happening, and found they were dying, shriveling up right before my eyes. It was the most painful sight I could ever behold."

"This is exactly what happened to us," Amariyn reflects solemnly. "And I was there."

"And I believe this gives us our answer," Thaelyn affirms. "At least as far as these trees are concerned and this alleged pain the High Elves were subjected to that allowed Sargeras to enter their minds."

"Those flaming bamboozlers," Relissa groans. "So, they came here four centuries ago, tried breaking us by dusting all the trees, and then snagged the High Elves. But why didn't they take us? I mean, we felt the same. Didn't he want us back then? Not that I would want him to take us, but, um, you know."

"You apparently held strong whereas we did not," Sehnisavain considers. "I guess we fell too far."

"And then," Amariyn reflects. "Everything you did after that was due to him inside your heads...maybe to say coercing you to follow his will?"

"Yes, precisely, coercing would be the word for it. We certainly didn't ask for it. We found ourselves driven to obey, and the Suuden-Aryku were the ones to give us our instructions."

"The Suuden-Aryku gave the instructions?" Thaelyn wonders. "Not Sargeras?"

"Sargeras motivates us with his songs, pushing us to follow along, but it's the Suuden-Aryku who govern most of our physical actions."

"How curious. Then, what is this mention I have heard from others about punishing you for disobeying?"

"Punishing? Where did you hear that?"

"We captured a small patrol south of your city not long ago, where at least one member mentioned something about the priests threatening punishment to the lessers if they did not behave themselves appropriately."

"Oh, that..." she ponders a moment. "Wait...a lost patrol, I heard about that. You did it? Where are they? Are they alright?"

"Yes, we redeemed them as well, and they are currently undergoing rehabilitation back home on Tae'Eladar."

"Then I should thank you for your kindness. Yes, these are essentially fear tactics ordered by that…creature…that seems to lead this military force that invaded our world, and they're intended to keep our younger generations in line to follow their orders. The younger ones tend to be more ambitious, and therefore, need restraint."

"Indeed, at least some small part of you still shines through even in such times as these."

"I remember when I first heard his songs," Tyshalis reminisces. "They started nagging at me. I couldn't concentrate on anything after that."

"Me too," Rhyvanith adds. "Even in my sleep… I would stay awake at night, wrapped in my blanket, wishing it would go away. It was so creepy, like someone you can't see whispering in your ear."

"You dear young Child," Amariyn mourns.

"What about that plague we have up in the city?" Marelle wonders.

"What plague?" Sehnisavain inquires.

"You know, that one we call the Withering Death."

"I don't know that name. What is it?"

Thaelyn once again sends a curious glare at the priestess, and on this occasion altering his posture to lean forward slightly. His arms, which were crossed before this, now drop to his sides. The alteration of his demeanor is noticed by virtually everyone in view.

"Oh great…" Marelle moans and shakes her head.

"I'm at a loss here…" Sehnisavain continues, realizing something vital is missing in the dialog. "You are saying you have a plague up there, and I'm going to guess at this moment, by everyone's reaction, that we are somehow implicated?"

"Marelle," Thaelyn asserts. "Describe for us again what this plague is about and where you think it came from. For this, we should recall Acolyte Sarens and what he said."

"Right," she nods. "First, it's described as a curse by the Flame Elves, and probably for as long as the war itself."

"What are the symptoms?" Sehnisavain asks.

"Headaches, then memory loss, and finally death, all usually in less than a month, and it only hits people fifty and above, give or take a few years."

"And you say it's a curse left by our people?"

"Not left by... It's a continual thing...still going, with no exceptions to who gets it."

"That's absolutely preposterous!" she screeches. "I would know if we were levying any sort of curse, and we don't do curses! Who tells you this rubbish?"

"Our Governor..." Marelle responds casually. "The same guy with the exclusive trade deal with the dwarves for all the iron we never get, and who apparently keeps our Guard patrols safe in Daanen-Aryku territory against Suuden-Aryku raids, and the rest of us boxed up inside our walls with stories of so many bad things out here."

"Really! And the rest of you actually listen to this?"

"Oh, but of course we do," she asserts ironically. "Along with all the stories of unholy rites you elves seem to be performing on a daily basis, and the...strange things...these unfortunate Daanen-Aryku are supposed to be conducting on their side," she glances at Padriyl. "It's all hand fed to us by the Dean of our academy, who by the way controls our education system a little like how Sargeras controlled all of you," she shrugs innocently. "And this also seems to include the loss of our old history, things like who we are and where we came from, along with who all our friends are supposed to be, so we can now accuse them of so much guff."

Sehnisavain held silent a moment as she pieced the image together.

"Yes, all right, I see it now. And this ultimately leads us up to your Governor. So, he must be the one overseeing your city. But I thought your city was governed by a Council."

"I don't personally know about that. It's always been a Governor from what I ever learned of it."

"These are indeed some dire accusations," Thaelyn accedes. "But justice will demand some form of evidence before we can move on it. Now that we are aware of this, we should try to move forward and find that evidence so we can take this proper action."

"Yeah," Marelle reflects. "And this would explain that assassin, and probably also that one Suuden-Aryku patrol."

"Indeed, I suspect it would," Thaelyn admits. "If he is in league with them, he might have received a report of some kind about Guard members out there."

"And what? Did he order the attack, or simply let them do it? If the Guard wasn't supposed to be out there, meaning to say he didn't order it, this was a message to…well, us, I guess, not to play the hero."

"And especially if they were using adamantium. This had to be a demonstration."

"What do you mean, Your Grace?" Sehnisavain wonders.

"A rogue Suuden-Aryku patrol dressed in adamantium armor and using swords, which is very unusual for their methods. We had some of our people out there in disguise as the Allegiance Guard, to offer cover for our early efforts. This rogue team came in and attacked our people directly. If it were a typical Guard deployment, they likely would have been shredded by the assault. But our people use the same materials, and are much better trained for this sort of combat, so we defeated them instead."

"The same materials? You have adamantium also?"

"My dear Priestess, did you not take notice of my soldiers here?" he waves his hand at the line-up.

Sehnisavain turned to examine the rows of soldiers in their glimmering armor. She follows the line all around the settlement, where many clusters of troops were standing in formation during the time of the interrogation.

"Dear Protector!" she gasps. "All of this?"

"Indeed, my full army, in one form or another, depending on profession, uses adamantium armor, and often mithril weapons and shields."

"And mithril?!" she shrieks. "Dearest, dearest Protector! You must be an exceptionally wealthy King to afford all this!"

"We are a prosperous people who have worked hard for our prestige. And I am not one to cut short the clear utility of this metal.

I suppose we could also say the issue of wealth is subjective, when you own the entire world," he smiles.

"Oh, but of course," she chuckles softly. "That would surely stand out. If only we could be so fortunate. We had a few precious pieces in our collection once, but now they are gone. It was such a terrible shame when we found them stolen from us, they were so vitally important to our religion."

"What?" Thaelyn mutters impulsively.

"Huh?" Marelle blurts spontaneously.

"Jiggers!" Relissa mumbles under her breath.

Amariyn stood there lost in a moment of thought, but it rolled around only once to find its nook.

"YOU LOST THEM?!" she screams abruptly.

The full assembly jumps, and then jerks around to stare at the elder Night Elf whose face was flushing with rage.

"It's not my fault, Amariyn," Sehnisavain pleads. "They were gone when I went to bring them out for our service after the tree was killed."

"Huh?" Thaelyn wheezes candidly.

"What?" Marelle murmurs bluntly.

"And more jiggers," Relissa mumbles again.

Aerlie was the only one among them holding her reaction, but she certainly shared the sensations Thaelyn and the others were feeling, both through her telepathic link with her husband, and her subtle empathic senses picking up from the rest.

"Amariyn, Sehnisavain…one moment!" she interjects sternly while raising her hand. "What is this about something stolen? And when did it actually occur?"

The two elven women glanced at Aerlie for a moment, and then it began to dawn on them for the timing of the event.

"We had four mithril holy symbols," Sehnisavain begins. "Our two societies shared them on a regular basis, trading them between the cities. We had them in Kynesoth when all this began. When our tree was killed, the people were in a near panic. It was unconscionable to think anyone would dare offend the sacred grove like this. So, I thought maybe I could bring some solace by offering these symbols in mass prayer. But when I went to the altar, they were gone."

"Were they there the night before?"

"Yes, I am sure of it, which is why I believe they were stolen from us. No one saw anything."

"What did you do after that?"

"Well, I recall speaking to several of the priests. We were all in great turmoil, but we decided, for the benefit of the people, that we should probably not let it out publicly until we could investigate further. Unfortunately, it got out anyway, and this brought even more horror to us."

"A compounding effect!" Thaelyn muses.

"And even MORE jiggers!" Relissa rants. "They got a double hit! That's why they went down."

"Worse than that, Relissa," Marelle intones cautiously. "These were mithril artifacts, the only known examples in this world. And where have we heard of a set of mithril artifacts in recent history?"

Relissa gawks at her friend at the suggestion.

"And double-bugger jiggers!" she screeches as she clamps her hands on her temples. "The mage academy!"

"And the Dean!" Marelle scowls.

"All right, wait," Thaelyn advises. "Before we come to any impromptu conclusions, let us make a test of this. Relissa, go to B.T. and find Haran…and also Acolyte Sarens. The two of them have been spending time together as apprentices, in large part due to the Acolyte's lack of proficiency in the local language. Order them to join us here, but do not tell them what this is about. I need their unknowing for this test."

"Right, I'll be back quick as a lick."

She rushes off to the gateway and jumps through to the guildhall.

"Now, as for the rest of you," Thaelyn asserts. "I wish to play this out in a specific manner, as with an interrogation. Sehnisavain, I will have you stand here in front. Amariyn, please move off to the side a bit. Aerlie and Marelle, kindly join her. When these two men come through, I will begin with a series of questions, and I wish to keep the answers short and precise, in order to ensure the integrity of our result. Sehnisavain, which of these four symbols did you have in your possession, and why only four?"

"These were all that we had left with us after our long journey," she mentions. "I am aware of stories where others were lost somewhere along the way."

"Very well, and which symbols were they?"

"Are you familiar with the elven gods, Your Grace?"

"More than you might think."

Marelle feels a compulsive giggle ushering up as she reflects on the implications of that statement. Thaelyn notices this and reaches out to pat her shoulder to help her regain her composure.

"Well," Sehnisavain recalls. "The first was in the shape of a crescent moon and represented the symbol of the Protector. The next one was a full moon with a halo around it, symbolizing the Lady of Dreams. The third one was a grand oak tree, the symbol of the Leaflord. And the last one we had was a heart of gold, for the goddess we call Lady Goldheart."

"Most excellent, I know them well. I am also noticing you still use the ancestral names for those gods. We have come a bit forward since then. Now, we will use this as a lure to see what sort of fish come to bite."

"Excuse me, but what do you mean by that?"

"I have two men in my employ that have essentially defected away from the academy up in Rolsklinde. They both claim to have seen mithril artifacts in the possession of the Dean. I want to see if there is any recognition while at the same time not directly giving away the details."

"This is a curious method, but as you wish."

They take up their positions and wait for Relissa to return with the two men. Several moments later, the three of them come into view through the portal.

"Ah, Haran! Acolyte Sarens! So nice of you to join us."

"My Lord!" Haran shouts as he rushes over to join the rest. "Is there something wrong? Relissa said you had an urgent need, and ordered the two of us to meet with you.”

“Indeed, but I think I do not need to tell you there is much afoul in this world.”

“Granted, but what is it you need from us?”

Haran and Willit both join by Thaelyn’s side. They take notice of the large assembly of people scattered all around, but their eyes settle on the three blonde-haired elves standing in front and reel back from it.

“Gracious! Are those Flame Elves?”

“Former Flame Elves, at this moment.”

“Former? I heard about this bit with the tree. Did it work?”

“It did, although it was a difficult affair to see it through. And we have been experiencing a rather curious conversation. I was just about to go into a new segment, and felt I needed a few extra witnesses for the occasion.”

Haran glares at Thaelyn, and then pans his view around the assembly of what could easily be hundreds of people standing in close proximity to the group.

“Really!” he smirks. “And we’re so privileged that you held the entire affair just for us?”

“But of course!” Thaelyn admits jovially. “After all, I feel you are an important member of our team. You were here with us when we first arrived, we shared a meal or two together, and we even slept by the same campfire. Is this not what good friends are for?” he finishes with a grin.

Both men stared at him, and then looked at each other.

“Um, my Lord,” Haran hesitates. “I get the distinct impression you are playing some sort of game with us.”

“Game or not, I still need your participation. I will have you stand just to the side here as I begin with our next series of questions.”

“All right...” he accedes warily.

Thaelyn now turns to the Priestess to begin this new sequence.

“Priestess Sehnisavain, now that we are more appropriately assembled, I should wish to ask you about this event you experienced.

You said you once had a number of holy symbols in your possession within your temple, is this correct?"

"Yes, it is."

"And how many are we speaking of?"

"There were four in all, Your Grace."

"Did they carry any distinguishing marks that one could easily identify them?"

"Actually, yes, they were all quite unique."

"Let us consider the first one, then. How did it appear?"

"The first of these was in the shape of a crescent moon."

"And which symbol did this represent?"

"This is the symbol of the Protector."

"In other words, if we translate to the elven pantheon of gods, we are speaking of Corellon Larethian."

"Gracious, you even know their names?"

"Indeed, I have a bit of experience with this. What about the second symbol, how did that one appear?"

"That one was in the shape of a full moon with a halo circling it."

"And it represented which god in this case?"

"A goddess, actually… We call her the Lady of Dreams."

"The goddess Sehanine Moonbow…yes, of course."

Haran and Willit both listened. Although the names meant nothing to them, the descriptions held meaning.

"Uh oh…" Haran mutters under his breath.

"Uh oh?" Willit retorts softly. "Is that all you can say?"

Thaelyn continued his session, ignoring their reactions for now.

"Now, the third symbol, how did this one appear?"

"As a grand oak tree…" she replies.

"That sounds like a fine one, and who was this for?"

"This was the symbol of the Leaflord."

"Ah, but of course, how silly of me… Rillifane Rallathil!"

"Yeah," Haran asserts softly. "Uh oh… He is playing a game on us. I'm starting to recognize his style."

"But on us?" Willit considers. "Are you sure? This is more like an 'oops' than an 'uh oh'. You know what those are, don't you?"

"Yes, and the reason why we're here, I'll bet."

Thaelyn glanced at the two of them as they carried their exchange, but he kept silent for any sort of reply, instead to continue with the last part of his inquiry.

"And lastly, Priestess Sehnisavain, the fourth and final of your artifacts, how did it appear?"

"It was in the form of a heart of gold."

"How lovely… And this represented…?" he raises his brow expectantly.

"This was the symbol of Lady Goldheart."

"Indeed, the Elven goddess known as Hanali Celanil, I believe. And where were these being kept the last time you saw them?"

"They were highly revered and kept on a special altar within our temple in Kynesoth."

"Very good, but now, to help us understand the timing of these last known to be in your possession, when did you first notice them missing?"

"On the day when our sacred Tree of Life was killed…"

"What?!" Haran yelps. "You had a Tree of Life?"

"Of course," she responds flatly. "Each of the elven cities did… all of us, both the High Elves and the Night Elves. It was a common feature. And these artifacts were passed between us regularly to share in their worship, as they were the only remaining links to our ancestors and their religion."

"And your tree was killed…when?"

"Four centuries ago."

"Gracious…" he mutters. "My Lord, what is going on here?"

"Ask her," he points at Sehnisavain.

"Oh, thank you…" he moans sarcastically.

Haran passes his gaze between the two of them, and then returns to the Priestess.

"Um, Priestess, what were these things made of?"

"A metal that is believed not to exist in this world, one called mithril. Have you ever heard of it?"

"Dear Madam," he relents humbly. "I think the answer is probably obvious by now. Yes, we've both seen these items in the possession of Dean Malorn in the mage academy up in Rolsklinde."

"Haran!" Amariyn steps forward. "Do you know how they came to be up there?"

"I only know that they came into our possession a long time ago. It's said to be on the order of centuries, maybe before the war. And given what Relissa and Marelle have brought back to me in their reports, I'm very suspicious for the timing."

"Worse than that, Haran," Marelle adds. "She says her people are under orders NOT to attack us at all because we have someone on the inside managing us."

"You're kidding! Who, do we know?"

"More than likely the Governor at this point, which could explain many of our problems by now."

"Yes, it would, actually, and so appropriate, to be sure."

"She also mentioned something about us having a council at one time. Do you know anything about this from your studies in there?"

"No, not a thing. But this sounds like a takeover now."

"Eh, Haran, is it?" Sehnisavain begins. "Do we know how or why he came into possession of these symbols?"

"I don't know the answer to this," he considers. "Only that he has always regarded them as priceless for their inherent magical properties, and he brings them out on occasion for study sessions."

"This is sacrilege!" Amariyn roars. "That man is defiling these symbols simply by touching them with his unclean hands, to say nothing of his contemptuous manners! I demand they be returned at once!"

"Lady Amariyn," Thaelyn offers. "I would most certainly agree, and I would desire just as much to see this through. But I think we should take this cautiously. It would seem both the Governor and the Dean are responsible for a number of criminal actions here. The Dean himself could not be responsible for their theft, and to see this in his possession causes me to wonder if he actually knows anything about their point of origin."

"Do you think he does not? Much like Haran and his opinions, I think that to be unlikely."

"Granted, it is clear he holds a close relationship with the Governor, especially if you consider the interactions with the dwarves, and let us not forget the Suuden-Aryku. But if we should move too quickly, we could find ourselves in a difficult situation, and on multiple fronts. I want to keep the advantage on my side, not give it to him."

"All right, I can agree on this, but then what? How do we find a solution to this?"

"By turning a few of these tables back on them."

TO BE CONTINUED